The Editor

J. GERALD KENNEDY is Boyd Professor of English at Louisiana State University. He is the author of *Imagining Paris: Exile, Writing, and American Identity* and coeditor (with Jackson R. Bryer) of *French Connections: Hemingway and Fitzgerald Abroad*. He was advisory editor of volumes 1–3 of the *Letters of Ernest Hemingway*, under the general editorship of Sandra Spanier, and he is coediting a forthcoming volume of Hemingway letters, the final years. He is also the author of a number of essays on Hemingway, Fitzgerald, and expatriate Paris, and he edited *Modern American Short Story Sequences: Composite Fictions and Fictive Communities*. His publications on nineteenth-century American literature include *Poe, Death, and the Life of Writing* and (with fellowships from the John Simon Guggenheim Foundation and the NEH) a cultural history, *Strange Nation: Literary Nationalism and Cultural Conflict in the Age of Poe*.

NORTON CRITICAL EDITIONS
Modernist & Contemporary Eras

ANDERSON, Winesburg, Ohio
AZUELA, The Underdogs
BURGESS, A Clockwork Orange
CATHER, My Ántonia
CATHER, O Pioneers!
CONRAD, Heart of Darkness
CONRAD, Lord Jim
CONRAD, The Secret Agent
CONRAD, The Secret Sharer and Other Stories
CUMMINGS, E. E. Cummings: Selected Works
Eight Modern Plays
ELIOT, The Waste Land and Other Poems
FAULKNER, As I Lay Dying
FAULKNER, The Sound and the Fury
FITZGERALD, The Great Gatsby
FORD, The Good Soldier
FORSTER, Howards End
FORSTER, A Passage to India
FREUD, Civilization and Its Discontents
FRIEDAN, The Feminine Mystique
HEMINGWAY, In Our Time
HEMINGWAY, The Sun Also Rises
JOHNSON, The Autobiography of an Ex-Colored Man
JOYCE, Dubliners
JOYCE, A Portrait of the Artist as a Young Man
KAFKA, Kafka's Selected Stories
KAFKA, The Metamorphosis
LARSEN, Passing
LARSEN, Quicksand
MANN, Death in Venice
MANSFIELD, Katherine Mansfield's Selected Stories
Modern African Drama
Modern and Contemporary Irish Drama
PROUST, Swann's Way
RHYS, Wide Sargasso Sea
RICH, Adrienne Rich: Poetry and Prose
SOYINKA, Death and the King's Horseman
STEIN, Three Lives and Q.E.D.
TOOMER, Cane
WATSON, The Double Helix
WHARTON, The Age of Innocence
WHARTON, Ethan Frome
WHARTON, The House of Mirth
WOOLF, Jacob's Room
WOOLF, Mrs. Dalloway
YEATS, Yeats's Poetry, Drama, and Prose

For a complete list of Norton Critical Editions, visit
wwnorton.com/nortoncriticals

A NORTON CRITICAL EDITION

Ernest Hemingway

IN OUR TIME

AUTHORITATIVE TEXT

CONTEXTS

CRITICISM

Edited by

J. GERALD KENNEDY
LOUISIANA STATE UNIVERSITY

W. W. NORTON & COMPANY
Independent Publishers Since 1923

In Memory of Mike Reynolds (1937–2000)
and Scott Donaldson (1928–2020)

W. W. Norton & Company has been independent since its founding in 1923, when William Warder Norton and Mary D. Herter Norton first published lectures delivered at the People's Institute, the adult education division of New York City's Cooper Union. The firm soon expanded its program beyond the Institute, publishing books by celebrated academics from America and abroad. By mid-century, the two major pillars of Norton's publishing program—trade books and college texts—were firmly established. In the 1950s, the Norton family transferred control of the company to its employees, and today—with a staff of five hundred and hundreds of trade, college, and professional titles published each year—W. W. Norton & Company stands as the largest and oldest publishing house owned wholly by its employees.

Manufacturing by Maple Press
Book design by Antonina Krass
Production manager: Brenda Manzanedo

Library of Congress Cataloging-in-Publication Data

Names: Hemingway, Ernest, 1899–1961, author. | Kennedy, J. Gerald, editor.
Title: In our time : authoritative text, contexts, criticism / Ernest Hemingway ;
    edited by J. Gerald Kennedy, Louisiana State University.
Description: First edition. | New York : W. W. Norton & Company, [2022] |
Series: A Norton critical edition | Includes bibliographical references.
Identifiers: LCCN 2021033757 | **ISBN 9780393543056 (paperback)**
Subjects: LCSH: Adams, Nick (Fictitious character)—Fiction. |
    Autobiographical fiction, American | Adventure stories, American. |
    Hemingway, Ernest, 1899–1961. Short stories. Selections (In our time) |
    LCGFT: Short stories. | Literary criticism.
Classification: LCC PS3515.E37 I5 2021b | DDC 813/.52—dc23
LC record available at https://lccn.loc.gov/2021033757

W. W. Norton & Company, Inc., 500 Fifth Avenue, New York, N.Y. 10110
        www.wwnorton.com
W. W. Norton & Company Ltd., 15 Carlisle Street, London W1D 3BS

1 2 3 4 5 6 7 8 9 0

Contents

Introduction

Published in 1925, *In Our Time* launched the international career of Ernest Hemingway and broached the themes of his first major novels. He gave the collection of stories and prose poems a loose continuity by tracing, in seven tales, the initiation of Nick Adams into the realities of adult life. But then and now, the book's arrangement produces unsettling discontinuities. The other seven stories depict different characters and odd circumstances quite unlike Nick's. Before and after the full-length stories, Hemingway also inserted italicized vignettes, called "Chapters," that captured brief, intense flashes of disconnected action. They mostly portray war and bull-fighting, along with crime scenes or executions. In range, the short stories somewhat mirror the author's life, from his Midwest boyhood to his war service, marriage, and expatriate life. Juxtaposed against the prose poems, however, they form a pastiche or cubist collage— an idea from modernist painting that Hemingway absorbed after arriving in Paris with his wife, Hadley, in late 1921. His volume title hints at a larger ambition: to represent in fiction the epochal changes produced by the First World War (1914–18). He drew the three-word phrase from the *Book of Common Prayer*: "Lord, give us peace in our time." But his stories depict instead a dramatic transition from prewar innocence to violent disillusionment in the postwar era. Wounded at the front as a Red Cross ambulance driver and canteen volunteer, Hemingway grasped the devastation of a war in which total combat deaths exceeded eight million, with twenty million more people dying from the flu pandemic of 1918–19. The twenties brought cultural energy and economic growth but no sense whatsoever that the "war to end all wars" had secured a lasting peace.

The volume evolved at first haphazardly. While working as a foreign correspondent for the *Toronto Star* in 1922–23, the author published a handful of stories, poems, and prose poems in avant-garde journals. In Paris, he produced two small, limited-edition chapbooks: *Three Stories and Ten Poems* (1923) and the eighteen short, jarring prose pieces he titled (lowercasing, in the manner of E. E. Cummings) *in our time* (1924). The cover design for the latter publication featured newspaper stories and headlines, suggesting Hemingway's effort to merge journalism with imaginative prose. Gradually, an idea for a composite larger volume emerged. After a short stay in Toronto, Hemingway abandoned journalism and in January 1924 returned to Paris. He soon began writing short stories at a furious pace, already envisioning an experimental design that would alternate full-length tales with his *in our time* pieces. As if to confuse future students, he gave the combined collection the same title as his 1924 chapbook but now capitalized it. *In Our Time*, the book published in New York in October 1925, made Hemingway a celebrity. Reviews hailed him as a rising star whose hard-edged style captured the cynicism of postwar culture.

Readers coming to the collection for the first time may wish to note a few basic strategies. One is the technique of juxtaposition, elaborated by Linda Wagner-Martin in an essay included in this Norton Critical Edition. Hemingway placed prose poems ("Chapters") between stories to produce jolting contrasts that sharpen recurrent ideas or images. In another essay included here, David Wyatt suggests that the Chapters represent the dreams (or nightmares) of characters in the stories. Hemingway evolved his much-discussed technique, omission, during the writing of *In Our Time*. He believed that a story could be made more suggestive by building the action around a concealed psychological or emotional problem. He later famously used an iceberg metaphor to imply heavy, submerged content. This principle helps explain the minimalist effect of several stories in which little appears to happen, including "Big Two-Hearted River." Hemingway's style accentuates this effect by relying on short, simple sentences, terse dialogue, and minimal exposition. A corollary of this stylistic minimalism is Hemingway's use of material objects to connote buried emotions. Several critical essays in this volume evoke the term "objective correlative" (a concept introduced by poet-critic T. S. Eliot) to describe personal feelings associated with an externalized object, such as the abandoned mill in "The End of Something." Throughout the volume, attentiveness to recurrent images (such as childbirth, violence, or death) helps readers recognize the larger patterns associated with a tumultuous time. Hemingway intuitively sensed that his experience epitomized that era.

Born in Oak Park, Illinois, in 1899, Hemingway grew up in a large, middle-class, churchgoing family, the son of an obstetrician and a music teacher. Like the fictional Nick Adams, he spent his summers boating, fishing, and hiking in northern Michigan, where the family owned a cottage on Walloon Lake. His father introduced him to outdoor sports and nurtured an interest in natural science; his mother taught him to play the cello and worried about his religious piety. Several stories in *In Our Time* offer glimpses of family dynamics in the Hemingway home. After graduating from high school in 1917,

Ernest decided not to attend college and took a job writing for *The Kansas City Star*. But after six months of reporting on crimes, accidents, and fires, he volunteered for the Red Cross ambulance service and sailed to Europe in May 1918. A few days after arriving in Italy, Hemingway viewed the scene of a factory explosion and found a site littered with decomposing corpses. It was a jolting introduction to the horrors of war. A month later, while delivering snacks to allied soldiers in an observation post, he was badly wounded in an Austrian mortar attack. He recovered from those injuries in a Milan hospital, where he became intimate with an attractive volunteer nurse. The romance was more serious for the 19-year-old Hemingway than for the 27-year-old American, Agnes von Kurowsky. After returning to Oak Park, he received her letter from Italy, calling their relationship a mere youthful flirtation and explaining that she was engaged to marry an Italian officer. From this rejection, Hemingway later composed "A Very Short Story," a sardonic piece that first appeared as a prose poem in *in our time*. His traumatic love affair would form the backstory of one novel, *The Sun Also Rises* (1926), and the principal plot in another, *A Farewell to Arms* (1929). Both his physical and his emotional wounds left residual pain.

Alone at Walloon Lake, Hemingway mended his broken heart by writing a handful of stories, all bad and destined for rejection by popular weekly or monthly magazines. Then, in Chicago, he found a job with a progressive newspaper, the *Cooperative Commonwealth*; he became acquainted with the writer Sherwood Anderson; and at age 21 he fell in love with Hadley Richardson, a 29-year-old from St. Louis. By September 1921, they were married, and three months later, they departed for Paris, where Ernest intended to become an author. He carried letters of introduction from Anderson to the literary innovator Gertrude Stein, the poet Ezra Pound, and the bookstore owner Sylvia Beach.

Although Hemingway later emphasized the poverty and hunger of the Paris years in his memoir, *A Moveable Feast*, postwar exchange rates boosted his income from the *Toronto Star* as well as Hadley's checks from a trust fund, making it possible for the couple to lease a flat, rent a piano, and enjoy lengthy sojourns in Switzerland, Italy, Germany, Austria, and Spain. In Paris, Hemingway and his wife became friends with Stein and her partner, Alice B. Toklas. In an apartment filled with paintings by Picasso, Matisse, and Cézanne, Stein tutored him in modern art and avant-garde prose; she explained her experiments with grammar and syntax, her uncoupling of words from meanings, and her use of repetition with variation. Beach offered a good lending library to Hemingway and introduced him to James Joyce, whose new book, *Ulysses*, she was then publishing. Pound, a former college teacher, advised Hemingway about what to read and how to write; he also introduced his protégé to the novelist Ford Madox Ford. Like Stein, Pound urged Hemingway to give up newspaper work.

Yet Hemingway's journalism formed a key part of his early literary apprenticeship, teaching him directness, accuracy of detail, and conciseness. His many articles for the *Toronto Star* reflect the scope of his reporting, which took him to Lausanne and Genoa for peace conferences, to Germany to cover the effects of postwar inflation as well as the French occupation of the Ruhr valley, and to Turkey to witness the forced retreat of the Greeks from Smyrna. He interviewed Prime Ministers Lloyd George of Great Britain and Benito Mussolini of Italy. He mastered "cablese" to economize on transatlantic telegram charges, omitting nonessential words and using innuendo. Not long after his journey to Asia Minor, perhaps moved by the spectacle of a refugee procession, Hemingway began to devise a hybrid prose form that fused journalism and fiction into short sketches, stark glimpses of misery or violence presented as eyewitness accounts.

Hemingway turned in a concerted way to writing prose poems after a railway theft in December 1922. Hadley planned to bring working manuscripts (including a war novel and several stories) to the conference in Lausanne, but a thief in the Gare de Lyon made off with the valise of material, igniting a marital feud as well as a literary meltdown. The outraged author returned to Paris by himself to investigate. Not until weeks later, when the couple traveled to Rapallo, Italy, to visit Pound, was Hemingway able to resume writing, aiming for verbal compression in the prose poem. Having urged Hemingway to innovate, Pound persuaded him to produce a short volume of experimental work for a cutting-edge series Pound was arranging for the American expatriate Bill Bird, who owned a printing press in Paris. Pound gave him another nudge by urging the editor Jane Heap to solicit Hemingway's new work for the April "Exiles" issue of *The Little Review*. In Rapallo, Hemingway dug into the task of creating something fresh, honing six vignettes, scenes from the war and the bullring, which he called "In Our Time."

During his stay in Italy, Hemingway also met Robert McAlmon, an expatriate writer and Pound admirer likewise about to become a publisher. McAlmon proposed to print a little book of Hemingway's stories and poems. He also offered to finance a summer trip to Spain, so that he and Hemingway could learn about bullfighting. Hemingway had based his only *Little Review* prose poem on bullfighting entirely on the account of his painter-friend Mike Strater, who was also in Rapallo. The book for McAlmon would include the story "My Old Man" (filed away in Paris as discarded) and "Up in Michigan," under review at *Cosmopolitan* when his other work was stolen. Hemingway later added a third tale, "Out of Season," that fictionalized an uneasy stay in Cortina after Hadley realized she was pregnant. Although the loss of his manuscripts had devastated Hemingway, he suddenly had two volumes forthcoming. As he revised the prose poems needed to complete *in our time*, he faced two inescapable realities: Mr. and Mrs. Hemingway were leaving Paris and would soon, in Toronto, become parents.

That June, Hemingway, McAlmon, and Bird followed the bull-fighting circuit from Madrid to Sevilla, Ronda, and Málaga. Fascinated by the culture that surrounded the ancient ritualized combat, Hemingway worked on several new prose poems and made notes for later *Toronto Star* feature stories. He would explain in July to his friend and fellow ambulance driver Bill Horne that watching bull-fights had a cathartic effect, something like being at the front, facing death, but from a safe vantage point: "It's just like having a ringside seat at the war with nothing going to happen to you."[1] That summer in Spain, he explored the emotional logic of the attraction. The thematic association of war and bullfighting would inform *In Our Time* and *The Sun Also Rises*. Hemingway was so entranced by bullfighting that when he returned to Paris, he told Hadley they were going to the July fiesta in Pamplona. Six months pregnant, Hadley went along because the trip seemed to be what Ernest needed. Before they departed for Toronto in August, Hemingway finished the last of the eighteen prose poems that made up *in our time*.

The move to Canada soon proved a terrible mistake. To be sure, Hadley had the benefit, in October, of delivering her son, John Hadley Nicanor Hemingway, in the care of an English-speaking medical staff in a fine Toronto hospital. But her husband was then absent in New York, pursuing a newspaper story. He was also trapped in a grueling routine of dull tasks assigned by an editor he despised. To Pound, Hemingway complained in expletive-laden letters about his woes, especially his inability to do any literary work. McAlmon's publication in Paris of *Three Stories and Ten Poems* provided some gratification, as did Edward O'Brien's publishing "My Old Man" in *The Best Short Stories of 1923* and then dedicating the volume to Hemingway. O'Brien (another Pound acquaintance from Rapallo) also asked when Hemingway would have enough stories to show a New York publisher. That query convinced Hemingway that he needed to return to Paris as soon as possible. In January, he and Hadley broke their lease, slipped out of Toronto with their infant son, and boarded a ship in New York.

Back in France, living in a new apartment near the great cafés of Montparnasse, Hemingway and Hadley adjusted to the whine of the

---

1. *The Letters of Ernest Hemingway*, Vol. 2: 1923–25 (Cambridge UP, 2013), p. 36.

sawmill beneath their apartment and to the crying of Mr. Bumby, as they lovingly called their son. Having resigned from the paper, Hemingway faced a make-or-break professional challenge, but his *Star* drudgery left him pent up with ideas and primed to write. That February, as his biographer Michael Reynolds has noted, he resumed work on a story begun in Toronto, a month after Bumby's birth, about a boy named Nick, Nick's doctor-father, and an Indian woman in labor. Hemingway's opening episode, a night scene, dramatized the boy's fear of death, but the author later omitted it, realizing that Nick's uneasiness and questions implied his anxiety. The almost spontaneous composition of "Indian Camp" triggered a flood of new work. Reynolds writes:

> They all went just like that, one story after another, exploding out of his head perfectly on to paper, needing little revision. It was like a mystical experience, an emotional rush that took him outside himself almost as if someone else were writing the stories. . . . [I]n less than three Paris months, Hemingway wrote eight of the best stories he would ever write, stories so spare and tense they outlasted his prime and later foolishness, outlasted the generation for which they were written, their publisher and their critics.[2]

At the lovely old café where he liked to work, La Closerie des Lilas, Hemingway discovered that stories became more suggestive when he resisted the urge to explain things. The stories that emerged from that season of manic creativity included (in addition to "Indian Camp") "Cat in the Rain," "The End of Something," "The Three-Day Blow," "The Doctor and the Doctor's Wife," "Soldier's Home," and "Cross-Country Snow." "Soldier's Home" used tricks he had learned from Stein (repetition) and Joyce (juxtaposition) to show the trauma of war, making shell shock seem more pervasive by shifting the focus from Nick to other soldiers. His output also included a nasty satire of an American poet whose sexual difficulties became the stuff of Paris gossip. Hemingway's slight acquaintance with the poet Chard Powers Smith, in 1922, inspired the title "Mr. and Mrs. Smith" until he learned in 1924 that the real Mrs. Smith had died in childbirth in an Italian hospital. Then he retitled the story "Mr. and Mrs. Elliot," probably to irritate Pound's friend T. S. Eliot.

This surge of productivity, which coincided with work as a subeditor for Ford's *Transatlantic Review*, encouraged Hemingway to update O'Brien on his progress. He was thinking, he said, of combining the *in our time* pieces with his new stories. But that gambit

---

2. Michael Reynolds, *Hemingway: The Paris Years* (Basil Blackwell, 1989), p. 167.

only complicated the problem of how to connect his diverse material. Recalling how deftly Joyce had gathered together the various threads of *Dubliners* in a resonant closing story called "The Dead," he began to write "Big Two-Hearted River," apparently intending it to link the Nick stories with his tales of war, wounding, and marital discord.

The troubled marriages in "Out of Season" and "Cat in the Rain," as well as Nick's hesitation about fatherhood in "Cross-Country Snow," suggest that Hemingway's domestic tensions may have aroused his nostalgia for Michigan fishing trips with male companions. The first version of "Big Two-Hearted River" reconstructed Hemingway's 1919 fishing expedition to the Fox River with two old buddies. But he soon saw that he needed a story about solitude; Nick would return alone to an unspoiled river, where the ritual of fishing would calm his unnamed anxieties. If the story *was* truly about returning from the war, as Hemingway later claimed, that subject would be insinuated by natural details such as blackened grasshoppers and charred trees. He worked on the story for several weeks and then set it aside to organize an excursion to Pamplona to watch bullfights and to fish. Leaving Bumby with a nanny, the Hemingways departed for Spain, where they would be joined by a group that included three fellow authors (McAlmon, Donald Ogden Stewart, and John Dos Passos). Though Hemingway fretted during the festivities that Hadley might be pregnant again, he enjoyed the action and camaraderie, wondering how he could turn the material into a novel.

Back in Paris, Hemingway picked up the story of Nick's fishing trip. All the talk in Spain about writing, painting, bullfighting, and fishing had apparently suggested a surreal ending. He drafted a conclusion implying that although Nick was revisiting Michigan, he was actually a married writer living in Paris, a friend of Pound, McAlmon, Joyce, and Stein. None of his literary pals understood Nick's appreciation of outdoor sports, and "Ezra thought fishing was a joke." When Nick thought about his fishing companions from Michigan, he admitted that before Helen became his wife, he was "married to fishing" (136 in this volume). But now, dedicated to becoming an author, he called writing "more fun than anything," even "the greatest pleasure." Nick then unexpectedly revealed that he wrote "My Old Man" and perhaps other stories in the collection. Conceivably, he had written the vignettes as well, for his admission that "his whole inner life had been bullfights all one year" neatly explained those six prose poems about bulls and matadors. But he also stoutly insisted that "Nick in the stories was never himself" (139) and that he had invented everything that happened. Giving the author-character relationship one last twist, however, the Nick of

"Big Two-Hearted River" described a life almost identical to Hemingway's, from the names of his Michigan friends and the places they fished to the location of his seat in the bullring. Like his author, Nick wanted to write the way Cézanne painted, to get the country exactly right. And at the end of the story as Hemingway drafted it that August and September (in the extract now known as "On Writing"), Nick closed his story about fishing by walking back to camp, holding something in his head, presumably the story that he would write—which Hemingway, his double, had already written.

This through-the-looking-glass maneuver—revealing that Nick Adams, the character in several early stories, is also perhaps the *author* of the entire collection—easily marked the most revolutionary move in the emerging work. Hemingway surely had in mind *A Portrait of the Artist as a Young Man*, the 1916 novel about the making of a young Irish novelist named Stephen Dedalus, whose travails roughly mirror those of his creator, James Joyce. Hemingway wanted to do something even more radically innovative. But flaunting the fictionality of a work of fiction (a practice theorists later dubbed "metafiction") was still, as Debra A. Moddelmog discusses in an essay included in this Norton Critical Edition, far ahead of its time. To make such a revelation in the volume's concluding story was a daring move that might have baffled readers of the 1920s. Hemingway's confidence in his own cleverness collapsed when Gertrude Stein read his story and told him to cut out the "mental conversation," bluntly observing (as she said in *The Autobiography of Alice B. Toklas*) that "remarks are not literature."[3]

Accepting Stein's judgment, Hemingway faced two problems. He first had to compose a more appropriate, understated conclusion. And then he had to swap that new ending for several pages he wished to delete from two copies of the manuscript possibly already under editorial review. He had earlier given one copy of his book to Dos Passos to show to Manhattan publishers; he had handed another copy to a Boni & Liveright talent scout visiting Paris. Also working on his behalf in New York was the humorist Don Stewart, to whom he wrote a desperate letter on November 3, revealing his misgivings about the talky ending of "Big Two-Hearted River," which, he suddenly recognized, amounted to "faecal matter."[4] He was sending Stewart a new ending, in which Nick decided not to wade into a dark, thickly wooded stretch of river because "there were plenty of days coming when he could fish the swamp" (129). Like his author, Nick finally elected not to take unnecessary risks. Hemingway obscured all evidence of Nick's literary life except a fugitive

3. *The Autobiography of Alice B. Toklas* (Literary Guild, 1933), p. 270.
4. *Letters*, 2:172.

reference to things left behind: "the need for thinking, the need to write, other needs" (112).

The manuscript that Dos Passos was carrying, as well as the one at Boni & Liveright, reflected other changes that Hemingway had made by mid-September. He had divided the longish "Big Two-Hearted River" into two parts, and (to better balance stories and prose poems) he had upgraded "A Very Short Story" and "The Revolutionist" (both included in *in our time*) to short stories, despite their brevity. At that point, though, the collection still began with "Up in Michigan," even though Stein had already advised him that his story of date rape was unpresentable, "*inaccrochable*" in the same way an offensive painting can't be hung on a wall. He had arranged the sequence so that the prose poems roughly followed the order of *in our time*, with the final sketch of the king of Greece forming a postscript, or "Envoi." After revising "Big Two-Hearted River" in November, Hemingway thought his work was done. But he was wrong.

During a skiing holiday in Schruns, Austria, Hemingway received word in February 1925 that Boni & Liveright had agreed to publish the book. They sent him a contract, but there was also a problem to fix: his opening story presented likely legal difficulties. It did not matter that "Up in Michigan" had already appeared in print in Paris. Its content was unpublishable in New York in 1925, and so Hemingway soon began devising a Nick Adams story to replace it.

He accomplished the work in Paris in late March and called that narrative "The Battler," inserting it among the early Nick stories after "The Three-Day Blow." The removal of "Up in Michigan" forced him to move "Indian Camp" to the opening story. It was a felicitous substitution, not only because "Up in Michigan" depicted a big blacksmith in the 1880s forcing himself on a naïve young woman, but also because it did not pertain to Nick Adams or to the twentieth century. "Indian Camp" aptly launches the story of Nick—which seems to culminate in the final tale—and more accurately associates *In Our Time* with the years bracketing the Great War. "The Battler," moreover, bridges the period between Nick's late adolescence ("The Three-Day Blow") and his war service (figured in Chapter VI). It was a fine repair job all around.

That spring, Hemingway was looking ahead to his story collection and to the novel he needed to write, but he was also mired in what Nick (in "On Writing") calls marital "discontent and friction." Depressed and making suicidal threats, he was also carrying on in Paris with the seductive Duff Twysden, a British expatriate and legendary drinker. His novel would eventually transform her into Lady Brett Ashley, a sexually liberated, utterly modern woman. In June, Hemingway began collecting another summer crew for Spain; in addition to Hadley, his entourage would include an old Michigan fishing pal, Bill Smith (enticed by Hemingway to visit Europe), and Don Stewart. A threesome would meet them in Pamplona: the novelist Harold Loeb, Twysden, and her drunken fiancé, Pat Guthrie. This time, the fishing preceded the fiesta, but it went badly because the Irati River had been spoiled by logging. The bullfighting was better: it hinged on the rivalry between a new star, Niño de la Palma, and the legendary Juan Belmonte. But among the expatriates, sexual rivalries complicated the revelry. Twysden's presence troubled Hadley, while Guthrie needled Loeb constantly. So too did Hemingway, when he realized that Twysden recently had a sexy tryst with Loeb. The two writers finally squared off, then apologized. After the fiesta, the Hemingways traveled around Spain, following the bullfights while Ernest worked on a novel that was quickly taking shape.

During those weeks in Spain, Hemingway received page proofs for *In Our Time* and a copy of the book's dull cover design, which featured blurbs by Dos Passos, Sherwood Anderson, and several others. The lavish promotional quotes convinced Hemingway that Boni & Liveright lacked confidence in the book. By the time the volume appeared, in early October, he was contriving to escape a contract that required him to give Boni & Liveright his next book. Hemingway knew he had better options: Knopf and Harcourt both showed interest in the bullfighting novel, and cordial letters from the editor Max Perkins assured him that Scribner's wanted to publish his next book. F. Scott Fitzgerald, who arrived in Paris in late April, added his urging. Scribner's had just released *The Great Gatsby* with an artful cover, strong promotion, and effective distribution. By late October, Hemingway realized that Boni & Liveright had no intention of pushing *In Our Time*. They were instead focused on promoting Anderson's current novel, *Dark Laughter*. Hemingway was irked that even enthusiastic reviewers of *In Our Time* kept noting his indebtedness to Anderson. Yes, Anderson had been helpful, and yes, "My Old Man" perhaps recalled Anderson's racetrack stories. But Hemingway wanted to be regarded as an original talent, not as someone's protégé.

While readers in the United States were first discovering *In Our Time*, Hemingway was thus hurriedly composing a short satirical novel that would be his "next" book. He wrote it in ten days, stealing his title—*The Torrents of Spring*—from the Russian author Turgenev, and he sent it to Boni & Liveright knowing that they could not possibly accept it, because it mocked their star author, Anderson, and *Dark Laughter*. The flimsy plot vaguely resembles a comic mashup of the "mental conversation" dropped from "Big Two-Hearted River": it tells the story of two sexually troubled men, a war veteran and a writer, who both work in Petoskey, Michigan, but long for Paris. One man is in love with two women; the other suffers from a lack of passion. The veteran knows where Gertrude Stein lives and wonders aloud, "Where were her experiments in words leading her?"[5] In several "author notes," Hemingway updates readers on his literary socializing in Paris and even invites them to visit him afternoons at the Café du Dôme. When Boni & Liveright rejected the parody, Hemingway handed it to Scribner's, all the while revising his serious novel, *The Sun Also Rises*.

The October 1925 publication of *In Our Time* triggered a succession of favorable reviews (eight reprinted in this volume) that continued well into 1926. The book's sales as a Boni & Liveright title, however, never matched its critical acclaim, which established Hemingway as a rising star. The back-and-forth pattern of stories and prose poems, which Hemingway once likened to looking at a coastline with the naked eye and then with high-powered binoculars, seemed a fresh tactic that underscored the volume's principal themes: birth, death, war, violence, sex, marriage, disillusionment, and resilience. "Indian Camp," "Soldier's Home," and "Big Two-Hearted River" emerged as the volume's best stories, and Nick Adams became a recurrent figure in Hemingway's subsequent collections of short stories, *Men Without Women* (1927) and *Winner Take Nothing* (1933). His contract-breaking parody, *The Torrents of Spring* (1926), stirred anger or perplexity but little else. *The Sun Also Rises* and *A Farewell to Arms*, in contrast, became successful and critically esteemed. When Scribner's bought the rights to *In Our Time* and reissued the volume in 1930, Hemingway wrote an introduction based on his 1922 visit to Turkey; he later titled it "On the Quai at Smyrna." He also restored language from "Mr. and Mrs. Elliot" that had appeared in the original 1924 magazine version but was softened in 1925 at the insistence of Boni & Liveright.

During the next thirty years, Hemingway established himself as one of the preeminent American writers of his generation. He wrote nonfictional books on the Spanish bullfight (*Death in the Afternoon* [1932]) and African game hunting (*The Green Hills of Africa* [1935]). In the mid-1930s, he published two superb short stories in *Esquire* magazine: "The Short Happy Life of Francis Macomber" and "The Snows of Kilimanjaro." With its parallel plot lines, his experimental novel, *To Have and Have Not* (1937), veered into the domain of working-class fiction. *For Whom the Bell Tolls* (1940) was a highly popular war novel and—after the critical panning of *Across the River and into the Trees* (1950)—*The Old Man and the Sea* (1952) also became a best seller, clinching Hemingway's selection for the Nobel Prize in Literature in 1954.

5. *The Torrents of Spring* (Scribner's, 1926), p. 74.

But a plethora of medical problems, aggravated by alcohol and multiple concussions, shortened Hemingway's career. After his death by suicide in 1961—following counterproductive electroshock therapy—Scribner's edited and published *A Moveable Feast* in 1964. In that memoir, Hemingway described his early years in Paris with Hadley, recalling his expatriate friendships and his apprenticeship as an author. He devised a myth of solitary self-instruction, of writing "true sentences" in a cold, rented room, thus minimizing his debts to Stein, Pound, Fitzgerald, and Joyce. He recounted the writing of "Big Two-Hearted River" in a café and helpfully explained why omitting any mention of war made the story work, but he said nothing about the experimental ending he likewise deleted. In recollecting the early years when he was writing his first great stories, Hemingway miraculously recovered the spare, stripped-down style of that work.

His first major publication, the 1925 collection of stories and prose poems showed the influence of modernist Paris in its inventive arrangement, and its content prefigured the direction of his future works. *In Our Time* marked the debut of a writer who truly changed the language of modern prose fiction.

Acknowledgments

Many friends in Hemingway studies have provided information or suggestions for this edition, including Sandra Spanier, Miriam Mandel, Robert Trogden, Fred Svoboda, Kirk Curnutt, Susan Beegel, Larry Grimes, Linda Patterson Miller, Carl Eby, Suzanne del Gizzo, Mark Cirino, Hilary Justice, David Wyatt, Don Daiker, Linda Wagner-Martin, Steve Paul, Chris Struble, Debra Moddelmog, and Michael Von Cannon. I have also felt a constant indebtedness to the scholarly work of several old friends now departed from the scene, Paul Smith, Bob Lewis, and especially Mike Reynolds, who long ago recommended me to Norton for this editorial project, and, more recently, Scott Donaldson. Louisiana State University continues to support my professional work, and I am grateful for the assistance of Emily Boimare in the Office of Research. Thanks as well to Andrew Sluyter for preparing the maps. At W. W. Norton I have enjoyed working with the incomparable Carol Bemis, and Rachel Goodman has provided smart, timely help and encouragement. Finally, I am most grateful to Sarah, my loving wife, travel companion, and partner in research.

A Note on the Text

The text in this volume reproduces not the 1925 Boni & Liveright edition but the 1930 Scribner's republication. At the request of his editor, Maxwell Perkins, Hemingway wrote an informal prologue, a sketch of the Greek-Turkish war that appeared as "An Introduction by the Author." In 1938, for the publication of the anthology *The Fifth Column and the First Forty-Nine Stories*, Hemingway inserted one of his early working titles for the piece: "On the Quai at Smyrna." That more familiar title and the sketch appear here with permission of Scribner's. Another story in the 1925 edition had been bowdlerized at the insistence of Horace Liveright. He forced Hemingway to remove the mild sexual innuendo used in the 1924 *Little Review* version, "Mr. and Mrs. Smith." In 1925, Hemingway suppressed those too-steamy references to the couple's "trying" to have a baby, renamed them "Mr. and Mrs. Elliot," and added a paragraph on famous Paris expatriates, calculated to titillate. In 1930, using the revised title, Hemingway restored the original 1924 language and content, reproduced here. This Norton Critical Edition thus represents the version of *In Our Time* readers have come to know and appreciate. A handful of original typos have also been silently corrected.

It also includes two episodes related importantly to key stories but deleted before their publication. These excerpts—included in *The Nick Adams Stories*, edited by Philip Young—offer vital insights into the composition process and illustrate the technique of omission, on which Hemingway later prided himself. The first, "Three Shots," marks the original opening of "Indian Camp" and exposes the onset of death anxiety in young Nick. Hemingway dropped the opening incident before the story's publication in the April 1924 issue of the *Transatlantic Review*. Possibly the review's editor, Ford Madox Ford, suggested the deletion.

The history of "On Writing" can be reconstructed more reliably (see xv–xvii above). This fragment gives us an extraordinary glimpse into the author's consciousness at the very moment he was launching his career. Several critical essays reprinted in this Norton Critical Edition illuminate this 1924 narrative experiment.

Abbreviations of Hemingway Works Cited

Thanks to Sandra Spanier, General Editor of the Cambridge Edition of *The Letters of Ernest Hemingway*, for permission to use these abbreviations, slightly modified for this edition.

ARIT   *Across the River and into the Trees*. New York: Scribner's, 1950.

BL   *By-Line: Ernest Hemingway: Selected Articles and Dispatches of Four Decades*. Ed. William White. New York: Scribner's, 1967.

CSS   *The Complete Short Stories of Ernest Hemingway: The Finca Vigía Edition*. New York: Scribner's, 1987.

DLT   *Dateline: Toronto: The Complete "Toronto Star" Dispatches, 1920–1924*. Ed. William White. New York: Scribner's, 1985.

DIA   *Death in the Afternoon*. New York: Scribner's, 1932.

DS   *The Dangerous Summer*. New York: Scribner's, 1985.

FC   *The Fifth Column and the First Forty-nine Stories*. New York: Scribner's, 1938.

FTA   *A Farewell to Arms*. New York: Scribner's, 1929.

FWBT   *For Whom the Bell Tolls*. New York: Scribner's, 1940.

GOE   *The Garden of Eden*. New York: Scribner's, 1986.

GHOA   *Green Hills of Africa*. New York: Scribner's, 1935.

iot   *in our time*. Paris: Three Mountains Press, 1924.

IOT   *In Our Time*. New York: Boni & Liveright, 1925. Rev. ed., New York: Scribner's, 1930.

IIS   *Islands in the Stream*. New York: Scribner's, 1970.

JFK/EH John F. Kennedy Library, Hemingway Collection, Boston, MA.

LEH 1   *The Letters of Ernest Hemingway, Vol. I: 1907–1922*. Eds. Sandra Spanier and Robert W. Trogdon. New York: Cambridge UP, 2011.

LEH 2   *The Letters of Ernest Hemingway, Vol. 2: 1923–1925*. Eds. Sandra Spanier, Albert J. DeFazio III, and Robert W. Trogdon. New York: Cambridge UP, 2013.

LEH 3   *The Letters of Ernest Hemingway, Vol. 3: 1926–1929.* Eds. Rena Sanderson, Sandra Spanier, and Robert W. Trogdon. New York: Cambridge UP, 2015.

LEH 4   *The Letters of Ernest Hemingway, Vol. 4: 1929–1931.* Eds. Sandra Spanier and Miriam Mandel. New York: Cambridge UP, 2017.

MAW   *Men at War.* New York: Crown Publishers, 1942.

MF   *A Moveable Feast.* New York: Scribner's, 1964.

MWW   *Men Without Women.* New York: Scribner's, 1927.

NAS   *The Nick Adams Stories.* New York: Scribner's, 1972.

OMS   *The Old Man and the Sea.* New York: Scribner's, 1952.

Poems   *Complete Poems.* Ed., with Introduction and Notes, by Nicholas Gerogiannis. Rev. ed., Lincoln: U of Nebraska P, 1992.

SAR   *The Sun Also Rises.* New York: Scribner's, 1926.

SL   *Ernest Hemingway: Selected Letters, 1917–1961.* Ed. Carlos Baker. New York: Scribner's, 1981.

SS   *The Short Stories of Ernest Hemingway.* New York: Scribner's, 1954.

TAFL   *True at First Light.* Ed. Patrick Hemingway. New York: Scribner's, 1999.

THHN   *To Have and Have Not.* New York: Scribner's, 1937.

TOS   *The Torrents of Spring.* New York: Scribner's, 1926.

TSTP   *Three Stories and Ten Poems.* Paris: Contact Editions, 1923.

UK   *Under Kilimanjaro.* Ed. Robert W. Lewis and Robert E. Fleming. Kent, OH: Kent State UP, 2005.

WTN   *Winner Take Nothing.* New York: Scribner's, 1933.

The Text of
IN OUR TIME

To
HADLEY RICHARDSON HEMINGWAY

CONTENTS

The Michigan of Nick Adams

0   50   100
miles

Cartographer: Andrew Sluyter, Professor of Geography and Anthropology, Louisiana State University.

4

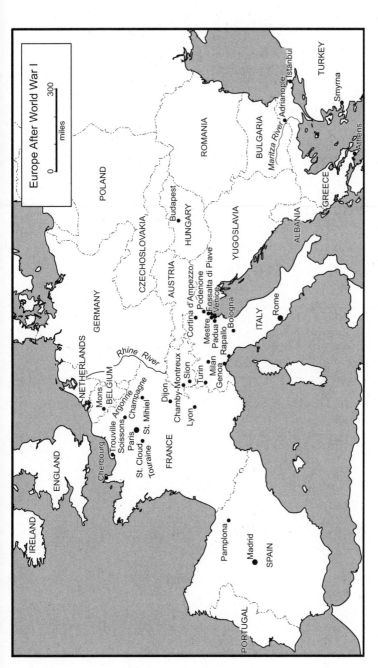

Europe After World War I

Cartographer: Andrew Sluyter, Professor of Geography and Anthropology, Louisiana State University.

ON THE QUAI AT SMYRNA†

The strange thing was, he said, how they screamed every night at midnight. I do not know why they screamed at that time. We were in the harbor and they were all on the pier and at midnight they started screaming. We used to turn the searchlight on them to quiet them. That always did the trick. We'd run the searchlight up and down over them two or three times and they stopped it. One time I was senior officer on the pier and a Turkish officer came up to me in a frightful rage because one of our sailors had been most insulting to him. So I told him the fellow would be sent on ship and be most severely punished. I asked him to point him out. So he pointed out a gunner's mate, most inoffensive chap.[1] Said he'd been most frightfully and repeatedly insulting; talking to me through an interpreter. I couldn't imagine how the gunner's mate knew enough Turkish to be insulting. I called him over and said, "And just in case you should have spoken to any Turkish officers."

"I haven't spoken to any of them, sir."

"I'm quite sure of it," I said, "but you'd best go on board ship and not come ashore again for the rest of the day."

Then I told the Turk the man was being sent on board ship and would be most severely dealt with. Oh most rigorously. He felt topping about it. Great friends we were.

The worst, he said, were the women with dead babies. You couldn't get the women to give up their dead babies. They'd have babies dead for six days. Wouldn't give them up. Nothing you could do about it. Had to take them away finally. Then there was an old lady, most extraordinary case. I told it to a doctor and he said I was lying. We were clearing them off the pier, had to clear off the dead ones, and this old woman was lying on a sort of litter. They said, "Will you have a look at her, sir?" So I had a look at her and just then she died and went absolutely stiff. Her legs drew up and she drew up from the waist and went quite rigid. Exactly as though she had been dead over night. She was quite dead and absolutely rigid. I told a medical chap about it and he told me it was impossible.

---

† From *In Our Time* (New York: Scribner's, 1930). Copyright © 1925, 1930 by Charles Scribner's Sons; copyright renewed 1953, 1958 by Ernest Hemingway. Reprinted with the permission of Scribner, a division of Simon & Schuster, Inc. All rights reserved. Smyrna, on the Aegean Sea in western Turkey, was originally Greek. Now called Izmir, it remained predominantly Greek after falling under Ottoman rule. In 1919, Greece invaded Turkey to overthrow the Islamic government. But Turkish forces under Mustafa Kemal Atatürk overwhelmed Smyrna in 1922. Hemingway never visited the city but read news reports and perhaps saw the newsreel *The Burning of Smyrna*.
1. The word "chap" identifies the speaker as British, probably an officer with the Allied peacekeeping forces passively observing the genocide of Greeks fleeing Smyrna.

They were all out there on the pier and it wasn't at all like an earthquake or that sort of thing because they never knew about the Turk. They never knew what the old Turk would do.[2] You remember when they ordered us not to come in to take off any more? I had the wind up when we came in that morning. He had any amount of batteries and could have blown us clean out of the water. We were going to come in, run close along the pier, let go the front and rear anchors and then shell the Turkish quarter of the town. They would have blown us out of water but we would have blown the town simply to hell. They just fired a few blank charges at us as we came in. Kemal came down and sacked the Turkish commander. For exceeding his authority or some such thing. He got a bit above himself. It would have been the hell of a mess.

You remember the harbor. There were plenty of nice things floating around in it. That was the only time in my life I got so I dreamed about things. You didn't mind the women who were having babies as you did those with the dead ones. They had them all right. Surprising how few of them died. You just covered them over with something and let them go to it. They'd always pick out the darkest place in the hold to have them. None of them minded anything once they got off the pier.

The Greeks were nice chaps too. When they evacuated they had all their baggage animals they couldn't take off with them so they just broke their forelegs and dumped them into the shallow water. All those mules with their forelegs broken pushed over into the shallow water. It was all a pleasant business. My word yes a most pleasant business.

---

2. "Old Turk" refers to the Turkish officer at the harbor, who commands artillery batteries to prevent Allied ships from aiding the Greeks. But he fires only blank charges, warning shots.

Chapter I

Everybody was drunk. The whole battery was drunk going along the road in the dark. We were going to the Champagne.[1] *The lieutenant kept riding his horse out into the fields and saying to him, "I'm drunk, I tell you, mon vieux.*[2] *Oh, I am so soused." We went along the road all night in the dark and the adjutant kept riding up alongside my kitchen and saying, "You must put it out. It is dangerous. It will be observed." We were fifty kilometers from the front but the adjutant worried about the fire in my kitchen. It was funny going along that road. That was when I was a kitchen corporal.*

1. The French region famous for sparkling white wine. East of Reims, French and German forces fought two major battles in 1915, the probable date of this action.
2. My old pal (French).

9

INDIAN CAMP

At the lake shore there was another rowboat drawn up. The two Indians[1] stood waiting.

Nick and his father got in the stern of the boat and the Indians shoved it off and one of them got in to row. Uncle George sat in the stern of the camp rowboat. The young Indian shoved the camp boat off and got in to row Uncle George.

The two boats started off in the dark. Nick heard the oarlocks of the other boat quite a way ahead of them in the mist. The Indians rowed with quick choppy strokes. Nick lay back with his father's arm around him. It was cold on the water. The Indian who was rowing them was working very hard, but the other boat moved further ahead in the mist all the time.

"Where are we going, Dad?" Nick asked.

"Over to the Indian camp. There is an Indian lady very sick."

"Oh," said Nick.

Across the bay they found the other boat beached. Uncle George was smoking a cigar in the dark. The young Indian pulled the boat way up on the beach. Uncle George gave both the Indians cigars.

They walked up from the beach through a meadow that was soaking wet with dew, following the young Indian who carried a lantern. Then they went into the woods and followed a trail that led to the logging road that ran back into the hills. It was much lighter on the logging road as the timber was cut away on both sides. The young Indian stopped and blew out his lantern and they all walked on along the road.

They came around a bend and a dog came out barking. Ahead were the lights of the shanties where the Indian bark-peelers lived.[2] More dogs rushed out at them. The two Indians sent them back to the shanties. In the shanty nearest the road there was a light in the window. An old woman stood in the doorway holding a lamp.

Inside on a wooden bunk lay a young Indian woman. She had been trying to have her baby for two days. All the old women in the camp had been helping her. The men had moved off up the road to sit in the dark and smoke out of range of the noise she made. She screamed just as Nick and the two Indians followed his father and Uncle George into the shanty. She lay in the lower bunk, very big under a

---

1. Native Americans. Hemingway's term, typical of his era, is now regarded as a slur by Indigenous People. The Michigan lake recalls Walloon Lake, where Hemingway's family owned a summer cottage. Nearby camps of Ojibwe remained there in the early 20th century, and Hemingway's father, a doctor, occasionally treated their medical problems.
2. Native "bark-peelers" stripped hemlock bark to make tannic acid, used to waterproof leather. Others worked at lumber mills, peeling bark to ready logs for milling.

quilt. Her head was turned to one side. In the upper bunk was her husband. He had cut his foot very badly with an ax three days before. He was smoking a pipe. The room smelled very bad.

Nick's father ordered some water to be put on the stove, and while it was heating he spoke to Nick.

"This lady is going to have a baby, Nick," he said.

"I know," said Nick.

"You don't know," said his father. "Listen to me. What she is going through is called being in labor. The baby wants to be born and she wants it to be born. All her muscles are trying to get the baby born. That is what is happening when she screams."

"I see," Nick said.

Just then the woman cried out.

"Oh, Daddy, can't you give her something to make her stop screaming?" asked Nick.

"No. I haven't any anæsthetic," his father said. "But her screams are not important. I don't hear them because they are not important."

The husband in the upper bunk rolled over against the wall.

The woman in the kitchen motioned to the doctor that the water was hot. Nick's father went into the kitchen and poured about half of the water out of the big kettle into a basin. Into the water left in the kettle he put several things he unwrapped from a handkerchief.

"Those must boil," he said, and began to scrub his hands in the basin of hot water with a cake of soap he had brought from the camp. Nick watched his father's hands scrubbing each other with the soap. While his father washed his hands very carefully and thoroughly, he talked.

"You see, Nick, babies are supposed to be born head first but sometimes they're not. When they're not they make a lot of trouble for everybody. Maybe I'll have to operate on this lady. We'll know in a little while."

When he was satisfied with his hands he went in and went to work.

"Pull back that quilt, will you, George?" he said. "I'd rather not touch it."

Later when he started to operate Uncle George and three Indian men held the woman still. She bit Uncle George on the arm and Uncle George said, "Damn squaw[3] bitch!" and the young Indian who had rowed Uncle George over laughed at him. Nick held the basin for his father. It all took a long time.

His father picked the baby up and slapped it to make it breathe and handed it to the old woman.

---

3. "Squaw" derives from the Narraganset language and means "woman" or "wife." Whites later used the term derisively, as does Uncle George.

"See, it's a boy, Nick," he said. "How do you like being an interne?"

Nick said, "All right." He was looking away so as not to see what his father was doing.

"There. That gets it," said his father and put something into the basin.

Nick didn't look at it.

"Now," his father said, "there's some stitches to put in. You can watch this or not, Nick, just as you like. I'm going to sew up the incision I made."

Nick did not watch. His curiosity had been gone for a long time.

His father finished and stood up. Uncle George and the three Indian men stood up. Nick put the basin out in the kitchen.

Uncle George looked at his arm. The young Indian smiled reminiscently.

"I'll put some peroxide on that, George," the doctor said.

He bent over the Indian woman. She was quiet now and her eyes were closed. She looked very pale. She did not know what had become of the baby or anything.

"I'll be back in the morning," the doctor said, standing up. "The nurse should be here from St. Ignace[4] by noon and she'll bring everything we need."

He was feeling exalted and talkative as football players are in the dressing room after a game.

"That's one for the medical journal, George," he said. "Doing a Cæsarian with a jack-knife and sewing it up with nine-foot, tapered gut leaders."[5]

Uncle George was standing against the wall, looking at his arm.

"Oh, you're a great man, all right," he said.

"Ought to have a look at the proud father. They're usually the worst sufferers in these little affairs," the doctor said. "I must say he took it all pretty quietly."

He pulled back the blanket from the Indian's head. His hand came away wet. He mounted on the edge of the lower bunk with the lamp in one hand and looked in. The Indian lay with his face toward the wall. His throat had been cut from ear to ear. The blood had flowed down into a pool where his body sagged the bunk. His head rested on his left arm. The open razor lay, edge up, in the blankets.

"Take Nick out of the shanty, George," the doctor said.

There was no need of that. Nick, standing in the door of the kitchen, had a good view of the upper bunk when his father, the lamp in one hand, tipped the Indian's head back.

---

4. A town at the southern tip of Michigan's Upper Peninsula, putting in question the fictional geography of the story. A hospital in Petoskey, near Walloon Lake, had been established in 1902.
5. Tapered fishing leader, then typically made of cat gut.

It was just beginning to be daylight when they walked along the logging road back toward the lake.

"I'm terribly sorry I brought you along, Nickie," said his father, all his post-operative exhilaration gone. "It was an awful mess to put you through."

"Do ladies always have such a hard time having babies?" Nick asked.

"No, that was very, very exceptional."

"Why did he kill himself, Daddy?"

"I don't know, Nick. He couldn't stand things, I guess."

"Do many men kill themselves, Daddy?"

"Not very many, Nick."

"Do many women?"

"Hardly ever."

"Don't they ever?"

"Oh, yes. They do sometimes."

"Daddy?"

"Yes."

"Where did Uncle George go?"

"He'll turn up all right."

"Is dying hard, Daddy?"

"No, I think it's pretty easy, Nick. It all depends."

They were seated in the boat, Nick in the stern, his father rowing. The sun was coming up over the hills. A bass jumped, making a circle in the water. Nick trailed his hand in the water. It felt warm in the sharp chill of the morning.

In the early morning on the lake sitting in the stern of the boat with his father rowing, he felt quite sure that he would never die.

Chapter II

Minarets stuck up in the rain out of Adrianople across the mud flats. The carts were jammed for thirty miles along the Karagatch road.[1] *Water buffalo and cattle were hauling carts through the mud. No end and no beginning. Just carts loaded with everything they owned. The old men and women, soaked through, walked along keeping the cattle moving. The Maritza was running yellow almost up to the bridge. Carts were jammed solid on the bridge with camels bobbing along through them. Greek cavalry herded along the procession. Women and kids were in the carts crouched with mattresses, mirrors, sewing machines, bundles. There was a woman having a kid with a young girl holding a blanket over her and crying. Scared sick looking at it. It rained all through the evacuation.*

1. On a 1922 stopover in Adrianapolis (present-day Edirne), Hemingway saw Greek Christians fleeing Turkey along the Karagatch road into Greece. Chapter II condenses his *Toronto Star* piece of October 20, 1922, included in this volume (145).

THE DOCTOR AND THE DOCTOR'S WIFE

Dick Boulton came from the Indian camp to cut up logs for Nick's father. He brought his son Eddy and another Indian named Billy Tabeshaw with him. They came in through the back gate out of the woods, Eddy carrying the long cross-cut saw. It flopped over his shoulder and made a musical sound as he walked. Billy Tabeshaw carried two big cant-hooks.[1] Dick had three axes under his arm.

He turned and shut the gate. The others went on ahead of him down to the lake shore where the logs were buried in the sand.

The logs had been lost from the big log booms[2] that were towed down the lake to the mill by the steamer *Magic*. They had drifted up onto the beach and if nothing were done about them sooner or later the crew of the *Magic* would come along the shore in a rowboat, spot the logs, drive an iron spike with a ring on it into the end of each one and then tow them out into the lake to make a new boom. But the lumbermen might never come for them because a few logs were not worth the price of a crew to gather them. If no one came for them they would be left to waterlog and rot on the beach.

Nick's father always assumed that this was what would happen, and hired the Indians to come down from the camp and cut the logs up with the cross-cut saw and split them with a wedge to make cord wood and chunks for the open fireplace. Dick Boulton walked around past the cottage down to the lake. There were four big beech logs lying almost buried in the sand. Eddy hung the saw up by one of its handles in the crotch of a tree. Dick put the three axes down on the little dock. Dick was a half-breed and many of the farmers around the lake believed he was really a white man. He was very lazy but a great worker once he was started. He took a plug of tobacco out of his pocket, bit off a chew and spoke in Ojibway to Eddy and Billy Tabeshaw.

They sunk the ends of their cant-hooks into one of the logs and swung against it to loosen it in the sand. They swung their weight against the shafts of the cant-hooks. The log moved in the sand. Dick Boulton turned to Nick's father.

"Well, Doc," he said, "that's a nice lot of timber you've stolen."

"Don't talk that way, Dick," the doctor said. "It's driftwood."

Eddy and Billy Tabeshaw had rocked the log out of the wet sand and rolled it toward the water.

"Put it right in," Dick Boulton shouted.

"What are you doing that for?" asked the doctor.

---

1. Tools for moving heavy slabs of wood.
2. Logs linked end to end as a floating barrier to collect timber.

"Wash it off. Clean off the sand on account of the saw. I want to see who it belongs to," Dick said.

The log was just awash in the lake. Eddy and Billy Tabeshaw leaned on their cant-hooks sweating in the sun. Dick kneeled down in the sand and looked at the mark of the scaler's hammer in the wood at the end of the log.

"It belongs to White and McNally," he said, standing up and brushing off his trousers knees.

The doctor was very uncomfortable.

"You'd better not saw it up then, Dick," he said, shortly.

"Don't get huffy, Doc," said Dick. "Don't get huffy. I don't care who you steal from. It's none of my business."

"If you think the logs are stolen, leave them alone and take your tools back to the camp," the doctor said. His face was red.

"Don't go off at half cock, Doc," Dick said. He spat tobacco juice on the log. It slid off, thinning in the water. "You know they're stolen as well as I do. It don't make any difference to me."

"All right. If you think the logs are stolen, take your stuff and get out."

"Now, Doc——"

"Take your stuff and get out."

"Listen, Doc."

"If you call me Doc once again, I'll knock your eye teeth down your throat."

"Oh, no, you won't, Doc."

Dick Boulton looked at the doctor. Dick was a big man. He knew how big a man he was. He liked to get into fights. He was happy. Eddy and Billy Tabeshaw leaned on their cant-hooks and looked at the doctor. The doctor chewed the beard on his lower lip and looked at Dick Boulton. Then he turned away and walked up the hill to the cottage. They could see from his back how angry he was. They all watched him walk up the hill and go inside the cottage.

Dick said something in Ojibway. Eddy laughed but Billy Tabeshaw looked very serious. He did not understand English but he had sweat all the time the row was going on. He was fat with only a few hairs of mustache like a Chinaman.[3] He picked up the two cant-hooks. Dick picked up the axes and Eddy took the saw down from the tree. They started off and walked up past the cottage and out the back gate into the woods. Dick left the gate open. Billy Tabeshaw went back and fastened it. They were gone through the woods.

---

3. Hemingway's stereotype associates Native facial features with those of Chinese men, perhaps to impugn the masculinity of both. "Row": quarrel.

In the cottage the doctor, sitting on the bed in his room, saw a pile of medical journals on the floor by the bureau. They were still in their wrappers unopened. It irritated him.

"Aren't you going back to work, dear?" asked the doctor's wife from the room where she was lying with the blinds drawn.

"No!"

"Was anything the matter?"

"I had a row with Dick Boulton."

"Oh," said his wife. "I hope you didn't lose your temper, Henry."

"No," said the doctor.

"Remember, that he who ruleth his spirit is greater than he that taketh a city," said his wife. She was a Christian Scientist. Her Bible, her copy of *Science and Health* and her *Quarterly*[4] were on a table beside her bed in the darkened room.

Her husband did not answer. He was sitting on his bed now, cleaning a shotgun. He pushed the magazine full of the heavy yellow shells and pumped them out again. They were scattered on the bed.

"Henry," his wife called. Then paused a moment. "Henry!"

"Yes," the doctor said.

"You didn't say anything to Boulton to anger him, did you?"

"No," said the doctor.

"What was the trouble about, dear?"

"Nothing much."

"Tell me, Henry. Please don't try and keep anything from me. What was the trouble about?"

"Well, Dick owes me a lot of money for pulling his squaw through pneumonia and I guess he wanted a row so he wouldn't have to take it out in work."

His wife was silent. The doctor wiped his gun carefully with a rag. He pushed the shells back in against the spring of the magazine. He sat with the gun on his knees. He was very fond of it. Then he heard his wife's voice from the darkened room.

"Dear, I don't think, I really don't think that any one would really do a thing like that."

"No?" the doctor said.

"No. I can't really believe that any one would do a thing of that sort intentionally."

The doctor stood up and put the shotgun in the corner behind the dresser.

"Are you going out, dear?" his wife said.

"I think I'll go for a walk," the doctor said.

4. *Christian Science Quarterly.* Founded by Mary Baker Eddy in the 1870s, Christian Science arose in opposition to medical science, and Eddy's book, *Science and Health with Key to the Scriptures* (1875), emphasized spiritual healing while discouraging medical treatment. "He who ruleth . . . taketh a city": Proverbs 16:31–32.

"If you see Nick, dear, will you tell him his mother wants to see him?" his wife said.

The doctor went out on the porch. The screen door slammed behind him. He heard his wife catch her breath when the door slammed.

"Sorry," he said, outside her window with the blinds drawn.

"It's all right, dear," she said.

He walked in the heat out the gate and along the path into the hemlock woods. It was cool in the woods even on such a hot day. He found Nick sitting with his back against a tree, reading.

"Your mother wants you to come and see her," the doctor said.

"I want to go with you," Nick said.

His father looked down at him.

"All right. Come on, then," his father said. "Give me the book, I'll put it in my pocket."

"I know where there's black squirrels, Daddy," Nick said.

"All right," said his father. "Let's go there."

Chapter III

We were in a garden at Mons.[1] *Young Buckley came in with his patrol from across the river. The first German I saw climbed up over the garden wall. We waited till he got one leg over and then potted him. He had so much equipment on and looked awfully surprised and fell down into the garden. Then three more came over further down the wall. We shot them. They all came just like that.*

1. This glimpse of the Battle of Mons (Belgium), on August 23, 1914, probably derives from the eyewitness account of Hemingway's friend Captain Eric Dorman-Smith, a British officer he met in Milan, Italy, in 1918.

THE END OF SOMETHING

In the old days Hortons Bay was a lumbering town.[1] No one who lived in it was out of sound of the big saws in the mill by the lake. Then one year there were no more logs to make lumber. The lumber schooners came into the bay and were loaded with the cut of the mill that stood stacked in the yard. All the piles of lumber were carried away. The big mill building had all its machinery that was removable taken out and hoisted on board one of the schooners by the men who had worked in the mill. The schooner moved out of the bay toward the open lake carrying the two great saws, the travelling carriage that hurled the logs against the revolving, circular saws and all the rollers, wheels, belts and iron piled on a hull-deep load of lumber. Its open hold covered with canvas and lashed tight, the sails of the schooner filled and it moved out into the open lake, carrying with it everything that had made the mill a mill and Hortons Bay a town.

The one-story bunk houses, the eating-house, the company store, the mill offices, and the big mill itself stood deserted in the acres of sawdust that covered the swampy meadow by the shore of the bay.

Ten years later there was nothing of the mill left except the broken white limestone of its foundations showing through the swampy second growth as Nick and Marjorie rowed along the shore. They were trolling[2] along the edge of the channel-bank where the bottom dropped off suddenly from sandy shallows to twelve feet of dark water. They were trolling on their way to the point to set night lines for rainbow trout.

"There's our old ruin, Nick," Marjorie said.

Nick, rowing, looked at the white stone in the green trees.

"There it is," he said.

"Can you remember when it was a mill?" Marjorie asked.

"I can just remember," Nick said.

"It seems more like a castle," Marjorie said.

Nick said nothing. They rowed on out of sight of the mill, following the shore line. Then Nick cut across the bay.

"They aren't striking," he said.

"No," Marjorie said. She was intent on the rod all the time they trolled, even when she talked. She loved to fish. She loved to fish with Nick.

---

1. The lumber mill at Horton Bay in Michigan was built in 1876 but closed soon after the turn of the century when the local timber was gone.
2. Here, fishing from a slow-moving boat. Marjorie Bump, a Michigan girl who fished and swam with Hemingway, became a temporary object of affection in late 1919, when he was in Petoskey, recovering from heartbreak and learning to write.

Close beside the boat a big trout broke the surface of the water. Nick pulled hard on one oar so the boat would turn and the bait spinning far behind would pass where the trout was feeding. As the trout's back came up out of the water the minnows jumped wildly. They sprinkled the surface like a handful of shot thrown into the water. Another trout broke water, feeding on the other side of the boat.

"They're feeding," Marjorie said.

"But they won't strike," Nick said.

He rowed the boat around to troll past both the feeding fish, then headed it for the point. Marjorie did not reel in until the boat touched the shore.

They pulled the boat up the beach and Nick lifted out a pail of live perch. The perch swam in the water in the pail. Nick caught three of them with his hands and cut their heads off and skinned them while Marjorie chased with her hands in the bucket, finally caught a perch, cut its head off and skinned it. Nick looked at her fish.

"You don't want to take the ventral fin out," he said. "It'll be all right for bait but it's better with the ventral fin in."

He hooked each of the skinned perch through the tail. There were two hooks attached to a leader on each rod. Then Marjorie rowed the boat out over the channel-bank, holding the line in her teeth, and looking toward Nick, who stood on the shore holding the rod and letting the line run out from the reel.

"That's about right," he called.

"Should I let it drop?" Marjorie called back, holding the line in her hand.

"Sure. Let it go." Marjorie dropped the line overboard and watched the baits go down through the water.

She came in with the boat and ran the second line out the same way. Each time Nick set a heavy slab of driftwood across the butt of the rod to hold it solid and propped it up at an angle with a small slab. He reeled in the slack line so the line ran taut out to where the bait rested on the sandy floor of the channel and set the click on the reel. When a trout, feeding on the bottom, took the bait it would run with it, taking line out of the reel in a rush and making the reel sing with the click on.

Marjorie rowed up the point a little way so she would not disturb the line. She pulled hard on the oars and the boat went way up the beach. Little waves came in with it. Marjorie stepped out of the boat and Nick pulled the boat high up the beach.

"What's the matter, Nick?" Marjorie asked.

"I don't know," Nick said, getting wood for a fire.

They made a fire with driftwood. Marjorie went to the boat and brought a blanket. The evening breeze blew the smoke toward the point, so Marjorie spread the blanket out between the fire and the lake.

Marjorie sat on the blanket with her back to the fire and waited for Nick. He came over and sat down beside her on the blanket. In back of them was the close second-growth timber of the point and in front was the bay with the mouth of Hortons Creek. It was not quite dark. The fire-light went as far as the water. They could both see the two steel rods at an angle over the dark water. The fire glinted on the reels.

Marjorie unpacked the basket of supper.

"I don't feel like eating," said Nick.

"Come on and eat, Nick."

"All right."

They ate without talking, and watched the two rods and the fire-light in the water.

"There's going to be a moon tonight," said Nick. He looked across the bay to the hills that were beginning to sharpen against the sky. Beyond the hills he knew the moon was coming up.

"I know it," Marjorie said happily.

"You know everything," Nick said.

"Oh, Nick, please cut it out! Please, please don't be that way!"

"I can't help it," Nick said. "You do. You know everything. That's the trouble. You know you do."

Marjorie did not say anything.

"I've taught you everything. You know you do. What don't you know, anyway?"

"Oh, shut up," Marjorie said. "There comes the moon."

They sat on the blanket without touching each other and watched the moon rise.

"You don't have to talk silly," Marjorie said. "What's really the matter?"

"I don't know."

"Of course you know."

"No I don't."

"Go on and say it."

Nick looked on at the moon, coming up over the hills.

"It isn't fun any more."

He was afraid to look at Marjorie. Then he looked at her. She sat there with her back toward him. He looked at her back. "It isn't fun any more. Not any of it."

She didn't say anything. He went on. "I feel as though everything was gone to hell inside of me. I don't know, Marge. I don't know what to say."

He looked on at her back.

"Isn't love any fun?" Marjorie said.

"No," Nick said. Marjorie stood up. Nick sat there, his head in his hands.

"I'm going to take the boat," Marjorie called to him. "You can walk back around the point."

"All right," Nick said. "I'll push the boat off for you."

"You don't need to," she said. She was afloat in the boat on the water with the moonlight on it. Nick went back and lay down with his face in the blanket by the fire. He could hear Marjorie rowing on the water.

He lay there for a long time. He lay there while he heard Bill come into the clearing walking around through the woods.[3] He felt Bill coming up to the fire. Bill didn't touch him, either.

"Did she go all right?" Bill said.

"Yes," Nick said, lying, his face on the blanket.

"Have a scene?"

"No, there wasn't any scene."

"How do you feel?"

"Oh, go away, Bill! Go away for a while."

Bill selected a sandwich from the lunch basket and walked over to have a look at the rods.

---

3. The character of Bill recalls Bill Smith, a summer friend from St. Louis and one of Hemingway's closest fishing companions.

Chapter IV

It was a frightfully hot day.[1] *We'd jammed an absolutely perfect barricade across the bridge. It was simply priceless. A big old wrought-iron grating from the front of a house. Too heavy to lift and you could shoot through it and they would have to climb over it. It was absolutely topping. They tried to get over it, and we potted them from forty yards. They rushed it, and officers came out alone and worked on it. It was an absolutely perfect obstacle. Their officers were very fine. We were frightfully put out when we heard the flank had gone, and we had to fall back.*

1. As described to Hemingway by Eric Dorman-Smith (see note 1 on 21).

THE THREE-DAY BLOW[1]

The rain stopped as Nick turned into the road that went up through the orchard. The fruit had been picked and the fall wind blew through the bare trees. Nick stopped and picked up a Wagner apple[2] from beside the road, shiny in the brown grass from the rain. He put the apple in the pocket of his Mackinaw coat.[3]

The road came out of the orchard on to the top of the hill. There was the cottage, the porch bare, smoke coming from the chimney. In back was the garage, the chicken coop and the second-growth timber like a hedge against the woods behind. The big trees swayed far over in the wind as he watched. It was the first of the autumn storms.

As Nick crossed the open field above the orchard the door of the cottage opened and Bill came out. He stood on the porch looking out.

"Well, Wemedge,"[4] he said.

"Hey, Bill," Nick said, coming up the steps.

They stood together, looking out across the country, down over the orchard, beyond the road, across the lower fields and the woods of the point to the lake. The wind was blowing straight down the lake. They could see the surf along Ten Mile point.

"She's blowing," Nick said.

"She'll blow like that for three days," Bill said.

"Is your dad in?" Nick said.

"No. He's out with the gun. Come on in."

Nick went inside the cottage. There was a big fire in the fireplace. The wind made it roar. Bill shut the door.

"Have a drink?" he said.

He went out to the kitchen and came back with two glasses and a pitcher of water. Nick reached the whisky bottle from the shelf above the fireplace.

"All right?" he said.

"Good," said Bill.

They sat in front of the fire and drank the Irish whisky and water.

"It's got a swell, smoky taste," Nick said, and looked at the fire through the glass.

"That's the peat," Bill said.[5]

---

1. Hemingway composed this story shortly after he wrote "The End of Something."
2. Correctly spelled "Wagener," a variety that originated in New York.
3. The references to "second-growth timber" allude to the history of Michigan deforestation; the short plaid wool jacket was popularized in the 1800s by lumberjacks around Mackinac City.
4. Nickname for Hemingway used by Bill Smith and other fishing friends.
5. Collected from bogs and cut into bricks, peat has long provided fuel for distilleries and gives Irish whiskey its smoky taste.

"You can't get peat into liquor," Nick said.

"That doesn't make any difference," Bill said.

"You ever seen any peat?" Nick asked.

"No," said Bill.

"Neither have I," Nick said.

His shoes, stretched out on the hearth, began to steam in front of the fire.

"Better take your shoes off," Bill said.

"I haven't got any socks on."

"Take them off and dry them and I'll get you some," Bill said. He went upstairs into the loft and Nick heard him walking about overhead. Upstairs was open under the roof and was where Bill and his father and he, Nick, sometimes slept. In back was a dressing room. They moved the cots back out of the rain and covered them with rubber blankets.

Bill came down with a pair of heavy wool socks.

"It's getting too late to go around without socks," he said.

"I hate to start them again," Nick said. He pulled the socks on and slumped back in the chair, putting his feet up on the screen in front of the fire.

"You'll dent in the screen," Bill said. Nick swung his feet over to the side of the fireplace.

"Got anything to read?" he asked.

"Only the paper."

"What did the Cards do?"

"Dropped a double header to the Giants."

"That ought to cinch it for them."

"It's a gift," Bill said. "As long as McGraw can buy every good ball player in the league there's nothing to it."

"He can't buy them all," Nick said.

"He buys all the ones he wants," Bill said. "Or he makes them discontented so they have to trade them to him."

"Like Heinie Zim," Nick agreed.

"That bonehead will do him a lot of good."[6]

Bill stood up.

"He can hit," Nick offered. The heat from the fire was baking his legs.

"He's a sweet fielder, too," Bill said. "But he loses ball games."

"Maybe that's what McGraw wants him for," Nick suggested.

"Maybe," Bill agreed.

---

6. Nick's question about the "Cards" (St. Louis Cardinals) raises the topic of the National League's New York Giants under manager John McGraw. The reference to Heinie Zim (Henry Zimmerman) seems to place the story in late 1917, after the Giants lost the World Series, thanks partly to Zimmerman's poor hitting and to a controversial "bonehead" play by the third baseman.

"There's always more to it than we know about," Nick said.

"Of course. But we've got pretty good dope for being so far away."

"Like how much better you can pick them if you don't see the horses."

"That's it."

Bill reached down the whisky bottle. His big hand went all the way around it. He poured the whisky into the glass Nick held out.

"How much water?"

"Just the same."

He sat down on the floor beside Nick's chair.

"It's good when the fall storms come, isn't it?" Nick said.

"It's swell."

"It's the best time of year," Nick said.

"Wouldn't it be hell to be in town?" Bill said.

"I'd like to see the World Series," Nick said.

"Well, they're always in New York or Philadelphia now," Bill said. "That doesn't do us any good."

"I wonder if the Cards will ever win a pennant?"

"Not in our lifetime," Bill said.

"Gee, they'd go crazy," Nick said.

"Do you remember when they got going that once before they had the train wreck?"[7]

"Boy!" Nick said, remembering.

Bill reached over to the table under the window for the book that lay there, face down, where he had put it when he went to the door. He held his glass in one hand and the book in the other, leaning back against Nick's chair.

"What are you reading?"

"*Richard Feverel.*"

"I couldn't get into it."

"It's all right," Bill said. "It ain't a bad book, Wemedge."[8]

"What else have you got I haven't read?" Nick asked.

"Did you read the *Forest Lovers?*"

"Yup. That's the one where they go to bed every night with the naked sword between them."

"That's a good book, Wemedge."

---

7. The Cardinals were playing well until July 11, 1911, when their train derailed in Bridge-port, Connecticut. Completely unscathed, the players helped pull victims—including fourteen fatalities—from the wreckage. The Cardinals finished fifth in the National League that year, with a mediocre record.

8. These English novels suggest possible influences on the Nick Adams stories, especially George Meredith's novel *The Ordeal of Richard Feverel: A History of Father and Son* (1859), which portrays sexual desire as uncontrollable. Other works cited here include Maurice Hewlett's first novel, *The Forest Lovers* (1898); Hugh Walpole's *Fortitude* (1913) and *The Dark Forest* (1916); and G. K. Chesterton's *The Flying Inn* (1914), a futuristic satire of temperance.

"It's a swell book. What I couldn't ever understand was what good the sword would do. It would have to stay edge up all the time because if it went over flat you could roll right over it and it wouldn't make any trouble."

"It's a symbol," Bill said.

"Sure," said Nick, "but it isn't practical."

"Did you ever read *Fortitude?*"

"It's fine," Nick said. "That's a real book. That's where his old man is after him all the time. Have you got any more by Walpole?"

"*The Dark Forest,*" Bill said. "It's about Russia."

"What does he know about Russia?" Nick asked.

"I don't know. You can't ever tell about those guys. Maybe he was there when he was a boy. He's got a lot of dope on it."

"I'd like to meet him," Nick said.

"I'd like to meet Chesterton," Bill said.

"I wish he was here now," Nick said. "We'd take him fishing to the 'Voix tomorrow."[9]

"I wonder if he'd like to go fishing," Bill said.

"Sure," said Nick. "He must be about the best guy there is. Do you remember the *Flying Inn?*"

> "'If an angel out of heaven
> Gives you something else to drink,
> Thank him for his kind intentions;
> Go and pour them down the sink.'"

"That's right," said Nick. "I guess he's a better guy than Walpole."

"Oh, he's a better guy, all right," Bill said.

"But Walpole's a better writer."

"I don't know," Nick said. "Chesterton's a classic."

"Walpole's a classic, too," Bill insisted.

"I wish we had them both here," Nick said. "We'd take them both fishing to the 'Voix tomorrow."

"Let's get drunk," Bill said.

"All right," Nick agreed.

"My old man won't care," Bill said.

"Are you sure?" said Nick.

"I know it," Bill said.

"I'm a little drunk now," Nick said.

"You aren't drunk," Bill said.

He got up from the floor and reached for the whisky bottle. Nick held out his glass. His eyes fixed on it while Bill poured.

Bill poured the glass half full of whisky.

---

9. I.e., to Charlevoix, probably to fish the Pine River or Round Lake, connecting Lake Charlevoix to Lake Michigan. The lyrics below are from Chesterton's poem "The Song of Right and Wrong," a defense of red wine.

"Put in your own water," he said. "There's just one more shot."

"Got any more?" Nick asked.

"There's plenty more but dad only likes me to drink what's open."

"Sure," said Nick.

"He says opening bottles is what makes drunkards," Bill explained.

"That's right," said Nick. He was impressed. He had never thought of that before. He had always thought it was solitary drinking that made drunkards.

"How is your dad?" he asked respectfully.

"He's all right," Bill said. "He gets a little wild sometimes."

"He's a swell guy," Nick said. He poured water into his glass out of the pitcher. It mixed slowly with the whisky. There was more whisky than water.

"You bet your life he is," Bill said.

"My old man's all right," Nick said.

"You're damn right he is," said Bill.

"He claims he's never taken a drink in his life," Nick said, as though announcing a scientific fact.

"Well, he's a doctor. My old man's a painter. That's different."

"He's missed a lot," Nick said sadly.

"You can't tell," Bill said. "Everything's got its compensations."

"He says he's missed a lot himself," Nick confessed.

"Well, dad's had a tough time," Bill said.

"It all evens up," Nick said.

They sat looking into the fire and thinking of this profound truth.

"I'll get a chunk from the back porch," Nick said. He had noticed while looking into the fire that the fire was dying down. Also he wished to show he could hold his liquor and be practical. Even if his father had never touched a drop Bill was not going to get him drunk before he himself was drunk.

"Bring one of the big beech chunks," Bill said. He was also being consciously practical.

Nick came in with the log through the kitchen and in passing knocked a pan off the kitchen table. He laid the log down and picked up the pan. It had contained dried apricots, soaking in water. He carefully picked up all the apricots off the floor, some of them had gone under the stove, and put them back in the pan. He dipped some more water onto them from the pail by the table. He felt quite proud of himself. He had been thoroughly practical.

He came in carrying the log and Bill got up from the chair and helped him put it on the fire.

"That's a swell log," Nick said.

"I'd been saving it for the bad weather," Bill said. "A log like that will burn all night."

"There'll be coals left to start the fire in the morning," Nick said.

"That's right," Bill agreed. They were conducting the conversation on a high plane.

"Let's have another drink," Nick said.

"I think there's another bottle open in the locker," Bill said.

He kneeled down in the corner in front of the locker and brought out a square-faced bottle.

"It's Scotch," he said.

"I'll get some more water," Nick said. He went out into the kitchen again. He filled the pitcher with the dipper dipping cold spring water from the pail. On his way back to the living room he passed a mirror in the dining room and looked in it. His face looked strange. He smiled at the face in the mirror and it grinned back at him. He winked at it and went on. It was not his face but it didn't make any difference.

Bill had poured out the drinks.

"That's an awfully big shot," Nick said.

"Not for us, Wemedge," Bill said.

"What'll we drink to?" Nick asked, holding up the glass.

"Let's drink to fishing," Bill said.

"All right," Nick said. "Gentlemen, I give you fishing."

"All fishing," Bill said. "Everywhere."

"Fishing," Nick said. "That's what we drink to."

"It's better than baseball," Bill said.

"There isn't any comparison," said Nick. "How did we ever get talking about baseball?"

"It was a mistake," Bill said. "Baseball is a game for louts."

They drank all that was in their glasses.

"Now let's drink to Chesterton."

"And Walpole," Nick interposed.

Nick poured out the liquor. Bill poured in the water. They looked at each other. They felt very fine.

"Gentlemen," Bill said, "I give you Chesterton and Walpole."

"Exactly, gentlemen," Nick said.

They drank. Bill filled up the glasses. They sat down in the big chairs in front of the fire.

"You were very wise, Wemedge," Bill said.

"What do you mean?" asked Nick.

"To bust off that Marge business," Bill said.

"I guess so," said Nick.

"It was the only thing to do. If you hadn't, by now you'd be back home working trying to get enough money to get married."

Nick said nothing.

"Once a man's married he's absolutely bitched," Bill went on. "He hasn't got anything more. Nothing. Not a damn thing. He's done for. You've seen the guys that get married."

Nick said nothing.

"You can tell them," Bill said. "They get this sort of fat married look. They're done for."

"Sure," said Nick.

"It was probably bad busting it off," Bill said. "But you always fall for somebody else and then it's all right. Fall for them but don't let them ruin you."

"Yes," said Nick.

"If you'd have married her you would have had to marry the whole family. Remember her mother and that guy she married."

Nick nodded.

"Imagine having them around the house all the time and going to Sunday dinners at their house, and having them over to dinner and her telling Marge all the time what to do and how to act."

Nick sat quiet.

"You came out of it damned well," Bill said. "Now she can marry somebody of her own sort and settle down and be happy. You can't mix oil and water and you can't mix that sort of thing any more than if I'd marry Ida that works for Strattons. She'd probably like it, too."

Nick said nothing. The liquor had all died out of him and left him alone. Bill wasn't there. He wasn't sitting in front of the fire or going fishing tomorrow with Bill and his dad or anything. He wasn't drunk. It was all gone. All he knew was that he had once had Marjorie and that he had lost her. She was gone and he had sent her away. That was all that mattered. He might never see her again. Probably he never would. It was all gone, finished.

"Let's have another drink," Nick said.

Bill poured it out. Nick splashed in a little water.

"If you'd gone on that way we wouldn't be here now," Bill said.

That was true. His original plan had been to go down home and get a job. Then he had planned to stay in Charlevoix all winter so he could be near Marge. Now he did not know what he was going to do.

"Probably we wouldn't even be going fishing tomorrow," Bill said. "You had the right dope, all right."

"I couldn't help it," Nick said.

"I know. That's the way it works out," Bill said.

"All of a sudden everything was over," Nick said. "I don't know why it was. I couldn't help it. Just like when the three-day blows come now and rip all the leaves off the trees."

"Well, it's over. That's the point," Bill said.

"It was my fault," Nick said.

"It doesn't make any difference whose fault it was," Bill said.

"No, I suppose not," Nick said.

The big thing was that Marjorie was gone and that probably he would never see her again. He had talked to her about how they would go to Italy together and the fun they would have. Places they would be together. It was all gone now.

"So long as it's over that's all that matters," Bill said. "I tell you, Wemedge, I was worried while it was going on. You played it right. I understand her mother is sore as hell. She told a lot of people you were engaged."

"We weren't engaged," Nick said.

"It was all around that you were."

"I can't help it," Nick said. "We weren't."

"Weren't you going to get married?" Bill asked.

"Yes. But we weren't engaged," Nick said.

"What's the difference?" Bill asked judicially.

"I don't know. There's a difference."

"I don't see it," said Bill.

"All right," said Nick. "Let's get drunk."

"All right," Bill said. "Let's get really drunk."

"Let's get drunk and then go swimming," Nick said.

He drank off his glass.

"I'm sorry as hell about her but what could I do?" he said. "You know what her mother was like!"

"She was terrible," Bill said.

"All of a sudden it was over," Nick said. "I oughtn't to talk about it."

"You aren't," Bill said. "I talked about it and now I'm through. We won't ever speak about it again. You don't want to think about it. You might get back into it again."

Nick had not thought about that. It had seemed so absolute. That was a thought. That made him feel better.

"Sure," he said. "There's always that danger."

He felt happy now. There was not anything that was irrevocable. He might go into town Saturday night. Today was Thursday.

"There's always a chance," he said.

"You'll have to watch yourself," Bill said.

"I'll watch myself," he said.

He felt happy. Nothing was finished. Nothing was ever lost. He would go into town on Saturday. He felt lighter, as he had felt before Bill started to talk about it. There was always a way out.

"Let's take the guns and go down to the point and look for your dad," Nick said.

"All right."

Bill took down the two shotguns from the rack on the wall. He opened a box of shells. Nick put on his Mackinaw coat and his shoes. His shoes were stiff from the drying. He was still quite drunk but his head was clear.

"How do you feel?" Nick asked.

"Swell. I've just got a good edge on." Bill was buttoning up his sweater.

"There's no use getting drunk."

"No. We ought to get outdoors."

They stepped out the door. The wind was blowing a gale.

"The birds will lie right down in the grass with this," Nick said.

They struck down toward the orchard.

"I saw a woodcock this morning," Bill said.

"Maybe we'll jump him," Nick said.

"You can't shoot in this wind," Bill said.

Outside now the Marge business was no longer so tragic. It was not even very important. The wind blew everything like that away.

"It's coming right off the big lake," Nick said.

Against the wind they heard the thud of a shotgun.

"That's dad," Bill said. "He's down in the swamp."

"Let's cut down that way," Nick said.

"Let's cut across the lower meadow and see if we jump anything," Bill said.

"All right," Nick said.

None of it was important now. The wind blew it out of his head. Still he could always go into town Saturday night. It was a good thing to have in reserve.

Chapter V

They shot the six cabinet ministers at half-past six in the morning against the wall of a hospital. There were pools of water in the court-yard. There were wet dead leaves on the paving of the courtyard. It rained hard. All the shutters of the hospital were nailed shut. One of the ministers was sick with typhoid. Two soldiers carried him down-stairs and out into the rain. They tried to hold him up against the wall but he sat down in a puddle of water. The other five stood very quietly against the wall. Finally the officer told the soldiers it was no good try-ing to make him stand up. When they fired the first volley he was sitting down in the water with his head on his knees.[1]

---

1. Hemingway drew the details of this vignette from a report in the Paris edition of the *Chicago Tribune* on November 28, 1922, of six Greek cabinet ministers executed by the military junta that seized government control when King Constantine abdicated upon Turkey's defeat of the Greek army.

THE BATTLER[1]

Nick stood up. He was all right. He looked up the track at the lights of the caboose going out of sight around the curve. There was water on both sides of the track, then tamarack swamp.[2]

He felt of his knee. The pants were torn and the skin was barked. His hands were scraped and there were sand and cinders driven up under his nails. He went over to the edge of the track down the little slope to the water and washed his hands. He washed them carefully in the cold water, getting the dirt out from the nails. He squatted down and bathed his knee.

That lousy crut of a brakeman. He would get him some day. He would know him again. That was a fine way to act.

"Come here, kid," he said. "I got something for you."

He had fallen for it. What a lousy kid thing to have done. They would never suck him in that way again.

"Come here, kid, I got something for you." Then *wham* and he lit on his hands and knees beside the track.

Nick rubbed his eye. There was a big bump coming up. He would have a black eye, all right. It ached already. That son of a crutting brakeman.

He touched the bump over his eye with his fingers. Oh, well, it was only a black eye. That was all he had gotten out of it. Cheap at the price. He wished he could see it. Could not see it looking into the water, though. It was dark and he was a long way off from anywhere. He wiped his hands on his trousers and stood up, then climbed the embankment to the rails.

He started up the track. It was well ballasted and made easy walking, sand and gravel packed between the ties, solid walking. The smooth roadbed like a causeway went on ahead through the swamp. Nick walked along. He must get to somewhere.

Nick had swung on to the freight train when it slowed down for the yards outside of Walton Junction. The train, with Nick on it, had passed through Kalkaska as it started to get dark. Now he must be nearly to Mancelona.[3] Three or four miles of swamp. He stepped along the track, walking so he kept on the ballast between the ties, the swamp ghostly in the rising mist. His eye ached and he was

---

1. Hemingway added this story to the volume belatedly to replace the objectionable "Up in Michigan."
2. The tamarack tree, a coniferous larch, thrives in swampy areas of Canada and the northeastern U.S.
3. Heading north, Nick has hopped the train at a desolate railway junction southeast of Traverse City and thirty miles later has been dropped near Mancelona, twenty-seven miles south of Walloon Lake. See map (4).

hungry. He kept on hiking, putting the miles of track back of him. The swamp was all the same on both sides of the track.

Ahead there was a bridge. Nick crossed it, his boots ringing hollow on the iron. Down below the water showed black between the slits of ties. Nick kicked a loose spike and it dropped into the water. Beyond the bridge were hills. It was high and dark on both sides of the track. Up the track Nick saw a fire.

He came up the track toward the fire carefully. It was off to one side of the track, below the railway embankment. He had only seen the light from it. The track came out through a cut and where the fire was burning the country opened out and fell away into woods. Nick dropped carefully down the embankment and cut into the woods to come up to the fire through the trees. It was a beechwood forest and the fallen beechnut burrs were under his shoes as he walked between the trees. The fire was bright now, just at the edge of the trees. There was a man sitting by it. Nick waited behind the tree and watched. The man looked to be alone. He was sitting there with his head in his hands looking at the fire. Nick stepped out and walked into the firelight.

The man sat there looking into the fire. When Nick stopped quite close to him he did not move.

"Hello!" Nick said.

The man looked up.

"Where did you get the shiner?" he said.

"A brakeman busted me."

"Off the through freight?"

"Yes."

"I saw the bastard," the man said. "He went through here 'bout an hour and a half ago. He was walking along the top of the cars slapping his arms and singing."

"The bastard!"

"It must have made him feel good to bust you," the man said seriously.

"I'll bust him."

"Get him with a rock sometime when he's going through," the man advised.

"I'll get him."

"You're a tough one, aren't you?"

"No," Nick answered.

"All you kids are tough."

"You got to be tough," Nick said.

"That's what I said."

The man looked at Nick and smiled. In the firelight Nick saw that his face was misshapen. His nose was sunken, his eyes were slits, he had queer-shaped lips. Nick did not perceive all this at once, he only saw the man's face was queerly formed and mutilated. It was like putty in color. Dead looking in the firelight.

"Don't you like my pan?"[4] the man asked.

Nick was embarrassed.

"Sure," he said.

"Look here!" the man took off his cap.

He had only one ear. It was thickened and tight against the side of his head. Where the other ear should have been there was a stump.

"Ever see one like that?"

"No," said Nick. It made him a little sick.

"I could take it," the man said. "Don't you think I could take it, kid?"

"You bet!"

"They all bust their hands on me," the little man said. "They couldn't hurt me."

He looked at Nick. "Sit down," he said. "Want to eat?"

"Don't bother," Nick said. "I'm going on to the town."

"Listen!" the man said. "Call me Ad."

"Sure!"

"Listen," the little man said. "I'm not quite right."

"What's the matter?"

"I'm crazy."

He put on his cap. Nick felt like laughing.

"You're all right," he said.

"No, I'm not. I'm crazy. Listen, you ever been crazy?"

"No," Nick said. "How does it get you?"

"I don't know," Ad said. "When you got it you don't know about it. You know me, don't you?"

"No."

"I'm Ad Francis."

"Honest to God?"

"Don't you believe it?"

"Yes."

Nick knew it must be true.

"You know how I beat them?"

"No," Nick said.

"My heart's slow. It only beats forty a minute. Feel it."

Nick hesitated.

"Come on," the man took hold of his hand. "Take hold of my wrist. Put your fingers there."

The little man's wrist was thick and the muscles bulged above the bone. Nick felt the slow pumping under his fingers.

"Got a watch?"

4. Face.

"No."

"Neither have I," Ad said. "It ain't any good if you haven't got a watch."

Nick dropped his wrist.

"Listen," Ad Francis said. "Take ahold again. You count and I'll count up to sixty."

Feeling the slow hard throb under his fingers Nick started to count. He heard the little man counting slowly, one, two, three, four, five, and on—aloud.

"Sixty," Ad finished. "That's a minute. What did you make it?"

"Forty," Nick said.

"That's right," Ad said happily. "She never speeds up."

A man dropped down the railroad embankment and came across the clearing to the fire.

"Hello, Bugs!" Ad said.

"Hello!" Bugs answered. It was a negro's voice. Nick knew from the way he walked that he was a negro. He stood with his back to them, bending over the fire. He straightened up.

"This is my pal Bugs," Ad said. "He's crazy, too."

"Glad to meet you," Bugs said. "Where you say you're from?"

"Chicago," Nick said.

"That's a fine town," the negro said. "I didn't catch your name."

"Adams. Nick Adams."

"He says he's never been crazy, Bugs," Ad said.

"He's got a lot coming to him," the negro said. He was unwrapping a package by the fire.

"When are we going to eat, Bugs?" the prizefighter asked.

"Right away."

"Are you hungry, Nick?"

"Hungry as hell."

"Hear that, Bugs?"

"I hear most of what goes on."

"That ain't what I asked you."

"Yes. I heard what the gentleman said."

Into a skillet he was laying slices of ham. As the skillet grew hot the grease sputtered and Bugs, crouching on long nigger[5] legs over the fire, turned the ham and broke eggs into the skillet, tipping it from side to side to baste the eggs with the hot fat.

"Will you cut some bread out of that bag, Mister Adams?" Bugs turned from the fire.

"Sure."

---

5. Although the narrator most often uses the word "negro," this slur (which recurs) exposes the racism of the era. The critical essay by Marc Kevin Dudley on race in "The Battler" (285) illuminates the story's cultural context.

Nick reached in the bag and brought out a loaf of bread. He cut six slices. Ad watched him and leaned forward.

"Let me take your knife, Nick," he said.

"No, you don't," the negro said. "Hang onto your knife, Mister Adams."

The prizefighter sat back.

"Will you bring me the bread, Mister Adams?" Bugs asked. Nick brought it over.

"Do you like to dip your bread in the ham fat?" the negro asked.

"You bet!"

"Perhaps we'd better wait until later. It's better at the finish of the meal. Here."

The negro picked up a slice of ham and laid it on one of the pieces of bread, then slid an egg on top of it.

"Just close that sandwich, will you, please, and give it to Mister Francis."

Ad took the sandwich and started eating.

"Watch out how that egg runs," the negro warned. "This is for you, Mister Adams. The remainder for myself."

Nick bit into the sandwich. The negro was sitting opposite him beside Ad. The hot fried ham and eggs tasted wonderful.

"Mister Adams is right hungry," the negro said. The little man whom Nick knew by name as a former champion fighter was silent. He had said nothing since the negro had spoken about the knife.

"May I offer you a slice of bread dipped right in the hot ham fat?" Bugs said.

"Thanks a lot."

The little white man looked at Nick.

"Will you have some, Mister Adolph Francis?" Bugs offered from the skillet.

Ad did not answer. He was looking at Nick.

"Mister Francis?" came the nigger's soft voice.

Ad did not answer. He was looking at Nick.

"I spoke to you, Mister Francis," the nigger said softly.

Ad kept on looking at Nick. He had his cap down over his eyes. Nick felt nervous.

"How the hell do you get that way?" came out from under the cap sharply at Nick.

"Who the hell do you think you are? You're a snotty bastard. You come in here where nobody asks you and eat a man's food and when he asks to borrow a knife you get snotty."

He glared at Nick, his face was white and his eyes almost out of sight under the cap.

"You're a hot sketch. Who the hell asked you to butt in here?"

"Nobody."

"You're damn right nobody did. Nobody asked you to stay either. You come in here and act snotty about my face and smoke my cigars and drink my liquor and then talk snotty. Where the hell do you think you get off?"

Nick said nothing. Ad stood up.

"I'll tell you, you yellow-livered Chicago bastard. You're going to get your can knocked off. Do you get that?"

Nick stepped back. The little man came toward him slowly, stepping flat-footed forward, his left foot stepping forward, his right dragging up to it.

"Hit me," he moved his head. "Try and hit me."

"I don't want to hit you."

"You won't get out of it that way. You're going to take a beating, see? Come on and lead at me."

"Cut it out," Nick said.

"All right, then, you bastard."

The little man looked down at Nick's feet. As he looked down the negro, who had followed behind him as he moved away from the fire, set himself and tapped him across the base of the skull. He fell forward and Bugs dropped the cloth-wrapped blackjack on the grass. The little man lay there, his face in the grass. The negro picked him up, his head hanging, and carried him to the fire. His face looked bad, the eyes open. Bugs laid him down gently.

"Will you bring me the water in the bucket, Mister Adams," he said. "I'm afraid I hit him just a little hard."

The negro splashed water with his hand on the man's face and pulled his ears gently. The eyes closed.

Bugs stood up.

"He's all right," he said. "There's nothing to worry about. I'm sorry, Mister Adams."

"It's all right." Nick was looking down at the little man. He saw the blackjack on the grass and picked it up. It had a flexible handle and was limber in his hand. It was made of worn black leather with a handkerchief wrapped around the heavy end.

"That's a whalebone handle," the negro smiled. "They don't make them any more. I didn't know how well you could take care of yourself and, anyway, I didn't want you to hurt him or mark him up no more than he is."

The negro smiled again.

"You hurt him yourself."

"I know how to do it. He won't remember nothing of it. I have to do it to change him when he gets that way."

Nick was still looking down at the little man, lying, his eyes closed in the firelight. Bugs put some wood on the fire.

"Don't you worry about him none, Mister Adams. I seen him like this plenty of times before."

"What made him crazy?" Nick asked.

"Oh, a lot of things," the negro answered from the fire. "Would you like a cup of this coffee, Mister Adams?"

He handed Nick the cup and smoothed the coat he had placed under the unconscious man's head.

"He took too many beatings, for one thing," the negro sipped the coffee. "But that just made him sort of simple. Then his sister was his manager and they was always being written up in the papers all about brothers and sisters and how she loved her brother and how he loved his sister, and then they got married in New York and that made a lot of unpleasantness."

"I remember about it."

"Sure. Of course they wasn't brother and sister no more than a rabbit, but there was a lot of people didn't like it either way and they commenced to have disagreements, and one day she just went off and never come back."

He drank the coffee and wiped his lips with the pink palm of his hand.

"He just went crazy. Will you have some more coffee, Mister Adams?"

"Thanks."

"I seen her a couple of times," the negro went on. "She was an awful good-looking woman. Looked enough like him to be twins. He wouldn't be bad-looking without his face all busted."

He stopped. The story seemed to be over.

"Where did you meet him?" asked Nick.

"I met him in jail," the negro said. "He was busting people all the time after she went away and they put him in jail. I was in for cuttin' a man."

He smiled, and went on soft-voiced:

"Right away I liked him and when I got out I looked him up. He likes to think I'm crazy and I don't mind. I like to be with him and I like seeing the country and I don't have to commit no larceny to do it. I like living like a gentleman."

"What do you all do?" Nick asked.

"Oh, nothing. Just move around. He's got money."

"He must have made a lot of money."

"Sure. He spent all his money, though. Or they took it away from him. She sends him money."

He poked up the fire.

"She's a mighty fine woman," he said. "She looks enough like him to be his own twin."

The negro looked over at the little man, lying breathing heavily. His blond hair was down over his forehead. His mutilated face looked childish in repose.

"I can wake him up any time now, Mister Adams. If you don't mind I wish you'd sort of pull out. I don't like to not be hospitable, but it might disturb him back again to see you. I hate to have to thump him and it's the only thing to do when he gets started. I have to sort of keep him away from people. You don't mind, do you, Mister Adams? No, don't thank me, Mister Adams. I'd have warned you about him but he seemed to have taken such a liking to you and I thought things were going to be all right. You'll hit a town about two miles up the track. Mancelona they call it. Good-bye. I wish we could ask you to stay the night but it's just out of the question. Would you like to take some of that ham and some bread with you? No? You better take a sandwich," all this in a low, smooth, polite nigger voice.[6]

"Good. Well, good-bye, Mister Adams. Good-bye and good luck!"

Nick walked away from the fire across the clearing to the railway tracks. Out of the range of the fire he listened. The low soft voice of the negro was talking. Nick could not hear the words. Then he heard the little man say, "I got an awful headache, Bugs."

"You'll feel better, Mister Francis," the negro's voice soothed. "Just you drink a cup of this hot coffee."

Nick climbed the embankment and started up the track. He found he had a ham sandwich in his hand and put it in his pocket. Looking back from the mounting grade before the track curved into the hills he could see the firelight in the clearing.

---

6. Here the racist epithet may signal, as Dudley suggests (294–95), a clever "posture" to manage Ad.

Chapter VI[1]

Nick sat against the wall of the church where they had dragged him to be clear of machine-gun fire in the street. Both legs stuck out awkwardly. He had been hit in the spine. His face was sweaty and dirty. The sun shone on his face. The day was very hot. Rinaldi, big backed, his equipment sprawling, lay face downward against the wall. Nick looked straight ahead brilliantly. The pink wall of the house opposite had fallen out from the roof, and an iron bedstead hung twisted toward the street. Two Austrian dead lay in the rubble in the shade of the house. Up the street were other dead. Things were getting forward in the town. It was going well. Stretcher bearers would be along any time now. Nick turned his head carefully and looked at Rinaldi. "Senta[2] Rinaldi. Senta. You and me we've made a separate peace." Rinaldi lay still in the sun breathing with difficulty. "Not patriots." Nick turned his head carefully away smiling sweatily. Rinaldi was a disappointing audience.

1. This vignette offers a brief glimpse of Nick in World War I, apparently attached to the Italian army and fighting in northern Italy against Austria.
2. Listen (Italian).

A VERY SHORT STORY

One hot evening in Padua they carried him up onto the roof and he could look out over the top of the town. There were chimney swifts in the sky. After a while it got dark and the searchlights came out. The others went down and took the bottles with them. He and Luz could hear them below on the balcony. Luz sat on the bed. She was cool and fresh in the hot night.

Luz stayed on night duty for three months.[1] They were glad to let her. When they operated on him she prepared him for the operating table; and they had a joke about friend or enema. He went under the anæsthetic holding tight on to himself so he would not blab about anything during the silly, talky time. After he got on crutches he used to take the temperatures so Luz would not have to get up from the bed. There were only a few patients, and they all knew about it. They all liked Luz. As he walked back along the halls he thought of Luz in his bed.

Before he went back to the front they went into the Duomo and prayed. It was dim and quiet, and there were other people praying. They wanted to get married, but there was not enough time for the banns, and neither of them had birth certificates. They felt as though they were married, but they wanted every one to know about it, and to make it so they could not lose it.

Luz wrote him many letters that he never got until after the armistice.[2] Fifteen came in a bunch to the front and he sorted them by the dates and read them all straight through. They were all about the hospital, and how much she loved him and how it was impossible to get along without him and how terrible it was missing him at night.

After the armistice they agreed he should go home to get a job so they might be married. Luz would not come home until he had a good job and could come to New York to meet her. It was understood he would not drink, and he did not want to see his friends or any one in the States. Only to get a job and be married. On the train from Padua to Milan they quarrelled about her not being willing to come home at once. When they had to say good-bye, in the station at Milan, they kissed good-bye, but were not finished with the quarrel. He felt sick about saying good-bye like that.

---

1. When this story was first published as a prose poem in *in our time*, the nurse's name was Ag and the hospital was in Milan, where Hemingway recovered from his July 8, 1918, wounds, attended by Agnes von Kurowsky. Hemingway later changed the location to Padua, a city west of Venice, and the nurse's name to Luz (Spanish for "light").
2. The armistice ending World War I was signed on November 11, 1918.

He went to America on a boat from Genoa. Luz went back to Pordenone[3] to open a hospital. It was lonely and rainy there, and there was a battalion of arditi[4] quartered in the town. Living in the muddy, rainy town in the winter, the major of the battalion made love to Luz, and she had never known Italians before, and finally wrote to the States that theirs had been only a boy and girl affair. She was sorry, and she knew he would probably not be able to understand, but might some day forgive her, and be grateful to her, and she expected, absolutely unexpectedly, to be married in the spring. She loved him as always, but she realized now it was only a boy and girl love. She hoped he would have a great career, and believed in him absolutely. She knew it was for the best.

The major did not marry her in the spring, or any other time. Luz never got an answer to the letter to Chicago about it.[5] A short time after he contracted gonorrhea from a sales girl in a loop department store while riding in a taxicab through Lincoln Park.[6]

---

3. A town northeast of Venice.
4. Literally, the daring ones (Italian); shock troops.
5. Hemingway received a letter from von Kurowsky like the one the narrator receives from Luz. He told another former ambulance driver, Bill Horne, that he was "just smashed" by the news (*LEH* 1:177).
6. "Loop" refers to the Chicago central business district, defined by an elevated railway line circling it. Lincoln Park extends along Lake Michigan above the Near North Side of Chicago.

Chapter VII

While the bombardment was knocking the trench to pieces at Fossalta,[1] he lay very flat and sweated and prayed oh jesus christ get me out of here. Dear jesus please get me out. Christ please please please christ. If you'll only keep me from getting killed I'll do anything you say. I believe in you and I'll tell every one in the world that you are the only one that matters. Please please dear jesus. The shelling moved further up the line. We went to work on the trench and in the morning the sun came up and the day was hot and muggy and cheerful and quiet. The next night back at Mestre he did not tell the girl he went upstairs with at the Villa Rossa about Jesus. And he never told anybody.

1. Fossalta di Piave, the site of Hemingway's wounding on the Italian front.

SOLDIER'S HOME[1]

Krebs went to the war from a Methodist college in Kansas. There is a picture which shows him among his fraternity brothers, all of them wearing exactly the same height and style collar. He enlisted in the Marines in 1917 and did not return to the United States until the second division returned from the Rhine[2] in the summer of 1919.

There is a picture which shows him on the Rhine with two German girls and another corporal. Krebs and the corporal look too big for their uniforms. The German girls are not beautiful. The Rhine does not show in the picture.

By the time Krebs returned to his home town in Oklahoma the greeting of heroes was over. He came back much too late.[3] The men from the town who had been drafted had all been welcomed elaborately on their return. There had been a great deal of hysteria. Now the reaction had set in. People seemed to think it was rather ridiculous for Krebs to be getting back so late, years after the war was over.

At first Krebs, who had been at Belleau Wood, Soissons, the Champagne, St. Mihiel and in the Argonne did not want to talk about the war at all.[4] Later he felt the need to talk but no one wanted to hear about it. His town had heard too many atrocity stories to be thrilled by actualities. Krebs found that to be listened to at all he had to lie, and after he had done this twice he, too, had a reaction against the war and against talking about it. A distaste for everything that had happened to him in the war set in because of the lies he had told. All of the times that had been able to make him feel cool and clear inside himself when he thought of them; the times so long back when he had done the one thing, the only thing for a man to do, easily and naturally, when he might have done something else, now lost their cool, valuable quality and then were lost themselves.

His lies were quite unimportant lies and consisted in attributing to himself things other men had seen, done or heard of, and stating as facts certain apocryphal incidents familiar to all soldiers. Even his lies were not sensational at the pool room. His acquaintances,

1. Written in April 1924, this story recalls Hemingway's return to Oak Park, Illinois, in 1919.
2. River separating France and Germany.
3. Krebs's late return probably means he arrived home after the national victory parade, in New York City, on September 10, 1919.
4. This list places Krebs in the thick of the heaviest U.S. fighting. In 1917, the Battle of Belleau Wood was the first engagement of the American Expeditionary Forces. The 1918 Battle of Soissons broke the German offensive drive. The Fourth Battle of the Champagne halted a diversionary attack near the Marne River. The Battle of St. Mihiel was the first Allied victory led by American forces. The Meuse-Argonne offensive involved 1.2 million U.S. forces and forced the German surrender.

who had heard detailed accounts of German women found chained to machine guns in the Argonne forest and who could not comprehend, or were barred by their patriotism from interest in, any German machine gunners who were not chained, were not thrilled by his stories.

Krebs acquired the nausea in regard to experience that is the result of untruth or exaggeration, and when he occasionally met another man who had really been a soldier and they talked a few minutes in the dressing room at a dance he fell into the easy pose of the old soldier among other soldiers: that he had been badly, sickeningly frightened all the time.[5] In this way he lost everything.

During this time, it was late summer, he was sleeping late in bed, getting up to walk down town to the library to get a book, eating lunch at home, reading on the front porch until he became bored and then walking down through the town to spend the hottest hours of the day in the cool dark of the pool room. He loved to play pool.

In the evening he practised on his clarinet, strolled down town, read and went to bed. He was still a hero to his two young sisters. His mother would have given him breakfast in bed if he had wanted it. She often came in when he was in bed and asked him to tell her about the war, but her attention always wandered. His father was non-committal.

Before Krebs went away to the war he had never been allowed to drive the family motor car. His father was in the real estate business and always wanted the car to be at his command when he required it to take clients out into the country to show them a piece of farm property. The car always stood outside the First National Bank building where his father had an office on the second floor. Now, after the war, it was still the same car.

Nothing was changed in the town except that the young girls had grown up. But they lived in such a complicated world of already defined alliances and shifting feuds that Krebs did not feel the energy or the courage to break into it. He liked to look at them, though. There were so many good-looking young girls. Most of them had their hair cut short. When he went away only little girls wore their hair like that or girls that were fast. They all wore sweaters and shirt waists with round Dutch collars. It was a pattern. He liked to look at them from the front porch as they walked on the other side of the street. He liked to watch them walking under the shade of the trees. He liked the round Dutch collars above their sweaters. He

---

5. Such feelings suggest why so many veterans were diagnosed with shell shock after the Great War. Battle trauma was one of the first disorders to be identified and treated by modern psychologists.

liked their silk stockings and flat shoes. He liked their bobbed hair and the way they walked.

When he was in town their appeal to him was not very strong. He did not like them when he saw them in the Greek's ice cream parlor. He did not want them themselves really. They were too complicated. There was something else. Vaguely he wanted a girl but he did not want to have to work to get her. He would have liked to have a girl but he did not want to have to spend a long time getting her. He did not want to get into the intrigue and the politics. He did not want to have to do any courting. He did not want to tell any more lies. It wasn't worth it.

He did not want any consequences. He did not want any consequences ever again. He wanted to live along without consequences. Besides he did not really need a girl. The army had taught him that. It was all right to pose as though you had to have a girl. Nearly everybody did that. But it wasn't true. You did not need a girl. That was the funny thing. First a fellow boasted how girls mean nothing to him, that he never thought of them, that they could not touch him. Then a fellow boasted that he could not get along without girls, that he had to have them all the time, that he could not go to sleep without them.

That was all a lie. It was all a lie both ways. You did not need a girl unless you thought about them. He learned that in the army. Then sooner or later you always got one. When you were really ripe for a girl you always got one. You did not have to think about it. Sooner or later it would come. He had learned that in the army.

Now he would have liked a girl if she had come to him and not wanted to talk. But here at home it was all too complicated. He knew he could never get through it all again. It was not worth the trouble. That was the thing about French girls and German girls. There was not all this talking. You couldn't talk much and you did not need to talk. It was simple and you were friends. He thought about France and then he began to think about Germany. On the whole he had liked Germany better. He did not want to leave Germany. He did not want to come home. Still, he had come home. He sat on the front porch.

He liked the girls that were walking along the other side of the street. He liked the look of them much better than the French girls or the German girls. But the world they were in was not the world he was in. He would like to have one of them. But it was not worth it. They were such a nice pattern. He liked the pattern. It was exciting. But he would not go through all the talking. He did not want one badly enough. He liked to look at them all, though. It was not worth it. Not now when things were getting good again.

He sat there on the porch reading a book on the war. It was a history and he was reading about all the engagements he had been in.[6] It was the most interesting reading he had ever done. He wished there were more maps. He looked forward with a good feeling to reading all the really good histories when they would come out with good detail maps. Now he was really learning about the war. He had been a good soldier. That made a difference.

One morning after he had been home about a month his mother came into his bedroom and sat on the bed. She smoothed her apron.

"I had a talk with your father last night, Harold," she said, "and he is willing for you to take the car out in the evenings."

"Yeah?" said Krebs,[7] who was not fully awake. "Take the car out? Yeah?"

"Yes. Your father has felt for some time that you should be able to take the car out in the evenings whenever you wished but we only talked it over last night."

"I'll bet you made him," Krebs said.

"No. It was your father's suggestion that we talk the matter over."

"Yeah. I'll bet you made him," Krebs sat up in bed.

"Will you come down to breakfast, Harold?" his mother said.

"As soon as I get my clothes on," Krebs said.

His mother went out of the room and he could hear her frying something downstairs while he washed, shaved and dressed to go down into the dining-room for breakfast. While he was eating breakfast his sister brought in the mail.

"Well, Hare," she said. "You old sleepy-head. What do you ever get up for?"

Krebs looked at her. He liked her. She was his best sister.

"Have you got the paper?" he asked.

She handed him *The Kansas City Star*[8] and he shucked off its brown wrapper and opened it to the sporting page. He folded *The Star* open and propped it against the water pitcher with his cereal dish to steady it, so he could read while he ate.

"Harold," his mother stood in the kitchen doorway, "Harold, please don't muss up the paper. Your father can't read his *Star* if it's been mussed."

"I won't muss it," Krebs said.

His sister sat down at the table and watched him while he read.

6. Michael Reynolds shows in *Hemingway's First War* (1976) that when Hemingway returned to Oak Park, he did extensive reading about the war (140).
7. Hemingway confected the name from Paris acquaintances: Harold Loeb, expatriate novelist and tennis partner; or Harold Stearns, well-published, hard-drinking critic of American shallowness and hypocrisy; and Krebs Friend, a shell-shocked veteran Hemingway knew in Chicago and Paris.
8. Hemingway worked for *The Star* from October 1917 to April 1918.

"We're playing indoor over at school this afternoon," she said. "I'm going to pitch."

"Good," said Krebs. "How's the old wing?"

"I can pitch better than lots of the boys. I tell them all you taught me. The other girls aren't much good."

"Yeah?" said Krebs.

"I tell them all you're my beau. Aren't you my beau, Hare?"

"You bet."

"Couldn't your brother really be your beau just because he's your brother?"

"I don't know."

"Sure you know. Couldn't you be my beau, Hare, if I was old enough and if you wanted to?"

"Sure. You're my girl now."

"Am I really your girl?"

"Sure."

"Do you love me?"

"Uh, huh."

"Will you love me always?"

"Sure."

"Will you come over and watch me play indoor?"[9]

"Maybe."

"Aw, Hare, you don't love me. If you loved me, you'd want to come over and watch me play indoor."

Krebs's mother came into the dining-room from the kitchen. She carried a plate with two fried eggs and some crisp bacon on it and a plate of buckwheat cakes.

"You run along, Helen," she said. "I want to talk to Harold."

She put the eggs and bacon down in front of him and brought in a jug of maple syrup for the buckwheat cakes. Then she sat down across the table from Krebs.

"I wish you'd put down the paper a minute, Harold," she said.

Krebs took down the paper and folded it.

"Have you decided what you are going to do yet, Harold?" his mother said, taking off her glasses.

"No," said Krebs.

"Don't you think it's about time?" His mother did not say this in a mean way. She seemed worried.

"I hadn't thought about it," Krebs said.

"God has some work for every one to do," his mother said. "There can be no idle hands in His Kingdom."

"I'm not in His Kingdom," Krebs said.

9. Madeleine ("Sunny") Hemingway asked her brother to watch her play indoor baseball in the spring of 1919.

"We are all of us in His Kingdom."

Krebs felt embarrassed and resentful as always.

"I've worried about you so much, Harold," his mother went on. "I know the temptations you must have been exposed to. I know how weak men are. I know what your own dear grandfather, my own father, told us about the Civil War and I have prayed for you. I pray for you all day long, Harold."

Krebs looked at the bacon fat hardening on his plate.

"Your father is worried, too," his mother went on. "He thinks you have lost your ambition, that you haven't got a definite aim in life. Charley Simmons, who is just your age, has a good job and is going to be married. The boys are all settling down; they're all determined to get somewhere; you can see that boys like Charley Simmons are on their way to being really a credit to the community."

Krebs said nothing.

"Don't look that way, Harold," his mother said. "You know we love you and I want to tell you for your own good how matters stand. Your father does not want to hamper your freedom. He thinks you should be allowed to drive the car. If you want to take some of the nice girls out riding with you, we are only too pleased. We want you to enjoy yourself. But you are going to have to settle down to work, Harold. Your father doesn't care what you start in at. All work is honorable as he says. But you've got to make a start at something. He asked me to speak to you this morning and then you can stop in and see him at his office."

"Is that all?" Krebs said.

"Yes. Don't you love your mother, dear boy?"

"No," Krebs said.

His mother looked at him across the table. Her eyes were shiny. She started crying.

"I don't love anybody," Krebs said.

It wasn't any good. He couldn't tell her, he couldn't make her see it. It was silly to have said it. He had only hurt her. He went over and took hold of her arm. She was crying with her head in her hands.

"I didn't mean it," he said. "I was just angry at something. I didn't mean I didn't love you."

His mother went on crying. Krebs put his arm on her shoulder.

"Can't you believe me, mother?"

His mother shook her head.

"Please, please, mother. Please believe me."

"All right," his mother said chokily. She looked up at him. "I believe you, Harold."

Krebs kissed her hair. She put her face up to him.

"I'm your mother," she said. "I held you next to my heart when you were a tiny baby."

Krebs felt sick and vaguely nauseated.

"I know, Mummy," he said. "I'll try and be a good boy for you."

"Would you kneel and pray with me, Harold?" his mother asked.

They knelt down beside the dining-room table and Krebs's mother prayed.

"Now, you pray, Harold," she said.

"I can't," Krebs said.

"Try, Harold."

"I can't."

"Do you want me to pray for you?"

"Yes."

So his mother prayed for him and then they stood up and Krebs kissed his mother and went out of the house. He had tried so to keep his life from being complicated. Still, none of it had touched him. He had felt sorry for his mother and she had made him lie. He would go to Kansas City and get a job and she would feel all right about it. There would be one more scene maybe before he got away. He would not go down to his father's office. He would miss that one. He wanted his life to go smoothly. It had just gotten going that way. Well, that was all over now, anyway. He would go over to the schoolyard and watch Helen play indoor baseball.

Chapter VIII

At two o'clock in the morning two Hungarians got into a cigar store at Fifteenth Street and Grand Avenue. Drevitts and Boyle drove up from the Fifteenth Street police station in a Ford. The Hungarians were backing their wagon out of an alley. Boyle shot one off the seat of the wagon and one out of the wagon box. Drevitts got frightened when he found they were both dead. Hell Jimmy, he said, you oughtn't to have done it. There's liable to be a hell of a lot of trouble.

—They're crooks, ain't they? said Boyle. They're wops, ain't they? Who the hell is going to make any trouble?

—That's all right maybe this time, said Drevitts, but how did you know they were wops when you bumped them?

Wops, said Boyle, I can tell wops a mile off.[1]

---

1. This vignette condenses a November 1917 report in *The Kansas City Star,* possibly filed by Hemingway. In *Hemingway's Paris Laboratory* (2005), Cohen shows (162) how Chapter VIII alters the *Star* account, making the police shooting ethnically motivated: an Irish cop kills two Hungarians, believing them to be Italians ("wops"). By the 1920s, resentment of foreigners pervaded white America. The Immigration Act of 1924 virtually excluded foreigners of undesirable "national origin."

THE REVOLUTIONIST[1]

In 1919 he was travelling on the railroads in Italy, carrying a square of oilcloth from the headquarters of the party written in indelible pencil and saying here was a comrade who had suffered very much under the Whites in Budapest and requesting comrades to aid him in any way.[2] He used this instead of a ticket. He was very shy and quite young and the train men passed him on from one crew to another. He had no money, and they fed him behind the counter in railway eating houses.

He was delighted with Italy. It was a beautiful country, he said. The people were all kind. He had been in many towns, walked much, and seen many pictures. Giotto, Masaccio, and Piero della Francesca he bought reproductions of and carried them wrapped in a copy of *Avanti*. Mantegna he did not like.[3]

He reported at Bologna, and I took him with me up into the Romagna[4] where it was necessary I go to see a man. We had a good trip together. It was early September and the country was pleasant. He was a Magyar, a very nice boy and very shy. Horthy's men had done some bad things to him. He talked about it a little. In spite of Hungary, he believed altogether in the world revolution.

"But how is the movement going in Italy?" he asked.

"Very badly," I said.

"But it will go better," he said. "You have everything here. It is the one country that every one is sure of. It will be the starting point of everything."

I did not say anything.[5]

At Bologna he said good-bye to us to go on the train to Milano and then to Aosta to walk over the pass into Switzerland.[6] I spoke to him about the Mantegnas in Milano. "No," he said, very shyly, he did not like Mantegna. I wrote out for him where to eat in Milano and the addresses of comrades. He thanked me very much, but his

---

1. Like "A Very Short Story," an *in our time* prose poem converted into a short story.
2. The backstory of this "Magyar" (Hungarian) Communist on the run alludes to an abortive Bolshevik revolution in Budapest, put down by the "Whites" of Miklós Horthy (1868–1957), a former naval officer who appointed himself regent.
3. The first three artists named were painters of religious subjects during the late Middle Ages or early Renaissance. Mantegna painted more naturalistic, sculptural figures and used darker coloring. The socialist newspaper *Avanti* was established in 1896.
4. Italian historical region southeast of Bologna toward the Adriatic; "up into the Romagna" suggests a journey into the Appenine Mountains.
5. In 1922, Hemingway witnessed the rise of the Italian fascist dictator Benito Mussolini (1883–1945).
6. I.e., by rail from one city to another, then by foot into Switzerland, probably through the same Great St. Bernard Pass that the Hemingways and Eric Dorman-Smith (see note 1 on 21) had hiked in 1922.

mind was already looking forward to walking over the pass. He was
very eager to walk over the pass while the weather held good. He
loved the mountains in the autumn. The last I heard of him the
Swiss had him in jail near Sion.[7]

7. Town in southern Switzerland.

Chapter IX[1]

The first matador got the horn through his sword hand and the crowd hooted him. The second matador slipped and the bull caught him through the belly and he hung on to the horn with one hand and held the other tight against the place, and the bull rammed him wham against the wall and the horn came out, and he lay in the sand, and then got up like crazy drunk and tried to slug the men carrying him away and yelled for his sword but he fainted. The kid came out and had to kill five bulls because you can't have more than three matadors, and the last bull he was so tired he couldn't get the sword in. He couldn't hardly lift his arm. He tried five times and the crowd was quiet because it was a good bull and it looked like him or the bull and then he finally made it. He sat down in the sand and puked and they held a cape over him while the crowd hollered and threw things down into the bull ring.

1. The first of six vignettes on bullfighting, this piece appeared in *The Little Review* in 1923 and was based on a firsthand account by Hemingway's friend Mike Strater.

MR. AND MRS. ELLIOT[1]

Mr. and Mrs. Elliot tried very hard to have a baby. They tried as often as Mrs. Elliot could stand it. They tried in Boston after they were married and they tried coming over on the boat. They did not try very often on the boat because Mrs. Elliot was quite sick. She was sick and when she was sick she was sick as Southern women are sick. That is women from the Southern part of the United States. Like all Southern women Mrs. Elliot disintegrated very quickly under sea sickness, travelling at night, and getting up too early in the morning. Many of the people on the boat took her for Elliot's mother. Other people who knew they were married believed she was going to have a baby. In reality she was forty years old. Her years had been precipitated suddenly when she started travelling.

She had seemed much younger, in fact she had seemed not to have any age at all, when Elliot had married her after several weeks of making love to her after knowing her for a long time in her tea shop before he had kissed her one evening.

Hubert Elliot was taking postgraduate work in law at Harvard when he was married.[2] He was a poet with an income of nearly ten thousand dollars a year. He wrote very long poems very rapidly. He was twenty-five years old and had never gone to bed with a woman until he married Mrs. Elliot. He wanted to keep himself pure so that he could bring to his wife the same purity of mind and body that he expected of her. He called it to himself living straight. He had been in love with various girls before he kissed Mrs. Elliot and always told them sooner or later that he had led a clean life. Nearly all the girls lost interest in him. He was shocked and really horrified at the way girls would become engaged to and marry men whom they must know had dragged themselves through the gutter. He once tried to warn a girl he knew against a man of whom he had almost proof that he had been a rotter at college and a very unpleasant incident had resulted.

Mrs. Elliot's name was Cornelia. She had taught him to call her Calutina, which was her family nickname in the South. His mother

---

1. First published in *The Little Review* in October 1924, Hemingway's story carried the title "Mr. and Mrs. Smith" to satirize a wealthy expatriate poet, Chard Powers Smith (1894–1977). But Hemingway later retitled the piece, either to avoid a libel suit or because he learned that the real Mrs. Smith had died in childbirth in 1924. When Boni & Liveright accepted *In Our Time*, they found the opening sentences too sexually suggestive and made Hemingway modify the language. The final title reflects Hemingway's scorn for T. S. Eliot, whom he had already insulted in the *Transatlantic Review*.
2. Smith received an undergraduate degree from Yale and a law degree from Harvard. Hemingway omits from his caricature Smith's service in the U.S. Army as an artillery captain.

cried when he brought Cornelia home after their marriage but brightened very much when she learned they were going to live abroad.

Cornelia had said, "You dear sweet boy," and held him closer than ever when he had told her how he had kept himself clean for her. Cornelia was pure too. "Kiss me again like that," she said.

Hubert explained to her that he had learned that way of kissing from hearing a fellow tell a story once. He was delighted with his experiment and they developed it as far as possible. Sometimes when they had been kissing together a long time, Cornelia would ask him to tell her again that he had kept himself really straight for her. The declaration always set her off again.

At first Hubert had no idea of marrying Cornelia. He had never thought of her that way. She had been such a good friend of his, and then one day in the little back room of the shop they had been dancing to the gramophone while her girl friend was in the front of the shop and she had looked up into his eyes and he had kissed her. He could never remember just when it was decided that they were to be married. But they were married.

They spent the night of the day they were married in a Boston hotel. They were both disappointed but finally Cornelia went to sleep. Hubert could not sleep and several times went out and walked up and down the corridor of the hotel in his new Jaeger[3] bathrobe that he had bought for his wedding trip. As he walked he saw all the pairs of shoes, small shoes and big shoes, outside the doors of the hotel rooms. This set his heart to pounding and he hurried back to his own room but Cornelia was asleep. He did not like to waken her and soon everything was quite all right and he slept peacefully.

The next day they called on his mother and the next day they sailed for Europe. It was possible to try to have a baby but Cornelia could not attempt it very often although they wanted a baby more than anything else in the world. They landed at Cherbourg and came to Paris. They tried to have a baby in Paris. Then they decided to go to Dijon where there was summer school and where a number of people who crossed on the boat with them had gone. They found there was nothing to do in Dijon. Hubert, however, was writing a great number of poems and Cornelia typed them for him. They were all very long poems. He was very severe about mistakes and would make her re-do an entire page if there was one mistake. She cried a good deal and they tried several times to have a baby before they left Dijon.

They came to Paris and most of their friends from the boat came back too. They were tired of Dijon and anyway would now be able

3. An expensive British brand.

to say that after leaving Harvard or Columbia or Wabash[4] they had studied at the University of Dijon down in the Côte d'Or. Many of them would have preferred to go to Languedoc, Montpellier or Perpignan[5] if there are universities there. But all those places are too far away. Dijon is only four and a half hours from Paris and there is a diner on the train.

So they all sat around the Café du Dome, avoiding the Rotonde across the street because it is always so full of foreigners,[6] for a few days and then the Elliots rented a château in Touraine[7] through an advertisement in the New York *Herald*. Elliot had a number of friends by now all of whom admired his poetry and Mrs. Elliot had prevailed upon him to send over to Boston for her girl friend who had been in the tea shop. Mrs. Elliot became much brighter after her girl friend came and they had many good cries together. The girl friend was several years older than Cornelia and called her Honey. She too came from a very old Southern family.

The three of them, with several of Elliot's friends who called him Hubie, went down to the château in Touraine. They found Touraine to be a very flat hot country very much like Kansas. Elliot had nearly enough poems for a book now. He was going to bring it out in Boston and had already sent his check to, and made a contract with, a publisher.[8]

In a short time the friends began to drift back to Paris. Touraine had not turned out the way it looked when it started. Soon all the friends had gone off with a rich young and unmarried poet to a seaside resort near Trouville. There they were all very happy.

Elliot kept on at the château in Touraine because he had taken it for all summer. He and Mrs. Elliot tried very hard to have a baby in the big hot bedroom on the big, hard bed. Mrs. Elliot was learning the touch system on the typewriter, but she found that while it increased the speed it made more mistakes. The girl friend was now typing practically all of the manuscripts. She was very neat and efficient and seemed to enjoy it.

Elliot had taken to drinking white wine and lived apart in his own room. He wrote a great deal of poetry during the night and in the morning looked very exhausted. Mrs. Elliot and the girl friend now

4. The phrase "Harvard or Columbia or Wabash" was calculated to tease Ezra Pound, who as a teacher of foreign languages had been fired by Indiana's Wabash College. But it also reflects Hemingway's scorn for Ivy League schools and academic credentials.
5. The Universities of Montpellier and Perpignan, in southern France, are among the country's oldest. For Cherbourg and Dijon, see map (5).
6. The Elliots frequent the part of Paris where Hemingway lived in 1924. For the 1925 *In Our Time* volume, as Paul Smith notes in his *Reader's Guide* (1989), Hemingway added a paragraph on Paris (77). In it, the Smiths cross paths with Ezra Pound, James Joyce, and Leo Stein (Gertrude's older brother, who no longer spoke to her).
7. The region around Tours in the Loire Valley.
8. Elliot's check to the Boston publisher implies a self-financed, vanity press edition.

slept together in the big mediæval bed. They had many a good cry together. In the evening they all sat at dinner together in the garden under a plane tree and the hot evening wind blew and Elliot drank white wine and Mrs. Elliot and the girl friend made conversation and they were all quite happy.

Chapter X

They whack—whacked the white horse on the legs and he kneed himself up. The picador twisted the stirrups straight and pulled and hauled up into the saddle. The horse's entrails hung down in a blue bunch and swung backward and forward as he began to canter, the monos whacking him on the back of his legs with the rods. He cantered jerkily along the barrera.[1] He stopped stiff and one of the monos held his bridle and walked him forward. The picador kicked in his spurs, leaned forward and shook his lance at the bull. Blood pumped regularly from between the horse's front legs. He was nervously wobbly. The bull could not make up his mind to charge.

---

1. Barrier (Spanish); red-painted wooden wall encircling the bull ring. Unlike Chapter IX, this vignette was written after Hemingway had seen a bullfight. The horse has been gored by the bull. In *DIA* (1932), Hemingway defines "*monos*," short for *monosabios*, as "red-shirted bull ring servants, who aid the picadors" (422).

CAT IN THE RAIN

There were only two Americans stopping at the hotel.[1] They did not know any of the people they passed on the stairs on their way to and from their room. Their room was on the second floor facing the sea. It also faced the public garden and the war monument. There were big palms and green benches in the public garden. In the good weather there was always an artist with his easel. Artists liked the way the palms grew and the bright colors of the hotels facing the gardens and the sea. Italians came from a long way off to look up at the war monument. It was made of bronze and glistened in the rain. It was raining. The rain dripped from the palm trees. Water stood in pools on the gravel paths. The sea broke in a long line in the rain and slipped back down the beach to come up and break again in a long line in the rain. The motor cars were gone from the square by the war monument. Across the square in the doorway of the café a waiter stood looking out at the empty square.

The American wife stood at the window looking out. Outside right under their window a cat was crouched under one of the dripping green tables. The cat was trying to make herself so compact that she would not be dripped on.

"I'm going down and get that kitty," the American wife said.

"I'll do it," her husband offered from the bed.

"No, I'll get it. The poor kitty out trying to keep dry under a table."

The husband went on reading, lying propped up with the two pillows at the foot of the bed.

"Don't get wet," he said.

The wife went downstairs and the hotel owner stood up and bowed to her as she passed the office. His desk was at the far end of the office. He was an old man and very tall.

"Il piove,"[2] the wife said. She liked the hotel-keeper.

"Si, si, Signora, brutto tempo. It's very bad weather."

He stood behind his desk in the far end of the dim room. The wife liked him. She liked the deadly serious way he received any complaints. She liked his dignity. She liked the way he wanted to serve

---

1. In a 1925 letter to F. Scott Fitzgerald, Hemingway identifies this couple as "a Harvard kid and his wife" whom Hemingway had met in Genoa (*LEH* 2:454). The tale also recalls the February–March 1923 stay of the Hemingways at the Hotel Splendide, in Rapallo, Italy. There, they visited the Pounds, and Hemingway first read T. S. Eliot's recently published *The Waste Land* (see note 1 on Smith, 330–36). During that stay, Hadley Hemingway probably began to suspect she was pregnant. Ernest told Fitzgerald he wrote the story in Rapallo when Hadley was "4 months pregnant" (*LEH* 2:455). In reality, he composed it in 1924, after the birth of his son.
2. It is raining (Italian).

her. She liked the way he felt about being a hotel-keeper. She liked his old, heavy face and big hands.

Liking him she opened the door and looked out. It was raining harder. A man in a rubber cape was crossing the empty square to the café. The cat would be around to the right. Perhaps she could go along under the eaves. As she stood in the doorway an umbrella opened behind her. It was the maid who looked after their room.

"You must not get wet," she smiled, speaking Italian. Of course, the hotel-keeper had sent her.

With the maid holding the umbrella over her, she walked along the gravel path until she was under their window. The table was there, washed bright green in the rain, but the cat was gone. She was suddenly disappointed. The maid looked up at her.

"Ha perduto qualque cosa, Signora?"[3]

"There was a cat," said the American girl.

"A cat?"

"Si, il gatto."

"A cat?" the maid laughed. "A cat in the rain?"

"Yes," she said, "under the table." Then, "Oh, I wanted it so much. I wanted a kitty."

When she talked English the maid's face tightened.

"Come, Signora," she said. "We must get back inside. You will be wet."

"I suppose so," said the American girl.

They went back along the gravel path and passed in the door. The maid stayed outside to close the umbrella. As the American girl passed the office, the padrone bowed from his desk. Something felt very small and tight inside the girl. The padrone made her feel very small and at the same time really important. She had a momentary feeling of being of supreme importance. She went on up the stairs. She opened the door of the room. George was on the bed, reading.

"Did you get the cat?" he asked, putting the book down.

"It was gone."

"Wonder where it went to," he said, resting his eyes from reading.

She sat down on the bed.

"I wanted it so much," she said. "I don't know why I wanted it so much. I wanted that poor kitty. It isn't any fun to be a poor kitty out in the rain."

George was reading again.

She went over and sat in front of the mirror of the dressing table looking at herself with the hand glass. She studied her profile, first one side and then the other. Then she studied the back of her head and her neck.

---

3. Have you lost something, madame? (Italian).

"Don't you think it would be a good idea if I let my hair grow out?" she asked, looking at her profile again.

George looked up and saw the back of her neck, clipped close like a boy's.[4]

"I like it the way it is."

"I get so tired of it," she said. "I get so tired of looking like a boy."

George shifted his position in the bed. He hadn't looked away from her since she started to speak.

"You look pretty darn nice," he said.

She laid the mirror down on the dresser and went over to the window and looked out. It was getting dark.

"I want to pull my hair back tight and smooth and make a big knot at the back that I can feel," she said. "I want to have a kitty to sit on my lap and purr when I stroke her."

"Yeah?" George said from the bed.

"And I want to eat at a table with my own silver and I want candles. And I want it to be spring and I want to brush my hair out in front of a mirror and I want a kitty and I want some new clothes."[5]

"Oh, shut up and get something to read," George said. He was reading again.

His wife was looking out of the window. It was quite dark now and still raining in the palm trees.

"Anyway, I want a cat," she said, "I want a cat. I want a cat now. If I can't have long hair or any fun, I can have a cat."

George was not listening. He was reading his book. His wife looked out of the window where the light had come on in the square.

Someone knocked at the door.

"Avanti," George said. He looked up from his book.

In the doorway stood the maid. She held a big tortoise-shell cat pressed tight against her and swung down against her body.

"Excuse me," she said, "the padrone asked me to bring this for the Signora."

4. Possibly an allusion to "La Garçonne," a short hairstyle popular in the 1920s. The French name feminizes the word for "boy."
5. Cf. *The Waste Land*, lines 77–93.

Chapter XI

The crowd shouted all the time and threw pieces of bread down into the ring, then cushions and leather wine bottles, keeping up whistling and yelling. Finally the bull was too tired from so much bad sticking and folded his knees and lay down and one of the cuadrilla leaned out over his neck and killed him with the puntillo.[1] The crowd came over the barrera and around the torero and two men grabbed him and held him and some one cut off his pigtail[2] and was waving it and a kid grabbed it and ran away with it. Afterwards I saw him at the café. He was very short with a brown face and quite drunk and he said after all it has happened before like that. I am not really a good bull fighter.

1. Dagger (Spanish). *"Cuadrilla"*: team (Spanish).
2. Traditionally worn by a bullfighter, or torero. "Barrera": see note 1 on 73.

OUT OF SEASON[1]

On the four lire[2] Peduzzi had earned by spading the hotel garden he got quite drunk. He saw the young gentleman coming down the path and spoke to him mysteriously. The young gentleman said he had not eaten but would be ready to go as soon as lunch was finished. Forty minutes or an hour.

At the cantina near the bridge they trusted him for three more grappas because he was so confident and mysterious about his job for the afternoon. It was a windy day with the sun coming out from behind clouds and then going under in sprinkles of rain. A wonderful day for trout fishing.

The young gentleman came out of the hotel and asked him about the rods. Should his wife come behind with the rods? "Yes," said Peduzzi, "let her follow us." The young gentleman went back into the hotel and spoke to his wife. He and Peduzzi started down the road. The young gentleman had a musette[3] over his shoulder. Peduzzi saw the wife, who looked as young as the young gentleman, and was wearing mountain boots and a blue beret, start out to follow them down the road, carrying the fishing rods, unjointed, one in each hand. Peduzzi didn't like her to be way back there. "Signorina," he called, winking at the young gentleman, "come up here and walk with us. Signora, come up here. Let us all walk together." Peduzzi wanted them all three to walk down the street of Cortina together.

The wife stayed behind, following rather sullenly. "Signorina," Peduzzi called tenderly, "come up here with us." The young gentleman looked back and shouted something. The wife stopped lagging behind and walked up.

Everyone they met walking through the main street of the town Peduzzi greeted elaborately. Buon' di,[4] Arturo! Tipping his hat. The bank clerk stared at him from the door of the Fascist café.[5] Groups of three and four people standing in front of the shops stared at the three. The workmen in their stone-powdered jackets working on the foundations of the new hotel looked up as they passed. Nobody spoke or gave any sign to them except the town beggar, lean and old, with a spittle-thickened beard, who lifted his hat as they passed.

---

1. Hemingway told Fitzgerald (see note 1 on 75) this story was "an almost literal transcription" (*LEH* 2:455) of what happened during a 1923 stay at Cortina d'Ampezzo, Italy, with his wife, Hadley.
2. Plural of *lira*, Italian currency 1861–2002.
3. A bag containing his fishing gear.
4. Good morning or hello (Italian).
5. See note 5 on 65.

Peduzzi stopped in front of a store with the window full of bottles and brought his empty grappa bottle from an inside pocket of his old military coat. "A little to drink, some marsala for the Signora, something, something to drink." He gestured with the bottle. It was a wonderful day. "Marsala, you like marsala, Signorina? A little marsala?"

The wife stood sullenly. "You'll have to play up to this," she said. "I can't understand a word he says. He's drunk, isn't he?"

The young gentleman appeared not to hear Peduzzi. He was thinking, what in hell makes him say marsala? That's what Max Beerbohm drinks.[6]

"Geld,"[7] Peduzzi said finally, taking hold of the young gentleman's sleeve. "Lire." He smiled, reluctant to press the subject but needing to bring the young gentleman into action.

The young gentleman took out his pocketbook and gave him a ten-lira note. Peduzzi went up the steps to the door of the Specialty of Domestic and Foreign Wines shop. It was locked.

"It is closed until two," someone passing in the street said scornfully. Peduzzi came down the steps. He felt hurt. Never mind, he said, we can get it at the Concordia.[8]

They walked down the road to the Concordia three abreast. On the porch of the Concordia, where the rusty bobsleds were stacked, the young gentleman said, "Was wollen sie?"[9] Peduzzi handed him the ten-lira note folded over and over. "Nothing," he said, "anything." He was embarrassed. "Marsala, maybe. I don't know. Marsala?"

The door of the Concordia shut on the young gentleman and the wife. "Three marsalas," said the young gentleman to the girl behind the pastry counter. "Two, you mean?" she asked. "No," he said, "one for a vecchio."[1] "Oh," she said, "a vecchio," and laughed, getting down the bottle. She poured out the three muddy looking drinks into three glasses. The wife was sitting at a table under the line of newspapers on sticks. The young gentleman put one of the marsalas in front of her. "You might as well drink it," he said, "maybe it'll make you feel better." She sat and looked at the glass. The young gentleman went outside the door with a glass for Peduzzi but could not see him.

"I don't know where he is," he said, coming back into the pastry room carrying the glass.

"He wanted a quart of it," said the wife.

---

6. Beerbohm, the legendary English dandy, critic, and caricaturist (1872–1956), was living near Ezra Pound in Rapallo, Italy, in 1922 when Hemingway, then covering the Genoa conference, joined fellow journalists in drinking a glass of marsala with him.
7. Money (German).
8. The hotel Concordia (named for the Roman goddess of peace).
9. What do you want? (German).
1. An old timer (Italian).

"How much is a quarter litre?" the young gentleman asked the girl.

"Of the bianco? One lira."

"No, of the marsala. Put these two in, too," he said, giving her his own glass and the one poured for Peduzzi. She filled the quarter litre wine measure with a funnel. "A bottle to carry it," said the young gentleman.

She went to hunt for a bottle. It all amused her.

"I'm sorry you feel so rotten, Tiny," he said. "I'm sorry I talked the way I did at lunch. We were both getting at the same thing from different angles."

"It doesn't make any difference," she said. "None of it makes any difference."

"Are you too cold?" he asked. "I wish you'd worn another sweater."

"I've got on three sweaters."

The girl came in with a very slim brown bottle and poured the marsala into it. The young gentleman paid five lira more. They went out the door. The girl was amused. Peduzzi was walking up and down at the other end out of the wind and holding the rods.

"Come on," he said, "I will carry the rods. What difference does it make if anybody sees them? No one will trouble us. No one will make any trouble for me in Cortina. I know them at the municipio.[2] I have been a soldier. Everybody in this town likes me. I sell frogs. What if it is forbidden to fish? Not a thing. Nothing. No trouble. Big trout, I tell you. Lots of them."

They were walking down the hill toward the river. The town was in back of them. The sun had gone under and it was sprinkling rain. "There," said Peduzzi, pointing to a girl in the doorway of a house they passed. "My daughter."

"His doctor," the wife said, "has he got to show us his doctor?"

"He said his daughter," said the young gentleman.

The girl went into the house as Peduzzi pointed.

They walked down the hill across the fields and then turned to follow the river bank. Peduzzi talked rapidly with much winking and knowingness. As they walked three abreast the wife caught his breath across the wind. Once he nudged her in the ribs. Part of the time he talked in d'Ampezzo dialect and sometimes in Tyroler German dialect.[3] He could not make out which the young gentleman and his wife understood the best so he was being bilingual. But as the young gentleman said, Ja, Ja,[4] Peduzzi decided to talk altogether in Tyroler. The young gentleman and the wife understood nothing.

2. Town hall (Italian).
3. In addition to Italian, Peduzzi uses the mountain dialect (Ladin) spoken around Cortina and the German of the Tyrolean Alps.
4. Yes, yes (German).

"Everybody in the town saw us going through with these rods. We're probably being followed by the game police now. I wish we weren't in on this damn thing. This damned old fool is so drunk, too."

"Of course you haven't got the guts to just go back," said the wife. "Of course you have to go on."

"Why don't you go back? Go on back, Tiny."

"I'm going to stay with you. If you go to jail we might as well both go."

They turned sharp down the bank and Peduzzi stood, his coat blowing in the wind, gesturing at the river. It was brown and muddy. Off on the right there was a dump heap.

"Say it to me in Italian," said the young gentleman.

"Un' mezz' ora. Piu d' un' mezz' ora."

"He says it's at least a half hour more. Go on back, Tiny. You're cold in this wind anyway. It's a rotten day and we aren't going to have any fun, anyway."

"All right," she said, and climbed up the grassy bank.

Peduzzi was down at the river and did not notice her till she was almost out of sight over the crest. "Frau!" he shouted. "Frau! Fräulein! You're not going."

She went on over the crest of the hill.

"She's gone!" said Peduzzi. It shocked him.

He took off the rubber bands that held the rod segments together and commenced to joint up one of the rods.

"But you said it was half an hour further."

"Oh, yes. It is good half an hour down. It is good here, too."

"Really?"

"Of course. It is good here and good there, too."

The young gentleman sat down on the bank and jointed up a rod, put on the reel and threaded the line through the guides. He felt uncomfortable and afraid that any minute a gamekeeper or a posse of citizens would come over the bank from the town. He could see the houses of the town and the campanile over the edge of the hill. He opened his leader box. Peduzzi leaned over and dug his flat, hard thumb and forefinger in and tangled the moistened leaders.

"Have you some lead?"

"No."

"You must have some lead." Peduzzi was excited. "You must have piombo. Piombo. A little piombo. Just here. Just above the hook or your bait will float on the water. You must have it. Just a little piombo."[5]

---

5. The lack of a lead fishing sinker (*piombo* in Italian) dooms bait fishing on a fast-moving stream.

"Have you got some?"

"No." He looked through his pockets desperately. Sifting through the cloth dirt in the linings of his inside military pockets. "I haven't any. We must have piombo."

"We can't fish then," said the young gentleman, and unjointed the rod, reeling the line back through the guides. "We'll get some piombo and fish tomorrow."

"But listen, caro, you must have piombo. The line will lie flat on the water." Peduzzi's day was going to pieces before his eyes. "You must have piombo. A little is enough. Your stuff is all clean and new but you have no lead. I would have brought some. You said you had everything."

The young gentleman looked at the stream discolored by the melting snow. "I know," he said, "we'll get some piombo and fish tomorrow."

"At what hour in the morning? Tell me that."

"At seven."

The sun came out. It was warm and pleasant. The young gentleman felt relieved. He was no longer breaking the law. Sitting on the bank he took the bottle of marsala out of his pocket and passed it to Peduzzi. Peduzzi passed it back. The young gentleman took a drink of it and passed it to Peduzzi again. Peduzzi passed it back again. "Drink," he said, "drink. It's your marsala." After another short drink the young gentleman handed the bottle over. Peduzzi had been watching it closely. He took the bottle very hurriedly and tipped it up. The gray hairs in the folds of his neck oscillated as he drank, his eyes fixed on the end of the narrow brown bottle. He drank it all. The sun shone while he drank. It was wonderful. This was a great day, after all. A wonderful day.

"Senta, caro!⁶ In the morning at seven." He had called the young gentleman caro several times and nothing had happened. It was good marsala. His eyes glistened. Days like this stretched out ahead. It would begin at seven in the morning.

They started to walk up the hill toward the town. The young gentleman went on ahead. He was quite a way up the hill. Peduzzi called to him.

"Listen, caro, can you let me take five lire for a favor?"

"For today?" asked the young gentleman frowning.

"No, not today. Give it to me today for tomorrow. I will provide everything for tomorrow. Pane, salami, formaggio,⁷ good stuff for all of us. You and I and the Signora. Bait for fishing, minnows, not

---

6. Listen, dear fellow (Italian).
7. Cheese (Italian). "Pane": bread (Italian).

worms only. Perhaps I can get some marsala. All for five lire. Five
lire for a favor."

The young gentleman looked through his pocketbook and took out
a two-lira note and two ones.

"Thank you, caro. Thank you," said Peduzzi, in the tone of one
member of the Carleton Club accepting the *Morning Post* from
another.[8] This was living. He was through with the hotel garden,
breaking up frozen manure with a dung fork. Life was opening out.

"Until seven o'clock then, caro," he said, slapping the young gentleman on the back. "Promptly at seven."

"I may not be going," said the young gentleman putting his purse
back in his pocket.

"What," said Peduzzi, "I will have minnows, Signor. Salami, everything. You and I and the Signora. The three of us."

"I may not be going," said the young gentleman, "very probably
not. I will leave word with the padrone at the hotel office."[9]

8. The Carlton Club, in London, is a members-only bastion of upper-class, conservative
   values. *The Morning Post* was a conservative London newspaper, published 1772–
   1937.
9. In *MF* (1964), Hemingway recalls evolving his technique of omission while writing this
   story (75). The detail he claimed to have omitted was that the guide hanged himself.
   But manuscript analysis (see Paul Smith's *Reader's Guide* [1989], 17) suggests that
   Hemingway had probably already drafted the piece before learning of the man's death.

Chapter XII

If it happened right down close in front of you, you could see Villalta[1] snarl at the bull and curse him, and when the bull charged he swung back firmly like an oak when the wind hits it, his legs tight together, the muleta trailing and the sword following the curve behind. Then he cursed the bull, flopped the muleta at him, and swung back from the charge his feet firm, the muleta curving and at each swing the crowd roaring.

When he started to kill it was all in the same rush. The bull looking at him straight in front, hating. He drew out the sword from the folds of the muleta and sighted with the same movement and called to the bull, Toro! Toro! and the bull charged and Villalta charged and just for a moment they became one. Villalta became one with the bull and then it was over. Villalta standing straight and the red hilt of the sword sticking out dully between the bull's shoulders. Villalta, his hand up at the crowd and the bull roaring blood, looking straight at Villalta and his legs caving.

1. Niçanor Villalta (1897–1980), Spanish bullfighter from Aragon, popular in the 1920s.

CROSS-COUNTRY SNOW[1]

The funicular car bucked once more and then stopped. It could not go farther, the snow drifted solidly across the track. The gale scouring the exposed surface of the mountain had swept the snow surface into a wind-board crust. Nick, waxing his skis in the baggage car, pushed his boots into the toe irons and shut the clamp tight. He jumped from the car sideways onto the hard wind-board, made a jump turn and crouching and trailing his sticks slipped in a rush down the slope.

On the white below George[2] dipped and rose and dipped out of sight. The rush and the sudden swoop as he dropped down a steep undulation in the mountain side plucked Nick's mind out and left him only the wonderful flying, dropping sensation in his body. He rose to a slight up-run and then the snow seemed to drop out from under him as he went down, down, faster and faster in a rush down the last, long steep slope. Crouching so he was almost sitting back on his skis, trying to keep the center of gravity low, the snow driving like a sand-storm, he knew the pace was too much. But he held it. He would not let go and spill. Then a patch of soft snow, left in a hollow by the wind, spilled him and he went over and over in a clashing of skis, feeling like a shot rabbit, then stuck, his legs crossed, his skis sticking straight up and his nose and ears jammed full of snow.

George stood a little farther down the slope, knocking the snow from his wind jacket with big slaps.

"You took a beauty, Mike,"[3] he called to Nick. "That's lousy soft snow. It bagged me the same way."

"What's it like over the khud?"[4] Nick kicked his skis around as he lay on his back and stood up.

"You've got to keep to your left. It's a good fast drop with a Christy at the bottom on account of a fence."[5]

"Wait a sec and we'll take it together."

"No, you come on and go first. I like to see you take the khuds."

---

1. The setting is near Chamby, above Lake Geneva in the Swiss Alps, where the Hemingways skied with the Dave O'Neil family in December–January 1922–23.
2. Young George Blackman O'Neil, Dave's son, skied with Hemingway, boxed with him in Paris, and at age 18 joined the author's entourage to film the Pamplona bullfights of 1924. See *LEH* 2:133.
3. The reference to Nick as "Mike" is an uncorrected error, the name used in an early draft.
4. A Hindi word for a steep slope or precipice. Hemingway likely acquired the term from the poem "Over the *Khud*," by the English writer Rudyard Kipling (1865–1936).
5. A "Christy," or Christie, is a turning technique developed in Austria. The skier forms a wedge by slanting the back of one ski in the direction of a turn, then bringing the other ski parallel to slide through the turn.

Nick Adams came up past George, big back and blond head still faintly snowy, then his skis started slipping at the edge and he swooped down, hissing in the crystalline powder snow and seeming to float up and drop down as he went up and down the billowing khuds. He held to his left and at the end, as he rushed toward the fence, keeping his knees locked tight together and turning his body like tightening a screw brought his skis sharply around to the right in a smother of snow and slowed into a loss of speed parallel to the hillside and the wire fence.

He looked up the hill. George was coming down in telemark position, kneeling; one leg forward and bent, the other trailing;[6] his sticks hanging like some insect's thin legs, kicking up puffs of snow as they touched the surface and finally the whole kneeling, trailing figure coming around in a beautiful right curve, crouching, the legs shot forward and back, the body leaning out against the swing, the sticks accenting the curve like points of light, all in a wild cloud of snow.

"I was afraid to Christy," George said, "the snow was too deep. You made a beauty."

"I can't telemark with my leg," Nick said.

Nick held down the top strand of the wire fence with his ski and George slid over. Nick followed him down to the road. They thrust bent-kneed along the road into a pine forest. The road became polished ice, stained orange and a tobacco yellow from the teams hauling logs. The skiers kept to the stretch of snow along the side. The road dipped sharply to a stream and then ran straight up-hill. Through the woods they could see a long, low-eaved, weather-beaten building. Through the trees it was a faded yellow. Closer the window frames were painted green. The paint was peeling. Nick knocked his clamps loose with one of his ski sticks and kicked off the skis.

"We might as well carry them up here," he said.

He climbed the steep road with the skis on his shoulder, kicking his heel nails into the icy footing. He heard George breathing and kicking in his heels just behind him. They stacked the skis against the side of the inn and slapped the snow off each other's trousers, stamped their boots clean, and went in.

Inside it was quite dark. A big porcelain stove shone in the corner of the room. There was a low ceiling. Smooth benches back of dark, wine-stained tables were along each side of the rooms. Two Swiss sat over their pipes and two decies[7] of cloudy new wine next to the stove. The boys took off their jackets and sat against the wall on the

---

6. The Telemark style, developed in Norway, requires great leg strength, both in the squatting, downhill position and in one-leg lunge turns.
7. Probably one-deciliter glasses, a standard serving size in Switzerland.

other side of the stove. A voice in the next room stopped singing and a girl in a blue apron came in through the door to see what they wanted to drink.

"A bottle of Sion,"[8] Nick said. "Is that all right, Gidge?"

"Sure," said George. "You know more about wine than I do. I like any of it."

The girl went out.

"There's nothing really can touch skiing, is there?" Nick said. "The way it feels when you first drop off on a long run."

"Huh," said George. "It's too swell to talk about."

The girl brought the wine in and they had trouble with the cork. Nick finally opened it. The girl went out and they heard her singing in German in the next room.

"Those specks of cork in it don't matter," said Nick.

"I wonder if she's got any cake."

"Let's find out."

The girl came in and Nick noticed that her apron covered swellingly her pregnancy. I wonder why I didn't see that when she first came in, he thought.

"What were you singing?" he asked her.

"Opera, German opera." She did not care to discuss the subject. "We have some apple strudel if you want it."

"She isn't so cordial, is she?" said George.

"Oh, well. She doesn't know us and she thought we were going to kid her about her singing, maybe. She's from up where they speak German probably and she's touchy about being here and then she's got that baby coming without being married and she's touchy."

"How do you know she isn't married?"

"No ring. Hell, no girls get married around here till they're knocked up."

The door came open and a gang of woodcutters from up the road came in, stamping their boots and steaming in the room. The waitress brought in three litres of new wine for the gang and they sat at the two tables, smoking and quiet, with their hats off, leaning back against the wall or forward on the table. Outside the horses on the wood sledges made an occasional sharp jangle of bells as they tossed their heads.

George and Nick were happy. They were fond of each other. They knew they had the run back home ahead of them.

"When have you got to go back to school?" Nick asked.

"Tonight," George answered. "I've got to get the ten-forty from Montreux."[9]

8. Wine from Sion, the capital of the Valais canton, a Swiss wine-producing region.
9. The train station closest to Chamby.

"I wish you could stick over and we could do the Dent du Lys[1] tomorrow."

"I got to get educated," George said. "Gee, Mike,[2] don't you wish we could just bum together? Take our skis and go on the train to where there was good running and then go on and put up at pubs and go right across the Oberland and up the Valais and all through the Engadine and just take repair kit and extra sweaters and pyjamas in our rucksacks and not give a damn about school or anything."

"Yes, and go through the Schwarzwald that way. Gee, the swell places."

"That's where you went fishing last summer, isn't it?"

"Yes."[3]

They ate the strudel and drank the rest of the wine.

George leaned back against the wall and shut his eyes.

"Wine always makes me feel this way," he said.

"Feel bad?" Nick asked.

"No. I feel good, but funny."

"I know," Nick said.

"Sure," said George.

"Should we have another bottle?" Nick asked.

"Not for me," George said.

They sat there, Nick leaning his elbows on the table, George slumped back against the wall.

"Is Helen going to have a baby?" George said, coming down to the table from the wall.

"Yes."

"When?"

"Late next summer."

"Are you glad?"

"Yes. Now."

"Will you go back to the States?"

"I guess so."

"Do you want to?"

"No."

"Does Helen?"

"No."

George sat silent. He looked at the empty bottle and the empty glasses.

"It's hell, isn't it?" he said.

---

1. A peak northeast of Chamby.
2. Another uncorrected error.
3. George projects a skiing itinerary crossing the Bernese Oberland, the more distant canton of Valais, and the remote Engadine, a high Alpine valley 250 kilometers east of Chamby. Nick suggests a detour through the Schwarzwald (the Black Forest) of Germany to reach the Engadine. The indirect itinerary enables Hemingway to mention his 1922 fishing trip there.

"No. Not exactly," Nick said.

"Why not?"

"I don't know," Nick said.

"Will you ever go skiing together in the States?" George said.

"I don't know," said Nick.

"The mountains aren't much," George said.

"No," said Nick. "They're too rocky. There's too much timber and they're too far away."

"Yes," said George, "that's the way it is in California."

"Yes," Nick said, "that's the way it is everywhere I've ever been."

"Yes," said George, "that's the way it is."

The Swiss got up and paid and went out.

"I wish we were Swiss," George said.

"They've all got goiter," said Nick.[4]

"I don't believe it," George said.

"Neither do I," said Nick.

They laughed.

"Maybe we'll never go skiing again, Nick," George said.

"We've got to," said Nick. "It isn't worth while if you can't."

"We'll go, all right," George said.

"We've got to," Nick agreed.

"I wish we could make a promise about it," George said.

Nick stood up. He buckled his wind jacket tight. He leaned over George and picked up the two ski poles from against the wall. He stuck one of the ski poles into the floor.

"There isn't any good in promising," he said.

They opened the door and went out. It was very cold. The snow had crusted hard. The road ran up the hill into the pine trees.

They took down their skis from where they leaned against the wall in the inn. Nick put on his gloves. George was already started up the road, his skis on his shoulder. Now they would have the run home together.

---

4. Goiter (thyroid enlargement) due to iodine deficiency long devastated certain parts of Switzerland. In 1922, the Swiss introduced iodized salt and soon remedied the problem, making Nick's crude stereotype an ironic nod to medical progress.

Chapter XIII

I heard the drums coming down the street and then the fifes and the pipes and then they came around the corner, all dancing. The street was full of them. Maera saw him and then I saw him. When they stopped the music for the crouch he hunched down in the street with them all and when they started it again he jumped up and went dancing down the street with them.[1] *He was drunk all right.*

You go down after him, said Maera, he hates me.

So I went down and caught up with them and grabbed him while he was crouched down waiting for the music to break loose and said, Come on Luis. For Christ's sake you've got bulls this afternoon. He didn't listen to me, he was listening so hard for the music to start.

I said, Don't be a damn fool Luis. Come on back to the hotel.

Then the music started up again and he jumped up and twisted away from me and started dancing. I grabbed his arm and he pulled loose and said, Oh leave me alone. You're not my father.

I went back to the hotel and Maera was on the balcony looking out to see if I'd be bringing him back. He went inside when he saw me and came downstairs disgusted.

Well, I said, after all he's just an ignorant Mexican savage.

Yes, Maera said, and who will kill his bulls after he gets a cogida?[2]

We, I suppose, I said.

Yes, we, said Maera. We kills the savages' bulls, and the drunkards' bulls, and the riau-riau *dancers' bulls. Yes. We kill them. We kill them all right. Yes. Yes. Yes.*

---

1. The traditional procession in Pamplona, Spain, a noisy march featuring drums, music, and dancing, with marchers singing the refrain "*riau-riau*." Maera is the famous bull-fighter Manuel Garcia López (1896–1924), also seen in Chapter XIV.
2. Tossing (by a bull) (Spanish).

MY OLD MAN[1]

I guess looking at it, now, my old man was cut out for a fat guy, one of those regular little roly fat guys you see around, but he sure never got that way, except a little toward the last, and then it wasn't his fault, he was riding over the jumps only and he could afford to carry plenty of weight then. I remember the way he'd pull on a rubber shirt over a couple of jerseys and a big sweat shirt over that, and get me to run with him in the forenoon in the hot sun. He'd have, maybe, taken a trial trip with one of Razzo's skins early in the morning after just getting in from Torino[2] at four o'clock in the morning and beating it out to the stables in a cab and then with the dew all over everything and the sun just starting to get going, I'd help him pull off his boots and he'd get into a pair of sneakers and all these sweaters and we'd start out.

"Come on, kid," he'd say, stepping up and down on his toes in front of the jock's dressing room, "let's get moving."

Then we'd start off jogging around the infield once, maybe, with him ahead, running nice, and then turn out the gate and along one of those roads with all the trees along both sides of them that run out from San Siro.[3] I'd go ahead of him when we hit the road and I could run pretty good and I'd look around and he'd be jogging easy just behind me and after a little while I'd look around again and he'd begun to sweat. Sweating heavy and he'd just be dogging it along with his eyes on my back, but when he'd catch me looking at him he'd grin and say, "Sweating plenty?" When my old man grinned, nobody could help but grin too. We'd keep right on running out toward the mountains and then my old man would yell, "Hey, Joe!" and I'd look back and he'd be sitting under a tree with a towel he'd had around his waist wrapped around his neck.

I'd come back and sit down beside him and he'd pull a rope out of his pocket and start skipping rope out in the sun with the sweat pouring off his face and him skipping rope out in the white dust with the rope going cloppetty, cloppetty, clop, clop, clop, and the sun hotter, and him working harder up and down a patch of the road. Say, it was a treat to see my old man skip rope, too. He could whirr it fast or lop it slow and fancy. Say, you ought to have seen wops[4] look at us sometimes, when they'd come by, going into town walking

---

1. One of Hemingway's earliest stories, "My Old Man" appeared in *Three Stories and Ten Poems* (1923) and reflects the influence of Sherwood Anderson (1876–1941), who also wrote about boys, horses, and racetracks.
2. Turin, an industrial city in northern Italy. "Skins": slang for "horses."
3. A famous racecourse near Milan, Italy, that hosts steeplechase events and flat-track racing. Hemingway saw races there in 1918 during his recovery from war wounds.
4. Slang for "Italians."

along with big white steers hauling the cart. They sure looked as
though they thought the old man was nuts. He'd start the rope whirring till they'd stop dead still and watch him, then give the steers a
cluck and a poke with the goad and get going again.

When I'd sit watching him working out in the hot sun I sure felt
fond of him. He sure was fun and he done his work so hard and he'd
finish up with a regular whirring that'd drive the sweat out on his
face like water and then sling the rope at the tree and come over
and sit down with me and lean back against the tree with the towel
and a sweater wrapped around his neck.

"Sure is hell keeping it down, Joe," he'd say and lean back and
shut his eyes and breathe long and deep, "it ain't like when you're a
kid." Then he'd get up and before he started to cool we'd jog along
back to the stables. That's the way it was keeping down to weight.
He was worried all the time. Most jocks can just about ride off all
they want to. A jock loses about a kilo every time he rides, but my
old man was sort of dried out and he couldn't keep down his kilos
without all that running.

I remember once at San Siro, Regoli, a little wop, that was riding
for Buzoni, came out across the paddock going to the bar for
something cool; and flicking his boots with his whip, after he'd just
weighed in and my old man had just weighed in too, and came out
with the saddle under his arm looking red-faced and tired and too
big for his silks and he stood there looking at young Regoli standing
up to the outdoors bar, cool and kid-looking, and I said, "What's the
matter, Dad?" cause I thought maybe Regoli had bumped him or
something and he just looked at Regoli and said, "Oh, to hell with
it," and went on to the dressing room.

Well, it would have been all right, maybe, if we'd stayed in Milan
and ridden at Milan and Torino, 'cause if there ever were any easy
courses, it's those two. "Pianola,[5] Joe," my old man said when he
dismounted in the winning stall after what the wops thought was a
hell of a steeplechase. I asked him once. "This course rides itself.
It's the pace you're going at, that makes riding the jumps dangerous, Joe. We ain't going any pace here, and they ain't really bad
jumps either. But it's the pace always—not the jumps—that makes
the trouble."

San Siro was the swellest course I'd ever seen but the old man
said it was a dog's life. Going back and forth between Mirafiore[6] and
San Siro and riding just about every day in the week with a train
ride every other night.

---

5. Self-playing piano.
6. Ippodromo di Mirafiori, a racetrack in Turin.

I was nuts about the horses, too. There's something about it, when they come out and go up the track to the post. Sort of dancy and tight looking with the jock keeping a tight hold on them and maybe easing off a little and letting them run a little going up. Then once they were at the barrier it got me worse than anything. Especially at San Siro with that big green infield and the mountains way off and the fat wop starter with his big whip and the jocks fiddling them around and then the barrier snapping up and that bell going off and them all getting off in a bunch and then commencing to string out. You know the way a bunch of skins gets off. If you're up in the stand with a pair of glasses all you see is them plunging off and then that bell goes off and it seems like it rings for a thousand years and then they come sweeping round the turn. There wasn't ever anything like it for me.

But my old man said one day, in the dressing room, when he was getting into his street clothes, "None of these things are horses, Joe. They'd kill that bunch of skates for their hides and hoofs up at Paris."[7] That was the day he'd won the Premio Commercio with Lantorna shooting her out of the field the last hundred meters like pulling a cork out of a bottle.

It was right after the Premio Commercio that we pulled out and left Italy. My old man and Holbrook and a fat wop in a straw hat that kept wiping his face with a handkerchief were having an argument at a table in the Galleria.[8] They were all talking French and the two of them was after my old man about something. Finally he didn't say anything any more but just sat there and looked at Holbrook, and the two of them kept after him, first one talking and then the other, and the fat wop always butting in on Holbrook.

"You go out and buy me a *Sportsman*, will you, Joe?" my old man said, and handed me a couple of soldi[9] without looking away from Holbrook.

So I went out of the Galleria and walked over to in front of the Scala[1] and bought a paper, and came back and stood a little way away because I didn't want to butt in and my old man was sitting back in his chair looking down at his coffee and fooling with a spoon and Holbrook and the big wop were standing and the big wop was wiping his face and shaking his head. And I came up and my old man acted just as though the two of them weren't standing there and said, "Want an ice, Joe?" Holbrook looked down at my old man and

---

7. Joe's father expresses scorn for slow horses, the "skates" at San Siro that would be butchered in Paris.
8. Galleria Vittorio Emanuele II, Italy's oldest active shopping mall and a popular meeting place.
9. Two coins (in the Italian currency of that era).
1. La Scala, a famous opera house.

said slow and careful, "You son of a bitch," and he and the fat wop went out through the tables.

My old man sat there and sort of smiled at me, but his face was white and he looked sick as hell and I was scared and felt sick inside because I knew something had happened and I didn't see how anybody could call my old man a son of a bitch, and get away with it. My old man opened up the *Sportsman* and studied the handicaps for a while and then he said, "You got to take a lot of things in this world, Joe." And three days later we left Milan for good on the Turin train for Paris, after an auction sale out in front of Turner's stables of everything we couldn't get into a trunk and a suit case.

We got into Paris early in the morning in a long, dirty station the old man told me was the Gare de Lyon. Paris was an awful big town after Milan. Seems like in Milan everybody is going somewhere and all the trams run somewhere and there ain't any sort of a mix-up, but Paris is all balled up and they never do straighten it out. I got to like it, though, part of it, anyway, and say, it's got the best race courses in the world. Seems as though that were the thing that keeps it all going and about the only thing you can figure on is that every day the buses will be going out to whatever track they're running at, going right out through everything to the track.[2] I never really got to know Paris well, because I just came in about once or twice a week with the old man from Maisons and he always sat at the Café de la Paix on the Opera side with the rest of the gang from Maisons and I guess that's one of the busiest parts of the town. But, say, it is funny that a big town like Paris wouldn't have a Galleria, isn't it?

Well, we went out to live at Maisons-Lafitte, where just about everybody lives except the gang at Chantilly, with a Mrs. Meyers that runs a boarding house. Maisons is about the swellest place to live I've ever seen in all my life. The town ain't so much, but there's a lake and a swell forest that we used to go off bumming in all day, a couple of us kids, and my old man made me a sling shot and we got a lot of things with it but the best one was a magpie. Young Dick Atkinson shot a rabbit with it one day and we put it under a tree and were all sitting around and Dick had some cigarettes and all of a sudden the rabbit jumped up and beat it into the brush and we chased it but we couldn't find it. Gee, we had fun at Maisons. Mrs. Meyers used to give me lunch in the morning and I'd be gone all day. I learned to talk French quick. It's an easy language.

---

2. Hemingway identifies many racetracks around Paris: the flat tracks of Chantilly, St. Cloud, and Tremblay, and the steeplechase tracks, Auteuil and Enghien. Both types of racing took place at Maisons-Lafitte, northwest of Paris, where Joe and his father stay.

As soon as we got to Maisons, my old man wrote to Milan for his license and he was pretty worried till it came.[3] He used to sit around the Café de Paris in Maisons with the gang, there were lots of guys he'd known when he rode up at Paris, before the war, lived at Maisons, and there's a lot of time to sit around because the work around a racing stable, for the jocks, that is, is all cleaned up by nine o'clock in the morning. They take the first bunch of skins out to gallop them at 5.30 in the morning and they work the second lot at 8 o'clock. That means getting up early all right and going to bed early, too. If a jock's riding for somebody too, he can't go boozing around because the trainer always has an eye on him if he's a kid and if he ain't a kid he's always got an eye on himself. So mostly if a jock ain't working he sits around the Café de Paris with the gang and they can all sit around about two or three hours in front of some drink like a vermouth and seltz and they talk and tell stories and shoot pool and it's sort of like a club or the Galleria in Milan. Only it ain't really like the Galleria because there everybody is going by all the time and there's everybody around at the tables.

Well, my old man got his license all right. They sent it through to him without a word and he rode a couple of times. Amiens, up country[4] and that sort of thing, but he didn't seem to get any engagement. Everybody liked him and whenever I'd come into the Café in the forenoon I'd find somebody drinking with him because my old man wasn't tight like most of these jockeys that have got the first dollar they made riding at the World's Fair in St. Louis in nineteen ought four. That's what my old man would say when he'd kid George Burns.[5] But it seemed like everybody steered clear of giving my old man any mounts.

We went out to wherever they were running every day with the car from Maisons and that was the most fun of all. I was glad when the horses came back from Deauville and the summer.[6] Even though it meant no more bumming in the woods, 'cause then we'd ride to Enghien or Tremblay or St. Cloud and watch them from the trainers' and jockeys' stand. I sure learned about racing from going out with that gang and the fun of it was going every day.

I remember once out at St. Cloud. It was a big two hundred thousand franc[7] race with seven entries and Kzar a big favorite. I went around to the paddock to see the horses with my old man and you never saw such horses. This Kzar is a great big yellow horse that

---

3. Joe's father must transfer his license to race in France.
4. I.e., at a track in Amiens, a city in northern France.
5. A fictional character, *not* the American comedian (1896–1996), who became famous in the 1930s.
6. At the fashionable beach resort of Deauville, summer races entertained vacationers.
7. French currency until the introduction of the Euro.

looks like just nothing but run. I never saw such a horse. He was being led around the paddocks with his head down and when he went by me I felt all hollow inside he was so beautiful. There never was such a wonderful, lean, running built horse. And he went around the paddock putting his feet just so and quiet and careful and moving easy like he knew just what he had to do and not jerking and standing up on his legs and getting wild eyed like you see these selling platers with a shot of dope in them.[8] The crowd was so thick I couldn't see him again except just his legs going by and some yellow and my old man started out through the crowd and I followed him over to the jock's dressing room back in the trees and there was a big crowd around there, too, but the man at the door in a derby nodded to my old man and we got in and everybody was sitting around and getting dressed and pulling shirts over their heads and pulling boots on and it all smelled hot and sweaty and linimenty and outside was the crowd looking in.

The old man went over and sat down beside George Gardner that was getting into his pants and said, "What's the dope, George?" just in an ordinary tone of voice 'cause there ain't any use him feeling around because George either can tell him or he can't tell him.

"He won't win," George says very low, leaning over and buttoning the bottoms of his breeches.

"Who will?" my old man says, leaning over close so nobody can hear.

"Kircubbin," George says, "and if he does, save me a couple of tickets."

My old man says something in a regular voice to George and George says, "Don't ever bet on anything I tell you," kidding like, and we beat it out and through all the crowd that was looking in, over to the 100 franc mutuel machine.[9] But I knew something big was up because George is Kzar's jockey. On the way he gets one of the yellow odds-sheets with the starting prices on and Kzar is only paying 5 for 10, Cefisidote is next at 3 to 1 and fifth down the list this Kircubbin at 8 to 1. My old man bets five thousand on Kircubbin to win and puts on a thousand to place and we went around back of the grandstand to go up the stairs and get a place to watch the race.

We were jammed in tight and first a man in a long coat with a gray tall hat and a whip folded up in his hand came out and then one after another the horses, with the jocks up and a stable boy holding the bridle on each side and walking along, followed the old guy. That big yellow horse Kzar came first. He didn't look so big when

8. "Selling platers": inferior horses drugged and sold in auction races.
9. A device for adding up bets in a pari-mutuel system, where all wagers are divided among the winners.

you first looked at him until you saw the length of his legs and the whole way he's built and the way he moves. Gosh, I never saw such a horse. George Gardner was riding him and they moved along slow, back of the old guy in the gray tall hat that walked along like he was a ring master in a circus. Back of Kzar, moving along smooth and yellow in the sun, was a good looking black with a nice head with Tommy Archibald riding him; and after the black was a string of five more horses all moving along slow in a procession past the grandstand and the pesage.[1] My old man said the black was Kircubbin and I took a good look at him and he was a nice-looking horse, all right, but nothing like Kzar.

Everybody cheered Kzar when he went by and he sure was one swell-looking horse. The procession of them went around on the other side past the pelouse[2] and then back up to the near end of the course and the circus master had the stable boys turn them loose one after another so they could gallop by the stands on their way up to the post and let everybody have a good look at them. They weren't at the post hardly any time at all when the gong started and you could see them way off across the infield all in a bunch starting on the first swing like a lot of little toy horses. I was watching them through the glasses and Kzar was running well back, with one of the bays making the pace. They swept down and around and came pounding past and Kzar was way back when they passed us and this Kircubbin horse in front and going smooth. Gee, it's awful when they go by you and then you have to watch them go farther away and get smaller and smaller and then all bunched up on the turns and then come around towards into the stretch and you feel like swearing and god-damming worse and worse. Finally they made the last turn and came into the straightaway with this Kircubbin horse way out in front. Everybody was looking funny and saying "Kzar" in sort of a sick way and them pounding nearer down the stretch, and then something came out of the pack right into my glasses like a horse-headed yellow streak and everybody began to yell "Kzar" as though they were crazy. Kzar came on faster than I'd ever seen anything in my life and pulled up on Kircubbin that was going fast as any black horse could go with the jock flogging hell out of him with the gad[3] and they were right dead neck and neck for a second but Kzar seemed going about twice as fast with those great jumps and that head out—but it was while they were neck and neck that they passed the winning post and when the numbers went up in the slots the first one was 2 and that meant that Kircubbin had won.

1. The weighing area for jockeys.
2. Lawn.
3. Horseracing whip.

I felt all trembly and funny inside, and then we were all jammed in with the people going downstairs to stand in front of the board where they'd post what Kircubbin paid. Honest, watching the race I'd forgot how much my old man had bet on Kircubbin. I'd wanted Kzar to win so damned bad. But now it was all over it was swell to know we had the winner.

"Wasn't it a swell race, Dad?" I said to him.

He looked at me sort of funny with his derby on the back of his head. "George Gardner's a swell jockey, all right," he said. "It sure took a great jock to keep that Kzar horse from winning."

Of course I knew it was funny all the time. But my old man saying that right out like that sure took the kick all out of it for me and I didn't get the real kick back again ever, even when they posted the numbers upon the board and the bell rang to pay off and we saw that Kircubbin paid 67.50 for 10.[4] All round people were saying, "Poor Kzar! Poor Kzar!" And I thought, I wish I were a jockey and could have rode him instead of that son of a bitch. And that was funny, thinking of George Gardner as a son of a bitch because I'd always liked him and besides he'd given us the winner, but I guess that's what he is, all right.

My old man had a big lot of money after that race and he took to coming into Paris oftener. If they raced at Tremblay he'd have them drop him in town on their way back to Maisons and he and I'd sit out in front of the Café de la Paix and watch the people go by. It's funny sitting there. There's streams of people going by and all sorts of guys come up and want to sell you things, and I loved to sit there with my old man. That was when we'd have the most fun. Guys would come by selling funny rabbits that jumped if you squeezed a bulb and they'd come up to us and my old man would kid with them. He could talk French just like English and all those kind of guys knew him 'cause you can always tell a jockey—and then we always sat at the same table and they got used to seeing us there. There were guys selling matrimonial papers and girls selling rubber eggs that when you squeezed them a rooster came out of them and one old wormy-looking guy that went by with post-cards of Paris, showing them to everybody, and, of course, nobody ever bought any, and then he would come back and show the under side of the pack and they would all be smutty post-cards and lots of people would dig down and buy them.

Gee, I remember the funny people that used to go by. Girls around supper time looking for somebody to take them out to eat and they'd speak to my old man and he'd make some joke at them in French and they'd pat me on the head and go on. Once there was an American woman sitting with her kid daughter at the next table to us and they were both eating ices and I kept looking at the girl and she was awfully good looking and I smiled at her and she smiled at me but that was all that ever came of it because I looked for her mother and her every day and I made up ways that I was going to speak to her and I wondered if I got to know her if her mother would let me take her out to Auteuil or Tremblay but I never saw either of them again. Anyway, I guess it wouldn't have been any good, anyway, because looking back on it I remember the way I thought out would be best to speak to her was to say, "Pardon me, but perhaps I can give you a winner at Enghien today?" and, after all, maybe she would have thought I was a tout instead of really trying to give her a winner.

We'd sit at the Café de la Paix, my old man and me, and we had a big drag with the waiter because my old man drank whisky and it cost five francs, and that meant a good tip when the saucers were counted up.[5] My old man was drinking more than I'd ever seen him, but he wasn't riding at all now and besides he said that whisky kept his weight down. But I noticed he was putting it on, all right, just the same. He'd busted away from his old gang out at Maisons and seemed to like just sitting around on the boulevard with me. But he was dropping money every day at the track. He'd feel sort of doleful after the last race, if he'd lost on the day, until we'd get to our table and he'd have his first whisky and then he'd be fine.

He'd be reading the *Paris-Sport* and he'd look over at me and say, "Where's your girl, Joe?" to kid me on account I had told him about the girl that day at the next table. And I'd get red, but I liked being kidded about her. It gave me a good feeling. "Keep your eye peeled for her, Joe," he'd say, "she'll be back."

He'd ask me questions about things and some of the things I'd say he'd laugh. And then he'd get started talking about things. About riding down in Egypt, or at St. Moritz[6] on the ice before my mother died, and about during the war when they had regular races down in the south of France without any purses, or betting or crowd or anything just to keep the breed up. Regular races with the jocks riding hell out of the horses. Gee, I could listen to my old man talk by the hour, especially when he'd had a couple or so of drinks. He'd tell me about when he was a boy in Kentucky and going coon[7] hunting, and the old days in the States before everything went on the

---

5. Paris waiters piled up saucers to count the drinks consumed. "Big drag": influence.
6. Alpine resort in Switzerland.
7. Raccoon.

bum there. And he'd say, "Joe, when we've got a decent stake, you're going back there to the States and go to school."

"What've I got to go back there to go to school for when every-thing's on the bum there?" I'd ask him.

"That's different," he'd say and get the waiter over and pay the pile of saucers and we'd get a taxi to the Gare St. Lazare and get on the train out to Maisons.

One day at Auteuil, after a selling steeplechase, my old man bought in the winner for 30,000 francs.[8] He had to bid a little to get him but the stable let the horse go finally and my old man had his permit and his colors in a week. Gee, I felt proud when my old man was an owner. He fixed it up for stable space with Charles Drake and cut out coming in to Paris, and started his running and sweat-ing out again, and him and I were the whole stable gang. Our horse's name was Gilford, he was Irish bred and a nice, sweet jumper. My old man figured that training him and riding him, himself, he was a good investment. I was proud of everything and I thought Gil-ford was as good a horse as Kzar. He was a good, solid jumper, a bay, with plenty of speed on the flat, if you asked him for it, and he was a nice-looking horse, too.

Gee, I was fond of him. The first time he started with my old man up, he finished third in a 2500 meter hurdle race and when my old man got off him, all sweating and happy in the place stall, and went in to weigh, I felt as proud of him as though it was the first race he'd ever placed in. You see, when a guy ain't been riding for a long time, you can't make yourself really believe that he has ever rode. The whole thing was different now, 'cause down in Milan, even big races never seemed to make any difference to my old man, if he won he wasn't ever excited or anything, and now it was so I couldn't hardly sleep the night before a race and I knew my old man was excited, too, even if he didn't show it. Riding for yourself makes an awful difference.

Second time Gilford and my old man started, was a rainy Sunday at Auteuil, in the Prix du Marat, a 4500 meter steeplechase. As soon as he'd gone out I beat it up in the stand with the new glasses my old man had bought for me to watch them. They started way over at the far end of the course and there was some trouble at the barrier. Something with goggle blinders on was making a great fuss and rear-ing around and busted the barrier once, but I could see my old man in our black jacket, with a white cross and a black cap, sitting up on Gilford, and patting him with his hand. Then they were off in a jump and out of sight behind the trees and the gong going for dear life

---

8. In this event, the winning horse is auctioned off.

and the pari-mutuel wickets rattling down.[9] Gosh, I was so excited, I was afraid to look at them, but I fixed the glasses on the place where they would come out back of the trees and then out they came with the old black jacket going third and they all sailing over the jump like birds. Then they went out of sight again and then they came pounding out and down the hill and all going nice and sweet and easy and taking the fence smooth in a bunch, and moving away from us all solid. Looked as though you could walk across on their backs they were all so bunched and going so smooth. Then they bellied over the big double Bullfinch and something came down.[1] I couldn't see who it was, but in a minute the horse was up and galloping free and the field, all bunched still, sweeping around the long left turn into the straightaway. They jumped the stone wall and came jammed down the stretch toward the big water-jump right in front of the stands. I saw them coming and hollered at my old man as he went by, and he was leading by about a length and riding way out, and light as a monkey, and they were racing for the water-jump. They took off over the big hedge of the water-jump in a pack and then there was a crash, and two horses pulled sideways out off it, and kept on going, and three others were piled up. I couldn't see my old man anywhere. One horse kneed himself up and the jock had hold of the bridle and mounted and went slamming on after the place money.[2] The other horse was up and away by himself, jerking his head and galloping with the bridle rein hanging and the jock staggered over to one side of the track against the fence. Then Gilford rolled over to one side off my old man and got up and started to run on three legs with his front off hoof[3] dangling and there was my old man laying there on the grass flat out with his face up and blood all over the side of his head. I ran down the stand and bumped into a jam of people and got to the rail and a cop grabbed me and held me and two big stretcher-bearers were going out after my old man and around on the other side of the course I saw three horses, strung way out, coming out of the trees and taking the jump.

My old man was dead when they brought him in and while a doctor was listening to his heart with a thing plugged in his ears, I heard a shot up the track that meant they'd killed Gilford. I lay down beside my old man, when they carried the stretcher into the hospital room, and hung onto the stretcher and cried and cried, and he looked so white and gone and so awfully dead, and I couldn't help feeling that if my old man was dead maybe they didn't need to have shot

9. Betting windows close at post time, just before the race starts.
1. A bullfinch is a hedge six feet high over which the horse jumps. A double bullfinch presents consecutive hedges.
2. Trying to finish second.
3. The broken and limp front leg.

Gilford. His hoof might have got well. I don't know. I loved my old man so much.

Then a couple of guys came in and one of them patted me on the back and then went over and looked at my old man and then pulled a sheet off the cot and spread it over him; and the other was telephoning in French for them to send the ambulance to take him out to Maisons. And I couldn't stop crying, crying and choking, sort of, and George Gardner came in and sat down beside me on the floor and put his arm around me and says, "Come on, Joe, old boy. Get up and we'll go out and wait for the ambulance."

George and I went out to the gate and I was trying to stop bawling and George wiped off my face with his handkerchief and we were standing back a little ways while the crowd was going out of the gate and a couple of guys stopped near us while we were waiting for the crowd to get through the gate and one of them was counting a bunch of mutuel tickets and he said, "Well, Butler got his, all right."

The other guy said, "I don't give a good goddam if he did, the crook. He had it coming to him on the stuff he's pulled."

"I'll say he had," said the other guy, and tore the bunch of tickets in two.

And George Gardner looked at me to see if I'd heard and I had all right and he said, "Don't you listen to what those bums said, Joe. Your old man was one swell guy."

But I don't know. Seems like when they get started they don't leave a guy nothing.

Chapter XIV

Maera lay still, his head on his arms, his face in the sand. He felt warm and sticky from the bleeding. Each time he felt the horn coming. Sometimes the bull only bumped him with his head. Once the horn went all the way through him and he felt it go into the sand. Some one had the bull by the tail. They were swearing at him and flopping the cape in his face. Then the bull was gone. Some men picked Maera up and started to run with him toward the barriers through the gate out the passageway around under the grandstand to the infirmary. They laid Maera down on a cot and one of the men went out for the doctor. The others stood around. The doctor came running from the corral where he had been sewing up picador horses. He had to stop and wash his hands. There was a great shouting going on in the grandstand overhead. Maera felt everything getting larger and larger and then smaller and smaller. Then it got larger and larger and larger and then smaller and smaller. Then everything commenced to run faster and faster as when they speed up a cinematograph film.[1] Then he was dead.[2]

1. Hemingway adopts emerging cinematic techniques to simulate dying—things getting larger for Maera (see note 1 on 95), then smaller, then speeding up, like a film in fast-forward.
2. Maera died in December 1924 from pneumonia contracted during the last stages of tuberculosis. Hemingway saw Maera fight in 1923 and described his prowess in a Sunday *Toronto Star* piece excerpted in this volume (147).

BIG TWO-HEARTED RIVER: PART I[1]

The train went on up the track out of sight, around one of the hills of burnt timber. Nick sat down on the bundle of canvas and bedding the baggage man had pitched out of the door of the baggage car. There was no town, nothing but the rails and the burned-over country. The thirteen saloons that had lined the one street of Seney had not left a trace. The foundations of the Mansion House hotel stuck up above the ground. The stone was chipped and split by the fire. It was all that was left of the town of Seney. Even the surface had been burned off the ground.[2]

Nick looked at the burned-over stretch of hillside, where he had expected to find the scattered houses of the town and then walked down the railroad track to the bridge over the river. The river was there. It swirled against the log spiles of the bridge. Nick looked down into the clear, brown water, colored from the pebbly bottom, and watched the trout keeping themselves steady in the current with wavering fins. As he watched them they changed their positions by quick angles, only to hold steady in the fast water again. Nick watched them a long time.

He watched them holding themselves with their noses into the current, many trout in deep, fast moving water, slightly distorted as he watched far down through the glassy convex surface of the pool, its surface pushing and swelling smooth against the resistance of the log-driven piles of the bridge. At the bottom of the pool were the big trout. Nick did not see them at first. Then he saw them at the bottom of the pool, big trout looking to hold themselves on the gravel bottom in a varying mist of gravel and sand, raised in spurts by the current.

Nick looked down into the pool from the bridge. It was a hot day. A kingfisher flew up the stream. It was a long time since Nick had looked into a stream and seen trout. They were very satisfactory. As the shadow of the kingfisher moved up the stream, a big trout shot upstream in a long angle, only his shadow marking the angle, then lost his shadow as he came through the surface of the water, caught the sun, and then, as he went back into the stream under the surface, his shadow seemed to float down the stream with the current, unresisting, to his post under the bridge where he tightened facing up into the current.

---

1. About this work, Hemingway wrote in *MF*: "The story was about coming back from the war but there was no mention of the war in it" (76).
2. Located in Michigan's Upper Peninsula, Seney grew during the logging boom of the 1880s. Once boasting 3,000 residents, it became a virtual ghost town by 1900, when the local timber was gone. Forest fires menaced Seney in the 1890s but did not destroy it.

Nick's heart tightened as the trout moved. He felt all the old feeling.

He turned and looked down the stream. It stretched away, pebbly-bottomed with shallows and big boulders and a deep pool as it curved away around the foot of a bluff.

Nick walked back up the ties to where his pack lay in the cinders beside the railway track. He was happy. He adjusted the pack harness around the bundle, pulling straps tight, slung the pack on his back, got his arms through the shoulder straps and took some of the pull off his shoulders by leaning his forehead against the wide band of the tump-line.[3] Still, it was too heavy. It was much too heavy. He had his leather rod-case in his hand and leaning forward to keep the weight of the pack high on his shoulders he walked along the road that paralleled the railway track, leaving the burned town behind in the heat, and then turned off around a hill with a high, fire-scarred hill on either side onto a road that went back into the country. He walked along the road feeling the ache from the pull of the heavy pack. The road climbed steadily. It was hard work walking up-hill. His muscles ached and the day was hot, but Nick felt happy. He felt he had left everything behind, the need for thinking, the need to write, other needs. It was all back of him.

From the time he had gotten down off the train and the baggage man had thrown his pack out of the open car door things had been different. Seney was burned, the country was burned over and changed, but it did not matter. It could not all be burned. He knew that. He hiked along the road, sweating in the sun, climbing to cross the range of hills that separated the railway from the pine plains.

The road ran on, dipping occasionally, but always climbing. Nick went on up. Finally the road after going parallel to the burnt hillside reached the top. Nick leaned back against a stump and slipped out of the pack harness. Ahead of him, as far as he could see, was the pine plain. The burned country stopped off at the left with the range of hills. On ahead islands of dark pine trees rose out of the plain. Far off to the left was the line of the river. Nick followed it with his eye and caught glints of the water in the sun.

There was nothing but the pine plain ahead of him, until the far blue hills that marked the Lake Superior height of land. He could hardly see them, faint and far away in the heat-light over the plain. If he looked too steadily they were gone. But if he only half-looked they were there, the far-off hills of the height of land.

Nick sat down against the charred stump and smoked a cigarette. His pack balanced on the top of the stump, harness holding ready,

---

3. Nick distributes the weight of his heavy pack using a tump-line, a strap across his forehead.

a hollow molded in it from his back. Nick sat smoking, looking out over the country. He did not need to get his map out. He knew where he was from the position of the river.

As he smoked, his legs stretched out in front of him, he noticed a grasshopper walk along the ground and up onto his woolen sock. The grasshopper was black. As he had walked along the road, climbing, he had started many grasshoppers from the dust. They were all black. They were not the big grasshoppers with yellow and black or red and black wings whirring out from their black wing sheathing as they fly up. These were just ordinary hoppers, but all a sooty black in color. Nick had wondered about them as he walked, without really thinking about them. Now, as he watched the black hopper that was nibbling at the wool of his sock with its fourway lip, he realized that they had all turned black from living in the burned-over land. He realized that the fire must have come the year before, but the grasshoppers were all black now. He wondered how long they would stay that way.

Carefully he reached his hand down and took hold of the hopper by the wings. He turned him up, all his legs walking in the air, and looked at his jointed belly. Yes, it was black too, iridescent where the back and head were dusty.

"Go on, hopper," Nick said, speaking out loud for the first time. "Fly away somewhere."

He tossed the grasshopper up into the air and watched him sail away to a charcoal stump across the road.

Nick stood up. He leaned his back against the weight of his pack where it rested upright on the stump and got his arms through the shoulder straps. He stood with the pack on his back on the brow of the hill looking out across the country, toward the distant river and then struck down the hillside away from the road. Underfoot the ground was good walking. Two hundred yards down the hillside the fire line stopped. Then it was sweet fern, growing ankle high, to walk through, and clumps of jack pines; a long undulating country with frequent rises and descents, sandy underfoot and the country alive again.

Nick kept his direction by the sun. He knew where he wanted to strike the river and he kept on through the pine plain, mounting small rises to see other rises ahead of him and sometimes from the top of a rise a great solid island of pines off to his right or his left. He broke off some sprigs of the heathery sweet fern, and put them under his pack straps. The chafing crushed it and he smelled it as he walked.

He was tired and very hot, walking across the uneven, shadeless pine plain. At any time he knew he could strike the river by turning off to his left. It could not be more than a mile away. But he kept on

toward the north to hit the river as far upstream as he could go in
one day's walking.

For some time as he walked Nick had been in sight of one of the
big islands of pine standing out above the rolling high ground
he was crossing. He dipped down and then as he came slowly up to
the crest of the bridge he turned and made toward the pine trees.

There was no underbrush in the island of pine trees. The trunks
of the trees went straight up or slanted toward each other. The
trunks were straight and brown without branches. The branches
were high above. Some interlocked to make a solid shadow on the
brown forest floor. Around the grove of trees was a bare space. It
was brown and soft underfoot as Nick walked on it. This was the
over-lapping of the pine needle floor, extending out beyond the width
of the high branches. The trees had grown tall and the branches
moved high, leaving in the sun this bare space they had once covered
with shadow. Sharp at the edge of this extension of the forest floor
commenced the sweet fern.

Nick slipped off his pack and lay down in the shade. He lay on his
back and looked up into the pine trees. His neck and back and the
small of his back rested as he stretched. The earth felt good against
his back. He looked up at the sky, through the branches, and then
shut his eyes. He opened them and looked up again. There was a
wind high up in the branches. He shut his eyes again and went to
sleep.

Nick woke stiff and cramped. The sun was nearly down. His pack
was heavy and the straps painful as he lifted it on. He leaned over
with the pack on and picked up the leather rod-case and started out
from the pine trees across the sweet fern swale, toward the river.
He knew it could not be more than a mile.

He came down a hillside covered with stumps into a meadow. At
the edge of the meadow flowed the river. Nick was glad to get to the
river. He walked upstream through the meadow. His trousers were
soaked with the dew as he walked. After the hot day, the dew had
come quickly and heavily. The river made no sound. It was too fast
and smooth. At the edge of the meadow, before he mounted to a
piece of high ground to make camp, Nick looked down the river at
the trout rising. They were rising to insects come from the swamp
on the other side of the stream when the sun went down. The trout
jumped out of water to take them. While Nick walked through the
little stretch of meadow alongside the stream, trout had jumped high
out of water. Now as he looked down the river, the insects must be
settling on the surface, for the trout were feeding steadily all down
the stream. As far down the long stretch as he could see, the trout
were rising, making circles all down the surface of the water, as
though it were starting to rain.

The ground rose, wooded and sandy, to overlook the meadow, the stretch of river and the swamp. Nick dropped his pack and rod-case and looked for a level piece of ground. He was very hungry and he wanted to make his camp before he cooked. Between two jack pines, the ground was quite level. He took the ax out of the pack and chopped out two projecting roots. That leveled a piece of ground large enough to sleep on. He smoothed out the sandy soil with his hand and pulled all the sweet fern bushes by their roots. His hands smelled good from the sweet fern. He smoothed the uprooted earth. He did not want anything making lumps under the blankets. When he had the ground smooth, he spread his three blankets. One he folded double, next to the ground. The other two he spread on top.

With the ax he slit off a bright slab of pine from one of the stumps and split it into pegs for the tent. He wanted them long and solid to hold in the ground. With the tent unpacked and spread on the ground, the pack, leaning against a jackpine, looked much smaller. Nick tied the rope that served the tent for a ridge-pole to the trunk of one of the pine trees and pulled the tent up off the ground with the other end of the rope and tied it to the other pine. The tent hung on the rope like a canvas blanket on a clothesline. Nick poked a pole he had cut up under the back peak of the canvas and then made it a tent by pegging out the sides. He pegged the sides out taut and drove the pegs deep, hitting them down into the ground with the flat of the ax until the rope loops were buried and the canvas was drum tight.

Across the open mouth of the tent Nick fixed cheesecloth to keep out mosquitoes. He crawled inside under the mosquito bar with various things from the pack to put at the head of the bed under the slant of the canvas. Inside the tent the light came through the brown canvas. It smelled pleasantly of canvas. Already there was something mysterious and homelike. Nick was happy as he crawled inside the tent. He had not been unhappy all day. This was different though. Now things were done. There had been this to do. Now it was done. It had been a hard trip. He was very tired. That was done. He had made his camp. He was settled. Nothing could touch him. It was a good place to camp. He was there, in the good place. He was in his home where he had made it. Now he was hungry.

He came out, crawling under the cheesecloth. It was quite dark outside. It was lighter in the tent.

Nick went over to the pack and found, with his fingers, a long nail in a paper sack of nails, in the bottom of the pack. He drove it into the pine tree, holding it close and hitting it gently with the flat of the ax. He hung the pack up on the nail. All his supplies were in the pack. They were off the ground and sheltered now.

Nick was hungry. He did not believe he had ever been hungrier.
He opened and emptied a can of pork and beans and a can of spaghetti into the frying pan.

"I've got a right to eat this kind of stuff, if I'm willing to carry it,"
Nick said. His voice sounded strange in the darkening woods. He
did not speak again.

He started a fire with some chunks of pine he got with the ax from
a stump. Over the fire he stuck a wire grill, pushing the four legs
down into the ground with his boot. Nick put the frying pan on the
grill over the flames. He was hungrier. The beans and spaghetti
warmed. Nick stirred them and mixed them together. They began
to bubble, making little bubbles that rose with difficulty to the surface. There was a good smell. Nick got out a bottle of tomato catchup
and cut four slices of bread. The little bubbles were coming faster
now. Nick sat down beside the fire and lifted the frying pan off. He
poured about half the contents out into the tin plate. It spread slowly
on the plate. Nick knew it was too hot. He poured on some tomato
catchup. He knew the beans and spaghetti were still too hot. He
looked at the fire, then at the tent, he was not going to spoil it all by
burning his tongue. For years he had never enjoyed fried bananas
because he had never been able to wait for them to cool. His tongue
was very sensitive. He was very hungry. Across the river in the
swamp, in the almost dark, he saw a mist rising. He looked at the
tent once more. All right. He took a full spoonful from the plate.

"Chrise," Nick said, "Geezus Chrise," he said happily.

He ate the whole plateful before he remembered the bread. Nick
finished the second plateful with the bread, mopping the plate shiny.
He had not eaten since a cup of coffee and a ham sandwich in the
station restaurant at St. Ignace.[4] It had been a very fine experience.
He had been that hungry before, but had not been able to satisfy it.
He could have made camp hours before if he had wanted to. There
were plenty of good places to camp on the river. But this was good.

Nick tucked two big chips of pine under the grill. The fire flared
up. He had forgotten to get water for the coffee. Out of the pack he
got a folding canvas bucket and walked down the hill, across the
edge of the meadow, to the stream. The other bank was in the white
mist. The grass was wet and cold as he knelt on the bank and dipped
the canvas bucket into the stream. It bellied and pulled hard in the
current. The water was ice cold. Nick rinsed the bucket and carried
it full up to the camp. Up away from the stream it was not so cold.

Nick drove another big nail and hung up the bucket full of water.
He dipped the coffee pot half full, put some more chips under the
grill onto the fire and put the pot on. He could not remember which

4. See map (4).

way he made coffee. He could remember an argument about it with Hopkins, but not which side he had taken. He decided to bring it to a boil. He remembered now that was Hopkins's way. He had once argued about everything with Hopkins.[5] While he waited for the coffee to boil, he opened a small can of apricots. He liked to open cans. He emptied the can of apricots out into a tin cup. While he watched the coffee on the fire, he drank the juice syrup of the apricots, carefully at first to keep from spilling, then meditatively, sucking the apricots down. They were better than fresh apricots.

The coffee boiled as he watched. The lid came up and coffee and grounds ran down the side of the pot. Nick took it off the grill. It was a triumph for Hopkins. He put sugar in the empty apricot cup and poured some of the coffee out to cool. It was too hot to pour and he used his hat to hold the handle of the coffee pot. He would not let it steep in the pot at all. Not the first cup. It should be straight Hopkins all the way. Hop deserved that. He was a very serious coffee drinker. He was the most serious man Nick had ever known. Not heavy, serious. That was a long time ago. Hopkins spoke without moving his lips. He had played polo. He made millions of dollars in Texas. He had borrowed carfare to go to Chicago, when the wire came that his first big well had come in.[6] He could have wired for money. That would have been too slow. They called Hop's girl the Blonde Venus. Hop did not mind because she was not his real girl. Hopkins said very confidently that none of them would make fun of his real girl. He was right. Hopkins went away when the telegram came.[7] That was on the Black River. It took eight days for the telegram to reach him. Hopkins gave away his .22 caliber Colt automatic pistol to Nick. He gave his camera to Bill. It was to remember him always by. They were all going fishing again next summer. The Hop Head[8] was rich. He would get a yacht and they would all cruise along the north shore of Lake Superior. He was excited but serious. They said good-bye and all felt bad. It broke up the trip. They never saw Hopkins again. That was a long time ago on the Black River.[9]

Nick drank the coffee, the coffee according to Hopkins. The coffee was bitter. Nick laughed. It made a good ending to the story. His mind was starting to work. He knew he could choke it because he

5. Charles H. Hopkins (1893–1956) was an editor in Kansas City when Hemingway worked for the *Star* in 1917. Hopkins joined the group Hemingway gathered for a final Michigan fishing trip before his Red Cross deployment in May 1918.
6. Hopkins's father ran an oil business in Oklahoma, but the story of Hopkins making millions was entirely fabricated.
7. The telegram reports that Hopkins's well has started producing oil. But in 1918, the message received by Hemingway during his fishing trip was that his ship for Europe was leaving soon from New York.
8. Slang for a drug user.
9. Hemingway likely refers to the Black River forty miles east of Walloon Lake, as shown on the map (4).

was tired enough. He spilled the coffee out of the pot and shook the grounds loose into the fire. He lit a cigarette and went inside the tent. He took off his shoes and trousers, sitting on the blankets, rolled the shoes up inside the trousers for a pillow and got in between the blankets.

Out through the front of the tent he watched the glow of the fire, when the night wind blew on it. It was a quiet night. The swamp was perfectly quiet. Nick stretched under the blanket comfortably. A mosquito hummed close to his ear. Nick sat up and lit a match. The mosquito was on the canvas, over his head. Nick moved the match quickly up to it. The mosquito made a satisfactory hiss in the flame. The match went out. Nick lay down again under the blanket. He turned on his side and shut his eyes. He was sleepy. He felt sleep coming. He curled up under the blanket and went to sleep.

Chapter XV

They hanged Sam Cardinella at six o'clock in the morning in the cor-
ridor of the county jail.[1] The corridor was high and narrow with tiers
of cells on either side. All the cells were occupied. The men had been
brought in for the hanging. Five men sentenced to be hanged were
in the five top cells. Three of the men to be hanged were negroes. They
were very frightened. One of the white men sat on his cot with his head
in his hands. The other lay flat on his cot with a blanket wrapped
around his head.

They came out onto the gallows through a door in the wall. There
were seven of them including two priests. They were carrying Sam
Cardinella. He had been like that since about four o'clock in the
morning.

While they were strapping his legs together two guards held him up
and the two priests were whispering to him. "Be a man, my son," said
one priest. When they came toward him with the cap to go over his
head Sam Cardinella lost control of his sphincter muscle. The guards
who had been holding him up both dropped him. They were both
disgusted. "How about a chair, Will?" asked one of the guards. "Better
get one," said a man in a derby hat.

When they all stepped back on the scaffolding back of the drop,
which was very heavy, built of oak and steel and swung on ball bear-
ings, Sam Cardinella was left sitting there strapped tight, the younger
of the two priests kneeling beside the chair.[2] The priest skipped back
onto the scaffolding just before the drop fell.

---

1. The execution of Chicago gangster Sam Cardinella took place April 15, 1921. Hemingway saw the crowd gathering at the Cook County jail that morning (*LEH* 1:280).
2. Cardinella's seeming inability to stand was part of a scheme to avoid being killed. The
   chair was supposed to keep his neck from breaking, with Cardinella feigning death. A
   waiting ambulance contained medical equipment as well as a doctor and nurse hired by
   the mob to revive him. But the ploy failed; Cardinella was already dead.

BIG TWO-HEARTED RIVER: PART II

In the morning the sun was up and the tent was starting to get hot. Nick crawled out under the mosquito netting stretched across the mouth of the tent, to look at the morning. The grass was wet on his hands as he came out. He held his trousers and his shoes in his hands. The sun was just up over the hill. There was the meadow, the river and the swamp. There were birch trees in the green of the swamp on the other side of the river.

The river was clear and smoothly fast in the early morning. Down about two hundred yards were three logs all the way across the stream. They made the water smooth and deep above them. As Nick watched, a mink crossed the river on the logs and went into the swamp. Nick was excited. He was excited by the early morning and the river. He was really too hurried to eat breakfast, but he knew he must. He built a little fire and put on the coffee pot.

While the water was heating in the pot he took an empty bottle and went down over the edge of the high ground to the meadow. The meadow was wet with dew and Nick wanted to catch grasshoppers for bait before the sun dried the grass. He found plenty of good grasshoppers. They were at the base of the grass stems. Sometimes they clung to a grass stem. They were cold and wet with the dew, and could not jump until the sun warmed them. Nick picked them up, taking only the medium-sized brown ones, and put them into the bottle. He turned over a log and just under the shelter of the edge were several hundred hoppers. It was a grasshopper lodging house. Nick put about fifty of the medium browns into the bottle. While he was picking up the hoppers the others warmed in the sun and commenced to hop away. They flew when they hopped. At first they made one flight and stayed stiff when they landed, as though they were dead.

Nick knew that by the time he was through with breakfast they would be as lively as ever. Without dew in the grass it would take him all day to catch a bottle full of good grasshoppers and he would have to crush many of them, slamming at them with his hat. He washed his hands at the stream. He was excited to be near it. Then he walked up to the tent. The hoppers were already jumping stiffly in the grass. In the bottle, warmed by the sun, they were jumping in a mass. Nick put in a pine stick as a cork. It plugged the mouth of the bottle enough, so the hoppers could not get out and left plenty of air passage.

He had rolled the log back and knew he could get grasshoppers there every morning.

Nick laid the bottle full of jumping grasshoppers against a pine trunk. Rapidly he mixed some buckwheat flour with water and stirred it smooth, one cup of flour, one cup of water. He put a handful of coffee in the pot and dipped a lump of grease out of a can and slid it sputtering across the hot skillet. On the smoking skillet he poured smoothly the buckwheat batter. It spread like lava, the grease spitting sharply. Around the edges the buckwheat cake began to firm, then brown, then crisp. The surface was bubbling slowly to porousness. Nick pushed under the browned under surface with a fresh pine chip. He shook the skillet sideways and the cake was loose on the surface. I won't try and flop it, he thought. He slid the chip of clean wood all the way under the cake, and flopped it over onto its face. It sputtered in the pan.

When it was cooked Nick regreased the skillet. He used all the batter. It made another big flapjack and one smaller one.

Nick ate a big flapjack and a smaller one, covered with apple butter. He put apple butter on the third cake, folded it over twice, wrapped it in oiled paper and put it in his shirt pocket. He put the apple butter jar back in the pack and cut bread for two sandwiches.

In the pack he found a big onion. He sliced it in two and peeled the silky outer skin. Then he cut one half into slices and made onion sandwiches. He wrapped them in oiled paper and buttoned them in the other pocket of his khaki shirt. He turned the skillet upside down on the grill, drank the coffee, sweetened and yellow brown with the condensed milk in it, and tidied up the camp. It was a good camp.

Nick took his fly rod out of the leather rod-case, jointed it, and shoved the rod-case back into the tent. He put on the reel and threaded the line through the guides. He had to hold it from hand to hand, as he threaded it, or it would slip back through its own weight. It was a heavy, double tapered fly line.[1] Nick had paid eight dollars for it a long time ago. It was made heavy to lift back in the air and come forward flat and heavy and straight to make it possible to cast a fly which has no weight. Nick opened the aluminum leader box. The leaders were coiled between the damp flannel pads. Nick had wet the pads at the water cooler on the train up to St. Ignace. In the damp pads the gut leaders had softened and Nick unrolled one and tied it by a loop at the end to the heavy fly line.[2] He fastened a hook on the end of the leader. It was a small hook; very thin and springy.

1. Popular long ago, a double tapered fly line began with a small-diameter tip and gradually increased in thickness to the long "belly" of the line before tapering down to a narrower gauge. This type of line allowed for better casting and a lighter touch presenting dry flies.
2. The semi-invisible leader connects the fishing line to the lure or bait. Leaders were then typically made of cat gut (the material Dr. Adams uses to stitch up the Ojibwe woman in "Indian Camp" [see 13]).

Nick took it from his hook book,[3] sitting with the rod across his lap. He tested the knot and the spring of the rod by pulling the line taut. It was a good feeling. He was careful not to let the hook bite into his finger.

He started down to the stream, holding his rod, the bottle of grasshoppers hung from his neck by a thong tied in half hitches around the neck of the bottle. His landing net hung by a hook from his belt. Over his shoulder was a long flour sack tied at each corner into an ear. The cord went over his shoulder. The sack flapped against his legs.

Nick felt awkward and professionally happy with all his equipment hanging from him. The grasshopper bottle swung against his chest. In his shirt the breast pockets bulged against him with the lunch and his fly book.

He stepped into the stream. It was a shock. His trousers clung tight to his legs. His shoes felt the gravel. The water was a rising cold shock.

Rushing, the current sucked against his legs. Where he stepped in, the water was over his knees. He waded with the current. The gravel slid under his shoes. He looked down at the swirl of water below each leg and tipped up the bottle to get a grasshopper.

The first grasshopper gave a jump in the neck of the bottle and went out into the water. He was sucked under in the whirl by Nick's right leg and came to the surface a little way down stream. He floated rapidly, kicking. In a quick circle, breaking the smooth surface of the water, he disappeared. A trout had taken him.

Another hopper poked his face out of the bottle. His antennæ wavered. He was getting his front legs out of the bottle to jump. Nick took him by the head and held him while he threaded the slim hook under his chin, down through his thorax and into the last segments of his abdomen. The grasshopper took hold of the hook with his front feet, spitting tobacco juice on it. Nick dropped him into the water.

Holding the rod in his right hand he let out line against the pull of the grasshopper in the current. He stripped off line from the reel with his left hand and let it run free. He could see the hopper in the little waves of the current. It went out of sight.

There was a tug on the line. Nick pulled against the taut line. It was his first strike. Holding the now living rod across the current, he brought in the line with his left hand. The rod bent in jerks, the trout pumping against the current. Nick knew it was a small one. He lifted the rod straight up in the air. It bowed with the pull.

He saw the trout in the water jerking with his head and body against the shifting tangent of the line in the stream.

---

3. Nick's equipment includes folding cases, or "books," for his hooks and flies.

Nick took the line in his left hand and pulled the trout, thumping tiredly against the current, to the surface. His back was mottled the clear, water-over-gravel color, his side flashing in the sun. The rod under his right arm, Nick stooped, dipping his right hand into the current. He held the trout, never still, with his moist right hand, while he unhooked the barb from his mouth, then dropped him back into the stream.

He hung unsteadily in the current, then settled to the bottom beside a stone. Nick reached down his hand to touch him, his arm to the elbow under water. The trout was steady in the moving stream, resting on the gravel, beside a stone. As Nick's fingers touched him, touched his smooth, cool, underwater feeling he was gone, gone in a shadow across the bottom of the stream.

He's all right, Nick thought. He was only tired.

He had wet his hand before he touched the trout, so he would not disturb the delicate mucus that covered him. If a trout was touched with a dry hand, a white fungus attacked the unprotected spot. Years before when he had fished crowded streams, with fly fishermen ahead of him and behind him, Nick had again and again come on dead trout, furry with white fungus, drifted against a rock, or floating belly up in some pool. Nick did not like to fish with other men on the river. Unless they were of your party, they spoiled it.

He wallowed down the stream, above his knees in the current, through the fifty yards of shallow water above the pile of logs that crossed the stream. He did not rebait his hook and held it in his hand as he waded. He was certain he could catch small trout in the shallows, but he did not want them. There would be no big trout in the shallows this time of day.

Now the water deepened up his thighs sharply and coldly. Ahead was the smooth dammed-back flood of water above the logs. The water was smooth and dark; on the left, the lower edge of the meadow; on the right the swamp.

Nick leaned back against the current and took a hopper from the bottle. He threaded the hopper on the hook and spat on him for good luck. Then he pulled several yards of line from the reel and tossed the hopper out ahead onto the fast, dark water. It floated down towards the logs, then the weight of the line pulled the bait under the surface. Nick held the rod in his right hand, letting the line run out through his fingers.

There was a long tug. Nick struck and the rod came alive and dangerous, bent double, the line tightening, coming out of water, tightening, all in a heavy, dangerous, steady pull. Nick felt the moment when the leader would break if the strain increased and let the line go.

The reel ratcheted into a mechanical shriek as the line went out in a rush. Too fast. Nick could not check it, the line rushing out, the reel note rising as the line ran out.

With the core of the reel showing, his heart feeling stopped with the excitement, leaning back against the current that mounted icily his thighs, Nick thumbed the reel hard with his left hand. It was awkward getting his thumb inside the fly reel frame.

As he put on pressure the line tightened into sudden hardness and beyond the logs a huge trout went high out of water. As he jumped, Nick lowered the tip of the rod. But he felt, as he dropped the tip to ease the strain, the moment when the strain was too great; the hardness too tight. Of course, the leader had broken. There was no mistaking the feeling when all spring left the line and it became dry and hard. Then it went slack.

His mouth dry, his heart down, Nick reeled in. He had never seen so big a trout. There was a heaviness, a power not to be held, and then the bulk of him, as he jumped. He looked as broad as a salmon.

Nick's hand was shaky. He reeled in slowly. The thrill had been too much. He felt, vaguely, a little sick, as though it would be better to sit down.

The leader had broken where the hook was tied to it. Nick took it in his hand. He thought of the trout somewhere on the bottom, holding himself steady over the gravel, far down below the light, under the logs, with the hook in his jaw. Nick knew the trout's teeth would cut through the snell of the hook. The hook would imbed itself in his jaw. He'd bet the trout was angry. Anything that size would be angry. That was a trout. He had been solidly hooked. Solid as a rock. He felt like a rock, too, before he started off. By God, he was a big one. By God, he was the biggest one I ever heard of.

Nick climbed out onto the meadow and stood, water running down his trousers and out of his shoes, his shoes squelchy. He went over and sat on the logs. He did not want to rush his sensations any.

He wriggled his toes in the water, in his shoes, and got out a cigarette from his breast pocket. He lit it and tossed the match into the fast water below the logs. A tiny trout rose at the match, as it swung around in the fast current. Nick laughed. He would finish the cigarette.

He sat on the logs, smoking, drying in the sun, the sun warm on his back, the river shallow ahead entering the woods, curving into the woods, shallows, light glittering, big water-smooth rocks, cedars along the bank and white birches, the logs warm in the sun, smooth to sit on, without bark, gray to the touch; slowly the feeling of disappointment left him. It went away slowly, the feeling of disappointment that came sharply after the thrill that made his shoulders ache. It was all right now. His rod lying out on the logs, Nick tied a new hook on the leader, pulling the gut tight until it grimped[4] into itself in a hard knot.

He baited up, then picked up the rod and walked to the far end of the logs to get into the water, where it was not too deep. Under and beyond the logs was a deep pool. Nick walked around the shallow shelf near the swamp shore until he came out on the shallow bed of the stream.

On the left, where the meadow ended and the woods began, a great elm tree was uprooted. Gone over in a storm, it lay back into the woods, its roots clotted with dirt, grass growing in them, rising a solid bank beside the stream. The river cut to the edge of the uprooted tree. From where Nick stood he could see deep channels, like ruts, cut in the shallow bed of the stream by the flow of the current. Pebbly where he stood and pebbly and full of boulders beyond; where it curved near the tree roots, the bed of the stream was marly and between the ruts of deep water green weed fronds swung in the current.

Nick swung the rod back over his shoulder and forward, and the line, curving forward, laid the grasshopper down on one of the deep channels in the weeds. A trout struck and Nick hooked him.

Holding the rod far out toward the uprooted tree and sloshing backward in the current, Nick worked the trout, plunging, the rod bending alive, out of the danger of the weeds into the open river. Holding the rod, pumping alive against the current, Nick brought the trout in. He rushed, but always came, the spring of the rod yielding to the rushes, sometimes jerking under water, but always bringing him in. Nick eased downstream with the rushes. The rod above his head he led the trout over the net, then lifted.

The trout hung heavy in the net, mottled trout back and silver sides in the meshes. Nick unhooked him; heavy sides, good to hold, big undershot jaw, and slipped him, heaving and big sliding, into the long sack that hung from his shoulders in the water.

Nick spread the mouth of the sack against the current and it filled, heavy with water. He held it up, the bottom in the stream, and the water poured out through the sides. Inside at the bottom was the big trout, alive in the water.

Nick moved downstream. The sack out ahead of him sunk heavy in the water, pulling from his shoulders.

It was getting hot, the sun hot on the back of his neck.

Nick had one good trout. He did not care about getting many trout. Now the stream was shallow and wide. There were trees along both banks. The trees of the left bank made short shadows on the

4. To draw up or become snug.

current in the forenoon sun. Nick knew there were trout in each shadow. In the afternoon, after the sun had crossed toward the hills, the trout would be in the cool shadows on the other side of the stream.

The very biggest ones would lie up close to the bank. You could always pick them up there on the Black. When the sun was down they all moved out into the current. Just when the sun made the water blinding in the glare before it went down, you were liable to strike a big trout anywhere in the current. It was almost impossible to fish then, the surface of the water was blinding as a mirror in the sun. Of course, you could fish upstream, but in a stream like the Black, or this, you had to wallow against the current and in a deep place, the water piled up on you. It was no fun to fish upstream with this much current.

Nick moved along through the shallow stretch watching the banks for deep holes. A beech tree grew close beside the river, so that the branches hung down into the water. The stream went back in under the leaves. There were always trout in a place like that.

Nick did not care about fishing that hole. He was sure he would get hooked in the branches.

It looked deep though. He dropped the grasshopper so the current took it under water, back in under the overhanging branch. The line pulled hard and Nick struck. The trout threshed heavily, half out of water in the leaves and branches. The line was caught. Nick pulled hard and the trout was off. He reeled in and holding the hook in his hand, walked down the stream.

Ahead, close to the left bank, was a big log. Nick saw it was hollow; pointing up river the current entered it smoothly, only a little ripple spread each side of the log. The water was deepening. The top of the hollow log was gray and dry. It was partly in the shadow.

Nick took the cork out of the grasshopper bottle and a hopper clung to it. He picked him off, hooked him and tossed him out. He held the rod far out so that the hopper on the water moved into the current flowing into the hollow log. Nick lowered the rod and the hopper floated in. There was a heavy strike. Nick swung the rod against the pull. It felt as though he were hooked into the log itself, except for the live feeling.

He tried to force the fish out into the current. It came, heavily.

The line went slack and Nick thought the trout was gone. Then he saw him, very near, in the current, shaking his head, trying to get the hook out. His mouth was clamped shut. He was fighting the hook in the clear flowing current.

Looping in the line with his left hand, Nick swung the rod to make the line taut and tried to lead the trout toward the net, but he was gone, out of sight, the line pumping. Nick fought him against the current, letting him thump in the water against the spring of the rod. He shifted the rod to his left hand, worked the trout upstream, holding his weight, fighting on the rod, and then let him down into the net. He lifted him clear of the water, a heavy half circle in the net, the net dripping, unhooked him and slid him into the sack.

He spread the mouth of the sack and looked down in at the two big trout alive in the water.

Through the deepening water, Nick waded over to the hollow log. He took the sack off, over his head, the trout flopping as it came out of water, and hung it so the trout were deep in the water. Then he pulled himself up on the log and sat, the water from his trouser and boots running down into the stream. He laid his rod down, moved along to the shady end of the log and took the sandwiches out of his pocket. He dipped the sandwiches in the cold water. The current carried away the crumbs. He ate the sandwiches and dipped his hat full of water to drink, the water running out through his hat just ahead of his drinking.

It was cool in the shade, sitting on the log. He took a cigarette out and struck a match to light it. The match sunk into the gray wood, making a tiny furrow. Nick leaned over the side of the log, found a hard place and lit the match. He sat smoking and watching the river.

Ahead the river narrowed and went into a swamp. The river became smooth and deep and the swamp looked solid with cedar trees, their trunks close together, their branches solid. It would not be possible to walk through a swamp like that. The branches grew so low. You would have to keep almost level with the ground to move at all. You could not crash through the branches. That must be why the animals that lived in swamps were built the way they were, Nick thought.

He wished he had brought something to read. He felt like reading. He did not feel like going on into the swamp. He looked down the river. A big cedar slanted all the way across the stream. Beyond that the river went into the swamp.

Nick did not want to go in there now. He felt a reaction against deep wading with the water deepening up under his armpits, to hook big trout in places impossible to land them. In the swamp the banks were bare, the big cedars came together overhead, the sun did not come through, except in patches; in the fast deep water, in the half light, the fishing would be tragic. In the swamp fishing was a tragic adventure. Nick did not want it. He did not want to go down the stream any further today.

He took out his knife, opened it and stuck it in the log. Then he pulled up the sack, reached into it and brought out one of the trout. Holding him near the tail, hard to hold, alive, in his hand, he whacked him against the log. The trout quivered, rigid. Nick laid him on the log in the shade and broke the neck of the other fish the same way. He laid them side by side on the log. They were fine trout.

Nick cleaned them, slitting them from the vent to the tip of the jaw. All the insides and the gills and tongue came out in one piece. They were both males; long gray-white strips of milt, smooth and clean. All the insides clean and compact, coming out all together. Nick tossed the offal ashore for the minks to find.

He washed the trout in the stream. When he held them back up in the water they looked like live fish. Their color was not gone yet. He washed his hands and dried them on the log. Then he laid the trout on the sack spread out on the log, rolled them up in it, tied the bundle and put it in the landing net. His knife was still standing, blade stuck in the log. He cleaned it on the wood and put it in his pocket.

Nick stood up on the log, holding his rod, the landing net hanging heavy, then stepped into the water and splashed ashore. He climbed the bank and cut up into the woods, toward the high ground. He was going back to camp. He looked back. The river just showed through the trees. There were plenty of days coming when he could fish the swamp.

L'Envoi

The king was working in the garden.[1] *He seemed very glad to see me. We walked through the garden. This is the queen, he said. She was clipping a rose bush. Oh how do you do, she said. We sat down at a table under a big tree and the king ordered whiskey and soda. We have good whiskey anyway, he said. The revolutionary committee, he told me, would not allow him to go outside the palace grounds. Plastiras*[2] *is a very good man I believe, he said, but frightfully difficult. I think he did right though shooting those chaps. If Kerensky*[3] *had shot a few men things might have been altogether different. Of course the great thing in this sort of an affair is not to be shot oneself!*

It was very jolly. We talked for a long time. Like all Greeks he wanted to go to America.[4]

1. Hemingway reduced his story in the *Toronto Star Weekly*, September 15, 1923, to a glimpse of the Greek monarch George II (1890–1947), "the newest king in Europe, and probably the most uncomfortable" (*Dateline: Toronto*, 296). In Paris, Hemingway got the details from newsreel cameraman Shorty Wornall, who had interviewed the king, then living under house arrest after the September 1922 Revolution.
2. Col. Nikolaos Plastiras (1883–1953), head of the revolutionary government.
3. Socialist Alexander Kerensky (1881–1970) led a moderate provisional Russian government after the abdication of Tsar Nicholas II (1894–1917), only to be overthrown by the Bolshevik Revolution.
4. Instead, George II lived in exile in Romania and Britain, until, after many changes of government in Greece, he returned as monarch by invitation in 1935.

Discarded Episodes[†]

Three Shots[1]

Nick was undressing in the tent. He saw the shadows of his father and Uncle George cast by the fire on the canvas wall. He felt very uncomfortable and ashamed and undressed as fast as he could, piling his clothes neatly. He was ashamed because undressing reminded him of the night before. He had kept it out of his mind all day.

His father and uncle had gone off across the lake after supper to fish with a jack light.[2] Before they shoved the boat out his father told him that if any emergency came up while they were gone he was to fire three shots with the rifle and they would come right back. Nick went back from the edge of the lake through the woods to the camp. He could hear the oars of the boat in the dark. His father was rowing and his uncle was sitting in the stern trolling. He had taken his seat with his rod ready when his father shoved the boat out. Nick listened to them on the lake until he could no longer hear the oars.

Walking back through the woods Nick began to be frightened. He was always a little frightened of the woods at night. He opened the flap of the tent and undressed and lay very quietly between the blankets in the dark. The fire was burned down to a bed of coals outside. Nick lay still and tried to go to sleep. There was no noise anywhere. Nick felt if he could only hear a fox bark or an owl or anything he would be all right. He was not afraid of anything definite as yet. But he was getting very afraid. Then suddenly he was afraid of dying. Just a few weeks before at home, in church, they had sung a hymn, "Some day the silver cord will break."[3] While they were singing the hymn Nick had

† From *The Nick Adams Stories* (New York: Scribner's, 1972), pp. 3–6, 241–49. Copyright © 1972 and renewed © 2000 by The Ernest Hemingway Foundation. Reprinted with the permission of Scribner, a division of Simon & Schuster, Inc. All rights reserved.

1. This fragment, as titled by editor Philip Young, represents the original opening of "Indian Camp," and manuscript evidence shows that Hemingway began writing the story in Canada in November 1923. As late as March 1924, when he gave "Indian Camp" to Ford Madox Ford to publish in the April *Transatlantic Review,* he was still opening the story this way. For more on EH and Ford see "Introduction," xxiii.
2. A lantern or flashlight, to attract fish.
3. Each stanza of the 1891 hymn "Saved by Grace," with lyrics by Fanny Jane Crosby, evokes the "someday" a person dies and experiences a heavenly awakening, in which the believer sees God "face to face" and "tell[s] the story—saved by grace." The image of a mortal "silver cord" comes from Ecclesiastes 12:6.

*realized that some day he must die. It made him feel quite sick. It was
the first time he had ever realized that he himself would have to die
sometime.*

*That night he sat out in the hall under the night light trying to read
Robinson Crusoe[4] to keep his mind off the fact that some day the silver cord must break. The nurse found him there and threatened to
tell his father on him if he did not go to bed. He went in to bed and as
soon as the nurse was in her room came out again and read under the
hall light until morning.*

*Last night in the tent he had had the same fear. He never had it
except at night. It was more a realization than a fear at first. But it was
always on the edge of fear and became fear very quickly when it started.
As soon as he began to be really frightened he took the rifle and poked
the muzzle out the front of the tent and shot three times. The rifle
kicked badly. He heard the shots rip off through the trees. As soon as
he had fired the shots it was all right.*

*He lay down to wait for his father's return and was asleep before his
father and uncle had put out their jack light on the other side of the lake.*

*"Damn that kid," Uncle George said as they rowed back. "What did
you tell him to call us in for? He's probably got the heebie-jeebies about
something."[5]*

*Uncle George was an enthusiastic fisherman and his father's younger
brother.*

"Oh, well. He's pretty small," his father said.

"That's no reason to bring him into the woods with us."

*"I know he's an awful coward," his father said, "but we're all yellow
at that age."*

"I can't stand him," George said. "He's such an awful liar."

"Oh, well, forget it. You'll get plenty of fishing anyway."

*They came into the tent and Uncle George shone his flashlight into
Nick's eyes.*

"What was it, Nickie?" said his father. Nick sat up in bed.

*"It sounded like a cross between a fox and a wolf and it was fooling
around the tent," Nick said. "It was a little like a fox but more like a
wolf." He had learned the phrase "cross between" that same day from
his uncle.*

"He probably heard a screech owl," Uncle George said.

*In the morning his father found two big basswood trees that leaned
across each other so that they rubbed together in the wind.*

"Do you think that was what it was, Nick?" his father asked.

"Maybe," Nick said. He didn't want to think about it.

---

4. The novel *Robinson Crusoe* (1719), by the English writer Daniel Defoe (ca. 1660–1731),
   depicts the survival of a castaway-narrator.
5. "Heebie-jeebies": extreme nervousness.

"You don't want to ever be frightened in the woods, Nick. There is nothing that can hurt you."

"Not even lightning?" Nick asked.

"No, not even lightning. If there is a thunder storm get out into the open. Or get under a beech tree. They're never struck."

"Never?" Nick asked.

"I never heard of one," said his father.

"Gee, I'm glad to know that about beech trees," Nick said.

Now he was undressing again in the tent. He was conscious of the two shadows on the wall although he was not watching them. Then he heard a boat being pulled up on the beach and the two shadows were gone. He heard his father talking with someone.

Then his father shouted, "Get your clothes on, Nick."

He dressed as fast as he could. His father came in and rummaged through the duffel bags.

"Put your coat on, Nick," his father said.

On Writing[1]

It was getting hot, the sun hot on the back of his neck.

Nick had one good trout. He did not care about getting many trout. Now the stream was shallow and wide. There were trees along both banks. The trees of the left bank made short shadows on the current in the forenoon sun. Nick knew there were trout in each shadow. He and Bill Smith had discovered that on the Black River one hot day. In the afternoon, after the sun had crossed toward the hills, the trout would be in the cool shadows on the other side of the stream.

The very biggest ones would lie up close to the bank. You could always pick them up there on the Black. Bill and he had discovered it. When the sun was down they all moved out into the current. Just when the sun made the water blinding in the glare before it went down you were liable to strike a big trout anywhere in the current. It was almost impossible to fish then, the surface of the water was blinding as a mirror in the sun. Of course you could fish upstream, but in a stream like the Black or this you had to wallow against the current and in a deep place the water piled up on you. It was no fun to fish upstream although all the books said it was the only way.

All the books. He and Bill had fun with the books in the old days.[2] They all started with a fake premise. Like fox hunting. Bill Bird's dentist

---

1. This fragment, so titled by editor Philip Young, represents the original ending of "Big Two-Hearted River." It begins with material from that story (compare 126–27), then deviates at the end of the third paragraph.
2. See Nick and Bill's discussion of novels mentioned in "The Three-Day Blow" (31–32).

in Paris said,[3] *in fly fishing you pit your intelligence against that of the fish. That's the way I'd always thought of it, Ezra said.*[4] *That was good for a laugh. There were so many things good for a laugh. In the States they thought bullfighting was a joke. Ezra thought fishing was a joke. Lots of people think poetry is a joke. Englishmen are a joke.*

Remember when they pushed us over the barrera *in front of the bull at Pamplona*[5] *because they thought we were Frenchmen? Bill's dentist is as bad the other way about fishing. Bill Bird, that is. Once Bill meant Bill Smith. Now it means Bill Bird. Bill Bird was in Paris now.*

When he married he lost Bill Smith, Odgar, the Ghee, all the old gang.[6] *Was it because they were virgins? The Ghee certainly was not. No, he lost them because he admitted by marrying that something was more important than the fishing.*

He had built it all up. Bill had never fished before they met. Everyplace they had been together. The Black, the Sturgeon, the Pine Barrens, the Upper Minnie, all the little streams. Most about fishing he and Bill had discovered together. They worked on the farm and fished and took long trips in the woods from June to October. Bill always quit his job every spring. So did he. Ezra thought fishing was a joke.

Bill forgave him the fishing he had done before they met. He forgave him all the rivers. He was really proud of them. It was like a girl about other girls. If they were before they did not matter. But after was different.

That was why he lost them, he guessed.

They were all married to fishing. Ezra thought fishing was a joke. So did most everybody. He'd been married to it before he married Helen. Really married to it. It wasn't any joke.

So he lost them all. Helen thought it was because they didn't like her.[7]

Nick sat down on a boulder in the shade and hung his sack down into the river. The water swirled around both sides of the boulder. It was cool in the shade. The bank of the river was sandy under the edge of the trees. There were mink tracks in the sand.

He might as well be out of the heat. The rock was dry and cool. He sat letting the water run out of his boots down the side of the rock.

Helen thought it was because they did not like her. She really did. Gosh, he remembered the horror he used to have of people getting married. It was funny. Probably it was because he had always been with older people, non-marrying people.

3. Bill Bird, an American newsman, ran Three Mountains Press in Paris and published *in our time* (1924). His dentist is unknown.
4. Pound lived in Paris 1920–24. He helped Hemingway publish his early work.
5. City in Spain. "Barrera": see note 1 on 73.
6. Including Bill Smith, Carl Edgar (Odgar), Jock Pentecost (the Ghee), and others.
7. Hemingway's wife, Hadley, met his fishing companions all together only once, at her wedding, where several served as ushers.

Odgar always wanted to marry Kate.[8] *Kate wouldn't ever marry anybody. She and Odgar always quarreled about it but Odgar did not want anybody else and Kate wouldn't have anybody. She wanted them to be just as good friends and Odgar wanted to be friends and they were always miserable and quarreling trying to be.*

It was the Madame planted all that asceticism.[9] *The Ghee went with girls in houses*[1] *in Cleveland but he had it, too. Nick had had it, too. It was all such a fake. You had this fake ideal planted in you and then you lived your life to it.*

All the love went into fishing and the summer.

He had loved it more than anything. He had loved digging potatoes with Bill in the fall, the long trips in the car, fishing in the bay, reading in the hammock on hot days, swimming off the dock, playing baseball at Charlevoix and Petoskey, living at the Bay,[2] *the Madame's cooking, the way she had with servants, eating in the dining room looking out the window across the long fields and the point to the lake, talking with her, drinking with Bill's old man, the fishing trips away from the farm, just lying around.*

He loved the long summer. It used to be that he felt sick when the first of August came and he realized that there were only four more weeks before the trout season closed. Now sometimes he had it that way in dreams. He would dream that the summer was nearly gone and he hadn't been fishing. It made him feel sick in the dream, as though he had been in jail.

The hills at the foot of Walloon Lake, storms on the lake coming up in the motorboat, holding an umbrella over the engine to keep the waves that came in off the spark plug, pumping out, running the boat in big storms delivering vegetables around the lake, climbing up, sliding down, the wave following behind, coming up from the foot of the lake with the groceries, the mail and the Chicago paper under a tarpaulin, sitting on them to keep them dry, too rough to land, drying out in front of the fire, the wind in the hemlocks and the wet pine needles underfoot when he was barefoot going for the milk. Getting up at daylight to row across the lake and hike over the hills after a rain to fish in Hortons Creek.

Hortons always needed a rain. Shultz's[3] *was no good if it rained, running muddy and overflowing, running through the grass. Where were the trout when a stream was like that?*

8. Bill Smith's sister, Kate.
9. Self-denial promoted by Kate's aunt, Mrs. Charles (the Madame), who raised Bill, Kate, and their brother Y. K. after the death of their mother.
1. Brothels.
2. Horton Bay, on Lake Charlevoix.
3. Presumably, the small creek that flows into Horton Creek in what is now called the Schulz Working Forest Preserve, Charlevoix County, Michigan.

That was where a bull chased him over the fence and he lost his pocketbook with all the hooks in it.

If he knew then what he knew about bulls now.[4] *Where were Maera and Algabeno now? August the Feria at Valencia, Santander, bad fights at St. Sebastien. Sanchez Mejias killing six bulls. The way phrases from bullfight papers kept coming into his head all the time until he had to quit reading them.* The corrida *of the Miuras. In spite of his notorious defects in the execution of the* pase natural. *The flower of Andalucia.* Chiquelín el camelista. *Juan Terremoto. Belmonte Vuelve?*

Maera's kid brother was a bullfighter now. That was the way it went.

His whole inner life had been bullfights all one year. Chink pale and miserable about the horses. Don never minded them, he said. "And then suddenly I knew I was going to love bullfighting." *That must have been Maera. Maera was the greatest man he'd ever known. Chink knew it, too. He followed him around in the* encierro.

He, Nick, was the friend of Maera and Maera waved at them from Box 87 above their sobrepuerta *and waited for Helen to see him and waved again and Helen worshipped him and there were three picadors in the box and all the other picadors did their stuff right down in front of the box and looked up and waved before and after and he said to Helen that picadors only worked for each other, and of course it was true. And it was the best pic-ing he ever saw and the three pics in the box with their Cordoba hats nodded at each good* vara *and the other pics waved up at them and then did their stuff. Like the time the Portuguese were in and the old pic threw his hat into the ring hanging on over the* barrera *watching young Da Veiga. That was the saddest thing he'd ever seen. That was what that fat pic wanted to be, a caballero en plaza. God, how that Da Veiga kid could ride. That was riding. It didn't show well in the movies.*

The movies ruined everything. Like talking about something good. That was what had made the war unreal. Too much talking.

Talking about anything was bad. Writing about anything actual was bad. It always killed it.

The only writing that was any good was what you made up, what you imagined. That made everything come true. Like when he wrote

4. Four paragraphs elaborate Nick's passion for bullfights (corridas) and festivals (ferias). He remembers cities (Valencia, Santander, St. Sebastien), gifted bullfighters (Maera, Algabeño, Sanchez Mejias), great bulls (the Miuras), bullfighting techniques (the *pase natural*), and colorful torero nicknames. Memories of Pamplona in 1924 include "Chink" Dorman-Smith's (see note 1 on 21) disgust at gored horses, the wit of the American writer Donald Ogden Stewart (1894–1980), and their shared admiration for Maera. Chink follows Maera in the *encierro*, the running of the bulls in Pamplona. Maera's wave to Nick's wife, Helen, in her *sobrepuerta* seat (above the main door) recalls his attentiveness to Hadley in 1924. Miriam Mandel documents (in her annotated edition of *DIA*) that at the same fiesta in Pamplona, Hemingway saw Simão da Veiga, the Portuguese mounted bullfighter. Nick also remembers the skilled picadors, their Cordoba hats with broad brims and flat crowns, and the varas, or steel-pointed pikes, used to wound the bull.

"My Old Man" he'd never seen a jockey killed and the next week Georges Parfrement was killed at that very jump and that was the way it looked.[5] *Everything good he'd ever written he'd made up. None of it had ever happened. Other things had happened. Better things, maybe. That was what the family couldn't understand. They thought it all was experience.*

That was the weakness of Joyce. Daedalus in Ulysses *was Joyce himself, so he was terrible. Joyce was so damn romantic and intellectual about him. He'd made Bloom up, Bloom was wonderful. He'd made Mrs. Bloom up.*[6] *She was the greatest in the world.*

That was the way with Mac.[7] *Mac worked too close to life. You had to digest life and then create your own people. Mac had stuff, though.*

Nick in the stories was never himself. He made him up. Of course he'd never seen an Indian woman having a baby. That was what made it good. Nobody knew that. He'd seen a woman have a baby on the road to Karagatch and tried to help her. That was the way it was.[8]

He wished he could always write like that. He would sometime. He wanted to be a great writer. He was pretty sure he would be. He knew it in lots of ways. He would in spite of everything. It was hard, though.

It was hard to be a great writer if you loved the world and living in it and special people. It was hard when you loved so many places. Then you were healthy and felt good and were having a good time and what the hell.

He always worked best when Helen was unwell. Just that much discontent and friction. Then there were times when you had to write. Not conscience. Just peristaltic action. Then you felt sometimes like you could never write but after a while you knew sooner or later you would write another good story.

It was really more fun than anything. That was really why you did it. He had never realized that before. It wasn't conscience. It was simply that it was the greatest pleasure. It had more bite to it than anything else. It was so damn hard to write well, too.

There were so many tricks.

It was easy to write if you used the tricks. Everybody used them. Joyce had invented hundreds of new ones. Just because they were new didn't make them any better. They would all turn into clichés.

He wanted to write like Cezanne painted.[9]

5. The Belgian jockey George Parfrement died on April 17, 1923, when his horse fell on him at the Enghien track in Paris. But Hemingway could not have seen that accident, because he was in Cortina, Italy. Moreover, Hemingway had written "My Old Man" seven months earlier.
6. Stephen Dedalus (not Daedalus) and Leopold and Molly Bloom are characters in James Joyce's novel *Ulysses* (1922).
7. The fiction writer Robert McAlmon (1895–1956).
8. On the claims in this paragraph, see "Indian Camp" (11) and "Chapter II" (15).
9. French painter Paul Cézanne (1839–1906) rendered scenes in Impressionist, Post-Impressionist, and Cubist styles.

Cezanne started with all the tricks. Then he broke the whole thing down and built the real thing. It was hell to do. He was the greatest. The greatest for always. It wasn't a cult. He, Nick, wanted to write about country so it would be there like Cezanne had done it in painting. You had to do it from inside yourself. There wasn't any trick. Nobody had ever written about country like that. He felt almost holy about it. It was deadly serious. You could do it if you would fight it out. If you'd lived right with your eyes.

It was a thing you couldn't talk about. He was going to work on it until he got it. Maybe never, but he would know as he got near it. It was a job. Maybe for all his life.

People were easy to do. All this smart stuff was easy. Against this age, skyscraper primitives, Cummings when he was smart, it was automatic writing, not The Enormous Room,[1] that was a book, it was one of the great books. Cummings worked hard to get it.

Was there anybody else? Young Asch[2] had something but you couldn't tell. Jews go bad quickly. They all start well. Mac had something. Don Stewart had the most next to Cummings. Sometimes in the Haddocks.[3] Ring Lardner,[4] maybe. Very maybe. Old guys like Sherwood.[5] Older guys like Dreiser.[6] Was there anybody else? Young guys, maybe. Great unknowns. There are never any unknowns, though.

They weren't after what he was after.

He could see the Cezannes. The portrait at Gertrude Stein's. She'd know it if he ever got things right.[7] The two good ones at the Luxembourg, the ones he'd seen every day at the loan exhibit at Bernheim's. The soldiers undressing to swim, the house through the trees, one of the trees with a house beyond, not the lake one, the other lake one. The portrait of the boy. Cezanne could do people, too. But that was easier, he used what he got from the country to do people with. Nick could do that, too. People were easy. Nobody knew anything about them. If it sounded good they took your word for it. They took Joyce's word for it.

He knew just how Cezanne would paint this stretch of river. God, if he were only here to do it. They died and that was the hell of it. They worked all their lives and then got old and died.

---

1. The 1922 novel by the American writer E. E. Cummings (1894–1962) was set in a French prison camp during World War I.
2. Polish-American fiction writer Nathan Asch (1902–1964).
3. *Mr. and Mrs. Haddock Abroad*, Stewart's 1924 novel.
4. American sports columnist and short-story writer (1885–1933).
5. Hemingway's mentor Sherwood Anderson (1876–1941), American fiction writer.
6. Theodore Dreiser (1871–1945), American novelist and champion of social realism.
7. Leo and Gertrude Stein's (see note 6 on 71) first art purchase was an 1878 portrait of Cézanne's wife. Until 1925, Hemingway appreciated Gertrude's criticism of his work. The Luxembourg refers to the art museum adjacent to the Luxembourg palace. Bernheim-Jeune was an important art gallery on the Boulevard de la Madeleine.

Nick, seeing how Cezanne would do the stretch of river and the swamp, stood up and stepped down into the stream. The water was cold and actual. He waded across the stream, moving in the picture. He kneeled down in the gravel on the bank and reached down into the trout sack. It lay in the stream where he had dragged it across the shallows. The old boy was alive. Nick opened the mouth of the sack and slid the trout into the shallow water and watched him move off through the shallows, his back out of water, threading between rocks toward the deep current.

"He was too big to eat," Nick said. "I'll get a couple of little ones in front of camp for supper."

He climbed the bank of the stream, reeling up his line and started through the brush. He ate a sandwich. He was in a hurry and the rod bothered him. He was not thinking. He was holding something in his head. He wanted to get back to camp and get to work.

He moved through the brush, holding the rod close to him. The line caught on a branch. Nick stopped and cut the leader and reeled the line up. He went through the brush now easily, holding the rod out before him.

Ahead of him he saw a rabbit, flat out on the trail. He stopped, grudging. The rabbit was barely breathing. There were two ticks on the rabbit's head, one behind each ear. They were gray, tight with blood, as big as grapes. Nick pulled them off, their heads tiny and hard, with moving feet. He stepped on them on the trail.

Nick picked up the rabbit, limp, with dull button eyes, and put it under a sweet fern bush beside the trail. He felt its heart beating as he laid it down. The rabbit lay quiet under the bush. It might come to, Nick thought. Probably the ticks had attached themselves to it as it crouched in the grass. Maybe after it had been dancing in the open. He did not know.

He went on up the trail to the camp. He was holding something in his head.

CONTEXTS

Hemingway's *Toronto Star* Journalism

A Silent, Ghastly Procession[†]

ADRIANOPLE.—In a never-ending, staggering march the Christian population of Eastern Thrace is jamming the roads towards Macedonia.[1] The main column crossing the Maritza River at Adrianople is twenty miles long. Twenty miles of carts drawn by cows, bullocks and muddy-flanked water buffalo, with exhausted, staggering men, women and children, blankets over their heads, walking blindly along in the rain beside their worldly goods.

This main stream is being swelled from all the back country. They don't know where they are going. They left their farms, villages and ripe, brown fields and joined the main stream of refugees when they heard the Turk was coming. Now they can only keep their places in the ghastly procession while mud-splashed Greek cavalry herd them along like cow-punchers driving steers.

It is a silent procession. Nobody even grunts. It is all they can do to keep moving. Their brilliant peasant costumes are soaked and draggled. Chickens dangle by their feet from the carts. Calves nuzzle at the draught cattle wherever a jam halts the stream. An old man marches bent under a young pig, a scythe and a gun, with a chicken tied to his scythe. A husband spreads a blanket over a woman in labor in one of the carts to keep off the driving rain. She is the only person making a sound. Her little daughter looks at her in horror and begins to cry. And the procession keeps moving.

[†] The *Toronto Daily Star* (October 20, 1922), rpt. in *By-Line: Ernest Hemingway* (New York: Scribner's, 1967; paperback, 1998), pp. 51–52. Copyright © 1967 by By-Line Ernest Hemingway Inc. Copyright renewed 1995 by Patrick Hemingway and John H. Hemingway. Reprinted with the permission of Scribner, a division of Simon & Schuster, Inc. All rights reserved. Founded in 1892, the *Star* published both the *Toronto Daily Star* and the Sunday supplement, the *Toronto Star Weekly*. Hemingway's articles, which include the following selections, were featured in both publications.

1. Geographic and administrative region of Greece. Adrianople, present-day Edirne, Turkey, is a city in Thrace, an area in southeastern Europe ruled by Turkey until it was partitioned in 1919 among Turkey, Greece, and Bulgaria. Eastern Thrace was heavily populated by Greek Orthodox Christians until the ethnic-religious purge of 1922. The Maritza River marked the boundary of Greek-controlled territory.

At Adrianople where the main stream moves through, there is no Near East relief[2] at all. They are doing very good work at Rodosto[3] on the coast, but can only touch the fringe.

There are 250,000 Christian refugees to be evacuated from Eastern Thrace alone. The Bulgarian frontier is shut against them. There is only Macedonia and Western Thrace to receive the fruit of the Turk's return to Europe. Nearly half a million refugees are in Macedonia now. How they are to be fed nobody knows, but in the next month all the Christian world will hear the cry: "Come over into Macedonia and help us!"

Bull Fighting a Tragedy[†]

Bull fighting is not a sport. It was never supposed to be. It is a tragedy. A very great tragedy. The tragedy is the death of the bull. It is played in three definite acts.

*   *   *

* * * And underneath it all is the necessity for playing the old tragedy in the absolutely custom bound, law-laid-down way. It must all be done gracefully, seemingly effortlessly and always with dignity. The worst criticism the Spaniards ever make of a bull fighter is that his work is "vulgar."

The three absolute acts of the tragedy are first the entry of the bull when the picadors[1] receive the shock of his attacks and attempt to protect their horses with their lances. Then the horses go out and the second act is the planting of the banderillos. This is one of the most interesting and difficult parts but among the easiest for a new bull fight fan to appreciate in technique. The banderillos are three-foot, gaily colored darts with a small fish hook prong in the end. The man who is going to plant them walks out into the arena alone with the bull. He lifts the banderillos at arm's length and points them toward the bull. Then he calls "Toro! Toro!" The bull charges and the banderillero rises to his toes, bends in a curve forward and just as the bull is about to hit him drops the darts into the bull's hump just back of his horns.

They must go in evenly, one on each side. They must not be shoved, or thrown or stuck in from the side. This is the first time

2. Relief supplies for the westernmost part of Asia (Thrace).
3. Now known as Tekirdag; a city in eastern Thrace, on the Sea of Marmara, west of Istanbul.
† The *Toronto Star Weekly* (October 20, 1923), rpt. in *By-Line: Ernest Hemingway* (New York: Scribner's, 1967; paperback, 1998), pp. 90, 95–98. Copyright © 1967 by By-Line Ernest Hemingway Inc. Copyright renewed 1995 by Patrick Hemingway and John H. Hemingway. Reprinted with the permission of Scribner, a division of Simon & Schuster, Inc. All rights reserved.
1. See note 4 on 138.

the bull has been completely baffled, there is the prick of the darts that he cannot escape and there are no horses for him to charge into. But he charges the man again and again and each time he gets a pair of the long banderillos that hang from his hump by their tiny barbs and flop like porcupine quills.

Last is the death of the bull, which is in the hands of the matador who has had charge of the bull since his first attack. Each matador has two bulls in the afternoon. The death of the bull is most formal and can only be brought about in one way, directly from the front by the matador who must receive the bull in full charge and kill him with a sword thrust between the shoulders just back of the neck and between the horns. Before killing the bull he must first do a series of passes with the muleta, a piece of red cloth he carries about the size of a large napkin. With the muleta the torero must show his complete mastery of the bull, must make the bull miss him again and again by inches, before he is allowed to kill him. It is in this phase that most of the fatal accidents occur.

The word "toreador" is obsolete Spanish and is never used. The torero is usually called an espada or swordsman. He must be proficient in all three acts of the fight. In the first he uses the cape and does veronicas[2] and protects the picadors by taking the bull out and away from them when they are spilled to the ground. In the second act he plants the banderillos. In the third act he masters the bull with the muleta and kills him.

Few toreros excel in all three departments. Some, like young Chicuelo, are unapproachable in their cape work. Others like the late Joselito are wonderful banderilleros. Only a few are great killers. Most of the greatest killers are gypsies.

Pamplona in July[†]

In Pamplona, a white-walled, sun-baked town high up in the hills of Navarre,[1] is held in the first two weeks of July each year the World's Series of bull fighting.

*   *   *

---

2. A risky pass with both hands holding the cape, feet fixed in place, drawing the bull past the torero's waist.
† The *Toronto Star Weekly* (October 27, 1923), rpt. in *By-Line: Ernest Hemingway* (New York: Scribner's, 1967; paperback, 1998), pp. 99, 102–03, 105–08. Copyright © 1967 by By-Line Ernest Hemingway Inc. Copyright renewed 1995 by Patrick Hemingway and John H. Hemingway. Reprinted with the permission of Scribner, a division of Simon & Schuster, Inc. All rights reserved.
1. Region in northern Spain.

There were rockets going up into the air and the arena was nearly full when we got into our regular seats. The sun was hot and baking. Over on the other side we could see the bull fighters standing ready to come in. * * * We picked out the three matadors of the afternoon with our glasses. Only one of them was new. Olmos, a chubby faced, jolly looking man, something like Tris Speaker.[2] The others we had seen often before. Maera, dark, spare and deadly looking, one of the very greatest toreros of all time. The third, young Algabeno, the son of a famous bull fighter, a slim young Andalusian with a charming Indian looking face. All were wearing the suits they had probably started bull fighting with, too tight, old fashioned, outmoded.

There was the procession of entrance, the wild bull fight music played, the preliminaries were quickly over, the picadors retired along the red fence[3] with their horses, the heralds sounded their trumpets and the door of the bull pen swung open. The bull came out in a rush. * * * He was Maera's bull and after perfect cape play Maera planted the banderillos.[4] Maera is Herself's favorite bull fighter. And if you want to keep any conception of yourself as a brave, hard, perfectly balanced, thoroughly competent man in your wife's mind never take her to a real bull fight. * * * You cannot compete with bull fighters on their own ground. If anywhere. * * *

Maera planted his first pair of banderillos sitting down on the edge of the little step-up that runs around the barrera. He snarled at the bull and as the animal charged leaned back tight against the fence and as the horns struck on either side of him, swung forward over the brute's head and planted the two darts in his hump. He planted the next pair the same way, so near to us we could have leaned over and touched him. Then he went out to kill the bull and after he had made absolutely unbelievable passes with the little red cloth of the muleta drew up his sword and as the bull charged Maera thrust. The sword shot out of his hand and the bull caught him. He went up in the air on the horns of the bull and then came down. Young Algabeno flopped his cape in the bull's face. The bull charged him and Maera staggered to his feet. But his wrist was sprained.

With his wrist sprained, so that every time he raised it to sight for a thrust it brought beads of sweat out on his face, Maera tried again and again to make his death thrust. He lost his sword again and again, picked it up with his left hand from the mud floor of the arena and transferred it to the right for the thrust. Finally he made

---

2. Tristram Speaker (1888–1958) was a Hall of Fame baseball center fielder. The resemblance to Speaker implies Olmos's smiling confidence.
3. See note 1 on 73 and note 4 on 138.
4. See in-text definition on 146.

it and the bull went over. The bull nearly got him twenty times. As he came in to stand up under us at the barrera side his wrist was swollen to twice normal size. I thought of prize fighters I had seen quit because they had hurt their hands.

There was almost no pause while the mules galloped in and hitched on to the first bull and dragged him out and the second came in with a rush. The picadors took the first shock of him with their bull lances. There was the snort and charge, the shock and the mass against the sky, the wonderful defense by the picador with his lance that held off the bull, and then Rosario Olmos stepped out with his cape.

Once he flopped the cape at the bull and floated it around in an easy graceful swing. Then he tried the same swing, the classic "Veronica,"[5] and the bull caught him at the end of it. Instead of stopping at the finish the bull charged on in. He caught Olmos squarely with his horn, hoisted him high in the air. He fell heavily and the bull was on top of him, driving his horns again and again into him. Olmos lay on the sand, his head on his arms. One of his teammates was flopping his cape madly in the bull's face. The bull lifted his head for an instant and charged and got his man. Just one terrific toss. Then he whirled and chased a man just in back of him toward the barrera. The man was running full tilt and as he put his hand on the fence to vault it the bull had him and caught him with his horn, shooting him way up into the crowd. He rushed toward the fallen man he had tossed who was getting to his feet and all alone—Algabeno grabbed him by the tail. He hung on until I thought he or the bull would break. The wounded man got to his feet and started away.

The bull turned like a cat and charged Algabeno and Algabeno met him with the cape. Once, twice, three times he made the perfect, floating, slow swing with the cape, perfectly, graceful, debonair, back on his heels, baffling the bull. And he had command of the situation. There never was such a scene at any world's series game.

There are no substitute matadors allowed. Maera was finished. His wrist could not lift a sword for weeks. Olmos had been gored badly through the body. It was Algabeno's bull. This one and the next five.[6]

He handled them all. Did it all. Cape play easy, graceful, confident. Beautiful work with the muleta. And serious, deadly killing. Five bulls he killed, one after the other, and each one was a separate problem to be worked out with death. At the end there was nothing debonair about him. It was only a question if he would last through or if the bulls would get him. They were all very wonderful bulls.

5. See note 2 on 147.
6. There were six bulls in total, so Algabeño actually has four to go, not five.

Hemingway's Correspondence

To Gertrude Stein and Alice B. Toklas, 15 August [1924]†

August 15.

Dear Friends—

* * *

I have finished two long short stories, one of them not much good, and the other very good and finished the long one I worked on before I went to Spain where I'm trying to do the country like Cezanne and having a hell of a time and sometimes getting it a little bit. It is about 100 pages long and nothing happens and the country is swell, I made it all up, so I see it all and part of it comes out the way it ought to, it is swell about the fish, but isn't writing a hard job though?[1] It used to be easy before I met you. I certainly was bad, Gosh, I'm awfully bad now but it's a different kind of bad.

* * *

Ernest Hemingway.

Yale, ALS

---

† The following letters are reprinted from *The Letters of Ernest Hemingway, Vol. 2: 1923–1925*, eds. Sandra Spanier, Albert J. DeFazio III, and Robert W. Trogdon (Cambridge: Cambridge UP, 2013), pp. 141, 154–55, 165–67, 285–86, 411–13, 442–44, 454–57. Reprinted by permission of the The Hemingway Foundation and Society. Unless otherwise indicated, notes and bracketed insertions are the original editors'. One of their notes has been relocated. Stein was a literary mentor of EH in from 1922 to 1925. Toklas was her companion. Stein likely drew EH's attention to the painting of Cézanne, as suggested in "On Writing" (see 139–42).

1. In the original ending to his long story "Big Two-Hearted River," EH wrote that Nick Adams "wanted to write like Cezanne painted." EH later followed Stein's advice and cut that ending, which was first published in 1972 as "On Writing" (NAS). EH also notes his admiration for postimpressionist painter Paul Cézanne in the chapters "Miss Stein Instructs" and "Hunger Was Good Discipline" in *MF*. Baker speculates that the "not much good" story might be "A Lack of Passion," which EH eventually abandoned (*SL*, 123); it was published posthumously, along with Susan F. Beegel's analysis, "'A Lack of Passion'; Its Background, Sources, and Composition History," *Hemingway Review* 9, no. 2 (Spring 1990): 50–56. However, Paul Smith asserts that another abandoned story, "Summer People" (NAS), is the weak one alluded to in this letter (395–96).

To Edward J. O'Brien,[1] 12 September 1924

113 Rue Notre Dame des Champs
Paris VI
September 12, 1924.

Dear O'Brien—

*   *   *

I have written 14 stories and have a book ready to publish. It is to be called In Our Time and one of the chapters of the In Our Time[2] I sent you comes in between each story. That was what I originally wrote them for, chapter headings. All the stories have a certain unity—the first 5 are in Michigan—starting with the Up In Michigan—which you know and in between each one comes bang! the In Our Time—It should be awfully good I think.[3] I've tried to do it so you get the close up very quietly but absolutely solid and the real thing but very close and then through it all between every story comes the rythm of the in our time chapters.

Some of the stories I think you would like very much—I wish I could show them to you—The last one in the book is called Big Two Hearted River, it is about 12,000 words and goes back after a skiing story[4] and My Old Man and finishes up the Michigan scene the book starts with. It is much better than anything I've done. What I've been doing is trying to do country so you dont remember the words after you read it but actually have the country. It is hard because to do it you have to see the country all complete all the time you write and not just have a romantic feeling about it. It is swell fun.

*   *   *

With best regards,
Your friend,
Ernest Hemingway.

UMD, ALS

1. Editor (1890–1941), notably of an annual anthology of best American short stories [Editor].
2. Hemingway here refers to *in our time*, the 1924 book of prose poems [Editor].
3. Nearly all the stories EH had finished at the time would be included in *IOT*, published by Boni & Liveright in 1925. However, Liveright deemed "Up in Michigan" objectionable, and EH would replace it with "The Battler." After its 1923 appearance in *TSTP*, "Up in Michigan" was not reprinted until 1938 (*FC*).
4. "Cross-Country Snow," which would appear in the December 1924 *Transatlantic Review*.

To Edmund Wilson,[1] 18 October 1924

113 Rue Notre Dame des Champs,
Paris VI
October 18, 1924.

Dear Wilson:

* * *

I've worked like hell most of the time and think the stuff gets better. Finished the book of 14 stories with a chapter of In Our Time between each story—that is the way they were meant to go—to give the picture of the whole in between examining it in detail. Like looking with your eyes at something, say a passing coast line, and then looking at it with 15X binoculars. Or rather, maybe, looking at it and then going in and living in it—and then coming out and looking at it again.

I sent the book to Don Stewart[2] at the Yale Club about three weeks ago. When he was here he offered to try and sell it for me. I think you would like it, it has a pretty good unity. In some of the stories since the In Our Time I've gotten across both the people and the scene. It makes you feel good when you can do it. It feels now as though I had gotten on top of it.

* * *

Very sincerely,
Ernest Hemingway.

Yale. ALS; postmark: PARIS 80 / R. DUPIN,
18 / x24. / 15 45

To Clarence Hemingway,[1] 20 March [1925]

March 20—

Dear Dad—
Thanks for your fine letter enclosing the K.C. Star review.[2] I'm so glad you liked the Doctor story. I put in Dick Boulton and Billy

---

1. Influential literary critic (1895–1972) and Princeton friend of F. Scott Fitzgerald (see 157) [*Editor*].
2. Hemingway's friend and fellow writer in Paris and part of his crew in Pamplona in 1924. See also note 4 on 138 [*Editor*].
1. Ernest's father (1871–1928) [*Editor*].
2. In his letter to EH of 8 March 1925 (JFK), Clarence enclosed a review of *TSTP* by Nelson Antrim Crawford (1888–1963) titled "A Little Book by Ernest Hemingway Shows

Tabeshaw as real people with their real names because it was pretty sure they would never read the Transatlantic Review.[3] I've written a number of stories about the Michigan country—the country is always true—what happens in the stories is fiction.

This Quarter—a new quarterly review is publishing a long fishing story of mine in 2 parts called Big Two Hearted River. It should be out the first of April. I'll try and get it for you. The river in it is really the Fox above Seney.[4] It is a story I think you will like.

The reason I have not sent you any of my work is because you or Mother sent back the In Our Time books. That looked as though you did not want to see any.[5]

You see I'm trying in all my stories to get the feeling of the actual life across—not to just depict life—or criticize it—but to actually make it alive. So that when you have read something by me you actually experience the thing. You cant do this without putting in the bad and the ugly as well as what is beautiful. Because if it is all beautiful you cant believe in it. Things arent that way. It is only by showing both sides—3 dimensions and if possible 4 that you can write the way I want to.

So when you see anything of mine that you dont like remember that I'm sincere in doing it and that I'm working toward something.

Promise," which appeared in the 20 December 1924 *Kansas City Star.* In it Crawford called EH "one of the most promising young writers in the English language" who finds "the essentials of an object or a person or an action in much the same way that contemporary painters are endeavoring to do" (6).

3. Clarence had read "The Doctor and the Doctor's Wife" in a copy of the December 1924 *Transatlantic Review* that he had been shown "by accident." Dick Boulton and his family lived in the Ojibway "Indian Camp" near Windemere Cottage, and the Tabeshaws lived near Horton Bay (Constance Cappell, *Hemingway in Michigan* [Petoskey, Michigan: Little Traverse Historical Society, 1999], 56–57). In his letter of 8 March, Clarence wrote to EH about the story, "I know your memory is very good for details and I surely saw that old log on the beach as I read your article—I got out the Old Bear Lake book and showed Carol and Leicester [younger siblings— *Editor*] the shots of Nic Boulton and Bill Tabeshaw on the beach sawing the big old beach log."

4. In August 1919 EH and his companions had fished the Fox River, which runs through the town of Seney in Michigan's Upper Peninsula. EH took the name for his story "Big Two-Hearted River" from another river to the northeast of Seney. [See map on 4—*Editor.*]

5. In his 8 March letter, Clarence lamented that he had only seen EH's story by chance and wrote, "Wish,—dear boy you would send me some of your work often." The record is murky as to the reason the elder Hemingways returned copies of *iot.* Unbeknownst to the other, EH's parents had each written to Pound [the poet Ezra Pound—*Editor*] in November 1922 to order five copies of *iot,* and they may have simply returned excess copies. Marcelline [EH's older sister—*Editor*] recalled that her parents had been "shocked and horrified" by the book and that her father returned to the publisher "all six" of the copies he had ordered [Marcelline Hemingway Sanford, *At the Hemingways* (U of Idaho P, 1999), 218–19—*Editor*]. For the confusion over Clarence and Grace's order of copies of *iot,* see EH to Hemingway Family, [c. 7 May 1924].

If I write an ugly story that might be hateful to you or to Mother the next one might be one that you would like exceedingly.

❊   ❊   ❊

With love and good luck,
Ernie

JFK, ALS

To Ezra Pound, 8 November [1925]

November 8, (Rent Day)

Dear Duce—[1]

❊   ❊   ❊

Have been getting some pretty good reviews. Some damn nice ones and a lot of guys who say the stories are not stories at all but psychological sketches or formless bits etc. etc. Don't know whether you would feel like doing a review or anything. Would be refreshing for me at any rate. Le Grand Gertrude Stein[2] warned me when I presented her with a copy not to expect a review as she thought it would be wiser to wait for my novel. What a lot of safe playing kikes. Why not write a review of one book at a time? She is afraid that I might fall on my nose in a novel and if so how terrible it would have been to have said anything about this book no matter how good it may be. These things help one very much. It is like the litmus paper test for acid mouth.[3]

You might, if you liked the goddam book, and I think you will because it is pretty good and hard and solid and they are all damning it for being hard boiled and cold and lacking in verbal beauty and felicity whatever the hell that is, do something for Elliot's thing. Eliot doesn't know whether I am any good or not. He came over and asked Gertrude if I were serious and worth publishing and Gertrude said it were best to wait and see—that I was just starting and there wasn't any way of knowing yet.

Oh well what the hell. I'm not asking you to review it and I won't be sore if you don't. But the way it works out is that the whole thing of the

1. Hemingway's salutation mocks Pound's support of Benito Mussolini, "Il Duce," meaning "The Leader," a title the Italian fascist dictator used informally many years before he made it his official national title in 1943 [Editor].
2. See 151 [Editor].
3. Stein's refusal to review IOT seems to have ended EH's friendship with her; any correspondence they may have exchanged after this point remains unlocated. [EH used the slur to appeal to Pound's antisemitism. A litmus test uses specially treated paper to determine whether a solution is acidic or alkaline—Editor.]

damned opposition is done on this goddam personal basis and why in hell shouldn't we from time to time stab them with their own knives.[4]

*   *   *

yrs. always.
Hem.

Yale, TL with typewritten signature

To Clarence Hemingway, 15 December 1925

December 15, 1925
Hotel Taube, Schruns, Vorarlberg,
Austria

Dear Dad:

*   *   *

* * * Glad you bought the In Our Time. Mother sent a review cut out of the New Republic. It's still getting splendid reviews. Some hate it; like a bird named Elmer Adams in Detroit News. Others seem to like it. Nobody seems very indifferent. I've written a funny book that they will hate or like even more violently.[1] I know what I'm doing and it doesn't make any difference either way what anybody says about it. Naturally it is nice to have people like it. But it is inside yourself that you have to judge and nothing anybody says outside can help you anymore than anybody can help you shoot when a partridge flies up. Either you hit them or you dont. Good instruction beforehand teaching you to shoot etc. is fine. But after a while it all depends on yourself and you have to be your own worst critic.

*   *   *

Best love,
Ernie

PSU, ALS; postmark: SCHRUNS / *a*, 16.XII.25

4. Pound did not review *IOT* for Eliot's *Criterion* [the literary magazine founded by the poet-critic T. S. Eliot in 1922—*Editor*] nor is he known to have reviewed any other of EH's works.
1. Clarence wrote in his letter: "I bought 'In Our Time,' and have read it with interest. Many press comments are published and Mother has collected and sent to you." Elmer Cleveland Adams (1885–1964) edited the column "Random Shots" for the *Detroit News*, a popular evening newspaper. [The new "funny book" is *TOS*—*Editor*.]

To F. Scott Fitzgerald,[1] [ca. 24 December 1925]

Dear Scott—

* * *

Your rating of I.O.T. stories very interesting. The way I like them as it seems now, without re-reading is Grade I (Big 2 hearted. Indian Camp. 1st ¶ and last ¶ of Out of Season. Soldier's Home)

Hell I cant group them. Why did you leave out My Old Man? That's a good story, always seemed to me, though not the thing I'm shooting for. It belongs to another categorie along with the bull fight story and the 50 Grand.[2] The kind that are easy for me to write.

Cat in the Rain wasnt about Hadley. I knew you and Zelda[3] always thought it was. When I wrote that we were at Rapallo but Hadley was 4 months pregnant with Bumby. The Inn Keeper was the one at Cortina D'Ampezzo and the man and girl were a harvard kid and his wife that I'd met at Genoa. Hadley never made a speech in her life about wanting a baby because she had been told various things by her doctor and I'd—. No use going into all that.

The only story in which Hadley figures is Out of Season which was an almost literal transcription of what happened. Your ear is always more acute when you have been upset by a row of any sort, mine I mean, and when I came in from the unproductive fishing trip I wrote that story right off on the typewriter without punctuation. I meant it to be tragic about the drunk of a guide because I reported him to the hotel owner—the one who appears in Cat In The Rain— and he fired him and as that was the last job he had in the town and he was quite drunk and very desperate he hanged himself in the stable. At that time I was writing the In Our Time chapters and I wanted to write a tragic story <u>without</u> violence. So I didnt put in the hanging. Maybe that sounds silly. I didnt think the story needed it.

* * *

Review of In Our Type from Chicago Post says all of it obviously not fiction but simply descriptive of passages in life of new Chicago Author.[4] God what a life I must have led.

---

1. Novelist and short-story writer (1896–1940), who by this time had become Hemingway's friend and confidant [*Editor*].
2. The bullfight story, "The Undefeated," had just appeared in *This Quarter*, and "Fifty Grand" is a boxing story that would first appear in *Atlantic Monthly* in July 1927 [*Editor*].
3. Fitzgerald's wife. "Hadley": See note 1 on 81 [*Editor*].
4. In "A New Chicago Writer," a review of *IOT* that appeared in the 27 November 1925 *Chicago Post*, Mary Plum wrote: "it seems absurd to speak of this book as fiction or its

*   *   *

Original ending of story had dose of clapp instead of gonorreaha but I didnt know whether clap had two ps or one, so changed it to gonoccoci. [*EH wrote in the right margin:*] referring to Very Short Story. The hell I did. Try and get it. (This is a piece of slang I invented down here)[5]

Hope you have a swell Christmas.

Yrs. always.
Yogi Liveright[6]

*   *   *

PUL, ALS

---

characters as fictitious. They are too obviously drawn from life" [165 in this volume—*Editor*].

5. EH drew an arrow from the closing parenthesis of this sentence to the phrase "Try and get it," which appears on the previous line in the letter. At the end of EH's "A Very Short Story" (*IOT*), the reader is told that the protagonist, having received a letter from the woman he loves saying that she plans to marry another man, "contracted gonorrhea from a sales girl in a loop department store while riding in a taxicab through Lincoln Park." [EH denies this actually happened ("the hell I did. Try and get it")—*Editor*.]

6. EH is conflating the names of Yogi Johnson, a character in *TOS*, and Horace Liveright [owner of Boni & Liveright, the publisher of *In Our Time*—*Editor*].

CRITICISM

Early Reviews

HERBERT J. SELIGMANN

In Our Time†

Ernest Hemingway is abrupt at times as only an American can be. He wants his moments direct. The fewer words the better. What words there are must yield explicitness. It is like people talking. His vocabulary is close to the happening. It fits the mood of young men who had to face war, who killed and were mutilated.

Mr. Hemingway's generation found their world one in which men sniveled of love and religion and blew each other to shreds on the battlefield. War experience Mr. Hemingway renders briefly. Death is made no more immediate by expatiating upon its horrors. You tell in a paragraph how a German soldier got his leg over a garden wall, how you "potted" him and he fell down looking awfully surprised. The flat, even banal declarations in the paragraphs alternating with Mr. Hemingway's longer sketches are a criticism of the conventional dishonesty of literature. Here is neither literary inflation nor elevation, but a passionately bare telling of what happened. It represents the impact of a young man loving waters, light, trees and fine horses upon the brutalities of childbirth, bull fights, jail, execution and shooting.

The Spoken Word

Suffering creates irony. Mr. Hemingway uses words more often spoken than printed. Why not? Life is not censored by those who decide what is fit to print. Not Mr. Hemingway's life. Did not James Joyce explore three minds during a day, in "Ulysses," unhampered by any consideration of what words are or are not permissible? As a matter of course the society that finds it proper to indulge in whole-sale murder outlaws "Ulysses."[1]

---

† From *The Sun* (New York: October 17, 1925): 17. Notes are by the editor of this Norton Critical Edition. Page numbers in brackets refer to this Norton Critical Edition.
1. Published in Paris, James Joyce's *Ulysses* (1922) was a highly innovative modernist novel that scandalized some readers through its sexual explicitness and shocking language. For a time it was banned in the United States.

Mr. Hemingway's brief delineations of men shot, horses gored in the bull ring, a hanging in jail, are the ironic commentary of a man avid of life. In the longer pieces he is often no less ironic. There is a contrast between the longer and shorter sketches. The short represent youth's defense against rawness, set down with intent care, seeming off-hand and brutally banal. The longer sketches, not long really, range autobiographically from childhood onward.

Both sets of alternating sketches have a bright declarative definiteness like boards neatly joined end to end. It was Sherwood Anderson [xi], I think, who found anew this way of using words. Like Anderson, Hemingway has a story about a jockey and horses. There is another about tramps. Anderson says of himself that he learned of [i.e., from] Gertrude Stein [xi]. Probably most writers have learned from literature to listen keenly to spoken language.

Surgical Precision

His attention to speech is only part of Mr. Hemingway's intentness upon exactitude. His intentness upon his job is like a surgeon's. When Nick baited a trout hook with a grasshopper "he took him by the head and held him while he threaded the slim hook under his chin, down through his thorax and into the last segments of his abdomen" [123]. Mr. Hemingway is no less direct when he writes of birth, of love coming to an end, of a returned soldier who finds clinging family sentiment intolerable, of the revealing moment when a young American girl wants a cat and gets it, not from her husband, but from their Italian landlord.

Mr. Hemingway comes close to people at such moments; he creates the moments by seeing them clear. So the artist creates his world, and himself. Mr. Hemingway's generation was partially destroyed, deeply hurt by war. He at least proposes not to relinquish the clarity so dearly bought. Like Nick, he does not want to rush his sensations any. Once attained, this clarity animates all things. Increasing refinement gives overtone and color to experience inaudible and invisible to any but the artist. On that so carefully and lingeringly observed solitary fishing expedition, Nick looks down the river toward a cedar swamp. ". . . in the fast deep water, in the half light, the fishing would be tragic. In the swamp fishing was a tragic adventure" [128].

A True Experimenter

There is delicacy in the writing of Mr. Hemingway, a fine sense of the word. To read his book is to feel something of life's ruthlessness. This young American's awareness is to be welcomed and enjoyed even by those who do not live in Paris and who hesitate to proclaim him the best American writer of his time. As yet Mr. Hemingway, admirable as is his achievement, seems to me still intent upon discovering his way, upon perfecting his formidable instrument. Varied though his experience, he has not yet the big movement, the rich content of such a book as "Dark Laughter."[2]

ANONYMOUS

Preludes to a Mood[†]

Ernest Hemingway has a lean, pleasing, tough resilience. His language is fibrous and athletic, colloquial and fresh, hard and clean; his very prose seems to have an organic being of its own. Every syllable counts toward a stimulating, entrancing experience of magic. He looks out upon the world without prejudice or preconception and records with precision and economy, and an almost terrifying immediacy, exactly what he sees. His short stories, sketches, anecdotes and epigrams are triumphs of sheer objectivity.

The items which make up the collection of "In Our Time" are not so much short stories, in the accepted meaning, as preludes to a mood, composed with accurate and acute finesse to converge in the mind of the reader. Mr. Hemingway is oblique, inferential, suggestive rather than overt, explicit, explanatory. His people and events emerge with miraculous suddenness and inevitability out of a timeless paradise of their own, to intimate their own especial and intrinsic incongruities and ironies and pathos out of an illimitable fabric of comedies and tragedies.

Mr. Hemingway packs a whole character into a phrase, an entire situation into a sentence or two. He makes each word count three or four ways. The covers of his book should strain and bulge with the healthful ferment that is between them. Here is an authentic energy and propulsive force which is contained in an almost primitive isolation of images as if the language itself were being made over in its early directness of metaphor. Each story, indeed, is a sort of expanded metaphor, conveying a far larger implication than its literal significations.

The first five stories are linked upon the personality of one Nick. In the seventy pages or so, Nick, his father a doctor, and his hypochondriacal Christian Science wife, his uncle, his friend, his first love affair, his fishing expeditions and his casual adventures serve

<hr>

2. Sherwood Anderson's 1925 novel was published by Boni & Liveright, the publisher of *In Our Time.*
† From *The New York Times Book Review* (October 18, 1925): 8. Notes are by the editor of this Norton Critical Edition. Page numbers in brackets refer to this Norton Critical Edition.

to give a unique and unmistakable portrait of a growing boy in a Michigan backwoods settlement. The first story might almost be a stripped, matter-of-fact account of a delicate, tricky surgical operation told with the scientific finality and reticence of a medical report. Mr. Hemingway does not worry at the young boy's symptoms, his "reactions" to this terrifying introduction to the mysteries of birth and death; he states: "Nick did not watch. His curiosity had been gone for a long time" [13].

"Cat in the Rain" concerns itself with an American couple in an Italian hotel, the attentive, ingratiating proprietor, the maid and the cat. The husband lies on the bed and reads. The wife presses her nose against the chill windowpane, and sees a cat crouched under a table to keep out of the wet. "Anyway, I want a cat," she said, "I want a cat. I want a cat now. If I can't have long hair or any fun, I can have a cat" [77]. She goes down to get the cat and finds it gone. The proprietor learns of it and sends her a cat. That is absolutely all there is, yet a lifetime of discontent, of looking outside for some unknown fulfillment is compressed into the offhand recital.

Mr. Hemingway can make the reader see a trout lying on the pebbles of a clear, swift, cold stream. He can show you the four-cornered mouth of a grasshopper and the sudden, disconcerting spurt of "tobacco juice" [123] over the restraining fingers. He can call up a whole bullfight, indeed an entire civilization, in a curt epigram. He can present the life and the preoccupations about a race course— the horses, the jockeys, the touts, the bettors.

Mr. Hemingway's most noteworthy gift, however, is for a delightful economy of dialogue. In "The Three-Day Blow," two boys sit over a wood fire and talk: the shanty, the gale outside, their convictions and habitual modes of being are fully revealed in irrelevant aimless snatches of conversation. It seems to be overheard, it is so compellingly actual, yet it gives evidence of Mr. Hemingway's severely schooled selectiveness. It is merely one afternoon when these two decided to get drunk, nothing more, yet it is a friendship of months and years, dense with common experiences and impressions. Their weighing of the relative values of baseball teams, of Hugh Walpole and G. K. Chesterton, of their respective fathers, and their philosophizings on life in general are priceless yet poignant with a hint of that fleeting, ephemeral quality, youth.

PAUL ROSENFIELD

Tough Earth[†]

Hemingway's short stories belong with cubist painting, Le Sacre du Printemps,[1] and other recent work bringing a feeling of positive forces through primitive modern idiom. The use of the direct, crude, rudimentary forms of the simple and primitive classes and their situations, of the stuffs, textures and rhythms of the mechanical and industrial worlds, has enabled this new American story teller, as it enabled the group to which he comes a fresh recruit, to achieve peculiarly sharp, decided, grimly affirmative expressions; and with these acute depictions and half-impersonal beats to satisfy a spirit running through the age. Hemingway's spoken prose is characteristically iron with a lyricism, aliveness and energy tremendously held in check. With the trip-hammer thud of Le Sacre his rhythms go. Emphatic, short, declarative sentences follow staunchly one upon the other, never precipitously or congestedly or mechanically, and never relenting. The stubby verbal forms are speeded in instances up to the brute, rapid, joyous jab of blunt period upon period. Hemingway's vocabulary is largely monosyllabic, and mechanical and concrete. Mixed with the common words, raw and pithy terms picked from the vernaculars of boys, jockeys, hunters, policemen, soldiers, and obscurely related to primitive impulse and primitive sex, further increase the rigidity of effect. There is something of Sherwood Anderson [363], of his fine bare effects and values coined from simplest words, in Hemingway's clear medium. There is Gertrude Stein [xiv–xvi] equally obvious: her massive volumes, slow power, steady reiterations, and her intuition of the life of headless bodies. The American literary generations are learning to build upon each other. This newcomer's prose departs from the kindred literary mediums as a youngling from forebears. Wanting some of the warmth of Anderson and some of the pathos of Gertrude Stein, Hemingway's style none the less in its very experimental stage shows the outline of a new, tough, severe and satisfying beauty related equally to the world of machinery and the austerity of the red man.

It comes on the general errand of the group, the realization of a picture of the elements of life caught in barest, intensest opposition. In the world of Hemingway's stories, characters and principles are boxers crouched and proposing fists. Stocky rudimentary passions

---

† *The New Republic* (November 25, 1925): 22–23. The note is by the editor of this Norton Critical Edition. Page numbers in brackets refer to this Norton Critical Edition.
1. Avant-garde ballet and orchestral work by Igor Stravinsky, first performed in Paris in 1913.

wrestle for a throw. The sport of the two youths snowshoeing in high Alps is brusquely, casually interrupted by consciousness of pregnancy and the responsibility seeking out the man. A lad sees his sensitive father beset by the active brutality of men and the passive brutality of women. Inside the hotel room in the rain male and female face each other for a swift passage of their eternal warfare. The sheer unfeeling barbarity of life, and the elementary humor and tenderness lying close upon it, is a favorite theme. The amazing single pages previously assembled in a booklet by the Three Mountains Press in Paris, sandwiched between the longer stories in the Liveright volume and connecting these with the doings of an epoch, bring dangerously close in instantaneous pictures of the War, of the bull-ring and the police-world, the excitement of combat, the cold ferocity of the mob, the insensibility of soldiering, the relief of nerves in alcoholic stupor, the naked, the mean, the comic brute in the human frame. Against these principles, set invariably in crude, simple, passionate opposition, the author plays the more constructive elements. We feel the absorption and fine helpfulness of the handicapped doctor performing a Cæsarean operation with a jack-knife and releasing a child; the tender, subtle feeling for woman's life found among certain of the ordinary people of Europe; the enjoyment of the body in the physical play of life; the seriousness in the young man making him accept responsibility and automatically limit his narcissistic impulse to freedom. And both these forces and the uglier ones are given sharp physiognomies by the dramatic counterpoint; and what certain of them owe Sherwood Anderson is made good by the personal intensification of the passionate opposition between them.

There is little analysis in this narrative art. We are given chiefly, at times with marvelous freshness and crispness, what the eye sees and the ear hears. The conflicting principles are boldly established without psychologizings. Yet Hemingway's acceptation of the æsthetic responsibility of getting his material into action in instances remains near gesturing. His units are not brought into actual opposition in all his pieces. Or, formally introduced, they remain at inadequate degrees of tension, while a youthfully insolent sense of the stereotype in life blinds the author. Soldier's Home is one of Hemingway's forms half left in the limbo of the stencil. The happy relief to this and other incompleted pieces is furnished by stories like Cat in the Rain, Indian Camp, and My Old Man. In these, plastic elements accurately felt are opposed point against point, and a whole brought into view. It is a whole this newcomer has to show. It is one from which the many beauties of his book are fetched. He shares his epoch's feeling of a harsh impersonal force in the universe, permanent, not to be changed, taking both destruction and construction up into itself and set in motion by their dialectic. With the blood and pain, he makes us know the toughness of the earth, able to meet desire, nourish life, and waken in man the power to meet the brutalities of existence. This bald feeling is the condition of an adjustment to life begun in men before the War, but demanded even more intensely of them by its ghastlier train, and natural at all times to the products of primitive America. Through it men are reconciled to perpetual struggle, and while holding themselves tight work in relation to something in the universe. This adjustment is not the sole possible one. It is not necessarily the one of next year or of the year to follow, for any. But it had and still has its reality; and the rhythms, and tempi which communicate it share in its permanence.

MARY PLUM

A New Chicago Writer[†]

Thru the mind of a drowning person are supposed to flash staccato glimpses of his past life. It is just such brief and vivid snatches of memory that Mr. Hemingway shows in the compact and vigorous sketches given in this volume. He alternates thruout the book extremely short and startlingly brutal vignettes, only a paragraph or two in length, with longer sketches, none of which, however, reach the proportions of the true short story. They are snapshots only, clear and accurate souvenirs of unforgettable moments, shown in the simplest and most economical manner. Some of the pictures are of big moments, more of them reveal mere incidents, temporary sensations, such as seem unimportant when they occur, but are apt to live in the back of their participant's memory. The feel of sandpapery snow against the face when skiing recklessly down a mountain side, the sun warm on the back when loafing by the river after fishing, thoughts under bombardment and that curious clearness of mind which comes after having well drunken of good whisky but before actual drunkenness; it is such sensations and temporary intensities of emotion which are photographed for the reader.

Mr. Hemingway is sparing with his adjectives, and his style is harsh and unadorned. Only when he uses the actual speech of one of his characters does it warm into human violence. The characters are alive; they are as honest and human creations as any in fiction. In fact, it seems absurd to speak of this book as fiction or its characters as fictitious. They are too obviously drawn from life. They are

† From *Chicago Post* (November 27, 1925). The note is by the editor of this Norton Critical Edition.

the sort of person that everyone knows, the Nick and Bill and Marjorie that you played with by the river and in the woods when you were young, and the boys are there that you met on an artillery-crowded road in France, or got drunk with in a little cafe behind the lines.

None of these unusual stories are pleasant ones; they are brutal, trenchant and terse. They have in them a fierce and compelling energy. Brief and concise as a memorandum, they are as vivid as Revelation.[1] If we may take this one volume as a criterion of his future work, Mr. Hemingway is likely to become one of the most original and vital short story writers in America.

SCHUYLER ASHLEY

Another American Discovers the Acid in the Language[†]

At 2 o'clock in the morning two Hungarians got into a cigar store at Fifteenth street and Grand avenue. Drevitts and Boyle drove up from the Fifteenth street police station in a Ford. The Hungarians were backing their wagon out of an alley. Boyle shot one off the seat of the wagon and one out of the wagon box. Drevitts got frightened when he found they were both dead. 'Hell, Jimmy,' he said, 'you oughtn't to have done it. There's liable to be a hell of a lot of trouble.'

"'They're crooks, ain't they?' said Boyle. 'They're wops, ain't they? Who the hell is going to make any trouble?'

"'That's all right maybe this time,' said Drevitts, 'but how did you know they were wops when you bumped them off?'

"'Wops,' said Boyle, 'I can tell wops a mile off.'" [63]

That amiable incident may have been drawn from the rich annals of Kansas City's streets. I am inclined to think that it was, although the author, Ernest Hemingway, is now an outstanding figure in the group of young writers who find the perspective afforded by a residence in Paris helpful in depicting the contemporary American scene. This curious and interesting collection of stories and sketches is distinguished by a discriminating use of modern idiom and argot. The short sentences bite like acid; the infrequent expletives snarl and rumble like loaded trucks under a viaduct.

---

1. The prophetic final book of the New Testament in the Christian Bible.
† From *The Kansas City Star* (Dec. 12, 1925): 6. Notes are by the editor of this Norton Critical Edition. Page numbers in brackets refer to this Norton Critical Edition.

Severely Objective

There are many adjectives which come easily to mind in an attempt to characterize the writing of Ernest Hemingway. Objective is one of the first of them; his stories are almost too artfully disanchored from his own emotions. Vital and astringent they are to a surpassing degree. His phrases are brittle, with mordant edges, and he has the inestimable gift of concrete visualization. In lean, spare sentences he always makes you *see* the thing he writes about. But what comes nearest to catching his peculiar quality is the everyday, vernacular term "hardboiled." This fellow is indubitably a hardboiled writer. He has a great feeling for the nonchalant, bleak-faced relish for life enjoyed by truck drivers and city detectives. He knows niggers,[1] prize fighters, ex-marines and lonely men who go fishing. He gets at the very essence of young, fairly tough, boys, and he writes with gusto of horse racing and bull fighting.

It is very hard to resist quoting Mr. Hemingway. One wishes to share with others the conviction that something worth while has come to American letters with the advent of a new man who can give to common words a corrosive quality like that in the following tiny etching: "The bull charged and Villalta charged and just for a moment they became one. Villalta became one with the bull and then it was over. Villalta standing straight and the red hilt of the sword sticking out dully between the bull's shoulders. Villalta, his hand up at the crowd and the bull roaring blood, looking straight at Villalta and his legs caving" [87].

Figures from Modern Life

With Sherwood Anderson and Ring Lardner this author shares a secret.[2] They have discovered a rich vein of linguistic ore that lies just below the surface of every traffic way and freight dock, and they are all realizing on the lode. They seek to let the old, worn, literary metaphors retire to amply earned repose, since from the lips of every irascible towboat captain or badly frightened coon[3] they hear vivid startling figures drawn from the complex mechanical civilization of today.

Yes, even at sea a new language is being born; the beautiful, die-hard picturesqueness of the days of sail is now found less often between decks than between book covers. But the new sea lingo is not without its savor. I remember one black and gray morning off

---

1. This offensive word reflects the ethos of much of white America in the 1920s.
2. For Anderson, see 97. Lardner (1885–1933) was a popular sports columnist and short-story writer.
3. White racial slur for a Black American, derived from "raccoon" and implying stealth.

the Orkneys,[4] when a squadron of 25,000-ton battle ships were making heavy weather of it against the vicious, short sea that runs in those latitudes. A little weasel-faced signalman, perched on watch at the end of a bridge wing, wrinkled his nose distastefully against the flying spray, while the huge steel hull beneath him pounded and slammed along. "Say!" he yelped to the windy universe, "seems to me like the springs on this old bus are weakenin'!"

It is to sources like that that Mr. Hemingway owes some of the vigor of his style. Of course, "In Our Time" is admittedly a slight and fragmentary enterprise. It is, however, a promise, almost an assurance, of richer and more important things to come. A pianist who supples his fingers before essaying a Brahm's sonata,[5] a pitcher warming up craftily in the bullpen, or a fighter shadow boxing under the arc lights before going to work in a cold ring; these are figures comparable to Ernest Hemingway in "In Our Time." By this collection he has established himself as a colorful and competent performer; when he tackles a real subject he should bring all the stands up cheering. More power to him!

DAVID MERRILL ANDERSON

Stories That Disclose An Artist[†]

Ernest Hemingway looks to us like an artist.

We are too fond of that word to use it often, and we have charged through his book several times before taking the word out of its special case for his benefit.

"In Our Time" is a collection of short stories that reek with life. They are not altogether "normal," nor do they, as Rupert Hughes once remarked in eulogizing Robert W. Chambers, portray "well-groomed men and women in their stately homes."[1] They deal with the Northern woods, with bull fights, with wars. Frontiers of emotion as well as of action.

Possibly Hemingway, like most sincere artists, has felt somewhat swamped by the tremendous annual rainfall of wax-flower romances, prettified sex stories and hop dreams of success.[2] At any rate, parts of

4. Islands northeast of Scotland.
5. Johannes Brahms (1833–1897), German composer of symphonic, instrumental, and choral music, including three piano sonatas.
† From *The Evening Sun* (Baltimore: December 12, 1925): 8. Notes are by the editor of this Norton Critical Edition. Page numbers in brackets refer to this Norton Critical Edition.
1. Rupert Hughes (1872–1956) was a novelist, composer, historian, film writer, and journalist. Robert W. Chambers (1865–1933) was a novelist and short-story writer. In a foreword to a 1938 edition of Chambers's supernatural stories, *The Yellow King*, Hughes used language similar to this remark, but the source of the "eulogizing" quoted by Anderson is unknown.
2. See note 8 on 117.

his work sound as if he had been forced to write for "The Epworth Era" or "Little Folks" for years,[3] and were now out to tell the polite world that the lid is blown to hell-an'-gone. In the entire book there is only one euphemism, and that is not news-printable. Except for that single lapse into reticence, Hemingway says exactly what he means.

Probably a fair proportion of the public will read this book in hopes of a shocking. Even the crowds of little he and she flappers that swarmed to the first Baltimore night of "Desire Under the Elms"[4] may hear of it, and be tricked into reading a good book. We frankly hope so.

Interspersed between the short stories are brief, vivid episodes of a page or so, quite unrelated to the main stories. A pungent vitality bristles through most of them—packed with about as much violence and brutality as words can carry. On the whole, the stories interest us more than these interludes.

But it is not fair to give the impression that Hemingway, like the average moviac,[5] needs a flock of hairbreadth escapes, murders, seductions and suicides to keep his stories moving. He can deal with subtler material, and several of his stories paddle along casually enough, with almost the Meander manner of Katherine Mansfield.[6]

It is our guess that a score of years from now the only aspect of this book that will seem "dated" (except to those who insist on outmoding everything they do not like) will be the style—and only certain passages, at that:

As an instance:

"His wife was silent. The doctor wiped his gun carefully with a rag. He pushed the shells back in against the spring of the magazine. He sat with his gun on his knees. He was very fond of it. Then he heard his wife's voice from the darkened room" [19].

This monotone with varying overtones, this sparse, staccato manner that seems at first glance to insist on the equal emotional value of unequal things, is at its height now with several of our best writers. Hemingway does not drive it too hard, and he usually has a reason for using it.

Keep this book off Grandma's Christmas list. But be sure that some one puts it on your own.

---

3. *The Epworth Era* was in the 1920s the official publication of the Methodist Epworth League, a youth group. *Little Folks* was a magazine for children, published in England and the United States.
4. "Flappers" were young people, usually female, of the 1920s who danced the Charleston, wearing fashions and hairstyles of that era. *Desire Under the Elms*, a tragedy by Eugene O'Neill, was first published in 1924.
5. A movie maniac.
6. Modernist short-story writer (1888–1923) from New Zealand, whose "meandering" prose style was distinctive.

LAWRENCE MORE

Daring Stories[†]

There's a new star in the literary firmament . . . a new star blinking savagely and laughing at us. It came out suddenly, at a time when we thought our celestial organization was pretty complete. It came crashing in, rude and laughing, bumped a couple of other stars and made them mad.

We're always skeptical of new stars. We looked at this one long and hard and then consulted the sages, those who had gazed deep into the astronomy of letters. We rather hoped it would disappear like stars do after you look at them quite a while. But it didn't.

One can imagine Ernest Hemingway, 25 years old, prematurely blase, a young man who went through the war and saw lots of life, handing his collection of short stories, "In Our Time," to the world. He did it with a sneer. Probably he didn't give a d—— what people thought of it.

But the young man handed us a red-hot penny. We took it and yelled and cursed him. The burn kept us thinking about him, however, and we did some inquiring. Ford Madox Ford (ne Hueffer), editor of the "transatlantic review," who collaborated with Conrad in writing two big stories, came out with such an ambitious statement as "the best writer in America at this moment (though for the moment he happens to be in Paris), the most conscientious, the most master of his craft, the most consummate, is Ernest Hemingway."[1] We always wanted to get back at Ford, however, because he didn't go and beg Conrad's pardon for mixing ink with him, and here's our chance to say that we think he's got an awful nerve. That's that.

Then along comes Sherwood Anderson and says that "although older writers do not much like to see young prosemen coming on in their own day," nevertheless "Mr. Hemingway can write, and I like his tales. The pen feels good in his hand. In his tales people come close."[2]

And Edward J. O'Brien, greatest living authority on the short story, says "I regard this volume as a permanent contribution to the American literature of our time—a brave book not only for us but

† From the St. Petersburg Times (February 28, 1926): 82. Notes are by the editor of this Norton Critical Edition. Page numbers in brackets refer to this Norton Critical Edition.
1. Ford made this assessment in the New York Evening Post, March 8, 1926 (cited in Reynolds, The Paris Years, 274). Earlier in his career, Ford had collaborated with Polish-British author Joseph Conrad (1857–1924) on two novels and a novella.
2. Hemingway's Chicago mentor, Anderson, made this comment for a Boni & Liveright advertisement in The New York Times Book Review, October 11, 1925.

for posterity."[3] And Gilbert Seldes, John Dos Passos, and Donald Ogden Stewart, and Waldo Frank, and many others join hands and applaud.

Hemingway's unusual book can be warmly admired, and violently disliked. It so happens that we have been fortunate enough to have made the acquaintance here in St. Petersburg of a personal friend of Hemingway's.[4] From him, whose contribution appears elsewhere on this page, we learn that a very large proportion of the material in the book is distinctly autobiographical. Ernest Hemingway, saucy, young, strong, full of laughter, walks right through the book, from cover to cover.

"In Our Time" is extraordinary in its courage, vividness, and brutality. It is to a great extent written in the deliberately unliterary modern style, and it leaves you gasping with such original grammar as "and the last bull he was so tired he couldn't hardly get the sword in," and "could not go further," and "had gotten," but you know those are pieces of studied negligence.

The book is a collection of short "stories," ranging in length from a half page to many pages. We hesitate to call them stories. Some of them are impressions only. You read one and you feel as if a gust of wind had rushed into the room and upset something, or you read another and you feel as if you were looking deep into a quiet pool of water. There's no trick to them, and they are written in a homely, unaffected style that at times recalls Anderson's easy informality.

Hemingway has been a newspaper man, but he escapes the sloppy, reportorial style so common to newspapermen who imagine themselves inspired. His is fevered, sometimes delirious writing, but always remarkable writing. It is quick, deliberate, indisputable. It is passionate. It is cold and brutal. It is consummate.

This reviewer is familiar with most of the ground that Hemingway takes his readers over, even up into the woods of northern Minnesota [sic], along the Lake Superior country. The war, and Italy, and France, and bull fights are dragged in, and crass scenes from domestic life.

One rainy night we find a cat "trying to make herself compact so she won't be dripped on" [75], a man "talking French just like English" [104], the old man who when killed in the steeple chase "looked so white and gone and awfully dead" [107]. Mrs. Elliott "became very much brighter after her girl friend came and they had

---

3. Editor and anthologist O'Brien's comment appeared as a promotional blurb on the cover of Boni & Liveright's edition of *In Our Time*. All the authors mentioned below contributed promotional comments for that cover.

4. More alludes to John Miller, a Red Cross ambulance driver in Italy who knew Hemingway during the war. Miller, a professional singer, was then spending the winter in St. Petersburg, Florida, and published a brief reminiscence that ran alongside More's review.

many good cries together" [71]. There is nothing better in modern literature than this: "They spent the night of the day they were married in a Boston hotel; they were both very disappointed" [70].

RUTH SUCKOW

Short Stories of Distinction[†]

Ernest Hemingway's first book is a collection of fifteen short stories interspersed with minute sketches. The most noticeable thing about them is the excellence of their technique. They are written in a hard, sure, clean style without an unnecessary word—sometimes in fact, without a few words that would be welcome if not actually necessary. This style is the natural outcome of a modern tendency toward compression, and—in a larger sense—toward inference rather than explanation. Except for occasional repetitions that seem to have been caught from Gertrude Stein, its taciturn firmness is unbroken throughout the volume.[1] Both in method and content, the book is essentially of our time. The best of the stories are concerned with the boy, Nick Adams, in whom, to judge from comments upon the volume, the literary youth of our day recognizes his own authentic portrait. They have a distinctly autobiographical cast. The other sketches are slight, although well-done. Two stories especially seem to me to have value: "Soldiers Return" ["Home"] which reminds one (although in no derivative sense) of another short story, the fruit of an earlier war, Hamlin Garland's "The Return of the Private";[2] and the last in the book, "Big Two-Hearted River." This is the most thoroughly distinctive piece of work in the volume. Externally, it is a description of a fishing party in the northern timber country taken by the now familiar Nick. Actually it is an embodiment in prose of the outdoor passion of our modern youth brought up to the cult of "back to nature" and of bodily excellence. Every one of its details is essential, for every one is informed with this passion. Plenty of other young men have expressed the disillusion of youth after the war. In this, "Soldiers Return" ["Home"] is better done than most, but not unique. It is in this other aspect, revealed in "Cross-Country Snow" and better still in "Big Two-Hearted River," that Mr. Hemingway's volume shows its most original side.

[†] From *The Des Moines Sunday Register* (September 12, 1926): 21. Notes are by the editor of this Norton Critical Edition.

1. Stein (see xiv) advised Hemingway on rhythm and repetition (see especially 56–57, where "like" is repeated).

2. Garland's story appeared in *Main-Travelled Roads* (1891) and depicts a soldier returning from the Civil War.

Critical Views of *In Our Time*

DAVID WYATT

A Second Will: *In Our Time* and *in our time*†

When Hadley Hemingway packed up her husband's papers and carried them in an overnight bag to the Gare de Lyon in December 1922, she set in motion a process that would have profound implications for the composition of *In Our Time*. After placing her valise in her overnight compartment, Hadley took a walk around the train station. When she returned to her compartment, her luggage was gone. It contained almost all of the work Hemingway had done since moving to Paris a year earlier. What survived the loss were poems already published or in the mail, a chapter of a long fishing story, and some Paris sketches, as well as two short stories, "Up in Michigan" and "My Old Man." Only one of these pieces, the story about a boy and his horse-riding father, would eventually be included in the sequence of stories and sketches that make up *In Our Time*.

✳   ✳   ✳

"Memory is the best critic," Ezra Pound had responded, when Hemingway wrote to him about the lost manuscripts. "The *point* is," Pound went on, "how much of it can you remember?" [But] Hemingway did not attempt any photographic recovery of the sentences that had been stolen. Instead, he turned to new work.

Within a month or two of Hadley's fateful train trip, Hemingway began writing the "series of short prose sketches" that became the foundation of *in our time*. Each new sketch "was the product of a score of crossed-out beginnings," as Carlos Baker writes (108). Once six of the sketches were completed Hemingway gave them to Jane Heap for publication in the April 1923 issue of *The Little Review*. In that month, he also wrote "Out of Season," his first attempt at a

---

† From *Hemingway, Style, and the Art of Emotion* (New York: Cambridge UP, 2015), pp. 27–46. Reprinted by permission of Cambridge University Press through the licensor, PLSclear. Parenthetical citations have been supplied. Page numbers in brackets refer to this Norton Critical Edition.

full-length story since the loss of the manuscripts. That summer, Robert McAlmon published Hemingway's first book, *Three Stories and Ten Poems*. The volume contained the remnant stories, "Up in Michigan" and "My Old Man," as well as the new "Out of Season."

Hemingway continued work on the prose sketches that would become *in our time* during the summer of 1923. By late August, when he and Hadley departed for Toronto, where their son was to be born, Hemingway had completed eighteen sketches and had given them to Pound for one final editing. Pound had earlier questioned whether "there was any controlling logic to the experiences" (Reynolds 140), and Hemingway had responded, "It has form all right" (*LEH* 2:41). On April 3, 1924, Shakespeare and Company sold its first copy of *in our time* for thirty francs.

The sketches took violence as their recurring subject. They dealt with potting Germans at forty yards, firing squads, Nick's wounding, bank robberies, bullfights, hangings. On their own, the sketches read as language games, experiments in tone and point of view. Read as part of *In Our Time*, where they would take their rightful place, they become something much more grave and disturbing, the iceberg cruising beneath.

Hemingway could not have known when he sailed for Toronto that the form he had found was to discover its final home as part of a larger form. Although he was later to claim to have written the vignettes of *in our time* as "chapter headings" for the stories in *In Our Time*, the great burst of creativity that began as early as November 1923 and continued on into the following fall was an act of working toward an encompassing form, not from an overall design imposed at the very start (*LEH* 2:154).

In this effort, Hemingway devoted considerable attention to how his book should begin and end: as manuscript evidence makes clear, "Indian Camp" and "Big Two-Hearted River" became the key pressure points. With the publication of Philip Young's *The Nick Adams Stories* in 1972, much of this evidence became widely available. Young did not attend, however, to the process of composition itself. Yet, as the papers at the Kennedy Library reveal, an understanding of *how In Our Time* took shape is crucial to any sense of *what* it might mean.

By late January 1924, when Ernest and Hadley returned to Paris from Toronto, it is likely that Hemingway had already begun "Indian Camp" since page nine of the earliest manuscript version of the story is typed on the back of an unfinished and unsent letter dated November 6, 1923. The story was in any case finished by mid-March, when Ford Madox Ford accepted it for publication in the April 1924 issue of *Transatlantic Review*. Hemingway's first paying short story appeared alongside a section from *Finnegans Wake*.

"I am writing some damn good stories," Hemingway told Pound, in the letter informing his friend of Ford's acceptance of "Indian Camp" (*LEH* 2:103). But "not even in his few moments of hope could he have predicted," Paul Smith writes, "the close to miraculous half-year of writing that started with this story" (35). The writing of "Indian Camp" marked the beginning of an outpouring of eight stories in three months: "Indian Camp," "Cat in the Rain," "The End of Something," "The Three-Day Blow," "The Doctor and the Doctor's Wife," "Soldier's Home," "Mr. and Mrs. Smith" (later "Mr. and Mrs. Elliot"), and "Cross-Country Snow." Still to come was "Big Two-Hearted River," begun in May 1924 and finished in November, as well as the final addition, "The Battler," a story written after Boni and Liveright objected to the explicit sexual content of "Up in Michigan," which contained sentences like, "Oh, it's so big and it hurts so. You can't. Oh, Jim. Jim. Oh" (*SS* 85). It turned out that Gertrude Stein had been right all along in finding the story *"inaccrochable"*—unhangable (*MF* 15).

By August 1924, Hemingway could count twelve completed stories as destined for *In Our Time*. There were the three from his first book, the eight written that spring, and the big fishing story now well under way. Thinking his new book needed to be longer, he began feathering into it the sketches from *in our time*. In the process, "A Very Short Story" and "The Revolutionist" were converted from vignettes into stories. The unity of the emergent book was one to be realized by zooming in and zooming out, Hemingway wrote to Edmund Wilson, "like looking with your eyes at something, say a passing coast line, and then looking at it with 15× binoculars. Or rather, maybe, looking at it and then going in and living in it—and then coming out and looking at it again. . . . I think you would like it, it has a pretty good unity" (*LEH* 2:166).

"What will I have to cut?" Hemingway asked the friend who cabled him in February 1925 with the news of the Boni and Liveright offer to publish *In Our Time* (*LEH* 2:259). One of the things he had to cut was the beginning. Hemingway had long imagined his book as commencing with "Up in Michigan." "All the stories have a certain unity," he wrote Edward J. O'Brien in the fall of 1924. "The first 5 are in Michigan, starting with the Up in Michigan" (*LEH* 2:154). Even at this late date, Hemingway was conceiving of the unity of his book as grounded in locale rather than in character. But "Up in Michigan" was not a Nick Adams story, and Nick, whether Hemingway quite yet knew it or not, was to provide the book's center of concern.

Once Hemingway wrote "The Battler" as a replacement story for "Up in Michigan," he began calling it "about the best I've ever written" (*LEH* 2:295). The story was unique in the volume in showing a working couple, despite their being a punch-drunk ex-boxer and his "negro" [44] partner. Bugs manages Ad's dementia with a tender-hearted violence, and the two men offer Nick a unique vision of civility and hospitality. It is hard to imagine any member of another couple in the book saying "I like to be with him" [47], as Bugs does about Ad. With the addition of "The Battler," completed in the winter of 1925, the opening sequence of five Nick Adams stories was now complete, one ending with the striking image of a young man looking back at a fire in the dark.

Although it was a publisher's resistance that forced Hemingway to uncover the true beginning of his book, he quickly recognized the logic of the change and acknowledged as much in a letter to Horace Liveright:

> The new story makes the book a good deal better. It's about the best I've ever written and gives additional unity to the book as a whole.
>
> You are eliminating the second story—Up in Michigan. The next three stories move up one place each and this new story—The ~~Great Little Fighting Machine~~ Battler—takes the place at present occupied by—The Three Day Blow. (*LEH* 2:295)

By March 1925, when this letter was written, Hemingway had experienced a crucial recognition: whether or not "Up in Michigan" was to remain a part of *In Our Time*, it could not be the first story in the book. That place, he had come to realize, was to be reserved for "Indian Camp," which was to take "its rightful place," in Paul Smith's words, "as the first story in that remarkable collection. For once then, a benighted and overly scrupulous publisher moved a Hemingway story to its perfect position" (36). *In Our Time* now began where Nick himself begins, at the lake shore where there was another rowboat drawn up.

There is an endless revelatory power to a literary archive. One fiction readily set aside after even a casual perusal of the Hemingway papers at the Kennedy Library is the fiction of the "one true sentence." Given the chiseled finish of the published work, it is easy to believe Hemingway's description of his writing process in *A Moveable Feast*, where the older man looks back upon the days of writing *In Our Time*:

> But sometimes when I was starting a new story and I could not get it going, I would sit in front of the fire and squeeze the peel of the little oranges into the edge of the flame and watch the sputter of blue that they made. I would stand and look out over the roofs of Paris and think, "Do not worry. You have always written before and you will write now. All you have to do is write

one true sentence. Write the truest sentence that you know."
So finally I would write one true sentence, and then go on from
there. (*MF* 12)

One of the illusions being entertained here is that true sentences
come to Hemingway fully formed. The surviving manuscripts reveal
instead a much more searching style and a writing practice devoted
to returning upon the already-written in order to revise it. And this
pattern obtains from the very beginning, in the opening words of
"Indian Camp."

I have made much of the force and effect of the adjective "another"
as it appears in the first sentence of the story. It was therefore a considerable shock to discover, on my second visit to the Hemingway
papers, that the word "another" does not appear in the earliest surviving version of "Indian Camp." The two sentences leading off the
story were originally combined into one. Without the crossings out
and the insertions so clearly visible on the manuscript page, that sentence reads as follows: "At the lake shore there was a white rowboat
drawn up with two indians standing beside it."

At some point in the revision process, Hemingway came to see
that he needed to add a key word and that his flaccid opening sentence needed to be broken up into two true ones. The manuscript
records this process:

> At the lake shore there
>
> was a ~~white~~ *nother* rowboat drawn up
> ~~with~~ x Two indians ~~standing~~ stood
> beside it   (JFK/EH 493, 9)

(The "x" is Hemingway's mark indicating a period. The word "another"
angles up the page after the word "a." The lower case "t" has been
revised into a capital "T.") As Hemingway reworked the sentence,
the letters "nother" were simply sutured onto the original word "a" and
were angled up the page to fit into the space above the word "white."
By the time "Indian Camp" appeared in the *Transatlantic Review*,
Hemingway had also come to see that the word "another" required
the reinforcing addition of the word "The":

> At the lake shore there was another
> row-boat drawn up. The two indians
> stood waiting.   (JFK/EH 96)

In replacing the words "beside it" with the word "waiting," Hemingway created an air of expectation. More importantly, the first two
sentences of *In Our Time* were now virtually intact: all that remained
was to drop the hyphen in "row-boat" and to capitalize the word
"indians."

That hard-won beginning was itself the result of another cut. Well before Hemingway began wrestling with Liveright over "excisions" (*LEH* 2:295), he had begun wavering on the question of how "Indian Camp" itself should begin. The dramatic cutting in "At the lake shore" was not, in fact, the original opening of the story. That opening can be found in Item 493 at the Kennedy Library.

Readers of *The Nick Adams Stories* will be familiar with this opening under the title "Three Shots" [134–35]. The eight pages of manuscript written as the original beginning for "Indian Camp" were eventually to be condensed into three and a half pages in Philip Young's 1972 compilation. In the fragment, Nick feels *"ashamed"* about his memory of the previous night [133]. Left alone in a tent by his father and Uncle George, Nick had been revisited by a fear he had felt before. *"He was afraid of dying"* [133]. Unable to subdue his fear, he picks up a rifle and fires a prearranged signal of three shots. When the two men return to the tent, Nick claims to have heard something. The next morning, Dr. Adams finds two trees that rub together in the wind, and he asks Nick if *"that was what it was?"* *"Maybe,"* Nick answers [134–35]. The fragment ends with Nick being told—he has been undressing for bed as he remembers—to put on his clothes so that he can set out across the lake for the Indian Camp.

Whether we view it as an omitting or as a *"deleting,"* as Paul Smith calls it, Hemingway's decision to cut his original beginning was one made for fairly obvious reasons (35). "Three Shots" makes Nick's shame and fear so explicit as to spare the reader the work of having to infer. It also indulges in "mental conversation," a phrase Hemingway applied to the original last nine pages of "Big Two-Hearted River," pages he also eventually cut (*LEH* 2:170). That ending was as unnecessary to the project of *In Our Time* as was opening with the scene of Nick in the tent. Both passages show a character thinking, and the life of the mind was an experience Hemingway chose to externalize rather than to represent directly in his early work. So, as Bernard Oldsey notes, Hemingway engaged in his "usual method of arriving at a true beginning by cutting" (38).

But the story of the beginning was not yet over. Anyone picking up a copy of *In Our Time* today will see that the volume begins not with "Indian Camp" but with "On the Quai at Smyrna." In the story, two unnamed narrators describe the consequences of the Turkish drive through Anatolia in 1922. As a structural addition to *In Our Time*, the story reaches forward to connect up with "L'Envoi" on the book's final page, a vignette dealing with the Greek king deposed after his country's defeat in the Greco-Turkish War. The net effect of the addition of "On the Quai at Smyrna" to *In Our Time* is to enclose the book within a circle bounded by a war fought directly *after* the war to end all wars.

"On the Quai at Smyrna" is a publisher's artifact. *In Our Time* was originally published by Boni and Liveright in New York on October 5, 1925. After being wooed by Max Perkins, an editor at Scribner's, Hemingway set out to break his contract with Boni and Liveright by writing *The Torrents of Spring*, a lampoon of Sherwood Anderson, one of B & L's leading authors. Once B & L declined to publish Hemingway's *inaccrochable* parody, he was free to sever his contract with them and to move to Scribner's. In the summer of 1930, as Perkins was making plans to reissue *In Our Time*, he asked Hemingway to provide it with an Introduction. Hemingway begged off the request but did send Perkins a story about the fall of Smyrna, one he had worked on in late 1926 and early 1927. It was offered to Scribner's as an "Introduction by the Author" and was published at the head of the reissued volume under that title. Only in the 1938 collection *The First Forty-Nine* did the story acquire the title it carries to this day, "On the Quai at Smyrna." The copyright page of subsequent editions of *In Our Time* contained the following sentence: "'On the Quai at Smyrna' was first published as the introduction to the 1930 edition of IN OUR TIME." The beginning that has come down to us seems to be saying: here is where we find ourselves, on the quai at Smyrna; now, in "Indian Camp," let me show you how we got there.

Hemingway possessed an affective theory of literary form: the "unity" of a book was an effect resulting from the experience of a carefully structured whole. His recurring use of the words "reading" and "reader" signals his commitment to writing as an act of appeal to the heart and mind of an audience. The gift on offer in Hemingway's early work, as he understood it, was to allow the reader to "feel more," a response usually provoked by his carefully managed art of omission.

The first time we see Nick after "Indian Camp" he is sitting with his back against a tree. He is "reading" [20]. One wonders whether Hemingway offers Nick this activity as an adaptive response to the overwhelming scene of instruction in which he has just participated. Reading will in any case perform such a function for Krebs. After returning from the war, he discovers that he has to lie in order to be listened to, gives up talking about the war, and begins "reading a book" about it. "It was the most interesting reading he had ever done. . . . Now he was really learning about the war" [58]. The husband in "Cat in the Rain" spends the entire story reading in bed, and Nick, confronted at the end of the book with the option of fishing the swamp, "wished he had brought something to read" [128]. In the final paragraph of "Big Two-Hearted River," Nick climbs the bank and cuts up into the woods toward the high ground. "He was going back to camp" [129]. In the manuscript, this sentence reads as follows: "He was going back to camp to read" (JFK/EH 277, 10; 278, unnumbered page). When the sentence was typed up, the phrase "to read" had been cut.

Through the figure of Krebs, Hemingway anticipates his upcoming program of reading as well, a course of study entered into in order to prepare for the writing of *A Farewell to Arms*. In the case of both character and author, the point worth making has to do with the relationship between experience and afterthought. Learning is only completed when the self returns upon the lived experience by way of "a second Will more wise," in Wordsworth's phrase, in an act of imaginative encounter (reading) or refiguration (writing) that discovers the shape and meaning of what the self has lived through (385). Through this process, private memories and fantasies are transformed into a shared and usable past. For Hemingway, the shaping and meaning-making process involved in writing was typically subjected to a further correction by a second will, as the words first put down on the page were themselves so often subjected to revision.

Despite Hemingway's claim that in *In Our Time* "everything hangs on everything else" (*LEH* 2:322), it can prove difficult for a reader of the volume to connect what lies "behind" with what lies "ahead." Hemingway's book asks us to infer, to search for patterns of continuity underlying seemingly disparate episodes. In the end, for one reader at least, as Edmund Wilson wrote in 1941, "the parts held together and produced a definite effect" (7).

One continuity to be discovered while reading *In Our Time* is the life history of a character who feels present even when absent, as in the suite of marriage stories in which Nick Adams does not appear but where the characters stand in for and act out the possibilities of love both in Nick's adulthood and "in our time." Nick's story culminates in "Big Two-Hearted River," where he returns to the landscape of "Indian Camp" in order to restart his story on his own terms. Between the beginning and the return, Nick sees his father humiliated, ends an affair, drinks and talks with a friend, confronts incest and homosexuality, is wounded in war, and then passes through a series of veiled avatars—a numb veteran, a friend of a jailed revolutionary, a partner in three troubled marriages—before re-entering the text as the anxious husband in "Cross-Country Snow" who plucks his mind out while skiing in lieu of confronting the "hell" of his wife's pregnancy [92].

Nick Adams had such a hold upon his author's imagination that Hemingway continued to write about him for eight more years after the publication of *In Our Time*. Nick appears in five of the stories in the 1927 *Men Without Women*, in five of the stories in the 1933

Winner Take Nothing, and again in a number of fragments—including an unfinished novel that Hemingway eventually chose not to publish. In the last completed Nick Adams story, "Fathers and Sons," the boy from "Indian Camp" has become a father himself, one who has learned from his father how not to treat a son. As Hemingway wrote in 1938, "there is a line in all the Nick stories that is continuous" (Bruccoli 267).

In his review of *In Our Time,* D. H. Lawrence made the case for Nick as a unifier: "It is a short book: and it does not pretend to be about one man. But it is. It is as much as we need know of the man's life" (311). One might add that by having Nick appear, disappear, and reappear, Hemingway succeeds in intensifying a reader's curiosity about his fate.

In constructing *The Nick Adams Stories,* Philip Young attempted to make Nick's story even more "continuous." Young arranged all the available stories about Nick "chronologically," in the order, that is, of the sequence of events in Nick's life (v). Since the order of the publication of the stories is read by Young as a "jumbled sequence," Hemingway's development as a writer is thereby subordinated to Nick's development as a character.

In Young's scheme, Nick's story becomes overarranged. Even then, Young appears to have gotten the sequence wrong. "The End of Something" and "The Three-Day Blow" are positioned after "Big Two-Hearted River" in Young's "over-all narrative" (vii). But Nick is clearly younger in these stories than he is in "Big Two-Hearted River," at most a boy in his late teens. Marjorie is one of Nick's early loves, and Bill is the confidant who fills out the triangle. "Big Two-Hearted River" is the story of an older man, now married, coming back from the war, although there is no mention of the war in it.

Young's arrangement of the Nick Adams stories pays no attention to a reader's experience of *In Our Time* as he moves through it. Deeply attentive to the logic of sequence, Hemingway created a book in which the reader's attempt to discover sequences would give the experience much of its meaning and its force. While Nick's life is offered up as the through-story, we are diverted from it by his disappearance from the text after his wounding in chapter VI and also by the continual intervening presence of the vignettes.

Yet, however disconcerting a reader might find them, the vignettes are where Hemingway believed they should be. As he wrote to Ernest Walsh in March 1925: "Book is called In Our Time like the little one. Is short stories, 15 of them, with a chapter of In Our Time between each story. That's what I originally wrote them for. It all hooks up" (*LEH* 2:277). When Max Perkins suggested grouping together all the vignettes for the 1930 reissue, Hemingway responded: "Max *please believe* me that those chapters are where they belong"

(*LEH* 4:335). Despite Hemingway's claim, it is not always possible to discern a clear connection between a vignette and the story it precedes or follows. The last vignette written for *in our time* did, however, find a place in *In Our Time* that is both necessary and overdetermined. How that vignette got written also reveals much about Hemingway's use of revision to give form to the overall structure of a book.

Ernest and Hadley Hemingway met Ezra Pound within a few months of their arrival in Paris in December 1921. By the period in which Hemingway was finishing up *in our time*, Pound had become a fast friend and a frequent correspondent: of the 247 letters published in the second volume of the Cambridge edition of *The Letters of Ernest Hemingway*, thirty-two are addressed to Pound. In a letter written in early August of 1923, Hemingway responded to Pound's critique of the vignette sequence. One change made involved shifting the death of Maera (chapter XIV in *In Our Time*) from a hospital room to the bullring. But the biggest change was the addition of a final vignette based on a story Hemingway had shared with Pound about the hanging of a Chicago gangster in 1921. Pound had liked the story and urged Hemingway to work it up into one more of his "frozen moments" (Reynolds 140).

Hemingway's letter to Pound about the emerging form of *in our time* reveals both his willingness to revise and his abiding concern with reconciling the way things "start" with how they "finish off":

> Dear Ezra,
> I will do the hanging. Have redone the death of Maera altogether different and fixed the others. The new death is good. * * *
> They should each one be headed Chapter 1, Chapter 2 etc. When they are read together they all hook up. It seems funny but they do. The bulls start, then reappear and then finish off. The war starts clear and noble just like it did, Mons etc., gets close and blurred and finished with the feller who goes home and gets clap. The refugees leave thrace, due to the Greek ministers, who are shot. The whole thing closes with the talk with the King of Greece and his Queen in their garden (just written), which shows the king all right. The last sentence in it is - - - Like all Greeks what he really wanted was to get to America. – – – My pal Shorty, movie operator with me in Thrace, just brings the dope on the King. Edifying.
> The radicals start noble in the young Magyar story and get bitched. America appears in the cops shooting the guys who robbed the cigar store. It has form all right.
> The king closes it in swell shape. Oh that king.

I will commence hanging. Then I think she rides. Will try
and drop in on you tomorrow a.m.

> Immer [German: Always,]
> Hem. (*LEH* 2:41–42)

The story of the hanging of Sam Cardinella was needed, then, in
order to make the thing ride. Two years later, as Hemingway began
interpolating the vignettes from *in our time* between his new short
stories, the question became: where would the hanging take its place
in the long structure of *In Our Time*?

Not, at first, in the place it finally assumed. Item 97A in the Kennedy Library contains a Cablogramme with a handwritten table of
contents of "Chapters from In Our Time" (JFK/EH 97A). It lists a
chapter, as the vignettes were to be called, and then a story. At the
end of the list, the story "My Old Man" is followed by "Chapter Fourteen," the Sam Cardinella vignette. Then Hemingway has listed
"Big Two-Hearted River." The last long story was to be printed without an intervening vignette.

Having given the matter a second thought, Hemingway then drew
an arrow down the page, one pointing from "Chapter Fourteen" to
the space between Part One and Part Two of "Big Two-Hearted
River." The revised list looks like this:

Chapter Fourteen x (They hanged

Sam Cardinella at six o'clock in the

Morning in the corridor of the county jail"

Big Two Hearted River

Part one

Insert chapter-Hanging-

Part two

In looking over the book's overall design, Hemingway came to see
that the hanging belonged between the two parts of the final story,
where it would become chapter XV.

"*They hanged Sam Cardinella at six o'clock in the morning in the
corridor of the county jail*" [119]. The condemned man has to be carried to the place of execution. He is attended by a priest who says,
"*Be a man, my son.*" In his fear, Sam Cardinella loses "*control of his
sphincter muscle.*" The disgusted guards strap him into a chair, and
the priest skips back from the scaffolding just before the drop falls.

The difficulty of sustaining the performance of being male, of
operating within what Thomas Strychacz calls "Hemingway's Theaters of Masculinity," is here given its most efficient treatment. Told
to "*be a man,*" a man shames himself in the most abject and public

way. In his reading of *In Our Time*, Strychacz draws a sharp contrast between Sam Cardinella and Nick Adams. Sam's "humiliation is intensified by his inability to control the theatricalization of his last moments" (222); a scaffold, after all, is also a stage. Nick, on the other hand, "postulates the existence of a self-possessed and non-theatrical masculinity, fashioned without an empowering audience. In this respect, Cardinella's heroic opposite must be said to be the Nick Adams of 'Big Two-Hearted River'" (223).

It is more accurate to say that Sam is Nick's dark familiar. The considered positioning of the Sam Cardinella vignette, coming as it does between the two parts of "Big Two-Hearted River," itself makes this case. Part I ends with Nick pitching camp, eating dinner, remembering Hopkins, crawling into his tent, executing a mosquito, and going "to sleep" [118]. On the facing and the following page is positioned the Sam Cardinella vignette. The reader reads the vignette, turns the page, and finds the first sentence of "Big Two-Hearted River: Part II": "In the morning the sun was up and the tent was starting to get hot" [121].

What happens to Sam Cardinella happens while Nick is asleep. We recognize the concerns of the vignette as Nick's concerns; he is less the heroic opposite of the condemned man than simply another character struggling to understand what it might mean to "be a man." Of course, these are thoughts Nick attempts not to think: "He felt he had left everything behind, the need for thinking, the need to write, other needs" [112]. "*He was not thinking,*" Hemingway wrote about Nick, in the concluding pages eventually cut from "Big Two-Hearted River." "*He was holding something in his head*" [141]. The last sentence of "On Writing," as Philip Young chooses to title these pages [in *NAS*], repeats the claim: "*He was holding something in his head.*" Sam's story is what fills Nick's head when he is not awake; Sam, that is, is Nick's nightmare.

Nick's nightmare of Sam Cardinella reverberates backward through the reading experience of *In Our Time* in the same way that the word "another" in the first sentence of "Indian Camp" anticipates what is to come. The linking of the vignette to Nick's inner life thus makes possible the following claim: in *In Our Time*, the vignettes are the dreams haunting the minds of the characters met in the stories.

In Our Time offers a reader an experience of two kinds of material, what might be called its manifest and its latent content. The book contains testimony about waking life as well as an account of the dream work arising in the nights that fall between the book's "plenty of days" [129]. In taking up the challenge of seeing how "it all hooks up," the reader is placed in a position of great difficulty and great dignity, since the role being assigned to him resembles nothing so much as that of the dedicated analyst. As Hemingway issues his call for an act of listening, one testifying to his trust in the capacity of his audience to confront "things" from which Nick himself will often turn away, Nick's unfinished education becomes an occasion for a reader's painful and potentially liberating effort of understanding.

The richest subject for analysis provided by *In Our Time* is the book's ending. Just as "Big Two-Hearted River" has two parts, so it can be read as having two endings: the scene in which Nick pitches his tent and the scene in which Nick confronts the swamp. Twoness can be said to be the subject here, as Hemingway's book refuses to end in just one way. Nick's behavior on his return to the landscapes of his youth is so layered and so complex as to have solicited an unending outpouring of critical speculation.

At the beginning of the story, Nick arrives at a place where "even the surface had been burned off the ground" [111]. Yet this return to his own personal waste land contains within it the possibility of a resurfacing. For Nick, the resurfacing takes two forms: given the utter effacement of the town he once knew, it remains for him to reinscribe with meaning the landscape he moves through. At the same time, he works hard to prevent certain kinds of thoughts and feelings from coming to the surface, works hard, as D. H. Lawrence has it, to keep himself "loose" (312).

"Big Two-Hearted River" opens with a third-person narrator describing Nick's return: "The train went on up the track out of sight, around one of the hills of burnt timber. Nick sat down on the bundle of canvas and bedding the baggage man had pitched out of the door of the baggage car" [111]. It is striking to discover the original manuscript of "Big Two-Hearted River" beginning quite differently: "We got off the train at Seney. There was no station" (JFK/EH 279, 1). The "We" would later be changed to a "They." These attempts at a beginning contain two quite unimaginable outcomes: Nick as not alone but accompanied, part of a "They"; and Nick as the first-person narrator of the story he is in, part of a "We" (Oldsey 43). In the end, Hemingway realized that the story had to be focalized through Nick but not narrated by him and that Nick had to be alone.

"The story was about coming back from the war but there was no mention of the war in it" (*MF* 76). This sentence about the meaning of "Big Two-Hearted River" can be found in chapter 8 of *A Moveable Feast*. Since the claim was made more than thirty years after the story was written, it has the status of after-wisdom. Hemingway's insight into what goes unmentioned was itself the result of second thought; the sentence about coming back from the war cannot be found in the manuscript version of the passage about writing "Big Two-Hearted River." The sentence was added quite late to a typescript of "Hunger Was Good Discipline" (JFK/EH 150, 8) and is interpolated in Hemingway's big, looping hand.

Nick's obsessively tidy mental and physical habits can certainly be read as a response to shell shock. His walk toward the campsite at the river is carefully calibrated. "He did not need to get his map out. He knew where he was from the position of the river" [113]. The landscape he walks through figures forth a concern with limits and boundaries: "Sharp at the edge of this extension of the forest floor commenced the sweet fern" [114]. Here, the vegetable world appears to create a neat pattern as if in response to a command issued by Nick's edginess. The alliterative "s's" and "t's" and "f's" also give an edge to the very sound of the sentence itself.

It was perhaps during the writing of "Big Two-Hearted River" that Hemingway came to realize that the mind needs a landscape, a set of physical contours through which to realize itself and to think things out, and so thinking becomes like a walk through an ever-materializing past, where the rememberer bumps up against his unavoidable spots of time. Later, in "A Way You'll Never Be," when Nick remembers the low house painted yellow by the canal, he knows that the scene means something to him, however much Hemingway's prose refuses to spell out those meanings. "That house meant more than anything" (SS 408), Nick thinks to himself. Not what the lay of the land means but *that* it means and continues to acquire meaning by way of Nick's repeated night thoughts—this is the crucial insight.

While Nick's war experience surely conditions much of his behavior in "Big Two-Hearted River," the first culmination provided by the story, the scene in which Nick pitches his tent, makes much more sense when read as his response to the awkwardness of beginnings as they are imagined in "Indian Camp." For Nick, I am arguing, the original traumatic event is not the Wound of War but the uncanny fact of having been originated—and even that trauma is one entirely mediated by how Nick chooses to take it.

Nick levels a piece of ground, smoothes out the sandy soil, unpacks his tent, pegs the sides taut, and then crawls in:

> Inside the tent the light came through the brown canvas. It smelled pleasantly of canvas. Already there was something mysterious and homelike. Nick was happy as he crawled inside the tent. He had not been unhappy all day. This was different though. Now things were done. There had been this to do. Now it was done. It had been a hard trip. He was very tired. That was done. He had made his camp. He was settled. Nothing could touch him. It was a good place to camp. He was there, in the good place. He was in his home where he had made it. Now he was hungry.

He came out, crawling under the cheesecloth. It was quite dark outside. It was lighter in the tent. [115]

The short four- and five-word sentences and the repeated sounding of the word "done" here lend to Hemingway's prose and the psyche being notated by way of it a quality of running in place. Nick has reached a kind of end, even perhaps the possibility of rest, and yet the overly insistent tone takes on, as so often with Nick, a sense of protesting too much. Sartre's description of the Hemingway style hits home here: "Each sentence refuses to exploit the momentum accumulated by preceding ones. Each is a new beginning" (116). While the phrase "new beginning" may sound promising, such an effect is the opposite of what Nick is trying to achieve—a resolved ending. The rhythm of the prose here conveys a sense that Nick's actions are still compelled rather than free and that the many efficient motions being made are unintegrated.

Three words in the passage capture what Nick has lost—or never had—and is hoping to refind: "the good place." Just as every bull has its "*querencia*," its "preferred locality" (*DIA* 150) in the ring, so Hemingway characters will continue to seek and to find and, more often than not, to lose again the good place. * * *

*   *   *

Nick creates a space, crawls into it, feels hungry, crawls out again. The desire to control beginnings here fulfills itself as Nick restages his birth on his own terms. But, of course, Nick's tent is sterile, empty except for his "things." Something crucial to any lasting recovery has been left out: the female body. Nick here indulges in a fantasy of autogenesis that attempts to supplant sexual genesis. The striving to fulfill such a fantasy can, for the male imagination, sometimes result in the making of art. Yet any enduring possibility of success in that kind of making, Hemingway comes to believe, depends upon taking the risk of creating a good place with an actual woman.

By the time of his culminating appearance in the Hemingway canon, Nick Adams appears to have worked things out. In "Fathers and Sons," published in 1933, Nick makes peace with his beginnings by remembering his father as both caring and limited, by acknowledging and celebrating his sexual history, and by instructing his son with a tact and protectiveness never shown him when he was young. Somehow, in the eight years between the writing of "Big Two-Hearted River" and the writing of "Fathers and Sons," Hemingway has been able to imagine Nick's growing up. That Nick has only begun to do so on his fishing trip at the end of *In Our Time* is indicated by the phrase still haunting his erection of the tent. For all his belief that things can be "smoothed out," the good place he has attempted to create remains, also, "mysterious and homelike" [115].

Part II of "Big Two-Hearted River" ends with the even more suggestive set piece of the swamp. No single passage in the Hemingway canon has occasioned so many symbolic readings. "It's a symbol," Bill says to Nick in "The Three-Day Blow," as they discuss the meaning of the sword in *Forest Lovers*. "'Sure' said Nick, 'but it isn't practical'" [32]. Symbolic readings of Hemingway's early work prove impractical largely because of that work's resistance to the notion that one thing can be compared to something else: it is a prose noticeably absent of metaphor. Hemingway's early avoidance of figurative language has the curious effect, however, of endowing everything noticed as somehow significant. Since so few details are elevated by figuration above any others, the entire field of experience comes to feel suffused with meaning and value. Every little detail can speak with what Richard Hovey calls "hallucinated urgency" (33). Or, as Hemingway himself put it, in *Death in the Afternoon*, his work aims to provide "the sequence of motion and fact which made the emotion" (*DIA* 2). In moving through a story like "Big Two-Hearted River," then, a reader can feel a continuous pressure to interpret its every fact and motion as somehow expressive of how Nick is feeling.

The swamp occupies, however, a different order of importance than the grasshoppers that have turned black after the fire or the fact that Nick likes to open cans. It occupies the place of an ending. And it is easy enough to see why *In Our Time* would come to rest here: not only does the swamp contrast with the tent in such a way as to indicate that Nick's work is not yet done, but it also conjures up, in its darkness and its wetness and its interweavings and in the motions required of those brave enough to move through it—"You would have to keep almost level with the ground to move at all"— the uncanny place that is the home of every one of us, once upon a time and in the beginning [128].

Whatever the swamp may be taken to be, a more pressing question is left open at the end: will Nick fish the swamp? As he considers whether or not to do so, Nick kills and cleans two male trout. "All the insides clean and compact, coming out all together." The cleanness and compactness of these "insides" evoke Nick's tent and contrast with the imbrications of the swamp. Nick's act of cutting and cleaning gives a kind of answer to the looming question; he, in any case, stands up, climbs the bank, and begins to return to camp. "He looked back. The river just showed through the trees. There were plenty of days coming when he could fish the swamp" [129]. With these sentences, the story ends.

The phrase "plenty of days coming" sounds forward across more than thirty years of writing to find its echo in Hemingway's

memory, one recorded in *A Moveable Feast*, of sitting in the Closerie des Lilas and writing "Big Two-Hearted River":

> When I stopped writing I did not want to leave the river where
> I could see the trout in the pool, its surface pushing and swell-
> ing smooth against the resistance of the log-driven piles of the
> bridge. The story was about coming back from the war but there
> was no mention of the war in it.
>
> But in the morning the river would be there and I must make
> it and the country and all that would happen. There were days
> ahead to be doing that each day. (*MF* 76–77)

Hemingway's story and the memory of it turn upon the repetition
of a single word. "There were days ahead to be doing that each day,"
he writes, later, about how he felt then. "Ahead the river narrowed
and went into a swamp," he wrote then, about what Nick finds himself facing at the end [128]. In the story, Nick is smoking and watching the river when this sentence abrupts into view. While it is often
difficult to see ahead and fearful to move ahead in *In Our Time*, it
is nevertheless the direction in which Nick and the reader are asked
to go. In the passage from *A Moveable Feast*, Hemingway accom-
plishes a revision of the force of the word "ahead," converting it from
a source of anxiety into a sense of promise. What lies ahead is the
possibility of writing more stories that express fears and apprehen-
sions but that also allow for an experience of working through. Of
course, as Hemingway remembers the promise of days ahead in his
memoir, he is actually looking back at a work already accomplished
and so assures himself that the promise made was a promise kept.

In this reading, the swamp does not symbolize the female body,
or mature sexuality, or the unconscious, or the stream of consciousness, or a regression to origins. It is, quite simply, the *ahead*. And
the meaning given in *A Moveable Feast* to what lies ahead, something the young Hemingway clearly apprehended as he wrote his
story in 1924, was the promise of a career.

But will that career achieve a reconciliation between Hemingway's
anxiety about the uncontrollability of beginnings and his obsession
with trying to control endings such that a character might be allowed
the experience of life, of a true middle? The beginning of an answer
can be found in an ending considered and rejected for "Big Two-
Hearted River."

In August of 1924 Hemingway wrote the editor of *The Little
Review* about his having "finished a swell story of 100 pages" (*LEH*
2:140). These were handwritten pages, and my count of the pages
in the manuscript of "Big Two-Hearted River" held at the Kennedy
Library puts the number at 113. It was a long story, and, at some point
in the next few months, Hemingway realized that it had to be cut.

In the story, as Hemingway wrote to Gertrude Stein and Alice B. Toklas, he had been "trying to do the country like Cezanne" (*LEH* 2:141). He even said so in the story itself. "*He, Nick, wanted to write about the country so it would be there like Cezanne had done it in painting*" [140]. This sentence can be found in the "On Writing" section of *The Nick Adams Stories*.

The pages printed by Philip Young mark a striking departure from Hemingway's chosen practice. Previously, whenever Nick's mind has begun "starting to work," Hemingway has chosen to "choke it" with various stylistic and narrative strategies [117]. Now, as he nears the end, Hemingway allows Nick's mind to range freely in both memory and thought. Nick thinks about "*writing that was any good*" [138], and then makes the connection to Cezanne, a painter who "*started with all the tricks*" and who then "*broke the whole thing down and built the real thing*" [140].

When shown these pages of "meditations," as Gertrude Stein was to describe them, she responded by saying, "Hemingway, remarks are not literature" (875). Stein's own remark may have prompted Hemingway to cut his meditations; by November of 1924 he was in any case writing Donald Ogden Stewart "that the last eleven pages of the last story I got you are crap" and that Stewart was to "detach" them and to "substitute the five pages enclosed" (*LEH* 2:172). Stewart had been circulating the manuscript of *In Our Time* to publishers in New York, and it was therefore imperative that the substitution be made quickly. "Wouldn't it be funny," Hemingway had written another friend a few days earlier, "if some publisher had accepted it because of the stuff that had to be cut?" (*LEH* 2:171).

So, a long passage of "mental conversation" was replaced by "just the straight fishing" (*LEH* 2:170). The material had to be cut because it violated a contract made with the reader involving the maintenance of a certain kind of dignity. "The dignity of the movement of an iceberg," like the dignity of Hemingway's early style, "is due to only one-eighth of it being above water." As he wrote in *Death in the Afternoon*,

> If a writer of prose knows enough about what he is writing about he may omit things that he knows and the reader, if the writer is writing truly enough, will have a feeling of those things as strongly as though the writer had stated them. The dignity of the movement of an ice-berg is due to only one-eighth of it being above water. A writer who omits things because he does not know them only makes hollow places in his writing. (*DIA* 192)

This passage, along with the sentences in *A Moveable Feast* describing "my new theory" of the "omitted," constitute Hemingway's most cogent defense of the purposes of his early style. Realizing that the final pages of "Big Two-Hearted River" had violated those purposes by giving his reader direct access to the motion of Nick's mind, Hemingway decided to cut them.

The decision not to include Nick's mental conversation has more to do with form than with content. What Nick thinks about is less striking—and disruptive of the Hemingway project—than is the fact that the reader is allowed to see a man thinking. To be able to go into the mind and to represent a character as feeling at home there is, at this point in the career, the undiscovered country. Hemingway will, however, eventually find the courage to explore it and, with a change of style, comes a change of subject. This, too, is anticipated in the closing paragraphs of "On Writing."

It happens when Nick stops thinking about how "*Cezanne would do the stretch of river and the swamp*" and decides to begin "*moving in the picture*" he has been imagining [141]. At this point in the passage, Nick does two things. He reaches for the one trout still in his sack, finds "*the old boy was alive*," and lets him go [141]. He then begins to walk back to camp. On the way, he runs into another animal, also alive. "On Writing" concludes with these sentences:

> Ahead of him he saw a rabbit, flat out on the trail. He stopped, grudging. The rabbit was barely breathing. There were two ticks on the rabbit's head, one behind each ear. They were gray, tight with blood, as big as grapes. Nick pulled them off, their heads tiny and hard, with moving feet. He stepped on them on the trail.
>
> Nick picked up the rabbit, limp, with dull button eyes, and put it under a sweet fern bush beside the trail. He felt its heart beating as he laid it down. The rabbit lay quiet under the bush. It might come to, Nick thought. Probably the ticks had attached themselves to it as it crouched in the grass. Maybe after it had been dancing in the open. He did not know.
>
> He went on up the trail to the camp. He was holding something in his head. [141]

* * *

What Hemingway was clearly holding in his head as he tried out and discarded the scenes with the trout and the rabbit was a new sense of an ending. The animal most in need of a reprieve, it would turn out, was the human animal. The motion apprehended as possible but not yet accepted as plausible was to imagine life as more than a movement without hope. The ending, like the beginning, could not change: "There is no end except death and birth is the only beginning" (*FTA* 305). But perhaps a heart could nevertheless be left "beating" at the end. This will be the gift offered to Robert Jordan in the final sentence of *For Whom the Bell Tolls* (*FWTBT* 471). In the

fifteen years between the sparing of the rabbit and the writing of
that sentence, the hard facts surrounding beginnings and endings
would not change. But Hemingway's attitude toward beginnings and
endings did change, and in that changing what was felt about love,
and time, and life itself changed as well.

Works Cited

Baker, Carlos. *Ernest Hemingway: A Life Story*. Scribner's, 1969.
Bruccoli, Matthew J., ed., with Robert W. Trogdon. *The Only Thing
    That Counts: The Ernest Hemingway–Maxwell Perkins Corres-
    pondence, 1925–1947*. Scribner's, 1996.
Hovey, Richard. *Hemingway: The Inward Terrain*. U of Washington
    P, 1968.
Lawrence, D. H. *The Works of D. H. Lawrence: Introductions and
    Reviews*. Cambridge UP, 2005.
Oldsey, Bernard. *Ernest Hemingway: The Papers of a Writer*. Garland,
    1981.
Reynolds, Michael. *Hemingway: The Paris Years*. Blackwell, 1989.
Sartre, Jean Paul. "An Explication of *The Stranger*." *Camus: A Collec-
    tion of Critical Essays*, ed. Germaine Brée, Prentice Hall, 1962,
    pp. 108–19.
Smith, Paul. *A Reader's Guide to the Short Stories of Ernest Heming-
    way*. G. K. Hall, 1989.
Stein, Gertrude. *Stein: Writings, 1903–1932*. Library of America, 1998.
Strychacz, Thomas F. *Hemingway's Theaters of Masculinity*. Louisi-
    ana State UP, 2003.
Wilson, Edmund. "Hemingway's Gauge of Morale." *Ernest Heming-
    way: Bloom's Modern Critical Views*, ed. Harold Bloom. Chelsea
    House, 2005, pp. 7–24.
Wordsworth, William. *Wordsworth: Poetical Works*. Oxford UP, 1974.

MICHAEL REYNOLDS

Hemingway's *In Our Time*:
The Biography of a Book[†]

If you were not there at the time, Hemingway insisted, you could
not possibly understand how things happened. He might have added

---

† From *Modern American Short Story Sequences*, ed. J. Gerald Kennedy (New York: Cam-
    bridge UP, 1995), pp. 35–51. Reprinted by permission of Cambridge University Press
    through the licensor, PLSclear. Unless otherwise indicated, notes are by the author;
    some of the author's notes have been omitted. Page numbers in brackets refer to this
    Norton Critical Edition.

that if you were there, you might be equally confused but in a different way. Of all the books in the Hemingway canon, none is more confusing than *In Our Time*, confusing now and then, confusing to reader and author, and particularly confusing to its bibliographers. It will remain that way forever, for its several parts—biographical, literary, editorial, and bibliographical—contain so many contradictions that any analysis will be flawed. Perhaps it is better that way, for so long as enigmas remain, the book lives; despite our proclaimed rage for order, there remains something about confusion that particularly delights us. Today the book and its attendant bibliography are a tangled ball of yarn. No matter which piece one selects to unravel first, the reader finds it snarled with another, and the unraveling becomes merely a rearrangement of the tangle.[1]

As an entry point, we might note that Hemingway published three volumes of short stories: *In Our Time* (1925), *Men Without Women* (1927), and *Winner Take Nothing* (1933).[2] Although all three titles imply a governing concept, only *In Our Time* has provoked numerous and divergent readings as a crafted sequence of stories with a sum larger than its parts. Neither the second nor the third volume evolved quite as complexly as did *In Our Time*, nor did Hemingway make any organizational claims for either of these volumes as he did for his first collection. From its earliest critical reading to the present day, *In Our Time* has provoked a wide range of response generated by the basic question: Is this book an interconnected sequence of stories to be read more like a novel, and if so, what is its governing principle? The easiest answer is, No, it is not. If the stories are read as discrete units, as they have been with great critical success, then *In Our Time* is no different structurally from several hundred other short story collections and, in fact, can be read as a predictable step in any young author's career. That response eliminates the need to ask more difficult questions, and as we shall see, the biography of the book in some ways supports such a view.

However, the collection's curious alternation of stories and vignettes, abetted by Hemingway's own remarks, has encouraged us to read, critique and teach the book as a conscious sequence of stories-as-novel in the tradition of Turgenev, Anderson, Stein, and Joyce. To do so forces one to ask: How could a barely educated, twenty-four-year-old writer produce a complex sequence of short fiction in his first book? If the reader replies, *impossible*, he or she is

---

1. Parts of this essay bring together fragments from my several previous publications. Without footnoting every point, I refer the reader to *Hemingway's Reading* (Princeton, NJ: Princeton University Press, 1981); and the indexes to *The Young Hemingway* (Oxford: Blackwell Publisher, 1986) and *Hemingway: The Paris Years* (Oxford: Blackwell Publisher, 1989).
2. Ernest Hemingway, *To Have and Have Not* (New York: Scribner's, 1937), which did begin as a series of stories, has been largely ignored as a failed novel worth small critical attention.

back to the first position: These are good stories, somewhat connected, but not a coherent sequence. Those determined for the sequence, but with no good answer to this question, might reply that Hemingway wrought better than he knew. This position allowed old New Critics and their children to treat the text as a discrete unit, uncomplicated by literary history or biography, while fostering the image of the dumb Hemingway who did not understand the depth of his own work.

There is, however, far too much evidence that Hemingway was intelligent, gifted, and well-read for the "Dumb Ox" epithet of Wyndham Lewis to apply any longer to Ernest. He may not have gone to an Ivy League college, as did most of his Paris literary friends, but by the time he was twenty-four, he had acquired a more useful literary education than most of today's college graduates and many of his early academic critics and literary friends. His Oak Park high-school curriculum, one of the most demanding in the country, included mostly the British classics but little American literature and almost nothing contemporary; but at sixteen he listed his favorite authors as O. Henry, Rudyard Kipling, and Stewart Edward White. When he returned to Chicago after the war, Hemingway fell in with a rather literary crowd, all of whom suggested new reading to him. Through his friends, Hemingway met and drank with Sherwood Anderson who loved to talk literary shop and give advice to young would-be writers. He directed Hemingway to the Russians: Dostoyevsky, Chekov, and Turgenev. He also told Ernest to read D. H. Lawrence and Gertrude Stein.

It was Anderson who sent Hemingway to Paris where one of his first stops was to join the lending library at Sylvia Beach's bookshop, Shakespeare and Company. In Paris, he quickly became a full-fledged member of one of the most literary crowds of the twentieth century. His friends and acquaintances included: Gertrude Stein, Ezra Pound, Ford Madox Ford, Robert McAlmon, Gerald Murphy, Louis Bromfield, James Joyce, Archibald MacLeish, and John Dos Passos. Had Hemingway been as ill-educated as many once believed, he could never have held his own with that group. When he died in 1961, his Cuban library held over eight thousand volumes. He may not have gone to college, but few American authors were any better read than Ernest Hemingway.[3]

Included in his reading were the now classic short story sequences: *Winesburg, Ohio, Dubliners, Three Lives, A Sportsman's Sketches,* and one might add, Eliot's *The Waste Land.* Of all Joyce's work,

---

3. For substantiation and more information on this subject, see James Brasch and Joseph Sigmund, *Hemingway's Library* (Boston: G. K. Hall, 1981) and my *Hemingway's Reading* and *The Young Hemingway* (Oxford: Blackwell Publisher, 1986).

Hemingway loved Molly Bloom, but it was *Dubliners* that he thought most likely to reach immortality.[4] To Turgenev's stories, Hemingway returned time and again, seeming never to tire of them. In 1927 he wrote himself a note: "Education consists in finding sources obscure enough to imitate so that they will be perfectly safe."[5] Certainly he learned that maxim at Pound's knee and reinforced it every time he picked up T. S. Eliot, all of whose books were in his library. My point, belabored as it may be, is now only too obvious: By the time Hemingway wrote the stories for *In Our Time*, he knew the genre of the short story sequence full well and was educated enough to challenge its masters. However it may rankle some ghosts of respected critics, we must finally admit that Hemingway knew what he was doing and that his craft does not depend upon the eye of its beholder. One might also note that over a period of sixteen years, Hemingway experimented more with the short story genre than almost any other American writer. From his "unwritten stories," which reduced the genre to a single paragraph, to his "The Snows of Kilimanjaro," which used a single story to hold a series of "unwritten stories," Hemingway continually stretched the limits of the genre.[6] If the stories of *In Our Time* form a sequence, then we must allow that Hemingway consciously crafted the collection that way.

However, the most cursory glance through the appended chronology of the book will raise interesting questions about Hemingway's authorial intentions, for the earliest parts of *In Our Time* were published in 1923, but the book did not reach its final form until 1955 when Scribner's reissued it with its 1930 "Introduction by the Author" retitled "On the Quai at Smyrna." With *Dubliners* or *Winesburg* there is ample evidence to support a governing plan for each of those books. *In Our Time* is different, with evidence to support both sides of the question. It may help to review the book's gestation before making any arguments for its coherence as a sequence of stories.

In February of 1923, Hemingway was in Rapallo, Italy, complaining about the meager surf and working on a series of sketches he called "unwritten stories." With most of his 1921–2 fiction lost when Hadley's valise was stolen in the Gare de Lyon the previous December, Hemingway was starting his career afresh. Having moved on from the "true" sentences of his "Paris 1922" sketches, he was now working on paragraphs done in different voices, for with his good ear,

4. Ernest Hemingway, item 489, undated note on back of February 1927 letter, Hemingway Collection, Kennedy Library, Boston, MA.
5. Hemingway, item 489.
6. One might also note that Hemingway's *To Have and Have Not* and *A Moveable Feast* are, in fact, sequences of connected short stories, and his *For Whom the Bell Tolls* is thirty-percent short stories told by embedded characters to the central character who is a writer.

he could imitate almost anyone who caught his attention. One such voice was that of his war buddy, Chink Dorman Smith, with whom he had skied only two months earlier. He used Chink's voice to tell about the garden in Mons when

> Young Buckley came in with his patrol from across the river. The first German I saw climbed up over the garden wall. We waited till he got one leg over then potted him. He had so much equipment on and looked awfully surprised and fell down into the garden. Then three more came over further down the wall. We shot them. They all came just like that. [21]

That's how they all went—detached voices speaking, describing tightly focused events, small pieces of modern times.

By March he had six sketches finished, enough to send to Jane Heap for her "Exiles" issue of *The Little Review*. Three centered on Western Front experiences in the Great War; one came from the 1922 retreat of the Greek army across Thrace; another described a bull fight in Spain; the last one detailed the firing-squad execution of the Greek ministers at the end of the Greco-Turkish war. Only the retreat across Thrace came from Hemingway's direct experience; the other five, including that of the bullfight, came from secondary sources. Taken as a group, their thematic center was violence; however, they were not written as a sequence but as an experiment, and Hemingway needed a title before sending them on to Jane Heap. He jotted down a page of possibilities:

> Unwritten Stories Are Better
> Perhaps You Were There At The Time
> That Was Before I Knew You
> Romance is Dead
> The Good Guys See A Thing Or Two
> In Our Time
>   subtitle
> I Am Not Interested In Artists[7]

The April 1923 issue of *The Little Review* grouped the six vignettes as "In Our Time" without the subtitle.

By mid-August 1923 when the Hemingways returned to Toronto, Ernest had completed eighteen of his "unwritten stories," which he left with his friend and publisher, William Bird, to be the final installment in Ezra Pound's "*Inquest* into the state of contemporary English prose." Hemingway titled the book *in our time*. The first six vignettes were revised versions of the *Little Review* publication. The twelve new sketches ranged just as freely as the first ones, following

---

7. Ernest Hemingway, item 92, Hemingway Collection, Kennedy Library, Boston, MA.

no chronologic or geographic principle of organization and coming most often from secondary sources or out of his imagination. Nine were war-related, but from two different wars and three different fronts. Six came from the Spanish bullfights;[8] two involved American gangsters; and one was an anomaly about a young revolutionist. While Hemingway was working on his last vignette, the hanging of Sam Cardinella, he wrote Ezra Pound that the sketches held together quite nicely.

> The bulls start, then reappear and then finish off. The war starts clear and noble just like it did, Mons etc., gets close and blurred and finish with the feller who goes home and gets clap. The refugees leave Thrace, due to the Greek ministers, who are shot. The whole thing closes with the talk with the King of Greece and his Queen in their garden (just written). . . . America appears in the cops shooting the guys who robbed the cigar store. It has form all right. . . . I will commence the hanging.[9]

But the form had not dictated content; rather the sketches created the form. If there was a principle involved, it came from the title, *in our time*, which itself had not appeared until the first six vignettes were finished. Done in several distinct voices, Hemingway's "unwritten stories" were more like Eliot's *Waste Land* than any recognizable prose model.

Between August 1923 and January 1924 while the Hemingways were in Toronto, Ernest did no creative writing. However, in February when they returned to Paris, pent up stories began to explode from his head. During the following three months while assisting part-time on the *Transatlantic Review*, Hemingway wrote eight new stories, five of which centered on Nick Adams, who first appeared simply as "Nick" in one of the vignettes.[1] On May 2 Hemingway wrote Edward O'Brien for advice on his publishing career. He said he had ten stories finished and needed to get them moving. "What I would like to do would be bring out a good fat book in N.Y. with some good publisher who would tout it and have In Our Time [sic *in our time*] in it and the other stories, My Old Man and about 15 or 20 others. How many would it take?"[2] It was an ingenuous question,

8. Having been twice to Spain since writing his first bullfight vignette, he now revised the one written from hearsay and wrote five new ones based loosely on what he had seen.
9. Ernest Hemingway, letter to Ezra Pound, c. 5 August 1923, *Ernest Hemingway, Selected Letters*, ed. Carlos Baker (New York: Scribner, 1981), 91.
1. The last name, Adams, first appeared in an unpublished vignette that Hemingway wrote during the spring of 1923, entitled "Did You Ever Kill Anyone." In it a soldier named Adams is shot by an "old boche [French slang: German] in a round cap and spectacles." Item 94a, Hemingway Collection, Kennedy Library.
2. Ernest Hemingway, letter to Edward O'Brien, 2 May 1924, *Selected Letters*, 116–17. The "ten stories" finished included "Up in Michigan," "Out of Season," and "My Old Man" from *Three Stories & Ten Poems* (Paris: Contact Publishing Co.: 1923).

for Hemingway knew full well how many stories were in *Winesburg* and *Dubliners,* and his projected totals were roughly correct only if he included the vignettes.

Looking over the material at hand, he could find no obvious relationships like location in Anderson or Joyce, or gender as in Stein's *Three Lives.* These were not stories about a particular place, a single character, or a point in time. But then they were not written to be a book; there was no unifying concept at their inception. It was at this point in May 1924, when he thought he had almost completed enough stories for a book, that Hemingway began to write "Big Two-Hearted River," which was going to anchor the collection, hopefully in the same manner that "The Dead" anchored *Dubliners.* But before he could finish the story, his work on the *Transatlantic* interrupted the flow, and then came Pamplona and the feria of San Fermin. It was not until July 20, when he and Hadley were finally alone at Burguete, that he returned to Nick where he had left him on the river. During the intervening two months, his life had been very literary. While Ford Madox Ford was in America raising money for the *Transatlantic,* Hemingway edited a complete issue of the periodical, soliciting manuscripts and eliminating what he considered dead wood, including one of Ford's own columns. Then, during and after the Pamplona celebration, Ernest was in the company of Chink Dorman Smith, Bill Bird, Robert McAlmon, and John Dos Passos, all of whom were current in literary gossip and ideas.

It was after these events that Hemingway returned to Nick on the river and wrote his original ending to "Big Two-Hearted River," a pre-Borgesian tour de force[3] that, had it worked, would have turned the collection of stories back on itself endlessly. Now he made Nick the author of all the stories in the collection, even those in which the character was Nick:

> Everything good he'd ever written he'd made up. None of it had ever happened. . . . That was the weakness of Joyce, the main one, except Jesuits. Daedalus in Ulysses was Joyce himself so he was terrible. Joyce was so damn romantic and intellectual about him. He'd made Bloom up. Bloom was wonderful. He'd made Mrs. Bloom up. She was the greatest in the world. . . . Nick in the stories was never himself. He made him up. Of course he'd never seen an Indian woman having a baby. That was what made it so good.[4]

3. A work of fiction that blurs the distinction between the story and its writing, in the manner of Jorge Luis Borges (1899–1986), Argentinian short-story writer and essayist [*Editor*].

4. Although this has been printed as "On Writing" in *The Nick Adams Stories,* I am quoting from the first, unrevised draft, item 274, Hemingway Collection, Kennedy Library, 91.

Thinking aloud to himself, his mind jumping erratically from past to present, now Nick had as part of his memories Hemingway's past three weeks in Spain and all of Paris, including the Cézanne paintings Ernest so much admired. Nick wanted to write about country the way Cézanne painted it, breaking it down into its basic parts and then building it back up. "It was deadly serious. You could do it if you would fight it out. It was a thing you couldn't talk about. He was going to work on it until he got it. Maybe never, but he would know as he got near it. It was a job, maybe for all his life."[5]

He ended it with Nick hurrying back to his fishing camp, holding a story in his head to write. By mid-August he told Gertrude Stein that the story was finished. It was "100 pages long and nothing happens and the country is swell, I made it all up, so I see it all and part of it comes out the way it ought to, it is swell about the fish, but isn't writing a hard job though? It used to be easy before I met you."[6] "Nothing happens," he said quite proudly, trying to write a fiction so pure that it minimized character and conflict, leaving only setting and style, the painterly elements. He did not achieve anything close to that degree of purity, but it is interesting that he was trying and that he thought Gertrude, with her continuous present tense, would approve. But then it was Gertrude who sent him to Cézanne, claiming that she composed all of *Three Lives* while seated before a Cézanne portrait. It was also Gertrude who brought Flaubert's idea of pure fiction to Hemingway's attention.

He was so sure of the story that he had it professionally typed and placed at the end of the *In Our Time* manuscript. Two of the longer vignettes were revised into stories, "A Very Short Story" and "The Revolutionist," and "Big Two-Hearted River" was split into two parts, all of which made the volume seem longer than it actually was. Having arranged and rearranged the sequence of stories, Hemingway included all his new fiction, plus the stories from *Three Stories & Ten Poems* and used the "unwritten stories" from *in our time* as a counterpoint between stories. The book had, he thought, "a certain unity," which he tried to explain to Edward O'Brien. "The first 5 are [set] in Michigan starting with Up in Michigan . . . and in between each one comes bang! the In Our Time [*in our time*]." Without further explaining the "unity," he said that his long fishing story "finishes up the Michigan scene the book starts with." He was now calling the terse vignettes chapter headings, claiming that was what he first wrote them to be. "You get the close up very quietly but

5. Item 274, p. 94.
6. Ernest Hemingway, letter to Gertrude Stein, 15 August 1924, *Selected Letters*, 122 [151]. Although we have no evidence that Hemingway had read the short stories of Henry James by 1924, Gertrude Stein, Ezra Pound, and Hadley Hemingway were all fans of James, who may have helped influence Hemingway's redefinition of what a short story was.

absolutely solid and the real thing but very close, and then through
it all between every story comes the rhythm of the in our time
chapters."[7] A month later Hemingway used a different metaphor to
explain to Edmund Wilson that the interchapters separated the stories because

> that is the way they were meant to go—to give the picture of
> the whole between examining it in detail. Like looking with
> your eyes at something, say a passing coast line, and then look-
> ing at it with 15 x [power] binoculars. Or rather, maybe, look-
> ing at it and then going in and living in it—and then coming
> out and looking at it again.[8]

A week after Hemingway wrote Wilson, Gertrude Stein returned to
Paris from her long summer at St. Remy; immediately he took her a
copy of "Big Two-Hearted River," which he was certain she would
appreciate. She returned it with the terse comment, "Remarks are
not literature."[9] It was the ending she objected to, the ending that
completely changed the collection, taking it to a different level of
complexity. He read back over his "remarks," which were already circulating among the publishing houses of New York. Not yet confident enough to ignore Gertrude's criticism, Hemingway hacked off
the last eleven pages of his typescript and added ten pages of new
manuscript, ending the story where it began with Nick, the river,
and the trout. Ahead of him, where the fishing would be "tragic,"
the river entered a swamp. As Nick moved back toward his camp,
Hemingway ended the story: "There were plenty of days coming
when he could fish the swamp" [129]. In mid-November 1924, he
told Robert McAlmon that he had "decided that all that mental conversation in the long fishing story is the shit and have cut it all out."
It would be humorous, he thought, if some New York publisher took
the book on the basis of that interior monologue.[1]

Thus did Hemingway's experiment with metafiction largely disappear beneath the surface of *In Our Time*. All that remained was
the now enigmatic statement, "He had left everything behind, the
need for thinking, the need to write, other needs" [112]. Had Nick-
as-writer remained in the ending, the reader would have been looped
back to the beginning to reassess the stories in a different light; such
an ending would also have borne similarities to Joyce's ending of

7. Ernest Hemingway, letter to Edward O'Brien, 12 September 1924, *Selected Letters*, 123
[152].
8. Ernest Hemingway, letter to Edmund Wilson, 18 October 1924, *Selected Letters*, 128
[153].
9. *Selected Writings of Gertrude Stein*, ed. Carl Van Vechten (New York: Random House,
1962), p. 207.
1. Ernest Hemingway, letter to Robert McAlmon, c. 15 November 1924, *Selected Letters*, 135.

Portrait of the Artist as a Young Man, where young Stephen Dedalus sets out to become the writer who may or may not be capable of writing *Portrait*.[2]

Hemingway's elimination of the obvious metafiction did not eliminate other unifying elements, nor did it completely erase the theme of the writer writing about a writer, which became a life-long obsession of Hemingway's. So many of his characters turn out to be writers, and their recurring concern is frequently the act of writing. In almost all of his novels, Hemingway keeps the reader continually aware of the writer in the rigging. *In Our Time's* only remaining writer is the pathetic poet, Hubert Elliot, but the experimental nature of the interchapters and the stories, with their remarkably understated style in which little happened on the surface of the fiction, reminded Hemingway's contemporary reader that he was on new ground. Combining all he had learned from Anderson, Stein, Turgenev, and Joyce, Hemingway had forged an American style for his age.

In Our Time, even without its deleted section, remains Hemingway's most writerly book, in which he not only uses what his tutors taught him, but also pays homage to them in the process. Why else did he include "My Old Man," as good an Anderson story as Sherwood ever wrote, imitating his voice but leaving out the sentimentality? In "Three Day Blow," Hemingway gave us upper Michigan as Turgenev might have treated it. "Mr. and Mrs. Elliot" was written in the style and manner of Gertrude Stein's *Three Lives*. And Joyce was everywhere in the stories, helping with the down-beat endings and informing the selection of detail. He was particularly there in "Soldier's Home" when "Krebs looked at the bacon fat hardening on his plate." Including, as it did, all of Hemingway's previous fiction, *In Our Time* was a covert literary biography, showing forth all its author had learned since arriving in Paris three years earlier.

However, before the book reached print, other elements came into play, forcing Hemingway to make still more changes in the contents and their arrangement. Since his letter to O'Brien, he had once more rearranged the sequence so that it now opened with Nick Adams and his father the Doctor at "Indian Camp." On 5 March 1925, Hemingway received Boni & Liveright's acceptance of *In Our Time*, including a promise of a two-hundred-dollar advance against royalties. When the contract arrived, its cover letter asked Hemingway to eliminate what was now his second story, "Up in Michigan," which would create censorship problems in the America of 1925. Did he

---

2. My reading of *In Our Time* and its potential for metafiction is completely indebted to Debra Moddelmog's seminal and provocative essay, "The Unifying Consciousness of a Divided Conscience: Nick Adams as Author of *In Our Time*," *American Literature* 60 (December 1988): 591–610. [See this volume, 209–25—*Editor*.]

have a replacement? In fact, Hemingway had in hand "The Undefeated," a newly written story about an over-the-hill bullfighter that would have tied in very neatly with the six corrida interchapters, but he did not use it. Instead of taking that easy solution, he wrote a completely new story about the Michigan education of Nick Adams and called it "The Battler." Instead of inserting it in the second position left blank by excising "Up in Michigan," he moved the next three Nick Adams stories forward one position and slipped "The Battler" into the fifth position without changing the sequence of the interchapters. Whatever relationship he once saw between the vignettes and their accompanying stories was arbitrarily changed, but the book was finished. No more revisions, he told Liveright.[3]

The advance check arrived with Horace Liveright's apology for making his own revisions to "Mr. and Mrs. Elliot," which "would surely have made the book immediately suppressible. . . . galleys will be sent you very soon, and then you can change what I've done to suit yourself, bearing in mind, though, that it would be a pretty bad thing all around if your first book were brought into court for obscenity."[4] When Hemingway received his butchered story, he could not believe the changes. In New York it was apparently obscene for a husband and wife to "try" to have a baby. His story once opened: "Mr. and Mrs. Elliot tried very hard to have a baby. They tried as often as Mrs. Elliot could stand it. They tried in Boston after they were married and they tried coming over on the boat. They did not try very often on the boat because Mrs. Elliot was quite sick!" [69].

Taking his future in his own hands, Hemingway revised his paragraph to read: "Mr. and Mrs. Elliot tried very hard to have a baby. They were married in Boston and sailed for Europe on a boat. It was a very expensive boat and was supposed to get to Europe in six days. But on the boat Mrs. Elliot was quite sick."

Bereft of babies the opening sounded silly, its humor dead. It remained that way until 1930, when Scribner's negotiated with Liveright to bring out a new edition in which they restored Mr. and Mrs. Elliot's attempts to have a baby.

In early August 1930, Hemingway's editor, Max Perkins, asked Ernest to write an introduction for Scribner's new edition of *In Our Time*. On 12 August, Hemingway replied that he was "too busy, too disinterested, too proud or too stupid" to do as Perkins asked. He said he would return the text "with a few corrections, the original Mr. and Mrs. Elliot, and with or without a couple of short pieces of the same period."[5] What he sent Perkins was a laconic narrative

3. Ernest Hemingway, letter to Horace Liveright, 31 March 1925, *Selected Letters*, 154–5.
4. Horace Liveright, letter to Ernest Hemingway, 1 May 1925, Hemingway Collection, Princeton University Library, NJ.
5. *Selected Letters*, 327.

done in a British voice describing the horrors at the 1922 Greek evacuation of Smyrna during their war with Turkey. Hemingway had not witnessed the event himself, but there had been graphic news coverage, and he had talked to men who were there. The style was "of the same period" as the interchapters, but the piece was probably written somewhat later, perhaps as late as 1926–7. There is no evidence to suggest that the piece was originally written with the other vignettes in 1923, nor is there evidence that Hemingway wrote the piece specifically for the "Introduction by the Author," as it was called. Nevertheless, in what was to be his penultimate chance to focus the book, he chose to place the sketch as an introduction. When his first forty-nine stories were collected in 1938, the "Introduction" was changed, apparently by Hemingway, to "On the Quai at Smyrna." It was not until 1955 that another edition of *In Our Time* was printed in which "On the Quai at Smyrna" was the opening story.[6]

Understanding this complex and lengthy evolution of *In Our Time* may help us account for our difficulty in reading the collection as a unified sequence, but our perplexity remains. We have Hemingway's various statements about the collection's unity, statements leaving us not much the wiser for them. We can say with some certainty that the stories of *In Our Time* were not written to fit a preconceived plan, nor were the interchapters written to complement their attendant stories. The more we know, however, the greater our discomfort. We know that "Up in Michigan" should have been part of the book, but in 1955 when Hemingway apparently had the opportunity to reinsert it, he did not. And yet who would take out "The Battler" to restore "Up in Michigan"?

Despite all this, despite last-minute changes and flawed texts, *In Our Time* still has a coherence, but that coherence is not narrative. We are not merely following a particular character's life; we are not listening to a single voice. Attempts to force these kinds of unity find the reader either ignoring "My Old Man" and "Mr. and Mrs. Elliot" or apologizing for their intrusion. The fault does not lie with the author but with us, his beholders. For years we tried to read *The Waste Land* as a narrative because any poem longer than a page had to tell a story. Those same nineteenth-century glasses have distorted our reading of more than one modernist piece. About 1906, painters stopped telling stories, to the continuing unhappiness of some whose tastes remain in the previous century. Painters like Picasso, Braque, Miró, and Gris, painters whom Hemingway knew and in some cases collected, those painters abandoned plot, narrative, and

6. Most of this paragraph is taken from Paul Smith, *A Reader's Guide to the Short Stories of Ernest Hemingway*, pp. 189–91.

most of character, flattened their canvases and continually called our attention to the artifice of their product. "This is not a pipe," says the clear label on Magritte's painting of a pipe. One might put a similar note—This is not a narrative—on the covers of *The Waste Land* and *In Our Time*.

Hemingway said once that he did not lead guided tours through his work, for the writing itself was difficult enough. He did, however, leave us a few clues to *In Our Time*. He eliminated Nick's interior monologue, but he left us the clue that Nick was a writer who had left the need for writing somewhere behind him. Hemingway also told us something by writing "The Battler" when he had another story in hand to complete his book. Both stories, "The Battler" and "The Undefeated," have a similar focus—an old, physically battered professional at the end of his career. The difference is the presence of Nick Adams in "The Battler" and his absence in the story of the bullfighter. Another clue was Hemingway's repositioning "Up in Michigan" from opening story to the second position, which moved "Indian Camp," a Nick Adams story, to the front so that the book opened and closed on Nick. All of these clues argue strongly that Nick is central to *In Our Time*, as we have always known, for he appears in half of the stories and in one vignette.[7] But those other seven stories prevent any narrative from forming, leaving us only certain that the "time" of *In Our Time* is that of Nick Adams, the period immediately before, during, and after the Great War.[8]

Our only other major clue is the "Introduction by the Author," for if Hemingway did not fully understand his book in 1924, he surely did by 1930. There, on the quai at Smyrna, the Greek refugees "screamed every night at midnight," and in the harbor there floated "plenty of nice things," such stuff as the narrator's dreams are made of. His detached, disembodied voice is British, his dark vision a sign of the times. It is not women giving birth in dark corners that disturbs him so much as the mothers refusing to give up their dead babies. In the end the Greeks break the legs of their baggage mules and dump them into the harbor to drown. "It was all a most pleasant business" [8]. Similarly, in all but one vignette, we never see the war, only its aftermath, only the effects of violence on the mind of the beholder.

What we are left with is the New Historian's picnic, a book that assumes the reader is cognizant of the major events of 1910–24, which is no longer "our" time. We are never told which war or what

---

7. In fact, the evidence seems so strong, that Philip Young rearranged the sequence of these and other episodes into *The Nick Adams Stories*, an almost coherent effort of the sort many wish Hemingway had written. But he did not.

8. One reason not to restore "Up in Michigan" was that it was set before the turn of the century. "He talked about . . . the Republican Party and about James G. Blaine." Blaine died in 1893.

front, but the clues are there. In 1925 the reader should have remembered the Greeks retreating across Thrace. It was in all the papers and on the newsreel screen. Hemingway assumes we understand the contemporary economics that allow his characters to live so idly in Europe, assumes we are familiar with the growing divorce rate. He assumes we remember the Russian revolution and have lived through the Palmer Acts that deported politically undesirable immigrants. He assumes we are living in Prohibition America. All of these assumptions are implicit in the title and embedded in most of the stories.

All of which takes us back to a qualification of our initial question: If the book is not a narrative then what holds it together as a coherent sequence? Let me suggest now obvious answers. *In Our Time* achieves its coherency in at least two ways, neither of them narrative. At its most subliminal level, the book is a literary biography of an American male learning to write in the postwar period. We see his homage to tutors—Turgenev, Joyce, Stein, and Anderson—and we see him moving beyond them in "Big Two-Hearted River," creating a style and attitude for his time. It is a young, brash writer showing us his "stuff," giving us an irreverent pastiche of styles and technique, a range of voices, blinding us at times with his brilliance. It is Hemingway at his most experimental, at a point in his career when he had nothing to lose and the world to gain.

At its more accessible level, the book is a series of long and short takes, close-ups and wide angles, creating a visual scrapbook of the age that spawned it. It is the repetition of thematic experiences that binds the collage together: war, violence, water, darkness, isolation, babies, and most centrally, failed relationships. Fathers fail their sons; lovers fail each other. In every story but one, the male–female relationship is either flawed, ruined, or missing. Nick ruins his relationship with Marge; the boxer is emotionally wrecked when his wife leaves him. The husband on the bed is not interested in his wife's identification with the poor kitty out in the rain. Unheroic, the enervated men accept disappointment as their inheritance and wounding as their inevitable due. In another part of the country, the jazz bands were playing hot music in the "speaks" where flappers strutted their stuff. It was the age of bathtub gin, bobbed hair, rolled stockings and sleek cars. But Hemingway's stories took a longer view of what was, in fact, an emotionally desperate period in our nation's history.

The opening story, "Indian Camp," set the tone and established the themes for all that followed: a father and son without a mother, a bloody Caesarian operation done without anesthetic, a wounded father cutting his own throat in the upper bunk; and Nick, watching it all, assuring himself later that he will never die. Played in different keys, almost every story is a variation on some thematic element of "Indian Camp" until we are alone with Nick isolated by his own choice on Big Two-Hearted River, trying to recover his poise. Behind him he has left, we're told, the needs to think and write, and he can stop his mind from working if he sufficiently tires his body. There the modernist and postmodernist come together: the writer writing about a writer who has temporarily killed the need to write. Beside the river, half afraid to face the swamp where fishing will be tragic, Nick Adams has nothing left to tell us about his era or its pitfalls. Unlike Gabriel Conroy at the end of Joyce's "The Dead," Nick is not in tears, but the two remain first cousins nonetheless. Both men, anchoring as they do the collections that house them, have come to realize the pathos of their situations. By 1930, when the music stopped and the jazz babies went on the dole, the rest of the country joined Nick to face the swamp, which had been waiting for them since the end of the war.[9]

APPENDIX: Chronology of In Our Time

August 1923	"My Old Man" and "Out of Season" are published by Robert McAlmon in Hemingway's *Three Stories & Ten Poems* (Paris: Contact Publishing Co.).
October 1923	*The Little Review* 10 (Spring 1923) publishes six sketches under the title "In Our Time."
January 1924	Edward O'Brien republishes "My Old Man" in his *Best Short Stories of 1923* (Boston: Small, Maynard & Co.).
March 1924	Bill Bird publishes eighteen sketches, including those in *The Little Review*, in book form as *in our time* (Paris: Three Mountains Press).
April 1924	"Indian Camp," *transatlantic review.*
October 1924	"Mr. and Mrs. Elliot," *The Little Review.*
December 1924	"The Doctor and the Doctor's Wife," *transatlantic review.*
January 1925	"Cross-Country Snow," *transatlantic review.*
May 1925	"Big Two-Hearted River," *This Quarter.*
June 1925	"Soldier's Home" is published by Robert McAlmon in *Contact Collection of Contemporary Writers* (Paris: Contact Publishing Co.).

9. There have been several thematic readings of the book, many of which are reprinted in my *Critical Essays on Hemingway's* In Our Time (Boston: G. K. Hall, 1983). * * *

October 1925	Boni & Liveright publish *In Our Time*, including sixteen *in our time* sketches as interchapters and another two converted to stories: "A Very Short Story" and "The Revolutionist." Of the fourteen stories, only four were previously unpublished: "The End of Something," "The Three-Day Blow," "The Battler," and "Cat in the Rain."
October 1938	Scribner's publishes *The Fifth Column* and the *First Forty-Nine Stories*, which includes all of the interchapters and stories from *In Our Time* but changes the "Introduction by the Author" to "On the Quai at Smyrna."
1955	Scribner's reissues *In Our Time*, opening with "On the Quai at Smyrna."[1]

Given the probability for printers' errors in each new edition and the authorial and/or editorial changes along the way, the comprehensive critic would do well to establish first that he is reading the correct text. Sad to say, we still do not have a standard edition of *In Our Time*.[2]

DEBRA A. MODDELMOG

[Nick Adams as Author of *In Our Time*][†]

In the lengthy passage that was Hemingway's original ending to "Big Two-Hearted River," Nick Adams, having caught "one good trout" [126], rests and reflects on many things, particularly his writing. For readers of *In Our Time*, who have arrived with "Big Two-Hearted River" at the book's final story, this interior monologue (had Hemingway kept it) would have revealed some interesting facts, but none more so than that Nick has written two of the stories we have just read: "Indian Camp" and "My Old Man." Indeed, in the final scene

---

1. The most reliable sources of bibliographic information are Audre Hanneman, *Ernest Hemingway: A Comprehensive Bibliography* (Princeton, NJ: Princeton University Press, 1967) and Paul Smith, *A Reader's Guide to the Short Stories of Ernest Hemingway* (G. K. Hall, 1989). See also my *Hemingway: The Paris Years*.
2. See, for example, E. R. Hagemann's two studies: "A Collation, with Commentary, of the Five Texts of the Chapters in Hemingway's *In Our Time*, 1923–38," *Papers of the Bibliographical Society of America* 75 (1979): 443–58; and "Only Let the Story End as Soon as Possible," *Modern Fiction Studies* 26 (Summer, 1980): 255–62.
† From "The Unifying Consciousness of a Divided Conscience: Nick Adams as Author of *In Our Time*," in *American Literature* 60.1 (Dec. 1988): 591–610. Copyright, 1988, Duke University Press. All rights reserved. Republished by permission of the copyright holder, Duke University Press. Some of the author's notes have been omitted. Page numbers in brackets refer to this Norton Critical Edition.

of this ending, Nick heads back to camp "holding something in his head" [141] and is apparently preparing to write "Big Two-Hearted River" itself. But lest we misunderstand these stories, Nick also explains his method of composition: "Nick in the stories was never himself. He made him up. Of course he'd never seen an Indian woman having a baby. That was what made it good. Nobody knew that. He'd seen a woman have a baby on the road to Karagatch and tried to help her. That was the way it was" [139].

Most critics who discuss this rejected conclusion generally assume that Hemingway lost control of his art here, identified too closely with Nick, and began writing autobiography rather than fiction.[1] In fact, both Hemingway's critics and biographers quote from this monologue as if Hemingway, not Nick, were the speaker. Even when a critic, like Robert Gibb, takes Hemingway at his word, he concludes that we need not worry finally about distinguishing between Nick and Hemingway. Whether a story has been written by "Hemingway the writer who wrote in the character of Nick Adams" or by "Nick Adams the writer who, by existing, shaped the idea of a man and his cosmos" matters not, according to Gibb: "Remembrance goes both ways."[2]

Remembrance may go both ways, but Gibb is finally wrong to suggest that our understanding of a story remains the same regardless of whom we see as its author. Obviously, all words lead back to Hemingway, and I would not wish to suggest that in the stories of *In Our Time* he is introducing the kinds of author-character confusions we have come to expect from many postmodern writers. However, as I hope to show, there are some good reasons for seeing Nick as the implied author of *In Our Time*, and doing so resolves many confusions about the book's unity, structure, vision, and significance. Moreover, such an approach also casts new light on Nick Adams as a character both separate from yet also an extension of Hemingway.

In his book-length study of Nick, Joseph Flora states, "No one would argue that 'Big Two-Hearted River' would gain from the inclusion of Nick's several memories and theories of writing."[3] I

---

1. Philip Young, for instance, asserts that "the 'he,' the consciousness of the piece, shifts from Nick to Hemingway back to Nick again"—"'Big World Out There': The Nick Adams Stories," in *The Short Stories of Ernest Hemingway: Critical Essays*, ed. Jackson J. Benson (Durham: Duke Univ. Press, 1975), p. 31. Paul Smith also criticizes this passage, citing as its most incriminating sentence: "He, Nick, had wanted to write about country so it would be there like Cézanne had done it in painting" [140]. Smith maintains that the unnecessary appositive here emphasizes the "autobiographical character" of this ending: "it is as if [Hemingway] had to remind himself he was writing a work of fiction"—"Hemingway's Early Manuscripts: The Theory and Practice of Omission," *Journal of Modern Literature*, 10 (1983), 282.
2. "He Made Him Up: 'Big Two-Hearted River' as Doppelganger," in *Critical Essays on Ernest Hemingway's In Our Time*, ed. Michael S. Reynolds (Boston: G. K. Hall, 1983), pp. 255, 256.
3. *Hemingway's Nick Adams* (Baton Rouge: Louisiana State Univ. Press, 1982), p. 181.

want to make clear from the start that I wholeheartedly agree with this statement. From the moment Nick arrives at Seney he does everything in his power to hold back his thoughts, yet in the nine pages that Hemingway finally rejected, Nick suddenly begins thinking and does so calmly and contentedly. This ending would have reduced the story's tension and given us a very different Nick Adams. That Hemingway realized this indicates how clear a vision he had formed of what he wanted to accomplish in his fiction. His letter to Robert McAlmon—written in mid-November 1924, about three months after he finished "Big Two-Hearted River" and two months after he had arranged and submitted *In Our Time* for publication—provides the fullest explanation of his reasoning: "I have decided that all that mental conversation in the long fishing story is the shit and have cut it all out. The last nine pages. The story was interrupted you know just when I was going good and I could never get back into it and finish it. I got a hell of a shock when I realized how bad it was and that shocked me back into the river again and I've finished it off the way it ought to have been all along. Just the straight fishing."[4] In brief, Hemingway recognized that "all that mental conversation" jarred aesthetically with the rest of his story and actually contradicted its point.[5] Wisely, he cut.

But just because Hemingway saved "Big Two-Hearted River" by removing Nick's monologue does not mean that we, like a jury commanded to disregard a witness's last remark, should automatically ignore all we learn here. Certainly critics are right that Hemingway comes close to crossing the boundary between fiction and experience in these pages, but that is a line he almost always approaches in his Nick Adams stories. As Flora notes, "Although Nick is not Hemingway, he reflects more of Hemingway than any other Hemingway hero,"[6] and Philip Young observes that Nick has "much in common" with his creator and was, for Hemingway, "a special kind of mask."[7] Significantly, Hemingway's letter to McAlmon discloses that he revised his conclusion because he was worried about the artistic integrity of his story, not about his artistic persona.

Ironically, it is actually *because* Hemingway was so close to Nick and yet not Nick that he was able to conceive of surrendering

---

4. In *Ernest Hemingway: Selected Letters 1917–1961*, ed. Carlos Baker (New York: Scribner's, 1981), p. 133.

5. * * * Gertrude Stein * * * alerted Hemingway to the problem with this ending. In *The Autobiography of Alice B. Toklas*, she recalls that in the fall of 1924, Hemingway "had added to his stories a little story of meditations and in these he said that The Enormous Room was the greatest book he had ever read * * *. It was then that Gertrude Stein had said, Hemingway, remarks are not literature"—(New York: Random House, 1933), p. 219.* * *

6. *Hemingway's Nick Adams*, p. 189.

7. *Ernest Hemingway: A Reconsideration* (University Park: Pennsylvania State Univ. Press, 1966), p. 62.

authorship to Nick without destroying the illusion of his fictional world. Of course, when he wrote "Big Two-Hearted River," Hemingway had already written almost every story in In Our Time (only "The Battler" and "On the Quai at Smyrna" came later), and so obviously he did not plan from the time he composed these stories to attribute any of them to Nick. However, Nick shared so much of Hemingway's personality and experience that turning him into the author of the stories *ex post facto* required very little work. All Hemingway had to do was supply Nick with the relevant background, specifically a writing career and some post-war history. This he was doing in the nine pages he eventually cut. And, as I indicated above, Hemingway actually gave Nick the background needed to be considered author of all of In Our Time, not just of the two stories he specifically mentions, "My Old Man" and "Indian Camp."

The evidence leading to this deduction begins with a sentence quoted earlier in which Nick tells us: "Nick in the stories was never himself." The use of the plural "stories" is significant. Because Nick is not in "My Old Man," he apparently has written other stories about himself besides "Indian Camp." This hypothesis is supported by Nick's references in this lengthy monologue to people and places that play a part in other Nick Adams stories. For example, Nick thinks about fishing at Hortons Creek [137], the scene of the breakup with Marjorie in "The End of Something," and he remembers "drinking with Bill's old man" [137], which calls to mind "The Three-Day Blow." He also mentions his wife, Helen, a figure whose existence we learn of in "Cross-Country Snow." Finally, Nick states that his family has misunderstood his stories, believing that they were all recountings of his experience [139]. One implication of this statement is that his relatives have been reading fiction in which Nick appears as a central character and have presumed that the other characters are themselves; the most likely candidate to provoke this reaction would be "The Doctor and the Doctor's Wife."

But Nick's memories of people and places are not limited to those who materialize in stories about himself. Many of his allusions also recall the non-Nick narratives of In Our Time. For instance, the woman giving birth on the road to Karagatch, the encounter from which Nick indicates that "Indian Camp" derives, is presented without change in chapter 2. Nick also states that too much talking had made the war unreal [138], an attitude shared by Harold Krebs in "Soldier's Home." The matador Maera figures prominently in Nick's thoughts (e.g., "Maera was the greatest man he'd ever known," [138]), as he does in chapters 13 and 14 of In Our Time. Nick even confesses that "His whole inner life had been bullfights all one year" [138], an obsession that could explain why six of the fifteen chapters deal with that subject. All of these connections between Nick's memories reviewed during his fishing trip to upper Michigan and the narratives of *In Our Time* support the premise that this original conclusion supplied the personal history necessary to see Nick as the author of this book.

To repeat what I said earlier, we need not assume that Nick lost all of this past when we lost this ending. In fact, a key sentence in the version of "Big Two-Hearted River" that was finally published implies that this background did not disappear forever but simply moved, so to speak, underground. Soon after Nick starts hiking away from Seney and towards the river, he discovers that "He felt he had left everything behind, the need for thinking, the need to write, other needs" [112]. Exactly why Nick feels so relieved to leave behind these three needs becomes clear when we see *In Our Time* as the product of his experiences and imagination. Although obviously we cannot pin down the precise date when Nick wrote any particular story in *In Our Time*—excluding perhaps "Big Two-Hearted River"— we can, I think, safely infer that he composed most of the book after World War I. Not only do most of the stories describe events of this war or shortly thereafter (the Greco-Turkish War, American couples visiting Europe, soldiers returning to the States), but also Nick admits that "He always worked best when Helen was unwell" [139], a condition that definitely arises after the war. By roughly dating the composition of these stories, we are able to connect them to that stage in Nick's life immediately following World War I, and they can, therefore, help us to understand the Nick Adams we meet in "Big Two-Hearted River."

In approaching the stories of *In Our Time* as if Nick were their author, we discover that it will, indeed, be easier to trace through them Nick's recent psychological history than his actual history. Because Nick has told us that he was never himself in his stories and because we lack the biographical evidence (letters, memoirs, interviews) that usually fill the gap between an author's life and his fiction, we are left wondering where we might find the real Nick Adams. The fact that Nick's family has taken his fiction for autobiography suggests that, like Hemingway, Nick was drawing heavily from life when he wrote his stories.[8] Still, we will have to guess, for the most part, at what Nick actually experienced, at "the way it was" [139]. But since our main interest is Nick's psyche, we need not worry too much about our inability to sort reality from imagination. By looking for repeated patterns and by studying the subjects that

8. Carlos Baker notes that during the decade when Hemingway wrote his first 45 stories, "he was unwilling to stray very far from the life he knew by direct personal contact, or to do any more guessing than was absolutely necessary"—*Hemingway: The Writer as Artist*, 4th ed. (Princeton: Princeton Univ. Press, 1972), p. 128.

Nick chooses to develop as well as his manner of presenting those subjects, we should uncover those fixations of his imagination that reveal his basic outlook on life.

Having established the parameters of our investigation, we find new fascination in one fact about Nick's history that we *do* know: "he'd never seen an Indian woman having a baby. . . . He'd seen a woman have a baby on the road to Karagatch and tried to help her" [139]. This confession about the source of "Indian Camp" indicates, first of all, that the woman Nick attempted to help has affected him deeply. As I have already noted, Nick reports this encounter directly in chapter 2 of *In Our Time*, a description which ends with the comment "Scared sick looking at it" [15]. Apparently neither version alone was enough to purge Nick of this memory, and the question is why he is so preoccupied with it.

Part of the answer could lie in the transformations Nick makes when turning the experience into fiction. Not only does he concentrate on the pain and suffering of childbirth, but he also changes the witness of the delivery from an adult immersed in war and evacuation to a child involved with family life and night-time adventures. Such a transference is psychologically symbolic. It implies, first, that the older Nick views his meeting with the woman on the road to Karagatch as an initiation of the innocent. By projecting himself as a young boy present at a difficult childbirth, Nick suggests that he feels victimized by the exigencies of the adult world ("It was an awful mess to put you through," his father says—[14]) and also reveals a lingering inability to accept suffering and dying ("[C]an't you give her something to make her stop screaming?" [12] "Do ladies always have such a hard time having babies?" "Do many men kill themselves?" "Is dying hard?"—[14]). A strong degree of self-pity thus permeates the story, especially its final scene, where the young Nick questions the all-knowing father. However, Nick also attacks that self-indulgence with self-irony by ending his story with the child's denial of his own mortality, a denial that he, a war veteran and writer, now knows to be a lie.

But "Indian Camp" discloses more about Nick than just the fact that he feels victimized and confused by life. It also reveals his despair, possibly even his guilt, over being unable to ease the suffering of the woman on the road to Karagatch. In describing the source of his story, Nick tells us that he "tried" to help this woman, a qualifier which implies failure. He reproduces that sense of helplessness and frustration in the person of the Indian father who commits suicide because he "couldn't stand things" [14]. But he also places the suffering Indian mother in the professional hands of Dr. Adams, who *does* stop her pain and delivers her child. Nick thereby completes in his imagination what he failed to do in reality. Fiction serves as wish fulfillment by enabling Nick to control a world that seems to deny all attempts at such control.

Feelings of horror and frustration and a desire not to enter the complex realm of adulthood help to explain why Nick has built two separate narratives out of his meeting with the woman in Asia Minor. But, in fact, this focus on pain and suffering—both experienced and observed, physical and mental—countered by a wish to escape or deny that vision actually forms a pattern found throughout the stories of *In Our Time*, especially those where Nick is a central character. In "The Doctor and the Doctor's Wife" we are witnesses to the marriage of incompetence and insularity, and find that its sole issue is incompatibility. The young Nick responds to the friction of his parents' relationship and the myopia of his mother by ignoring the latter's summons for that of black squirrels. In "The End of Something" and "The Three-Day Blow," Nick discovers for himself the agony of relationships and reacts to that pain, first, by retreating from all companionship, even that of his friend Bill, and then by retreating from the home, the conventional domain of woman, to the woods, where "the Marge business was no longer so tragic. It was not even very important. The wind blew everything like that away" [37]. Nick learns in "The Battler" about the cruelty of society and the viciousness of insanity, a lesson which ends, once again, in confused escape. And, finally, in chapter 6, the violence of war so shatters Nick's spine and peace of mind that he vows to make "a separate peace" [49], to desert not only the battlefield but also the patriotism that led him to that destructive arena.

A quick glance at the six non-Nick stories which follow chapter 6— our last look at Nick until he reappears in "Cross-Country Snow"— is enough to confirm the paradigm. In fact, although the flight from pain is not depicted as regularly in these stories, the vision they present is so similar to that found in the Nick narratives that we can have no doubt that their author is the same. In "A Very Short Story" a soldier who wants to marry his girlfriend-nurse "to make it so they could not lose it" [51] does lose "it." The woman jilts him and he subsequently loses his health when he contracts gonorrhea from a salesgirl in the backseat of a cab. Harold Krebs, the soldier come home, loses touch with the reality of World War I and his own identity: by lying he "lost everything" [56]. The revolutionist, failing to comprehend the political reality of the world, is captured by the Swiss and loses his freedom; the narrator of his story has already lost his own political idealism. And the couples in "Mr. and Mrs. Elliot," "Cat in the Rain," and "Out of Season" all dramatize loss of understanding, communication, and love; in place of these things they substitute reading, a cat, writing reams of poetry, a lesbian affair, fishing.

This consistency of vision found throughout the stories we have examined so far suggests that Nick has a fairly inflexible, troubled way of seeing the world. No matter what or whom he writes about, he tends to view life as a losing proposition. Gertrude Stein's "You are all a lost generation" describes *In Our Time* as aptly as it describes *The Sun Also Rises* in this sense:[9] Nick seems to believe that the things most worth having and caring about—life, love, ideals, companions, peace, freedom—will be lost sooner or later, and he is not sure how to cope with this assurance, except through irony, bitterness, and, sometimes, wishful thinking. Although we cannot determine definitely when such a belief was formed, the most likely candidate to have precipitated this change is, of course, Nick's involvement in two wars—WWI and the Greco-Turkish war of 1922—which brought him face to face with many kinds of losses, especially of life and ideals. As I have already discussed, Nick was so shaken by his encounter with the pregnant woman on the road to Karagatch, an encounter that certainly included violent pain and possibly death, that he created two stories out of it. The several other narratives of *In Our Time* depicting the violence and senselessness of war ("On the Quai at Smyrna" and chaps. 3, 4, 5, and 7) emphasize Nick's obsession with these matters.

And as if we needed further evidence, the bullfighting chapters (9–14) reinforce the extent and nature of Nick's fixation. Nick, we recall, has declared that "His whole inner life had been bullfights all one year" [138], and thus he implies that these narratives represent his inner experience as much as his actual experience. In general, these six chapters repeat themes and images found in the earlier war chapters: men and animals being maimed and killed, cowardice, fear, rare stoicism in the face of death, even rarer triumphs over the enemy, be it man or beast. However, the most interesting chapter in terms of Nick's mental state is the last one, in which Nick "kills off" his friend, the matador Maera, a man who, as Nick's monologue makes clear, is still living. By projecting Maera's death, Nick seems to be preparing himself for the inevitable, the loss of another comrade like Rinaldi, whose situation in chapter 6 closely resembles Maera's: both men lie face down, silent, still, unable to defend themselves, waiting for stretchers to carry them off the field.

In "Big Two-Hearted River," we find another hint at how much Nick is bothered by losing friends when he thinks about Hopkins, a memory associated with bitterness and one he is glad exhaustion prevents him from contemplating further. Hopkins seems to have disappeared suddenly from Nick's circle of comrades—because of either death or wealth—for "They never saw Hopkins again," despite

---

9. See the epigraph to *TSAR* [*Editor*].

plans for a fishing trip the next summer [117]. As Nick says in the excised conclusion to "Big Two-Hearted River"—in a statement that refers to artists but seems to have more general applications— "They died and that was the hell of it. They worked all their lives and then got old and died" [140]. In sum, part of what brought Nick to the Big Two-Hearted River is the same thing that brought him to writing: a need to come to terms with all the loss he has experienced in the last few years and, equally important, the loss he has come to expect.

That Nick takes his trip to upper Michigan to restore both his mind and spirit debilitated by war has, of course, been the accepted reading of "Big Two-Hearted River" ever since critics began to assess the story formally. Hence, my analysis so far has primarily enabled me to clarify the state of Nick's mind, the memories which are troubling him. However, an important question regarding Nick's trip which has never been satisfactorily settled is why he waits so long after the war to take it. Many readers of *In Our Time* have assumed that its Nick stories are arranged chronologically so that the Nick who appears in "Cross-Country Snow," the husband and soon-to-be father, is slightly younger than the Nick who appears in "Big Two-Hearted River." But if this chronology is correct, then we somehow have to explain why Nick, who seems healthy in "Cross-Country Snow," could suddenly become so unstable that he must take off to the Michigan woods to escape "the need for thinking, the need to write, other needs."

In 1972, Philip Young resolved Nick's apparent about-face by reversing the order of these two stories in *The Nick Adams Stories*. "Big Two-Hearted River" takes place, he asserted, immediately after World War I; "Cross-Country Snow" follows, displaying the success of Nick's recuperative journey to the river.[1] Yet Hemingway's original conclusion to "Big Two-Hearted River" disputes this rearrangement, for in it Nick mentions Helen and discusses the reactions his friends have had to his marriage. Obviously, when Hemingway wrote this story he saw Nick as a married man, someone who had been back from the war for some time. But even without this external evidence, we should still, I think, date "Big Two-Hearted River" several years after the war. Support for this proposal lies in the stories that Nick has written, especially in those that come after chapter 6 describing Nick's wounding.

The non-Nick stories that follow this chapter might seem, simply by virtue of their point of view, to be based less on Nick's actual experience and more on his imagination than those narratives in

---

1. See the Preface to *The Nick Adams Stories* [New York: Bantam, 1973; subsequently, in this essay, *NAS*], p. v.

which his namesake plays a central role. However, without biographical evidence we cannot prove this. Given some of the parallels
between Nick's ideas stated in the excised "Big Two-Hearted River"
monologue and those presented in the non-Nick stories, it appears
that Nick is still drawing heavily from his life. To repeat an earlier
example, Nick claims that the war was made unreal by too much
talking, an assertion that sounds very similar to Harold Krebs's discovery that "to be listened to at all he had to lie, and after he had
done this twice he, too, had a reaction against the war and against
talking about it" [55].

Why Nick should choose to present some of his experiences through
the medium of his alter ego and other experiences through varying
viewpoints could have to do, therefore, with his sensitivity to certain
subjects. In other words, Nick might romanticize a protagonist named
after himself yet be willing to describe his most painful, embarrass-
ing, and passionate experiences when safely shielded—from both his
readers and himself—behind a more opaque persona. Young maintains that this is the approach Hemingway took in his writing: "he
tended to smuggle certain things away in his fiction; if they were com-
promising or shameful and he wanted to get rid of them he chose
masks much less transparent than Nick's."[2] In a classic psychoana-
lytic paradox, the closer the matter is to Nick the writer, the further
away Nick the character is likely to be. The non-Nick stories can
thus hold the key to Nick's innermost secrets and fears.

The area of chronology provides the first clue that the non-Nick
stories reflect those anxieties that trouble Nick most deeply. As we
have seen, the first half of *In Our Time* traces the growth of Nick's
alter ego from a young boy to a young man, almost qualifying it as
a bildungsroman. However, throughout the rest of the stories, except
for "My Old Man," the age of the male protagonist remains steady,
from late teens to mid twenties, or approximately Nick's age at the
time he wrote these narratives. And while an age correspondence
between the male characters in the non-Nick stories and Nick himself does not definitely prove that the former are fictional alter egos,
it does seem more than just a coincidence that Nick has written so
many stories about men who are basically his age or a bit younger.

Moreover, these men share more with Nick than simply his age.
Excluding the narrator of "The Revolutionist" (whose story may or
may not be founded in Nick's history), all of these men are pictured
in situations which we know—from the discarded conclusion to "Big
Two-Hearted River"—that Nick himself has recently experienced,
specifically, returning from the war and getting married. Once again,

2. "'Big World Out There': The Nick Adams Stories," p. 43.

we cannot be sure how directly Nick has drawn from his own life in creating these stories, and so the more general patterns and attitudes are what most concern us.

In the two stories about recovering soldiers, "A Very Short Story" and "Soldier's Home," the protagonists attempt to engage in normal civilian life, yet find this participation difficult. The anonymous soldier's plans for such a life are foiled when Luz jilts him; Harold Krebs is simply repulsed by the hypocrisy of post-war America and its middle-class lifestyle. However, both men react, rather than act, and consequently lose the chance to control their own destinies. The soldier rebounds from Luz into the arms of a nameless salesgirl who gives him not love but gonorrhea. Krebs surrenders to his family's demands to lie and to get a job, and thereby contributes to the hypocrisy he detests. These stories thus show us men who are greatly confused about their futures after returning from the war.

Significantly, the problems that the soldier and Krebs have adjusting to life-after-the-war center as much on women as on making the transition from a military to a civilian lifestyle. The soldier had been ready to change his life radically upon returning to America. He was going to give up both alcohol and his friends; all he wanted was to get a job and get married. He blames Luz for destroying that dream. Krebs "would have liked to have a girl" [57], but he dreads the consequences, i.e., the complications involved in close relationships. The difficulties that these two men have with women prepare us for the three non-Nick stories preceding "Cross-Country Snow," the so-called marriage group of *In Our Time*. In these stories— "Mr. and Mrs. Elliot," "Cat in the Rain," and "Out of Season"—we observe the disintegration of three marriages. And although each relationship is falling apart for its own reason, the disintegration always hinges on an awareness of the disparity between the ideal and the real.

This awareness is revealed directly in "Mr. and Mrs. Elliot," for both partners had kept themselves "pure" [69] but were equally disappointed on their wedding night. The physical insufficiency of their lovemaking is more than just sexual frustration. Despite their efforts, they cannot conceive what they most desire: a child. In "Cat in the Rain" and "Out of Season," the general cause of the couples' discontent is more subtly conveyed, but a key phrase indicates that, once again, it comes down to unfulfilled expectations. The wife in the former story compares herself to the cat outside her hotel window when she declares, first, that "It isn't *any fun* to be a poor kitty out in the rain" and, then, that "If I can't have long hair or *any fun*, I can have a cat" [77]; my emphasis). Like the cat in the rain, she feels shut out, unwanted, unnoticed, unloved; she and her husband do not make each other happy anymore. In "Out of Season" the husband voices a similar sentiment when he sends his wife back to the hotel with: "It's a rotten day and we aren't going to have *any fun*, anyway" ([84]; my emphasis). The concentration in both stories on a lack of fun recalls Nick's reason for breaking up with Marjorie in "The End of Something": "It isn't fun any more" [25]. "Isn't love any fun?" Marjorie asks. "No," Nick answers; and so might the couples in "Mr. and Mrs. Elliot," "Cat in the Rain," and "Out of Season."

Thus, the marriage group, "A Very Short Story," and "Soldier's Home" present us with a series of portraits of failed love and/or overall dissatisfaction with male-female relationships. Such a consistently unflattering picture of love calls into question the state of Nick's own marriage. In the dropped ending to "Big Two-Hearted River," Nick says that when he married Helen he lost all his old friends "because he admitted by marrying that something was more important than the fishing" [136]. Although this sounds like a positive statement about his marriage, Nick contradicts himself when he says that he loved his fishing days "more than anything" and admits that he has nightmares about missing a fishing season: "It made him feel sick in the dream, as though he had been in jail" [137].

Nick makes one other seemingly positive remark about marriage in this monologue, when he says that he remembers the horror he once had of marriage: "It was funny. Probably it was because he had always been with older people, nonmarrying people" [136]. But even this confession does not indicate Nick's true feelings; marriage may not be a horror, but it also might not be a piece of cake. In "Cross-Country Snow" Nick's alter ego is similarly ambiguous. When George says—about life in general, including marriage, parenthood, responsibility—"It's hell, isn't it?" Nick responds, "No. Not exactly" [92–93]. Not exactly? Why not "Definitely not"?

In fact, the most important thing we learn about Helen may be that she's never about. In "Cross-Country Snow" Nick and George ski the mountains of Switzerland without Helen. In "Big Two-Hearted River" Nick takes his fishing trip alone. This habitual absence of Helen combined with the attitude toward relationships revealed in Nick's stories suggests that Nick's marriage is one of those "other needs" which has motivated his journey to the Michigan woods in "Big Two-Hearted River." Significantly, a later Nick Adams story, "Now I Lay Me," ends with Nick thinking, "He was going back to America and he was very certain about marriage and knew it would fix up everything" (*NAS*, p. 134). This piece of anachronistic evidence substantiates the patterns implied by and within *In Our Time*: upon Nick's return from Europe to America, he jumped into marriage, viewing it (at least in part) as a salve for his mental war wounds. However, he has since discovered that, far from healing anything, marriage has actually aggravated his pain. Nick's feelings about Helen thus make up the darker depths of the swamp he must one day fish.

In Our Time reveals one final other need which has possibly sent Nick to the river and which seems to be among those darker depths of his own mental swamp: the duties of fatherhood. As I have noted, Nick was greatly upset by his meeting with the pregnant woman on the road to Karagatch, and the horror of that scene is, of course, enough to explain Nick's preoccupation with it. But, in fact, the several other references to pregnancy and children in the book indicate that this preoccupation has expanded into a generalization. The British narrator of "On the Quai at Smyrna" cannot forget the Greek women who were having babies, particularly those who refused to give up their dead babies. They were the worst, he declares [7]. Mr. and Mrs. Elliot try, without success, to have a child, even though Mrs. Elliot obviously finds sex with her husband distasteful or painful—or both. In "Cross-Country Snow" Nick assumes the German waitress is unhappy because she is pregnant but unmarried. Nowhere in *In Our Time* are the joys of pregnancy and young children described. Whenever mentioned, children and having babies are associated with suffering, unhappiness, an end of freedom and innocence, even death. As Jackson J. Benson puts it, "we are brought back again and again to pain, mutilation and death in connection with birth, sex, and the female."[3]

A likely source of this association for Nick was his encounter with the woman in Asia Minor, but given this view, he would certainly face the prospect of fatherhood with great trepidation. "Cross-Country Snow" exhibits that fear both directly and obliquely. Nick tells George that he is glad *now* about Helen's pregnancy, a distinction which points to his initial displeasure. However, the lie of that assertion is shown in his reaction to the pregnant waitress: he fails to notice her condition immediately and wonders why. The psychological answer is that to do so would mean allowing the reality of his married life to interfere with the happiness of his skiing excursion. Once again, in writing about himself, Nick reveals a desire to avoid those adult responsibilities which inhibit freedom and complicate life. To have a child means one can no longer be a child.

Neither "Big Two-Hearted River" nor its original conclusion contains any explicit evidence that Nick is or is about to become a father. Yet if we see these various references to children as representative of Nick's feelings about fatherhood and if we assume that "Cross-Country Snow" is based in Nick's experience, then perhaps the lack of evidence itself is important. In other words, through his silence,

---

3. "Ernest Hemingway as Short Story Writer," in *The Short Stories of Ernest Hemingway*, ed. Benson, pp. 287–88.

Nick could be revealing just how painful the whole matter of children has become; he does not even trust himself to think or talk about it. Thus, his impending or actual fatherhood is the most recent need that urged Nick's trip to the Michigan woods, even the one that may have directly motivated it. Interestingly, "Big Two-Hearted River" is immediately preceded by "My Old Man." Although this story depicts a strong father-son relationship, the positive image is offset by the story's conclusion with the father dead and the son feeling assaulted by life's realities. The characters form a composite of Nick, who seems near to a spiritual death, burdened by anxieties that include his memories of war, married life, and fatherhood. He thus turns to the one great pleasure which has never failed him, the one activity he knows will allow him to escape the world that is too much with him: fishing.

This explanation of Nick's actions in "Big Two-Hearted River" may make him sound much like the character he writes about who shares his name: constantly running away from suffering and responsibility. And Nick definitely possesses that desire; his fiction shows that he wishes there were some kind of escape hatch, a way out, a way back to a more carefree, careless time. However, we must be careful not to confuse Nick the writer with Nick the character. And here is where approaching *In Our Time* as if Nick were its author begins to change our understanding of both the book and Nick Adams. In "Fathers and Sons," a later Nick Adams story—both in terms of when it was written and when it takes place—Nick announces, "If he wrote it he could get rid of it. He had gotten rid of many things by writing them" (*NAS*, p. 237). Although this confession is anachronistic in reference to my present study, writing often serves as catharsis. If we view Nick's work as partly an act of exorcism, then we can assume that the Nick who has written a story is one step further on the road to health than the Nick who writes the story and two steps ahead of the Nick who is described in the story.

But we should not be overly generous in formulating this assumption, for the patterns I have found throughout *In Our Time* indicate that Nick also has not been able to heal himself in the space of one or two tales. In fact, what begins as an act of purging can end as an act of control, an attempt to contain the emotions that are playing havoc with one's insides. The repetitions of loss, suffering, violence, and general unhappiness in Nick's fiction suggest that his recent experiences have dug so deeply into his psyche that he must continually bring them out, look them in the face, and thereby convince himself that by controlling them, they are not controlling him. And even though Nick has yet to admit to others—and possibly even to himself—that he fears such things as marriage and fatherhood, his fiction reveals that at some level he recognizes these anxieties. Such awareness is the first step toward conquering his fears.

The escape that he typically shows his namesake seeking is, therefore, not a real option for Nick the writer. Nick's fiction is his greatest effort to face life and himself. In fact, had Hemingway kept the original ending to "Big Two-Hearted River," we would have had a much clearer picture of the artist as hero. In the last scene of this conclusion, Nick returns to camp to write a story which will describe the country like Cézanne had painted it, a story very similar to the one we have just read. Lest we underestimate the significance of that enterprise—and with Nick's announcement that he writes because "It was really more fun than anything" [139] it would be easy to do so—we should remember that writing is not only one of those needs from which Nick was seeking relief, but it is also an activity that will undoubtedly engage him in another need he had hoped to escape: thinking. To put this another way, in the act of writing, Nick will *have* to fish that symbolic mental swamp, an effort which, in the final version of "Big Two-Hearted River," he is not quite ready to make. Of course, just how honestly and fully Nick will confront what troubles him (especially those "other needs" which are so new and sensitive that he cannot even name them, as if to do so would be to admit their reality and his own limitations) is another matter and one we cannot gauge since it occurs outside the pages and time period of *In Our Time*. The book is a record of how Nick has been and is, not how he will be.

As this record of Nick's recent mental history, *In Our Time* should thus be seen as a novel, not merely a collection of short stories. D. H. Lawrence, one of the book's first reviewers, came close to making this assessment when he called *In Our Time* a "fragmentary novel," and Young once proposed that it was "nearly a novel" about Nick.[4] However, as I have argued, although Nick's mind is fragmented, confused to pieces by his accelerated entry into adulthood, *In Our Time* is not at all fragmentary. It is a complete work, unified by the consciousness of Nick Adams as he attempts to come to terms through his fiction with his involvement in World War I and, more recently, with the problems of marriage and his fear of fatherhood. Furthermore, reading the book from this perspective removes our focus from Hemingway's biographical sources, a focus which has too often caused critics to juggle the sequence of the stories in an attempt to make their chronology match the order of events in Hemingway's life or to state simply that *In Our Time* lacks structural unity. To the contrary, the stories are ordered precisely to

4. *Ernest Hemingway: A Reconsideration*, p. 32.

reflect the actual history and the psychological state of Nick Adams. As F. Scott Fitzgerald suggested in 1926, *In Our Time* does not pretend to be about one man, but it is.[5]

Finally, though, we do come back to Hemingway. For while this analysis of *In Our Time* has separated Nick Adams' history from Hemingway's in ways that are important to our understanding of the book, it has also revealed that Nick's inner life is similar to that of his creator in areas that readers have often failed to notice. First of all, although two of Hemingway's most recent biographers, Jeffrey Meyers and Kenneth Lynn, challenge earlier conclusions about the effects of Hemingway's participation in World War I on his psyche, there can be no doubt that at some level he was significantly affected.[6] Both point out that Hemingway was obsessed by the fear of loss; as Lynn puts it, Hemingway always sank into a depression "whenever he lost anything, whether good or bad."[7] It seems possible that this obsession grew out of his experiences in the war, or at least increased after that time. Second, and just as important, Meyers and Lynn both show that Hemingway was afraid that marriage and fatherhood would change his life drastically, and for the worse. According to Meyers, "he was too emotionally immature (despite his wide experience) to accept domestic and paternal responsibility."[8] Thus we can claim for Hemingway what we have claimed for Nick, that, as Lynn argues, "Uncertain to the point of fear about himself, he was compelled to write stories in which he endeavored to cope with the disorder of his inner world by creating fictional equivalents for it."[9]

Yet it is Hemingway's initial inclination to turn over his stories to Nick that gives us our most fascinating look into his psyche. Besides the possibility that Hemingway recognized that making Nick the author of his stories would help unify *In Our Time*, we can also infer that by this plan he could add another layer of insulation between himself and the truths contained in his stories. Apparently the distance provided by a fictional persona was not enough room for a man whose greatest fiction was rapidly becoming the lies he passed off

5. Fitzgerald's exact words are that the book "takes on an almost autobiographical tint"— "How to Waste Material: A Note on My Generation," *Bookman*, 63 (1926), 264.
6. Meyers states that "Hemingway's wound, far from being psychologically traumatic (as Philip Young has argued in an influential book), had an extraordinarily positive effect on his life," although he also proposes that after Agnes von Kurowsky jilted him, Hemingway probably "lost his perilous balance and began to suffer the delayed psychological effects of shell shock"—*Hemingway: A Biography* (New York: Harper & Row, 1985), pp. 35, 46. Lynn argues that Hemingway's anxiety about his wounding in World War I did not occur until after World War II, when he was suffering deep depression and thinking of suicide (p. 106).
7. *Hemingway*, p. 160. Meyers simply states that the sense of loss was one of Hemingway's great themes (p. 145).
8. *Hemingway: A Biography*, p. 182.
9. *Hemingway*, p. 10.

to friends, relatives, critics, and himself as the truth about his life.[1] Hence, in his original conclusion to "Big Two-Hearted River," Hemingway was engaging Nick Adams in the new capacity of author to run interference for him, to block out what he had disclosed about himself to himself (and others) in the writing of his fiction.

However, despite Hemingway's desire, which increased as he got older, to deny that he was troubled, immature, or anything less than a courageous man, *In Our Time* suggests—as it does for Nick—that finally he could not deceive himself. Norman Mailer once said that "It may even be that the final judgment on [Hemingway's] work may come to the notion that what he failed to do was tragic, but what he accomplished was heroic, for it is possible he carried a weight of anxiety within him from day to day which would have suffocated any man smaller than himself."[2] Hemingway's public image still persists as that of a brave man constantly proving himself in battles with both men and animals. *In Our Time* reveals, through the unifying consciousness of Nick Adams, a more substantial kind of bravery, for it indicates that the greatest opponent he wrestled with was himself.

LINDA W. WAGNER

Juxtaposition in Hemingway's *In Our Time*[†]

Hemingway's first collection of stories and vignette interchapters is perhaps his most striking work, in terms of both personal involvement and technical innovation. Thematically, all the later Hemingway writing is here in embryo—the fruitless if still polite marriages, the understated agony of war (both military and personal), veneration for the old but unbeaten, censure for the uncaring and unjust, and the fascination with the way man meets death. The Nick Adams/ Hemingway persona, regardless of his fictional name, is as effective in these early stories as he is ever to be; and Malcolm Cowley, for

---

1. Nearly all of Hemingway's biographers have emphasized his tendency to lie about his life. For example, Carlos Baker notes that this inclination began early: "Since the age of four he had delighted in tall tales, usually with himself as hero. Now that he was nineteen, the content had merely become a little more worldly"—*Ernest Hemingway: A Life Story* (New York: Scribner's, 1969), p. 56. Michael Reynolds states simply that Hemingway found that writing allowed him to "create his life exactly as he wished it to be, and eventually come to believe it"—*The Young Hemingway* (Oxford: Blackwell, 1986), p. 149.
2. "Punching Papa," *New York Review of Books*, 1 (Special Issue, 1963), 13.
† From *Studies in Short Fiction* 12.3 (Summer 1975): 243–52. Reprinted with permission of Copyright Management Services, LLP on behalf of *Studies in Short Fiction*. Some of the author's notes have been omitted. Page numbers in brackets refer to this Norton Critical Edition.

one, thinks this collection may be Hemingway's best, most fully realized, work.[1]

Technically, too, the book is a masterpiece of that most intriguing device, juxtaposition. Brought to artistic attention early in the century through movies and graphic art, this practice of essentially omitting transition, of placing one concrete image against another, edge on edge, was also an outgrowth of Joyce's *Ulysses* and Pound's *Cantos*. The position of each story, and its relationship to what surrounds it, is crucial in creating the total effect of *In Our Time*, just as it had been in Hemingway's 1924 vignette collection, the lower case *in our time*. Situating his longer stories within the vignettes of this earlier book was effective partly because it placed the burden of association on the reader, and partly because the more formal stories—which usually concerned personal and relatively slight happenings—were thus coupled with the pieces that focused on war, honor, man against death. As Hemingway had explained to Edmund Wilson, the arrangement was intended "to give the picture of the whole between examining it in detail. Like looking with your eyes at something, say a passing coast line, and then looking at it with 15x binoculars."[2]

Hemingway's progression in *IOT* combines a chronological arrangement (the stories) with a largely thematic one (the vignettes). The shorter sketches move from World War I to bullfighting, thus taking the reader from the question of man's honor as determined by the relatively impersonal forces of war, to man's honor as self-determined. The order of the vignettes varies somewhat from their sequence in the earlier *iot*; Chapter IX, for example, originally appeared as Chapter II, as bullfighting was paired with war in order to give what were presumably the author's first views of each: war, in Chapter I, appears at first to be a huge, unruly drunk to the new kitchen corporal; bullfighting, conversely, seems to be an unpleasant blood ritual.[3] Successive glimpses of each, however, educate the observer more fully.

The studies of war emphasize death and the way men, including Nick, prepare to meet it. But another theme in *iot* is that of man's fear, stemming often from his ignorance—the soldier's fear during the shelling, Sam Cardinella's and the typhoid victim's, the Chicago policeman's fear of the very "wops" Hemingway admired so greatly. And a further connecting theme is that of man's responsibility. It is

1. Cowley's comment on the CBC [Canadian Broadcasting Corporation] radio broadcast, aired 1970. * * *
2. Quoted in *The Shores of Light* (New York: Farrar, Straus and Young, Inc., 1952), p. 122. Letter dated October 18, 1924 [see 153].
3. * * * In the 1925 collection, two of the earlier vignettes were titled and used as stories proper, "The Revolutionist" and "A Very Short Story." Names and places in the latter were changed for the 1925 publication.

the bull that gores Maera, but *men* let him die. All the deaths that Hemingway records in the vignettes occur because of men, whether they are performing under the guise of patriotism or justice.

In the 1925 *IOT*, the stories trace these same themes but more obliquely. The first stories reflect Nick's boyhood response to his parents, then his broken romance; Hemingway takes us briefly to war, then to a marriage, and finally to Nick's trying in "Big Two-Hearted River" to re-establish himself, ostensibly after his war experience but perhaps too after his years of battering loves. At the end of *IOT*, Nick is alone, happily alone. And it is this essential tranquility that in retrospect heightens the tension and sorrow of the preceding pieces. By finally seeing what is possible for Nick, we can better understand the real torment of Krebs, Nick, or Maera. The calm of "River" would be much less moving were it not surrounded by the deaths of Maera and Sam Cardinella: Nick is managing to save himself; other men— for various reasons—could not. A further dimension to Nick's endurance in this two-part story is given in the recently-published section "On Writing," which was once included as the ending of "River," Part II. Here Nick speaks movingly of his future life as writer [138–40] and we see that as much of his composure comes from his belief in his writing as in his pleasure from fishing.

What occurs in *IOT*, as in the best collections of fiction, is that the powerful cumulative effect of the prose obscures the force of many single pieces. The book is unified, finally, by its organ base[4] of tone—a mood of unrelieved somberness if not outright horror. The mood is even more striking because it is given the reader so objectively, with such control that he is caught in the tension resulting from the discrepancy between what is said and how it is said. The short reportorial nature of the prose in the vignettes is particularly effective in creating the objective tone.

Throughout the collection, Hemingway's arrangement contributes a great deal to the creation of this mood. "On the Quai at Smyrna," the preface vignette that was added in the 1930 edition, makes explicit both the devastation of war/life and man's protective coldness toward it. This detached recounting of incredible human misery during evacuation intensifies the tragedy, once the reader realizes the gap between what is meant and the understatement of the narrator. Here Hemingway doubles on his irony; the speaker is not one of Hemingway's heroes but a refined dolt—British, as in Chapter V— who may not really see the horror. His detachment is consequently open to question, unlike the self-protective attitudes of Krebs or Nick later. "You couldn't get the women to give up their dead babies. They'd

---

have babies dead for six days. Wouldn't give them up. Nothing you could do about it" [7]. The effect here of death and bereavement *en masse* prepares the reader for the close-up stories to follow, and for their parallel tone.

While the vignettes deal with death, and subconsciously make us search for our joys, most of the stories proper deal with kinds of love—yet, because their outlook is often so bleak, we realize that the stories too are studies of death. In "Indian Camp" and "The Doctor and the Doctor's Wife," the opening stories, Hemingway portrays the death of Nick's feeling for his parents. The pompous answers of the doctor—who should understand men but doesn't—are played against the Indian husband's unspoken act of contrition, and Uncle George's unspoken hatred. Nick's mock delusion at the end of the story (knowing he will never die) is modified in the next tale when he comes to understand the fantasy worlds of both his parents, working against each other and making him their only point of contact, and contest.

After this introduction, Nick comes of age. The next two stories, "The End of Something" and "The Three-Day Blow," recount his broken romance, his chagrin at not being his own man, and his subsequent drunk. Slight stories, they reinforce Nick's isolation, and prepare for stories like "The Battler" and the sequence of four marriage stories where Hemingway observes what can happen to people who live without real love. Ad Francis, "the battler," lives in delusion not because he's been beaten so much, but because his wife has left him ("He was busting people all the time after she went away" [47]). The Elliots' perversion occurs seemingly because they are too selfish to care about each other, as are many of the characters in the more suggestive love stories. The Marjorie stories also, ironically, prepare the reader for the haunting sense of disbelief in "Cat in the Rain," "Out of Season," and "Cross-Country Snow" as the hero grows out of his earlier illusions about love and marriage just as he had earlier grown out of his illusions about his parents and Bill. As Nick was to say in analyzing the problems of the people around him, "You had this fake ideal planted in you and then you lived your life to it" [137].

Fittingly, at the very center of the book Hemingway has placed "Soldier's Home," the powerful story that so well summarizes his primary theme in *IOT*, one man's alienation from his culture, even from—or especially from—those who love him. Yet the story is not a romantic hero-against-society indictment; the values of the parents and the culture are not entirely to blame for his isolation. Krebs is himself bewildered; it is too soon after his war experience; he recognizes the games he will have to play, but he is not yet ready to play them. Krebs needs time. And Hemingway gives him time by placing Nick's resolution in "River" as far away as possible, at the end of the book. What Krebs sees as tentative—that he will some-day have to find a job and a girl and a place in this world—Nick has accepted. (He *will* carry those heavy cans of spaghetti and beans so that he can enjoy them for supper, knowing he has paid the price.)

"Soldier's Home" is a central story too in that Hemingway here first expresses his ethic of virtue: "All of the times that had been able to make him feel cool and clear inside himself when he thought of them; the times so long back when he had done the one thing, the only thing for a man to do, easily and naturally, when he might have done something else . . ." [55]. * * * Each man acts as he needs to act.

Similarly, Hemingway uses the idea of choice to draw negative characters. In "Cat in the Rain," George goes back to his book, instead of giving his wife the love she so apparently needs; Nick breaks up with Marjorie, but because Bill wants him to, not because he wants to. * * * It is interesting that Hemingway's characterization grows more positive in the later writing: he spends less time and effort drawing characters who are not in some way valuable.

Even in this tendency to interrelate characters, Hemingway shows an awareness of the cumulative effects of his writing. Knowing one novel prepares us to understand another, just as we can more fully understand a single story in *IOT* by seeing the way it fits into, and participates in, the whole.

Yet, the collection is a whole, and not merely a collection, and like any novel, it gains strength from likely beginnings and endings. Just as Hemingway was to use epigraphs as a means of clarifying his intention in his novels, and "On the Quai" as preface piece to this book, so he closed *IOT* with another purposeful vignette.

"L'Envoi" completes the emptiness of the collection for, even though Hemingway has seemingly ended on a positive note with "River," the victory that exists there is a victory only for Nick—and a partial one at that. The victory is meaningless for the culture, the times, or for any other character in Hemingway's fiction. "L'Envoi" repeats the limitation, with a more ironic slant: the king finds his happiness on a very limited basis (physically limited as well as emo-tionally), resting on his fallacious dream to retain his optimism and contentment. The last lines suggest that delusions are all we have, but perhaps they are better than nothing. That this "meaning" is itself irony, and that Hemingway disagrees with the king's outlook, is clear only when we read the stories as a unit: neither Krebs nor Nick deludes himself. Krebs will not say the right things to his mother, just as Nick will not yet try the swamp. * * *

Crucial as juxtaposition is in creating the whole of *IOT*, it is per-haps even more important as a device within each story, particularly in achieving the suggestive quality Hemingway admired. In "Indian Camp," for example, he uses only a single passage of juxtaposition to tell the reader, with no direct statement, why the Indian husband was superior to the white doctor:

> Just then the woman cried out.
> "Oh, Daddy, can't you give her something to make her stop screaming?" asked Nick.
> "No. I haven't any anaesthetic," his father said. "But her screams are not important. I don't hear them because they are not important."
> The husband in the upper bunk rolled over against the wall. [12]

Carefully, as in all his writing, Hemingway has prepared us for this effect: we have seen Nick's earlier, more objective reaction against the woman suddenly change when she screams. We have been convinced with the doctor's scientific explanations for everything; now the question of "Why no anaesthetic?" rears its head, and we are no longer reassured even though he repeats, as if to mesmerize Nick, that her screams are not important. In the next passage Hemingway is to blacken the doctor further with his apparently justifiable attention to washing his hands. Because he describes the washing operation three times, our suspicions are aroused, only to be confirmed when he tells us, in another masterful juxtaposition, both how dirty the surroundings are and that his father's cleanliness is more obsessive than practical:

> When he was satisfied with his hands, he went in and went to work.
> "Pull back that quilt, will you, George?" he said. "I'd rather not touch it." [12]

The responses of the other men in the story—Uncle George's distance from the doctor, the husband's rolling silently in his humane empathy—are necessary to the story so that we can more clearly understand the rightness of Nick's instinctive responses and the weakness of his father's. Through juxtaposition, Hemingway compares the reactions of these four characters even before the more definite resolution of the story.

In "Soldier's Home," Krebs' reaction against his mother's cloying platitudes is never expressed. It is conveyed only through a graphic one-line description:

> "I've worried about you so much, Harold," his mother went on. "I know the temptations you must have been exposed to. I know how weak men are. I know what your own dear grandfather, my own father, told us about the Civil War and I have prayed for you. I pray for you all day long, Harold."

> Krebs looked at the bacon fat hardening on his plate.
> "Your father is worried, too," his mother went on . . . [60]

Similarly, in "Cat in the Rain," Hemingway uses the kindly old hotel padrone as a contrast to the young husband, George. This story has a less apparent resolution, Hemingway working almost entirely through juxtaposition:

> They went back along the gravel path and passed in the door. The maid stayed outside to close the umbrella. As the American girl passed the office, the padrone bowed from his desk. Something felt very small and tight inside the girl. The padrone made her feel very small and at the same time really important. She had a momentary feeling of being of supreme importance. She went on up the stairs. She opened the door of the room. George was on the bed, reading. [76]

In six words, Hemingway tellingly dims the warm glow he has worked so hard to establish. The rest of the story only reinforces our knowledge of the dulling relationship between husband and wife.

"Cat in the Rain," "The End of Something"—many of the stories in *IOT* are sometimes maligned because of their lack of "plot," of resolution. The problem again seems to be one of terminology. *Plot* to mean prescriptive action, action that points to a moral, was too artificial to appeal to either Ezra Pound or Hemingway. As Pound had written, "Life for the most part does not happen in neat little diagrams and nothing is more tiresome than the continual pretence that it does."[5] Hemingway would favor using *plot* to mean motion. He seldom wrote a static story. Its movement might be circular, might bring the reader back—or at least close to—its initial mood, but the very motion would be the means of telling the story, just as the fact that the story did circle would be integral to its "meaning." The exhilaration of skiing in "Cross-Country Snow" both opens and closes the story, yet within its brief compass Hemingway has conveyed the tension in the young marriage because of the coming of the child (a situation so expertly foreshadowed in the behavior of the pregnant waitress). The story suggests the change in life style, the change in the marriage, and the change in Nick and George's friendship, all through the objective correlative of skiing. That act itself is described by Hemingway as the epitome of physical freedom in its "rush and sudden swoop," the very freedom that in other ways forms the theme of the story. In 1955 Hemingway described his concept of movement in fiction: "Everything changes as it moves. That is what makes the movement which makes the story. Sometimes the

---

5. Ezra Pound, *Literary Essays of Ezra Pound* (Norfolk, Conn.: New Directions Press, 1935), p. 401.

movement is so slow it does not seem to be moving. But there is always change and always movement."[6]

With Hemingway, there is also always a reason for his inclusion—as, above, the fact that the surly waitress was pregnant, and that it was Nick in his sensitivity to the situation who was aware of her pregnancy. No character, no scene, no line of description remains in a story without some credible justification (the chief difference between his fiction and nonfiction seems to be the discursiveness of the latter). He often complained about some modern writing as being "crude and defective in art": "Many of their novels are without unity of plot and action. The story is at times tediously spun out, running on and on like the tale of a garrulous storyteller. They seem to have little idea of what the next chapter of their novel will contain. And sometimes they drag in strange and unnecessary scenes with no apparent reason whatever."[7]

Hemingway's insistence on justifying everything in the story can also be seen in his choice of titles. Titles are of two kinds: either they signal the objective focus of the fiction, or they contain definite and expressible irony, as with "The Revolutionist," who is shy and gentle, or "The Battler," pathetic instead of fierce. With deeper irony, Hemingway chooses "Indian Camp" so that he can play on the connotations of the supposedly dirty and insensitive Indians in the opening of the story, and thus reverse our expectations of their behavior in the course of the action. That his father had no anaesthesia (as well as no sympathy) for the woman surely stemmed in part from his reaction against her race. And "Soldier's Home" with its echo of "old folks' home" or "veterans' home" catches the reader off-balance twice—first when he realizes that Krebs is in his own home, where people love him, and therefore better off than someone in a "home"; and again, when he realizes that his first take is wrong, and that in Krebs' home love is used—albeit unintentionally—to control instead of to protect.

Such separation in kinds of titles is, with Hemingway, arbitrary at best, for even the simpler titles carry double weight. "Three-Day Blow" and "Cross-Country Snow" refer to Nick's emotional state as well as to the weather, just as "The End of Something" describes three things, the mill, the love affair, and Nick's illusions; and "Cat in the Rain," both the woman and the animal.

The result of this extremely tight writing is that the reader must value every word, every scene, every character in his reaction to the fiction. Hemingway's comment about his writing being "suggestive"

6. *Writers at Work*, p. 226.
7. *The Uncollected Prose of Ernest Hemingway*, ed. Clinton Burhans (Michigan State University, 1967), p. 255.

is, of course, helpful; so too is his remark to William Seward that his short stories were of two kinds, "tough" and "as delicate as they come."[8] What he meant by *tough* were stories like "The Light of the World," "Indian Camp," or the Paco story, "The Capital of the World," where the sensational characters or actions nearly obliterate any less pleasant philosophical meaning. Hemingway always felt called to defend these "unpoetic" kinds of subjects, even though he was constantly using them to capture the most basic of truths.

In contrast, the "delicate" stories are the relationship stories— "The End of Something," "The Doctor and the Doctor's Wife," "Out of Season"—and Hemingway is again accurate in his choice of term: *delicate* in the sense of suggestive (although even his tough stories are primarily suggestive); but *delicate* also in his approach to subject matter. What easier focus in stories of love and marriage than sex scenes, yet there is almost no sex anywhere in *IOT*. What easier means of characterization than a conflict between two characters, but Hemingway instead presents two characters' reactions to an outside force, as with George and the doctor to the Indians, or with Bill and Wemedge to literature and romance. Such an approach is oblique perhaps, but it is also much closer to reality, where everyday events comprise the fabric of most lives. Yet from mundane and trivial happenings, something dramatic does happen: lives are formed, as Hemingway's stories so expertly show. His selection of episodes in a way parallels his objective presentation. What easier way to draw character than to tell a reader what a man is like? Hemingway instead relies almost entirely on dialogue and action. The short dialogue between Krebs and his "best" sister presents in miniature the story's theme of using love for one's own ends:

> "Am I really your girl?"
> "Sure."
> "Do you love me?"
> "Uh, huh."
> "Will you love me always?"
> "Sure."
> "Will you come over and watch me play indoor?"
> "Maybe."
> "Aw, Hare, you don't love me. If you loved me, you'd want to come over and watch me play indoor." [59]

With Hemingway, dialogue can convey information, establish character, present theme, and create tempo—even while it appears to be only repeating itself.

---

8. Seward quotes Hemingway's remark made in October, 1957, in *My Friend Ernest Hemingway* (New York: A. S. Barnes and Co., 1969), pp. 24–25.

In "Cat in the Rain," the differences in the apparently repetitious dialogue pattern signal the quickening pace of the story. Early scenes used generally short speeches and relatively polite responses; here the wife's longer, more impassioned sentences provoke George's more abrupt answers.

> "I want to pull my hair back tight and smooth and make a big knot at the back that I can feel," she said. "I want to have a kitty to sit on my lap and purr when I stroke her."
> "Yeah?" George said from the bed.
> "And I want to eat at a table with my own silver and I want candles. And I want it to be spring and I want to brush my hair out in front of a mirror and I want a kitty and I want some new clothes."
> "Oh, shut up and get something to read," George said. He was reading again. [77]

Like the varying pace of "Cat," the pace of IOT as a whole slows as it progresses, moving as it has from the war deaths and the shock of "Indian Camp" to these relationship stories where very little happens, except under the surface. Lest we miss the real tension, Hemingway employs his masterful juxtaposition; the stories occur amid bullfighting vignettes, which in themselves stress man's choice of the life and death struggle. The bullfighter struggles to live with honor; similarly, the marriage in question struggles to live—also with honor. But the bullfighting sequence goes on to an end with the great Maera dead, whereas Hemingway spares us the end of this marriage and swings back to an earlier period for the last three stories, "My Old Man" and the two parts of "Big Two-Hearted River." By ending with these stories, Hemingway broadens his interest in romantic love to include different kinds of love—one man's responsibility for another (man for son in "My Old Man" and for himself in "River" as Nick searches again to find his separate peace). The stories also remind us of the opening and recurring motifs of death. That the deaths in IOT are as often figurative ones, resulting from love as frequently as from war, foreshadows one part of the enduring Hemingway vision. And that Nick is able to find his life even after experiencing some of the inevitable dying foreshadows another side of his composite.

Critical Views of
in our time and *In Our Time*

E. R. HAGEMANN

[Time-and-History in Ernest Hemingway's
In Our Time Vignettes]†

The sixteen italicized Chapters in *In Our Time* are in five states with some ninety variant readings and total 2,552 words but only 759 different words.[1] Because Ernest Hemingway expended so much care in so few words, we should expend equal care (but not in so few words) to examine the Interchapters as an artistic unit: time-and-history, hyphenated; time-and-history as record *and* imagination, for not every detail or event is verifiable. No less than fiction, history is in direct proportion of the writer, a rearrangement of reality and, above all, time. Time-and-history is a product of memory and desire and necessarily fragmented and *dis*arranged.

These Interchapters, drypoints * * * Edmund Wilson once astutely called them, haphazard as to time as printed in *In Our Time*, become an entity when rearranged chronologically (see Appendix on page [243] for chart); for what Hemingway has done is to reconstruct a decade, 1914–1923. His choice is not random. The Great War and its aftermath were, collectively, *the* experience of his generation, the experience that dumped his peers and his elders into graves, shell-holes, hospitals, and onto gallows. These were "in our time," Hemingway is saying, and he remarks the significant and the insignificant.

---

† From "'Only Let the Story End as Soon as Possible': Time-and-History in Ernest Hemingway's *In Our Time*," in *Modern Fiction Studies* 26.2 (Summer 1980): 255–62. © 1980 The Purdue Research Foundation. Reprinted with permission of Johns Hopkins University Press. Unless otherwise indicated, notes are by the author. Some of the author's notes have been omitted. Page numbers in brackets refer to this Norton Critical Edition.

1. Without going into too much detail, the five states are "In Our Time," *Little Review*, 9 (Spring 1923), 3–5, six chapters; *in our time* (Paris: Three Mountains Press, 1924), eighteen chapters; *In Our Time* (New York: Boni & Liveright, 1925), fifteen chapters and L'Envoi, First American Edition; *In Our Time* (New York: Charles Scribner's Sons, 1930), fifteen chapters, L'Envoi, and "Introduction by the Author," pp. 9–12, Second American Edition; and *The Short Stories of Ernest Hemingway* (New York: The Modern Library, 1942).

And time, to quote the best definition I have ever read, is "the system of those relations which any event has to any other as past, present, or future. This relationship is realistically conceived as a sort of self-subsistent entity, or object of contemplation" (*The Century Dictionary and Cyclopedia* [1897]). Hemingway moves about in time and gives us sixteen vignettes for our "contemplation."

To iterate: the decade is from 1914 to 1923 inclusive. I will reconstruct it and present the what, the where, and the when so that the reader can conceive of the years as Hemingway does: "a stream flowing through the field of the present," to quote again from *Century*'s definition.

Time-and-history begins in *In Our Time* with Chapter IV ("It was a frightfully hot day") and Chapter III ("We were in a garden in Mons"). The terse narrator is Lieutenant Eric Edward Dorman-Smith, Royal Northumberland Fusiliers (Fifth Fusiliers), First Battalion, dedicatee of the 1924 edition, and a personal friend of Hemingway.

It is Sunday, 23 August 1914; the place is Mons, Belgium, where the British Expeditionary Force has set up defense along a sixteen-mile stretch of the ruler-straight Mons-Condé Canal, spanned by eighteen bridges. (Hemingway errs when he calls it a "river" in Chapter III.) Dorman-Smith's battalion is responsible for the Mariette Bridge, which he so jollily speaks of in Chapter IV. The German right wing under Alexander von Kluck went after the bridge early, despite the barricade, and sustained fearful losses as the Tommies "potted" them from "forty yards." The skirmish at the "absolutely perfect barricade" occurred prior to 5 p.m., at which time the English had to fall back and Dorman-Smith and his fellow Fusiliers were "frightfully put out" [27].

The location of the garden, Chapter III, is unclear and unverifiable, nor is it known when the incident occurred during the battle. It is possible the garden was in Mons, but the city was not in the Fifth's sector. Unfortunately, it is not mentioned in official dispatches; but then, neither is Dorman-Smith. What is important is that Hemingway introduces one of the controlling metaphors in the Chapters: The Wall. "The first German . . . climbed up over the garden wall. We waited till he got one leg over and then potted him" [21].

Mons at once entered the realm of the Glorious in English history; to the BEF, however, it was to be but the first battle in four years of Pyrrhic warfare which drained England of her manhood.

The French were drained over and over again, and Chapter I ("Everybody was drunk") points to the Champagne. The identity of the kitchen corporal will never be known, but in 112 words this hapless *poilu* [French soldier] relates a desperately comical incident as he heads for slaughter. The Champagne was not a wine but a frontal assault against an intricate German defense. After a terrific artillery preparation on 25 September 1915, the French attacked and engaged the enemy until Christmas Day. In three months they lost 145,000 men, 120,000 in the first three weeks. The Germans suffered as heavily. A French tactical victory, military experts call it. This depends on one's viewpoint; plainly, the Champagne was mass execution.

"Everybody was drunk" and no one can blame them, while the insignificant kitchen corporal wrestles with his mess in the dark, and the drunken lieutenant tells him to put it out. It can be seen. "'It was funny going along that road'" [9], muses the corporal, the road that led to the Champagne.

From execution in battle, Hemingway switches to execution in the streets of corrupt Kansas City, Missouri, in Chapter VIII ("At two o'clock in the morning two Hungarians got into a cigar store"). Maybe Hungarians did at some time but not on 19 November 1917, when two Italians, "Cap" Gargotta and Joe Musso, were killed by the cops as they fled after robbing the Parker-Gordon Cigar Company at 1028 Broadway. "They were shot on the seat of a covered wagon in which they had cigars valued at $3,000. . . . The men attempted to drive their team over the detectives ["Jack" Farrell and Carl Grantello] when ordered to stop," reported the *Kansas City Star* later the same day, not on page one but page three, so unimportant were the executions. Like Boyle says: "'They're crooks, ain't they? . . . They're wops, ain't they? Who the hell is going to make any trouble?'" [63].

Why Hemingway, who was in Kansas City working as a cub reporter on the evening *Star*, changed the ethnic origin of the robbers, although the cops in Chapter VIII do not, can be partially explained as a thematic tactic. The piece leads directly to the cryptic story "The Revolutionist," which considers a Hungarian Red who is a political refugee from Regent-Admiral Miklós Horthy's arch-reactionary regime in Hungary. If this is so, this direct carry-over, then it is the only time that such occurs in *In Our Time*.[2]

Out there on our Western home front, Italians were dead on the pavement. Wops! Out there on the Italian war front thousands upon thousands of Italians—Wops! to connote the lowly victims and not to impart ethnic slurs—were dead on the ground defending the tawdry House of Savoy on the throne of Italy in the unimpressive person of Victor Emmanuel III, Prince of Naples.

---

2. Not only did Hemingway change the ethnicity, he also changed the Kansas City street geography. The police station was not on 15th Street but at 1420 Walnut; the cigar store was not at 15th and Grand, although there were three stores elsewhere on Grand.

In Chapter VII ("While the bombardment was knocking the trench to pieces") the final Austrian offensive of the war in Italy has just begun, 15 June 1918, and initial success brings them to Fossalta on the west bank of the Piave River on the 16th; their heavy mortars batter the Italians, and the narrator (*not*, I insist, Nick Adams) madly prays to "dear jesus" to keep him "from getting killed" [53]. He has every reason to, for the Austrians were well equipped to reach their ultimate objective, the industrial heart of Italy. They failed. Perhaps the prayer helped. Whatever, the narrator never tells of Jesus when he is safe in Mestre and ascends the stairs with a whore in the Villa Róssa (Red Villa), the officers' brothel. "And he never told anybody" [53].

The time is early July 1918 in Chapter VI ("Nick sat against the wall of the church"); the place is still the Piave; but now the Italians' counterattack is underway ("Things were getting forward in the town"). Nick Adams is seriously wounded, and from his quasi-articulate words to his felled Italian comrade, Rinaldo Rinaldi, comes the germ of *A Farewell to Arms*: "'You and me we've made a separate peace. . . . Not patriots'" [49]. This is the sole appearance of the word "peace" in the Chapters. And this is the only time Hemingway permits one of his characters to speechify, if that is it, about The War. As he observed in his "Introduction" to *Men at War* (New York: Crown Publishers, 1942): "They [the various writers] had learned to tell the truth without screaming. Screaming, necessary though it may be to attract attention at the time, reads badly in later years" (p. xvi).

The incident is fictional; the battle is actual. The Austrians sustained, overall, 200,000 killed and wounded, 25,000 prisoners; the "victorious" Italians, 90,000. In his brief combat duty in 1918, Hemingway served at Fossalta di Piave and was badly shot-up during the night of 8 July.

In Chapter VIII, the Irish cops called the Hungarians Wops; in Chapter VI, Rinaldi, an Italian if not a Wop, is close to death, "breathing with difficulty" [49]; and in Chapter XV ("They hanged Sam Cardinella at six o'clock in the morning") there is another Italian, doomed long before [119]. "They" hanged him in Chicago not at six but shortly after nine in the morning on 15 April 1921, and it required eleven minutes for him to die of a broken neck. He died for the murder of one Andrew P. Bowman not quite two years previous. Cardinella was thirty-nine years old, the leader of a gang operating out of a pool room at 22nd and Clark Streets, and the father of six children. Hanged with him, but not members of his gang, were Giuseppe Costanzo and Salvatore Ferrara; a fourth victim, Antonio López, had been awarded a temporary reprieve. No Negroes died that day, Chapter XV to the contrary; rather, they died the following week. "They" hanged people in those days in Illinois, but not so many at one time since 1912 as "they" did on 15 April.

"When the death march time arrived," said the *Chicago Tribune* on the 16th, "[Cardinella] fought his guards like a maniac. . . . Finally he was carried to the scaffold in a chair, unable to stand erect, and gibbering insanely in Italian. . . . [S]till cringing in the chair, he was executed." So Hemingway does not exaggerate Cardinella's physical collapse.[3] The *Trib* does not mention the two priests, and we can surmise that Sam's final prayers (the "gibbering"?) went unrecognized by a man of God; but there was no one to respond to the young *ufficiale's* prayers in the Fossalta trench, either.

In this episode Hemingway alludes to a procession and a wall— "they came out onto the gallows through a door in the wall" [119]— and in Chapter II ("Minarets stuck up in the rain") he expands his processional metaphor. Evacuation of Eastern Thrace began on 15 October 1922, pursuant to an armistice signed at Mudania between the Turks and the Greeks. Turks would occupy the district within forty-five days. Terrorized Greek Christians—*giaours* to the Muslim Turks—thousands of them, spilled onto the road through Adrianople and beyond to Karagatch, on the other side, the western side, of the Maritza River in Western Thrace, Greek territory.

Hemingway, on assignment for the *Toronto Star*, arrived in Constantinople on 29 September. Some time subsequent to 15 October, the 16th is a safe guess, he was in the melee on the Karagatch road: "twenty miles [thirty miles in the Chapter] of carts drawn by cows, bullocks and muddy-flanked water buffalo. . . . It is a silent procession," he wrote for the paper, 20 October [145]. Greek cavalry herded the Christians along like "cow-punchers driving steers," not dissimilar to the lieutenant herding his *poilus* in Chapter I. Hemingway walked in the rain for five miles, dodging camels. Under the bridge the Maritza was running "a brick-red [yellow in the Chapter] quarter-mile wide flood."[4] And behind them "minarets stuck up in the rain."

Greeks again appear in Chapter V ("They shot the six cabinet ministers at half-past six"), and Hemingway ingeminates the "wall" in the Cardinella vignette. As elsewhere in *In Our Time* what he recounts is true and less than true, an impression based on fact; fact, in turn, readjusted to respond to memory and time, "in our time." On 22 November 1922, at approximately 11 a.m., Demetrios Gounaris, Petros Protopapadakis, and Nicholas Stratos, former prime ministers;

---

3. Oddly, Hemingway does not describe Cook County Jail but Jackson County Jail in Kansas City, and this may have led Fenton and others astray when they say that Cardinella was hanged there. In 1917, capital punishment was forbidden by law in Missouri.

4. William White, ed., *By-Line: Ernest Hemingway* (New York: Charles Scribner's Sons, 1967), * * * p. 59; the dispatch [is] headled * * * "Refugees from Thrace," 14 November 1922.

George Baltatzis, Nicholas Theotokis, former ministers; and George Hadjanestis, former military commander in chief in Ionia, were shot as they stood against a wall of the new Municipal Hospital in Athens, having been removed from the prison where they had heard the death-verdict by a military court martial which adjudged them guilty of high treason and responsible for the debacle in Asia Minor.

Accounts differ and none agrees precisely with Hemingway, who was not a witness. Gounaris was stricken with typhoid and had to be supported to the wall, but he was not sitting in the rain water with "his head on his knees" [39]. Hadjanestis, having been degraded, stood at attention. The six of them were slain from a distance of six meters, one infantry firing-squad per victim; and *coups de grace* were administered to all by pistol-shots through their heads. They were hastily buried by their families that afternoon in an Athens cemetery. "They" shot people in those days in Greece like "they" hanged people in Cook County.

Chapters IX through XIV translate us from the hospital wall to the *barrera*, the red wood fence (wall) around the bull ring in Spain. Grouped together as they are, these six Chapters comprise a miniature *tauromaquia* [bullfighting guide] derived ultimately from Francisco Goya's thirty-three etchings of 1816. There are three subgroups of two Chapters each: IX–X (the kid, the horse, and the bull; all perform but not brilliantly), XI–XII (the bad *torero* and the good *torero*), and XIII–XIV (the drunken *torero* and the "death" of Maera). Every one is tripartite. This structural device, not used any other place, is significant in that the bull ring is divided into three imaginary concentric circles and the fight itself into *tercios*, thirds. As Hemingway once wrote in the *Toronto Star*, 20 October 1923, "Bull fighting is not a sport. . . . It is a tragedy. A very great tragedy . . . played in three definite acts" [146].

Although new to *El Toreo*, he knew what he was about here. He experiences the *afición* (passion) for it; he acknowledges the underside of it. He employs a modicum of technical language and analysis and foreshadows the Romero-Belmonte *corrida* in *The Sun Also Rises* three years later. By implication, the season (*temporada*) is 1923.

Chapter IX ("The first matador got the horn") appeared in the Spring 1923 issue of *Little Review* before he had ever seen a *corrida de toros*. (His very first was that summer in Spain.) Therefore, I tentatively conclude (1) that he describes a fight that never took place and (2) that he describes the same mythical fight in his dispatch to the *Toronto Star Weekly*, dated 27 October 1923.[5] There are those

---

5. This mystery had been resolved when Kenneth S. Lynn published *Hemingway* (Simon and Schuster, 1987). See p. 197 of that volume [*Editor*].

who would disagree, but nowhere in José María de Cossío's massive *Los Toros: Tratado Técnico e Histórico* (Madrid: Espasa-Calpe, 1960; 3 vols.) is such a *corrida* narrated, although Cossio does tell of the legendary Joselito (born José Gómez) killing six bulls on six different occasions in 1915, when he was just twenty years old.

It is reasonable to assume that Chapter X ("They whack-whacked the white horse") is a scene Hemingway witnessed with Hadley [73]. Certainly the incident occurred long before the introduction in 1928 of the *peto*, the mattress-like covering to protect horses in the ring. It was an innovation Hemingway disapproved of and said so in *Death in the Afternoon*. Chapter XI ("The crowd shouted all the time") similarly is another bit of action from 1923 and a sad one, for the *torero* is self-admittedly bad: "'I am not really a good bull fighter'" [79].

"If it happened right down close in front of you" opens Chapter XII, wherein Nícanor Villalta Sérres executes a flawless kill with the *estoque* [sword] [87]. He was one of Hemingway's favorites that first summer in Spain. He nicknamed him "The Basque Telephone-Pole" and named his first son after him. The twenty-five-year-old Villalta was one of the best; in July he was awarded the coveted *Oreja de Oro* [Golden Ear] in Madrid, the supreme achievement in *Los Toros*. His unsurpassed killing ("the bull charged and Villalta charged [*a un tiempo*] and just for a moment they became one" [87]) was to gain him thirty-two ear-trophies by 1931.[6] Strange to report, though, that some of the details in XII seem to come from a *corrida* in which Chicuelo (born Manuel Jiménez Moreno) fought.

Chapter XIII ("I heard the drums coming down the street") and Chapter XIV ("Maera lay still, his head on his arms") have as protagonist the then famous *matador de toros* Manuel García López, known as Maera [95, 109]. In 1923, he was twenty-seven and was to have fifty *corridas*; many *aficionados* regarded him as the potential champion of them all, now that Joselito was dead, killed in the ring on 16 May 1920, now that Juan Belmonte had retired the year before. It is impossible to identify the soused Luis in XIII. His antics are indicative of the underside of *El Toreo*. But he was Mexican and therefore regarded contemptuously by Maera. A Mexican bullfighter had many obstacles to overcome in Spain. Much more to the point is the fact that not only is Luis drunk but "Everybody was drunk" going to the Champagne.

That Chapter XIV is fiction is common knowledge. Maera did not die of a *cornada* (horn wound), did not die as Hemingway tells it.

6. Villalta was born on 11 November 1898. He received the *alternativa*, the ceremony in which a *matador de novillos* graduates to *matador de toros*, at San Sebastián on 6 August 1922. It was confirmed in Madrid a little over six weeks later. See Barnaby Conrad, *La Fiesta Brava* (Boston: Houghton Mifflin Co., 1953), p. 176, and throughout the work.

He died of tuberculosis on 11 December 1924.[7] However, artistry triumphs. The bullfighting Chapters begin with a *cornada* and end with one, and Maera, inert in the sand awaiting the *coups de grace* of the horns, is no different from the Greek politicos, fallen before the wall of the hospital, or the bull after the kill.

L'Envoi, Chapter XVI ("The king was working in the garden"), is the postscript [131]. Hemingway never saw King George II, who has ascended the throne of the Hellenes a year previous; nor did he ever see his queen, Elizabeth of Roumania, great-granddaughter of Victoria. But his friend, Shorty Wornall, a movie-news cameraman, had, and he told about his audience with the royal pair in the palace garden ("She was clipping a rose bush"); and Hemingway expropriated the gossip for the *Star Weekly*, 15 September 1923. His picture of an affable, cynical, inept King, nice enough but no *King*, even though he considered himself to be "divinely annointed," is not excessive.

Colonel Nicholas Plastiras and his Revolutionary Committee, now in control of the government and distrusting the royal personages, had made virtual prisoners of them, confining them to the palace grounds. On 18 December 1923, at Plastiras's "request," George and Elizabeth went into exile, not to return for twelve years. "Like all Greeks he wanted to go to America" [131]. This is true. George wanted to come over here to California and observe agricultural methods in a climate and terrain very similar to Greece.

It was planned for 1924.

He never made it; the political climate was unseasonable.

Time-and-history in these sixteen Chapters begins in a garden in Mons and terminates artistically in a garden in Athens; begins with the Tommies shooting Germans and ends with George II saying that Plastiras "did right . . . shooting those chaps" [131], that is, the six Greeks in Chapter V. The decade begins with death and ends with death, but as George so cheerfully puts it, "'The great thing in this sort of an affair is not to be shot oneself'" [131]. He was "frightfully" accurate and "frightfully" lucky. Luckier by far than the bulls, the horses, the Greeks, the Hungarians, the Germans, the bullfighters, the Italians. "Geue peace in oure time, O Lorde"; so goes the beseechment in Edward VI's First Prayer-Book. The only problem is that there is no peace *In Our Time*; nor is there a "separate peace" unilaterally declared by Nick Adams as he sat against the wall of the church. "'Only let the story end as soon as possible,'" pleaded Demetrios

---

7. Maera was born in 1896. Before his success as a matador, he had worked as a *banderillero* for Juan Belmonte. His *alternativa* came on 28 August 1921 at Puerto de Santa María; it was confirmed in Madrid on 15 May 1922. Bullfighting details have been derived from Cossio, cited above.

Gounaris before he was shot down. The only problem is that story as time-and-history never ends; for, indeed, time as defined in the commencement of this article is "the system of those relations which any event has to any other as past, present, or future," and Ernest Miller Hemingway knew it, young as he was.[8]

Appendix

Interchapters:

IV–III:	23 August 1914; Mons, Belgium
I:	Late September–Early October 1915; Champagne, France
VIII:	19 November 1917; Kansas City, Missouri
VII:	16 June 1918; Fossalta di Piave, Italy
VI:	Early July 1918; Fossalta
XV:	15 April 1921; Chicago, Illinois
II:	16 October 1922; Eastern Thrace
V:	22 November 1922; Athens, Greece
IX–XIV:	Summer 1923; Spain
L'Envoi:	August 1923; Athens

MILTON A. COHEN

[The Fate of Hemingway's Experiments]†

* * *

Those murky, half-hidden narrators, so typical of *in our time*, illustrate how Hemingway adapted his experiments to conventional genres. * * * The experiments with ambiguous narrative voices and contexts taught Hemingway how to create immediacy by beginning in medias res yet cloud the context to focus the reader's attention on the narrator's tone, on journalistic details ("at six o'clock in the morning in the corridor of the county jail") [119], on the quality of the action ("They whack-whacked the white horse on the legs and he knee-ed himself up") [73], or on suggestive images ("against the wall of a hospital") [39]. But where *in our time* often maintains that

---

8. I wish to acknowledge the pioneering work by Michael S. Reynolds in his article, "Two Hemingway Sources for *In Our Time*," *Studies in Short Fiction*, 9 (Winter 1972), 81–86.
† From *Hemingway's Laboratory: The Paris* in our time (Tuscaloosa: U of Alabama P, 2005), pp. 206–14, 248. Reprinted by permission of the publisher. Unless otherwise indicated, notes are by the author; some of the author's notes have been omitted. Page numbers in brackets refer to this Norton Critical Edition.

ambiguity throughout a chapter—for example, the unidentified first-person narrators in chapters 2 ("the kid" kills five bulls) and 13 (the bad bullfighter)—the stories * * * clarify it relatively soon.

Controlling narrative distance in these brief chapters concerned Hemingway as much as characterizing the narrative voice. The positioning of this voice was therefore crucial to the kinesthetic, psychological, and expressive effect of each scene: If the narrator is an observer, as in many of the bullfight chapters, how close to the action is he? How knowledgeable (in delineating the bullfighter's technique) or impressionistic (in reporting the crowd's hijinks)? If a participant, what could he reasonably know or see from the middle of an action? The officer in chapter 4 never tells us *why* the Germans came over the wall so ill-advisedly. Presumably, he does not know. The kitchen corporal in chapter 1 *reports* the bizarre and drunken antics of his battery, but he has no way of knowing at the time where these events are taking him. And as the perspective in chapter 3 narrows from a distant view to the plodding Greek civilians, the procession really seems to have "No end and no beginning" for the narrator.

The risks Hemingway took working within these distances did not always succeed, as when the point of view in chapter 16 briefly shifts from Maera's consciousness to an external view of the hurrying doctor. But the stories that followed *in our time* show how much he learned from these exercises in controlling narrative perspective and distance. * * *

Just as the *in our time* chapters establish the narrator's perceptual distance, so they explore varieties of tone to establish the narrator's expressive distance from other characters or from the action. In particular, Hemingway tried out undercutting tones through irony, satire, and parody. To be sure, some of these methods badly needed adjustment, notably the malicious irony of chapter 10 (the recovering soldier and Ag). More subtly, the narrators of chapters 8, 11, 13, 15, and 18 put skeptical distance between themselves and the characters they describe—the praying soldier, the blinkered revolutionist, the incompetent and irresponsible bullfighters, the ineffectual king—by presenting their self-incriminating statements without comment or by changing the subject. Positioning a narrator apart from or between significant characters or ideologies became one of Hemingway's most effective devices to achieve irony, sometimes through direct comment, but often by merely juxtaposing these contrasting stances and having them, in effect, cancel each other out, as did the drunken lieutenant's antics and the nervous adjutant's fears in chapter 1. * * *

Hemingway continued to write in the subversive genres of satire and parody * * *. A direct descendent of the fairy tale parody of chapter 10 is "Mr. and Mrs. Elliot," * * * which satirizes Victorian sexuality and aesthetics and parodies the fairy tale in its closing: "and they were all quite happy." More relentlessly satirical than chapter 10, it shares that chapter's style of heavily narrated storytelling with little action or dialogue. Like chapter 10, it also relies on complex sentences to compress the historical past of this couple—only here, even the subordinating conjunctions seem to smirk as Hemingway satirizes the style itself in its Victorian (Jamesian?) turgidity:

> She had seemed much younger, in fact she had seemed not to have any age at all, *when* Elliot had married her *after* several weeks of making love to her *after* knowing her for a long time in her tea shop *before* he had kissed her one evening. (*In Our Time* [69], emphasis mine)

From chapter 11, which depicted the revolutionist, "Mr. and Mrs. Elliot" borrows another undercutting device, the inflated intensives *very* and *quite*, which the story joins to repeated key words—*tried* and *sick*—in the opening paragraph to establish the Elliots' view of married sex (solely for procreation and sickening drudgery in practice) and the narrator's mocking contempt for them:

> Mr. and Mrs. Elliot tried very hard to have a baby. They tried as often as Mrs. Elliot could stand it. They tried in Boston after they were married and they tried coming over on the boat. They did not try very often on the boat because Mrs. Elliot was quite sick. She was sick and when she was sick she was sick as Southern women are sick. That is women from the Southern part of the United States. Like all Southern women, Mrs. Elliot disintegrated very quickly under sea sickness. (*In Our Time* [69])[1]

As these passages suggest, Hemingway typically blended varieties of narrative mode, voice, and sentence rhythm—elements he intensively explored in *in our time*—to capture the right distance, tone, and "sequence of motion and fact."[2] * * *

[The] techniques [of] imagistic repetition and contrasting sentence structure to highlight a key fact come straight from the chapters. Their purposes have not changed: to re-create action, suggest theme, evoke psychological and emotive states. But here they achieve a

---

1. Because Horace Liveright felt that this passage might cause the book to be suppressed, he deleted it and invited Hemingway to revise it. Hemingway docilely complied—[an] index of his eagerness to have the book published "by a good publisher." He restored the opening for the first Scribner's edition in 1930.
2. Here and later Cohen quotes EH's formula for capturing "the real thing" in *DIA*, 2 [*Editor*].

fluidity far beyond the journeyman's explorations of *in our time*. What Hemingway taught himself about writing sentences in that book matured into a style that could employ virtually any combination of sentence structures to suggest multiple types of meaning. * * * [For example,] the abrupt, simple sentences that begin "The Battler"— "Nick stood up. He was all right" [41]—do more than start the story as if the narrative itself were abruptly thrown off a train. They convey Nick's psychic shock and instinctive rebound in recognizing what has just happened to him and reassuring himself that he is still "all right." Remarkably, both the action and [the] diction thematically foreshadow the central theme of outsiders getting physically busted and not being "all right."

Compound sentences—the rhythm in which Hemingway most naturally composed—appear everywhere in his mature prose. Even the self-conscious run-ons of chapters 2 ("the kid" kills five bulls) and 13 (the bad bullfighter) have a place. * * *

* * * Hemingway was [chary] of complex structures: their explanatory potential runs counter to his evolving techniques of understatement and omission. Yet composing the chapters also taught him the value of complex sentences, not just to convey information efficiently, but to arrange related actions into a hierarchy in which the lesser images or actions both subserve and build to the key image. In "Indian Camp," when Dr. Adams discovers that the Indian father has slit his throat, the doctor orders his own young son removed from the shanty: "There was no need of that. Nick, standing in the door of the kitchen, had a good view of the upper bunk when his father, the lamp in one hand, tipped the Indian's head back" [13]. As Nick's positioning compels him to witness this grisly scene, so the precise arrangement of clauses and phrases does not release the crucial action—"tipped the Indian's head back"—until the end. The sentence closes with a click, forcing the reader to visualize what Nick sees. A more dramatically complex sentence in "Cross-Country Snow" self-reflexively points to the author's obsession with capturing exactly "the sequence of motion and fact which creates the emotion":

> George was coming down in telemark position, kneeling: one leg forward and bent, the other trailing; his sticks hanging like some insect's thin legs, kicking up puffs of snow as they touched the surface and finally the whole kneeling, trailing figure coming around in a beautiful right curve, crouching, the legs shot forward and back, the body leaning out against the swing, the sticks accenting the curve like points of light, all in a wild cloud of snow. [90]

The Steinian participles (*coming, trailing, hanging, kicking, kneeling, trailing, coming, crouching, leaning, accenting*) create simultaneous and parallel actions, just as they do in the Villalta chapter: "the muleta trailing and the sword following the curve behind."

*   *   *

In a remarkably short time, Hemingway polished and developed the thematic potential of techniques he had tried out in the short chapters. Consider the technique of presenting the sensation before explaining the conditions that create it:

> Nick sat against the wall of the church where they had dragged him to be clear of the machine gun fire in the street. Both legs stuck out awkwardly. He had been hit in the spine. (chapter 7)

Hemingway could easily have reversed sentences 2 and 3, making the legs sticking out awkwardly a clear consequence of Nick's having been hit in the spine. Instead, he gives us the physical fact ("stuck out awkwardly") before providing the explanatory cause. Experience is sensory—for characters and readers alike—before it is contextualized and understood.

The same technique appears often—and memorably—in the stories and novels. In "Indian Camp," for example, when Dr. Adams checks on the Indian father, "He pulled back the blankets from the Indian's head. His hand came away wet" (*In Our Time* [13]). Not for another two sentences do we find out what this wetness signifies. In "Cross-Country Snow" the "sensations first" technique acquires thematic implications: "The rush and the sudden swoop as he dropped down a steep undulation plucked Nick's mind out and left him only the wonderful flying, dropping sensation in his body" (*In Our Time* [89]). "Plucked Nick's mind out" ironically anticipates the story's conclusion, when paternal responsibilities now weigh on that mind and eliminate skiing's opportunities for lightening it in a rush of sensations. "The Battler" further develops the "sensations first" technique into an objective correlative [x] for Nick's emotions. Having barely escaped a bad beating from ex-prizefighter Ad Francis, Nick heeds Bugs's advice to leave: "Nick climbed the embankment and started up the track. He found he had a ham sandwich in his hand and put it in his pocket" [48]. "He found" perfectly conveys Nick's dazed condition at this point, while the second action—"put it in his pocket"—reinforces this mental numbness with a mechanical action. Following his violent rescue by Bugs, Nick's questions about Ad gradually fade, while Bugs's answers expand to monologue. The physical fact of the sandwich in his hand thus establishes itself in his mind as a new reality but also conveys (along with Nick's growing silence) a mind that is still reacting to a powerful shock. In sum, a technique used to heighten the reader's physical perception in *in our time* evolves in stories written only a year or two later into a subtle method of suggesting a theme or conveying a character's psychological state.

The techniques discussed above were all legacies of the *in our time* experiments. Hemingway refined them in his stories and novels, extended their variety, deepened their complexity and subtlety, combined and recombined them in his prose to form a mature, intricate style of apparent simplicity. That style had not yet coalesced in *in our time*—the book explores too many directions to represent "the" Hemingway style. But the components of that style were clearly present. The characteristic rhythm of simple sentences intermingling with compounds and occasionally a complex sentence; the plain diction and precise rendering of physical details; the closely observed actions conveyed through calculated sentence rhythms; the narrative emphasis on sensation before context, on showing over telling; the unblinking stare at violent actions and previously unmentionable conditions, yet the calculated reluctance to describe emotions or state themes directly—all create a freshness and intensity of experience, both physical and psychological, that the earliest readers and critics of these chapters immediately felt. *in our time* provided the raw material for this style in a self-consciously avant-garde form that imposed rigorous discipline on these laboratory experiments. Hemingway's most distinctive achievement in moving from these chapters to the stories and novels that followed was not to retreat from the experiments of *in our time*, but to shape them into a style and technique that was simultaneously popular and modernist—his own style.

Critical Views of Individual Stories

"INDIAN CAMP"

JOSEPH M. FLORA

[Hard Questions in "Indian Camp"]†

* * *

*** Hemingway's *** "Indian Camp" *** not only [was] the first Nick story to appear in print, but also ranks among Hemingway's best.[1] It touches keys that haunt the reader in ways Hemingway could not have anticipated when he completed it: in the beginning, suicide receives a kind of justification. But personal implications of Hemingway's life and death aside, it is clear that Nick is Adamic in the story, thereby raising some of the most basic questions that man has always pondered. From that perspective, too, the title "Work in Progress," under which it was first published, seems apt.

In "Indian Camp" Nick, roused from his tent for a night ride across the lake to the Indian camp, is the archetypal innocent. Hemingway tells us nothing about Nick that would make us qualify our sympathetic feeling for his youthful entry into a complex world. Throughout the Nick stories, journey (psychological and spiritual more than physical) usually helps define meaning. The first words of the story and the first we hear from Nick are natural, but also symbolic: "Where are we going, Dad?" [11]. The story suggests that Nick is too young to realize the real answer to his question, for it is larger than he knows. (It turns out that his father does not fully know either.)

Nick is very young during the time of "Indian Camp." Not only is he the questioner of the story, but he receives answers that make his

† From *Hemingway's Nick Adams* (Baton Rouge: Louisiana State UP, 1982), pp. 22–31. Reprinted by permission of Louisiana State University Press. Some of the author's notes have been omitted. Page numbers in brackets refer to this Norton Critical Edition.

1. "Indian Camp" appeared in *Transatlantic Review*, 1 (April, 1924) under the heading "Work in Progress," a title that reveals Hemingway's perception of Nick in a larger context, of Nick as protagonist in something like a novel.

extreme youth clear. "There is an Indian lady very sick," says his father [11]. A teenager or adult would have received more exact information in syntax less formal. But the answer satisfies the doctor's son, who is leaning back "with his father's arm around him." Hemingway's technique in the story may be described in large part as catechetic. The questions are profound, beyond the comprehension of the questioner ultimately, and so are the answers. Yet the answers, if uncomprehended, carry authority and assurance.

Nick seems to sense that the night's journey is to take him into totally new experiences. It is dark and there is mist over the lake. The opening sentences of the story immediately signal the sense of action to come—and action in a world far beyond the secure one Nick has known as a doctor's son: "At the lake shore there was another rowboat drawn up. The two Indians stood waiting" [11].

The reader may wonder why Nick, so obviously young, is going on this night journey. It is clear that he is already in surroundings at least once removed from the normal life of a doctor's son. There is a "camp" rowboat—so Nick with his father and Uncle George have already taken a journey to the more primitive, the more basic. By design, theirs is a group of men without women.

When the doctor's party gets into the boats for the row across the lake, no one gives instructions about who should get into which boat. Nick and his father quite naturally get into one boat, Uncle George into the other. From the beginning of the story, George's presence sets off an ideal obligation in the relationship between father and son. Furthermore, the narrative evokes something of an aura from the tradition of Indian culture: fathers give instructions to sons as they are initiated into manhood. The doctor is the important man of the hour—for the Indian lady and for Nick. Nick has a guide who is assured—or seems to be—and can give him answers that are reassuring. One's father—and not one's uncle—should be, and here is, that reassuring voice.

But almost as soon as Hemingway has set the stage for the important father-son focus, he indicates that Uncle George will have a symbolic role. (George and Nick never speak to each other in the story—further creating the sense of the doctor's primacy for the initiate.) "Functionless" on the journey across the lake, Uncle George smokes a cigar "in the dark" [11]. When his boat is beached, he gives the Indians cigars. The gesture, as a remnant of Indian rituals, reinforces the sense of the white man's arrival into the Indian world. The fact that there are cigars offered by the white man rather than a pipe by the Indian hints at the changed position of the Indian in the white world. The Indians of the story have lost much of their power and pride. They live in shanties and make their livelihood through an enterprise (logging) of the white man.

Indians had become associated with cigars mainly in the phenomenon of the wooden Indian statue commonly placed outside tobacco shops: tobacco had been their gift.

But as Nick enters this Indian world, he will discover that the life of the more ["primitive"] people can teach him a great deal, for the ["primitive"] contains values that the doctor's son needs to discover. A journey to "Indian Camp" may be far more useful to the young boy than a camping trip with his father and uncle, however good that might be. For there is light in the Indian camp. As the doctor, Nick, and Uncle George make their way through a meadow, they follow the young Indian "who carried a lantern." Ahead it is "much lighter" on the logging road, and the Indian is able to blow out his lantern. Light comes from the shanties, and in the shanty nearest the road there is "a light in the window" and an old woman stands in the doorway "holding a lamp" [11].

Even though the white visitors will get jarred from some of their assumptions before the story ends, it is also clear that the Indian has had to reach out to the technology of the whites. A young Indian woman has been in labor for two days. The old women in the camp have been assisting her, but they must finally admit they can be of no further use. The theme of the separation between men and women with which the story mutedly began is made more important. The Indian men, helpless to aid the woman, have moved up the road where they cannot hear her screams, where they sit to smoke "in the dark" [11]. In this story, as in many of the Nick stories, and in much of Hemingway's work, there is the stark sense that the world is a hospital. A common response to the pain of the world is to sit "in the dark" far from the screams.

We typically characterize the Indian as possessing an admirable stoicism. Hemingway emphasizes the pain involved in merely getting into the world by making the Indian woman no passive sufferer. Everything in "Indian Camp" is complex and tends towards ambiguity; the stereotypes will not hold. The woman is screaming as the doctor arrives, and she continues screaming, quite unsettling Nick. The doctor tries to assure Nick that the screams "are not important" [12]. If the woman is to be helped, someone has to discipline himself and not hear the screams. That is what doctors commonly do. Nick has to admire his father as he goes about his business—certainly a part of him takes consolation from the explanations that his father gives. Probably the doctor's professional stance gives Nick the courage not to buckle during the primitive Caesarian operation he partly watches and assists.

Nick can also observe how those not trained to work in a hospital react. Since the doctor has no anaesthesia in his camp, he needs Uncle George and the three Indians (not privileged to join the other men) to hold the woman down. When the woman's pain becomes so great that she bites Uncle George, he instinctively curses, "Damn squaw bitch!" [12], and the young Indian who had rowed him over laughs. The event is useful for guarding against reading too much into George's later indictment of the doctor. George is quite human in his reaction, and the young Indian's response to George is further instructive on human behavior. Only the implied narrator (to use the distinction of Wayne C. Booth's *The Rhetoric of Fiction*) outside the story has demonstrated the compassion that the woman's suffering demands.

However traumatic the event of birth can sometimes be (the doctor later reassures Nick that the case has been exceptional), getting out of life can also be a gruesome event. The overriding irony of "Indian Camp" is that the doctor, who has thought to educate his son on the ways of birth, has brought him also to witness death. For although the Indian men have removed themselves from the sound of the woman's screams (save for the three who assist the doctor), one has been unable to do so because of bad luck. The Indian woman's husband is in the bunk above her because he had cut his foot badly with an ax three days before. While the woman screams and the doctor instructs Nick and then operates, the husband does act the part of the stoical Indian. Hemingway makes his lesson in stoicism forcefully. Just after the doctor has told Nick that he does not hear the woman's screams "because they are not important" a one-sentence paragraph makes a stark contrast: "The husband in the upper bunk rolled over against the wall" [12]. Obviously to him the screams are important, and he does hear them. The Indian male is taught to endure pain. In part, he measures his manhood by his ability to demonstrate an indifference to excruciating pain. The husband has been enduring his own pain, but finally his wife's pain is more than he can bear, and he cuts his throat—quietly but efficiently.

Doctor Adams understandably takes satisfaction from the fact that he is able to deliver the woman's baby, saving her life and the baby's. But he increasingly loses the reader's approval—and Uncle George's—as he talks about his achievement. Hemingway tells us that the doctor "was feeling exalted and talkative as football players are in the dressing room after a game" [13]. This has not been a football game, however. Uncle George is the average, fallible man in the story, and although he respects the doctor's knowledge, he finds the doctor's self-esteem distasteful. He defines for us the vast difference between the way a child regards the superior wisdom of the parent and the way the rest of humanity regards the wise one. The time after this birth should be a time to refrain from talking, but the doctor talks on, using the clichés of the approved bedside manner: "Ought to have a look at the proud father. They're usually the worst sufferers in these little affairs" [13].

The man of words is then brought down hard when he discovers how the husband "took it." Nick, too, has seen something he will never forget, and the doctor is left to repent.

Hemingway restores the doctor to favor as he and Nick make the journey back across the lake together. The dialogue contrasts markedly with the professional tone the doctor has been using in the shanty. He is here father, not doctor; and Nick is glad to get back to that relationship. The doctor shows that he is also glad to return to this level of experience as he addresses his son with the diminutive: "I'm terribly sorry I brought you along, Nickie" [14]. Nick seems eager to be reassured: he uses *Daddy* four times in addressing his father. Nick is still the questioner, and his father still has the answers. We note that only the first question has to do with the birth, however, for the suicide has obviously impressed Nick more profoundly. Finally he asks the climactic question that relates all of the events of the experience to his own life: "Is dying hard, Daddy?" [14].

The question and the answer ("No, I think it's pretty easy, Nick. It all depends") produce a marked resonance in the story since the Indian has been a major element in it. Traditionally the value of the good death was one instilled in the Indian boy from earliest years. Dying was not something to be feared; rather, to die ignobly would be the disaster. In the white culture death seems to be more fearful, but for the time being, Nick is reassured by his father's answer. Nick has returned from the night experience to the comforting day world: "The sun was coming up over the hills. A bass jumped, making a circle in the water. Nick trailed his hand in the water. It felt warm in the sharp chill of the morning" [14].

Hemingway indicates how much of the night's experience is beyond the boy in the famous end line of the story: "with his father rowing, he felt quite sure that he would never die" [14]. A major theme of the Nick stories is Nick's coming to grips with the idea of death, especially his own death—something Nick briefly in "Indian Camp" catches a glimpse of, but then dismisses. The Indian's death, while vivid, does not touch Nick personally, nor is Nick unusual in this ability to dismiss death. This ability of the young is not necessarily soon outgrown, or the change necessarily welcomed. * * * Nick's strange journey to the Indian camp will haunt him on other nights, and his later recollections of his father's superficial explanations will make him doubt his tutor's wisdom even as Uncle George has.

Sherwood Anderson defined the line into manhood in the penultimate story of *Winesburg, Ohio*; it comes when the boy "for the first time takes the backward view of life."[2] Anderson's George Willard has been led to this position through his mother's death when he was eighteen. The point here is not to suggest an influence but to define a problem for Nick's progress, to see where Nick has to go. Nick's coming to terms with death will be decidedly more difficult than it was for George Willard. Nick's premature initiation in "Indian Camp" has not led him to take "the backward view of life."

The grimness of death and the questions about the meaning of death—not to mention the strong sense of the universe as an arena of pain—come so forcefully to Nick and to the reader that it is possible to miss the positive implications of "Indian Camp." There is, of course, the upbeat at the end of the story that comes with the doctor's recognition that he has taken Nick into waters way over his head, his apology to Nick, and the image of their love as they row back together. That Nick will later reflect on the mistakes of his father-guide is clear from his question about Uncle George's whereabouts, for George—overwhelmed by the events of the night, including his disgust for the doctor but probably some disgust at his own inadequacies in the face of them—has remained behind. Nick has not missed the challenge to his father in George's ironical line: "Oh, you're a great man, all right" [13]. But there is a bond of love between Nick and his father that gives the boy something he needs and will never forget.

The bond between father and son is an important dimension of the light that ends the story. And the doctor, who has witnessed birth and death many times before, is frank and truthful as he answers Nick's questions. Although some critics have dwelt on the doctor's weaknesses, the doctor has some real wisdom and convincing humanity. His humanity is much in evidence at the story's end. He empathizes with the Indian husband: "He couldn't stand things, I guess," he explains to Nick. The doctor's last speech of the story is the admission to Nick that under certain circumstances dying can be easier than living. That is a lesson that Nick cannot totally comprehend, but it helps dissipate the horror that he had earlier felt in his first confrontation with a violent human death.

In addition to this light—literal, emotional, and symbolic—that ends "Indian Camp," there are other lights in the story, the lights of the Indian camp itself. Other stories reveal that the most shocking of the visits to the Indian camp was not the only one Nick made. Presumably the later visits would cause him to reflect on matters of dying and birth, but they would also clarify other dimensions of Indian experience. The Indians were a vanishing race and for that

2. Sherwood Anderson, "Sophistication," *Winesburg, Ohio* (New York: B. W. Huebsch, 1919), 286.

reason often judged inferior, but "Indian Camp" conveys a great sense of their humanity, of their suffering and ability to love, and of their solidarity. The need of the Indian wife has mobilized the entire camp, although there are specialized roles.

But although Nick would come to sense a good deal about the value in Indian culture and although he could understand that under certain conditions suicide was understandable and that sometimes birth is very hard, the story raises hard questions about the relationship between men and women who love, questions about obligations that the Nick of "Indian Camp" could hardly begin to verbalize. What sort of bond is marriage if it would lead a husband to kill himself because his wife suffered? * * * "Indian Camp" indicates that even if two people love each other, the penalty for loving may be too great. By aligning his destiny with that of a woman, the Indian husband has accepted her pain. The husband has been able to bear his own pain, but her pain in addition is too much for him. His suicide suggests that he was dying in his wife's place. Loving between man and woman and between father and son are matters that Nick will pause over, time and time again.

*   *   *

AMY STRONG

[The Violence of Race in "Indian Camp" and "The Doctor and the Doctor's Wife"]†

In her recent work of literary criticism, *Playing in the Dark*, Toni Morrison calls our attention to the way critics have ignored an abiding Africanist presence that weaves its way through the works of white American authors:

> There seems to be a more or less tacit agreement among literary scholars that, because American literature has been clearly the preserve of white male views, genius, and power, those views, genius, and power are without relationship to and removed from the overwhelming presence of black people in the United States. . . . The contemplation of this black presence is central to any understanding of our national literature and should not be permitted to hover at the margins of the literary imagination. (5)

† From "Screaming through Silence: The Violence of Race in 'Indian Camp' and 'The Doctor and the Doctor's Wife,'" in *The Hemingway Review* 16.1 (Fall 1996): 18–32. Copyright © 1996. Reprinted by permission of The Ernest Hemingway Foundation. All rights reserved. Some of the author's notes have been omitted. Page numbers in square brackets refer to this Norton Critical Edition.

While my focus in this essay will be on the lack of an Indian (rather than Africanist) presence, I will explore the ways Hemingway negotiates the matter of "race" and racial difference in two short stories from *In Our Time*. Like recent readings of Hemingway's fiction which have begun to outline issues of "gender trouble,"[1] my work will center on two of his earliest short stories, "Indian Camp" and "The Doctor and the Doctor's Wife," to examine how Hemingway represents the instability of racial identity. In the first story, he presents race simply as a biological feature, but then in the second revises this model to create a complex, shifting depiction of race that anticipates the essentialist/constructionist debates waged today.[2] Secondarily, I hope this study might begin to uncover the ways his work has interrogated power relations built on racial identity, and even exposed the instability of power based on such a system of inequality.

Critics have long been aware of the Edenic and, more specifically, Adamic longings to be found in Hemingway's work, longings he shares with American writers such as Whitman, Hawthorne, and Melville. The Nick Adams stories, with their obvious gesture toward this tradition, have generated a number of comments on the symbolism of the name "Adams," but most critics seem to have internalized R. W. B. Lewis's formulation in *The American Adam* that to be Adamic is to efface racial history.[3] Quoting from an 1839 *Democratic Review*, Lewis defines the Adamic myth: "Our national birth was the beginning of a new history . . . which separates us from the past and connects us with the future only" (5). Traditionally, "Indian Camp" and "The Doctor and the Doctor's Wife" have been read as tales of initiation, focusing heavily on the final scene in "Indian Camp" and Nick's musing that "he felt quite sure that he would never die" [14], and/or on the unity between father and son in "The Doctor and the Doctor's Wife" when they choose to seek out black

---

1. The term is taken from Judith Butler's *Gender Trouble: Feminism and the Subversion of Identity*. For readings that explore the instability of gender categories, see J. Gerald Kennedy, "Hemingway's Gender Trouble"; Debra Moddelmog, "Reconstructing Hemingway's Identity: Sexual Politics, the Author, and the Multicultural Classroom"; Mark Spilka, *Hemingway's Quarrel with Androgyny*; and Nancy R. Comley and Robert Scholes, *Hemingway's Genders: Rereading the Hemingway Text*.
2. Diana Fuss outlines the parameters of this debate in *Essentially Speaking: Feminism, Nature and Difference*. Chapter Six, "'Race' Under Erasure? Poststructuralist Afro-American Literary Theory," specifically focuses on the category of race, questioning whether racial identity can be seen as *either* a "question of morphology, of anatomical or genetic characteristics" *or* as a "psychological, historical, anthropological, sociological, legal" construct (73). Fuss argues that the essentialist/constructionist opposition is "largely artificial" (119) because the two categories depend on each other for meaning, and we will see that Hemingway's stories sustain exactly this tension between the two categories in a way that destabilizes our grasp of racial identity.
3. See R. W. B. Lewis, *The American Adam*, for "the first tentative outlines of a native American mythology" (1), covering the period between 1820 and 1860, where "Adamic imagery is altogether central and controlling" (6). By "native American," Lewis does not refer to Indians; on the contrary, he refers to the "birth in America of a clear conscience unsullied by the past" (7).

squirrels together.[4] To be sure, the Indians in these stories have been characterized, often as symbols of darkness and primitivism, but even this characterization functions primarily to offset Nick's character. My argument is not specifically with the way critics have characterized the Indians (although that racial subtext should be examined). It is rather that Hemingway's stories do, in fact, present an Adamic figure whose identity cannot be fully understood without historicizing his relation to these Indians—a relation based on racial domination. What takes place within these two stories is a male-male rivalry, white male against Indian male, where the endangered territory returns to eerily familiar historical subjects/catalysts for violence: the woman's body and the land. In the opening scene of "Indian Camp," we find Nick, Dr. Adams, and Uncle George being ferried across a lake through a gloomy, misty darkness. Joseph DeFalco points out that "the classical parallel is too obvious to overlook, for the two Indians function in a Charon-like fashion in transporting Nick, his father, and his uncle from their own sophisticated and civilized world of the white man into the dark and primitive world of the camp" (161). The Hades metaphor not only seems "too obvious to overlook," but other details add further support to his reading, such as the dogs "rushing out" at the men once they reach the other side of the lake. "A dog came out barking. . . . More dogs rushed out at them" [11]. This seemingly gratuitous appearance recalls Cerberus, the many-headed dog who challenged spirits trying to enter or leave Hades. Furthermore, if a Charon-like figure ferries the men across the lake, we may imagine the river Styx, but as the men return, now with Dr. Adams at the oars, we may be reminded of another famous river in Hades. Lethe, the river of forgetfulness, works well in this context for two reasons: it helps illuminate Nick's final thoughts of immortality at the end of the story, and it implicates both father and son in a larger historical pattern of forgetting. At the end of "Indian Camp," Nick and his father have a brief but pointed catechistic interchange about death, and because we have just witnessed Nick's "initiation" into the world of pain and death, his final thought surprises some readers. Trailing his hand in the water as his father rowed them back across, Nick "felt quite sure that he would never die" [14]. Even if we abandon the mythic

---

4. I am indebted to readings by Paul Smith, *A Reader's Guide to the Short Stories of Ernest Hemingway*, Joseph M. Flora's *Hemingway's Nick Adams*, Philip Young's *Ernest Hemingway: A Reconsideration*, and Joseph DeFalco's *The Hero in Hemingway's Short Stories*. Young highlights "Nick's initiation to pain, and to the violence of birth and death" in "Indian Camp," while "The Doctor and the Doctor's Wife" "teaches Nick something about the solidarity of the male sex" (32, 33); Joseph DeFalco asserts that "the major focus of ["Indian Camp"] is Nick's reaction to these events," and "the central conflict that emerges [in "The Doctor and the Doctor's Wife"] reveals a further step in the learning process that Nick undergoes" (28, 34).

elements here and simply see a boy being rowed across the lake by his father, we must admit some element of willful forgetfulness and an enormous amount of psychical distancing from his experience at the Indian camp. The goal of this particular reading is not meant to encourage discussion of Hemingway's familiarity with Orphic mythology, or even to presume that he was referring to Greek myth in "Indian Camp." Rather, it serves as a metaphor for the ways Hemingway's story has been read; readers have also trailed their hands in the river of forgetfulness, overlooking the Indians' role not only in this story, but in the making of American identity. I believe we have not fully engaged with "Indian Camp" or "The Doctor and the Doctor's Wife" unless we come to terms with the way the identities of Nick and his father are constructed in relation to the Indians' presence, and vice versa.

One of the most perplexing issues in "Indian Camp" springs from the moment when Dr. Adams has successfully completed his crude operation on the Indian woman and reaches up into the bunk to check on the father, only to find—to his undisguised horror—that the Indian has slit his throat "from ear to ear" [13]. We may simply wish to accept the explanation given by Dr. Adams: "He couldn't stand things, I guess" [14]. It does seem true that the Indian "couldn't stand things," but does this simply mean he couldn't stand his wife's physical pain? However astounding the woman's pain, the doctor has arrived, and the two days of pain should be alleviated very soon. Which then raises a different question: is it the doctor's *presence* that drives the Indian husband to suicide? I believe "Indian Camp" tells a different kind of initiation story, one that, like the Orphic myth, shows how a purified and initiated identity cannot be constructed without the binary opposition of unpurified and fallen selves.

The imagery surrounding Dr. Adams, Uncle George, and Nick's entry into the opposing camp is permeated by structures of domination. Once across the lake, Uncle George's first action is to offer cigars to the Indians who have rowed them across. It is not clear why Uncle George gives the Indians two cigars; it would not be a form of payment for rowing them across, because the doctor is obviously doing the Indian family a favor. It must be a gift, either in the form of a traditional 'peace' offering, or as a congratulatory gesture for the newborn baby. We have no signs, however, that the Indians will give any gift in return. Gayle Rubin's work explains that "gifts were the threads of social discourse, the means by which . . . societies were held together in the absence of specialized governmental institutions" (172). She further suggests that "gift exchange may also be the idiom of competition and rivalry" (172), using the example of the "Big Man" who humiliates another by giving more than can be reciprocated. This first form of exchange between cultures establishes a subtle, unequal dynamic of dominator/dominated.

Jürgen C. Wolter's article "Cæsareans in an Indian Camp" describes the word *Cæsarean* as "highly ambiguous; in addition to being a technical term in surgery, it connotes authority, imperialism, assumption of power, and even tyrannical dictatorship" (92). After introducing this formulation, however, Wolter reverts to the familiar theme of the father-son relationship: "through the unintentionally violent (Cæsarean) initiation of his son, the pompous and omniscient Cæsar-doctor is reborn as a responsible and humanly imperfect father" (93). Despite this gesture toward metaphoric imperialism, Wolter reiterates the same story of initiation, adding the Cæsarean component to complicate our reading of Nick's father. But the "violent" Cæsarean is not performed on the doctor's son; it is performed, without anesthetic, on a screaming Indian woman. And while the location of this story may alleviate a severe condemnation of the doctor and his methods per se, because he saves the life of mother and child in an Indian camp distant from "civilization" (where, for example, anesthetic would be available) it is precisely the story's location that highlights the racial inequality between the two cultures with its insistent juxtaposition of light/dark, civilization/wilderness, clean/dirty. Dr. Adams's "Cæsarean" assumption of power implicates both father and son in a violent history with relevance far beyond the realm of familial bonds. As Hemingway draws the scene, the doctor appears to be the only person who can remain oblivious to the Indian woman's screams. All others who do not have to assist in the operation have moved up the road out of earshot. When Nick asks his father to quiet her screams, he responds: "But her screams are not important. I don't hear them because they are not important" [12]. Some have read this as callousness, others as professional distance; either way, Dr. Adams psychically distances himself from the woman to the point that she loses her markers of humanity (this psychical distancing is repeated in Nick's belief that he will never die). Dr. Adams chooses to envision her body as a territory without agency or voice, a kind of uninhabited land he takes possession of and must get under control (what Stephen Greenblatt, in *Marvelous Possessions*, refers to as "*terrae nullius*" [60]). Once the doctor begins working on the Indian woman, her pain is so great—"Uncle George and three Indian men held the woman still" [12]—she bites Uncle George on the arm, resisting, fighting back. * * * Certainly we cannot say that "Indian Camp" here depicts a rape; the doctor and the men holding this woman down are attempting to deliver a baby and save the mother's life. But what we can see, and perhaps more importantly, what the Indian husband sees, is a woman's body as a territory under complete control of white men.[5] The Indian husband, we must not forget, had endured the most painful part of his wife's suffering, when she had been attended by "all the old women in the camp" [11]. His suicide comes later, when the Indian women mysteriously leave the birthing to be replaced by three Indian men, Uncle George, Nick, and Dr. Adams.

When Dr. Adams finishes the operation, he feels "exalted and talkative as football players are in the dressing room after a game" [13].

> "That's one for the medical journal, George," he said. "Doing a Cæsarian with a jack-knife and sewing it up with nine-foot, tapered gut leaders." [13]

Uncle George's sarcastic response, "Oh, you're a great man, all right" [13], not only reinforces the insidious connection between Dr. Adams and Cæsar ("a great man"), but the doctor's immediate desire to have the operation written down in the medical journals recalls Stephen Greenblatt's research on ways explorers conquered the "new world." In *Marvelous Possessions*, Greenblatt explains that early settlers of the "new world" established themselves and gained property almost exclusively by means of speech acts: "For Columbus taking possession is principally the performance of a set of linguistic acts: declaring, witnessing, recording. The acts are public and official" (57). In addition to the verbal testimony, the speaker would take care that "everything would be written down and consequently have greater authority" (57). These documents would then provide both 'truth' and 'legality' for the procedure, "ensuring that the memory of the encounter is fixed, ensuring that there are not competing versions of what happened" (57). After the Cæsarean, Dr. Adams feels "exalted," a word that not only means elated, but also connotates a rise in "status, dignity, power, honor, wealth" (*Webster's New World Dictionary*). He is "talkative," defining and declaring his accomplishment before witnesses. Dr. Adams feels like a "football player in the dressing room after a game," and when we consider football as a sanctioned form of violence between men, the dressing room represents a space where the winning team revels in a victory [13]. Finally, there is Dr. Adams's wish to have this event written down in a medical journal. His medical journals represent an ultimate authority: a removed, consecrated sign of medical, legal, and institutional power, not unlike the proclamations sent back to the crown by Columbus as a form of institutional domination over the colonies.

---

5. See Annette Kolodny's *The Lay of the Land: Metaphor as Experience and History in American Life and Letters*. Kolodny outlines the American metaphor of "the land as woman" and its attendant imagery of "eroticism, penetration, raping, embrace, enclosure, and nurture, to cite only a few" (150).

Greenblatt further points out that Indians were unable to contradict the colonizers' proclamations, "because only linguistic compe-
tence, the ability to understand and to speak, would enable one
to fill in the sign" (60). "Indian Camp" does not offer a single Indian
voice, only the pregnant Indian woman's screams. Elaine Scarry's
The Body in Pain explains the way extreme physical pain will "bring
about an immediate reversion to a state anterior to language, to the
sounds and cries a human being makes before language is learned"
(4). The Indian woman loses her ability to make sense through language, and she is ultimately rendered altogether senseless: "She did
not know what had become of the baby or anything" [13]; moreover,
when her screams are acknowledged in this story, we find that the
men have purposefully devised ways to screen them out. First, we
find that the Indian men "moved off up the road . . . out of range of
the noise she made" [11], specifically removing to a place where
they need not hear her screams. Second, when Nick asks his father
to quiet her screams, Dr. Adams instructs his son outright that he
does not hear them. Third, as suggested earlier, we cannot defini-
tively assert that even the Indian husband is directly reacting to his
wife's screams, because he must know that after enduring them for
so much time, they will soon cease. Hemingway's juxtaposition of
Dr. Adams's insistent discourse and the woman's pre-literate or illiterate state shows how her body becomes her only identity. Her body
literally gets hollowed out in this story; the figurative metaphor of
terrae nullius has become a reality in the hands of Dr. Adams, much
like Greenblatt's description of early settlers and their official claims
for territory in the "new world":

> [Y]ou shall make before a notary public and the greatest possi-
> ble number of witnesses, and the best known ones, an act of
> possession in our name, cutting trees and boughs, and digging
> or making, if there be an opportunity, some small building. (56)

Dr. Adams has cut into the woman, like the early settlers leaving a
gash in a tree, and her scar will serve as a marker (just as the scaler's
mark of "White and McNally" signifies ownership of the logs in the
second story). Because "Indian Camp" offers no anesthetic, offers
a jack-knife rather than a scalpel, offers biting and screams of pain,
the line between healing and violence becomes blurred. "The Doctor
and the Doctor's Wife" also carries themes of gendered violence and
bodily pain into a racially charged context. The opening scene hints
at connections with "Indian Camp," both in the representation of
landscape and similarity in themes:

> Dick Boulton came from the *Indian camp* to *cut up* logs for
> Nick's father. He brought *his son* Eddy and another Indian

named Billy Tabeshaw with him. They came in through the
back gate *out of the woods*, Eddy carrying the long *cross-cut
saw.... . .*

He turned and shut the gate. The others went on ahead of
him down to *the lake* shore where the logs were buried in the
sand. (italics mine, [17])

The allusions to "Indian Camp" are impossible to overlook. Again,
we have an Indian camp, a father and son pair, a cross-cutting saw,
an entry-way, the woods, the lake. Paul Strong's article "The First
Nick Adams Stories" offers a clear and startling summary of parallels between the two stories:

"Doc" arrives at the Indian camp with his jack-knife to deliver
a baby trapped in its mother's womb; unless he is successful, it
will probably die. "Dick" arrives at the Adamses' with cant-
hooks to free up logs trapped in the sand; unless he does, the
wood will probably rot. "Doc" heats water, washes his hands,
delivers the baby and announces its identity—"it's a boy." Eddie
and Billy Tabeshaw deliver a log, wash it, and "Dick" determines
its identity—"It belongs to White and McNally." The Cæsarean
ends with "Doc" "sewing it up"; because of the set-to, "Dick"
never does "saw it up." (86)

"The Doctor and the Doctor's Wife" almost serves as a reply to the
doctor's Cæsarian hubris in "Indian Camp," for here the roles
between the white man and the Indian have reversed. In this story,
the doctor now needs the Indian men to help him dislodge the logs
and saw them up. Here one Indian speaks—has the last word, in
fact—while the doctor is silenced, though the Indians "could see
from his back how angry he was" [18]. Dr. Adams's verbal threat, "If
you call me Doc once again, I'll knock your eye teeth down your
throat," is returned with "Oh, no, you won't, Doc" [18]. Not only
does Dick Boulton make the doctor back down, but he uses Ojibway, a language unfamiliar to Dr. Adams, to mock him. This scene
presents an utter reversal of power relations, where the dominant
language, or, the language of dominance, has lost its force. The
threat of violence centers on the half-buried logs that lie along the
lake's shore. One is reminded again of Kolodny's work, which shows
a clear link between the land (virgin woods) and the female body as
a primary site of contestation. Dick Boulton, described as a "half-
breed," dares to accuse Dr. Adams of stealing the logs.

"Well, Doc," he said, "that's a nice lot of timber you've stolen."
"Don't talk that way, Dick," the doctor said. "It's driftwood."
[17]

Dr. Adams chooses to re-name the wood, altering its status from "timber," which entails value and ownership, to "driftwood," implying a freedom from the rules of legal possession. Dick counters this with a kind of textual evidence, the ultimate source of "truth" and "legality."

> "Wash it off. Clean off the sand on account of the saw. I want to see who it belongs to," Dick said.
>
> The log was just awash in the lake. Eddy and Billy Tabeshaw leaned on their cant-hooks sweating in the sun. Dick kneeled down in the sand and looked at the mark of the scaler's hammer in the wood at the end of the log.
>
> "It belongs to White and McNally," he said, standing up and brushing off his trousers' knees.
>
> The doctor was very uncomfortable. [18]

Just as the doctor's mark was left on the Indian woman's body and could later be further consecrated in the medical journals, the log in this scene bears the mark of its possessor—White and McNally. The symbolic value of the name, White, should not be lost in our reading. Thomas Strychacz's article "Dramatizations of Manhood in Hemingway's *In Our Time* and *The Sun Also Rises*" offers a useful reading of the scene's significance:

> The mark of the scaler's hammer in the log shows that it belongs to "White" and McNally. In the same way, the fence around the white doctor's garden marks the extent of his domain in the forest, the Indian's traditional space, from which the three Indians appear and into which they disappear. The recognition that the land is stolen as well as the logs deepens the significance of the doctor's shame—it becomes his culture's shame too—and begins to explain why he fails to protect the integrity of his space. The doctor has no ground to stand on because the ground is, morally speaking, not his; the fence around the garden is as morally indefensible as stealing the logs. (250)

Thus Dick Boulton uses a "textual" reference, the institutional imprint of a company's legal right, to support his shaming attack on Dr. Adams, and if we think back to "Indian Camp," Dick's success should not take us by surprise. When Dr. Adams wished to applaud his achievement in performing the Cæsarean section under such primitive conditions, he immediately exclaimed that the procedure would be "one for the medical journal" [13]. So when Dick Boulton refers to the text for *his* authority, the doctor can only back down. This may also explain the doctor's subsequent irritation when he re-enters the cottage: "In the cottage the doctor, sitting on the bed in his room, saw a pile of medical journals on the floor by the bureau. They were still in their wrappers unopened. It irritated him" [19].

These same journals had once been the textual representation and affirmation of his great power, but in this scene they lie on the floor, unread, impotent and useless to him.

The "Big Man" dynamic described earlier is also reversed here. In "Indian Camp," Uncle George distributes cigars, a gift that does not get reciprocated; but in "The Doctor and the Doctor's Wife," when the confrontation begins, we find that "Dick was a big man. He knew how big a man he was" [18]. The previously sanctioned forms of competition and rivalry have at last given way to overt threats and potential violence. For if we read these two stories as a unit, then the progression of violence from "Indian Camp" to "The Doctor and the Doctor's Wife" moves from the obscured to the overt; "Doc" sits on his bed cleaning a shotgun: "he pushed the magazine full of the heavy yellow shells and pumped them out again. They were scattered on the bed" [19]. Strychacz has pointed out that "the rifle . . . signifies the technological superiority that hastened the appropriation of the Indian lands" ("Trophy-Hunting" 36). More obviously, we can easily decode the sexual metaphor of shells pumped through a shaft and then left scattered on the bed, wasted and impotent. The scene where violent, sexual, and racial markers all coincide most completely is during the climactic confrontation between "Dick" and "Doc":

> "If you think the logs are stolen, leave them alone and take your tools back to the camp," the doctor said. His face was red.
> "Don't go off at half-cock, Doc," Dick said. [18]

This scene contains not only a sexual, but also a racial metaphor that finally dislodges the most stubborn racial marker of all—skin color. During the confrontation, the doctor's face, presumably because of his embarrassment and anger, has turned red. A fight, ostensibly between Dick, the Indian, and Doc, the white man, must also be read in reverse: as a confrontation between Dick, "many of the farmers around the lake really believed he was a *white* man," and Doc, whose "face was *red*" (italics mine, [18]). A climactic scene between the "great man" and the "big man" forces social relations into the realm of violence, at once exposing and challenging the artificiality of power relations based on essentialist notions of racial difference, like those presented in "Indian Camp." Here, in the second story, the racial markers continually shift, and we in turn must shift our perceptions of race in Hemingway's stories.

Borrowing from Michael Omi and Howard Winant, I would suggest that Hemingway's stories represent race as an "unstable and 'decentered' complex of social meanings constantly being transformed by political struggle" (55). "Indian Camp" does present a biologically based view of racial difference and implies almost unwavering success for power relations that rely on white male dominance. The only crack in the veneer comes with Uncle George's sarcasm, which deflates Dr. Adams's self-aggrandizement, but George's remark loses its force in the wake of Nick's final musing that he will never die. Returning once again to Nick's final words in "Indian Camp," George Monteiro has suggested that the words reflect a belief he will never die "that way" (155), as the Indian has died. This reading again foregrounds Nick's extreme psychical distancing between self and other, a pattern of distancing he learned from his father, to whom the woman's screams are "not important." But "The Doctor and the Doctor's Wife" seriously complicates Nick's hyper-essentialist notion (that we are so different, even the ultimate leveler of humanity—death—divides the races). Dick defies racial categorization, co-opts forms of literacy valued by Dr. Adams, challenges him based on the law, and therefore reverses the power relations based in an authority ordinarily accessible only to whites. All of this simultaneously highlights the social constructedness of racial difference, undoing the hierarchy of power in "Indian Camp," and creating overt parallels between Dick/Doc, and to some extent, between Dr. Adams and the Indian husband.

The brief interchange in the cottage between Dr. Adams and his nameless wife serves as yet another reference to the doctor's earlier authority in "Indian Camp":

> "Remember, that he who ruleth his spirit is greater than he that taketh a city," said his wife. She was a Christian Scientist. Her Bible, her copy of *Science and Health* and her *Quarterly* were on a table beside her bed in the darkened room. [19]

The depiction of the doctor's wife, in pain, lying in a room described twice as "darkened" and twice as "with the blinds drawn," may at first seem to present another helpless, colonized woman, whose nameless identity stems from her role as wife and mother. But her religion relies on divine law in times of sickness, disregarding medical means of healing. Almost a direct attack on the value of medical journals, her textual authority comes in the form of a Bible, *Science and Health,* and the *Quarterly*, books entirely devoted to a faith which "denies the necessity of [Dr. Adams's] professional function" (DeFalco 165). Furthermore, her quote from scripture draws a stark contrast between the Cæsar-doctor of "Indian Camp" ("he that taketh a city") and the diminutive "Doc" who turns his back on a petty fight ("he who ruleth his spirit"); the husband's power is productive here only when directed inward. Of course, this form of power is the only kind afforded to the Indian husband as well.

As Dana Nelson has written, drawing on Foucault, "it is wrong to see power as only oppressive. It can be productive and progressive— both by the intentions of those who exercise it, and unintentionally, in the gaps left by its constant failure to create a total, seamless system" (xii). For power to be total, or invulnerable, the object of that power would have to remain static and silent. While "Indian Camp" gives the impression of total domination, the seams begin to show even within that story (Uncle George's sarcasm, the Indian woman's biting back, Nick's tenuous immunity from death). In the second story, "The Doctor and the Doctor's Wife," the forms of domination in the first story come back to be co-opted and reinscribed by Dick, a man whose racial markings will not hold. The non-speaking have become bilingual; those without access to institutionalized literacy now rely on legal fine print; the woman's body has been colonized by a higher power; the doctor cannot control even the color of his skin. The conflict between Dick and Dr. Adams becomes an almost entirely discursive one, implying yet again that power relations depend on the social or cultural construction of "race," a construction that must remain variable, in flux. But Hemingway's stories do not allow such a simplified resolution, and if we take up Joyce A. Joyce's charge that to deconstruct race is to diminish or negate black identity (341), we cut to the heart of my interest in these two stories as a unit, because Hemingway does not deny the essentialist notion that some kind of inherent racial identity remains lodged in the body. The jack-knife cuts a woman's womb open; the razor slits a man's throat from ear to ear. These bodies are real; pain has marked them.

Without denying the corporeal reality of lived racial experience, these stories also demonstrate that individuals can slide back and forth between the larger categories of race. In the first story, racial essentialism comes from the fact that characters are clearly defined as white or Indian, and their roles do not shift or change in any way. White dominates and the Indian remains silent, passive, and under control of the whites. The only hint of role reversal comes when the Indian woman bites Uncle George's arm and the other Indian laughs at him, conscious of the incongruity and unexpectedness of her act. This laugh, however, is translated in the second story into outright mockery. The roles have been reversed, but in order to represent this, Hemingway actually has his characters' faces change color—to be humiliated is to be red and to be victor is to be white. In this scenario, then, the tag "race" remains stable, because "white" equates with power and "red" equates with submission, but the individuals move fluidly between these markers.

In an interview with George Plimpton in the *Paris Review*, Hemingway spoke of a writer's "unexplained knowledge which could come from *forgotten racial or family experience*" (italics mine, 85). His stories may have been spurred by an autobiographical "family experience," but we cannot ignore their relation to a larger "forgotten racial experience" in American history. What happens in the confrontation between Dick and Doc represents nothing less than a crisis of authority that betrays the unstable foundation upon which the white man has built his power. When relying on the institutional authority of the medical profession, Dr. Adams works on stable ground. But in the second story, his power rests on the speech act, a threat, and Dick derails its authority with the simple but devastating retort, "Oh, no, you won't." The beauty of this reply is that it not only offers an implicit counter-threat, but it exposes the creaky machinery behind the doctor's earlier dominance. Stripped of institutional authority, textual authority, or witnesses, the doctor's standard mechanisms of power are laid bare: without complicity, power cannot be effective. And this brings us full circle, because that, I believe, is the moral of Toni Morrison's story as well. The "more or less tacit agreement among literary scholars" (5) requires a complicity that, despite its hold on our literary imagination, can be controverted.

Works Cited

Butler, Judith. *Gender Trouble: Feminism and the Subversion of Identity*. New York: Routledge, 1990.

Comley, Nancy R. and Robert Scholes. *Hemingway's Genders: Rereading the Hemingway Text*. New Haven: Yale UP, 1994.

DeFalco, Joseph. *The Hero in Hemingway's Short Stories*. Pittsburgh: U of Pittsburgh P, 1963.

————. "Initiation ('Indian Camp' and 'The Doctor and the Doctor's Wife')." *The Short Stories of Ernest Hemingway: Critical Essays*. Ed. Jackson J. Benson. Durham, NC: Duke UP, 1975. 159–67.

Flora, Joseph M. *Hemingway's Nick Adams*. Baton Rouge: Louisiana State UP, 1982.

Fuss, Diana. *Essentially Speaking: Feminism, Nature and Difference*. New York: Routledge, 1989.

Greenblatt, Stephen. *Marvelous Possessions: The Wonder of the New World*. Chicago: U of Chicago P, 1991.

Hemingway, Ernest. "The Art of Fiction XXI: Ernest Hemingway." *Paris Review* 18 (1958): 61–89.

————. "The Doctor and the Doctor's Wife." *In Our Time*. 1925, 1930. New York: Scribner's, 1958. 23–27.

————. "Indian Camp." *In Our Time*. 1925, 1930. New York: Scribner's, 1958. 15–19.

————. "A Way You'll Never Be." *The Short Stories of Ernest Hemingway*. 1938. New York: Scribner's, 1966. 402–14.

Joyce, Joyce A. "The Black Canon: Reconstructing Black American Literary Criticism." *New Literary History* 18 (1987): 335–44.

Kennedy, J. Gerald. "Hemingway's Gender Trouble." *American Literature* 63:2 (1991): 187–207.

Kolodny, Annette. *The Lay of the Land: Metaphor as Experience and History in American Life and Letters.* Chapel Hill: U of North Carolina P. 1975.

Lewis, R. W. B. *The American Adam: Innocence, Tragedy, and Tradition in the Nineteenth Century.* Chicago: U of Chicago P, 1955.

Moddelmog, Debra. "Reconstructing Hemingway's Identity: Sexual Politics, the Author, and the Multicultural Classroom." *Narrative* 1:3 (October 1993): 187–206.

Monteiro, George. "The Limits of Professionalism: A Sociological Approach to Faulkner, Fitzgerald and Hemingway." *Criticism* 15 (Spring 1973): 145–55.

Morrison, Toni. *Playing in the Dark: Whiteness and the Literary Imagination.* New York: Vintage, 1992.

Nelson, Dana. *The Word in Black and White: Reading 'Race' in American Literature, 1638–1867.* Oxford: Oxford UP, 1992.

Omi, Michael, and Howard Winant. *Racial Formation in the United States from the 1960s to the 1980s.* New York: Routledge, 1994.

Rubin, Gayle. "The Traffic in Women: Notes on the 'Political Economy' of Sex." *Toward an Anthropology of Women.* Ed. Rayna R. Reiter. New York: Monthly Review, 1975. 157–210.

Scarry, Elaine. *The Body in Pain: The Making and Unmaking of the World.* New York: Oxford UP, 1985.

Smith, Paul. *A Reader's Guide to the Short Stories of Ernest Hemingway.* Boston: G. K. Hall, 1989.

Spilka, Mark. *Hemingway's Quarrel with Androgyny.* Lincoln: U of Nebraska P, 1990.

Strong, Paul. "The First Nick Adams Stories." *Studies in Short Fiction* 28:1 (Winter 1991): 83–91.

Strychacz, Thomas. "Dramatizations of Manhood in Hemingway's *In Our Time* and *The Sun Also Rises.*" *American Literature* 61:2 (May 1989): 245–60.

———. "Trophy-Hunting as a Trope of Manhood in Ernest Hemingway's *Green Hills of Africa.*" *The Hemingway Review* 13:1 (Fall 1993): 36–47.

Tanselle, G. Thomas. "Hemingway's Indian Camp." *Explicator* 20 (February 1962): Item 53.

Wolter, Jürgen C. "Cæsareans in an Indian Camp." *The Hemingway Review* 13:1 (Fall 1993): 92–94.

Young, Philip. *Ernest Hemingway: A Reconsideration.* University Park: Pennsylvania State UP, 1966.

"THE END OF SOMETHING"

LISA TYLER

From An Ecofeminist Reading of Hemingway's "The End of Something"†

* * * Ecofeminists argue that the domination of women and the domination of the environment are parallel if not in many ways identical. As Catherine Roach observes, * * * "Women are perceived to merge with nature, to be part of the nonhuman surround and only semihuman. Similarly, nature is perceived as female, as virgin resource to be exploited or raped, as sharing in woman's semihuman quality" (56).[1] More recently, in *Feminism and the Mastery of Nature*, Val Plumwood has articulated the philosophical underpinnings of this stance. She contends that in Western culture, a white, largely male elite, which she terms the "master model," dominates and excludes both nature and women. As with women, nature and the environment are valuable to this "master model" only insofar as they are resources available for the master's use—a philosophy she calls "instrumentalism." As Plumwood goes on to explain:

> Instrumentalism is a mode of use which does not respect the other's independence or fullness of being, or acknowledge their agency. Its aim is to subdue the other maximally within the sphere of the user's own agency. It recognises no residue or autonomy in the instrumentalised other, and strives to deny or negate that other as a limit on the self and as a center of resistance. (142)

Plumwood further associates instrumentalism with "the individual who stands apart from an alien other and denies his own relationship to and dependency on this other" (142).

In Ernest Hemingway's short story "The End of Something," the long introductory passage describing the demise of Hortons Bay as a logging town establishes an implicit parallel with the romantic

---

† *The Hemingway Review* 27.2 (Spring 2008): 60–73. Copyright © 2008. Reprinted by permission of The Ernest Hemingway Foundation. All rights reserved. Some of the author's notes have been omitted. Page numbers in brackets refer to this Norton Critical Edition.

1. Sherry B. Ortner in "Is Female to Male as Nature Is to Culture?" and Annette Kolodny, in *The Lay of the Land: Metaphor as Experience and History in American Life and Letters*, were in the mid-1970s the first to point out the sobering consequences of such blurring of women and nature.

breakup at the heart of the story,[2] a parallel that illustrates what Plumwood has described as the master model's instrumentalism of women and nature. Thus, the loggers in the story have used the forest until it can no longer provide them with anything they can exploit for profit. They reject the denuded land they have left behind as if they stand apart from it and as if denying their relationship to it will somehow cancel their dependence upon it for subsistence. Similarly, Nick, arguably the protagonist of "The End of Something," rejects Marjorie because she "isn't any fun any more" [25]—she is no longer useful in providing him with entertainment. He rejects her as if he stands apart from her and as if denying their relationship will somehow cancel his emotional dependence on her—a false hope, as his later misery over their breakup indicates.

Hemingway critic Horst H. Kruse * * * goes so far as to say of the story's problematic introduction: "In that it is taken from nature it implies that the course which Nick's love for Marjorie has taken is a natural one and as relentless as it is inevitable" (214). He concludes, "all things run their natural course, and submission and acceptance are the only sensible responses" (214). But logging a forested area until "there were no more logs to make lumber" is hardly a *natural* course.

Sheldon Grebstein makes a similar point but defines "nature" rather differently than most readers might. Grebstein contends that Hortons Bay becomes "a paradigm for the romance of Nick and Marjorie, once-thriving like Horton's Bay yet now about to perish"—so far, so good. "It will appear that it, too, has fallen victim to nature," he then explains rather illogically, offering a peculiar elaboration that nature means "man's nature to chafe under female domination and reject it" (158). How has Hortons Bay fallen victim to man's nature to chafe under female domination and reject it?

Rather than fall into these thickets of tortured logic, I want to suggest an alternative, ecofeminist approach to "The End of Something," one informed by both Susan Beegel's application of Michigan's environmental history to *In Our Time* ("Second Growth") and Laura Gruber Godfrey's call for us to attend to the "landscape of logging" in the short story's cultural geography. "The End of Something" is

---

2. I have chosen to adopt Hemingway's usage of "Hortons Bay" except where I am quoting someone else; the town is officially "Horton Bay," but "Horton's Bay" is also widely (if incorrectly) used.

   On the parallels between Nick and Marjorie's relationship and the former logging town of Hortons Bay, see for example Flora, *Ernest Hemingway: A Study of the Short Fiction* (28–29) and *Hemingway's Nick Adams* (54), as well as Godfrey (51–52), Parker (157), Stewart (49), Strychacz (66), and Whitt (156). Most critics accept the parallel but do not go on to develop its implications.

* * *

Hemingway's elegy for both a place and a relationship (Stoneback 66). In his view, the loggers have wantonly destroyed trees, the natural beauty of the Point, and the economy of the small town of Hortons Bay. Similarly, Nick has deliberately hurt a young woman who loves him and destroyed their relationship. In both cases, the damage is irreparable, and Hemingway is mourning the loss.

Despite bluntly stated condemnations by Paul Smith (53) and Matthew Stewart (49), the long opening passage succinctly summarizing the history of logging in Hortons Bay is artistically valuable, because the abandoned logging town represents a vivid (if disturbing) metaphor for the relationship Nick and Marjorie share. The town is abandoned for a very specific reason: the virgin forest that the timber industry relied on for its existence has been despoiled. Michigan no longer has any old-growth trees available for the loggers to exploit. Marjorie's virginity has also been despoiled, and the relationship is over once she, too, no longer has her virginity for Nick to exploit. Just as the loggers abandon the town to search for other virgin timber they can use, Nick, too, is ready to move on, presumably to other girls who can give him what Marjorie no longer has to offer.

Her actions early in the brief story suggest that Marjorie does not anticipate Nick's decision. Hemingway foreshadows her shock when he writes of their "trolling along the edge of the channel bank where the bottom dropped off suddenly from sandy shallows to twelve feet of water" [23]. For Marjorie, the bottom drops off very suddenly indeed. Marjorie calls the ugly abandoned sawmill "our old ruin" and tells Nick, "It seems more like a castle" [23]. She romanticizes the mill, seeing it as something they share ("*our* old ruin") and an idealized image from a fairy tale, just as she has romanticized their relationship, which she also sees as something they share and idealizes in fairy-tale terms. She fondly, foolishly believes they are in love with each other. Nick's response to her romanticizing of the mill's shabby remains is his trademark silence of disagreement: "Nick said nothing" [23]. But when she romanticizes the relationship, Nick finally, bluntly, even cruelly, sets her straight:

> "Isn't love any fun?" Marjorie said.
> "No," Nick said. [26]

The mill is not a romantic ruin, and Nick at least is apparently no longer in love.

When Nick goes on to insist that "It isn't fun any more. Not any of it," Marjorie clearly does not agree: "She didn't say anything" [25]. Sadly for her, the feeling isn't mutual. In rejecting Marjorie, Nick is clearly rejecting their emotional closeness: ". . . [T]he growing intimacy between them, and therefore Nick's own emotional dependency on her, had become too intense for him to handle" (Boker 186). Marjorie's sensitivity to Nick's emotional state is evident in the story. She is so attuned to his feelings that she asks, "What's the matter, Nick?" [24] before he even says anything about breaking up. She recognizes his insistence that she "knows everything" for what it is: "'You don't have to talk silly,' Marjorie said. 'What's really the matter?'" [25]. Bill, on the other hand, is so emotionally illiterate, so hopelessly out of touch with the feelings of others, that he anticipates a scene from the impeccably dignified Marjorie and, evidently oblivious to Nick's pain, blithely asks him how he feels [26].

When Nick proposes as his reason for the breakup the complaint that "You know everything. That's the trouble. You know you do" [25], Marjorie responds with the same silence Nick repeatedly uses throughout this collection of short stories to signal complete disagreement: "Marjorie did not say anything" [25]. When he repeats his claim, she says, "Oh, shut up" and asks him again what's wrong, a strong sign that she does not believe in the truth of this pretext for Nick's behavior. And Hemingway backs her up, implying that she erred in cleaning her fish. Nick corrects her, saying "You don't want to take the ventral fin out" [24] after looking at her fish. She *doesn't* know everything, after all. By falsely claiming that there is nothing left to teach Marjorie, Nick is deliberately provoking an argument, just as Dick Boulton has in the short story "The Doctor and the Doctor's Wife," that appears before "The End of Something" in *In Our Time* (in [an] example of Hemingway's juxtaposition of parallel themes in this collection). As readers soon learn, Nick was determined to end this relationship on some pretext no matter what Marjorie said (Montgomery 134).

The subsequent story in the collection, "The Three-Day Blow," reveals that what initially seems like the spontaneous and bittersweet ending of a teenaged couple's summer romance is actually an orchestrated event—yet oddly, many critics accept at face value Nick's facile excuse for ending what the story's title suggests he is too immature even to recognize as a relationship. Perhaps, like the naive Mrs. Adams in "The Doctor and the Doctor's Wife," such readers find it hard to believe a man would pick a fight intentionally so as to avoid having to work out what he owes someone.

While some critics might like to see Nick as "floundering," to borrow one critic's term (Stewart 55), or merely "confused about what he wants," as another benignly suggests (Ferrero 25), the parallels Hemingway draws in this story between Nick's treatment of Marjorie and the loggers' treatment of the virgin forests of Michigan indicate that Nick, like the loggers, is all too aware of the damage he is doing. It is instructive here to examine *Waiting for the Morning*

Train: An American Boyhood, a memoir written by the Pulitzer Prize–winning Civil War historian Bruce Catton (1899–1978), a contemporary of Hemingway's who spent his boyhood in Benzonia, Petoskey, and Boyne City, all in northern Michigan. Catton, who titled one of his chapters "Whatever Is, Is Temporary" and another "Death of a Wilderness," explains carefully what the loggers knew and when they knew it:

> People in Boyne City subscribed to Michigan's most cherished delusion: they thought that the supply of lumber was inexhaustible. The word *inexhaustible* had been on men's lips since before the Civil War, and by 1906 most of the state had stopped using it because most of the virgin timber had in fact been exhausted long since, so that big sawmill towns like Saginaw and Muskegon and Manistee were desperately looking for some other way to stay alive. But in Boyne City, the word was still good.
>
> Or at least it still seemed to be good. The men who owned the mills and the lumber camps and the railroad doubtless had a clear idea of the real situation, and they were prepared to follow the lumberman's oldest rule—*cut and get out*. But to everybody else the setup looked permanent. (88, his emphasis)

To Marjorie, the setup with Nick looked permanent (or at least potentially permanent). She had dreamed with him of going to Italy together, and they were going to get married, according to Nick's own admission in "The Three-Day Blow" [36]. But Nick "had a clear idea of the real situation" and was equally prepared to get what he wanted "*and get out.*" Hemingway judged Nick—and very likely himself, as Nick is autobiographical—much more harshly than some Hemingway critics would like. As "The Three-Day Blow" reveals, the chief difference between Nick and the loggers is that unlike the loggers, who fasten canvas securely over the "open hold" of the schooner that takes away "everything that had made the mill a mill," Nick has not yet learned how to keep his emotions "lashed tight" [23].

In "The End of Something," the image of the mill now reduced to "the broken white limestone of its foundations" further suggests that very little remains of the relationship Nick and Marjorie once shared [23]. More specifically, the word "broken" implies permanent damage to the relationship (and perhaps to Marjorie, as well) while the whiteness connotes the purity and innocence lost. The "acres of sawdust" are now all that remains of the old-growth forest the loggers exploited [23]. Hemingway's condemnations of second-growth forest as "swampy" in "The End of Something" [23] and as "an abandoned country with the heart gone out of it" in the manuscript of *Death in the Afternoon* (qtd. in Beegel, *Hemingway's Craft* 52–53) don't bode well for Nick's chances of resurrecting his relationship with Marjorie. The analogy with Michigan's forests implies that what has been destroyed is irreplaceable and that the damage done is irreparable. Presumably, a second-growth relationship, like a second-growth forest, would have no heart and would therefore be a pale imitation of the real thing.

Lest this interpretation seem all too woolly and ecofeminist for the supposedly ultra-macho or even reactionary Hemingway, it's important to note that this reading of "The End of Something" is entirely consistent with imagery he uses in his posthumously published memoir, *A Moveable Feast*, where through metonymy he specifically links a relationship that he believes he has betrayed and irreparably damaged to the metaphor of trees turned into so much timber: "When I saw my wife again standing by the tracks as the train came in by the piled logs at the station, I wished I had died before I ever loved anyone but her" (*MF* 210).

Michael Seefeldt has warned us against the folly of criticizing Hemingway's work on the basis of "anachronistically applied environmentalism" (122). Certainly Hemingway's astonishing hunt totals demonstrate that we cannot in good conscience argue that he was an "environmentalist" if the word is to retain its usual meaning. Nevertheless, Gerald Locklin and Charles Stetler concluded, as early as 1981, that "far from ecological villainy, Hemingway's life and works give powerful evidence of an early and exemplary concern for the preservation of the environment, and . . . those who share that concern can come to his works not as enemies but as allies" (24).[3] To avoid the peril of "anachronistically applied environmentalism," however, it might be best to ask ourselves how Hemingway (not 21st century readers of Hemingway) would perceive the logging of Michigan's virgin forests. And here we are in luck, for Hemingway wrote about his feelings toward the timber industry surprisingly often throughout his life.

Hemingway certainly did not see the loggers' destructiveness as natural. "Indiana was once a timber country. So was the lower peninsula of Michigan. Today there is hardly a patch of virgin timber in the upper peninsula of Michigan," Hemingway wrote in a newspaper article as early as 1923 ("More Game" 264). Many years later, he told his youngest son bedtime stories about "how beautiful the virgin forests were before the loggers came" (Gregory Hemingway 62).

---

3. For more recent ecocritical readings of Hemingway's work, see Beegel ("Eye and Heart" and "Second Growth"), Schmidt, and the essay collection *Hemingway and the Natural World*, edited by Robert Fleming.

According to biographer Carlos Baker, Hemingway was particularly disheartened by the change he witnessed in Spain's Irati River region from one year to the next:

> *** The dark stream bed of the Irati was filled with loggers' trash. . . . In four days of trying they did not take a single fish. "Fish killed, pools destroyed, dams broken down," said Ernest. "Made me feel sick." (149)

In 1925 he wrote about his disappointment to Gertrude Stein and Alice B. Toklas, "We found our best stream which was full of trout last year ruined by logging and running logs down—all the pools cleaned out—trout killed" (SL 167). Seven years later, when he published *Death in the Afternoon*, he was evidently still haunted by the destruction: ". . . if your memory is good you may ride still through the forests of the Irati with trees like drawings in a child's fairy book. They cut those down. They ran logs down the river and they killed the fish, or in Galicia they bombed and poisoned them; results the same; so in the end it's just like home . . ." (*DIA* 274).

He was even blunter in nine paragraphs of material he later cut from the conclusion of *Death in the Afternoon*:

> Michigan I loved very much when I lived in it, and when I was away from it, but as I grew up each time I returned to it it was changed. . . . They cut down the forests, the streams lost their water, the lakes had their levels lowered and raised by the taking or not taking of water to float sewerage from Chicago down the drainage canal; they built concrete motor roads across all the country and around the lakes; the motorists caught all the fish out of the streams and, as the boys went to Flint or Detroit to work and prices made it impossible to make a living, they abandoned the farms. Now the second growth is coming back where the forests were slashed . . . and people seeing the second growth believe that they know what the forest was like. But it was not like that and you will never know what it was like if you did not see it. Nor will you know what the heart of a country was after it is gone. (qtd. in Beegel, *Hemingway's Craft* 52–53)

Later in the same passage, he described his experience as "[s]eeing northern Michigan ruined" (qtd. in Beegel, *Hemingway's Craft* 55).

It seems evident from his own writings that Hemingway did not view logging in the morally neutral or even warmly benevolent terms which many Hemingway critics use to describe the activities of the timber industry. According to his own testimony, its effects on the landscape made him sick, and he was devastated by the loss of virgin forests and undisturbed rivers. As Constance Cappel Montgomery notes, most of the pine forests were already gone from Michigan by the turn of the century (27). If anything, Hemingway *exaggerated* the damage caused by the loggers during his lifetime, heightening their destructive impact on Michigan's landscape (Svoboda 19).

Still, other sources confirm that the end of the forests did bring change and loss to Michigan communities. As Theodore J. Karamanski notes in *Deep Woods Frontier: A History of Logging in Northern Michigan*, "During the hardwood era, the interior of the Upper Peninsula was more thickly settled than it would ever be again. For when the forest thinned, the railroads were closed, the towns decayed, and the backwoods farms, like a plant without roots, withered and died" (93). And towns like Hortons Bay *did* disappear: "Some of them simply evaporated, leaving hardly trace enough to make a traveler say: Ghost town. Others went into a long decline, surviving . . . as a couple of houses, a filling station, and a barbecue stand" (Catton 120).

It is difficult to comprehend the massive scope of the ecological damage the state sustained, but Catton suggests it indirectly:

> By 1897, in less than half a century, Michigan as a whole had turned out more than a hundred and sixty billion feet of pine boards. . . . [T]hat is enough lumber to build ten million six-room houses. One fanciful statistician once estimated that it was enough to build a solid pine floor over the entire state of Michigan, with enough left over to floor all of Rhode Island as well; or, such ventures being ruled out, to build fifty plank roads, each fifty feet wide, from New York to San Francisco. (111)

Susan Beegel has called what happened to Michigan a holocaust in American forestry.

We need to read (and reread) "The End of Something" in that context in order to see that it cannot be dismissed (as it sometimes has been) as a slight, purely autobiographical story about a long-ago teenage breakup. Rather we should read it as an important statement linking ecological trauma to the many other 20th century traumas represented in the collection. In "The End of Something," Hemingway considers men's (and perhaps his own) sexual exploitation of women as analogous to what he considered the logging industry's desecration of Michigan, and by placing the story in this collection, he links both to the patriarchal violence of World War I. The story hints at the long-lasting damage caused by Nick's refusal to examine the permanent consequences of his own choices, and we are implicitly cautioned that we, too, need to reexamine the choices we are making. Nick's vacillations and immaturity are our own; we want what we want when we want it, and we don't really care to confront the results of that kind of self-centeredness. Like Nick in

"The Three-Day Blow," we can always persuade ourselves that the damage (to our relationships, to our environment, to the nations of Europe) can still be reversed.

Throughout *In Our Time*, Harbour Winn notes that "the spoiled environment" is a recurring motif, citing not simply "The End of Something," but also the references to logging in "Indian Camp," the yellowed snow in "Cross-Country Snow," and the blackened countryside and carelessly killed trout in "Big Two-Hearted River" (131). In theorizing an ecofeminist peace politics, Karen Warren, one of the founders of ecofeminist philosophy, has termed such environmental damage a form of violence:

> Feminists can begin to develop analyses of violence and nonviolence which show the connections among kinds of violence: violence against the self (e.g. anorexia and bulimia, suicide); violence against others (e.g. spousal and child abuse, rape); violence against the earth (e.g. "rape of the land"); perhaps even global, systemic, economic violence (e.g. poverty). This would involve showing ways in which *patriarchalism* underlies all such kinds of violence and itself breeds violence. (194)

Anticipating this and other later ecofeminist theories linking war and violence against nature, Hemingway in *In Our Time* implicitly draws parallels between suicide, rape (in "Up in Michigan," the story which would have opened the collection but was deemed too explicit to be publishable in 1920s America), the psychological and emotional spousal abuse in "The Doctor and the Doctor's Wife," the despoilation of the earth, and the global, systemic, patriarchal violence of the First World War. Winn convincingly proposes that for Hemingway, "the exploitation of human beings in war is analogous to the spoiled environment" (131). Hemingway uses the imagery of an irreparably damaged environment in "The End of Something" and elsewhere throughout the stories of *In Our Time* to link violence against nature with the other forms of violence depicted in that collection, including violence against animals, women, underprivileged men, and enemy soldiers, suggesting that he was more ecofeminist in his sympathies than his readers have yet acknowledged.

Works Cited

Baker, Carlos. *Ernest Hemingway: A Life Story*. New York: Scribner's, 1969.

Beegel, Susan F. "Eye and Heart: Hemingway's Education as a Naturalist." In *A Historical Guide to Ernest Hemingway*. Ed. Linda Wagner-Martin. New York: Oxford UP, 2000. 53–92.

———. *Hemingway's Craft of Omission: Four Manuscript Examples*. Ann Arbor: UMI Research P, 1988.

————. "Second Growth: The Ecology of Loss in 'Fathers and Sons.'" In *New Essays on Hemingway's Short Fiction*. Ed. Paul Smith. New York: Cambridge UP, 1998. 75–110.

Boker, Pamela A. *The Grief Taboo in American Literature: Loss and Prolonged Adolescence in Twain, Melville, and Hemingway*. New York: New York UP, 1996.

Catton, Bruce. *Waiting for the Morning Train: An American Boyhood*. 1972. Detroit, MI: Wayne State UP, 1987.

Ferrero, David J. "Nikki Adams and the Limits of Gender Criticism," *The Hemingway Review* 17.2 (Spring 1998): 18–30.

Fleming, Robert F., ed. *Hemingway and the Natural World*. Moscow: U of Idaho P, 1999.

Flora, Joseph. *Ernest Hemingway: A Study of the Short Fiction*. Boston: Twayne, 1989.

————. *Hemingway's Nick Adams*. Baton Rouge: Louisiana State UP, 1982.

Godfrey, Laura Gruber. "Hemingway and Cultural Geography: The Landscape of Logging in 'The End of Something.'" *The Hemingway Review* 26.1 (Fall 2006): 47–62.

Grebstein, Sheldon Norman. *Hemingway's Craft*. Carbondale: Southern Illinois UP, 1973.

Hemingway, Ernest. *Death in the Afternoon*. New York: Scribner's, 1932.

————. "The End of Something." *The Short Stories of Ernest Hemingway*. New York: Scribner's, 1938. 107–111.

————. "Fathers and Sons." *The Short Stories of Ernest Hemingway*. New York: Scribner's, 1938. 488–499.

————. *Green Hills of Africa*. New York: Scribner's, 1935.

————. "More Game to Shoot in Crowded Europe than in Ontario." *Toronto Star Weekly*, 3 Nov. 1923: 20. Rpt. as "Hunting on the Continent." *The Wild Years*. Ed. Gene Z. Hanrahan. New York: Dell, 1967. 259–264.

————. *A Moveable Feast*. New York: Scribner's, 1964.

————. "The Snows of Kilimanjaro." *The Short Stories of Ernest Hemingway*. New York: Scribner's, 1938. 52–77.

————. "The Three-Day Blow." *The Short Stories of Ernest Hemingway*. New York: Scribner's, 1938. 115–125.

Hemingway, Gregory H. *Papa: A Personal Memoir*. Boston: Houghton Mifflin, 1976.

Karamanski, Theodore J. *Deep Woods Frontier: A History of Logging in Northern Michigan*. Detroit: Wayne State UP, 1989.

Kolodny, Annette. *The Lay of the Land: Metaphor as Experience and History in American Life and Letters*. Chapel Hill: U of North Carolina P, 1975.

Kruse, Horst H. "Ernest Hemingway's 'The End of Something': Its Independence as a Short Story and Its Place in the 'Education of Nick Adams.'" *Studies in Short Fiction* 4 (Winter 1967): 152–56. Rpt. in *The Short Stories of Ernest Hemingway: Critical Essays.* Ed. Jackson J. Benson. Durham, NC: Duke UP, 1975. 210–222.

LeGuin, Ursula K. "Women/Wilderness." *Healing the Wounds: The Promise of Ecofeminism.* Ed. Judith Plant. Philadelphia: New Society, 1989. 45–47.

Locklin, Gerald, and Charles Stetler. "Ernest Hemingway: 'Best of all he loved the fall.'" *Hemingway Notes* 6.2 (Spring 1981): 20–24.

Montgomery, Constance Cappel. *Hemingway in Michigan.* New York: Fleet, 1966.

Ortner, Sherry B. "Is Female to Male as Nature Is to Culture?" In *Woman, Culture, and Society.* Ed. Michelle Zimbalist Rosaldo and Louise Lamphere. Stanford, CA: Stanford UP, 1974. 67–87.

Parker, Alice. "Hemingway's 'The End of Something.'" *Explicator* 10 (March 1952): Item 36. Rpt. in Michael Reynolds, ed. *Critical Essays on Ernest Hemingway's In Our Time.* Boston, G. K. Hall, 1983. 157–158.

Plumwood Val. *Feminism and the Mastery of Nature.* London: Routledge, 1993.

Roach, Catherine. "Loving Your Mother: On the Woman-Nature Relation." In *Ecological Feminist Philosophies.* Ed. Karen J. Warren. Bloomington: Indiana UP, 1996. 52–65.

Schmidt, Susan. "Ecological Renewal Images in 'Big Two-Hearted River': Jack Pines and the Fisher King." *The Hemingway Review* 11.2 (Spring 1990): 142–144.

Seefeldt, Michael. Letter. *The Hemingway Review* 17.1 (Fall 1997): 120–123.

Smith, Paul. *A Reader's Guide to the Short Stories of Ernest Hemingway.* Boston: G. K. Hall, 1989.

Stewart, Matthew. *Modernism and Tradition in Ernest Hemingway's In Our Time: A Guide for Students and Readers.* Rochester, NY: Camden House, 2001.

Stoneback, H. R. "'Nothing Was Ever Lost': Another Look at 'That Marge Business.'" In *Hemingway: Up in Michigan Perspectives.* Ed. Frederic J. Svoboda and Joseph J. Waldmeir. East Lansing: Michigan State UP, 1995. 59–76.

Strychacz, Thomas. *Hemingway's Theaters of Masculinity.* Baton Rouge: Louisiana State UP, 2003.

Svoboda, Frederic J. "False Wilderness: Northern Michigan as Created in the Nick Adams Stories." In *Hemingway: Up in Michigan Perspectives.* Ed. Frederic J. Svoboda and Joseph J. Waldmeir. East Lansing: Michigan State UP, 1995. 15–22.

Warren, Karen J. "Toward an Ecofeminist Peace Politics." In *Ecological Feminism*. Ed. Karen J. Warren. New York: Routledge, 1994. 179–199.

Whitt, Joseph. "Hemingway's 'The End of Something.'" *Explicator* 9 (June 1951): Item 58. Rptd. in *Critical Essays on Ernest Hemingway's* In Our Time. Ed. Michael Reynolds. Boston: G. K. Hall, 1983. 155–156.

Winn, Harbour. "Hemingway's *In Our Time*: 'Pretty Good Unity.'" *The Hemingway Review* 9.2 (Spring 1990): 124–141.

"THE THREE-DAY BLOW"

WENDOLYN E. TETLOW

[Tonal Structure in "The Three-Day Blow"]†

Although "The Three-Day Blow" is a sequel to "The End of Something," each story is complete itself. The three-part tonal structure of "The Three-Day Blow," however, is more subtle than that of "The End of Something" because of its more dramatic form (there is very little exposition and narration).[1] But its preoccupations with the difficulty of understanding and expressing feelings, the focus on the loss of love, and on the relationships between men and women (as well as between men) connect the story to the former part of the sequence. The comic effects in "Three-Day Blow" make it unique, however, as does the predominance of dialogue to produce emotional flow.

Like "The End of Something," the story opens with an elegiac tone, but instead of a mill town it presents an autumn scene as the objective correlative [x] for Nick's feelings about the end of his relationship with Marjorie.[2]

> The rain stopped as Nick turned into the road that went up through the orchard. The fruit had been picked and the fall wind blew through the bare trees. Nick stopped and picked up a Wagner apple from beside the road, shiny in the brown grass

† From *Hemingway's* In Our Time: *Lyrical Dimensions* (Lewisburg, PA: Bucknell UP, 1992), pp. 61–65, 135. Reprinted by permission of Associated University Presses. One of the author's footnotes has been omitted. Page numbers in brackets refer to this Norton Critical Edition.

1. On the contrary, James M. Mellard argues that there are seven scenes within the story as in a one-act drama, "all contained within the ceremonial pattern of the drinks Nick and Bill take" (Four *Modes*, 287).

2. "The Three-Day Blow," Philip Young points out, relates among other things how "The End of Something" felt to Nick: "the end of the affair with Marjorie felt like the autumnal three-day wind storm that is blowing . . ." (*Reconsideration*, 34–35).

from the rain. He put the apple in the pocket of his Mackinaw coat.

The road came out of the orchard on to the top of the hill. There was the cottage, the porch bare, smoke coming from the chimney. In back was the garage, the chicken coop and the second-growth timber like a hedge against the woods behind. The big trees swayed far over in the wind as he watched. It was the first of the autumn storms. [29]

The details of a season's end—the picked fruit, the bare trees, the fall wind, and the brown grass—give the scene a sense of something having passed away, something over or lost. In particular, the fallen apple in the grass, though "shiny," suggests an innocence that is no more.[3] Likewise, the bare porch and the "smoke coming from the chimney" suggest a kind of winter seclusion and barrenness [29]. But the "second timber growth" keeps the danger of the "woods" beyond it from taking over. The storm Hemingway speaks of is "Only the first of the autumn storms," and it anticipates other losses in the latter half of the sequence [29].

A long section of dialogue between Nick and Bill then follows; it begins with a solemnity that suggests something is troubling them:

"Well, Wemedge," he said.
"Hey, Bill," Nick said, coming up the steps.
They stood together, looking out across the country, down over the orchard, beyond the road, across the lower fields and the woods of the point to the lake. They could see the surf along Ten Mile point.
"She's blowing," Nick said.
"She'll blow like that for three days," Bill said.
"Is your dad in?" Nick said.
"No. He's out with the gun. Come on in."
Nick went inside the cottage. There was a big fire in the fireplace. The wind made it roar. Bill shut the door.
"Have a drink?" he said. [29]

Even though Nick and Bill address each other informally by nickname, the slow, deliberate salutations, the remarks about the weather, Nick's asking about Bill's father, and Bill's invitation into the cabin and offering Nick a drink make their exchange seem more a ritual than the casual greeting of two old friends.[4] After their salu-

---

3. Kenneth Johnston, however, says that "the fact that he has not yet eaten of the forbidden fruit suggests the essential innocence of his affair of the heart." Johnston supports this in a note saying, "A scene set in the same orchard in 'Summer People' lends support to this interpretation. An hour before Nick has physical relations with Kate, he takes a bite from a green apple" ("'Three-Day Blow': Tragicomic Aftermath of a Summer Romance," *Hemingway Review* 2 [Fall 1982]: 21–25), 22.
4. Cf. Mellard, *Four Modes*, 285–89.

tations, Nick's disagreements about McGraw's purchase of Heinie Zim, about the books *Richard Feverel* and *Forest Lovers*, and about Walpole and Chesterton reveal that Nick is the one who is troubled by something.[5]

After each of Nick's disagreements, however, he comes around to Bill's point of view. This rhythm of conflict and reconciliation in the second movement of the story builds to a point of revelry as the two men proceed to get drunk. Thus, after the disagreement about McGraw's purchasing Heinie Zim, Nick concludes that "There's always more to it than we know about," as if this drinking rite must be closed with a formal propitiation [31]. And following their disagreement about Walpole and Chesterton, Nick says, "I wish we had them both here. . . . We'd take them both fishing to the 'Voix tomorrow" [32].

The more Nick and Bill drink, the more personal their conversations become. In their disagreement about their fathers, Nick insists his father has "missed a lot" because "He claims he's never taken a drink in his life" [33]. But Bill defends Nick's father, the doctor, and says, "You can't tell. . . . Everything's got its compensations" [33]. To smooth out this difference in opinion, Nick says, "It all evens up" [33].

This second movement of the story builds comically on waves of reconciliation to the point where Nick and Bill are so drunk that Nick has difficulty being "practical," a word Hemingway repeats four times (three times in the passage below) to emphasize the contrast between Nick's intention and his actions. Earlier, Nick did not think Hewlett's lovers in *Forest Lovers* terribly "practical" for having a naked sword between them in bed at night to keep them apart. In the following passage, however, Hemingway uses the scene of the spilled apricots to counterpoint Nick's opinion about the *Forest Lovers* and to parallel Nick's later self-deluded conclusion that he can always mend his relationship with Marjorie:

> "I'll get a chunk [of wood] from the back porch," Nick said. He had noticed while looking into the fire that the fire was dying down. Also he wished to show he could hold his liquor and be practical. Even if his father had never touched a drop Bill was not going to get him drunk before he himself was drunk.
>
> "Bring one of the big beech chunks," Bill said. He was also being consciously practical.
>
> Nick came in with the log through the kitchen and in passing knocked a pan off the kitchen table. He laid the log down and picked up the pan. It had contained dried apricots, soak-

---

5. For a discussion about Hemingway's reference to these particular baseball teams, novels, and authors, see Kenneth G. Johnston, "Tragicomic Aftermath," 21–25.

ing in water. He carefully picked up all the apricots off the floor, some of them had gone under the stove, and put them back in the pan. He dipped some more water onto them from the pail by the table. He felt quite proud of himself. He had been thoroughly practical. [33]

Part of the humor of this section is the deadpan tone in which Hemingway relates the incident, and part of the humor derives from the point of view—third person limited through Nick's inebriated consciousness. The repetition of the words "fire," "drunk," "apricots," "water," "practical," "log," and "table" among others, give the section a simple rhythmical quality which reflects Nick's state of mind. He is exaggeratedly deliberate and aware of his actions because he is trying to keep control while drunk, just as he tries to control his emotions elsewhere in the sequence, particularly in "Indian Camp," "The End of Something," and later in "Big Two-Hearted River." The central irony in the story is that Nick's primary practicality—his breaking up with Marjorie—has made him miserable. But for the time being, Nick feels only the pleasure alcohol has provided; both men drink to Chesterton and Walpole, Bill saying, "Gentlemen . . . I give you Chesterton and Walpole." "Exactly, gentlemen," Nick agrees [34].

A sudden shift in tone from a drink-induced loquaciousness to sober gravity comes as Bill tells Nick he was "very wise" (i.e. practical) "To bust off that Marge business" [34]. Nick's noncommittal responses to Bill's comments that Nick would be working now if he were married to Marjorie, that he would be fat, and that he would be struggling to cope with Marjorie's mother suggest that he agrees with Bill's point of view.[6] Even when Bill says Marjorie is not of his class, Nick assents in silence. While Nick may agree on these points, they are not causes for his breaking up with Marjorie. Nick's problem is that his love for Marjorie has disappeared "suddenly" and for no comprehensible (at least to him) reason.

The second movement of the story reaches a crescendo of disappointment after Bill says Marjorie is now able to marry someone "of her own sort and settle down and be happy" (35):

Nick said nothing. The liquor had all died out of him and left him alone. Bill wasn't there. He wasn't sitting in front of the fire or going fishing tomorrow with Bill and his dad or anything. He wasn't drunk. It was all gone. All he knew was that he had once had Marjorie and that he had lost her. She was gone and he had sent her away. That was all that mattered. He

6. Kruse notes that it is improbable "that the interpretation [Bill's reasons for Nick's breaking up with Marjorie] furnishes the true motive for Nick's behavior in 'The End of Something.' It is more likely that Hemingway is exploiting a favorite theme of his, that of failure of communication" (152–66).

> might never see her again. Probably he never would. It was all
> gone, finished. [35]

The short, staccato sentences and the repetition of negatives such
as "wasn't" and "never," and words that suggest loss such as "gone,"
"finished," "alone," and "lost" provide a somber contrast to earlier
notes of revelry. But the closest Nick comes to understanding and
articulating his loss is his analogy of his feelings to a three-day blow:
"I couldn't help it. Just like when the three-day blows come now and
rip all the leaves off the trees" [35]. Hemingway's use of this simile
for Nick suggests the capriciousness of love and its devastating
effects. The inexplicability of Nick's loss of love parallels the suddenness and irrationality of death at other points in the sequence.

As in "Indian Camp," the story closes with self-deception. After
Nick says, "I oughtn't to talk about it," Bill says, "You don't want to
think about it. You might get back into it again" [36]. But this
thought triggers another response in Nick and pulls him out of
depression, for suddenly he feels happy:

> Nothing was finished. Nothing was ever lost. He would go into
> town on Saturday. He felt lighter, as he had felt before Bill
> started to talk about it. There was always a way out. . . . It was
> not even very important. The wind blew everything like that
> away. [36–37]

Drinking plays a large part in the way Nick perceives his loss, for
when he goes outside he feels that "the Marge business was no longer so tragic. It was not even very important. The wind blew everything like that away. . . . Still he could always go into town Saturday
night. It was a good thing to have in reserve" [37].

"The Three-Day Blow," like "Indian Camp," "The Doctor and the
Doctor's Wife," and "The End of Something," is less concerned with
character development and plot than it is with a progression of tonal
centers that build toward a moment of heightened awareness. Characters are not developed; as embodiments of feelings, characters
present certain sets of feelings, often very limited. Thus, in "The
Three-Day Blow," as in "Indian Camp," Nick denies his awareness
of evil in the world. In "Indian Camp" the evil is death. In "The
Three-Day Blow" Nick denies his loss of love for Marjorie. Nick's
loss is treated in the same way that the awareness of death is treated
in the rest of the sequence—as casual, unimportant, often comic.

Works Cited

Kruse, Horst H. "Ernest Hemingway's 'The End of Something'": Its
    Independence as a Short Story and Its Place in the 'Education of
    Nick Adams.'" *Studies in Short Fiction* 4 (1967): 152–66.

Mellard, James M., ed. *Four Modes: A Rhetoric of Modern Fiction.*
New York: Macmillan, 1973.
Young, Philip. *Ernest Hemingway: A Reconsideration.* University Park:
Pennsylvania State UP, 1966.

"The Battler"

MARC KEVIN DUDLEY

[Race in "The Battler"]†

In the summer of 1908, up became down, black became white, and
the world as many knew it changed forever. In that year, Jack Johnson became the first African American heavyweight boxing world
champion. Some seven years later, Johnson would lose that title
to the last of several so-called great white hopes looking to knock
the defiant smile from the black man's face. In the spring of 1915,
Jess Willard became that man, seizing the crown for himself, and
reclaiming it for all of white America. It was a moment etched into
the national consciousness, and a reality that Ernest Hemingway
subtly infuses as backstory into the narrative threads of * * * "The
Battler." * * *

During the first two decades of the twentieth century, racial tensions in America were palpable. World war, increased foreign immigration, and a sizable African American migration from the South
to the North all marked the American landscape during the new
century's first decades. So did increased xenophobia and related
immigration laws, a resurgence of the Ku Klux Klan, and lynching
and race riots. And, as any good social realist would, Hemingway
imbibed what he saw. What many scholars and general readers alike
seem to overlook in assessing the author's modern vision is that
Hemingway, the voice of Anglo American masculinity, saw the world
in more than shades of white. And in "The Battler" * * * he explores
blackness and the gray spaces where black and white collide. For
Hemingway, the allusive boxing ring * * * becomes an appropriate
metaphor for the violent energy both holding together and threat-
ening to tear apart the present social order, an order predicated on
understood rules of racial construction.

Hemingway's "The Battler" is a fine entrée into the realm of
his black-and-white tales, * * * with a young white male protagonist

† From *Hemingway, Race, and Art* (Kent, OH: Kent State UP, 2011), pp. 69, 71–81, 172–
74. Used by permission of Kent State University Press. Some of the author's notes have
been omitted. Page numbers in brackets refer to this Norton Critical Edition.

being initiated into a world of violent racial negotiation. However, here the minority presence works to both indirectly illuminate the Anglo character and properly educate the reader.[1] *** Published in [1925] as part of the *** Nick Adams collection and included in *In Our Time*, it is an early reflection of Hemingway's awareness of the African American presence. Hemingway's prospective descriptions of the tale before its publication casually suggest the proper racial lens through which the story's principal players should be viewed.[2] *** "The Battler" forecasts and anticipates nicely this and other ancillary motifs visited repeatedly in the author's later works ***. Here Hemingway consciously underscores then deconstructs the fault(y) lines separating the races.

"The Battler" opens in line with reader expectation as Hemingway introduces us to a harsh landscape and a young, impressionable naïf, Nick Adams. The story unfolds amid violent environs with Nick battered and bruised, much the worse for wear after a scuffle with a train's brakeman. His pants, Hemingway tells us, are torn and "the skin was barked." His hands prove to be in no better shape, as "there were sand and cinders driven up under his nails" [41]. Nick has been tossed from a train for playing (rather poorly) the part of a stowaway intent on riding the rails for free. The brakeman has other ideas and passes along the lesson to Nick.

The greater lesson for Nick, though, is not necessarily one of economy or ethics; it is one of racial negotiation, and the story, which transpires at the foot of the embankment below the rails, follows Nick's brief encounter with the brakeman. Nick suddenly comes across a wandering duo: a white ex-prizefighter and his African American ex–jail mate and traveling companion. Hemingway's story begins ostensibly with Nick's meeting of this roving twosome, and the narrative's true racial implications are not readily apparent until well into the text. Hemingway does not disclose the tale's narrative import until the last sequence unfolds and Nick Adams wanders onward: "He must get to somewhere" [41]. The physical site then

1. In *Playing in the Dark*, Morrison suggests that much of the American literary canon, even texts seemingly devoid of a minority presence, has at its core a dependency on some (often phantom) minority presence to help define itself. In "The World and the Jug," Ralph Ellison seems to anticipate, some thirty years earlier, Morrison's assertions, as he suggests that "Southern whites cannot walk, talk, sing, conceive of laws or justice, think of sex, love, the family or freedom without responding to the presence of Negroes" (*Shadow and Act* 116).

2. In a letter to his friend and fellow expatriate John Dos Passos dated April 25, 1925, Hemingway describes the story as "a swell new Nick story about a busted down pug and a *coon* called The Battler" (*Selected Letters* 157, my emphasis). Race clearly marks the story. However, Hemingway's epithets, littering both the printed page and private conversation, demonstrate a marked struggle with and ambivalence toward matters of race and certainly complicate and cloud the picture of modernity.

becomes secondary to the encounter itself as a site of newfound racial knowledge.

Hemingway chooses a darkened clearing underneath the rails as his site of conveyance, carefully crafting a new Gothic space within which to divide then conquer old myths. Nick happens upon a fire burning for one Ad Francis, former boxing champion, and his black compatriot and former cell mate, Bugs. Bugs, we quickly learn, acts as caretaker and confidant to the former fighter; further pertinent details are revealed later. However, the narrative's initial sequences involving the two strangers serve to underscore white reader expectation as we quickly get typology at its strongest. Nick meets Ad first: "The fire was bright now, just at the edge of the trees. There was a man sitting by it. Nick waited behind the tree and watched. The man looked to be alone. He was sitting there with his head in his hands looking at the fire. Nick stepped out and walked into the firelight" [42]. The man in deep thought is Ad Francis. Immediately, the narrative forges an associative linkage of sorts among Nick, the former boxer, and the thriving fire. The connection is bolstered by the seemingly automatic bond between young Nick and the fighter, contrary to Joseph Flora's perceived disjuncture between the two figures.[3]

The point of convergence for the two is the evidence Nick sports as proof of his encounter with the train's brakeman—his black eye—as Nick's "Hello!" is followed by "Where did you get the shiner?" [42]. The connection between the nameless man and the fire, and soon enough Nick himself, is significant in that fire stands as the first sign of civilization for Nick as he walks through the darkness with "three or four miles of swamp" between himself and the next town, Mancelona [41]. In this sequence, Hemingway elicits unspoken racial typology as shared images of whiteness and civilization conflate in the form of the fire. And as Ad and Nick rail against the brakeman ("The bastard!"), man and boy forge an alliance against a system seemingly intent on constricting them both. They implicitly share an understanding of violence's place in this world:

> "You're a tough one, aren't you?"
> "No," Nick answered.
> "All you kids are tough."
> "You got to be tough," Nick said.
> "That's what I said." The man looked at Nick and smiled. [42]

---

3. Flora suggests that the initial encounter between the boy and the ex-prizefighter produces no "communal fellowship," and later that the real connection is between Nick and Bugs (88).

They both know that this brand of violence is best left relegated to the realm of tough talk and hard-boiled machismo. This violence is born of a mythical kind of bravado celebrated in the ring and the back alleys of crime fiction lore. Confined to tough talk, theirs is a violence of story. It stands in stark contrast to the actual violence we get with our introduction to Bugs, Ad's African American side-kick, whose brand of violence promises to be both unexpected and terrifying.

A bit later, the ex-fighter touts his toughness and insists that the strange boy call him by his first name, Ad. Conversely, his friend of several years, Bugs, never moves beyond the formalities of surname. The bond between white men appears to be instantaneous, and the black man immediately moves outside the circle. In fact, he shows deference to both white figures with a last name address for each. In keeping with the racial constrictions separating the men, at work even in this space, even young Nick is afforded the title of "Mister." When asked by Bugs who he is, Nick offers his last name first to convey the lineage and history denied the black man; it is important to note that Hemingway's narrative never grants Bugs those entitle-ments. All demonstrations of respect are reserved for Ad.

On the surface, Ad is the epitome of the great white hero and the Hemingway code hero. Anticipating white reader expectation, Hemingway initially casts the boxer as the embodiment of white mas-culinity (Early).[4] Fittingly, his original working title for the story was "The Great Man." The former champion has apparently weathered a life's storm, and he has endured; his battered body and psyche (he admits to being "not quite right") stand as testament to this. Even in his worn state, though, he assumes quasi-mythic proportions as a man with a storied past. And this story is not lost on Nick, who instantly recognizes the name. He was once a fighter of some renown and comes to us as a conqueror of men. Nick's reaction is one of earnest awe as he credulously verifies the former boxer's identity ("Honest to God?"), just knowing that "it must be true" [43]. Ad names no opponent, cites no particular fight, as he recounts his past glory; instead, Hemingway gives us mythical allusion to a boundless name-less corpus of slain warriors. His success, he says, is due in part to an unnaturally slow-beating heart, the marker of fine physicality.

> "You know how I beat them?"
> "No," Nick said.
> "My heart's slow. It only beats forty a minute. Feel it."
> Nick hesitated.

---

4. In *Tuxedo Junction: Essays on American Culture*, Early underscores the importance of the sport's Anglo roots in tracing the history of its apparent "appropriation" by nonwhites. * * *

"Come on," the man took hold of his hand. "Take hold of my wrist. Put your fingers there."

The little man's wrist was thick and the muscles bulged above the bone. Nick felt the slow pumping under his fingers. [43]

Nick counts his pulse to quantify that prowess. Joe Flora asserts that "the touch leads to no epiphany or communal fellowship" (88). To the contrary, the sequence demonstrates a young white boy's hero worship and evinces his connection to this white superman as something that is both race-based and immediate.

White reader expectation is met yet again as the focus shifts to the boxer's black traveling companion and confidant, Bugs. Juxtaposed, at least initially, with a pronounced Anglo masculine model is the African American type. Again, Nick's initial encounter with this apparent secondary figure is one of blatant typology and fulfilled narrative expectation. Nick's first impressions of the black man exemplify this point best: "A man dropped down the railroad embankment and came across the clearing to the fire" [44]. Immediately, the black man's presence is phantom-like and Gothic, bearing all the markings of "otherness." He comes to the fire from the void of brush, darkness, and night. But even under the shroud of darkness, Bugs reveals enough of himself to Nick for the boy to make a race-based identification, to know him as an African American man: "It was a negro's voice." Nick listens, watches, then knows: "Nick knew from the way he walked that he was a negro." Later as he cooks for the group, Bugs "crouch[es] on long nigger legs over the fire" [44]. In each instance, Hemingway paints a picture of crafted racial difference.

Further, Hemingway tells us that Nick immediately recognizes the voice coming from the fire at the story's outset as that of a Negro. Race bears sensory marks, and Hemingway knows it, and he appropriately plays on this association. Type suggests that the Negro is meekness incarnate. In fact, the narrative subtly interchanges name with racial manner and racial manner with racial epithet as Bugs becomes the "polite negro," and the polite "negro" becomes "nigger." Bugs speaks with a Negro's voice, walks with a Negro's gait, and often is simply "the negro." As he warns Nick against handing the former boxer his knife, he is "the negro"; as he tends to the cooking requests, he is "the negro"; as he and Nick speak of the former champion's bouts with the press, the public, and the law, he is "the negro"; and he is "the negro" again as Nick finally takes leave of the duo at story's end. Hemingway cunningly refuses to allow the reader to forget that this is a story of racial exchange and difference.

The relationship between the two vagabonds initially fails to escape this polar paradigm. At first, the dynamic appears to be anything but complex. Anticipating reader expectation, Hemingway simplifies the complexities with an exaggerated color line. Bugs is deference and servility embodied, and outside his sense of allegiance to the former fighter, we know little about the man as the story begins. Bugs has no discernable past of his own. What we glean is through association and manner only. Whereas Ad is brash and purposeful in his exchange with Nick, Bugs is all quiet deference. The black man clearly knows his place. Financial support is apparently Ad's domain, while Bugs's is primarily domestic. Appropriately, once the proper introductions have been made, Bugs immediately launches into meal preparation for both friend and guest: "When are we going to eat, Bugs?" With a quick "Right away," the black man's response is automatic [44].

The narrative's racial divide further reveals itself in the short history the two vagabonds share. Their paths crossed, Nick learns from Bugs, in prison. Both men were prosecuted for violent crimes, and both paid their debts to society with time served. However, Hemingway makes clear a very important distinction between the two men, a distinction demonstrated through connotation. The former jail mates are men with similar fates, but altogether different guiding principles. Hemingway's narrative goads ever so slightly, coaxing both Nick and the (white) reader to judge the two men differently. Bugs's terse recount of Ad's collapse after his wife's desertion is telling: "'I met him in jail' the negro said. 'He was busting people all the time after she went away and they put him in jail. I was in for cuttin' a man'" [47]. Immediately, nuanced division overshadows any solidarity between the two mates. And that difference is notably one of racial association. Hemingway paints Ad as a man of brawn and bodily might (he "bust[s]" people with his fists), Bugs as seemingly less than a man, requiring a blade to even the score. The narrative links white with might and fair play, and blackness with inadequacy and cheating. * * * Hemingway intentionally drives a wedge between characters with racial discourse.

However, * * * division is only one part of the Hemingway racial equation; revelation is the other. Bugs's purpose here is more complicated than a typological reading suggests. In "The Battler," the racially charged narrative—especially its descriptions of the black man—both demonstrates Nick's race consciousness or hypercognizance and reveals the very new and often terrific realities of a color line in constant flux. These are realities Hemingway exposes with relish.

The first racial myth dispelled by Hemingway is perhaps the greatest of them all, and one that toppled quickly with the fall of Tommy

Burns [beaten by Johnson in the 1908 fight] and the rise of Jack Johnson: that of the indomitable white hero. We have a hero in this tale who is in fact unheroic. When we meet him, the fighter's best days are behind him. From the story's inception, Ad Francis is very much a diminished figure: "In the firelight Nick saw that his face was misshapen. His nose was sunken, his eyes were slits, he had queer-shaped lips. Nick did not perceive all this at once, he only saw the man's face was queerly formed and mutilated. It was like putty in color. Dead-looking in the firelight." Later in the same exchange, Nick sees that Ad "only had one ear. It was thickened and tight" [43]. Note that the emphasis is on exteriority, on the physical marker. Hemingway all but dehumanizes Ad with his beaten, almost monstrous countenance; the prizefighter becomes a grotesque, offering the wayward kid wisdom and a new racial truth. At its core, Hemingway's story is about a fluctuating color line and shifting racial authority, seen first in markers of physicality and then, more importantly, in characterization and action. Hemingway's corporeal focus furthers his experiment with the grotesque * * *.

Hemingway's narrative explores the grotesque in its exaggerated characterization: characters are super-masculine ("the muscles bulged above the bone") and overtly racialized as black or white ("his face was white," "crouching on long nigger legs"). In each instance, the distortion approaches the absurd. With a form and figure severely misshapen, the ex-champion is the grotesque incarnate * * *. However, Hemingway goes beyond the initial physical distortion to expose and exploit the incongruities of race. And the true incongruity, the true distortion, Hemingway shows us, is the one between racial mythos and racial reality. When viewed through the racial lens, the encounter between Nick and the two vagabonds shifts from one of pure typology and a clearly marked racial divide to one of floating definitions and an unraveling construct. Hemingway's original title, "The Great Man" (*Selected Letters* 155), thus becomes one of marked irony, not nostalgia, and one that challenges, rather than satisfies, white reader expectations.[5]

Ad Francis is a former ring warrior, a pugilist of some repute whose muscular wrists, scarred face, and seemingly perpetual income are proof of a man with history and legacy. However, the case of Ad Francis is also one of loss and degeneration, not of greatness (regained). Hemingway repeatedly employs the word "little" in his descriptions of the former fighter, suggesting a narrative deliberateness. Twelve times the former slayer of men and great white hope is cast as "the

---

5. Hemingway's working title, as he negotiated his contract with Horace Liveright in March of 1925 and put the finishing touches on the collection that would become *In Our Time*, was "The Great Little Fighting Machine." Clearly notions of greatness were something Hemingway wished to explore, define, and challenge as he honed this work.

little man." Hemingway's cognizance of racial construction becomes clear as he (de)constructs the character.

When he first meets Ad, Nick confirms the great man's claims to "superhuman" conditioning: "Feeling the slow hard throb under his fingers Nick started to count. He heard the little man counting, slowly, one, two, three, four, five, and on—aloud" [44]. Ad's physical prowess is undeniable. However, at a key point in the narrative, Ad asks to hold Bugs's knife and is summarily denied his request. Appropriately, the former champion asserts himself, and at the moment of his supposed resurgence, the narrative tells us that "the little man" glared at Nick, and then "came toward him slowly, stepping flat-footed forward, his left foot stepping forward, his right dragging up to it" [46]. Even in this moment of apparent self-affirmation, Hemingway marks Ad's attempted rise with diminution. The former champion is ultimately met with a knockout blow from Bugs. As Nick departs, with Ad prostrate on the ground and Bugs nursing him after having struck him down, he listens to the private conversation between the two men and notes Bugs's low soft voice and "the little man" complaining of a terrible headache. Thus, from beginning to end, whiteness is made small time and again.

While attention to exteriority (and its disintegration) allows for the beginnings of a subversive reading, there is another, more profound truth hidden in the grotesque face and form of Ad Francis. The image of the powerful white champion whose money sustains him years after he has left the ring is supplanted by the reality of an *ex*-champion with one foot squarely planted in the soil of a past that is anything but glorious. This former great white hope is also a convict and a degenerate. If he is a master of men when in the ring, outside it, Ad Francis is conversely an irrational law breaker and an unbridled slave to his emotions. Outside the ring, he is effectively feminized: unable to control himself, he goes to jail for "busting people all the time [after his wife] went away and they put him in jail" [47]. Bugs refuses to expound upon the known, simply suggesting that Ad's wife deserted him. The desertion poses, for us, a greater question of dubious (white) manhood.

With his wife's departure and his release from prison, Ad becomes an "other" of the Anglo imagination—bereft of his livelihood and his glory, he is a vagabond dependent on the personal kindness of his former cell mate and the monetary support of a former spouse who sends him money. Further, he is a man whose sanity ("I'm not quite right," he posits) becomes increasingly questionable as the narrative progresses [43]. Most importantly, he is a man who, in spite of his white skin, is clearly *not in control of himself*, let alone those around him. Thus Ad Francis is a man robbed of any and all authority. Gone with the glory, Hemingway seems to suggest, are the clear markers of racial primacy.

Hard on his luck, very much at the mercy of a black man, and only a shell of his former (supposedly greater) self, Ad Francis is the great white hope dashed. As such, he is living testament to the illusionary nature of racial configuration. If boxing is a crafted manhood, then dark dominance in the ring by Jack Johnson—whose capture of the heavyweight championship galvanized the race issue in America decades after Reconstruction—becomes a metaphor for a palpable black volition and an encroachment of white authority outside the ring. For Hemingway, the advent of Johnson's world championship marked the opening of a new epoch in American social history. The perpetuation of clearly debunked myths—the white reign over the square jungle—is the greater absurdity to which Hemingway seems to point.

Ad's traveling companion, Bugs—not Ad himself—becomes the true agent of action and control here and Hemingway's ultimate site of subversion. The black man effectively commandeers white authority while the white male subject becomes pliable and putty-like, at the mercy of those around him. Once more, focus on exteriority, the white man's "dead-looking" color, underscores this malleability [43]. We get the ultimate moment of white diminution at story's end with Ad's complete physical submission to Bugs, who stands over him as he lies prostrate and small on the ground. Hemingway gives us a racial inversion as he morphs and even transposes black and white bodies. To that end, Ad's realization of his own marked impotence, of the fact that he, Ad Francis, former world champion and white agent, is in reality no better than the seemingly simple dark figure frying his eggs, is enough to drive him to lunacy. Black has become white, up has become down. Truth be told, the only thing separating white master and black servant here are illusory racial truths, a consciously imposed color line, and a contained violent will.[6]

From the outset, Bugs is deceptively cast as the essence of dark typology: he is servile, he is genial, and he is gentle. He invites Nick to sup with him, he cooks for the group, he even serves the gathering. And he does all this with a gentle smile, a smile that belies a

---

6. Bugs represents that spectacle of wonderment and fear: the willful minority figure. Hemingway's narrative works to demonstrate how Bugs astutely exposes the Anglo's vulnerabilities and effectively beats him at his own game, referencing the Anglo rule book. This is the essence of social subversion. Miscegenation, as a general racial commingling in its broadest sense, becomes a black supplanting of white as the African American literally looms large over a prostrate "little white man" [45]. Bugs's general facility, coupled with his white comrade's inability to operate within this same framework, becomes the greater horror and the point of greater significance. And it all begins with a smile.

latent knowledge and power. George Monteiro, drawing a correlation
to Benito Cereno [victim of a slave rebellion], says of Bugs's smile,
"That smile, I would venture, is Melvillean. It is the smile of a black
who, too, would be seen as 'less a servant than a devoted companion'"
(128). I would amend Monteiro's statement and suggest that this
smile is less hopeful than knowing. While inexplicable rage incapaci-
tates Ad, a tempered violence empowers Bugs. Bugs becomes the
new danger. He relates to Nick how he served time for cutting a man,
recounting his crimes in clinical fashion. Thus, in the "cowardly"
razor lies actual empowerment. Ad's amusement at Nick's enthusiasm
("Hear that, Bugs?") elicits from his dark companion a telling response:
"I hear most of what goes on" [44]. Here Hemingway paints Bugs as
shrewd and adept at reading the racial landscape. Even as he dons
the garb of servility, Bugs directs the exchange, propels the narrative, and becomes the oracle of personal history for the crew.

Hemingway bestows upon Bugs the story's true agency and power.
The blow Bugs delivers to his friend at story's end instantly orders
the rage and squelches any resurgence of white might: "I have to do
it to change him when he gets that way" [46]. Black dictates pre-
dominate. After relaying to Nick some personal history regarding the
ex-champion and himself, Bugs again becomes the forceful agent as
he ushers Nick out, suggesting that it would be best if he were not
around when the little man awakes: "I don't like to not be hospitable, but it might disturb him back again to see you. I hate to have to
thump him and it's the only thing to do when he gets started. I have
to sort of keep him away from people" [48]. There is a method to the
apparent madness, as he suggests most tellingly: "I know how to do
it" [46]. In the tense exchange just prior to the knockout blow, Ad's
refusal to respond to Bugs's request draws a suggestive rebuke from
the black man: "I spoke to you, Mister Francis" [45]. Again, the
minority voice boldly asserts itself. All this, Hemingway shows us—
the dialogic authority, the self-assertion, the minority's physical
dominion—is in each instance carried out willfully and skillfully
within the parameters of the established order itself.

To this effect, civility and gentility color Bugs's words and actions.
Bugs's insistence on an answer from his ignorant and violently preoccupied crony is tempered with deference ("Mister Francis"). After
striking the white man, Bugs almost immediately resumes the servile posture, caring for his now-ailing friend, "pick[ing] him up, his
head hanging, and carry[ing] him to the fire . . . and la[ying] him
down gently" [46]. And as he tends to his friend, Bugs addresses
Nick in subservient phrases littered with "Misters," "all this in a
low, smooth, polite nigger voice" [48]. Just as quickly as the violence

commences, it ceases, and suddenly Bugs is nurse and companion again. Master of his rage, he sips coffee and smiles.

Unlike his compatriot, Bugs proves himself to be a master of tempered violence. Joseph Flora also notes the temperamental divide between the two figures and suggests that "the difference between Bugs and Ad is seen in the cool efficiency of Bugs" (89). The key to Bugs's "cool efficiency" is control. Here Hemingway inverts the tried-and-true model wherein—as critic Gerald Early posits in a marked criticism of Norman Mailer's overdependence on such tropes—"the black male is metaphorically the white male's unconsciousness personified" (138). In "The Battler," Hemingway toys with the natural order and Ad is the id-driven primordial figure, Bugs the rational being constrained by ego/superego. The unexpected literal blow to whiteness is a metaphor for the greater anticipated racial violence of Hemingway's day.

These social prescriptions were being tested during the last years of the nineteenth century and early part of the twentieth century. Lynchings were rampant as the ruling order desperately tried to reassert itself and to erase meager minority gains following Reconstruction. The second decade of the new century, especially after the First World War's conclusion, was marred by racial unrest and a black community in active revolt. It was revolution on a national level, sparked in part by the rise of an American icon. And within the pages of his boxing stories, Hemingway gives voice to a national conscience troubled by the rise of Jack Johnson.

Johnson's successful title defense against Jim Jeffries on July 4, 1910, set off racial strife all over the country. There were riots in cities nationwide following the fight, leaving no doubt as to the correlation between racial strife and violence.[7] Many cities around the country, fearing more violence, enacted a moratorium prohibiting the official fight reel from being shown in theaters. Local and state administrators feared a reignition of racial passion (not so much on the part of whites, but blacks), passion stoked by ideas of racial equality and personal value—ideas internalized, lived, and symbolized by Jack Johnson.

Johnson played on Hemingway's psyche as well: the author once again revisits the Gothic as he infuses a national angst in the subtext of "The Battler." Bugs comes to symbolize the reprehensible Jack Johnson: the willful minority. Ad conversely comes to symbolize white degeneration and self-deception. Both men—especially Ad, in his freakish ghoulishness—are monstrous Gothic operators within

---

7. See Hine, Hine, and Harrold as well as Franklin for excellent histories of the nation's racial tenor during these years.

Hemingway's benighted world. We see this in Bugs's forays across the color line, in his apparent Jekyll-and-Hyde racial negotiation, and in his eerily proffered truths; we see this, too, in Ad's ravaged body and exaggerated diminution, his lost dominion and lost sanity, his helplessness before the knife-wielding black man. Bugs's proffered truths and racial realities are written all over the white man's ghastly countenance.

Further, the Bugs-Ad commingling and conflation is representative and expressive of racial mixing's nightmarish potential. Bugs, after all, says he "like[s] living like a gentleman" [47] and tellingly, more than his white cohort, he has *mastered* the art of the civilized. Hemingway crafts a black character who skillfully negotiates that color line and shows us several key things: that the clearly defined separator between primitive and civilized is illusory, that the color line's transgression is *not* a unilateral exercise, that checked violence is often the only thing maintaining such an order, and that white primacy is a myth. A physically deformed Ad bears the markings, as a grotesque, of this new truth.

Works Cited

Early, Gerald. *Tuxedo Junction: Essays on American Culture*. New York: Ecco, 1989.

Ellison, Ralph. *Shadow and Act*. New York: Quality Paperback Book Club, 1994.

Flora, Joseph. *Hemingway's Nick Adams*. Baton Rouge: Louisiana State UP, 1982.

Franklin, John Hope. *From Slavery to Freedom: A History of American Negroes*. New York: Knopf, 1974.

Hemingway, Ernest. *Selected Letters, 1917–1961*, ed. Carlos Baker. New York: Scribner's, 1981.

Hine, Darlene et al., eds. *The African-American Odyssey*. Upper Saddle River, NJ: Prentice Hall, 2000.

Monteiro, George. "'This Is My Pal Bugs': Ernest Hemingway's 'The Battler.'" *Studies in Short Fiction* 23.2 (1986): 179–83.

Morrison, Toni. *Playing in the Dark: Whiteness and the Literary Imagination*. Cambridge, MA: Harvard UP, 1992.

"A VERY SHORT STORY"

SCOTT DONALDSON

From "A Very Short Story" as Therapy†

Other than a 1971 linguistic analysis and Robert Scholes's fine discussion in *Semiotics and Interpretation,* "A Very Short Story" has been largely ignored in Hemingway scholarship.[1] One reason is its relative lack of merit when measured against the best Hemingway short fiction, for reasons that are analyzed below. Yet as a study in the process of composition, "A Very Short Story" well repays close scrutiny.

Ernest Hemingway met Agnes von Kurowsky in the Red Cross hospital in Milan, where he had been taken to recuperate from his July 1918 wounding on the Austrian front. She was 26, a Red Cross nurse, very attractive, and not without experience in affairs of the heart. He was barely 19, good-looking, charming in his eagerness to confront life, and innocent in the ways of courtship. Despite the difference in their ages, they fell in love. When he sailed for the States from Genoa in early January, it was understood that he would get a job, she would follow, and they would be married. That did not happen, however. Agnes soon transferred her affections to an Italian officer, and wrote Ernest the bad news less than two months after his departure from Italy.

When the letter arrived at Oak Park in mid-March 1919, young Hemingway was devastated. If, as he wrote his friend Howell Jenkins, he then attempted to cauterize her memory "with a course of booze and other women,"[2] the therapy was not entirely successful. A residue of pain filled the hollow place that had housed his love for the Red Cross nurse and would not go away until he could write about it. "You'll lose it if you talk about it,"[3] Jake Barnes warned, and the obverse of the maxim was that you could get rid of it by talking or writing about it. When Ernest left [his first wife,] Hadley Hemingway, it took him only two months to put the tale into fictional form in

† From *Hemingway's Neglected Short Fiction: New Perspectives,* ed. Susan F. Beegel (Tuscaloosa: U of Alabama P, 1989), pp. 99–105. Reprinted by permission of the publisher. Unless otherwise indicated, notes are by the author. Page numbers in brackets refer to this Norton Critical Edition.
1. Emile Benveniste, *Problems in General Linguistics,* trans. Mary Elizabeth Meek (Coral Gables: U of Miami P, 1971) 223–30; Robert Scholes, "Decoding Papa: 'A Very Short Story' as Word and Text," *Semiotics and Interpretation* (New Haven: Yale UP, 1981) 110–26.
2. Ernest Hemingway to Howell G. Jenkins, 16 June 1919, *Ernest Hemingway: Selected Letters, 1917–1961,* ed. Carlos Baker (New York: Charles Scribner's Sons, 1981) 25.
3. Ernest Hemingway, *The Sun Also Rises* (New York: Charles Scribner's Sons, 1926) 245. [Jake Barnes, the impotent narrator of the novel, offers sardonic advice to his former war nurse, Brett Ashley, about her affair with a bullfighter—*Editor.*]

"A Canary for One."[4] When Agnes von Kurowsky rejected him, it took him four years to write a story about it.

Actually the story went through at least three versions: the pencil draft headed "Personal" or "Love" (version A), Chapter 10 of *in our time* (1924) (version B), and "A Very Short Story" of *In Our Time* (1925) and the collected stories (version C).[5] Most of the changes Hemingway made between the first draft and final copy worked to render the account at once more impersonal and more bitter. In the two-page, handwritten draft (version A), the love affair is depicted tenderly, and little blame is directed at Agnes. In this version she is called "Ag," the narrator is unambiguously "I," and the two of them are often "we," as in the straightforward "We loved each other very much." Those six little words do not appear in either subsequent version, nor does the following account of letter writing inside the hospital: "Daytimes I slept and wrote letters for her to read downstairs when she got up. She used to send letters up to me by the charwoman."

Using the first person pronoun and the name "Ag," together with placing the story in Milan, conformed to the practice Hemingway often followed in his early career: beginning with names drawn from experience but later changing the names as the experience became transformed from reportage to fiction. There were legal as well as artistic reasons for such changes. The female character here remained "Ag" in Chapter 10 of *in our time*, but became "Luz" in *In Our Time* upper case. That was the way it should stay, Hemingway instructed Max Perkins when *The First Forty-nine Stories* were in preparation in 1938: "Ag is libelous. Short for Agnes."[6] But version A's accuracy in the matter of names may also have reflected Hemingway's attempt to indicate how he felt about the broken affair. The subject was love, after all, and the tone of the piece in the first draft is unmistakably romantic.

Version A was originally headed "Personal" and began "There were flocks of chimney swifts in the sky. The searchlights were out and they carried me. . . ." Then this broke off, and was crossed out in favor of the new heading "Love" and the remainder of the story. Since Chapter 10 of *in our time* (version B) is also called "Love" in early typescripts, the presumption is strong that version A functioned as a preliminary draft for the *in our time* chapter published in 1924. Apparently he was trying during the interim to find the right

4. See Scott Donaldson, "Preparing for the End: Hemingway's Revisions of 'A Canary for One,'" *Studies in American Fiction* 6 (Autumn 1978): 203–11.
5. The three versions of the story are located in folders 633, 94, and 94A at the Kennedy library: *Catalog of the Ernest Hemingway Collection at the John F. Kennedy Library* (Boston: G. K. Hall, 1982) 13, 102.
6. Ernest Hemingway to Maxwell Perkins, 12 July 1938, *Letters*, 469.

way to approach the subject of lost love. In version A he even pen-ciled in one sexually suggestive passage—"I said, 'I love you, Ag,' and pulled her over hard against me. And she said, 'I know it, Kid,' and kissed me and got all the way up onto the bed." But this was deleted.

The most significant difference between version A and the two that followed was that the first draft did not censure Agnes in its closing section, either overtly or through the sarcasm that pervades the later versions. Ag had not kept the faith, of course, but in ver-sion A Hemingway provided her with an excuse for this failure. After the armistice, he wrote, "I went home to get a job so we could get married and Ag went up to Torre di Mosto to run some sort of a show. It was lonely there, and there was a battalion of Arditi quar-tered in the town. When the letter came saying ours had been only a kid affair I got awfully drunk. The major never married her, and I got a dose of clap from a girl in Chicago riding in a Yellow Taxi." The loneliness made her do it, and Ag got her due punishment when "the major" failed to marry her. These extenuating circumstances persist (and are even adumbrated on) in versions B and C, but they are outweighed there by a sardonic resentment of Ag's faithlessness.

Each version begins with the wounded protagonist on the roof with Ag (or Luz) beside him on the bed, "cool and fresh in the hot night." * * * In each version, too, the nurse "stayed on night duty for three months" and the patient, once on crutches, took the tempera-tures so that she would not have to "get up from the bed"—his bed [51]. All three versions have the lovers praying together in the Duomo, along with the declaration that they wanted to get married. But the particulars of these scenes changed substantially from ver-sion A to versions B and C. What Hemingway chose to change had considerable effect on the story that resulted.

Most of the revisions involve additions rather than deletions, a pat-tern, as Paul Smith has demonstrated,[7] that is often characteristic of Hemingway's working method. The only important omissions are "We loved each other very much," the business about writing letters to each other during Ag's three months of night duty, and the con-fessional "I got awfully drunk." In the way of substitutions, Milan becomes Padova in version B and is Anglicized to Padua in "A Very Short Story" itself, where Ag is changed to Luz. More important, the "I" of the first draft gives way to the seemingly more objective third person "he" in versions B and C (in no case is the protagonist given a name). This objectivity is more apparent than real, as Rob-ert Scholes demonstrates in "Decoding Papa: 'A Very Short Story' as Word and Text."[8] The sketch reads perfectly, Scholes points out,

7. Reader's Guide, 25–29 [Editor].
8. Scholes, 110–26.

if the "he" of the text is transposed to "I" and makes no sense if the "she" is converted to the first person. In other words, the "I" voice continues to speak from behind the facade of the "he." Moreover, most of the other changes Hemingway made are in the form of addenda designed to sharpen awareness that the "he" of the story has been done wrong. The deck has been stacked against Luz.

Version A contains only four paragraphs. Versions B and C—the story as it appeared in *in our time* and *In Our Time*—run to seven paragraphs and about twice as many words as the first draft. The first three versions of version A are substantially transferred to subsequent versions, and the first paragraph itself (other than the change in pronouns and place name) remains fixed throughout. In paragraphs two and three, however, Hemingway makes some important additions. Paragraph two of version A deals with Ag on night duty, her preparing him for his operation, the joke about "friend or enema" [51], and his taking temperatures so she could stay in his bed. The same paragraph in the printed story contains four additional sentences that strongly imply a sexual bond between them. After the friend or enema joke, for instance, versions B and C have "He went under the anaesthetic holding tight onto himself so he would not blab about anything during the silly, talky time" [51]. Not in front of the doctors and other nurses, that is, for as the other added sentences reveal, their affair was not a secret to his fellow patients. After the sentence about taking temperatures, versions B and C go on to reveal that "There were only a few patients, and they all knew about it. They all liked Ag. As we walked back along the halls he thought of Ag in his bed" [51]. These thoughts, in the context of the patients' all knowing about it, were presumably carnal. This was no casual nurse-patient infatuation, the story is insisting.

Paragraph three, about praying in the Duomo before he returns to the front and about their wanting to get married, is fleshed out by the addition of one clause and one full sentence. The clause places other people in the Duomo, and so tends to dispel the romantic aura of the two wartime lovers alone in the great cathedral. The sentence expands on their desire to get married. "They felt as though they were married, but they wanted everyone to know about it, and to make it so they could not lose it" [51]. Once they were really married, they could tell the world—doctors, nurses, her Red Cross superiors, his parents, everyone—about their love. Marriage would not only validate their love but fix it in concrete, "make it so they could not lose it" [51]. Again Hemingway's revisions stress the seriousness of their affair, but now he foreshadows the danger that what they have together might be lost.

Such foreshadowing is more appropriate in a short story than in a sketch, and in the process of composition Hemingway was uncertain which of the two he was creating. The corrected proofs of *in our time* use the heading "Chapter 10," crossed out but restored by an authorial "Stet." Beneath that another title, "A Short Story," is crossed out but not restored. So the piece appeared as yet another "chapter" or sketch among those collected in the 1924 *in our time*. The following year, however, he converted the piece from sketch to full status as "A Very Short Story" among the much larger ones of *In Our Time*. In its earliest version even that diminutive title would have claimed too much. Hemingway must have sensed that he had broken off version A too abruptly and without sufficient directions to guide his readers, for from the fourth paragraph on almost everything in "Chapter 10" and "A Very Short Story" (versions B and C) is new.

The fourth paragraph of versions B and C takes up the love letter motif, but in revision it is as if only Ag is writing them, hence giving him every reason to expect her undying love:

> Ag wrote him many letters that he never got until after the armistice. Fifteen came in a bunch and he sorted them by the dates and read them all straight through. They were about the hospital, and how much she loved him and how it was impossible to get along without him and how terrible it was missing him at night. [B]

The fifth paragraph is concerned with their parting in Italy, and the understanding they reached at that time. They "agreed he should go home," and she "would not come until he had a good job and could come to New York to meet her" [51], but on this latter point they were in anything but agreement. "On the train from Padova to Milan they quarreled about her not being willing to come home at once. When they had to say good-bye in the station . . . they kissed good-bye, but were not finished with the quarrel. He felt sick about saying good-bye like that" [B]. Still, the unnamed narrator—perhaps by this time we can call him Ernie, as Ag did—was willing to accept this condition and any other she imposed. "It was understood he would not drink, and he did not want to see his friends or any one in the States" [51]. What was understood between them, in other words, was that he should give up all vices and entertainments, including friendship, and not get involved with anyone else. No such conditions were exacted of her.

The sixth paragraph, after presenting expository details about his going back to America and Ag's opening a hospital in Torre di Mosto, proceeds to develop at length two topics barely touched on in version A: Ag's seduction by the Italian major and the contents of her good-bye letter. In versions B and C, it was not only lonely for Ag, but lonely "and rainy" as well:

> Living in the muddy, rainy town in the winter, the major of the battalion made love to Ag, and she had never known Italians before, and finally wrote a letter to the States that theirs had been only a boy and girl affair. She was sorry, and she knew he would probably not be able to understand, but might someday forgive her, and be grateful to her, and she expected, absolutely unexpectedly, to be married in the spring. She loved him as always, but she realized now it was only a boy and girl love. She hoped he would have a great career, and believed in him absolutely. She knew it was for the best. [B]

This long addition traces a curious emotional course. In the beginning it provides Agnes with still more valid excuses for her inconstancy. She had only succumbed after the rain and mud and the loneliness and the wiles of the Italian major conspired to diminish her resistance. Again this emphasizes the seriousness of the love between the narrator/protagonist and his nurse: she did not easily break the faith.

Once the paragraph switches to what she wrote in her final letter, however, the tone changes abruptly. The trigger to this change seems to be the phrase "boy and girl affair," later repeated as "boy and girl love." Following this phrase, the story launches into that long periodic sentence about how sorry she was and so on that ends with the sarcastic revelation that "she expected, absolutely unexpectedly, to be married in the spring" [52]. Here the full weight of her perfidy, built up previously by her love letters and the conditions she'd insisted on before they could be married, is expressed by the snide "expected, absolutely unexpectedly."

In the final paragraph, version B omits mention of his getting drunk on receipt of the letter about theirs having been a "kid affair," but otherwise elaborates on the consequence of the breakup. The major "did not marry her in the spring," the story reads, and then rather nastily adds, "or any other time" [52]. Nor did the narrator demean himself by replying to the letter she wrote him about *her* jilting by the major. He did not get drunk, either. Instead he followed a foolish and costly course of male assertiveness. "A short time after he contracted gonorrhea [changed from "got a dose of the clap" in the typescript for "Chapter 10"] from a salesgirl from the Fair "riding in a taxicab through Lincoln Park" [52].

The few alterations Hemingway made in version B, "Chapter 10," to version C, "A Very Short Story," are of minor significance. Most are made to suggest the fictitiousness of people and places. Milan is Padua, Torre di Mosto is Pordenone, "The Fair" becomes "a loop department store," and Ag becomes Luz [51–52]. The most important revision inserts three words in the fourth paragraph. Fifteen of Luz's

letters came in a bunch, Hemingway wrote, "to the front" [51].
Those words conjure up a picture of a harried soldier perusing the
letters from his loved one during a respite from combat. In fact, it
was Agnes who went off to various "fronts" on behalf of the Red
Cross, while Hemingway was recovering in hospital, first from his
wounds and then—after a very brief visit, not on duty, to the front—
from jaundice. The attempt here is obviously to arouse sympathy
for the male narrator, and nearly all the revisions from version A on
aim for a similar result. In effect, that is what is wrong with "A Very
Short Story." The narrator is too good, too noble, too unfairly
wronged. He is too close to Hemingway himself, or at least to that
Hemingway who—four years later—was still bitterly resentful of his
rejection by Agnes von Kurowsky.

"A Very Short Story" ranks as one of Hemingway's least effective
stories. Behind a pretense of objectivity, it excoriates the faithless
Agnes. Even four years after the jilting, he was too close to his subject matter to achieve the requisite artistic distance. But he does
seem to have dissipated his bitterness against her in the process.
Twice again—in "Along with Youth," his 1925 beginning-of-a-novel,
and in A Farewell to Arms (1929)—he explored the subject of love
between a wounded soldier and his nurse, but in both cases the ran-
cor is gone. In "A Very Short Story," apparently, Hemingway did
manage to get rid of it by writing about it.

"SOLDIER'S HOME"

ROBERT PAUL LAMB

[Form, Argument, and Meaning in Hemingway's "Soldier's Home]"[†]

Because it is Hemingway's only story about a First World War veteran's homecoming *and* a story that portrays a conflicted mother-son
relationship, "Soldier's Home" has been, along with "Big Two-Hearted
River" and "Now I Lay Me" [1927], a highly contested text in the debate
between critics who, following Philip Young, locate war trauma at
the heart of Hemingway's fiction and those who focus instead on

† From "The Love Song of Harold Krebs: Form, Argument, and Meaning in Hemingway's 'Soldier's Home,'" in *The Hemingway Review* 14.2 (Spring 1995): 18–36. Copyright
© 1995. Reprinted by permission of The Ernest Hemingway Foundation. All rights
reserved. Some of the author's notes have been omitted. Page numbers in brackets refer to
this Norton Critical Edition.

the author's unhappy childhood.[1] One early "war wound" critic, Frederick Hoffman, speaking of the "unreasonable wound" Hemingway suffered in 1918 and his consequent repetition compulsion, sees the story as the "sharpest portrait" in 1920s fiction of the returning veteran. "In the absence of any clearly defined reasons for having fought," according to Hoffman, "the returned soldier felt hurt, ill at ease, uncertain of his future, 'disenchanted'" (98). Like other veterans, Hemingway's Harold Krebs is unable to "adjust to the life he had left" for the war; he no longer loves anyone and can not "bring himself to enjoy or respect his family, his home" (98). And so he must go away.[2]

The principal "childhood wound" critic, however, thinks Krebs's wartime experiences barely worth noting. Instead, Kenneth Lynn sees the story as a transmutation into fiction of Hemingway's own troubled postwar response to his family and as an attack by the author on his mother, akin to the one in "The Doctor and the Doctor's Wife," in which Hemingway's home town of Oak Park has been changed to a "town in Oklahoma" (258). Observing that Krebs's last name derives from Hemingway's comrade, Krebs Friend, "who had married a woman fully old enough to be his mother" (258), but ignoring in his analysis of the story that Friend was also a shell-shocked veteran, Lynn focuses on the "portrayal of Mrs. Krebs's tyranny" (259) that he regards as the story's triumph.[3] He concludes with this assessment:

1. For a historical summary of the controversy between what I have labeled the "war wound" thesis and the "childhood wound" thesis, see Lamb (162–63).
2. Young does not address "Soldier's Home" in his book, in which his main interest is confined to stories about either Nick Adams or the "Hemingway code." Nevertheless his war wound thesis is echoed nearly everywhere among Hemingway critics. Robert Penn Warren observes that "the battlefields of A Farewell to Arms" explain young Krebs, "who came home to a Middle-Western town to accept his own slow disintegration" (76). In accord with a conclusion drawn earlier by Sheridan Baker (27), Richard Hasbany states that Nick Adams's trauma in "Big Two-Hearted River" can be better understood in light of Krebs's wartime experiences (237). Leo Gurko declares that "Hemingway's particularly bad case of postwar jitters was described with special delicacy and insight" in "Soldier's Home" (13). Arthur Waldhorn sees Krebs as having been "shocked into psychic disorientation . . . by the demands of a society whose values" he rejects. Krebs's "silence is a wordless metaphor expressing outrage against the chaos of the universe and the isolation of the individual" (37). Scott Donaldson contrasts Krebs's world as formed by his wartime experiences with the world of his hometown, and concludes that his "world was full of unreasonable pain and unconscionable suffering and inexplicable violence" (225). James Mellow calls the story "a classic in the literature of alienation following World War I, a definition of a generation returned from the war, dissatisfied with the goals and values of American life" (122). And Joseph DeFalco asserts that Krebs's war experiences have made him unable to accept the old norms: "Church, family, and society no longer command allegiance from the individual who has experienced the purgatorial initiation of war" (138).
3. Carlos Baker was the first to observe that Harold Krebs's name is a compound of the first names of Harold Loeb, soon to be "immortalized" as Robert Cohn in The Sun Also Rises, and Krebs Friend (585n). The information about Friend being a victim of shell shock is also in Reynolds (189), Smith (70), and Mellow (263). To be fair, Lynn also mentions this fact (236), but he does not emphasize it as he does the age difference

> 'Soldier's Home' is the story of a young man's struggle to sepa-
> rate from home, and Hemingway packed it with a lifetime of
> revulsion and outrage. Nevertheless, the utterly unrelenting,
> utterly unqualified characterization of Mrs. Krebs as a monster
> revealed that the author was in fact still in thrall to her flesh-
> and-blood counterpart. (260)[4]

As these conflicting interpretations demonstrate, "Soldier's Home"
is a complex story. But it is a structurally divided one as well, bifur-
cated into two nearly equal parts of summary exposition and scenic
development in which the war wound interpretation (here mani-
fested in the theme of a veteran's postwar alienation) derives from
the first half of the text and the childhood wound interpretation
from the second half. Therefore, unless one is foolish enough to
insist on a determinate or predominant meaning, both interpretations have merit. I cannot fault Hoffman; anyone writing about
literary responses to the war would be remiss not to see this story
as a textualization of postwar disillusionment. Nor can I blame
Lynn for searching out the biographical relevance of the text (he
is, after all, writing a biography), even if the use of fiction as biographical evidence can lead to a misunderstanding of that fiction
as fiction (e.g., how can the characterization of Mrs. Krebs be
"utterly unqualified" unless we regard her only as a depiction of
Mrs. Hemingway?).

On the other hand, no story can be satisfactorily interpreted by
de-emphasizing half of its text. In addition, by neglecting the story's
form and merely mining it for sociological and biographical content,
these critics have missed the manner of Hemingway's narrative argument as well as the considerable art that underlies it, for what "Soldier's Home" really means depends on how it means. Despite the
story's neat division into summary exposition that points to one interpretation and scenic development that points to another, there must
exist the relationship that normally obtains between these two
elements of a realist text (certainly, at least, of a non-postmodernist

---

between Friend and his wife (236, 258), and he does not bring it up, despite its manifest relevance, when examining "Soldier's Home."

4. Although Lynn's relatively recent perspective has influenced fewer critics of "Soldier's
Home" than has Young's, it has led to a number of non–war wound interpretations.
Hemingway's most perceptive biographer observes that "far beneath its surface" the
story is, among other things, "about Hemingway's anticipation of his parents' inability
to accept his fiction" (Reynolds 191). The story may also represent, perhaps consciously,
Hemingway's attempt to declare his literary independence from his maternal surrogate
and mentor, Gertrude Stein, whose experimental *Geography and Plays* he deliberately
signifies in a sentence about the Rhine not showing. On this, see the excellent article
by Kennedy and Curnutt. Perhaps somewhat less persuasively, J. F. Kobler questions
the extent of Krebs's combat experience in order to view the story as Hemingway's
"carefully constructed *mea culpa* for the lies he had told and for the truths he had
allowed the press to distort regarding his own role, duties, and injury on the Italian
front in 1918" (378).

text). That is, exposition provides us with the informational context necessary to understand development, and development illustrates and formally flows from exposition. Were this not so, then one or the other would be gratuitous and the story would make no sense. Any adequate interpretation of the story must therefore take into account these elements—exposition and development, summary and scene—because each is an indispensable part of how the story functions: its particular structure, its narrative argument, and its terrain of potential meaning. In other words, the "either/or" attitude that critics have brought to this story needs to be replaced by a "both/and" reading that subsumes the war wound and childhood wound interpretations within a more inclusive perspective exploring the aesthetic and cultural consequences of the entire text.

I

Summary exposition raises inherent epistemological questions more severely than scene, especially scene that is mostly dialogue—how reliable is the narrator? This is particularly true when exposition is lengthy and unsubstantiated by scene with dialogue, which, by convention, is generally considered reliable when presented in the third person. Because exposition, or diegesis, is by its nature less convincing than scene, or mimesis, and because it raises these epistemological questions, Hemingway employs narrative strategies to make the exposition more convincing and also to raise questions about the reliability of the scenes. He thereby balances the story's conflicting exposition and scenic development, as well as the interpretations that derive from them.

This equilibration of meaning begins in the deliberate ambiguity of the story title. With Hemingway's penchant for symbolic, poetic, and allusive or intertextual titles—as opposed to neutral, descriptive ones (e.g., "Krebs's Home")—he begins his narrative argument by specifically categorizing Krebs as "soldier" rather than as son, ex-soldier, student, Oklahoman, American, or just Krebs. "Soldier" points to the exposition and the war trauma thesis, "Home" to the scenes and the conflicted mother-son relationship. The two words, and the interpretations they signify, are linked by an apostrophe and an "s." But the nature of this construction is purposefully ambiguous. If it indicates the possessive case, then the title can be restated as "Home of the Soldier," which emphasizes the home. But if it is merely a contraction, then the title could be rewritten as "Soldier Is Home," highlighting the soldier. And of course there is even a third possibility to increase the ambiguity; the term "soldier's home" has been since the Civil War a common vernacular expression for a chronic care facility for physically or emotionally incapacitated veterans.

Throughout the story, Hemingway's sympathies are with Krebs, but he disguises this in the exposition in order to hide his bias from the reader, making the exposition, and the war veteran interpretation that derives from it, more persuasive. In the first three paragraphs he adopts an "objective" and distant narrative voice in which he appears to be presenting just some "facts" in a random fashion:

> Krebs went to the war from a Methodist college in Kansas. There is a picture which shows him among his fraternity brothers, all of them wearing exactly the same height and style collar. He enlisted in the Marines in 1917 and did not return to the United States until the second division returned from the Rhine in the summer of 1919.
>
> There is a picture which shows him on the Rhine with two German girls and another corporal. Krebs and the corporal look too big for their uniforms. The German girls are not beautiful. The Rhine does not show in the picture.
>
> By the time Krebs returned to his home town in Oklahoma the greeting of heroes was over. He came back much too late. The men from the town who had been drafted had all been welcomed elaborately on their return. There had been a great deal of hysteria. Now the reaction had set in. People seemed to think it was rather ridiculous for Krebs to be getting back so late, years after the war was over. [55]

A war wound critic could make much of these two photographs. In the prewar photograph, Krebs is pictured in a male social organization and no women are present; he attends a denominational educational institution; and he fits in easily, his conformity implied by the collars that mark the fraternity brothers as indistinguishable. The second photograph pictures him quite differently in a way that suggests the changes he has undergone during the war. The first sentence of the second paragraph presents a fairly common image: two soldier-buddies on the Rhine with a couple of German women. But the next three sentences quickly undercut that image. Although he is in uniform, it fits him less well than the clothing of the prewar photograph. This suggests that he has become more individualistic and, since he is too big for his uniform, that he has "grown" in some sense as a result of his wartime experiences. The presence of the German women suggests a sexual involvement that was lacking in the earlier picture. However, the women are not beautiful and the Rhine does not show. Like a man who is trying to recall a pleasant dream upon awakening but who is fighting a losing battle with the dreamwork of his psyche, Krebs is trying to hang onto the good feelings he once had as a soldier in Europe: what it was like to have enjoyed soldierly comradeship, to have been with a woman, and to have won a war. But the photograph makes these memories elusive by problematizing the referents to which they are attached.

Continuing this line of inquiry, we could speculate that if there were a third photograph, one taken in the story present, it would show Krebs casually dressed, sitting by himself on his mother's front porch, and watching the young women walk by on the other side of the street. He would be a part of no social organization (college fraternity or army); he would have no woman (his sisters and mother would be the only females in his life); and he would be on a street in his home town. What resonates in this hypothetical picture is that he is isolated and inert, without function or goal. His wartime experiences, both good and bad, have therefore in some way incapacitated him; he feels alienated from the home front and this has somehow vitiated his energy.

What this exposition says is fairly clear, and one must assume that Hemingway wants the reader to believe it because a third person narrator perceived from the start as unreliable would wreck this story. Therefore, what is most significant from a technical viewpoint is not what the exposition says, but the strategies of narrative argumentation the author employs to get us to believe it. The emotional distance and apparent disinterestedness of the prose in the first two paragraphs give the reader no cause to suspect that the narrator has didactic motives. The device of the two photographs further supports this matter-of-fact exposition, so that the reader will not stop to think that the author is deliberately choosing which pictures to present as well as what details to report. Lastly, the first paragraph seems disjointed, as though the narrator is merely listing a number of facts: information, a description of a picture, and some additional information. If Hemingway is planning something, it is not immediately discernible.

The third paragraph, which introduces the first explicit evidence of the disillusioned veteran theme, seems narrated in an equally dispassionate manner, even though the narrator makes a number of subjective observations. Because of the presentation, however, the reader accepts the following "facts": the drafted men were elaborately welcomed on their return home; this hysterical greeting of heroes subsequently led to a reaction against further celebrations; Krebs returned much too late for a hero's welcome; and the townspeople thought it ridiculous for him to have come back so late. From these facts the reader infers that drafted men returned before enlisted men. The passage also suggests, in the way it singles out Krebs, that his late return resulted from his having enlisted and that enlisting was atypical.

But let us take a closer look at the logic employed in the third paragraph. Krebs returned to the United States with the second division in the summer of 1919, seven to nine months after the Armistice of November 1918. Yet, if years have passed between the end of the war and his return to his hometown, then he did not come home for at least a year after his return stateside. If he was mustered out upon his arrival in the United States, then he chose to remain away from home for another year. Even if, having enlisted, he still had another year to serve, certainly he would have had a furlough coming to him before that. Moreover, the implication that men who were drafted came home before those who volunteered is ludicrous, as is the suggestion that enlisting was unusual. In the First World War, forty-two percent of America's soldiers were enlistees (Hawley 21).

If the last sentence of the above passage is literally true, and Krebs returned "years after the war was over" [55], then both the alienated veteran thesis and the unhappy son thesis could use this as supporting evidence by asking why he stayed away and coming up with different answers to this question. But it would be an act of extreme bad faith for an author to leave such critical information out of his exposition. It would be a matter not of artistic omission but of the suppression of vital information. Therefore, the last sentence cannot be read literally. Instead, it should be viewed as the narrator's mimicking in free indirect speech Krebs's sense of the townspeople's response to him. This mimicking, or merging of the voices of character and narrator, and the dubious suggestions about why Krebs missed out on the celebrations show just how strongly Hemingway identifies with his protagonist. The lengths to which he went to disguise this fact demonstrate how important it was for him to make the exposition convincing enough to hold its own with the later scenes.

Even if the reader were inclined to wonder about this exposition, to step back for a moment and examine Hemingway's persuasive attempts, the next paragraph, which discusses how Krebs was compelled to lie about his war experiences in order to be heard, begins with some further expository information tossed into the story by way of an inertly constructed, nonrestrictive clause—Krebs "had been at Belleau Wood, Soissons, the Champagne, St. Mihiel and in the Argonne" [55]. These were among the bloodiest battles in which American troops fought; in 1924 this list would evoke an immediate visceral sympathy for Krebs in the reader. * * * The purpose of both the dispassionate presentation and the grim list of battles is to get the reader to sympathize with Krebs, and to establish the credibility of the exposition well enough so that the reader will not look too closely at how this effect is being accomplished.

Once Hemingway gets the reader past the third paragraph the rest of the exposition unfolds with an impressive tightness of argument. Each of the five main sections of exposition leads smoothly into the next, often with the first sentence of each providing a graceful transition. The first three paragraphs establish Krebs's background and introduce the theme of alienation. The second section shows more specifically how the townspeople's failure to understand him produced this alienation. Forced to lie to the insensitive townspeople about his wartime experiences, Krebs "acquired the nausea in regard to experience that is the result of untruth or exaggeration" [56]. He is compelled to pose, and in "this way he lost everything" [56]. The third section focuses on Krebs's daily activities and illustrates the behavior of a man who has lost everything. The reader believes that Krebs's passive, desultory behavior has resulted from the process of alienation described in the previous section. Before the war, Krebs was not allowed to use his father's car; the third section ends: "Now, after the war, it was the same car" [56]. This suggestion about how his rights to the car have not changed leads to the lengthy fourth section, which begins: "Nothing was changed in the town except that the young girls had grown up" [56]. In this section, we see Krebs's desires for the "young girls" wax as he contemplates them and wane as he thinks about the effort he would have to expend to get them. The narrator makes full use of his access to Krebs's consciousness as the free indirect speech of the passage approaches interior monologue. Krebs rationalizes his passivity, but because the exposition is so firmly established by this point, the reader attributes that passivity to a veteran's alienation and buys Krebs's rationalizations. The section concludes with Krebs deciding that the hometown women are not worth the effort: "Not now when things were getting good again" [57]. This sentence leads into the final section of the exposition, in which Krebs is reading about the war. He is learning what happened to him and this makes him feel better. The exposition thus leaves off with Krebs still fighting his demons, the inner conflicts caused by the war.

However persuasively the exposition points to the disillusioned veteran thesis, a childhood wound critic could point out that Hemingway deliberately offers a prewar photograph of Krebs at college in Kansas in order to avoid showing us any image of the soldier at home before he was a soldier. Our knowledge of his prewar experiences in his home must therefore be deduced from the scenes presented later in the story—scenes that seem to demonstrate Mrs. Krebs's unsuitability as a mother and the ease with which she can manipulate and infantilize her son. Three gestures from the climactic breakfast scene capture the nature of Krebs's relationship with his mother, a relationship that surely had a long background before the war.

In the first gesture, Mrs. Krebs removes her glasses after asking him if he has made a decision about his future. On the one hand, this gesture seems to imply that she either cannot, or does not want to "see" him, even though she seems "worried" and does not ask him questions "in a mean way" [59]. From another perspective, Mrs. Krebs's removal of her glasses is better viewed as an attention-getting, dramatic gesture in which she aggressively pins her emotionally-wriggling and sprawling son with her gaze and formulated phrases—"Have you decided what you are going to do yet, Harold?" [59] and "God has some work for every one to do" [59].

A few lines later, after his mother has spoken about God's Kingdom, revealed her worries about the "temptations" he must have been exposed to during the war ("I know how weak men are"), and stated that she prays for him "all day long," he makes his own significant gesture: "Krebs looked at the bacon fat hardening on his plate" [60]. The hardening bacon fat is an objective correlative [x] of Krebs's feelings toward his mother. The image is especially effective because it is associated with the act of a mother feeding her son; Mrs. Krebs's nourishment is unnurturing.[5] * * *

The final significant gesture occurs after Krebs's statement that he does not love her causes his mother to cry. She refuses to accept his explanations and buries her head in her hands. First he holds her, then kisses her hair. She puts her face up to him and reminds him of how she held him next to her heart when he was a baby. He feels "sick and vaguely nauseated," calls her "Mummy," and promises to "try and be a good boy" for her [61]. Having stripped him of his adulthood, she then manipulates him into kneeling beside her on the floor while she prays for him. These three gestures, then, seem to typify their relationship: her inability to see him for who he is and her visual-verbal assault on him, his resentment of her, and his inevitable capitulation to her demands. As Krebs has only been home for a month, it would appear that this is what their relationship has been like for a long time, an assumption borne out by such sentences as "Krebs felt embarrassed and resentful *as always*." ([60], my emphasis)

In order that the exposition and the scenes might be equally convincing, rendering it impossible for a reader to make the alienated veteran or the unhappy son interpretation paramount, Hemingway found ways to make the former more persuasive; he also worked to undermine the latter somewhat, mainly by bringing his sympathies for Krebs out into the open, where no reader could miss them. The presence of the narrator's sympathies for his protagonist is pervasive

5. Peter L. Hays points out that Hemingway's "hardening bacon fat" may have been influenced by similar images in Ford Madox Ford's *Some. Do Not* and in James Joyce's "A Painful Case" and *Portrait of the Artist as a Young Man*, where they are used to express disgust regarding conventional sexual morality. Assessing Hays's observation, Paul Smith suggests that "the image of hardening grease seems to have taken on in those years an almost iconic association with a stultifying, normal, and homey morality" (70).

in the scenic passages, but rather than engage in a full-blown explication of these passages I will merely point out two instances where
the narrator employs diegetic commentary to decrease the
mimetic effectiveness of the scenes.

The first of these comments occurs after Mrs. Krebs says that
everyone is in God's Kingdom. To this point, Krebs has responded
to her speeches with either silence or unenthusiastic monosyllabic
replies. But here the response is an observation by the narrator:
"Krebs felt embarrassed and resentful as always" [60]. After her
next speech, the response is: "Krebs looked at the bacon fat hardening on his plate" [60]. Although the first response is entirely appropriate since Hemingway has legitimate access to the mind of his
central consciousness, the second response renders it superfluous.
The second employs an objective correlative to show Krebs's feelings
with a perfectly selected detail; the first merely tells about it. A psy-
chobiographer might call this a slip and conclude that Hemingway's
hatred of his mother caused him to intrude, but from a functional
point of view the sentence, whether or not it was a slip, serves the
purpose of slightly decreasing the effectiveness of the scene by
directing the reader's attention toward the narrator and away from
Krebs.

Another such sentence occurs a page later. After his mother tells
Krebs how she held him next to her heart when he was "a tiny baby,"
the response is: "Krebs felt sick and vaguely nauseated" [61]. As
before, the commentary is unnecessary (the entire scene is already
making the reader feel sick and vaguely nauseated) and it again turns
the reader's attention toward the narrator. With the narrator's sympathies now out in the open, the identification between narrator and
character is complete. The denouement is Krebs's decision to go
away, and the free indirect prose of that final passage fully merges
the narrator's and Krebs's voices.

If Hemingway's second diegetic comment is, as I believe it to be,
deliberate, so too is his use of the word "nauseated." It helps to link
the scene with the earlier exposition. Krebs feels nauseous because
his mother "made him lie" [61] about his feelings. In the second
section of the exposition, lying about his war experiences gives him
"nausea." Moreover, the reason he does not actively seek one of the
hometown "girls" is because he cannot abide any more lying, which
would lead, one must assume, to more nausea:

> Vaguely he wanted a girl but he did not want to have to work to
> get her. He would have liked to have a girl but he did not want to
> have to spend a long time getting her. He did not want to get into
> the intrigue and politics. He did not want to have to do any court-
> ing. He did not want to tell any more lies. It wasn't worth it. [57]

This passage follows one in which the young women are introduced as a "pattern" that he likes: their good-looks, youth, "round Dutch collars above their sweaters," "silk stockings and flat shoes," "bobbed hair and the way they walked" under "the shade of the trees" on the other side of the street [56–57]. In that passage, the word "like" is repeated six times and then countered by a sentence in which he "did not like them." In the quoted passage, he at first "wants" one of these young women, but this is followed by four uses of "did not want." The second sentence of the passage essentially reiterates the first, but expands it through a deliberate verbosity that mimics the "chore" of having to get a woman. That bloated sentence then collapses into four progressively shorter declarative statements leading to the free indirect "It wasn't worth it."

In these two passages, the one describing his attraction to the young women, the other his revulsion at the effort of getting a woman, Krebs's feelings are conveyed by Hemingway's use of "like" and "did not want" respectively. As the fourth section proceeds he wavers between these opposing feelings more and more rapidly until, at the end of the section, his ambivalence at last turns maddening:

> He would like to have one of them. But it was not worth it. They were such a nice pattern. He liked the pattern. It was exciting. But he would not go through all the talking. He did not want one badly enough. He liked to look at them all, though. It was not worth it. Not now when things were getting good again. [57]

Like T. S. Eliot's hollow men [in the poem so titled], Krebs finds that "Between the idea / And the reality / Between the motion / And the act / Falls the Shadow" (58). The shadow that renders Krebs incapable of action and that lies at the crux of the story is stated in three sentences that follow immediately after his first statement that the young women are not worth it: "He did not want any consequences. He did not want any consequences ever again. He wanted to live along without consequences" [57]. Buried in the exposition, placed between the passage that describes his ambivalence toward the women and a passage in which he rationalizes that ambivalence, these three sentences underlie Krebs's thoughts and actions throughout both the exposition and the scenes, and thus form the main thread that unites the two parts of the story.

His desire to avoid consequences is his single overriding motivation. He fondly recalls the French and German women because relationships with them were uncomplicated and without consequence; there was no need even to talk. He wants the hometown women but does not act on these desires because they are too complicated and not worth the consequences. He is attracted to his little sister because he can shrug off her demands and she will still love him.

But his mother repels him because her demands are complex and unavoidable. His father he avoids altogether. He lies because it is the easiest way to avoid complications, but his lies make him nauseous by alienating him from his own experiences, and thereby cause him even more complications.

In college and in war Krebs did not have to think or make decisions; he merely did "the one thing, the only thing for a man to do, easily and naturally" [55]. At home he wants to create a similar kind of world, one without complications and consequences, but he cannot. So he tries to disappear into his bed, or a book, or the sports page, or "the cool dark of the pool room" [56]. Yet, just when "things were getting good again" [57], reality impinges and flushes him out. When things get too complicated, "Hare"—his sister Helen's nickname for him—bolts; the road to Kansas City is the path of least resistance. The story ends:

> There would be one more scene maybe before he got away. He would not go down to his father's office. He would miss that one. He wanted his life to go smoothly. It had just gotten going that way. Well, that was all over now, anyway. He would go over to the schoolyard and watch Helen play indoor baseball. [61]

The "illustrative stamp"[6] of the story will take place after the narrative is over. It consists of the poignant image of Krebs, in his futile attempt to escape life's complications, halting just long enough to peer into a world from which he is irrevocably cut off, the seemingly simple world of childhood. This is the point to which both his wartime experiences and his filial experiences have brought him, the logical denouement of his story, beyond which this text and its intrinsic interpretive terrain cannot go.

II

"Soldier's Home," then, is a tale about a disillusioned war veteran and a conflicted mother-son relationship. But it is also, of course, much more. Having examined the story's form and argument, I would like to conclude with some comments on its larger cultural significance. The two parts of the text are linked by Krebs's desire to avoid complications, but they are also linked by a recurrent rhet-

---

6. The "illustrative stamp" is my own concept, which derives from an observation by Robert Louis Stevenson: "The threads of a story come from time to time together and make a picture in the web; the characters fall from time to time into some attitude to each other or to nature, which stamps the story home like an illustration. . . . Other things we may forget . . . but these epoch-making scenes, which put the last mark of truth upon a story and fill up, at one blow, our capacity for sympathetic pleasure, we so adopt into the very bosom of our mind that neither time nor tide can weaken or efface the impression" (256–57). * * * This aspect of the short story is an inextricable part of the reader's sense-making process, and readers will remember a story's stamp long after they have forgotten nearly everything else about that story.

orical strategy in which a popular normative image is presented and then immediately problematized. These images are found in both the exposition and the scenes, and speak to an important cultural issue—the way in which fundamental social constructs seemed to be everywhere disintegrating in the mid-1920s.[7] "Soldier's Home" thus expresses not only the "social reality" of the veteran's postwar alienation and the personal reality of its author's resentment of his mother, but also * * * what Raymond Williams has described as a "structure of feeling that is lived and experienced but not yet quite arranged" (192)—the "social experience" of a society that in the mid-1920s was perceived to be losing its coherence.[8]

The photograph in the second paragraph presents one such popular image—two triumphant American soldiers in Germany with their comely *fräuleins*, the symbolic fruits of military victory—but the image is immediately undercut as the women are not beautiful and the Rhine does not show.[9] The fruits of the war America supposedly waged to "make the world safe for democracy" were proving equally bitter. Between the Armistice of 1918 and the spring of 1924, when Hemingway was writing "Soldier's Home," the United States turned its back on the League of Nations, France and Belgium invaded the Ruhr, bloody civil insurrections in Spain and Italy were followed by military coups, the Russian civil war led to an ominous treaty between Russia and Germany, and yet another savage Greco-Turkish War erupted. On the home-front during that same short span of time, democratic hopes had been mocked by the Volstead Act, the Red Scare, the Palmer raids,[1] urban race riots, the outrage of a presidential candidate forced to campaign from a federal penitentiary for having criticized the war, several government corruption scandals, the Black Sox scandal (the sports page that provides Krebs with one of his few pleasures was, that summer, charting the course of Hemingway's hometown team on its way to throwing the

7. My understanding of the American 1920s derives from numerous sources, of which the fullest account is Perrett. Particularly valuable are Fass, Hawley, and, for literary history, Hoffman. The best account of the American home front during the war is David M. Kennedy.
8. The approximately five-year difference between the time when the story is set and the time when it is narrated contributes to its meaning. That is, the story represents a textual dialogue of sorts between Hemingway's retrospective construction of social reality as it was in 1919 and his personal experience of the intervening half decade. The popular normative images that dissolve or are problematized in "Soldier's Home" represent the social institutions that seemed to be disintegrating or in transition by the mid-1920s, and derive from the text's double perspective.
9. James Mellow shrewdly observes that in Hemingway's fictions a river generally "serves as a cleansing baptism, an absolution for past sins, a healing experience," as is the case with the Big Two-Hearted, the Irati (in *The Sun Also Rises*) and the Tagliamento (in *A Farewell to Arms*). But in "Soldier's Home" the "absence of the Rhine is, perhaps, a signal that there is no redemptive symbol in Krebs's circumstances—or in the story" (124–25).
1. The Volstead Act enforced Prohibition; the Red Scare—popular fear of immigrants with leftist sympathies—led to the Palmer raids, in which thousands were arrested and hundreds deported [*Editor*].

World Series in the fall), the first half of a decade-long farm depression, the rise of the Ku Klux Klan to political power in the South
and Midwest (leading to the collapse of civil government in Krebs's
Oklahoma in the fall of 1923), pervasive xenophobia, the immigration restriction acts, and a torrent of religious fanaticism (so nicely
captured in the character of Mrs. Krebs). In "Soldier's Home" and
the change in Krebs from military conqueror to enervated son we
see in miniature what Marc Dolan has identified as the "narrative
transit of mood" that underlies the myth of the Lost Generation—a
transit "from joy to dissipation" in a decade that "began with exhilaration and ended in deflation" (50).

Another qualified normative image is that of the "good-looking
young girls" [56] with their odd combination of the morally conventional (Dutch collars, sweaters, flat shoes) and the shockingly new
(bobbed hair, silk stockings). The appeal of this image is seen in
Krebs's normal healthy desire for these young women, but the
image is problematized by his anxious avoidance of them and his
rationalization of his failure to act. Krebs returns from the war to
find an incipient sexual and gender revolution taking place, and the
"nice pattern" [57] he silently observes is, as he suspects, a good
deal more complicated than it appears. These young women, who
have grown up while Krebs was in Europe, are on the verge of open
rebellion against the society into which they have been born; they
are a significant part of the work force, eager to escape the stultifi-
cation of small town life, and openly questioning the imprisoning
sex and gender roles to which Krebs's mother still clings.

Aping the dress of their flapper sisters in the speakeasies of the
big cities, this generation of "nice girls" would in the 1920s engage in
hitherto unheard of promiscuity and inaugurate a new era of wide-
spread birth control, rampant venereal disease, and increased divorce
rates. Although their cultural codes elude Krebs—who cannot read
the mixed signifiers of their attire and can only sense in them a complicated system of "already defined alliances and shifting feuds" that
he does not possess the "energy or the courage" [56] to penetrate—
nevertheless his attitude typifies the general male response to a phenomenon that surprised, excited, baffled, and frightened.

What is most interesting about the description of the young
women in "Soldier's Home" is their dialogical textualization. It is
highly improbable that young women in a town in Oklahoma in 1919,
where reactionary social attitudes prevailed, would have bobbed
their hair and worn silk stockings. Bobbed hair, according to Paula
Fass, was the very "badge of flapperhood"—perceived as "a symbol
of female promiscuity, of explicit sexuality, and of a self-conscious
denial of respectability and the domestic ideal" (93, 280). Such styles,
though, were already appearing on college campuses [or] in big

cities, and making their way into suburbs like Oak Park, the home to which Lieutenant Hemingway returned after the war. On the other hand, by 1924 these styles had spread to the hinterland, promoted by the proliferation of a whole new set of slick magazines that were, like so many other consumer items in this period, targeted at the young. The bobbed hair and silk stockings of the young women in "Soldier's Home" are thus an incongruous textual displacement, a projection across space (from Oak Park to a town in Oklahoma) and time (from 1924 to 1919) that endows the text's *fabula* and its protagonist with a preternatural sense of what was in the offing.

A third aspect of social experience in "Soldier's Home" pertains to an especially cherished image—the American family. In Krebs's dysfunctional American family, the father is absent, represented synecdochically by the car that stands outside his second floor office, which itself represents the autonomy Krebs desires but paradoxically can have only if he becomes an accomplice to his own infantilization. There is no small degree of irony in Mrs. Krebs's statement: "Your father does not want to hamper your freedom. He thinks you should be allowed to drive the car" [60]. This irony is compounded when she then adds: "If you want to take some of the nice girls out riding with you, we are only too pleased" [60]. Krebs's favorite sister, the only family member to show him unconditional affection, is summarily dismissed by his mother before the breakfast confrontation that will cause him to leave home for good. The domestic breakfast scene, a wholesome centripetal image of family life, is in this story a scene of absence, dispersal, manipulation, resentment, capitulation, and passive-aggressive self-abnegation. The text, then, expresses the anxieties, pervasive by the mid-1920s, that the American family—for over a century an indispensable fortress of prevailing cultural values—was on the verge of collapse.[2] Moreover, this development was taking place in a society in which a culture based on production was giving way to one based on consumption, and where an ethos of self-denial was increasingly turning to self-indulgence, as evidenced by an alarming rise in alcoholism and drug addiction.

Krebs, in his own idiosyncratically situated, self-indulgent torpor, represents a larger cultural malaise gripping many Americans during the 1920s and forming a significant part of the decade's social experience. Disappearing into a cool, dark pool room, reading newspapers and war books, and anxiously watching young women from his mother's porch, this awkward child of the new consumer culture

---

2. These anxieties were particularly acute during the 1920s and are part of the social experience of the period. In reality, of course, the family was not collapsing, but rather undergoing fundamental changes as "emotional ties of warmth and amicability replaced [former ties of] respect and authority" and the family became less hierarchical and more democratic (Fass 93).

has become an uncertain spectator in a transitional society where the disappearance of old norms precludes his participation. Caught between the already obsolete world of his parents and a new world he is not equipped to enter, [he can only] observe passively as he practices on his clarinet, metonymically associated with the "Jazz Age" and the new. As Krebs drifts ever farther from his familial matrix, his clarinet-playing, like all of his other activities, significantly devolves into lethargy and retreat: "In the evening he practiced on his clarinet, strolled down town, read and went to bed" [56]. Like the yellow fog of Eliot's "The Love Song of J. Alfred Prufrock," that after its "sudden leap" curls once about the house and falls asleep (4), Krebs's impulse toward action inevitably winds down into inertia.

From his vantage point in Europe, Hemingway, in one of the relatively few pieces of fiction he would set on the American mainland, sensed the larger social experience of his age and expressed it through a character whose more specific, preliminary problems were, by their biographical relevance, compelling enough to engage the attention of readers and critics for seven decades. But "Soldier's Home" was one of many texts published in 1925—*The Great Gatsby, The Professor's House, Bread Givers, Manhattan Transfer, Barren Ground, Arrowsmith, An American Tragedy,* "The Hollow Men,"[3] and, of course, [the rest of *In Our Time*]—that captured the experience of a people in painful transition: their failed institutions, their confused and often tragic attempts to hold onto past ideals and ideologies, and their inevitable failure. In the mid-1920s, Hemingway could allow his hero to escape to Kansas City, just as Nick Adams escapes to the Big Two-Hearted, [and, in *SAR*,] Jake Barnes to the bullfight arena, and Brett Ashley into hedonism. Escape was still possible then. But soon, all too soon, the bill would come due.

Works Cited

Baker, Carlos. *Ernest Hemingway: A Life Story.* New York: Scribner's, 1969.

Baker, Sheridan. *Ernest Hemingway.* New York: Holt, Rinehart & Winston, 1967.

DeFalco, Joseph. *The Hero in Hemingway's Short Stories.* Pittsburgh: U of Pittsburgh P, 1963.

Dolan, Marc. "The (Hi)story of their Lives: Mythic Autobiography and the 'Lost Generation.'" *Journal of American Studies* 27 (1993): 35–56.

Donaldson, Scott. *By Force of Will: The Life and Art of Ernest Hemingway.* New York: Viking, 1977.

---

3. Literary works of 1925 by F. Scott Fitzgerald, Willa Cather, Anzia Yezierska, John Dos Passos, Ellen Glasgow, Sinclair Lewis, Theodore Dreiser, and T. S. Eliot, respectively [*Editor*].

Eliot, T. S. *The Complete Poems and Plays 1909–1950*. New York: Harcourt Brace, 1962.

Fass, Paula. *The Damned and the Beautiful: American Youth in the 1920s*. New York: Oxford UP, 1977.

Gurko, Leo. *Ernest Hemingway and the Pursuit of Heroism*. New York: Crowell, 1968.

Hasbany, Richard. "The Shock of Vision: An Imagist Reading of *In Our Time*." In Wagner 224–40.

Hawley, Ellis W. *The Great War and the Search for a Modern Order: A History of the American People and Their Institutions, 1917–1933*. New York: St. Martin's, 1979.

Hays, Peter L. "'Soldier's Home' and Ford Madox Ford." *Hemingway Notes* 1 (1971): 21–22.

Hemingway, Ernest. "Soldier's Home." *In Our Time*. 1925. New York: Scribner's, 1970. 69–77 [55–61].

Hoffman, Frederick J. *The Twenties: American Writing in the Postwar Decade*. 1955. New York: Free Press, 1965.

Kennedy, David M. *Over Here: The First World War and American Society*. Oxford: Oxford UP, 1980.

Kennedy, J. Gerald, and Kirk Curnutt. "Out of the Picture: Mrs. Krebs, Mother Stein, and 'Soldier's Home.'" *The Hemingway Review* 12.1 (Fall 1992): 1–11.

Kobler, J. F. "'Soldier's Home' Revisited: A Hemingway *Mea Culpa*." *Studies in Short Fiction* 30 (1993): 377–85.

Lamb, Robert Paul. "Fishing for Stories: What 'Big Two-Hearted River' Is Really About." *Modern Fiction Studies* 37 (1991): 161–82.

Lynn, Kenneth S. *Hemingway*. New York: Simon and Schuster, 1987.

Mellow, James R. *Hemingway: A Life without Consequences*. Boston: Houghton Mifflin, 1992.

Perrett, Geoffrey. *America in the Twenties: A History*. New York: Simon and Schuster, 1982.

Reynolds, Michael. *Hemingway: The Paris Years*. Oxford: Basil Blackwell, 1989.

Smith, Paul. *A Reader's Guide to the Short Stories of Ernest Hemingway*. Boston: G. K. Hall, 1989.

Stevenson, Robert Louis. *Memories and Portraits*. New York: Scribner's, 1887.

Wagner, Linda Welshimer, ed. *Ernest Hemingway: Five Decades of Criticism*. East Lansing: Michigan State UP, 1974.

Waldhorn, Arthur. *A Reader's Guide to Ernest Hemingway*. New York: Farrar, Straus, Giroux, 1972.

Warren, Robert Penn. "Ernest Hemingway." 1951. In Wagner 75–102.

Williams, Raymond. *The English Novel from Dickens to Lawrence*. 1970. London: Hogarth, 1984.

Young, Philip. *Ernest Hemingway: A Reconsideration*. 1952. University Park: Pennsylvania State UP, 1966.

J. GERALD KENNEDY AND KIRK CURNUTT

Out of the Picture: Mrs. Krebs, Mother Stein, and "Soldier's Home"†

> Brother, brother, here is mother.
> We are all very well.
> —Gertrude Stein
> "Accents in Alsace"

To preface the story of Harold Krebs, the alienated veteran of World War I, Hemingway opens "Soldier's Home" with a brief description of two photographs. One portrays Krebs at a Methodist school in Kansas, among his fraternity brothers, each wearing "exactly the same height and style collar" in a scene of male solidarity. The other captures him in Europe, presumably after the Armistice: "There is a picture which shows him on the Rhine with two German girls and another corporal. Krebs and the corporal look too big for their uniforms. The German girls are not beautiful. The Rhine does not show in the picture" [55]. Intended as a generic war photo of victorious troops posing with comely women in a vivid foreign setting, the picture fails to produce the intended effect. None of the visual signs quite conveys the notion of military or romantic conquest. Instead, the picture betrays Krebs's chronic inability to live up to expectations or to play the role of hero: the uniforms are ludicrously small, the girls are less than ravishing, and the legendary river—calculated to certify the landscape as foreign—is nowhere to be seen. The juxtaposition of the two photos subtly implies a change in Krebs himself from a conventional, Midwestern college boy to a clownish figure posturing with "German girls" in a parody of male dominance.

Hemingway's wry comment about the Rhine indeed epitomizes the bathetic quality of Krebs's personal dilemma in "Soldier's Home." The young man has come home "years after the war was over," a circumstance that townspeople find "rather ridiculous." The photo in which the Rhine "does not show" metaphorizes Krebs's ongoing inability to represent and validate his war experience in a small town that has "heard too many atrocity stories to be thrilled by actualities" [55]. His lack of recognition within the community parallels the more humiliating situation that he faces at home: his failure to be accepted as an adult by his suffocating parents. He has returned from the bloodiest battles of the war to have his mother ask him not to "muss up" the newspaper because his "father can't read his *Star* if it's been

† *The Hemingway Review* 12.1 (Fall 1992): 1–11. Copyright © 1992. Reprinted by permission of The Ernest Hemingway Foundation. All rights reserved. Page numbers in brackets refer to this Norton Critical Edition.

mussed" [58]. The inadvertently comic photo of Krebs in uniform exemplifies his awkward struggle to be regarded *at home* as a good soldier, a Marine who has endured the slaughter of the Western front.

The clever sentence summing up Krebs's predicament must have occurred to Hemingway in 1924 in a moment of complex irony, for he conjured it up not from his own sardonic imagination but from Gertrude Stein's "Accents in Alsace," an experimental composition in *Geography and Plays* (1922). Since February 1922 Stein had been functioning as Hemingway's Parisian mentor, communicating (as he later conceded) "many truths about rhythms and the uses of words in repetition" (*MF* 17). He had reviewed *Geography and Plays* in 1923 for the Paris *Tribune* and so presumably recalled (or referred back to) the closing section of "Accents in Alsace," which reads:

> Sweeter than water or cream or ice. Sweeter than bells of roses. Sweeter than winter or summer or spring. Sweeter than pretty posies. Sweeter than anything is my queen and loving is her nature.
>
> Loving and good and delighted and best is her little King and Sire whose devotion is entire who has but one desire to express the love which is hers to inspire.
>
> In the photograph the Rhine hardly showed.
>
> (*Geography and Plays* 415)

Like Stein, Hemingway calls attention to a picture in order to note what has eluded the photographer; in "Soldier's Home," the river indeed no longer shows at all. But what is the object of this esoteric allusion to *Geography and Plays*? Is Hemingway thus acknowledging a debt or, conversely, indulging in parody? Or does he mean by this subtle revision of Stein's line to call attention to something else just out of sight in "Soldier's Home": the increasingly strained relationship between the brash young Hemingway and a garrulous female writer old enough to be his mother? When we reconsider the circumstances under which he composed the story and reexamine those fictional traces of Stein's style, the narrative takes on a new aspect, indicative of Hemingway's determination in the spring of 1924 to throw off the influence of his mentor.

The salient facts of the Hemingway-Stein friendship, familiar to most scholars, require only brief summary here. Suffice it to say that when Hemingway arrived in Paris in 1921, a letter of introduction from Sherwood Anderson enabled him to make the acquaintance of Stein and her companion Alice B. Toklas. During the spring of 1922, Hemingway must have paid several visits to the famous atelier on the rue de Fleurus, admiring the paintings, tasting the liqueurs, and receiving instruction from the author of *Three Lives* and *Tender Buttons*. Like Anderson, Stein initially treated Hemingway as a protégé and (according to *MF*) lectured him on money, food, clothing, art, literature, and sex. She read his early stories and offered blunt criticism; she let him read her own compositions to illustrate the effects that she was trying to create. For a while, Hemingway welcomed this attention. Stein's ideas about writing challenged him, and his regard for her literary opinion persisted into 1923, when he confessed to her: "I've thought a lot about the things you said about working and am starting that way at the beginning" (*SL* 79). As he learned his craft and began to publish stories, however, he grew impatient with Stein's imperious manner and looked to establish his literary independence.

As Michael Reynolds remarks, by early 1924, Hemingway "no longer needed Gertrude Stein," since his stories were virtually writing themselves (*Paris Years* 41). When Ford Madox Ford invited him in February to lend a hand at the editorial office of the *transatlantic*, Hemingway suddenly found himself in a position to do Stein a favor, persuading Ford to publish sight unseen part of her long narrative *The Making of Americans*. If Hemingway admired the work (as he professed to do), he also recognized an opportunity to twit Ford for his stuffiness, to repay Stein for her tutelage, and to demonstrate his own professional ascendancy. That winter he spent precious hours retyping and copyediting the manuscript for serialization in Ford's little magazine. But he carried out this labor, it would appear, less to promote Stein's work than to amass the necessary credit to cancel his own debt. His letter of 17 February 1924 manages to be both deferential and patronizing: addressing her (as usual) as "Miss Stein," he assumes the role of agent as he lightly counsels her to accept Ford's offer of thirty francs per magazine page. "Be haughty but not too haughty," he admonishes, hinting that she should not question the terms that he himself has negotiated. Hemingway further implies that he has manipulated Ford to gain her this royalty: "I made it clear it was a remarkable scoop for his magazine obtained only through my obtaining genius" (*SL* 111). But we know that Hemingway talked Ford into publishing *The Making of Americans* only by suppressing the fact that the manuscript ran to nine hundred pages, even as he allowed Stein to believe that the entire work would be serialized. By stretching the truth to both parties, he brokered a deal that (in his mind) enabled him to settle his account with Stein.

But as "Soldier's Home" attests, other tensions complicated the situation. Although Hemingway needed to break away from Stein to assert his autonomy and mark the end of his apprenticeship, psychic attachments made the process difficult. Recent biographers agree that he had discovered in Stein both a teacher and a surrogate for Grace Hemingway, the strong-willed mother from whom he had revolted during the angry summer of 1920. Kenneth Lynn characterizes Stein as "Grace's most encompassing replacement," noting similarities in age, weight, voice, and manner (168); Reynolds calls Stein "the Paris mother" whom Hemingway needed (*Paris Years* 35). Jeffrey Meyers notes that both women "were frustrated artists who felt irritated by their thwarted careers and lack of recognition" (76). To both, Hemingway attributed an emotional instability linked to menopause. Estranged from Grace, he felt a peculiar need for Stein's approval and affection, yet the very resemblance that drew him to her produced a recurrent, subconscious resentment of her solicitude.

From the outset, Stein's androgynous manner provoked in Hemingway an uncertain gendered response. "Gertrude Stein and me are just like brothers" he wrote to Sherwood Anderson in March 1922, asserting a fraternal bond. By the summer of that year, however, a physical attraction had moved Alice B. Toklas to jealousy; Stein acknowledged a "weakness" for Hemingway, while the younger writer toyed with the outrageous notion of seducing his gay mentor (*SL* 62, 79, 650). With Stein, Hemingway felt something very like a masculine bond; yet he also wanted to bed her, perhaps in his mind to feminize her. He moreover felt a filial affection, having discovered a nurturing mother to foster and validate his literary work. But the relationship cooled during the four months that Hemingway and his wife spent back in Toronto for the birth of their son. Perhaps the writer's brief visit to his Oak Park home in December 1923 allowed him to recognize the Oedipal tug in his attraction to Stein; or, perhaps, the birth of Bumby gave him a different perspective on the relation of mothers and sons. Whatever the reason, when he returned to Paris in January, he began to redefine his friendship to Stein.[1]

As if to rehearse a scene he now anticipated, he began in late March or early April to write "Soldier's Home," a story about a son's need to escape from parental authority and domestic routine. If the events were fictional, many of the specific details derived, of course, from Hemingway's uncomfortable return to Oak Park in early 1919, after his own war service as an ambulance driver in Italy. Although he had not fought on the Western Front like his protagonist, he had seen the effects of war, sustained a wound, and developed a cynical outlook. Back home he too had trouble readjusting to civilian life: he quarreled with his mother, pored over books about the war, and somewhat ironically entertained his admiring sisters. There he also

---

1. Hemingway did, however, ask Stein and Toklas to stand as godmothers for the March 1924 christening of his son, a gesture which underscores Stein's maternal function in Hemingway's Paris life. It is worth mentioning the odd coincidence that long before meeting Stein, Hemingway had assumed the nickname "Hemingstein" or simply "Stein," and that he also referred to his mother as "Mrs. Stein." See Lynn (64).

stooped to misrepresenting his wartime activities and felt the shame of exaggerating an entirely respectable record.[2]

But whatever imaginative grist Hemingway salvaged from those troubled months in Oak Park five years earlier, his situation in Paris gave immediacy to the story. While preparing Stein's text for the *transatlantic*, he conceived a narrative about a son too confused to remain obedient and respectful, a son who deliberately hurts his mother by telling her that he does not love her. With Stein's prose rhythms and repetitions filling his head and perhaps still scrolling out of his typewriter, Hemingway developed the confrontation between the prescriptive Mrs. Krebs and the disaffected Harold, who feels the emptiness of her language and feigns contrition to avoid a scene. Throughout "Soldier's Home," echoes of Stein's rhythms and repetitions infuse Hemingway's style. These are nowhere more apparent than in the paragraph depicting Krebs's voyeuristic interest in the local girls:

> He liked to look at them from the front porch as they walked on the other side of the street. He liked to watch them walking under the shade of the trees. He liked the round Dutch collars above their sweaters. He liked their silk stockings and flat shoes. He liked their bobbed hair and the way they walked. [56–57]

Hemingway subsequently works variations on a more revealing phrase: "He did not want any consequences. He did not want any consequences ever again. He wanted to live without consequences." Krebs wants to protect himself from emotional wounds, to escape ridicule. The same passage introduces an antiphonal phrase: "He did not want to tell any more lies. It wasn't worth it. . . . It was not worth the trouble. . . . But it was not worth it. . . . It was not worth it" [57]. Hemingway learned from Stein that repetition with variation could convey the insistence of a fixed idea without invoking psychoanalytical terms. He had heard her talk about repetition many times, and typing *The Making of Americans* clarified for him the possibilities and excesses of her method.[3]

While he thus emulated her prose effects in a seeming act of stylistic homage, Hemingway also explained, through the dilemma of Harold Krebs, why a son might need to throw off a stifling maternal influence. As if to signal a private project, he inserted into the opening paragraphs of "Soldier's Home" the photo reference that would have had peculiar significance for Stein. Among contemporary

---

2. See Reynolds, *The Young Hemingway* (36–64). For Hemingway's lies, see especially 55–57.
3. For an insightful examination of the contrast between the two, see Perloff, who argues that Stein uses abstract repetition as a means of analyzing changes in feeling. She contends that this technique is fundamentally unlike the concrete, "natural" language used by Hemingway (682–83).

readers, perhaps she alone recognized the sentence as a reformula-
tion of her own ironic line in *Geography and Plays*. An equivocal
gesture, Hemingway's allusion calls attention to what is now out of
the picture, to what has been excluded by the very act of rewriting
that it signals. What the author seems intent to show is his capacity to move beyond or away from the stylistic influence of Stein
through a parodic appropriation that at once simulates and sub-
verts the language of an influential text.

The composition evoked by Hemingway in fact has some relevance
to the subject of "Soldier's Home," for "Accents in Alsace" also
explores (in its fashion) the effects of the Great War upon family
relationships. Set in the Rhineland, this experimental pseudo-drama
(Stein divides the piece into acts and scenes) loosely reflects the
clash between French and Germanic cultures in Alsace during and
after the war. The opening section introduces the Schemils [, their
daughter,] and [a] son, who has run away to join the French Foreign
Legion.[4] * * * [Later,] the story * * * fades * * * after two lines that possibly refer to a photograph the sister has sent to her soldier-
brother: "Brother brother here is mother. / We are all very well."
Anticipating the son's desire to carry a picture of his mother, the
sister presents the photo and reports on the domestic scene in the
banal language of wartime censorship.

Another photograph forms the likely subject of the final section
of "Accents," "The Watch on the Rhine," which portrays a post-war
euphoria in which conflict has yielded to sweetness and pleasure.
This closing passage declares Stein's love for her "queen," Alice
B. Toklas, and points to the autobiographical basis of the work. Stein
and Toklas had toured Alsace in 1919 and served in a civilian relief
program in Mulhouse; "Accents" registers the sights and sounds of
the local scene as it commemorates their volunteer work. James
R. Mellow suggests that the closing section marks Stein's attempt
to capture the "burgeoning" mood of "the first spring of the peace"
(286). Stein here observes that "in the photograph the Rhine hardly
showed," probably alluding to an actual picture of herself and Alice,
contented and indifferent to the strategic significance of the Rhine
(then being guarded by Allied troops).[5] Indeed, she closes the composition by announcing that "in the midst of our happiness we were
very pleased."

Hemingway's revision of this scene with Krebs, the other corporal,
and the German girls thus turns an image of lesbian felicity into a
putative sign of heterosexual desire. In this way Hemingway seems

4. Toklas recalls how she and Stein met this family in *What is Remembered* (103).
5. Many thanks to Noreen O'Connor of Yale University Press for locating the 1919 picture
of Stein and Toklas [published in the 1992 *Hemingway Review* article] at the Beinecke
Rare Book Library, Yale University.

to locate the action of "Soldier's Home" within the domain of conventional, middle-class mores; yet he does so only to cast doubt on the sexual prowess implied by the photo of Krebs. After returning home (presumably from the 1919 "Watch on the Rhine"), Krebs sits on the porch watching local girls, but he discovers that "their appeal to him was not very strong"; he even convinces himself that "he did not really need a girl" [57]. He also remembers boasting, however, that "he could not get along without girls, that he had to have them all the time." Caught between desire and denial, Krebs decides (in a line taken from Anderson's "The Untold Lie") that "it was all a lie both ways": he both does and does not need women. His conflict apparently stems from a fear of being emotionally wounded, for he suspects that women cannot understand what he has been through: "The world they were in was not the world he was in" [57].

At the same time, Krebs's anxiety and apparent confusion may betray another sort of nervousness: Hemingway's uncertain response to Stein's lesbianism. If he has in mind an actual photo of Stein and Toklas on a riverbank in Alsace, what he also leaves out of the picture in "Soldier's Home" is his simultaneous fascination and discomfort with sapphic relations. Hemingway must have recognized in "Accents" Stein's covertly androgynous passion for Toklas, figured in the "devotion" of the king for his queen. Lynn suggests that Hemingway viewed the bond between Stein and Toklas as a "bolder, Parisian variation" of his mother's relationship with Ruth Arnold, the vocal student whose open affection for Grace sparked so many rumors in Oak Park that Clarence Hemingway finally banned her from the family home (168).[6] Through a curious pattern of association perhaps tied to the gender ambivalence precipitated (we now suspect) by his mother, Hemingway worked his way from the photo of Stein and Toklas to an exploration of the young soldier's sexual uncertainties. The picture in which the Rhine "does not show" anticipates the latent gender anxiety that complicates Krebs's relations with local girls, with the sister who calls him her "beau," and with the mother who wants him to find a "nice girl" and marry.

In yet another sense, Hemingway's reaction to the picture of Stein and Toklas in Alsace may betray his perception that playful compositions like "Accents" tended to trivialize the war. While Stein regarded many pieces in *Geography and Plays* as "political compositions" (*Autobiography* 188), war typically provides a pretext for what Richard Bridgman calls the "rhymed gaiety" of the poetry (158). Although Stein and Toklas performed wartime service for the American Fund for French Wounded (distributing care packages to

6. Lynn (168). See also Reynolds, *Hemingway: The Paris Years* (36–37), for insight into Hemingway's interest in lesbianism.

wounded "doughboys"), the author kept a careful distance from the fighting. Only once, during her post-armistice visit to Alsace, did she actually observe a battlefield. In *The Autobiography of Alice B. Toklas* she recalls that spectacle with disbelief: "To anyone who did not see it as it was then it is impossible to imagine it. It was not terrifying it was strange. We were used to ruined houses and even ruined towns but this was different. It was landscape. And it belonged to no country" (187). For Stein, the war was "strange," unreal, and literally unimaginable. Even her later narrative *Wars I Have Seen* (1945) displays her relative innocence of the horrors of battle. On the other hand, Hemingway's service on the Italian front in 1918 produced a lifelong preoccupation with warfare. His professional identity emerged from that violent episode, and he developed a proprietary attitude toward combat that informed his fictional program. In 1925 he argued that for the writer "war is the best subject of all. It groups the maximum of material and speeds up the actions and brings out all sorts of stuff that normally you have to wait a lifetime to get" (*SL* 176). Stein's elision of brutality in her writing must have struck him as willful escapism, a refusal to confront the harshness of life and death. Hemingway later observed that Stein always "wanted to know the gay part of how the world was going; never the real, never the bad" (*MF* 25).

In fact, Hemingway had reason to suspect that Stein found his preoccupation with war not only distasteful but ludicrous. In December 1923 she published in *Ex Libris* the verse fragment now known as "He and They, Hemingway," which Hemingway surely saw upon his return to Paris that winter.[7] Like "Accents," the poem is a collage of conversational gambits, the most intelligible of which perhaps alludes to Hemingway's arrivals and departures ("How do you do and good-bye. Good-bye and how do you do"). The piece also pokes fun at the young writer's pretensions, including a ponderous line that he possibly uttered in conversation: "Is there any memorial of the failure of civilization to cope with extreme savagedom?" (*Portraits* 193). The poem prefigures Stein's later comment that Hemingway "went the way so many other Americans have gone before. He became obsessed with sex and violent death" (quoted in Preston 191). Though Hemingway's response to the portrait is unknown, Stein's barely concealed parody suggests that she took a dim view of "savagedom" as a literary subject.

7. The poem's original title was "Hemingway: A Portrait." Stein added the new title in 1934 for publication in [her book] *Portraits and Prayers*. In a February 1924 letter to Anderson, Stein claims to have shown the poem to Hemingway before he returned to Toronto in the fall of 1923. If so, Hemingway did not mention it in the published correspondence. See White (36). [*Ex Libris* was a quarterly published by the American Library in Paris—*Editor*.]

The widening rift between Stein and Hemingway thus places the conflict between mother and son in "Soldier's Home" in a new light. Reynolds claims that the story projects the inability of Hemingway's parents to understand his work: "By that spring of 1924 he was writing stories that he knew his parents could not read without being deeply hurt. Deep within him he needed their approval and support, but a part of him continually raised barricades to prevent the possibility" (*Paris Years* 191). Similarly, "Soldier's Home" may represent Stein's inability to appreciate narratives informed by the savagery of battle: "His mother asked him to tell her stories about the war, but her attention always wandered" [56]. Hemingway could cut loose symbolically from Grace's expectations by portraying her as a one-dimensional "devouring mother" (DeFalco 143); yet he could not quite imagine complete liberation from Stein. Krebs tries to declare his independence by telling his mother that he does not love her. But when Mrs. Krebs breaks into tears, Harold recognizes that his strategy has failed: "It wasn't any good. He couldn't tell her, he couldn't make her see it. It was silly to have said it" [60]. What Krebs cannot make his mother see is that he is no longer her little boy; combat has changed him. In this sense, "Soldier's Home" is not only the story of a soldier's struggle to recuperate from battle; it also portrays a son's need to achieve autonomy and respect. What nauseates Krebs is not his mother's piety but the ease with which she reduces him to a child who promises his "Mummy": "I'll try and be a good boy for you" [61]. Krebs's capitulation reveals a dependence on his mother that persists despite his effort to deny it.

After Mrs. Krebs prays for Harold, he plans to leave home, thinking that he can escape to Kansas City with "one more scene maybe." The brave tone of the conclusion masks its irony, for though Krebs believes that the scene has not touched him, he lies to himself. His mother's reminder that she held him as a baby has evoked nausea and shame. His ambivalence may betray Hemingway's anxiety that no matter how rapidly his writing developed or how coolly he posed as Stein's agent, he remained dependent upon her approval.[8]

Such a recognition may explain why he chose an esoteric allusion to his mentor to signal his independence. Elsewhere in *In Our Time*, Oedipal conflicts with artistic predecessors reveal Hemingway's struggle to establish his "vocational integrity" against the stifling expectations of literary tradition (Renza 674).[9] The most obvious of

---

8. *The Autobiography of Alice B. Toklas* suggests that Hemingway's fear of being the eternal pupil was not unfounded: Stein claims that her "weakness" for him arose because "he takes training and anybody who takes training is a favorite pupil" (216). * * *
9. Among the writers that Renza finds Hemingway challenging are Twain, Thoreau, Henry Adams, and Anderson. Stein is mentioned only in biographical asides, and her

these encounters, "My Old Man," projects a revolt against his first patron, Sherwood Anderson, in a story that literally culminates with the death of the father. An explicit allusion to "The Untold Lie" likewise associates Anderson with Mr. Krebs, the patriarch of "Soldier's Home"; the father's absence may imply that Hemingway had already thrown off the weight of Anderson's expectations by the spring of 1924. Yet, unprepared to defy Stein's authority, Hemingway perhaps dreaded the impending scene that would produce a break with her.

What finally compelled Hemingway to declare his independence were reviews of *In Our Time* that exaggerated the influence of Stein and Anderson, lumping the three of them into an "expatriate school."[1] During a hurried ten days in late 1925 he wrote *The Torrents of Spring*, a travesty of Anderson's *Dark Laughter* that also lampooned his mentor's style: "All that in Paris. Ah, Paris. How far it was to Paris now. Paris in the morning. Paris in the evening. Paris at night. Paris in the morning again. Paris at noon, perhaps. Why not?" (*TS* 116). The jibe is curious, for recently Hemingway had praised Stein's technique, telling one friend that she could "take [language] apart and see what makes it go. Maybe she don't get it together again. But she's always getting somewhere" [*LEH* 2:258]. The contradiction suggests that, though he had rehearsed the break with Stein in "Soldier's Home," his conflicted feelings toward her remained. Wanting to be regarded as an original, he perhaps feared that Stein would leave the imprint of her style on every line he wrote. In this sense, "Soldier's Home" prefigures an action Hemingway would repeat throughout his career—trying to push Stein out of the picture because he could not get her out of his prose.

Works Cited

Bridgman, Richard. *Gertrude Stein in Pieces*. New York: Oxford UP, 1970.

Brinnan, John Malcolm. *The Third Rose: Gertrude Stein and Her World*. Boston: Little, Brown and Co., 1959.

DeFalco, Joseph. *The Hero in Hemingway's Short Stories*. 1963. Folcroft, PA: Folcroft Library Editions, 1978.

Hemingway, Ernest. "The Autobiography of Alice B. Hemingway." Item #256. Hemingway Collection. John F. Kennedy Library.

———. *Ernest Hemingway: Selected Letters, 1917–1961*. Ed. Carlos Baker. New York: Scribner's, 1981.

---

absence from the list of misprisioned figures exemplifies the paternal biases of Renza's Bloomian model.

1. Hemingway also attacked Stein because she refused to write a review of *In Our Time*. See his November 8, 1925, letter to Ezra Pound, *LEH* 2:412 [*Editor*].

————. *The Letters of Ernest Hemingway.* Ed. Sandra Spanier et al., Vol 2. Cambridge, Eng.: Cambridge UP, 2013.

————. *A Moveable Feast.* New York: Scribner's, 1964.

————. *The Torrents of Spring.* New York: Scribner's, 1926.

Lynn, Kenneth. *Hemingway.* New York: Simon and Schuster, 1987.

Mellow, James R. *Charmed Circle: Gertrude Stein and Company.* New York: Avon, 1974.

Meyers, Jeffrey. *Hemingway: A Biography.* New York: Harper and Row, 1985.

Perloff, Marjorie. "'Ninety-Percent Rotarian': Gertrude Stein's Hemingway." *American Literature* 62 (December 1990): 668–83.

Preston, John Hyde. "A Conversation." *Atlantic* 156 (August 1935): 187–94.

Renza, Louis A. "The Importance of Being Ernest." *South Atlantic Quarterly* (Spring 1989): 661–90.

Reynolds, Michael. *Hemingway: The Paris Years.* Oxford: Basil Blackwell, 1989.

————. *The Young Hemingway.* Oxford: Basil Blackwell, 1986.

Stein, Gertrude. *The Autobiography of Alice B. Toklas.* New York: Random House, 1933.

————. *Geography and Plays.* Boston: Four Seas, 1922.

————. "He and They, Hemingway." *Portraits and Prayers.* New York: Random House, 193. Originally published as "Hemingway: A Portrait" in 1923.

————. *Wars I Have Seen.* New York: Random House, 1945.

Toklas, Alice B. *What is Remembered.* 1963. San Francisco: North Point, 1985.

White, Ray Lewis. Ed. *Sherwood Anderson/Gertrude Stein: Correspondence and Personal Essays.* Chapel Hill: U North Carolina P, 1972.

"MR. AND MRS. ELLIOT"

PAUL SMITH

From the Waste Land to the Garden with the Elliots[†]

"Mr. and Mrs. Elliot" has been both more *and* less neglected than it deserves to be. One might wish that those biographers who found in it yet another instance of Hemingway's bad taste, callous contempt,

---

† From *Hemingway's Neglected Short Fiction: New Perspectives*, ed. Susan F. Beegel (Tuscaloosa: U of Alabama P, 1989), pp. 123–29. Reprinted by permission of the publisher. Some of the author's notes have been omitted. Page numbers in brackets refer to this Norton Critical Edition.

and occasional stylistic infelicity had neglected the story altogether; one might also wish for a larger company of critics who thought of it as, possibly, a short story. Never a story to attract much critical notice, once the object of its satire was revealed, there was little more to say except to regret its triviality.[1]

Now, of course, everyone knows that it was originally titled "Mr. and Mrs. Smith," that Hemingway had Chard Powers Smith in his sights, and that the two exchanged angry and characteristic letters in 1927, two years after the story's publication. Smith called Hemingway "a worm who attempted a cad's trick, [and] a contemptible shadow"; Hemingway, of course, threatened to knock him down.[2]

Most biographers have followed Carlos Baker in dismissing the satire as a "malicious gossip-story" ridiculing the Smiths' "alleged sexual ineptitudes."[3] We are not told who, other than Hemingway, made that allegation, or with what evidence if it was not common knowledge. But for Hemingway, Chard Powers Smith was an easy mark and natural enemy, several times over: he was independently wealthy; he had degrees from both Harvard and Yale; he lingered in Latin Quarter cafés, rented chateaux along the Loire, and wrote poetry in perfect classical meters with perfect Petrarchan emotions; and Yale published his first volume in 1925.

By the spring of 1924 Hemingway was writing at an astounding pace, nearly half his titles had been published and republished—six poems, six *in our time* chapters, and "My Old Man"—and he turned again to Edward O'Brien. He wrote that he had "quit newspaper work," was "about broke," and needed an agent to "peddle" the ten stories he had written. He enclosed three, one of which he was sure would not sell but which O'Brien could keep "as a souvenir." This story was titled "Mr. and Mrs. Smith."[4]

I suspect that Hemingway sent the story partly as an appreciative memento to the publisher who first accepted "My Old Man" and partly to pass on literary gossip—but not to be published, for soon after that he sent a typescript of the same story to Jane Heap for publication in *The Little Review*'s winter issue of 1924–25 with the name Smith crossed out and Elliot inserted.

Hemingway's motive for changing the name from Smith to Elliot might have arisen from his inordinate fear of a libel suit. Or perhaps,

1. Carlos Baker and Charles A. Fenton are typical of those who dismiss the story; Joseph DeFalco is the only critic who has analyzed it at some length. See Baker, *Ernest Hemingway: A Life Story* (New York: Charles Scribner's Sons, 1969); Fenton, *The Apprenticeship of Ernest Hemingway* (New York: Farrar, Straus, Young, 1954); and DeFalco, *The Hero in Hemingway's Short Stories* (Pittsburgh: U of Pittsburgh P, 1963).
2. Chard Powers Smith to Ernest Hemingway, 2 January 1927, John F. Kennedy Library, and Hemingway to Smith, ca. 21 January 1927, in *Ernest Hemingway: Selected Letters, 1917–1961*, ed. Carlos Baker (New York: Charles Scribner's Sons, 1981) 242.
3. Baker, *Life*, 133.
4. Hemingway to Edward O'Brien, 2 May 1924, *Letters*, 117.

sometime in the late spring of 1924, his original satiric intent was deflected by the news that Mr. and Mrs. Smith's "alleged sexual ineptitudes" had been overcome, tragically, for Mrs. Smith died in childbirth in Naples on 11 March 1924, a month before Hemingway wrote his story and sent it to O'Brien as a souvenir. Perhaps, finally, submitting the story to the very literary *Little Review*, Hemingway decided to direct his satire against another poet, one with more fame than Chard Powers Smith: T. S. Eliot, who had been published in that journal since 1917 and was by Hemingway's lights even more deserving of contempt.

Why Eliot? Consider the ways in which Hubert Elliot's career in the story is similar to the poet Hemingway most envied and whose success he could not abide. Like Hubie—in the annals of history or gossip—T. S. Eliot came from Boston, was a graduate student at Harvard, wrote long poems, was a virgin, was enticed (in the polite phrase) by his wife on the dance floor, and by all biographers' accounts, suffered through a loveless marriage of "sexual ineptitude."[5]

Hemingway was always and in several ways one step behind Eliot. He arrived in Paris in December 1921 at about the time that Eliot returned from his six-week stay in a sanatorium above Vevey in Switzerland, retrieved his wife from another sanatorium near Paris, gave Ezra Pound some 1,000 lines of the draft of *The Waste Land*, and returned to London. In their month in Paris the Hemingways set up digs on the rue Cardinal Lemoine and then departed for two weeks of skiing at Chamby, above Montreux, only a few miles from the sanatorium Eliot had left.[6]

When Hemingway returned to Paris and belatedly presented his letter of introduction to Ezra Pound, the poet might well have shown him "The Waste Land" manuscripts he was editing, if only to impress this young, arriviste writer with his editorial authority. And Pound, as given to gossip as Hemingway, must have passed on the tales of the Eliots' troubled marriage, of which, by several accounts, "everyone within miles of it was aware."[7] Vivien Eliot's marginal note on the typescript of the "Game of Chess" section of the poem—she wrote "Wonderful"—may be no more than innocent literary praise,[8] but rumor overcame that benign notion to whisper that, of course, she recognized herself as the harried and neurotic woman in those lines. So did Hemingway when he crossed out Smith's name, wrote

5. See Eliot's biographers—Peter Ackroyd, *T. S. Eliot* (London: Hamish Hamilton, 1984); Caroline Behr, *T. S. Eliot: A Chronology of His Life and Works* (New York: St. Martin's P, 1983); Lyndall Gordon, *Eliot's Early Years* (Oxford: Oxford UP, 1977); and T. S. Matthews, *Great Tom: Notes towards the Definition of T. S. Eliot* (New York: Harper, 1974).
6. Baker, *Life*, 84–85.
7. Matthews, 45.
8. Ackroyd, 115.

first "Eliot," then "Elliott," then finally dropped the last *t*—leaving, as in all his occasional satires, a clue to identify his victim.

So one returns to the now-delightful exchange of letters between Chard Powers Smith and Hemingway in January 1927. Smith noted, with good reason, that the story "suggests my wife at no point" and delicately implied that neither he nor his wife was sterile. But he went on to charge that Hemingway still had to learn the difference between writing like a "reporter" from motives of "petty malice" and writing like a true artist. That must have stung Hemingway to respond with his typical barroom invitation to step outside, but buried in his response are a backhanded apology and explanation. Hemingway wrote that he recalled the contempt he had for Smith, but he admitted that it was a "very cheap emotion and one very bad for literary production."[9] Hemingway did not contradict Smith's assertion that the story had nothing to do with his wife—by 1927 he could not—but he could, lamely, imply he had a larger literary object in mind, namely (as it were) T. S. Eliot.

One of the more persuasive arguments for Eliot as the object of this satire is Hemingway's deep indebtedness to the older and more famous poet—a paradox in any other writer than Hemingway. "Mr. and Mrs. Elliot" is one of Hemingway's three early responses to either the manuscripts of Eliot's poem he saw in Paris in March 1922 or the published version Pound showed him in Rapallo in February 1923. The two other stories completed before this one reflect the poem: "Out of Season" of April 1923, with its setting by a turbid river by a dump heap and other testimony of sterility; and "Cat in the Rain" of March 1924, with its frenetic dialogue and the direct allusions to Sweeney and Mrs. Porter in its preliminary notes.[1]

Hubert and Cornelia Elliot of Hemingway's story are so like the deracinated figures of Eliot's poems that they would have been unnoticed along the shores of the Starnbergersee or chatting in the Hofgarten with those who "read, much of the night, and go south in the winter."[2] And, like the neurotic and sickly women and their indifferent companions in the poem, the Elliots' union is as barren and rootless as the landscape through which they aimlessly drift. These evident literary origins lift the story above the merely occasional: it is to Eliot's "Burial of the Dead" what "Cat in the Rain" is to Eliot's "Game of Chess."

9. Hemingway to Smith, 21 January 1927, *Letters*, 242.
1. Items 670–74, John F. Kennedy Library. [Sweeney and Mrs. Porter: *Waste Land* characters—*Editor.*]
2. T. S. Eliot, "The Waste Land," in *The Waste Land and Other Poems* (New York: Harcourt, 1934) 29. [Eliot's memories of Germany include the Starnbergersee, a large lake in Bavaria, and the Hofgarten, a formal garden in Munich—*Editor.*]

There are inviting bits of biography that tempt us to return to the personal experiences behind the story. Nothing in the lives of the Smiths or the Eliots quite fully accounts for some of the story's details, and so we might add a third couple to this composite portrait: Mr. and Mrs. Hemingway. Like Hubert and Cornelia Elliot, the Hemingways sailed to Europe soon after their marriage (not so the Tom Eliots); for all Hemingway's claims of poverty, he was living well on Hadley's not insubstantial trust fund. Ernest, like Hubert, was 25 in 1924; and, although he was no virgin, he had married an older woman. And consider this passage on the Elliots' arrival in Paris, added to the 1925 version of the story: "Paris was quite disappointing and very rainy. . . . [E]ven though someone had pointed out Ezra Pound to them in a café and they had watched James Joyce eating in the Trianon and almost been introduced to Leo Stein . . . , they decided to go to Dijon"[3] [70]. The Hemingways arrived in a rain-swept Paris, may have seen but did not meet Pound and Joyce, and left three weeks later. Or consider this passage on the Parisian cafés: "So they all sat around the Café du Dome, avoiding the Rotonde across the street because it is always so full of foreigners, . . . and then the Elliots rented a chateau in Touraine" [71]. One of Hemingway's earliest *Toronto Star* articles of 1922 similarly condemns the Rotonde as a "showplace for tourists in search of atmosphere."[4] While the Elliots fled to a chateau on the Loire, the Hemingways left for a chalet in Chamby.

If the story reflected this much of the three years before it was written, it was uncannily prophetic of the next three. It was in the Loire valley of Touraine in the spring of 1926 that Hadley, motoring with Pauline and Jinny Pfeiffer, first recognized her competition. By June, Ernest and Hadley and Pauline were at a hotel in Juan-les-Pins, where, in Carlos Baker's nice phrase, "there were three of everything."[5] Hemingway's story had ended:

> Elliot had taken to drinking white wine and lived apart in his own room. He wrote a great deal of poetry during the night and in the morning looked very exhausted. Mrs. Elliot and the girl friend now slept together in the big mediaeval bed. They had many a good cry together. In the evening they all sat at dinner together in the garden under a plane tree and the hot evening wind blew and Elliot drank white wine and Mrs. Elliot and the

---

3. Hemingway, "Mr. and Mrs. Elliot," *In Our Time* (New York: Boni & Liveright, 1925) 112.
4. Hemingway, "American Bohemians in Paris," in *Dateline: Toronto, Hemingway's Complete* Toronto Star *Dispatches, 1920–1924*, ed. William White (New York: Charles Scribner's Sons, 1985) 114.
5. Baker, *Life*, 168, 171.

girl friend made conversation and they were all quite happy. [72]

David Bourne in *The Garden of Eden* [a novel published posthumously in 1986] did his writing in the mornings, of course, for he was otherwise engaged at night, although the regimen of his threesome was as exhausting as Hubert's. The dinner in the garden, the white wine, the hot evening wind, and the bisexual arrangement sketched in the story all find interminable variations in that late, bruised, and windfallen novel. Perhaps even the conflict between Catherine Bourne's jealousy and Marita's admiration of David's writing is suggested in Cornelia and her girlfriend's typing: with the touch system, Mrs. Elliot "found that while it increased the speed it made more mistakes. The girl friend was now typing practically all of the manuscripts. She was very neat and efficient and seemed to enjoy it" [71].

With the longer view of Hemingway's career and the literary history of his times, "Mr. and Mrs. Elliot" deserves another reading. I would argue that it is one of his best and most sophisticated satires, better than anything in *The Torrents of Spring*, as good as the satiric passages in *The Sun Also Rises*, and a satire that transcends its seminal gossip to reveal the social and literary pretensions among the elite expatriates who knew enough to frequent the Café du Dome rather than the Rotonde, but not much more.

Certainly the story should be read again for its importance in the Hemingway canon: it is his first portrait, if not a self-portrait, of the artist; it begins his long and sometimes querulous consideration of the relationship between the artist's sexual and creative impulses; and it should take its place, first with the "marriage tales" of the 1920s and then with the last, so far, of his posthumously published novels.

Finally, the story confirms the depth of Hemingway's indebtedness to T. S. Eliot. Sometime in late 1927 Hemingway listed on the back of an envelope his literary borrowings. The first was to "everybody" for his early imitations, and the second was to Elliot (note the spelling) with the phrase "watered the waste land and made it bloom like a rose."[6]

I am certain Hemingway recognized some similarity between the Chard Powers Smiths, the Elliots, and the figures in "The Waste Land." At least one other in that cast of the living and the literary did—Mrs. Smith. In a holograph dedication to the volume of poems Chard Powers Smith wrote as a memorial to his dead wife, he

6. Item 489, John F. Kennedy Library.

described her death: "Olive Cary Macdonald died in childbirth in Naples on March 11, 1924. 'Good-night, ladies, good-night, good-night,' she whispered."[7] To which one can only reply: "Goodnight Tom. Goonight Chard. Goonight Ernest. Ta ta. Goodnight, sweet ladies, good night, good night."[8]

"CAT IN THE RAIN"

JOHN V. HAGOPIAN

Symmetry in "Cat in the Rain"[†]

After an introductory paragraph that sets the scene and mood, "Cat in the Rain" is as formally and as economically structured as a classic ballet. It is probably Hemingway's best made short story. Every detail of speech and gesture carries a full weight of meaning.

In the opening paragraph we are told that the two Americans are isolated people: "they did not know any of the people they passed" [75], and their hotel room looks out on an empty square. In this isolation they are about to experience a crisis in their marriage, a crisis involving the lack of fertility, which is symbolically foreshadowed by the public garden (fertility) dominated by the war monument (death). "In the good weather there was always an artist," but the rain, ironically, inhibits creativity; there are no painters here, but the war monument "glistened in the rain" [75].

There follows a movement of departure and return in five symmetrically arranged scenes: the hotel room, the passage through the lobby, outdoors in the rain, return through the lobby, and back in the hotel room.

In the first scene, the American wife standing at the window sees a cat crouched under an outdoor table to avoid the rain and her compassion is aroused: "the poor kitty . . . I'll get it" [75]. At this stage of the story her underlying motives are not yet clear, but significant is the fact that she refers to the cat as a "kitty," sees it as a diminutive fluffy creature needing help and protection. The husband, lying on the bed reading a book, offers to get it for her, but does not rise.

As she passes through the lobby, the hotel-owner, an old man and very tall, rises and bows. There is obviously a great contrast between

---

7. Chard Powers Smith, holograph "Dedication to OCM," Bancroft Library, U California/ Berkeley. Intended for *Along the Wind* (New Haven: Yale UP, 1925).
8. The last line of the essay adapts the language of *The Waste Land*, especially the concluding lines of the "Game of Chess" section, ll. 170–71 [*Editor*].
† From *College English* 24.3 (Dec. 1962): 220–22. Page numbers in brackets refer to this Norton Critical Edition.

him and the husband, and five times the narrator repeats "She liked" [75–76] followed by attributes of the old man that powerfully appealed to her—he was serious, he had dignity, he wanted to serve her, he enjoyed his work, and he had an old heavy face and big hands. It would appear that these are traits lacking in her husband, but an explicit comparison does not occur to her. The story is told from her point of view, and only that which she is consciously aware of finds expression. Nevertheless the great attraction of this man is indicated by the repetitions of *she liked*. Since Hemingway is preeminently the artist of implications, we must try to discover what is implied here, a process which involves considerable speculation. We note that the old man is probably old enough to be her father and presumably arouses in her at a time of distress the feelings of comfort and protection that her father did. More immediately, he rises while her husband remained supine; he expresses himself with a gesture of masculine service that her husband had denied her. The further implications of this contrast become clear in the final scenes.

As she looks out into the wet empty square, she sees a man in a rubber cape crossing to the cafe in the rain. The critical reader seeking significance for every detail (as he must when working with a story so short and so economical as this) is encouraged again to speculate on possible meanings. The rubber cape is protection from rain, and rain is a fundamental necessity for fertility, and fertility is precisely what is lacking in the American wife's marriage. An even more precise interpretation is possible but perhaps not necessary here. At the moment she discovers that the cat is gone, she is no longer described as "the American wife," but as "the American girl"; it is almost as if she were demoted in femininity by failing to find a creature to care for.

But it is not the girl's fault. "Oh," she says to the maid sent by the padrone to assist her, "I wanted it so much. I wanted a kitty" [76]. Disappointed, she again enters the lobby and again the padrone rises to bow to her, a gesture which makes her feel "very small and tight inside . . . really important . . . of supreme importance," all phrases that might appropriately be used to describe a woman who is pregnant [76]. The conscious thought of pregnancy never enters her mind, but the feelings associated with it sweep through her.

As she returns to her room, her husband takes a moment to rest his eyes from reading to talk with her, but only briefly. He certainly does not rise or bow. The intensity of the repetitions of "she liked" in the lobby scene is here replaced by the even greater intensity of "I wanted" and "I want," phrases which occur no less than sixteen times in this very short story. And again what she really wants never reaches consciousness, but the sum total of the wants that do reach consciousness amounts to motherhood, a home with a family, an end to the strictly companionate marriage with George. She wants her hair, which is "clipped close like a boy's" to grow out, but George says, "I like it the way it is" [77]. Since the close-cropped hair styles of the twenties were preceded by matronly buns, it would appear that the American girl wants to be like her mother when she says, "I want to pull my hair back tight and smooth and make a big knot at the back that I can feel" [77]. Interwoven with this symbol of maternal femininity is her wish for a kitty, now an obvious symbol for a child. But George apparently prefers the world of fiction to the real world of adulthood: "Oh, shut up and get something to read" [77]. Darkness descends and the rain continues to fall.

The story might have ended here, but Hemingway adds a final, ironic coda. The girl's symbolic wish is grotesquely fulfilled in painfully realistic terms. It is George, and not the padrone, by whom the wife wants to be fulfilled, but the padrone has sent up the maid with a big tortoise-shell cat, a huge creature that swings down against the maid's body. It is not clear whether this is exactly the same cat that the wife had seen from the window—probably not; in any case, it will most certainly not do. The girl is willing to settle for a child-surrogate, but the big tortoise-shell cat obviously cannot serve that purpose.

Hemingway has succeeded in rendering an immensely poignant human experience with all the poetry that pure prose can achieve. The simple language and brittle style simultaneously conceal and reveal a powerful emotional situation without the least trace of sentimentality. The delicacy and accuracy of the achievement are magnificent.

"OUT OF SEASON"

WILLIAM ADAIR

Hemingway's "Out of Season": The End of the Line[†]

In *A Moveable Feast* Hemingway said that the first story he wrote after "losing everything"—that is, after most of his story manuscripts had been stolen—was "Out of Season" and that the "real end" of the story (based on his new theory of omission) was that "the old man

---

† From *New Critical Approaches to the Short Stories of Ernest Hemingway*, ed. Jackson J. Benson (Durham, NC: Duke UP, 1990), pp. 341–46, 498–99. Copyright, 1991, Duke University Press. All rights reserved. Republished by permission of the copyright holder, Duke University Press. Page numbers in brackets refer to this Norton Critical Edition.

hanged himself" after the story's conclusion.[1] But the statement hasn't met with universal belief; it's been argued instead that Hemingway is creating a fictionalized version of his past.[2] To some extent he probably was, but I want to suggest that he was telling the truth when he said that the real end, the omitted part, of the story was that the old fishing guide hanged himself.

In a December 1925 letter to F. Scott Fitzgerald, written almost two years after the completion of "Out of Season"—a story composed during a holiday in Cortina, Italy—Hemingway said,

> When I came in from the unproductive fishing trip I wrote that story right off on the typewriter without punctuation. I meant it to be a tragic [sic] about the drunk of the guide because I reported him to the hotel owner—the one who appears in Cat in the Rain—and he fired him and as that was the last job he had in town and he was quite drunk and very desperate, hanged himself in the stable. At that time I was writing the In Our Time chapters and I wanted to write a tragic story *without* violence. So I didn't put in the hanging. Maybe that sounds silly. I didn't think the story needed it.[3]

It seems incredible of course that Hemingway wrote a story and that during the writing, or immediately afterward, his fishing guide of that afternoon hanged himself and, further, that this became what the story was "about." But even if we assume that a hanging didn't take place (then, and as a consequence of Hemingway's complaint to the hotel owner), this isn't enough to invalidate his statement that the Peduzzi *of the story* hangs himself or that the story is "about" Peduzzi and is an early attempt at the omission style of composition.

Perhaps Hemingway had *heard* a story about a village drunk losing his job and hanging himself. (Other of his short stories and many of his vignettes were based on stories heard.) Or he might have *imagined* the hanging after reporting the old man. So if he considered it part of the story—and I see no good reason to doubt that he did—then it's something he must have known or imagined before writing the story, not something that happened *then*.

Nor does Hemingway's remark to Fitzgerald that the story doesn't need the hanging suggest that it was a dramatic afterthought and not originally in the story. The comment implies instead that the hanging is something that can be omitted yet felt by the reader. (Indeed, we may think that a story like "A Canary for One" [in his

---

1. *A Moveable Feast* (New York: Scribner's, 1964), p. 75. Further references will be to this edition and will be included in the text.
2. See Paul Smith's "Some Misconceptions of 'Out of Season,'" in *Critical Essays on Hemingway's* In Our Time, ed. Michael S. Reynolds (Boston: Hall, 1983), pp. 235–51.
3. *Ernest Hemingway: Selected Letters, 1917–1961,* ed. Carlos Baker (New York: Scribner's, 1981), pp. 180–81.

1927 volume, *Men without Women*] might have been better if its punch-line ending had been omitted. And if the war had been mentioned in "Big Two-Hearted River," it would have reduced that story to a kind of clinical illustration of war trauma.) So it's omitted—but it's a rare reader who "feels" it.

Also of interest is Hemingway's comment to Fitzgerald that he was trying to write a tragic (he uses the word loosely) story without violence. Hemingway had written to Gertrude Stein about this time telling her that he was following her advice about writing and asking for more help.[4] And it's likely that she discouraged him from writing stories violent and shocking—pictures *inaccrochable* or unhangable, as we hear in *A Moveable Feast* (15). Also, Hemingway had recently been visiting Ezra Pound, and as a Pound critic puts it, Pound often "scolded that part of Hemingway that seemed eager for violence."[5] So that Hemingway was trying to write a tragic story with no violent, dramatic action in it—the marital tension and its omitted source hardly seems enough for a story, unless the omission was of something major—makes good sense.[6]

Perhaps Stein also suggested to Hemingway that he try for a kind of autobiographical realism in his writing; and the cantos (viii–xi) that Pound was then working on include not only that "factive personality," Sigismundo Malatesta, but also fragments of speeches and of a letter once stolen from Malatesta's mail. If Hemingway were writing from life, then it may be fruitful to consider the background, because both "Out of Season" and "Cat in the Rain"—for which he had taken notes shortly before writing "Out of Season"—seem to a great extent to be autobiographical stories; they both seem painterly arrangements, so to speak, of current experiences in Hemingway's life.

After spending Christmas and the early part of the following year (1923) in Chamby, Switzerland, Hemingway and his wife went to Rapallo, Italy, to visit Pound and Mike Strater.[7] Again, in Rapallo Hemingway made notes for what was later to be "Cat in the Rain." And the story seems close to life. For instance, Strater was then

4. *Selected Letters*, p. 79.
5. George Kearns, *Guide to Ezra Pound's 'Selected Cantos'* (New Brunswick, N.J.: Rutgers University Press, 1980), p. 75.
6. Kenneth G. Johnston's "Hemingway's 'Out of Season' and the Psychology of Errors" argues that the couple is quarreling over an abortion; this essay is collected in *Critical Essays on Hemingway's* In Our Time (cited above), pp. 227–34; Smith's article provides a convincing reply. My suggestion is that the story is "about" Peduzzi, as Hemingway said in his letter to Fitzgerald; the topic of the couple's quarrel—perhaps it is about the young man's extended trips as a news correspondent, if he is one (Hemingway and wife quarreled on this subject some four months previous to the trip to Cortina, where "Out of Season" was written)—seems of no importance.
7. The background information in this paragraph, and the next four paragraphs, comes from Carlos Baker's *Ernest Hemingway: A Life Story* (New York: Scribner's, 1981), pp. 105–9.

painting seascapes, and in the story's opening paragraph we hear about painters working in Rapallo. And the short, blunt sentences of most of the opening paragraph seem comparable to the rough, textured brush strokes of a Cézanne painting. (Stein had made attempts to model fiction on modern painting, by the way, and Hemingway told her that in "Big Two-Hearted River" that he was trying to do the country like Cézanne.)[8] The story itself has a painterly quality. "Cat in the Rain" is largely a matter of composition or arrangement, balance and repetition: a trip down and up the stairs, the story ending as it begins, two cats, two pairs of characters, etc. Physical posture is also important: we have six vertical figures (if we include the statue of the soldier on the war memorial) and a seventh figure reclining, the young husband. Also, in Rapallo Hemingway got his first look at T. S. Eliot's new poem, "The Waste Land," and we find in "Cat in the Rain" a restless, unhappy lady sitting at her mirror, as we do in the "Game of Chess" section of Eliot's poem. In fact, the entire story seems to have a wasteland mood and theme.[9] Carlos Baker says that Hemingway saw two cats playing on a green table in the hotel garden and wrote a poem about them which mocked Eliot's poem and that the cats and table get into "Cat in the Rain." The tall hotel owner seems drawn from life—he's in the background of "Out of Season," Hemingway told Fitzgerald. Hemingway also told Fitzgerald that the young man in "Cat in the Rain" was a "Harvard kid" that he had met at a conference the year before in Genoa—that is, the young husband (except for the college degree) in the story is like Hemingway, a newspaper correspondent.[1]

From Rapallo Hemingway and his wife went with the Pounds on a walking tour of Piombino and Orbetello, where Malatesta (again, Pound was then working on the Malatesta cantos) had defeated Alphonse of Aragon in 1448. Hemingway showed Pound how Malatesta probably had fought there. And no doubt Pound filled him in on this remarkable Italian Renaissance figure, a soldier and patron of the arts.

Then Hemingway and his wife went to Cortina. And there, as he said, after an unproductive day of fishing, he came in and quickly wrote "Out of Season," which was "an almost literal transcription of what happened." Like "Cat in the Rain," it too is drawn from life (with the likely exception of the suicide).

8. Cézanne's "The House of the Hanged Man," which is simply a picture of a house by a road, was at the Louvre during the 1920s; it may have been an influence on "Out of Season."
9. The function of the statue of the soldier (assuming there is one) on the war memorial has always seemed to me comparable to the function of Michael Furey in James Joyce's "The Dead": a reminder in the wasteland of all the dead heroes, to be contrasted with the prone husband of "Cat in the Rain."
1. Selected Letters, p. 180.

And "Out of Season" is, we notice, a story much like "Cat in the Rain." In both stories we have a young couple not communicating very well (a lack of communication and mixed signals is general in both stories). Each story presents an unsuccessful quest, for fish, for a cat. Each story has, in addition to the young couple, an old man (the fishing guide in one, the hotel owner in the other) and a second girl (the girl at the Concordia who serves the marsalas and the maid with the umbrella). "Cat in the Rain" ends with the hotel owner sending a cat up to the young couple's room; "Out of Season" ends with the young man about to leave word with the "same" hotel owner. It rains in one story and sprinkles in the other. Both stories take place on holiday at an "out of season" place.[2] They both seem "Waste Land" stories (Peduzzi is a kind of aging, unsuccessful fisher king, a digger of frozen manure), with the hint of World War I hovering in the background (the war memorial, Peduzzi's claim of having been a soldier and his military jacket). Also, the "young gentleman"— perhaps he too is a Harvard grad—of "Out of Season" may be a newspaper correspondent, like the young man of "Cat in the Rain" (the Harvard man Hemingway had met at the Genoa conference): he thinks about Max Beerbohm drinking Marsala, a fact that Hemingway had picked up at the Genoa conference a year before. In fact it may be the same young man (and young couple) in both stories, and the same quarrel being carried on. The similarity of the two stories again suggests that Hemingway was writing from life.

And if both these stories are taken from the writer's life, then Hemingway's visit to Piombino (which came between his stays in Rapallo and Cortina) and perhaps the example of Malatesta may have some interpretive bearing on "Out of Season."

Malatesta, one-time captain of Venice, *condottiere* (not unlike the modern Arditi young Hemingway so admired), lover, and well-known patron of the arts, may have fired Hemingway's imagination; indeed, he is a "romantic" and finally defeated figure somewhat like General Ney, another Hemingway hero.[3] Perhaps Hemingway associated Peduzzi with Malatesta. Peduzzi, a former soldier, is now, like Malatesta, a man who has seen the final ruin of all his hopes; he is a man at the end of his luck, humiliated at the end of his life. (Hemingway's penchant for silently evoking the reader's pity also implies that the story is essentially "about" Peduzzi, not the young man and wife.)

---

2. Frederic and Catherine at Stresa [in *A Farewell to Arms*] and Col. Cantwell in Venice [in *Across the River and Into the Trees*] are staying at "out of season" hotels.

3. Hemingway refers to Malatesta twice in *Selected Letters*, pp. 375, 654: first in a 1932 letter, where he says that Malatesta's name in twenty years will sound more honest than Stalin's; second in a 1948 letter, where he recalls his walking trip with Pound.

More important I think is the word "Piombino." The word means plummet, plumb line.[4] Perhaps lead, *piombo*, was got from the earth at Piombino. Be that as it may, landscape was always significant to Hemingway, in and out of his fiction; it's easy to imagine him asking the learned Pound the meaning of "piombino" and "piombo" and getting in reply a long list of meanings (some of which are given below). As it turns out, the word *piombo* is associated not only with Malatesta (and the terrain of his battle) but with old Peduzzi too.

As "cat" (and "kitty") is repeated often in "Cat in the Rain," so toward the end of "Out of Season" "piombo" (and "lead") is used in rapid repetition: it appears nine times in less than half a page [84–85]. It is likely that this repetition means something in addition to Peduzzi's disappointment and excitement.

The word has various meanings that may have some relation to the story: *piombare nella miseria* means to sink into poverty; a *piombone* is a lazy man; a *piombonatore* is a cesspool emptier (Peduzzi spades frozen manure); *cadere di piombonatore* means to fall suddenly, violently; *piombo* is a dressmaking term meaning to hang or fall; *i Piombi* (the Leads) is a prison in the Doges' palace in Venice (the young wife mentions jail); *piombo* can mean both bullet and kingfisher.

In the story, of course, it means the lead used to hang at the end of a fishing line (a small sinker). And it seems likely that the repetition of the word—like a splash of red paint on a gray canvas or a Stein-like repetition that calls for readerly attention—implies the hanging: Peduzzi ("ped" may imply "at the foot of") hanging from a rope, as a lead sinker hangs from the end of a fishing line.

Also, just before this repetition of the word "piombo," the young wife mentions "the game police," and the young man fears that a gamekeeper or a "posse" (a hanging posse?) of citizens may suddenly come after them. We hear about a high campanile (which would have a rope hanging from the bell) seen over the edge of a hill. We even get a sudden close-up shot of Peduzzi's neck (after he finds that they have no *piombo*): "The gray hairs in the folds of his neck oscillated as he drank" [85]. Seven lines later come the words "stretched out." Perhaps we should also notice that at the story's beginning Peduzzi is twice called "mysterious."[5] "Mystery" is a word Hemingway sometimes associated with his omission theory.

---

4. This definition, and the ones two paragraphs below, come from *The Cambridge Italian Dictionary* (New York: Cambridge Press, 1962).
5. In the article cited in note 2 [on p. 339] above, Paul Smith suggests (p. 239) that there must have been at least three stages in the story's composition: (1) the original typed version, along with its typed revisions; (2) the later penciled revisions, made on the original typescript; and (3) final revisions incorporated in the setting copy for publication.

So it's a matter of words: "mysterious," "posse," "neck," "stretched out," and the suddenly and oft repeated "piombo," a weight to hang at the end of a line.

Apparently this is why Hemingway thought that the story didn't need the hanging (*in* the story). He thought it well enough implied that the "quite drunk and very desperate" [157] and humiliated old man, whose mood quickly goes down, then up, and then down again near the story's end (and down to rock bottom later when he is fired) hangs himself.

And the story's final words ("I will leave word with the padrone at the hotel office" [86], the young gentleman tells Peduzzi), words that lead to the suicide, give us an ironic ending, for the word left with the hotel owner has quite a different effect than the young gentleman imagines—as the cat sent up to the room by the "same" hotel owner in "Cat in the Rain" has a different effect than he supposed it would.[6]

THOMAS STRYCHACZ

From In Our Time, Out of Season[†]

If there is one central story in the bundle of whipsaw-keen narratives, terse vignettes, and fragmentary epiphanies of Ernest Hemingway's *In Our Time* (1925), it may be "Out of Season." The story probes the paradox of the book's title by asking, What does it mean to be in our time but out of season? The phrase "in our time" promises both relevance and revelation. It suggests that the book will deal

---

In the original version "mysteriously" has been typed in as an interlinear addition. But the "mysterious" of the second paragraph does not appear in the story until the final version for publication.

In the original version "piombo" appears eight times. With the penciled revisions we find that the word has been added twice: in the sentences "We must have piombo" and "Your stuff is all clean and new but you haven't [sic] any piombo." In the final, for publication version this second sentence replaces "piombo" with "lead": "Your stuff is all clean and new but you have no lead." Obviously, Hemingway is using these words with great care, which may suggest that they are intended to imply something below the story's surface.

See Hemingway's typescript (EH/ts. 644) and carbon for setting copy (EH/ts. 203) in the Kennedy Library's Hemingway collection.

6. If "Cat in the Rain" and "Out of Season" are really "twin" stories, then it may be worth noticing that at the end of the first one the big cat brought up to the room by the maid (sent by the hotel owner who is "in" both stories) is in a sense "hanging": the cat "pressed tight against her and swung down against her body." The drop on the scaffolding from which Sam Cardinella is to be hung "swung" on ball bearings. Again it's a matter of words.

† From *The Cambridge Companion to Hemingway*, ed. Scott Donaldson (Cambridge, Eng.: Cambridge UP, 1996), pp. 55–57, 85–86. Reprinted by permission of Cambridge University Press through the licensor, PLSclear. Page numbers in brackets refer to this Norton Critical Edition.

with contemporary historical circumstances, perhaps record valuable collective wisdoms, and certainly stake a claim to documenting the entire epoch. Moreover, by echoing the plea in the English *Book of Common Prayer* to "Give us peace in our time, O Lord," the phrase invites a new descent of the Holy Spirit into the era following the World War I apocalypse. But "Out of Season," like all the stories of *In Our Time*, presents a world of thorough disorientation. Spiritual deadness, anomie, aimless wandering, conflict between genders and cultures, and miscommunication—these define the relationship between the expatriate American couple and their guide Peduzzi, and emerge more broadly as Hemingway's concerns in *In Our Time*, his first major inquiry into the state of the lost generation. The story suggests powerfully that we may only understand our time as the communal loss of temporal, geographical, and cultural certainties; and it focuses *In Our Time's* often ironic and sometimes funny quests for adequate guides, codes of conduct, and manly actions in a world where the old, communal prayers seem to have lost their power.

The Americans of "Out of Season" lack both a cohesive sense of time and a language in which to express its loss. Peduzzi intends the Americans to fish before the season officially opens; the young gentleman is tardy at the beginning of the story; the Specialty of Domestic and Foreign Wines shop is "closed until two" [82] when Peduzzi tries to purchase marsala; and Tiny, the young wife, may herself be "past her time"—that is, pregnant.[1] Narrative chronology, too, seems oddly truncated. In the first paragraph, for instance, the statement that the "young gentleman went back into the hotel and spoke to his wife" segues directly into "He and Peduzzi started down the road" [81]. The narrative suspends the familiar logic of sequential events—the young gentleman speaking to his wife, then coming out of the hotel, then starting down the road. Momentary and fragmentary actions appear out of a continuum we can only intuit. To be out of season is to experience time as other, to see it as separate from the normal processes and aspirations of human life. Narrative gaps in time and action suggest that dissociation from commonplace logic.

If temporal dislocations characterize "our time," how much more ironic sounds the prayer to "give us peace . . . O Lord." For the intercessor—the Holy Spirit—of "Out of Season" is the war veteran Peduzzi, who tries to intercede between the warring couple but proves hilariously inept at setting things right. Though the Holy Spirit bestows the gift of tongues on Christ's disciples, Peduzzi merely confuses his charges as he speaks "[p]art of the time in d'Ampezzo dialect and sometimes in Tyroler German dialect," and

1. The supposition that the wife is pregnant rests in part on her misapprehension of "Tochter" (daughter) for "Doctor" and the many references in the story to "carrying."

sometimes in Italian, while the "young gentleman and the wife understood nothing" [83]. Yet Peduzzi, clownish as he seems, is the one character who is not ruled entirely by disrupted chronologies. For Peduzzi, unlike the American couple, the duration of time spent does not alter the significance and value of the experience. "It is good half an hour down. It is good here, too," says Peduzzi in response to the young gentleman's baffled inquiry about why they are not moving on [84]. And though on discovering they have no *piombo* (lead) Peduzzi's day seemed to be "going to pieces before his eyes," the bottle of marsala restores lost harmony: "It was wonderful. This was a great day, after all. A wonderful day," and the "sun shone while he drank" [85]. The day and Peduzzi together experience rebirth along with the resurrected sun; time cycles back, reminding us of the seasonal return of life, light, sun, and spring. And perhaps the tipped bottle reminds us of the rites practiced from generation to generation to celebrate that return. Though we should not miss the irony of Peduzzi's heroic stature—"Life was opening out," he promises himself when accepting four lire from the young gentleman at the end of the story, which reminds us that to begin with "On the four lire Peduzzi had earned by spading the hotel garden he got quite drunk"—for a moment he lives in transcendent or mythic time [81]. He experiences briefly the unchangingness of seasonal change.

Peduzzi's bumbling efforts to save the day appear painfully (though comically) representative of our time and *In Our Time*, for Hemingway, like many other modernist writers, saw the disruption of time and mythic experience as at once a pressing reality and a pertinent metaphor for the entire angst- and anomie-ridden post–World War I landscape. Like other modernists, Hemingway understood that such a drastic reshaping of temporal experience demanded new narrative strategies. T. S. Eliot put the case most strikingly, claiming that others would follow James Joyce in finding ways of "controlling, of ordering, of giving a shape and a significance to the immense panorama of futility and anarchy which is contemporary history."[2] Works like *The Waste Land* (1922) and *In Our Time* register the decay of what must once have seemed fundamental verities: religion, intimate human relationships, hierarchies of culture and class, masculine authority. New strategies of fragmentation, temporal discontinuity, and abrupt juxtaposition would be pressed into service as attempts to define and respond to a terrifyingly denatured and devitalized landscape of alienation, lostness, and emptiness. The wanderers of Hemingway's stories, out of season and beset with impotent guides like Peduzzi, are at once empty and revelatory of these profound changes.

2. T. S. Eliot, "*Ulysses*, Order, and Myth," *Dial* 75 ([November] 1923): 480.

* * *

In Our Time * * * concludes with a dry reminder ["L'Envoi"] that its time offers little hope of fairy-tale endings, even one attempted with the anguished determination of a nearly broken Nick Adams. But the book also rejects the apocalyptic finality we might have expected. Though an epic style might have befitted this Greek king, caught like the Agamemnons and Priams of old in the aftermath of colliding empires, his story of displacement and disenfranchisement is actually common among the many stories that document the travails of the lost generation in *In Our Time*. His fate is no more auspicious than Peduzzi's in "Out of Season," who on accepting four lire from the young American feels momentarily like a "member of the Carleton Club" [86] and who also awaits (futilely) his bright tomorrow. It is fitting that Peduzzi, grimy, self-deluding, and scorned in his own village, should rise on occasion to near-heroic stature, for *In Our Time*, like Joyce's *Ulysses* (1922), concerns ordinary people who feel the reverberation of uncontrollable forces yet participate most fully in what W. B. Yeats called the "casual comedy" of life. Hemingway's work is perhaps most astonishing in its capacity to evoke within its small compass such a rich variety of human predicaments and significant but often costly achievements. And it does so with a fervor for experimental writing that never obscures but only intensifies the pathos of the work's struggling survivors, whether Peduzzi, Nick Adams, or a displaced monarch. For our own time of cultural conflicts and inadequate codes of conduct, the work has never seemed so enduring, so relevant, or, though out of its own historical season, so timely.

"Cross-Country Snow"

DONALD A. DAIKER

Hemingway's Neglected Masterpiece: "Cross-Country Snow"[†]

Of Hemingway's seven Nick Adams stories in *In Our Time*, none has been so widely ignored as "Cross-Country Snow," the story of Nick's skiing in the Alps with his friend George and their discussing the pregnancy of Nick's partner, Helen, during a break at a Swiss inn.

† From *MidAmerican* XLI (2014): 23–38. Reprinted by permission of The Society for the Study of Midwestern Literature. One of the author's notes has been omitted. Page numbers in brackets refer to this Norton Critical Edition.

"Cross-Country Snow" has been so slighted that it is not the focus of a single essay in Jackson J. Benson's *New Critical Approaches to the Short Stories of Ernest Hemingway* (1990), although twenty-seven other stories are named by title in its table of contents. Nor did it qualify for inclusion in Susan F. Beegel's *Hemingway's Neglected Short Ficton: New Perspectives* (1989). Except for Joseph M. Flora, whose three excellent books on Hemingway's short stories constitute required reading, most commentators have accepted the verdict of Paul Smith that the story is "trivial," in part because it seems to Smith "manifestly offhand" and "hastily written" (84).

The critics who follow Smith tend to dismiss "Cross-Country Snow" with little more than a mention of its autobiographical associations and its connection to Hemingway's series of "marriage tales," his stories of conflicts between married or almost-married couples. In this essay I move beyond the story's biographical associations to offer a close reading of "Cross-Country Snow" in the context both of its unpublished manuscripts and of the collection *In Our Time*. My goal is to show that the story is an undisputed masterpiece—fully unified, brilliantly structured, highly significant, and one of Hemingway's best.

As in most Nick Adams stories, the first and last sentences of "Cross-Country Snow" are exceptionally important. Here is its beginning: "The funicular car bucked once more and then stopped" [89]. It is instructive that the story many critics mistakenly believe to be about freedom[1] opens with its opposite: restriction. This initial sense of restriction is reinforced through repetition in the story's second sentence: "It could not go further, the snow drifted solidly across the track." The third sentence underscores the reason the funicular car can go no further: "The gale scouring the exposed surface of the mountain had swept the snow surface into a wind-board crust." It is only after the story's first three sentences establish the conditions of restraint, the limitations upon freedom and choice, that Hemingway introduces Nick, who is "waxing his skis in the baggage car."

Although it is not clear at this point why we find Nick in the baggage car rather than a passenger car, we can infer that Nick is busy waxing his skis and then putting them on in anticipation that the funicular, which had bucked earlier, might soon come to a full, final stop. When it does, Nick is prepared for immediate action: "He jumped from the car sideways onto the hard wind-board, made a jump turn and crouching and trailing his sticks slipped in a rush down the slope" [89]. Nick's skiing prowess here—the jump turn,

---

1. Stephen Cooper writes that the "ski run that opens this story epitomizes the exhilaration of freedom" (25). But Flora recognizes that the skiing represents other than freedom, serving Hemingway "in a complex way," including as "a tremendous challenge" (*Nick Adams* 191).

the crouching posture, the trailing sticks—demonstrates that he is a competent professional. But what is equally important is what Nick does *not* do: he does not moan or complain or lament his bad luck in not reaching the top of the slope. He gets on with it.

Once on the slope, Nick sees his friend George skiing ahead of him. The two have evidently not exchanged a word—George seems not to have been in the baggage car with Nick—but the two friends apparently know each other so well that they anticipate each other's moves: George has jumped off the stopped funicular moments before Nick. In his opening five sentences Hemingway has subtly suggested several of the story's most important themes: the need to act in positive ways in the face of life's inevitable limitations, the necessity of professionalism, and the value of friendship. There follows one of the richest and most remarkable passages in all of Hemingway:

> The rush and the sudden swoop as he dropped down a steep undulation in the mountain side plucked Nick's mind out and left him only the wonderful flying, dropping sensation in his body. He rose to a slight up-run and then the snow seemed to drop out from under him as he went down, down, faster and faster in a rush down the last, long steep slope. Crouching so he was almost sitting back on his skis, trying to keep the center of gravity low, the snow driving like a sand-storm, he knew the pace was too much. But he held it. He would not let go and spill. Then a patch of soft snow, left in a hollow by the wind, spilled him and he went over and over in a clashing of skis, feeling like a shot rabbit, then stuck, his legs crossed, his skis sticking straight up and his nose and ears jammed full of snow. [89]

The passage begins with a moment of exhilaration, physical ecstasy, as Nick—his mind "plucked . . . out"—becomes pure body, pure sensation. Hemingway's description invites us to experience vicariously the wonderfully intense, if necessarily short-lived, pleasure of the downhill run; perhaps we have had a comparably ecstatic physical experience in white-water rafting, hang gliding, parasailing, skydiving, mountain climbing, roller-coaster riding, or—even—orgasmic sex. Hemingway later in the story invites us to embrace Nick's statement that "[t]here's nothing really can touch skiing. . . . The way it feels when you first drop off on a long run." George agrees: "It's too swell to talk about" [91]. Nick is echoing words Hemingway himself had earlier written for the *Toronto Star Weekly*: there is "no sensation in the world that can compare" with the "long, dropping, swooping, heart-plucking rush" down an Alpine slope (*Dateline* 422). The sheer unmitigated pleasure of skiing stands as an ultimate value in the story, and nothing that occurs later qualifies that pleasure or diminishes its value.

Like most activities that produce exhilarating moments, downhill skiing involves risks. For Nick and George it is particularly risky—and even dangerous—because the "wind-board" they encounter, as Hemingway wrote in a *Toronto Star Weekly* column, "is treacherous stuff to ski on. It is a hard layer of snow that lies precariously on the main field" (*Dateline* 453). But downhill skiing is always risky because you are not in full control of what happens; when Nick jumped from the funicular, he immediately "slipped" down the slope. As he gains more and more speed, suggested by the repetition of "down" and "faster" and by the series of free modifiers, two participles followed by an absolute, control becomes increasingly harder to maintain. "But he held it." This short simple sentence, the shortest thus far in the story, shows Nick's determination not to lose control. "He would not let go and spill." Nick does not let go, but he spills anyway—a sure sign that external forces sometimes triumph over even strong will. Nick spills not because he lacks determination or knowledge or skill but because of chance: he hits "a patch of soft snow, left in a hollow by the wind." The paragraph's closing cluster of free modifiers, two participles and three absolutes again points to the absence of full control.

But it is not Nick's fall but his reaction to it that tells us most about Nick—and about Hemingway's values. The carefully selected details of Nick's spill—the tumbling "over and over," the clashing of skis, the comparison to a shot rabbit, the snow jamming his nose and ears—all tell us that Nick's fall has been excruciatingly painful. But Nick, now fully in control, does not allow himself to register the pain. Like his older self in "Big Two-Hearted River," he is able to "choke" [117] his mind to prevent it from dwelling on the pain he has suffered. Nor does he bemoan his bad luck in encountering the patch of soft snow. Even while lying flat on his back, he dismisses the painful fall by looking ahead: "What's it like over the khud?" he asks George [89].

As Nick stands up and skis past George toward the final slope, Hemingway refers to him for the first and only time in the story by his full name: "Nick Adams." In both the story's typescript manuscript (#344) and its second typescript (#346), Hemingway had three times earlier called the story's protagonist by his last name only—"Adams." But perhaps realizing the greater appropriateness of first names in a story focusing on friendship and relationships—we never know George's last name—Hemingway changed all three of these early references from "Adams" to "Nick." By the same token, Hemingway substitutes the warmer and more personal George "called to Nick" for the more distant and impersonal George "called at Adams" (344,1). The significance of the full "Nick Adams" is that by this point in the story Hemingway has already firmly established Nick's identity: he is an accomplished skier, a competent professional, a good friend, and a man who accepts with grace and without complaint the natural conditions and restraints—the wind-board crust and the soft snow along with the accompanying risks and pains—of life's endeavors in order to experience its most intense pleasures.

"Cross-Country Snow" makes clear that another keen source of pleasure for Nick is his mutual and noncompetitive friendship with George. Once they arrive at an inn, Nick dominates, but on the slopes Nick follows George's lead. It is George who comments on the soft snow and who suggests that Nick go first down the next hill. George knows more about skiing in the Alps, so he advises Nick to "keep to your left. It's a good fast drop with a Christy at the bottom on account of a fence" [89]. Nick closely follows George's sound advice, holding to his left and then executing a Christy that brings him parallel to the fence. Nick's descent of the first hill is exhilarating, but George's descent of the second is a thing of heart-thumping beauty:

> He looked up the hill. George was coming down in telemark position, kneeling; one leg forward and bent, the other trailing; his sticks hanging like some insect's thin legs, kicking up puffs of snow as they touched the surface and finally the whole kneeling, trailing figure coming around in a beautiful right curve, crouching, the legs shot forward and back, the body leaning out against the swing, the sticks accenting the curve like points of light, all in a wild cloud of snow. [90]

Exhilaration, excitement, and beauty, all creating "points of light": this is what Nick and George experience together.

Unlike the adolescent boastfulness and competitiveness of Nick and Bill in "The Three-Day Blow," George and Nick relate to each other comfortably and noncompetitively. George compliments Nick—"You made a beauty"—and Nick acknowledges that he cannot do what George did: "I can't telemark with my leg." Later, they "slapped the snow off each other's trousers" [90]. The downhill-skiing segment of the story ends with another clear sign of the mutuality of their friendship: "Nick held down the top strand of the wire fence with his ski and George slid over" [90]. With this third reference to a "fence," the segment also ends on the same note it began: the presence of limitations and restraints. Even on the slopes, boundaries must be acknowledged and observed. Alpine skiing is not the place of unbridled freedom and irresponsibility, nor, as some commentators would have it, is "Cross-Country Snow" a celebration or condemnation of youthful freedom.

As Nick follows George in cross-country skiing to a Swiss inn, it becomes clear—although no commentator I've read has mentioned this—that Nick and George have been the only two skiers on the slopes. No one else is there. Unlike the "seemingly endless stream" of skiers that dot the same hills in Hemingway's 1923 *Toronto Star Weekly* article, "Christmas on the Roof of the World" (*Dateline* 422), Nick and George are alone and by themselves. Now we understand why Nick had earlier been sitting in the baggage car: with no skiers on the funicular except George and Nick, and therefore no skis to hold, the baggage car is empty and thus available for Nick's waxing his skis and readying himself to jump off at a moment's notice.

Why are the slopes deserted? Apparently because of the severe weather. Not only is it "very cold" [93] but there is a "gale scouring" the mountain with the snow "driving like a sand-storm" [89]. It is what Hemingway, looking back on a like occasion, called a "Gawd awful storm and blizzard" (*Selected Letters* 84). Evidently the cold and the wind and the driving snow have deterred all other would-be skiers. So it is a sign of their hardiness and courage and resolve that George and Nick chose to hit the slopes when others shied away. Their skiing under such adverse conditions makes it less like the relaxed fishing of Jake and Bill on the Irati River in *The Sun Also Rises* and more like the challenges Nick faces in "Big Two-Hearted River." When Nick and George begin their cross-country trek to the inn, Hemingway pays them the supreme compliment of referring to them as "the skiers" [90], his first use of a plural personal noun in the story. Just as Nick Adams has earned his full name, just as Nick's father in "Indian Camp" earns the title of "the doctor" only after he has prepared himself to perform "a Caesarian with a jack-knife and sewing it up with nine-foot, tapered gut leaders" [13], so George and Nick earn the title of "the skiers" because of their professional skills, courage, and resilient attitude: their ability to slough off disappointment and pain.

As Nick and George ski cross-country from the slopes to the inn, they encounter the first sign of the presence of others: "The road became polished ice, stained orange and a tobacco yellow from the teams hauling logs" [90]. At the inn they see some of the Swiss workers who produce and transport those logs, "a gang of woodcutters" who drink wine, smoke, and rest quietly—and who offer a sharp contrast to Nick and George. Whereas Nick and George arrive by ski, the workers come by "wood sledges" pulled by teams of horses. Whereas Nick and George drink wine by the bottle, the workers get theirs by the liter. Whereas Nick and George talk with each other, the workers sit quietly at their tables. And whereas Nick and George can stay almost as long as they please, the workers are reminded that they must return to work by the "occasional sharp jangle of bells" as the horses outside toss their heads [91].

It is a mistake to think that these contrasts are meant to criticize Nick and George, that the presence of the Swiss woodcutters somehow constitutes an indictment of George and Nick for enjoying what Richard Hovey mislabels "the irresponsible happiness of a skiing holiday" (14). Instead, the Swiss woodcutters "symbolize the world of work and responsibility" (Flora, *Study*, 43) that Nick and George recognize and acknowledge, the world to which, following this final day of skiing, both men will immediately return—George back to school and Nick back to the United States with Helen. Nick and George are acutely aware of this practical world of duty and responsibility, honoring it through their careful attention to detail when the woodcutters enter the inn, "stamping their boots and steaming in the room" and then sitting "smoking and quiet, with their hats off" [91]. It is at this precise moment that Hemingway tells us that "George and Nick were happy. They were fond of each other. They knew they had the run back home ahead of them" [91]. Their happiness comes from enjoying each other's company and anticipating the cross-country skiing to come even as they acknowledge, through their continuing attention to the woodcutters—they know exactly when the woodcutters "got up and paid and went out"—that their skiing trip will end soon. The jangling bells and tossing heads of the horses outside the inn call both the woodcutters and the skiers back to the world of responsibility and work.

Soon after their arrival at the inn, Hemingway, who had once earlier called Nick and George "[t]he skiers," refers to them, again just once, as "[t]he boys" [90], prompting several critics to suggest that the term implies not only their youth but their immaturity. "The description of the Alpine skiing enjoyed by Nick and George is boyish in its delight; and the dialogues with its 'Gee's' is kiddish," Hovey writes (14). But like his predecessors Mark Twain in *Adventures of Huckleberry Finn* and Sherwood Anderson in *Winesburg, Ohio*, especially in "Sophistication," Hemingway believed that the youthful perspective need not imply naïveté or immaturity. "Gee" was one of the young Hemingway's favorite expressions, almost always evincing happiness or excited anticipation. "Gee I wish I were with you" (*SL* 73), Hemingway wrote to his wife, Hadley, in Paris when he was on assignment in Lausanne, Switzerland. Nick and George each say "Gee" only once, and it is when they excitedly imagine traveling throughout Europe together.

Hemingway's revisions of his earliest draft of "Cross-Country Snow" follow a clear pattern in relation to dialogue: he makes George's speech less boyish and more adult. He does so by eliminating several instances of George's profanity. The "damn" soft snow becomes the "lousy" soft snow (#344, 1), the "damn sharp Christy" becomes simply the "Christy" (#344, 2), and "goddamn" is softened to "damn" (#344, 5). Hemingway also replaces three instances of slang with more formal and conventional language. George's "you've gotta keep to your left" is replaced by "got to," and "Gotta get educated" becomes "I got to get educated." Hemingway systematically revised George's utterances by inserting a subject when one was missing. Thus "Got to get the ten-forty from Montreux" becomes "I've got to" (#344, 5), and "Might as well carry 'em up here" is changed to "We might as well carry them up here" (#344, 2, 3). The change from "'em" to "them" in this last example typifies Hemingway's efforts to make George sound less juvenile and more adult. He does the same for Nick at one point as well, replacing the slangy "Yeah" with "Yes" (#344, 5). Hemingway tries to make sure that his readers do not dismiss either George or Nick as immature.

But their maturity is most persuasively demonstrated at the inn through what they do—especially in the quality of their friendship. As George assumed leadership on the slopes—jumping first from the funicular, leading the way down the first hill, advising Nick how to take the second hill, requesting that Nick go first, and then showing him the way to the inn—so Nick quietly takes charge once they arrive there. It is Nick who orders Sion wine after first checking with George, and it is Nick who helps when the waitress has trouble with the cork. Nick now becomes the teacher that George had been on the slopes: "Those specks of cork in it don't matter," Nick tells him [91]. Of course it doesn't take a wine connoisseur to know that specks of cork do in fact matter: they discolor the wine and they impair its taste. Nick's point to George is that you cannot permit the cork specks to matter; you cannot allow them to diminish your enjoyment, especially since there's nothing to be done about them. Bemoaning their presence makes no more sense than getting upset about soft snow or a stalled funicular. Perhaps Nick had learned this lesson from his father, Dr. Adams, in "Indian Camp," the first Nick Adams story in *In Our Time*. When young Nick asks his father to administer anesthesia to a woman screaming in labor, Dr. Adams replies that he has no anesthetic but that "her screams are not important. I don't hear them because they are not important" [12]. The doctor cannot allow himself to "hear" her screams—he cannot let them "matter"—because to do so might distract his attention, unsteady his hands, botch the operation, and further endanger the woman's life.

The maturity of Nick and George, as well as the quality of their friendship, is again illustrated when Nick asks, "Should we have another bottle?" of wine and George declines [92]. Then after a silent moment, George asks Nick if Helen is going to have a baby. But that's not the way it happens in a three-page manuscript fragment

that Hemingway considered adding to his story and then rejected
(#345). In the rejected fragment, Nick does not simply ask George
if they should order a second bottle of wine. He pushes it: "Let's
have another bottle." When George demurs with "I don't know," Nick
responds with a superior, belittling "Come on. It won't hurt you"
(#345, 6). Nick's condescending tone recalls his competitive relationship to Bill in "The Three-Day Blow," where Nick resolves "Bill
was not going to get him drunk before he himself was drunk" [33].
That Hemingway chose not to incorporate the manuscript fragment into his story may be a sign that he did not want to undermine
the mutuality he had established between the friends nor did he
want to suggest, through Nick's juvenile comment or George's
eventual acquiescense, the immaturity of either.

Perhaps because Nick and George had earlier shared dreams of
skiing other Alpine slopes and traveling through "swell places"
[92] like the Schwarzwald and perhaps even more because Nick
does not insist that George join him for a second bottle of wine,
George now feels equal to asking Nick a series of very personal
questions:

> "Is Helen going to have a baby?" George said, coming down to
> the table from the wall.
> "Yes."
> "When?"
> "Late next summer."
> "Are you glad?"
> "Yes. Now."
> "Will you go back to the States?"
> "I guess so."
> "Do you want to?"
> "No."
> "Does Helen?"
> "No." [92]

This conversation between these two good friends is one of the most
frank and open in all of Hemingway. To understand its openness and
the quality of friendship it bespeaks we need only compare it with
similar instances in "The Three-Day Blow," written a month earlier.
When Bill raises the issue of Nick's having broken up with Marjorie—
significantly not by asking questions like George but by making
assertions—Nick responds, not as he does to George with candor
and honesty, but first by saying "nothing" and then "nothing" and
then by nodding and then by sitting quietly and then again by saying "nothing" until he surrenders with "Let's have another drink"
and then "Let's get drunk" [35–36]. Nick is both more comfortable
and more forthcoming in answering George's questions; the period

in "Yes. Now" frankly acknowledges that it had taken Nick some time to accept his partner's pregnancy. Nick is completely honest with George, helping him understand the edge to Nick's earlier comment about the pregnant waitress, "Hell, no girls get married around here till they're knocked up" [91].

Nick's revelations, especially the news that neither he nor Helen want to leave Europe, touch George deeply:

> George sat silent. He looked at the empty bottle and the empty glasses.
> "It's hell, isn't it?" he said.
> "No. Not exactly," Nick said.
> "Why not?"
> "I don't know," Nick said. [92–93]

Empathizing with his friend, George takes the "empty" bottle and glasses as a sign that Nick's future life will be one of deprivation, even a "hell." But Nick kindly, gently, yet firmly dispels that notion: "No. Not exactly." In saying "I don't know" and then repeating that exact phrase two sentences later, Nick distances himself from Hemingway people, often juveniles, whose certainties mark them as dead wrong. No one is more certain and few are more mistaken than Bill in "The Three-Day Blow," who believes that "Once a man's married he's absolutely bitched. . . . He hasn't got anything more. Nothing. Not a damn thing. He's done for" [34]. The same certainty—and wild exaggeration—characterizes Luz in "A Very Short Story," who "expected, absolutely unexpectedly" to be married to an Italian major in the spring but never marries him at all [52]. Here is still another lesson Nick has apparently learned from his father, who tells his son in "Indian Camp," "I don't know, Nick" [14] and then offers tentative, conditional answers to Nick's ensuing questions. As Flora has observed, Nick "is learning to accept the uncertainties" of life (*Nick Adams* 196).

Nick and George have also learned that the world sometimes frustrates our hopes and disappoints our expectations. Both men agree that the mountains in the United States are too rocky, too timbered, and too distant for good skiing:

> "Yes," said George, "that's the way it is in California."
> "Yes," Nick said, "that's the way it is everywhere I've ever been."
> "Yes," said George, "that's the way it is."
> The Swiss got up and paid and went out.
> "I wish we were Swiss," George said.
> "They've all got goiter," said Nick.
> "I don't believe it," George said.
> "Neither do I," said Nick.
> They laughed. [93]

The three consecutive utterances beginning with "Yes" make clear that Nick and George share essentially the same philosophy of life: this world is not designed to accommodate human wishes or to effect human happiness, a philosophy which means that it makes little sense to turn bitter or resentful in the face of specks of cork, soft snow, a bucking funicular, or an unexpected pregnancy. It also means that the rare moments of unmitigated pleasure out on the slopes or inside with friends are to be savored and cherished. When the Swiss woodcutters that Nick and George have been closely observing get up and leave, George momentarily indulges in fantasy—"I wish we were Swiss"—a statement that lends credence to George's being younger than Nick and casts Nick once again in the role of George's teacher. Nick punctures George's fantasy not through direct refutation but through a statement that matches George's in its unreality: "They've all got goiter." Although the Swiss were known for their susceptibility to goiter, Nick knows, and George recognizes, that his blanket statement including "all" Swiss is foolish, intentionally comical. "They laughed" is one of the most important paragraphs in the story: after a frank discussion of sensitive issues Nick and George come together in shared laughter.

Their warm friendship prompts George to become a little sentimental: "Maybe we'll never go skiing again, Nick" [93]. When Nick responds twice with a positive "We've got to," George makes his third and final wish of the story: "I wish we could make a promise about it" [93]. Like his earlier wishes that he and Nick "could just bum together" and that he and Nick "were Swiss," George's third wish is unrealistic—and Nick knows it. But Nick does not immediately challenge George. First he "stood up"—exactly as he "stood up" [89, 93] when he had spilled on the slopes—then he buckled his jacket, picked up his ski poles, and stuck one pole into the floor to punctuate the story's final spoken words, a lucid statement of Nick's—and Hemingway's—mature philosophy: "There isn't any good in promising." Nick has learned from experiencing falls on and off the slopes that life is unpredictable: babies are not born as they should, some fathers commit suicide and others cannot answer your questions, love sometimes just goes "to hell inside" [25] you, a "friendly" brakeman tosses you off a moving train [41], a "friendly" ex-boxer threatens you with "a beating" [46], you get shot in the spine during a military offensive that is "going well" [49], and the woman you love and plan to marry sleeps with an Italian major and tells you that yours "had been only a boy and girl affair" [52]. In the face of life's uncertainties and unpredictabilities, there can hardly be any "good" in promising.

As the skiers leave the inn, George assumes the lead as he had earlier on the slopes: "George was already started up the road, his

skis on his shoulder" [93]. The story's final line is its most important: "Now they would have the run home together." In this culminating sentence, which remained unchanged from typescript/
manuscript (#344) through typescript (#346) to publication,
Hemingway unites the central themes of his story. Its emphasis, as
it should be, is on the present, the "Now." George may have to "get
the ten-forty from Montreux" [91] to return to school and Nick may
have to return to the States with Helen, but these future responsibilities will not be allowed to interfere with the pleasures of the
moment. Appropriately, a story that celebrates friendship through
the warm and affectionate relationship between Nick and George,
two men who are "fond of each other" [91], ends with the word
"together" [93].

But the word "home" may be equally significant, as it is throughout *In Our Time*, especially in "Big Two-Hearted River," the final
and climactic Nick Adams story in that volume. The key passage
occurs after Nick has hiked through "burned-over country" [111] to
his camp site and erected a tent:

> Inside the tent the light came through the brown canvas. It
> smelled pleasantly of canvas. Already there was something mys-
> terious and homelike. Nick was happy as he crawled inside the
> tent. He had not been unhappy all day. This was different
> though. Now things were done. There had been this to do. Now
> it was done. It had been a hard trip. He was very tired. That
> was done. He had made his camp. He was settled. Nothing
> could touch him. It was a good place to camp. He was there, in
> the good place. He was in his home where he had made it. Now
> he was hungry. [115]

Home for Nick is the "good place." It's where you can be "settled."
It's where you can be "happy." That's why "Now they would have the
run *home* [my italic] together" is so important to "Cross-Country
Snow." Wherever Nick and George are skiing together at the end of
the story, to a Swiss pension or chalet or even hotel, it is the "home"
that they have "made," however temporary that home may be. For
Nick and Hemingway, then, home is not necessarily a stable location; it may not even be a place at all. It is an enclave, an oasis pro-
tected from the things that can "touch" you, what Hemingway
almost ten years later would call "A Clean Well-Lighted Place." Thus
"Cross-Country Snow" and "Big Two-Hearted River," the final two
Nick Adams stories in *In Our Time*, each end on a note of optimism
and affirmation as Nick looks ahead excitedly: he has the run home
together with George in the first story and "plenty of days coming
when he could fish the swamp" [129] in the second.

As "Cross-Country Snow" concludes, we are now better able to appreciate the significance of the story's opening sentence: "The funicular car bucked once more and then stopped" [89]. Hemingway himself had ridden on a funicular at least once, and he obviously knew something about its workings. Unlike a simple ski lift, a funicular—also known as an incline or funicular railway—operates on the principle of counterweight or counterbalance. Using cables and pulleys, two cars are attached to each other so that as one car goes down an incline, it helps pull the other car up a second, parallel set of tracks. That is, the descending and ascending vehicles are complementary: they counterbalance each other. The car descending the slope minimizes the energy needed to lift the ascending car. It is this principle of the counterbalancing of opposites that, as Barbara Sanders has observed, helps structure "Cross-Country Snow." The counterbalancing forces within the story are the excitement of alpine and cross-country skiing and the social pleasures of drinking and eating on the one hand and the responsibilities and obligations of parenthood and schooling on the other. What makes the funicular the perfect metaphor for the competing claims of pleasure and responsibility is that the funicular cars are *attached together* by a cable. Thus there is of necessity a give-and-take, a reciprocating relationship between the opposing forces. The story suggests, then, that it is the looming obligations of parenthood—necessitating Nick's and Helen's return from Europe to the States—which enhance and perhaps even make possible the intense pleasures of the slopes and the inn. Moreover, the funicular cars are *permanently* attached to each other, suggesting that the competing yet reciprocating claims of excitement and pleasure versus responsibility and duty may be ongoing throughout a lifetime, each enabling and enriching the other.

When in the final sentence of the story Nick looks forward to the "run home together," Hemingway brilliantly merges the complementary opposites. The cross-country skiing with his good friend George resumes the physical and emotional pleasures the two men had enjoyed first on two slopes and then in their earlier "run" to the inn. But the word "home" evokes the responsibilities of parenthood because Helen, who is expecting their first child "[l]ate next summer," will apparently be waiting when Nick and George arrive at their pension. Just as Hadley Hemingway had accompanied her husband to Chamby sur Montreux the winter before the couple [moved] from Paris to Toronto to take advantage of superior North American medical facilities, so Helen, too, is in Europe with Nick and, like him, would rather not leave. Thus "the run home together" unites the pleasures of skiing with the responsibilities of parenthood.

Sherwood Anderson's "Sophistication," the wistful climactic chapter of *Winesburg, Ohio*, involves another "Helen," another "George," and another slope. Here is its wonderful final paragraph:

> It was so they went down the hill. In the darkness they played like two splendid young things in a young world. Once, running swiftly forward, Helen tripped George and he fell. He squirmed and shouted. Shaking with laughter, he rolled down the hill. Helen ran after him. For just a moment she stopped in the darkness. There was no way of knowing what woman's thoughts went through her mind but, when the bottom of the hill was reached and she came up to the boy, she took his arm and walked beside him in dignified silence. For some reason they could not have explained they had both got from their silent evening together the thing needed. Man or boy, woman or girl, they had for a moment taken hold of the thing that makes the mature life of men and women in the modern world possible. (242–243)

In "Sophistication," as in "Cross-Country Snow," growth and maturity depend upon our capacity to play, to get excited, to laugh, to get tripped up and fall and then get up again, to reach out and take hold of others, to delight in physical and even childlike pleasures—to become like Nick and George alone on the whitened wind-swept Alpine slopes "splendid young things in a young world." By the end of "Cross-Country Snow" Nick has achieved what Flora calls his "new maturity" (*Nick Adams* 198), and together with his young friend George he is happily and responsibly headed homeward.

Works Cited

Anderson, Sherwood. *Winesburg, Ohio: Text and Criticism*. 1919. Ed. John H. Ferres. NY: Viking, 1966.

Beegel, Susan F. Ed. *Hemingway's Neglected Short Fiction: New Perspectives*. Tuscaloosa: U of Alabama P, 1991.

Benson, Jackson J. Ed. *New Critical Approaches to the Short Stories of Ernest Hemingway*. Durham, NC: Duke UP, 1990.

Cooper, Stephen. *The Politics of Ernest Hemingway*. Ann Arbor: UMI Research Press, 1987.

Flora, Joseph M. *Ernest Hemingway: A Study of the Short Fiction*. Boston: Twayne, 1989.

———. *Hemingway's Nick Adams*. Baton Rouge: Louisiana State UP, 1982.

———. *Reading Hemingway's* Men Without Women: *Glossary and Commentary*. Kent, OH: Kent State UP, 2008.

Hemingway, Ernest. *The Complete Short Stories of Ernest Hemingway*. The Finca Vigía Edition. NY: Scribner's, 1987.

———. "Cross-Country Snow." Drafts. Files 344, 345, 346, 696. Hemingway Collection. John F. Kennedy Library, Boston.

———. *Dateline: Toronto: The Complete Toronto Star Dispatches, 1920–24.* Ed. William White. NY: Scribner's, 1985.

———. *Ernest Hemingway: Selected Letters, 1917–1961.* Ed. Carlos Baker. NY: Scribner's, 1981.

———. *The Sun Also Rises.* 1926. NY: Scribner's, 1954.

Hovey, Richard B. *Hemingway: The Inward Terrain.* Seattle: U of Washington P, 1968.

Sanders, Barbara. "Linguistic Analysis of 'Cross-Country Snow.'" *Linguistics in Literature* 1:2 (1976): 43–52.

Smith, Paul. *A Reader's Guide to The Short Stories of Ernest Hemingway.* Boston: G. K. Hall, 1989.

Twain, Mark. *Adventures of Huckleberry Finn.* 1884. Berkeley and Los Angeles: U of California P/ Mark Twain Library, 2001.

"My Old Man"

MATTHEW STEWART

From "My Old Man": A One-Story Interlude[†]

"My Old Man" temporarily puts the reader on hold with Nick. Of all the stories in [*In Our Time*], its placement is the most problematic: it focuses on a boy, but the volume's generic protagonist has already progressed into the first years of adulthood. A partial answer to the placement problem—and it is one that we can be sure that Hemingway considered, even if we are not satisfied with his decision[1]—lies not in the narrative focus but in the narrative voice, which is that of the boy, now grown into a man, looking back on the disillusioning experience of his father's death. Yet this answer is only partly satisfactory, because, although it is clear that the narrator is telling his story from a mature perspective, he occasionally adopts the "Gee" and "Say" mannerisms of his boyhood. The time referred

---

† From *Modernism and Tradition in Ernest Hemingway's* In Our Time (Rochester, NY: Camden House, 2001), pp. 80–84. Used by permission of Boydell & Brewer, Inc. Page numbers in brackets refer to this Norton Critical Edition.

1. Paul Smith writes [in his *Reader's Guide*; see 406 below] that in a preliminary arrangement of the volume Hemingway "considered switching the places of 'The Three-Day Blow' and 'My Old Man'" (118, JFK Collection item 97A). This would seem an odd place to consider inserting the story as opposed to one story earlier, for the boy in "My Old Man" is clearly a preteen, while Nick is in his late teens in "The End of Something," which would have preceded it if this provisional order had been adopted. Placing the story before "The End of Something" would have solved this problem of chronology as well as avoided splitting up "The End of Something" and its companion piece, "The Three Day Blow."

to by the "now" in the first sentence is never made exact: "I guess looking at it, now, my old man was cut out for a fat guy . . ." [97]. Based on the story's placement in the volume and on the sort of retrospective judgment the story implies, "now" should be taken to refer to the narrator speaking as a young adult.

The story begins with Joe Butler remembering the period his father spent as a jockey in Italy. Staying in shape is not easy for Joe's dad, but he has the self-discipline to work out daily to keep his weight down. His keeping in professional trim and his work with the horses are set at odds with a less distinguished facet of his character: in the past he has helped to fix races. At some point, however, he decided to change his ways, so when he wins the Premio Commercio, it is not a moment of clear and clean triumph for him because he had apparently been instructed not to win. This double-crossing of the race fixers leads to the father and son leaving Italy for Paris. Still, it is not correct to see Joe's father as a now-honest man struggling in a corrupt sport—not yet. He has cheated in the past; he had agreed to cheat at the Premio Commercio but changed his mind, and this decision may have been an attempt to turn over a new leaf but equally may have been odds-tampering or double-dealing to his own advantage—cheating within cheating. In Paris the elder Butler will buy his own horse and attempt to win on the up and up, but not before betting on inside tips on fixed races. One such race is described in detail. A magnificent horse named Kzar could have walked away with the race but is purposely held back to place. "It sure took a great jock to keep that Kzar horse from winning," Joe's father says. Joe describes this race as a moral turning point for himself, but just why this is so is not precisely clear:

> Of course I knew it was funny [a fixed race] all the time. But my old man saying that right out like that sure took the kick all out of it for me and I didn't get the real kick back ever again. . . . [104]

The moral crisis is dependent on Joe's admiration for Kzar and comes to a head when his father actually utters the words about cheating. That the horse's nobility is cheapened is easy to understand, but it is unclear why Joe's father's words wound him more deeply than his active participation in the plot to prevent the horse from winning. In the end Joe's father puts together a stake and wins a horse, Gilford, which he rides in a race in which he intends to compete honestly. He is doing well in the race when he is killed in a fall. As Joe is being escorted from the track by George Gardner, he overhears two men disparaging his father for the cheating in which the latter had engaged in the past. In the last lines of the story Joe thinks, "But

I don't know. Seems like when they get started they don't leave a guy with nothing" [108]. First the father had helped to betray Kzar; now, attempting to ride cleanly and do his honest best, he has fallen victim to circumstances. Ironically, George Gardner had been the jockey who rode Kzar in the fixed race, and from his untrustworthy lips come the words intended for comfort: "Don't listen to what those bums said, Joe. Your old man was one swell guy" [108].

While I would argue that *In Our Time* might be a stronger volume without "My Old Man," the story does maintain topical and thematic consistency with the stories that immediately precede it. All of them, beginning with "The Revolutionist," treat the disillusionment of expatriates adrift in the modern world. The story also recalls "Indian Camp" and "The Doctor and the Doctor's Wife" in its depiction of the imperfect father brought to bay by his weaknesses. In this respect it is closer to "Indian Camp," since in both stories the father is brought low in the act of doing good. The story also continues the theme that has followed Nick since "The Three-Day Blow," the impossibility of going back. In "Cross-Country Snow" Nick knows enough not to make any promises about "going back" to skiing. He has learned that it may not always be possible to return to that which you have loved. Joe's father tries to return to clean racing after fixing races, only to be thrown from his horse and killed. There is no cause-and-effect relationship between his past dishonesty and the accident, for contrived "poetic justice" is not part of Hemingway's stock in trade. To the young Joe his father's death must have seemed capricious. The older, narrating Joe may realize, along with the reader, that once one has sold out something that is dear, once one has betrayed his craft, he may not get a second chance. In a world where winners and losers alike may take nothing, where each person must struggle to develop his own moral center, that center, once obtained, should not be put at risk. This theme will be worked out with great poignancy in *The Sun Also Rises* in the contrastive relationship between Jake Barnes and Pedro Romero.

"My Old Man," more directly than any other story in the volume, shows the influence of Sherwood Anderson, who had already published his famous "I Want to Know Why," which also treats a boy who loves horse racing and culminates in the boy's disillusionment with a man. But one can also see why Hemingway began to bridle when critics compared him to Anderson, however well intended the comparisons may have been. Despite the Andersonesque qualities of "My Old Man," it is clear that even this early in his career Hemingway had begun to outdistance his mentor. Picking up on Anderson's use of the vernacular, Hemingway achieves a more informal, more fluid voice. He more fully effaces what Pound meant by the "licherary" [literary]. Anderson's stories often retain a flavor, however faint,

of the nineteenth century, and he can be prone to a sort of senti-
mentalism that Hemingway's taut style and more uncompromising
irony all but eliminate from the latter's earliest work. Even though
the story is narrated in the first person, it retains the show-don't-tell
methodology typical of the volume. Joe does not explain his feelings,
either at the time of his father's death or "now," but leaves them for
the reader to infer. This task is made ambiguous by the fact that Joe
seems alternately innocent and wise in the story, at once unable to
explain exactly what went on in Italy but able to say that he knew
about his father getting in on the fixed Kzar race. What we do know
is that one disreputable adult receives the compliments of another
at the end of the story, and that this is cold comfort to Joe.

"BIG TWO-HEARTED RIVER"

ANN PUTNAM

[On Defiling Eden: The Search for the Feminine in "Big Two-Hearted River"]†

> Nicholas Adams drove on through the town along the empty, brick-
> paved street . . . on under the heavy trees of the small town that
> are a part of your heart if it is your own town and you have walked
> under them, but that are only too heavy, that shut out the sun and
> that dampen the houses for a stranger.
> —Ernest Hemingway, "Fathers and Sons"[1]

In *The Green Breast of the New World: Landscape, Gender, and
American Fiction*, Louise H. Westling examines Hemingway's story
"Big Two-Hearted River" in the context of both feminist and eco-
critical theory, an approach that is beginning to open up Hemingway's works in new and invigorating ways. Eco-critical approaches
to Hemingway are long overdue, and her work is a fine example of
the richness of this synthesis. Her reading of "Big Two-Hearted
River," for example, places Hemingway's treatment of nature within
a paradigm of the use of the feminine in the depiction of nature from
antiquity to the present.

† From *Hemingway and Women: Female Critics and the Female Voice*, ed. Lawrence R.
Broer and Gloria Holland (Tuscaloosa: U of Alabama P, 2002), pp. 109–30, 304–05.
Reprinted by permission of the publisher. Some of the author's notes have been omitted. Page numbers in brackets refer to this Norton Critical Edition.
1. This epigraph is taken from *Winner Take Nothing* (New York: Charles Scribner & Sons,
1933), p. 151. Copyright © 1933 by Charles Scribner's Sons. Copyright renewed 1961
by Mary Hemingway. Reprinted with the permission of Scribner, a division of Simon &
Schuster, Inc. All rights reserved.

But finally she concludes that "at least half of us are not likely to see ourselves" in works by Hemingway, because he has "pared away so much of the world from his fiction, retreating into such a narrow and primitive masculinity, that there was nothing left for him [or the female reader] but death" (100–101). This world is too narrow, too exclusionary, too hostile to the feminine presence, to speak to the lives of both men and women. Of course it's the old familiar complaint. But reading it this time I'm stopped in my tracks. Suddenly theory and feeling, sense and sensibility collide in disturbing, complicated ways I have never articulated before. Where was my female sensibility? My feminist edge? What contradictions have blindsided me just now? The synthesis of these theories is so rich and has been so useful that I wonder if there is a way to acknowledge the power of the theory and the text as well as the response of many female readers of Hemingway to this apparently masculine, stripped-down world edged so precariously and uncompromisingly against death.

But it brings me to the question this essay seeks to answer: how do female readers who have always been moved by Hemingway's works— for whom those trees have never shut out the sun—negotiate theories that insist upon the exclusionary quality of the Hemingway world? * * *

✶   ✶   ✶

I want to focus on "Big Two-Hearted River" specifically because it establishes, as Westling points out, the "modern American hero in an emblematic Great Good Place" for generations of readers (91). But it is also a work that is wonderfully prescient, presenting in an almost uncanny way the conflict at the heart of so many works by Hemingway set in the natural world. Though for many readers "Big Two-Hearted River" is Hemingway's greatest short story triumph, it has always confounded interpretation. Yet its utter resistance to paraphrase is the source of both its difficulty and greatness. Explaining it is like trying to describe the wonder or terror of a dream, for what we remember most about it is its dreamlike quality and our own sense of astonishment that this simple story could have produced such power.

Readers first knew "Big Two-Hearted River" in the Paris magazine *This Quarter*, published in May of 1925, before it became part of *In Our Time*. This is important to remember, because although it has been widely anthologized, most readers know it in the contexts of the stories of *In Our Time*, and such stories as "Now I Lay Me" and "A Way You'll Never Be," and have felt that it does not achieve coherence outside of this context. Indeed, it is almost impossible to give the story a genuinely pure reading after having first read it as the last story of *In Our Time*. And it is true that it both informs and is informed by those other stories in rich as well as complicating ways. Reading it in the context of *In Our Time*, "Big Two-Hearted

River" holds the accumulation of all the sorrows from the stories that came before it—a rich reading to be sure, but one often merged with biography, and the backstory provided in "On Writing."

But the allegorical, metaphorical shape of the story becomes clearer, more resonant when it is read independently. My own sense here is to attempt to read it independently first and then see how the story plays out the patterns of gender and the natural world that emerge in works to come.

But what is the conflict in this story where nothing seems to happen? Where is the story? What is the trouble? What is the progression? And indeed, read on its own, "Big Two-Hearted River" would seem to be a story utterly without any conflict at all until the last page, when a shadow gathers over Nick's heart. "He did not feel like going on into the swamp. . . . Nick did not want to go in there now. . . . In the swamp fishing was a tragic adventure" [128].

In order to satisfy our need for a sense of storiness, there must be a progression of some sort. The events must cohere at some place and point toward a pattern of meaning. The challenge "Big Two-Hearted River" presents is whether it is possible to discover this from the text alone. At any rate, an independent reading highlights the extraordinary achievement this story represents. In this long account of a single character to whom nothing at all extraordinary happens, who talks to no one, not even himself, and who does not allow himself even to think, Hemingway stretches the concept of story to its very limits. Using only narration, relieved briefly by interior monologue and a few lines of speech, Hemingway creates a story that carries more risks than any story he ever wrote.

Writing about it in 1926, F. Scott Fitzgerald said that he had read it with "the most breathless unwilling interest" (qtd. in Baker, *Writer* 36). But it was not until Malcolm Cowley's exploration of the murky regions of the story that its depths were acknowledged. Since Cowley, no critic could afford to ignore the possibility of the story's underside. Yet he reads "Big Two-Hearted River" in the context of "Now I Lay Me," the war story in which fishing is the dream. Following Cowley's lead, critics have worked the dark parameters of "Big Two-Hearted River" and have caught some pretty strange fish. Lost in the murkiness they often miss the story's compelling sense of wonder. Carlos Baker suggests that "if we read the river-story *singly* looking merely at what it says, there is probably no more effective account of euphoria in the language" (Baker 125). If so, then where in the story's *underside* is the "nightmare at noonday" (Cowley 41)?[2] A number of recent readings of the story have

2. Cowley, of course, extends Edmund Wilson's reading five years earlier (see "Ernest Hemingway: Bourdon Gauge of Morale"). Recent biographical criticism has called into

suggested that there is no nightmare at all: that the story is a magnificent rendering of just what it seems—the story of a day's fishing. In his classic study of Hemingway, Philip Young states that the story "cannot be read with comprehension unless one understands the earlier stories. One would think it no more than . . . a story about a man fishing—and it would be, as readers have often complained, quite pointless" (* * * 2–3).

And readers have interpreted that vague sense of foreboding or dread in a number of ways, depending on the context. One of the more recent and more controversial readings has been Kenneth Lynn's, in which he acknowledges the tension in the story, but attributes it to the antipathy between Nick and his mother, not the war: "Not a single reference to war appears in the story, and it is highly doubtful . . . that panic is the feeling that [Nick] is fending off" (104).[3] The trouble here is that there are no specific references to the mother either. Lynn stumbles into the biographical fallacy, reading the story in the context of Hemingway's strained familial relations in 1919, the summer of his trip to the Fox River, ignoring the fact that Hemingway *wrote* the story some five years later when the memory of those touchy months may very well have faded in importance.

In addition to the threat of the maternal that Lynn proposes, other readers have found entanglements, feminine and otherwise, in the swamp—that place which, for whatever reason, the hero Nick cannot face.[4] For Westling the swamp is fearful because it "epitomizes the feminine characteristics" (98–99). For other readers, coming at the story through the context of *In Our Time*, it has been the threat of impending fatherhood, marriage itself, familial strife, the war and its wounds both physical and psychic. Is the swamp—that confounding, bewildering metaphor that suggests everything and guarantees nothing—the dark place that holds the entanglements of the feminine? Is it all things "fearful, gloomy, [and] entangling" (Westling, 99)? In general, is there a repudiation of the feminine in Hemingway's works that are set in the natural world? Particularly, is there such a repudiation in this work? Or is the feminine erased altogether?

These readings describe the encounter with the feminine as an encounter with a fearful otherness and not the feminine as reflection of some aspect of the self. But there are two senses of nature in Hemingway's fiction that always compete in strange and complicated

question whether or not it is the *war* that is the "thing left out." See for example Kenneth Lynn's interpretation of the story (102–08).

3. Again, the difficulty with Lynn's premise that the thing left out is [the] conflict with Hemingway's mother is that there is no more *textual* evidence for this than for the war.

4. For example, see William Bysshe Stein, and for the idea that the entrapment of marriage is what is in the swamp, see Moddelmog, "Unifying Consciousness."

ways. There is the sense of nature as bountiful mother, which leads to the pastoral moment, and there is the sense of nature as mistress, as an eroticized other who must be mastered, which leads away from the pastoral moment and toward the "tragic adventure." For Hemingway, however, both senses of nature ultimately come to reflect desires of the self—desires that conflict in ultimately tragic ways. And the collision between these two senses forms the heart of this two-hearted story. For the feminine is not erased at all, but is ever-present in both the idyllic surface story set in the pastoral landscape and the buried story with its well-guarded secrets that dare not be told outright. It is here, in the collision between these two, that the tension of "Big Two-Hearted River" lies.

Even so, we get the sense that the narrator is always measuring life's terror and dread against its wonder and beauty. But in this story it is a paradox presented imagistically rather than through a dramatic progression. Hemingway uses image clusters to construct two opposing sets of values—one fraught with complications and sorrow, the other ordered and compellingly beautiful. *What happens* in the story is that this paradox is revealed to the reader, slowly, intuitively, as it is acknowledged by the protagonist. But this conflict is not presented through action. It is given in a description of a journey across a landscape, which contains images of both wonder and dread. For the basic structural principle underlying "Big Two-Hearted River," as many readers have noted, is not linear, but imagistic. Hemingway's strategy was to let the reader supply the things left out, though always guided by a careful structure of repetition, image clusters, juxtapositions, oppositions, and strange, mysterious silences. Increasingly it becomes clear that if we are to find meaning it will not come from plot but from the story's configuration of images, and from the mysterious intensity of this story in which "nothing happens."

The structure of the story itself invites multiple and conflicting interpretations, an iceberg that dazzles readers with its glittery surface yet hides its meanings within impenetrable depths. Hemingway's theory of omission describes not only the way his stories are constructed, but also the way we read them. For one thing, it points out how much he depends upon his readers to supply the things he left out. He put his theory to the supreme test in "Big Two-Hearted River," which he later said was about "coming back from the war" but with "no mention of the war in it" (*MF* 76).

This story, which in Baker's words is so "oddly satisfying" (*Writer* 126), carries a vision of order and beauty so powerful that it unfolds in strangely compelling ways. It is important to recall that Hemingway remembers the writing of the story, not in terms of exorcising unspoken terrors, but with love and a sense of wonder at the country he was trying to render like Cézanne:

When I stopped writing I did not want to leave the river where I could see the trout in the pool, its surface pushing swelling smooth against the resistance of the log-driven piles of the bridge. . . . Some days it went so well that you could make the country so that you could walk into it through the timber . . . and feel the weight settle on your back and feel the pine needles under your moccasins as you started down for the lake. (*MF* 91)

In "Big Two-Hearted River" the landscape carries the sole burden of meaning. For Nick the landscape provides a sense of order; for the reader it represents the only way to meaning that the story offers. There is a natural order, which Nick finds with his wondering eye, and there is a created order, in the familiar sequence of details Nick follows in making his camp and fishing the river.

Right from the beginning Hemingway positions the images that are the paradox at the center of the story. Although Seney is burned, Nick knows "[it] could not all be burned. He knew that" [112]. If he walks far enough, he will come to the green hills again. This positioning of landscapes gives the story a *progression*, and it defines the values that are juxtaposed. At the beginning of the journey Nick finds the "fire-scarred hill" and the blackened earth. At the end he finds the dark, mysterious swamp. In between, Nick comes to the middle ground of the pastoral landscape.[5] It is this vision of nature as beckoning and maternal, the source of both salvation and rapture, that is also the vision of the perfect self. It is where he needs to go in order to hold steady in fast current. But the progression and meaning of the story is bound up in the juxtaposition of all *three* places and the values they represent.

The whole point of the journey has been to reach a place that had not changed, a place beyond the spread of the fire. Nick has earned the right to occupy such a place through the hard conditions that he had set for himself—going as far as he could go, carrying as heavy a pack as his endurance would allow. Nick sees that the grasshoppers have turned black from living in the burned-over country. And it is clear to any reader that Nick too has been burned by some kind of fire, although we cannot discover its source, not from the text, not from biography, nor from the other stories to which it seems allied. By going unnamed, it becomes the sorrow of all those who have one way or the other been broken by the world. Yet Nick comes to this middle ground

---

5. The term comes from Leo Marx's *The Machine in the Garden*, in which he describes that midpoint between savage nature and civilization, an oasis and temporary stay against the encroachments from either side. * * * "River" fits nicely into this tradition, with civilization on one side—with its railroad and blackened town of Seney—and the swamp on the other. Most of the story takes place in the area of the *green*: the middle position.

where nature is generous, where good fish can be caught through skill, order, and love, where he can feel "all the old feeling" [112].

This is the vision at the center of all works set in the natural world—that middle ground, edged on one side by civilization, on the other by wildness and haste. It reappears again and again—in the green hills of Africa and the blue waters of the Gulf; it is always strange and familiar, a landscape given in such luminous images that they shimmer with the power of the dream. For in the landscape of the dream, one can repeat the sequence of action across familiar terrain, and get "all the old feeling." The pastoral landscape is washed over with a radiant ever-presentness over which the hero journeys with a stillness of soul, and a "first chastity of sight" (*FTA* 239 qtd. in Tanner 242). Read purely by itself this is a narrative so wished for, so desired that it becomes the universal dream of reverence and stillness of heart. It becomes a landscape anyone can know.

The journey across the paradisal terrain becomes also the search for order and for meaning—some way of getting things to have "a definite end" (*SAR* 167), to have a meaning in themselves that will offer a stay against the darkness of the vision of *nada*, which is the unspeakable part of the story. But Hemingway insists that his protagonists search for meaning in the same world that holds both the wonder *and* the dread. The story moves from the town of Seney, across the landscape, but it ends with the swamp. Here there would be none of the clarity and light of the grove or the order of the camp. Here branches hang low in tangled knots and the sun comes through only "in patches" [128]. Hemingway introduces the swamp as part of a general description of the landscape, but through repetition it becomes an image of great power, drawing to it other dark images. It is the place insects come from, a place where the mist hovers:

> Nick did not want to go in there now. He felt a reaction against deep wading with the water deepening up under his armpits, to hook big trout *in places impossible to land them*. In the *swamp* the banks were bare, the big cedars came together overhead, the sun did not come through, except in patches; in the fast deep water, in the half light, the fishing would be tragic. In the *swamp* fishing was a tragic adventure. Nick did not want it. He did not want to go *down the stream* any further today. (my emphasis, [128])

For now, the "tragic adventure" must be avoided. "There were plenty of days coming when he could fish the swamp" [129].

In *The Old Man and the Sea* Hemingway shows what it means to have the "tragic adventure," what it means to hook fish in places impossible to land them. But here it is important to note that

Hemingway avoids a tragic telling by blunting the impact of the story through a structure that submerges the dread in the presentation of a landscape full of light and vague, mysterious shadows.

Yet perhaps one of the reasons this story seems so satisfying is because the details the narrator so lovingly gives are so costly. The pastoral moment, which is wrapped in a luminous sense of timelessness, includes also the pull and tug of longing. In fact for both writer and protagonist, the intensity of the present moment is fueled by desire. "All I wanted to do was get back to Africa," Hemingway writes in *Green Hills of Africa*. "We had not left it, yet, but when I would wake in the night, I would lie, listening, homesick for it already" (72). For Hemingway every country is the "last good country." Every landscape is washed over with a sense of both timelessness and impending loss. It is a paradox at the heart of this story and of all Hemingway's fiction. This poignancy and discontent is played out again and again in the figure of a solitary protagonist travelling across paradisal landscapes. Memory itself is hunger, Hemingway explains in *A Moveable Feast*. Thus it is the hunger that comes from the past that Nick cannot bear. He denies himself the poignancy of memory and instead intensifies his physical hunger only to satisfy it at last with exquisite deliberateness. It is the way longing itself is beckoned that creates such intensity in those seemingly simple descriptions of landscapes at once new and familiar, wrapped in timelessness and steeped in time.

By controlling sensation through parceling out experience, Nick creates a stay against the chaos that lies on either side of this middle ground he occupies. Nick employs a conscious deliberation, an exquisite sense of timing, such that he knows just when to eat, sleep, cast the next line. It involves a careful management of deprivation and satisfaction, a deliberate heightening of sensation by withholding gratification for as long as possible. The temptation is always to rush things, but by holding back, the sensation can be exquisitely controlled. So Nick deliberately parcels out his pleasures, saving and then spending them with compelling care. Life holds many pleasures, which can be heightened through a meticulous sense of timing, but perhaps its delights are numbered. In this, Hemingway reveals how fragile is the sense of wonder and how close at hand the sense of dread.

This exquisite sense of timing that all Hemingway protagonists know is rendered in prose rhythms so piercing and deliberate that each gesture becomes an incantation against unspoken things and proof of the narrator's "first chastity of sight." It is a vision rendered so lovingly it is removed from all ego and self-interest, captured by the "wondering, wandering eye" and rescued from the rush of history (Tanner 240). The cadence of the narration, emphasizing the integrity

of each separate gesture, results in a sequence so incantatory it
finally gathers him into perfect sleep.

> Nick knew it was too hot. He poured on some tomato catchup.
> He knew the beans and spaghetti were still too hot. He looked
> at the fire, then at the tent, he was not going to spoil it all by
> burning his tongue. For years he had never enjoyed fried
> bananas because he had never been able to wait for them to
> cool. . . . He was very hungry. Across the river in the swamp, in
> the almost dark, he saw a mist rising. He looked at the tent once
> more. All right. He took a full spoonful from the plate. "Chrise,"
> Nick said, "Geezus Chrise," he said happily. [116]

*   *   *

In the pastoral setting, through an imagination fired by longing,
every landscape becomes a clean, well-lighted place, luminous and
ever-present. But in the end it is only a temporary stay for those protagonists driven by restlessness and a discontent they do not understand, which forces them out of the pastoral moment and toward
the "tragic adventure." But it is a discontent that electrifies those
descriptions with a shimmering sense of place. The deliberate slow-
ness of the pastoral world, with its sense of timelessness and mysterious silences, is edged against the sure knowledge that the lesson
of the past is the certainty of loss.

But where is the past, in this story of a man alone in nature who
experiences no challenges from without? In such a story wouldn't
any writer include internal conflicts of some kind? Yet, what is obviously left out are all those things we might expect, memories, dreams,
and recollections given in narrative flashbacks if not character remi-
niscences. In other words, what is missing is the *past*, which holds
the memory of loss, which holds the hunger that would devour him,
which is present through its brooding absence. Thus the search for
the *story* becomes a reader's search for the past. Instead we are given
one long, glorious rendering of the *present* in all its stunning immediacy. Nostalgia may be wonderful for the narrator of *A Moveable
Feast*, who recollects the pleasure in writing "Big Two-Hearted River,"
but for Nick, its hero, remembering is full of menace. "Big Two-
Hearted River" is a story about the balancing of present and past,
wonder and dread, mastery and reverence, sound and silence. The
absence of the past is signaled by the absence of words, by the interior silence of the main character.

The overwhelming beauty of the world is balanced against terrors
that must not be told. Because Hemingway refuses to name them
they become more terrible yet, for we feel their presence in the prose

rhythms, and in the jarring of image against image. We sense that there are hidden stories lurking in the shadows throughout "Big Two-Hearted River," and the reader must be like Nick as he watches the stream for the big trout at the bottom, sometimes seeing them, sometimes not.

But Hemingway gives us clues in several ways: in a few direct but puzzling references to the past, through imagaic equivalents, and through an implied sense of the past in the overriding emphasis given the present. The story begins with a sense of loss and change. The first image we notice is the town of Seney, blackened from fire such that "Even the surface had been burned off the ground" [111]. Nick is first seen watching the train behind "one of the hills of burnt timber." "Nick looked at the burned-over stretch of hillside, *where he had expected* to find the scattered houses of the town" (my emphasis, [111]). In coming to the river Nick is attempting to re-create a part of the past that had nourished him. But the country is black, not green, and it presents as devastating an image as any scene of war could provide. The whole point of the journey is to find a place, a landscape, which has not changed. So in a real sense the story is about the search for permanence in an impermanent world—the search for the green hills, a pastoral landscape impervious to time, and perfect reflection of a self wrapped in a transcendent and abiding present.

Nick walks to the bridge and looks down at the river. *"The river was there"* (my emphasis, [111]). That short sentence contains all of Nick's joy for this return to a place that has not been burned away. Nick looks into the water, watching the trout. Again, Hemingway gives the astonishment and joy of his return, and by inference the deprivation of the past. "It was a long time since Nick had looked into a stream and seen trout" [111]. Here as always, the present moment gains in intensity, refracted as it is through the images of loss, the shadow of time. Though Hemingway packs great poignancy in that simple line, we do not know where Nick has come from or why he has been so long from the river. But through the use of incremental repetition, Hemingway begins to build images of the emotions that are left out of the story and define its emotional curve:

> Nick looked down into the clear, brown water . . . and watched *the trout keeping themselves steady in the current.* . . . As he watched them they changed their positions by quick angles, *only to hold steady in the fast water again.* . . .
> At the bottom of the pool were the big trout. Nick did not see them at first. Then he saw them at the bottom of the pool, big trout looking *to hold themselves* on the gravel bottom. . . .
> A big trout shot upstream . . . and then . . . he *tightened* facing up into the current.
> Nick's heart *tightened* as the trout moved. (my emphasis, [111–12])

Here Hemingway identifies Nick with the fish at the bottom of the stream, heart touching heart in the striving required to hold steady in fast current. It is part of the iceberg strategy that we are never told why holding steady is so difficult, yet we know that it is. As Nick puts on his pack and sets off across the land, we sense that holding steady is part of what this story is about. But the pack is heavy. So he takes some of the pull off his shoulders by "leaning his forehead against the wide band of the tumpline" [112]. In the heat, up the "fire-scarred hill," Nick's solitary figure against that blackened landscape creates an image so wrenching it becomes a mythic journey any reader knows.

"Big Two-Hearted River" is a story wrapped in silence. It depicts an Edenic world—a prelapsarian world that exists before the need for words. Nick moves through a beckoning silence, a passive, maternal landscape, which requires nothing but perfect assent. It is a world wrapped in mystery and wordlessness, a universe where every breath is a prayer of gratitude. But in the description of Nick making the coffee toward the end of Part I, Hemingway creates the odd presence of a story that is never told. It is the solitary excursion into words and the solitary journey into the past. Nick cannot remember the way he makes coffee. What he can remember is "an argument about it with Hopkins, but not which side he had taken. He decided to bring it to a boil. He remembered now that was Hopkins's way. He had once argued about everything with Hopkins. . . . They said goodbye and all felt bad. It broke up the trip. They never saw Hopkins again. That was a long time ago on the Black River" [117]. It is the only extended memory Nick allows himself, and just at the end of it the narrator reveals that it has made Nick's mind begin to work.

But who is Hopkins and what is he doing in this story that does not mention a single other character besides Nick? Hemingway leaves out the war, perhaps, or whatever terrors hold him, but includes a long description of someone named Hopkins and how he made coffee. So we bump into Hemingway's iceberg—the tip of it, anyway. By describing at length what seems to be a trivial anecdote, Hemingway brilliantly reveals the paucity of memory Nick allows himself, and how quickly he stops even such an innocuous-seeming recollection as this. This one excursion into the past is pleasant enough, yet even that becomes too dangerous and Nick must finally "choke it." The coffee turned out to be bitter anyway. Better to stay with ritual that re-enacts the past through action rather than thought. This is the only narrative offered in this seemingly plotless story, and Nick must stop it before he comes to the part that makes his "mind [start] to work" [117]. Yet this narrative fragment shows just how dangerous telling can become.

*　*　*

In his essay "Reading Hemingway Without Guilt," Frederick Busch describes "how [Hemingway] listened and watched and invented the language—using the power, the terror, of silences with which we could name ourselves" (3). Westling, however, insists that "Busch is wrong to assert that Hemingway's is the language with which we can name ourselves." Or "at least [for] half of us" (100). I would like to push beyond the description of the "silence[s]" Busch praises and the sound Westling dismisses to ask: what is this wordlessness for? Is it presence or absence? And what does it mean to speak? What does it mean to tell?

In "Big Two-Hearted River," it is clear that Nick must hold his tongue. Like the fish at the bottom of the fast moving current, he must hold on tight. At any moment words can slip free of the tongue and rush into dangerous places. The past is held in words that once spoken conjure it up. Better to stay with things, better to stay with masculine rituals enacted in sacramental places in ways that avoid words altogether. Better to create narratives of silence, wordless landscapes washed over in golden light and struck with green, landscapes shimmering in that original stillness. Better to remain in the paradisal world where no words are necessary and everything is bathed in an ever-present and luminous reality.

But one of the progressions of "Big Two-Hearted River" is the journey from speechlessness to sound. In one sense the story is a journey through a pastoral silence toward the rush of words, which, in this story, is a rush into the swamp and toward the tragic adventure. Perhaps what is in the swamp that for now must be avoided is words. But words are what Nick most fears and most desires. It is the world he must both avoid and ultimately enter, when silence finally erupts into the dangerous rush of sound. For in the end it is the sacred obligation of the writer to tell the tale no matter the cost the universe exacts. For the act of telling breaks the male code of silence and surrenders to words truths too fragile to hold.

In the coda, "On Writing," Nick tries to explain the passion of fishing. "They were all married to [it]," he says, "It wasn't any joke" [136]. Some readers over the years have suggested that it is fishing and its exclusionary male world that is threatened by adulthood, by marriage, by the feminine. It is fishing that is the real marriage, perhaps a better marriage, particularly in those works that depict an eroticized landscape as feminine terrain to be taken. In this view, the feminine is always an "other" that threatens the essential male self, depicted in this story as the lure and danger that lurks in the swamp. It is an immaturity, in Leslie A. Fiedler's view, a literature of adolescence, of boys who do not want to be men.[6]

---

6. See especially Fiedler's chapter, "The Failure of Sentiment and the Evasion of Love," in *Love and Death in the American Novel* (337–90).

But I'm going to suggest a different way to interpret what it means to fish the swamp, looking at the text alone. Nick said, "he felt he had left everything behind, the need for thinking, the need to write, other needs" [112]. The "other needs" that he refers to but does not name remain in the iceberg, though readers over the years have gained an intriguing sense of the possibilities from the biography and many of the other works, as I have mentioned earlier. The two things Nick cannot think about doing in this story are fishing the swamp and writing. In this story they are the same thing. Here is the first example of what was to become Hemingway's gathering metaphor for the life of the writer. In work after work, the story of the hunt becomes the writer's story. The metaphor of the hunter-artist—or here in "Big Two-Hearted River," the artist as fisher—is firmly established by the time he wrote *Green Hills of Africa*, and reaches its most allegorical expansion in *The Old Man and the Sea*, which becomes almost a parable of the writer's quest. In *Green Hills of Africa* Hemingway writes,

> The way to hunt is for as long as you live against as long as there is such and such an animal; just as the way to paint is as long as there is you and colors and canvas; and to write as long as you can live and there is pencil and paper or ink . . . or anything you care to write about. (*GHOA* 12)

Both hunter and artist seek to enter the timeless world of the pastoral dream in order to stop the remorseless rush of time, yet both are finally "caught by time" (*GHOA* 12), as they enter the time-driven narratives of the hunt. The hunter's story is the story of the writer's struggle to know and fix the truth, fought against the remorseless rush of time that would only destroy it.

But is writing, like fishing and hunting, the exclusively male activity always threatened by incursions from the feminine? What about this way of talking about writing? Does this metaphor of the writer as hunter necessarily exclude the feminine? Is this metaphor as exclusionary for women as the authorial, pen/phallus metaphor or as problematic as the birth metaphor?

Women have historically found it difficult to express the dangers that creation has meant to them. The difficulties with the former are perhaps self-evident, but as for the second metaphor, the act of writing framed in images of giving birth has always been too literal a metaphor for women not to be fraught with complications—both in terms of the writing process (the act of giving birth and the potential for suffering and death), as well as the uncertainties and insecurities of authorship itself. * * * Perhaps the most natural metaphor for the female writer remains the most problematic.

But what about writing as a killing out of season? To be sure, there are other ways to speak of writing, but I believe that Hemingway's metaphor does not exclude women and that it points to a certain sense many writers of both genders have felt to be true. * * *

* * * The dark is the swamp that Nick, whose heart has broken apart, cannot face. Nick knows there is something dangerous in the swamp—something forbidden and fraught with potential sorrow.

Earlier in the day, Nick had hooked a huge trout, a trout "broad as a salmon," "the biggest one [he] ever heard of" [125]. But the leader finally breaks under the strain and he loses him.

> There was a long tug. Nick struck and the rod came alive and dangerous, bent double, the line tightening, coming out of water, tightening, all in a heavy dangerous, steady pull. . . . He had never seen so big a trout. There was a heaviness, *a power not to be held.* (my emphasis, [124–25])

It is a presentiment of what would happen if he fished the swamp, how he would "hook big trout in places impossible to land them." In the treacherous light, where the "sun did not come through, except in patches . . . the fishing would be tragic" [128]. This fish, both caught and lost, is a *type* of other animals in other stories, too brave and strong and beautiful to be taken, but pursued nonetheless by other Hemingway protagonists who become figures of the hunter-artist. The spirit animal is what the writer is always seeking to catch, pursued finally into dark, tangled places—the swamp, the deep forest, the sea beyond all people. The vision the hunter seeks to capture is embodied in an animal so elusive and unearthly it is a vision seen only in flickering light and mysterious shadows—the visionary kudu, the mythical elephant, the otherworldly marlin. This animal is always taken against the rules, slain out of season by trick and by treachery, caught in forbidden places, in forbidden ways.[7]

And what of that moment of tightening, that sudden, cool detachment as one takes aim? What of that pulling away, that of taking notes on the scene before the release of words? The imagery is unarguably masculine. * * *

* * *

Perhaps the tightening I have been describing is the masculine mind taking aim; the feminine mind is the release of words that must tell the tale no matter how untellable. * * *

7. A fuller discussion of the concept of the spirit animal and what it means to slay it can be found in my essays "Across the River and into the Stream" and "Memory, Grief, and the Terrain of Desire."

* * *

* * * The time-driven adventure that awaits the narrator of "River," and all hunter-artists, will propel him out of silence into sound, and the solitary sin of art. For once set loose these words cannot be called back.

I fear the pleasures are all dark ones. Would that we could stay in the pastoral dream forever—that timeless moment that is the rush and stillness of love, the rush and stillness of death flung forever into a luminous ever-present. But Nick cannot. * * *

It seems like such a dark tale, a world rendered with such precision and love, a world so defiled, and the divided heart that has created them both. The ecological implications are enormous. But the pull of the swamp, in all its contradiction, is so strong, so irresistible that it is where I have to go. My response to the dividedness at the center of Hemingway's work is complex, disturbing, and rich in ways impossible to say. How to explain this beauty at the heart of loss, this beauty in the shadow of violence, this heart touching heart? There is a poignancy here that draws me in, over and over, and becomes the closest thing to an explanation of how theory reconciles with feeling that I know. Yet I go as no stranger to these parts. The heavy old boughs of those trees have never shut out the sunlight for me.

Works Cited

Baker, Carlos. *Hemingway: The Writer as Artist*. Princeton: Princeton UP, 1972.

Busch, Frederick. "Reading Hemingway Without Guilt." *New York Times Book Review* (Jan. 12, 1992): 3, 17–19.

Cowley, Malcolm. "Nightmare and Ritual in Hemingway." *Hemingway: Collection of Critical Essays,* ed. Robert P. Weeks. Englewood Cliffs, NJ: Prentice Hall, 1962, pp. 40–51.

Fiedler, Leslie. *Love and Death in the American Novel*. New York: Stein, 1982.

Hemingway, Ernest. *Green Hills of Africa*. New York: Scribner's, 1935.

———. *A Moveable Feast*. New York: Scribner's, 1964.

Lynn, Kenneth. *Hemingway*. New York: Fawcett, 1987.

Marx, Leo. *The Machine in the Garden: Technology and the Pastoral Idea in America*. New York: Oxford UP, 1964.

Moddelmog, Debra A. "The Unifying Consciousness of a Divided Conscience: Nick Adams as Author of *In Our Time*." *American Literature* 60 (Dec. 1988): 591–610 [209–25].

Putnam, Ann. "Across the River and into the Stream: Journey of the Divided Heart." *North Dakota Quarterly* 63.3 (1996): 90–98.

————. "Memory, Grief, and the Terrain of Desire." *Hemingway and the Natural World*, ed. Robert Fleming. Moscow: U of Idaho P, 1999, pp. 99–110.

Stein, William Bysshe. "Ritual in Hemingway's 'Big Two-Hearted River.'" *Texas Studies in Language and Literature* 1 (Winter 1960): 555–61.

Tanner, Tony. *The Reign of Wonder: Naivety and Reality in American Literature*. Cambridge, Eng.: Cambridge UP, 1965.

Westling, Louise H. *The Green Breast of the New World: Landscape, Genre, and American Fiction*. Athens: U of Georgia P, 1996.

Young, Philip. *Ernest Hemingway*. New York: Holt, 1952.

MARK CIRINO

Hemingway's "Big Two-Hearted River": Nick's Strategy and the Psychology of Mental Control[†]

At this point in Hemingway studies, it is well understood that in "Big Two-Hearted River" Nick Adams seeks a return to simplicity after his harrowing experience in World War I and that Hemingway's prose replicates the veteran's internal quest for manageable simplicity. At story's end, Nick avoids the physical swamp at the edge of the stream, and by doing so keeps at bay the metaphorical swamp of his own psyche. But * * * a crucial question remains unasked: Is Nick's strategy—to return to the Michigan woods of his youth, by himself, systematically replacing the thoughts of the trauma of the war with immediate stimulation from nature and camping—benign and productive or self-defeating and doomed from the start?

* * * Nick's strategy of rehabilitation depends upon focused self-distraction—to consider a more agreeable topic instead of confronting the source of his unpleasant memories. "Big Two-Hearted River" is a drama of metacognition; in his solitude, Nick's thoughts are occupied by his own thoughts. Therefore, the condition of Nick's consciousness becomes the narrative's primary concern. In ways unsurpassed in all of Hemingway, the text presents extended external metaphors to illuminate psychological corollaries.

Mental control, a slippery concept in the philosophy of mind, describes when people "suppress a thought, concentrate on a sensation, inhibit an emotion, maintain a mood, stir up a desire, squelch a craving, or otherwise exert influence on their own mental states"

[†] *Papers on Language & Literature* 47.2 (Spring 2011): 115–40. Reprinted by permission of the publisher. Some of the author's notes have been omitted. Page numbers in brackets refer to this Norton Critical Edition.

(Wegner and Pennebaker 1). Inherent in this definition is an implicit anxiety with the way a person feels, has felt, or soon might feel. If a person knew he would remain permanently and unalterably content, he would not exert energy trying to maintain positive feelings or alter negative ones. Likewise, in the unconscious thought avoidance that Freud analyzed, he found that "the motive and purpose of repression was nothing else than the avoidance of unpleasure" (153). Therefore, in their endeavors to control their mental states, Hemingway's heroes possess a level of introspection and self-awareness not always granted them. "Big Two-Hearted River" demonstrates the subtlety and complexity with which Hemingway understood mental control in that Nick wishes to adjust his cognitive activity as neatly as one might manipulate sound levels on the equalizer of a stereo. In his metacognitive drama, Nick is forced to ask: Am I satisfied with my thoughts? Are they pleasant? Are they productive? If so, how can I sustain them? Or, are they painful and harmful? If so, how might I eliminate them?

Once Nick disembarks the train in Seney, he is not just able to access the actual stream that is full of trout, but he can also better monitor the internal stream of his thoughts. Beside the helpful baggage man, who is referred to but unseen, and his old friend Hopkins, who appears only in the story's single extended reminiscence, Nick is alone. The only other characters spring from nature, and Nick relates to each one differently: grasshoppers, trout, a mosquito, a mink, a kingfisher. These creatures elicit telling reactions from Nick, but he has made the crucial decision to fish and camp alone. In an early draft of the story, which more closely adheres to its autobiographical inspiration, Nick is accompanied by a group of friends. By changing the narrative to one man's solo journey, Hemingway allows Nick to focus more meticulously upon his stated objective: escaping "the need for thinking, the need to write, other needs" [112]. Nick's quest to control his surroundings and his preference for solitude is clear: "Nick did not like to fish with other men on the river. Unless they were of your party, they spoiled it" [124]. And in this extreme setting, even if they were members of his party, they would be not a welcome distraction but an unpredictable variable to which he was not willing to expose his vulnerable state of mind.

In a note to himself during the 1924 drafting of "Big Two-Hearted River," Hemingway sketched the story, tracing the protagonist's crisis: "He thinks [. . .] gets uncomfortable, restless, tries to stop thinking, more uncomfortable and restless, the thinking goes on, speeds up, can't shake it—comes home to camp—hot before storm—storm—in morning creek flooded, hikes to the railroad" (qtd. in Reynolds 209). As Hemingway's outline makes apparent, and as the published narrative bears out, the story's concern was never the setting, the contrived antagonists of the trout, the chores of hiking and cooking, or conforming to any kind of behavioral code for constructing a proper camp. There is hardly a narrative to speak of. Hemingway confessed to Gertrude Stein and Alice B. Toklas that "nothing happens" (*Selected Letters* 122).[1] The issue that does justify the narrative is Nick's tortured consciousness, his struggle to control it—Nick "*tries* to stop thinking"—and the depiction of his failure when he "can't shake it." This description suggests a psyche out of control.

In the published story, Nick feels his mind begin to activate, but he "knew he could choke it" [117], having sufficiently exhausted himself. Although Nick is comforted to know he can ultimately dominate his thoughts, it is nevertheless revealing for a man to view his own mind so antagonistically, and even violently. Healthy individuals do not need to choke their thoughts to control them. "One of the most compelling occasions for mental control is in the face of mental turmoil," write Daniel M. Wegner and James W. Pennebaker. "When the mind is reeling in response to some traumatic event . . . it is natural to attempt to quell the storm by dimming sensation, stopping thought, or blocking the emotion" (5–6). To appreciate the ominous use of "choking" in Hemingway, one need only to be familiar with *A Farewell to Arms*, in which choking causes the stillbirth of Frederic Henry's son and is also the verb that describes the bombing death of Passini as well as Frederic's succumbing to general anesthesia (327, 55, 107).

In "Big Two-Hearted River," Nick Adams's journey to the woods and the river is a retreat to a setting filled with happy distractions, a quest for familiar simplicity and manageable complexity. Nick's hope is that if the external world can be managed, it will grant a period of stability to the chaotic thoughts and traumatic memories that persistently plague his mind. Nick's project should not be imputed to reflect Hemingway's philosophy of life, a systematic renunciation of thought, or devaluation of consciousness. Nick, after all, is in an emotionally extreme situation that is so compelling to explore in fiction. Philip Young speaks forcefully to this point, describing Nick's compulsive routine as suggesting "much less that he is the mindless primitive the Hemingway hero was so often thought to be than that he is desperately protecting his mind against whatever it is that he is escaping" (45). Sheldon Norman Grebstein seconds this view of "Big Two-Hearted River," confirming that the style "has sometimes been interpreted or misconstrued by hostile critics as the writer's incapacity for complex thought and his distrust

---

1. Likewise, when Hemingway submitted the piece to *This Quarter* in 1925, Christian Gauss and F. Scott Fitzgerald accused Hemingway of "having written a story in which nothing happened" (Baker 125).

of intellection" (83). To extend Grebstein's point, the prevailing premise that a protagonist who avoids thought is therefore uninterested in
thought is utterly illogical. If Nick Adams were not predisposed to
think, then the narrative would have no tension and no point. If a
non-thinker chooses to abandon thought, it is a non-story. Nick, however, has a fiction writer's curiosity and sensitivity to experience. The
simmering conflict in "Big Two-Hearted River" stems from Nick's
powerful impulse to think and his determination to restrain himself.

   When Nick prepares his tent before dinner, Hemingway's language eerily mimics his protagonist's consciousness.

> Now things were done. There had been this to do. Now it was
> done. It had been a hard trip. He was very tired. That was done.
> He had made his camp. He was settled. Nothing could touch
> him. It was a good place to camp. He was there, in the good
> place. He was in his home where he had made it. Now he was
> hungry. [115]

In this extraordinarily crafted passage, sixty-three of the sixty-seven
words (94%) are monosyllabic. Twelve of the thirteen sentences
(92%) have zero punctuation marks other than a period at the end,
and the other has but one comma. The first twenty-two words of the
excerpt are monosyllabic; before the "hungry" that ends the excerpt,
there is another stretch of thirty. The four disyllabic words are themselves far from complex: "very," "settled," "nothing," and "hungry."[2]
Matthew Stewart comments on the above passage, concluding similarly: "Here style is in absolute service to content, the short declarative sentences echoing both Nick's methodical construction of the
camp and his continued need for simplicity and controlled action.
By keeping things simple, the repetitions drive home Nick's self-
created domestic ease" (91). The omission of advanced vocabulary
gestures towards the central omission of the story, which Hemingway would explain later in his career. In *A Moveable Feast*, Hemingway refers to "Big Two-Hearted River" as a story "about coming back
from the war but there was no mention of the war in it" (72). Even
Hemingway's sentence summarizing "Big Two-Hearted River" contains the word "war" two times, which is twice more than it appears
in the story. In "Soldier's Home," a story almost three times shorter
than "Big Two-Hearted River," the word "war" is mentioned nine
times, including in the first sentence.

   Although William Faulkner would later charge that Hemingway
"never used a word where the reader might check his usage by a
dictionary" (Blotner 2: 1233), readers can imagine how ridiculous a

---

2. Elizabeth Wells, using her own statistical criterion of "substantive words only" (62),
   calculates that "Big Two-Hearted River" is comprised of 72% monosyllabic words and
   4% words over two syllables (62, 67).

narrative about a quest for simplicity would be if it were described in the vocabulary of Faulkner's Quentin Compson (or his father), or Joyce's Stephen Dedalus. In "Big Two-Hearted River," with its thematic focus on mental control, a similar control had to be mimicked by the vocabulary, syntax, and grammar of the writer. The avoidance of even a single exclamation point suggests that the vulnerable mind of the protagonist could not withstand such excitement.

Nick's fishing expedition as an exercise in mental control is represented vividly from the moment he steps off the train. All his activities and sensations become modulated, measured, and analyzed as being not enough, too much, or just right. Mostly, Nick is guarding against excess, against any unwieldy stimulation that will overwhelm the makeshift defenses erected to guard his fragile psyche. Readers are prepared for this cautious behavior at the beginning of Part Two of the narrative, when Nick finds "plenty of good grasshoppers" that will serve as bait. Out of all those grasshoppers, his selection is telling: "Nick picked them up, taking only the medium-sized brown ones, and put them into the bottle" [121]. After Nick lifts a log and sees several hundred more grasshoppers, he repeats the behavior: "Nick put about fifty of the medium browns into the bottle" [121]. Virtually every activity on the camping trip follows this approach, a hypersensitivity to the necessity of his tentativeness. Nick controls his excitement and eagerness to fish immediately by not skipping breakfast; he decides against the more flamboyant technique of "flopping" flapjacks; although he makes two big flapjacks and a third small one, he eats only a big and a small, saving the second big one until later; he is content to secure one trout as opposed to many; and most significant—and this may be the insight Nick gleans from the camping trip—Nick concludes that it would be reckless to enter the swamp.

Whenever Nick acts contrary to this compulsively controlled, carefully modulated behavior, he gets a harsh reminder of his current incapacities. When he ventures into the Big Two-Hearted itself, the description is unambiguous: "He stepped into the stream. It was a shock. . . . The water was a rising cold shock" [123]. Surely, the word "shock" is not used—much less repeated—to describe Nick without the added psychological connotation attached to the physical sensation. Furthermore, the specificity in narration is telling, that the *water* is responsible for the shock and not anything more abstract or internal. After catching and releasing a too-small trout, Nick leaves the shallows, knowing he could catch no big ones there. Predictably, when Nick leaves the sure terrain of the shallows, he is at the mercy of the rude stream and, hence, the anarchic rapids of his own stream of consciousness. Nick hooks the biggest trout he has ever seen, which ends up breaking his leader and escaping. As the too-cold water provides too-heightened emotions, so does this battle that was unwise, an anathema to Nick's prior (and subsequent) self-control during the camping trip: "Nick's hand was shaky. He reeled in slowly. The thrill had been too much. He felt, vaguely, a little sick, as though it would be better to sit down. . . . He went over and sat on the logs. He did not want to rush his sensations any" [125]. A "reeling" Nick's corrective behavior is to traverse the logs "where it was not too deep" [126].

The discourse of measurement and excess is made evident by Nick's acute awareness [of] the several similar occasions when things are too much. Readers are told when Nick's backpack is "too heavy . . . much too heavy" [112]; the inefficacy of looking "too steadily" at hills in the distance [112]; the river running "too fast and smooth" to make a sound [114]; the beans and spaghetti being "too hot" and, even after ketchup, "still too hot" [116]; he knows when the coffee is "too hot to pour" [117]; in the morning he is "really too hurried" [121] for breakfast; with the big trout, the line rushes out "[t]oo fast" [125]; battling the trout, Nick feels when "the strain was too great; the hardness too tight," and sums up the ill-advised encounter: "The thrill had been too much" [125]. The solution to this entire adventure, during which he must guard against too much of everything and too much of anything, soon emerges: to carry on fishing in waters "where it was not too deep" [126]. The story enacts the aphorism from Blake's "Proverbs of Hell": "you never know what is enough unless you know what is more than enough" (37). By the end of the narrative, Nick knows his limits and will not risk ceding mental control to the Big Two-Hearted River or to the similarly unpredictable stream of his consciousness.

The notion of modulation, of Nick's incessant gauging of the volume of his sensory intake and emotional reactions, is extended into the gauging of mental activity, of the psychological exertion of a brain, an act of self-monitoring that calls for intense introspection, self-scrutiny, and self-knowledge. When Nick notices the "sooty black" grasshoppers [113], he identifies with their traumatized state, the grasshoppers having "turned black from living in the burned-over land" [113]. Despite this grim realization, Nick must maintain the objective of his mission to avoid thoughts of war and the "need for thinking" entirely [112]. Nick is focused on mental control so intensely, however, that he finds a way to process his observation about the grasshoppers: "Nick had wondered about them as he walked, without really thinking about them" [113]. He continues, comprehending their state and the cause, but never brooding over it, or responding in an overly emotional way: "He wondered how long they would stay that way" [113]. For Nick, to "wonder" equals thinking diminished. It skims the surface of a perception, taking notice of it with innocent, superficial speculation and quickly processing it, without allowing it the full depth of exploration that the topic might ordinarily merit.

In the long chapter devoted to "Will" in *The Principles of Psychology*, William James describes the concept of thought avoidance. James outlines a behavioral phenomenon that is consistent with Nick's central struggle in the story. James argues that for a man who is in a dominant frame of mind it takes an overwhelming "effort of attention" (2: 562) to undo the body's tendency to sustain the prevailing mood. "When any strong emotional state whatever is upon us," James writes, "the tendency is for no images but such as are congruous with it to come up. If others by chance offer themselves, they are instantly smothered and crowded out" (563). In this sense, the short story treats the challenge posed to Nick's will, his determination to break out of the mental condition that has suffocated him since his return from the war. A central difference between "Soldier's Home" and "Big Two-Hearted River" is that Krebs's victory comes when he ultimately decides to move to Kansas City, a change in environment that will afford him the opportunity to recuperate on his own terms; in "Big Two-Hearted River," Nick arrives in the temporary sanctuary of his choosing, and the limit of his mental willpower plays itself out.

The confrontation between focusing on external or internal objects calls to mind philosopher Henri Bergson's analysis of the idea of "nothing." Although Nick's temporary ideal would be to think about nothing—to be completely beyond "the need for thinking" and literally to have it "all back of him" [112]—a complete annihilation of thought, memory, sensation, and perception is impossible for any thinking organism. Bergson describes an experiment where he tries to reduce his thoughts to nothing, to eliminate his sensations and recollections, and to reduce the consciousness of his body to zero. Ultimately, Bergson realizes the project's futility:

> But no! At the very instant that my consciousness is extinguished, another consciousness lights up—or rather, it was already alight: it had arisen the instant before, in order to witness the extinction of the first; for the first could disappear only for another and in the presence of another. I see myself annihilated only if I have already resuscitated myself by an act which is positive, however involuntary and unconscious. So, do what I will, I am always perceiving something, either from without or from within. . . . I can by turns imagine a nought of external perception or a nought of internal perception, but not both at once, for the absence of one consists, at bottom, in the exclusive presence of the other. (278–79)

Bergson is affirming William James's first fundamental rule of consciousness, which is that thought is constant and unavoidable.

Although seemingly intuitive, establishing consciousness as a perpetual feature of a sentient being must be accepted as a given. Bergson has described a volatile competition between internal and
external stimuli, but this interplay is not typically a centerpiece for
an entire work of fiction. Hemingway's confession to Gertrude Stein
and Alice B. Toklas that "nothing happens" in "Big Two-Hearted
River" is self-deprecatory and misleading, because something does
happen; the arena of activity has merely turned inward from the Italian front to the consciousness of a shell-shocked veteran [SL 122].

James also imagines a situation similar to Bergson's, of the complete eradication of thought. "It is difficult not to suppose," James
writes, "something like this scattered condition of mind to be the
usual state of brutes when not actively engaged in some pursuit.
Fatigue, monotonous mechanical occupations that end by being
automatically carried on, tend to produce it in men" (1: 404). James's
image is precisely the accusation that has been incorrectly applied
to Hemingway's characters. Hemingway is unequivocally not writing about unthinking brutes. Hemingway's sensitive, introspective
characters often perversely envy and emulate the limited mental
state of brutes because they feel that their own excessively cognitive inclinations distract and impede them from completing a task
or maintaining a pleasant existence. They are unable to reconcile
the competing demands of the internal and external worlds. In the
reductive, false dichotomy between the "man of thought" and the
"man of action," Hemingway posits the unhappy compromise that
the man of action can act effectively only by pretending that he is
not a man of thought. The man of thought can protect himself only
by immersing himself in action that will absorb his attention.

The idea of "nothing" introduces two integral aspects of Hemingway's writing: his "iceberg principle" of writing, in which whatever
the writer knows is omitted in order to provide the unseen tension
of the story, and also the theme of "*nada*," the depressed, nihilistic
state that haunts the characters in "A Clean Well-Lighted Place" and
other narratives. Bergson argues that the concept of nothing "is, at
bottom, the idea of Everything, together with a movement of the
mind that keeps jumping from one thing to another, refuses to stand
still, and concentrates all its attention on this refusal by never deter-
mining its actual position except by relation to that which it has
just left" (296). Bergson's point introduces a whole new slant to the
old waiter's "*nada*" prayer in "A Clean Well-Lighted Place": if the old
waiter is commenting on nothing and giving it a name, can he, by
definition, be living in the state of nothing to which critics have
always consigned him and he has consigned himself?

In "Big Two-Hearted River," although the word "war" does not
appear in the story, the text was preceded by the intentional authorial

decision to excise the word, which means it first entered the consciousness of the writer who chose not to write it. By preventing the word from appearing, it becomes pervasive despite its absence and exists as the text's unspoken obsession. Likewise, Nick Adams chose to take the trip to the woods for a specific reason: to avoid thought. But within the motivation itself exists the very thought Nick was determined to avoid in the first place. Thus, just as Hemingway made war more present by omitting its mention, by erasing the unpleasant memories, paradoxically, Nick could have unintentionally made those memories the axis around which his life revolves. By trying to reduce his thoughts and memories to nothing, they risk becoming everything and all consuming.

One of Daniel M. Wegner's central contributions to the psychology of mental control has been his claim that suppressing a thought often leads to its "hyperaccessibility," an ironic effect whereby, for example, the pleasant distraction of the Big Two-Hearted River might in the future remind Nick that it had served as a distraction for the war and instead become an unhappy reminder. Nick might begin to consider the woods not as an Edenic paradise, but as a secret refuge to avoid thoughts of the war. The distracter creates, Wegner writes, "associations between the unwanted thought and all the various distracters" ("You Can't Always Think" 214). * * * As Bergson points out, "To represent 'Nothing,' we must either imagine it or conceive it" (278). It is impossible to suppress a thought without first planning to suppress it (although it could be buried by an unconscious Freudian repression), therefore to plan to avoid a thought must inherently involve thinking of the thought on some level of cognition.

Nick's strategy, however, involves more than turning himself off and entirely eliminating his consciousness. He does not attempt simply to banish the thoughts of war from his mind but more sensibly to *replace* these unpleasant thoughts. While on the surface "concentration" and "distraction" seem antonymous, the relationship between those words is actually more nuanced. If "concentration" means "to pay attention to one thing," we might usefully define "distraction" as "paying attention to something else," T. S. Eliot's notion in "Burnt Norton" of "Distracted from distraction by distraction" (120). When Nick is paying attention to making coffee, he is in essence tricking himself into paying attention to not paying attention to his war memories. As Wegner phrases it in his study *White Bears and Other Unwanted Thoughts*, "We cannot concentrate well without suppressing, and we cannot suppress well without concentrating" (12). Therefore, when Nick suggests that he stop the need for *thinking*, it represents shorthand for "unpleasant thinking," or "thinking about the war." Consciousness is not a faucet to be turned off any more than the current of a stream can be stopped. Both can, however, with much effort, be redirected. To extend the metaphor of the stereo equalizer, consciousness is like a stereo where the individual can adjust sound levels on the equalizer but is forbidden to turn the power off.

Wegner writes of psychological experiments that support Nick's project of distraction, of suppressing one thought and concentrating on a more favorable one. Wegner devotes a chapter to the importance of choosing surroundings that are more conducive to thought control. Nick's deliberate trip into the woods confirms Wegner's argument: "we must go to places that will allow us to see and hear what we want to hold in consciousness; we must retain those objects that remind us of what we truly wish to think" (98). Once Nick * * * carries out Wegner's first stage—removal—he fastidiously engages in what Wegner considers to be the best strategy for defending oneself against unwanted thoughts: focused distraction. Since we cannot entirely avoid thought, we must redirect our attention. The title of Wegner's book refers to a famous psychological experiment where the subject is instructed not to think of a white bear, which becomes impossible once the idea is introduced. "If we wish to suppress a thought," Wegner writes, "it is necessary to become absorbed in another thought. The distracter we seek should be something intrinsically interesting and engaging to us. . . . The things that interest people most are the things that provide good exercise for their abilities" (70). Nick's engagement in the rudimentary mechanics of camping suggests he has chosen well.

A literary counterpoint might well be the fourth chapter of James Joyce's *Ulysses*, a veritable textbook for the representation of consciousness in fiction and a novel to which Nick Adams refers explicitly in "On Writing" [139], the excised ending to "Big Two-Hearted River." The Calypso episode of *Ulysses* depicts Leopold Bloom engaged in a mundane activity—preparing breakfast in bed for his wife, Molly. The benefit of habitual behavior is that it frees one's mind to ruminate. Bloom, therefore, is able to brood about his wife's infidelity, his daughter's emerging sexuality, and his son's untimely death. By performing the routine action, he is able to attend to the thoughts that are troubling him. Nick does precisely the opposite. He, too, is executing a routine that he has done countless times, yet unlike Bloom he does not want to ruminate, so his concentration unnecessarily adheres to the tasks that he performs. He is occupying his consciousness with a challenge he might ordinarily accomplish unconsciously, thus defeating the economizing function of habit.

William James, explaining habit, writes, "The more of the details of our daily life we can hand over to the effortless custody of automatism, the more our higher powers of mind will be set free for their own proper work" (1: 122). Later, James writes of the automaton: "A low brain does few things, and in doing them perfectly forfeits all other use" (1: 140). Indeed, in discussing "Big Two-Hearted River," Larry Andrews picks up on James's term: "it is through assuming the role of the automaton," he writes, "that Nick hopes to recover" (3). Nick knows the function of habit and the function of mind, and yet it would be his greatest nightmare to allow the higher powers of his mind to be, in James's phrase, "set free." His goal is to choke, not to release. Although consciousness does not exert effort on that which is habitual, Nick luxuriates in the familiar details of the present moment, and he is able to engage in behavior that is not at all risky, as well as to contemplate habitual stimuli that are also comparatively safe. When Leopold Bloom makes tea, for instance, it is hardly the elaborate process that Nick considers crafting a cup of coffee to be. Bloom's summation of the tea-making process: "Cup of tea soon. Good. Mouth dry" (4.14). While he would appreciate Bloom's monosyllabism, Nick's act of brewing a pot of coffee becomes a rare—actually singular—moment of reverie and retrospection.

James calls living creatures "bundles of habits" (1: 104) and explains that "*habit simplifies the movements required to achieve a given result, makes them more accurate, and diminishes fatigue*" (1: 112, italics original). In "Big Two-Hearted River," however, Nick is not interested in diminishing fatigue. Quite the opposite. Nick intentionally avoids striking the river early in his hike, instead carrying his heavy pack deeper into the woods. As Nick settles down at the end of Part One, he realizes, "He could have made camp hours before if he had wanted to" [116]; later, he feels his mind "starting to work. He knew he could choke it because he was tired enough" [117–18]. Nick does not want to consign all his activity to habit, keeping his mind alert and refreshed. He intentionally exhausts himself, increases rather than diminishes fatigue, which he knows will allow him to sleep. * * * Nick expends all of his cognitive powers on simple, safe, or irrelevant things so that he will have no mental energy for rumination, retrospection, or introspection.

If Leopold Bloom can reduce his tea-making to monosyllabic grunts, for Nick it is a more complex task. In the superficial puzzle of the narrative, the question becomes how to prepare a pot of coffee in the proper manner. Every other activity was done precisely and expertly, and Nick wants to make sure the coffee will be executed with the same care. At the minimum, Nick invests exaggerated importance in this issue, preferring to engage in an internal debate over coffee preparation rather than face the struggle of coming to terms with his war experience. Furthermore, Hemingway's presentation of Nick's organization of his external surroundings as a metaphor for the desire to replicate that order internally would become a hallmark of his fiction. When a Hemingway character immerses himself in external sensory details, it often signals a desire to avoid the messy business of introspection. In *The Sun Also Rises*, for example, rather than disclose what Jake Barnes sees in the mirror when he looks at his injured bare body and how he feels about it, he muses about the Frenchness of his room's interior decoration.

The brief coffee-making episode in "Big Two-Hearted River" has attracted so much critical curiosity because it stands as the only reverie in the story. * * * As memories go, Nick's reminiscence of Hopkins is fairly unrevealing when compared with the gravity of the thoughts he is trying to avoid. The very inclusion of this memory, though, is telling. Directly leading up to the coffee episode, Nick on three separate occasions forgets to do something with respect to dinner: to eat bread with his first plateful; to get water for the coffee; and to follow the proper procedure to make coffee. "He could remember an argument about it with Hopkins," we are told, "but not which side he had taken" [117]. This episode that may seem extraneous in fact contains a key to reading Hemingway's career-long obsession with detailing the types of drinks his characters order, how the drinks are made, how his drinkers like them, what food the drinks accompany, who pays for it all, and how much they pay. By investigating the external detail, the character is relieved of performing a similar, more imperative inventory of the mind. The brief passage reveals Nick's glee in trying to recall inconsequential nostalgia as opposed to the struggle of trying to forget a tremendously important traumatic memory.

As Robert Gibb, who refers to the memory of Hopkins as "pleasant but insufficient," phrases it, "nostalgia for the middle past is no match for the horrors of the immediate past" (256). Nick is defusing the power of memory by training it onto a comparatively harmless topic. Psychologist James W. Pennebaker observes a similar phenomenon in his interviews with traumatized subjects: "the interviewee either changes the topic to something superficial or focuses on minutiae surrounding the topic," pointing out that "when under stress, the person focuses more narrowly or superficially on the stressful topic and/or is concerned with superficial issues unrelated to it" (90–91). Therefore, the overemphasis on the unpleasantness of the memory of Hopkins ignores the context; although a marginally unhappy incident in Nick's life, compared to the emotions of being blown up in Italy, it is, as Pennebaker phrases it, "moving to a *lower level of analysis*" (91, italics original). Hemingway's intuitive grasp of this phenomenon of human consciousness makes the Hopkins memory in "Big Two-Hearted River" so crucial precisely because of its triviality.

The analysis of the proper way to make coffee eventually wanes, and as the coffee boils, Nick eats:

> While he waited for the coffee to boil, he opened a small can
> of apricots. He liked to open cans. He emptied the can of apri-
> cots out into a tin cup. While he watched the coffee on the fire,
> he drank the juice syrup of the apricots, carefully at first to keep
> from spilling, then *meditatively*, sucking the apricots down.
> ([117], italics mine)

Hemingway has given Nick Adams his madeleine episode. If what
makes Marcel's madeleine moment so quintessentially Proustian is
its lavish exploration of involuntary memory triggered by the little
cake, then what makes Nick's apricot juice moment so quintessentially Hemingwayesque is its language of omission, the iceberg theory manifest. Assigning the description "meditatively" to the act of
drinking is a stunning adverbial choice in this context. Paired with
the prior adverb "carefully," they represent the psychological
extremes of the camping trip. For the vast majority of the story,
Nick's intent is to be careful not to meditate; when Nick eats the
apricots, though, Nick surrenders to careful meditation. As in
Proust, when the combination of food and beverage provokes an
associative memory, Nick is transported to wartime, when consuming canned fruit was a necessity. Unlike Proust, however, Hemingway does not expose the content of the meditation, and refuses to
pursue its source. Since Marcel's memory is a warm and wonderful
sensation, Proust has no qualms about exploring its source in detail.
The involuntary memory in *Swann's Way* is an "exquisite pleasure"
and an "all-powerful joy" (60). Too many of Nick Adams's memories,
of course, are dreadful. All Hemingway reveals, therefore, is the
meditative quality of the fruit, as in Proust's madeleine. The writer's aesthetic restraint matches the protagonist's mental control by
withholding the information from the reader, which mimics the way
the character would not verbalize it and instead seeks to refuse its
entry into consciousness. Hemingway gives only Nick's judgment of
the strictly sensory detail of this drinking: "They were better than
fresh apricots" [117]. The comment is inane, a wholly inadequate
replacement of the content of the memory, which serves Hemingway's thematic purpose.
    Nick's attempt to control his cognitive functioning, his endeavor
to manage his sensory intake, ultimately determines how "Big Two-
Hearted River" is interpreted. In the excised addendum posthumously published as "On Writing," Nick's fragile victory is more
explicitly stated. The conclusion of the "mental conversation" that
Hemingway (and Stein) deemed extraneous reads, "He was holding
something in his head" [141]. This final line echoes another from
earlier: "He climbed the bank of the stream, reeling up his line and
started through the brush. He ate a sandwich. He was in a hurry

and the rod bothered him. He was not thinking. He was holding something in his head. He wanted to get back to camp and get to work" [141]. The phrase "holding something in his head" is an apt poetic rendering of mental control; Nick has gained mastery of an idea, harnessed a thunderbolt of inspiration, and he is holding it rather than being held by it. He is controlling it rather than being hostage to it. Furthermore, the significance of Nick "holding" something in his head rather than having to "choke it" demonstrates a less violently antagonistic relationship with his own mind. The verb "hold" signals the holding pattern and demonstrates Nick's confidence that he will eventually have a more stable relationship with his memory, that the "plenty of days coming when he could fish the swamp" promises a period of painful self-searching and reconciliation with the horrors of war [129]. "Big Two-Hearted River" is certainly progress, a first step, no matter how tentative. "Big Two-Hearted River" must not be seen as a gloomy example of a young man who has surrendered. Nick's decision to "quell the storm" swirling in his psyche—perhaps the same storm Hemingway drew up in his manuscript sketch of the story's movement—is the equivalent of a surgeon who waits until his patient's swelling subsides before performing an operation.

For Nick to be "not thinking" while also "holding something in his head" in consecutive sentences appears paradoxical. It is apparent, however, that at this moment, Nick equates "thinking" to tortured rumination upon the past, while "holding something" is the Bergsonian idea of acting upon inspiration, of thought as action. The "work" Nick is anxious to begin is the quest to compose immortal fiction. If "On Writing" might be considered as a conclusion to *In Our Time*, the accepted reading of the collection as a Bildungsroman must be modified to consider the volume a Künstlerroman, the narrative of an artist's maturation. This artistic exorcism gestures towards a more clinical way to avoid painful cognition over a traumatic event. Daniel Gold and Wegner explain that "ruminations often occur following traumatic events. We think and stew, trying to make sense of the unsensible. Based on a cathartic view of expression, until we talk about and release those thoughts, they will continue. Like a pressure cooker that needs to let off steam, it is beneficial, if not necessary, to express our thoughts" (1251). This human need, after all, brought forth psychotherapy, and probably confession in general.

The last line of "Big Two-Hearted River"—"There were plenty of days coming when he could fish the swamp" [129]—signals knowing discipline. Nick understands he has a future, and one that promises more than his current capabilities permit. The last line is not naïve and a signal of the futility of the journey to the river. The acknowledgement of the "plenty of days coming" is something Nick could not have asserted during the war. His present belief that in the future he will be capable of more adventurous, unpredictable activity is the most self-aware, mature moment any Hemingway protagonist experiences. The camping trip serves as a gauge to test Nick's limits, the capacity of his sensations, emotions, and thought. It may be a disappointment, but it is not a defeat to find that his limitations are more constricting than they were when he was a boy, or will be in the future. "Big Two-Hearted River" represents progress toward the final destination, not an easy answer that solves all Nick's problems.

As a first step, however, Nick is on dangerous ground even as he walks his familiar paths. He has unwittingly created associations between his reliable childhood hangout and World War I. Furthermore, by suppressing his thoughts, he has exacerbated them. Psychologists studying mental control show that subjects derive an initial excitement by suppressing "exciting thoughts" and then receive a more powerful effect by those thoughts when they eventually resurface (Wegner et al. 409). The phenomenon of sexual suppression leading to flamboyant and unexpected articulations of these submerged emotions has become commonplace, even in Hemingway's work; the same phenomenon is produced by the suppression of trauma. The cautionary tale of this story, then, is that Nick has left plenty of unfinished business and has not left this business in the most secure position. * * * Nick cannot fish his way out of his shock. Nick knows that there are plenty of days coming when he will be able to fish the swamp, but he may not understand that there are plenty of days coming when he must.

Works Cited

Andrews, Larry. "'Big Two-Hearted River': The Essential Hemingway." *Missouri English Bulletin* 25 (May 1969): 1–7. Print.

Baker, Carlos. *Hemingway: The Writer as Artist.* 4th ed. Princeton: Princeton UP, 1972. Print.

Bergson, Henri. *Creative Evolution.* 1911. Trans. Arthur Mitchell. New York: Dover, 1998. Print.

———. *L'évolution créatrice.* Paris: F. Alcan, 1908. Print.

Blake, William. *The Complete Poetry and Prose of William Blake.* Ed. David V. Erdman. Berkeley: U of California P, 1982. Print.

Blotner, Joseph. *Faulkner: A Biography.* 2 vols. New York: Random House, 1974. Print.

Eliot, T. S. "Burnt Norton." *The Complete Poems and Plays, 1909–1950.* New York: Harcourt, Brace & World, 1952. 117–122. Print.

Freud, Sigmund. *The Complete Psychological Works of Sigmund Freud.* Vol. 14. Trans. and ed. James Strachey. London: Hogarth Press, 1957. Print.

Gibb, Robert. "He Made Him Up: 'Big Two-Hearted River' as Doppleganger." *Critical Essays on Ernest Hemingway's In Our Time.* Ed. Michael S. Reynolds. Boston: G. K. Hall, 1983. 254–59. Print.

Gold, Daniel B., and Daniel M. Wegner. "The Origins of Ruminative Thought: Trauma, Incompleteness, Nondisclosure, and Suppression." *Journal of Applied Social Psychology* 25 (1995): 1245–61. Print.

Grebstein, Sheldon Norman. *Hemingway's Craft.* Carbondale: Southern Illinois UP, 1973. Print.

Hemingway, Ernest. *A Farewell to Arms.* 1929. New York: Scribner's, 1995. Print.

———. *A Moveable Feast: The Restored Edition.* Ed. Séan Hemingway. New York: Scribner's, 2009. Print.

———. *The Nick Adams Stories.* 1972. New York: Scribner's, 1999. Print.

———. *Selected Letters, 1917–1961.* Ed. Carlos Baker. New York: Scribner's, 1981. Print.

———. *The Short Stories.* New York: Scribner's, 2003. Print.

———. *The Sun Also Rises.* 1926. New York: Scribner's, 2003. Print.

James, William. *The Principles of Psychology.* 2 vols. 1890. New York: Dover, 1950. Print.

Joyce, James. *Ulysses.* 1922. New York: Random House, 1986. Print.

Pennebaker, James W. "Traumatic Experience and Psychosomatic Disease: Exploring the Roles of Behavioural Inhibition, Obsession, and Confiding." *Canadian Psychology* 26.2 (1985): 82–95. Print.

Proust, Marcel. *Swann's Way.* 1913. Trans. C. K. Scott Moncrieff and Terence Kilmartin, Rev. D. J. Enright. New York: Modern Library, 2004. Print.

Reynolds, Michael. *Hemingway: The Paris Years.* Cambridge, MA: Basil Blackwell, 1989. Print.

Stewart, Matthew. *Modernism and Tradition in Ernest Hemingway's In Our Time: A Guide For Students and Readers.* Rochester, NY: Camden House, 2001. Print.

Wegner, Daniel M. *White Bears and Other Unwanted Thoughts: Suppression, Obsession, and the Psychology of Mental Control.* New York: Guilford Press, 1994. Print.

———. "You Can't Always Think What You Want: Problems in the Suppression of Unwanted Thoughts." *Advances in Experimental Social Psychology.* Vol. 25. Ed. Mark Zanna. San Diego: Academic Press, 1992. 193–225. Print.

Wegner, Daniel M., and James W. Pennebaker, eds. *Handbook of Mental Control*. Englewood Cliffs, NJ: Prentice Hall, 1993. Print.

Wegner, Daniel M., Joann W. Shortt, Anne W. Blake, and Michelle S. Page. "The Suppression of Exciting Thoughts." *Journal of Personality and Social Behavior* 58.3 (1990): 409–18. Print.

Wells, Elizabeth. "A Comparative Statistical Analysis of the Prose Styles of F. Scott Fitzgerald and Ernest Hemingway." *Fitzgerald/Hemingway Annual* 1 (1969): 47–67. Print.

Young, Philip. *Ernest Hemingway: A Reconsideration*. University Park: Pennsylvania State UP, 1966. Print.

Ernest Hemingway / *In Our Time*: A Chronology

1899	EH born July 21, in Oak Park, IL, to Grace Hall Hemingway and Dr. Clarence "Ed" Hemingway; family builds summer cottage at Walloon Lake, MI.
1914	World War I (WWI) begins.
1915	EH writes for *Trapeze*, high school newspaper.
1916	EH writes stories for *Tabula*, high school literary magazine. Plays varsity football.
1917	EH graduates from Oak Park High School; moves to Kansas City, MO, joins staff of *Kansas City Star*.
1918	EH leaves *Star* staff; joins Red Cross Ambulance Corps; leaves via New York and Paris, begins ambulance duty in Milan, Italy; wounded at Fossalta di Piave on canteen duty; in Milan hospital, falls in love with nurse Agnes von Kurowsky (AvK); WWI ends.
1919	EH returns to Oak Park; AvK breaks engagement; in MI, EH fishes Fox River with two friends; writes stories; dates Marjorie Bump.
1920	Prohibition begins; EH in Toronto, writes occasional pieces for *Toronto Star*; in MI, summer clash with mother; moves to Chicago; meets Hadley Richardson (HR); writes for *Cooperative Commonwealth* (CC).
1921	EH meets Sherwood Anderson, who, after befriending expatriate authors in Paris, urges EH to move to France; EH and HR wed in Horton Bay, MI, move to Chicago; CC folds; Anderson writes letters of introduction; EH, HR (now HH) arrive in Paris, meet Sylvia Beach, join Shakespeare and Co. lending library.
1922	EH writes for *Toronto Star*; EH, HH rent apartment in Latin Quarter; Beach publishes Joyce's *Ulysses*; EH writes "Up in Michigan"; EH, HH meet Stein, Alice B. Toklas, then Pound and wife; EH meets Joyce, befriends John Dos Passos; EH covers Genoa peace conference; EH, HH, Chink Dorman-Smith hike Great St. Bernard Pass, visit Milan;

EH writes "My Old Man"; travels to Constantinople, covers Greek-Turkish peace talks, observes refugee crisis; meets Ford Madox Ford; reports on peace talks in Lausanne; HH joins EH in Switzerland, reveals theft of his manuscripts at Gare de Lyon; EH, HH in Chamby, skiing, bobsledding.

1923   EH, HH in Chamby; HH becomes pregnant; EH, HH visit Pounds in Rapallo, Italy, meet painter Mike Strater there; EH also meets Edward O'Brien, who selects "My Old Man" for *Best Stories of 1923*; also in Rapallo meets Robert McAlmon, who offers to publish EH's first book; EH, HH ski, fish in Cortina d'Ampezzo; EH writes "Out of Season"; EH publishes six prose poems (called "In Our Time") in *Little Review*; McAlmon, EH see bullfights in Spain; EH, HH attend Pamplona bullfights in July; McAlmon's Contact Editions publishes *TSTP*; EH, HH sail for Canada; EH joins staff of *Toronto Star*; son John H. N. Hemingway ("Bumby") born October 10; EH begins "Indian Camp"; visits Oak Park; resigns from *Star*.

1924   EH, HH return to France, rent apartment near Montparnasse cafés; EH helps edit Ford's *Transatlantic Review*; Bill Bird's Three Mountains Press publishes *iot*; EH writes "Cat in the Rain," "The End of Something," "The Three-Day Blow," "The Doctor and the Doctor's Wife," "Soldier's Home," "Mr. and Mrs. Elliot," and "Cross-Country Snow"; EH meets poets William Carlos Williams, Archibald MacLeish; EH edits July, August *Transatlantic* issues; begins "Big Two-Hearted River"; EH, HH watch Pamplona bullfights with Dos Passos, Don Stewart; in *Transatlantic*, EH publishes Stein, insults T. S. Eliot; EH closes "Big Two-Hearted River" with surprise twist; Stein reads "Big Two-Hearted River," warns against "mental conversation"; EH writes new ending; EH, HH, Bumby in Schruns, Austria.

1925   In Schruns, EH accepts Boni & Liveright (B & L) contract to publish *IOT*, agrees to give B & L next book; in Paris, EH writes "The Battler" to replace "Up in Michigan"; helps edit *This Quarter*; meets Duff Twysden, Pauline Pfeiffer (PP); fishing pal Bill Smith comes to Paris; Scribner's editor Max Perkins contacts Hemingway; EH meets F. Scott Fitzgerald (FSF); *This Quarter* publishes "Big Two-Hearted River"; EH, HH watch Pamplona bullfights with Bill Smith, Duff Twysden, Harold Loeb, Pat Guthrie, Don Stewart; EH begins writing *SAR* in Madrid, Valencia, San Sebastien, Hendaye; completes draft in

Paris; B & L publishes *IOT*; EH meets wealthy expatriate Gerald Murphy (GM), sees his painting *Watch* [cover art]; writes *TOS* in ten days, mails "satire" to B & L; EH, HH, Bumby in Schruns; PP joins them; B & L rejects *TOS*.

1926   EH sees PP in Paris, sails to New York; breaks with B & L, signs Scribner's contract for *TOS, SAR*; returns to HH in Austria; in Paris, mails *SAR* typescript to Scribner's; in Madrid for bullfights; Scribner's publishes *TOS*; HH, Bumby travel to Antibes; PP arrives in Antibes; EH joins them, rents villa near Murphys and Fitzgeralds; FSF reads *SAR*, advises cuts; EH attends Pamplona fiesta with Murphys, HH, PP; EH, HH return to Antibes, agree to separate; in Paris studio of GM, EH writes new stories; HH, Bumby relocate; PP returns to U.S.; *SAR* published in October; EH dedicates book to HH and Bumby, royalties to HH; EH writes "On the Quai at Smyrna"; files for divorce.

1927   PP rejoins EH in Europe; divorce from HH granted; PP, EH marry May 10, Paris; EH submits manuscript of *MWW*; writes "Hills Like White Elephants"; EH, PH watch Pamplona bullfights; visit Valencia, Madrid, La Coruña, Santiago de Campostella, Hendaye; find Paris apt. near Luxembourg Gardens; Scribner's publishes *MWW*.

1928   PH pregnant; accident gashes EH's forehead; EH begins *FTA*; EH, PH move to Key West, FL; EH drives PH to Kansas City, MO, for Caesarian birth of Patrick, June 28; EH fishes in WY, works on *FTA*; father commits suicide; EH attends funeral, returns to Key West.

1929   EH, PH in Paris, Spain; Scribner's publishes *FTA*; stock market crashes; EH, PH ski in Gstaad with Murphys, Fitzgeralds, Dos Passoses.

1930   EH begins *DIA*; Scribner's acquires *IOT*, EH refuses to reorder stories, restores "Mr. and Mrs. Elliot," adds "Introduction" describing Smyrna evacuation; EH family in WY; EH car wreck in MT.

1931   EH buys home in Key West; EH, pregnant PH in Paris, Spain; EH writes new stories; Gregory born in Kansas City by Caesarian delivery November 12; EH completes draft of *DIA*.

1932   EH writes stories for *WTN*; fishes in Cuba, revisits WY; publishes *DIA*; writes "Fathers and Sons" and "A Clean, Well-Lighted Place."

1933   EH writes more stories, returns to Cuba; EH, PH in Spain; Scribner's publishes *WTN*; EH, PH on two-month safari in Africa.

1934	EH hospitalized in Africa; EH buys fishing boat *Pilar*; in Cuba, drafts *GHOA*.
1935	Hurricane kills 259 vets building road to Key West; EH helps collect bodies; Scribner's issues *GHOA*.
1936	EH writes "Snows of Kilimanjaro," "Francis Macomber"; Spanish Civil War begins; EH drafts *THHN*; meets Martha Gellhorn (MG).
1937	EH, MG in Madrid as war correspondents; Guernica, Spain, bombed; EH works with Joris Ivens on film *The Spanish Earth*; Scribner's publishes *THHN*.
1938	EH lives with PH in FL and WY, with MG in Paris and Madrid; Scribner's publishes *FC*. EH, PH in Key West.
1939	EH begins *FWBT*; EH, MG rent Finca Vigía (Cuba); EH in WY, seeks divorce from PH; with MH in Sun Valley, ID.
1940	MG in Europe covering World War II; EH completes *FWBT*; Germans occupy Paris; Scribner's publishes *FWBT*; PH divorces EH; EH, MG marry, buy Finca, visit Sun Valley with EH's sons; FSF dies.
1941	James Joyce dies; EH, MG in China, MG on assignment; EH, MG in Cuba, then have lengthy stay at Sun Valley; Japan attacks Pearl Harbor.
1942	EH prepares anthology, *MAW*; MG on assignment; EH patrols Gulf Stream for German submarines aboard *Pilar*.
1943	EH continues submarine surveillance; MG accepts *Collier's* assignment, goes to England; EH at Finca alone.
1944	MG visits Cuba; MG, EH quarrel; EH takes *Collier's* assignment, meets journalist Mary Welsh (MW) in London; on D-Day troop ship; enters liberated Paris; with MW at Ritz; covers battle of Hürtgenwald.
1945	EH returns to Cuba; MW joins EH at Finca; EH begins "sea book," *IIS*; in serious car crash; atomic bombs end WWII.
1946	EH divorces MG, marries MW in Havana; MW (now MH) soon pregnant; Gertrude Stein dies; EH saves MH's life in WY hospital, in emergency that ends pregnancy.
1947	EH awarded Bronze Star; Max Perkins dies; car accident kills Katy (Smith) Dos Passos; EH, MH in Ketchum, ID.
1948	EH, MH return to Cuba; sail to Italy, visit Venice; EH meets Adriana Ivancich; skiing in Cortina.
1949	EH begins Venice novel; EH, MH return to Cuba; EH works on *ARIT*; EH, MH sail to France, return to Venice, visit Ivancich family.
1950	*Cosmopolitan* serializes *ARIT*; EH, MH return to Cuba; Scribner's publishes *ARIT*; critics pan novel; EH completes *IIS*.

1951	EH writes first draft of *OMS*; revises *IIS*; mother dies; Gregory arrested in CA; EH, PH quarrel by phone; PH dies next day.
1952	Hemingway's publisher, Charles Scribner III, dies; EH begins final Nick Adams story, "Last Good Country"; also begins novel, *GOE*; Scribner's publishes *OMS*.
1953	EH wins Pulitzer Prize for *OMS*; EH, MH attend Pamplona fiesta; revisit Paris, then depart for safari in Africa.
1954	EH, MH in successive plane crashes; EH badly injured; wins Nobel Prize; attends bullfights in Madrid before sailing to Cuba; EH receives Nobel medal at Finca.
1955	Depression, illness keep EH in Cuba; begins new African book.
1956	Works on African book (*TAFL*); watches filming of *OMS*; EH, MH attend fiestas in Spain; at Paris Ritz, EH finds notebooks, manuscripts from 1920s.
1957	In Cuba, EH continues *GOE*, suffers depression; begins *MF*; Cuban revolutionary Fidel Castro builds army.
1958	EH works on *TAFL* and *MF*; violent revolution in Cuba; EH helps secure Pound's release from DC mental hospital; in Ketchum works on *MF*, *GOE*.
1959	Castro routs Batista; EH, MH buy Ketchum home, sail to Spain for bullfights; EH begins *DS*, hires Valerie Danby-Smith as assistant; in November, gives *MF* manuscript to Scribner's; drives to ID with bullfighter Ordóñez and wife; paranoid, depressed.
1960	EH prepares *DS* manuscript; EH, MH return to Cuba; EH withdraws *MF* to revise; meets Castro; EH fears crack-up; flies to Spain to complete bullfighting article; Cuba breaks ties with U.S.; *Life* serializes *DS*; friend and collaborator A. E. Hotchner brings EH back to U.S.; EH in Ketchum suffers paranoia, confusion; undergoes electroshock therapy at Mayo Clinic.
1961	U.S. severs ties with Cuba; at Mayo, EH unable to attend inauguration of John F. Kennedy; in Ketchum, depression, paranoia halt work on *MF*; U.S. invasion of Cuba (Bay of Pigs) a debacle; EH distraught by loss of Finca, manuscripts; threatens suicide; at Mayo receives more electroshock therapy; released as "improved," returns to Ketchum; takes life July 2, buried in Ketchum July 5; MH returns to Cuba late July with Valerie Danby-Smith to pack and ship EH's papers to NY.
1961–65	In a Scribner's office, Danby-Smith sorts material to form core of Ernest Hemingway Collection at JFK Library.
1964	Scribner's publishes *MF*.

1970   Scribner's publishes *IIS*.
1972   Scribner's publishes *NAS*; first EH materials arrive at JFK Library, Boston.
1980   Opening of Ernest Hemingway Collection, JFK Library.
1981   Scribner's publishes *SL*.
1986   Scribner's publishes *GOE*.
1999   Scribner's publishes *TAFL*.
2005   Kent State UP publishes *UK*, scholarly edition of *TAFL*.
2009   Scribner's publishes Restored Edition of *MF*.
2011   Cambridge UP publishes first volume of *LEH* (1907–22).
2013   Cambridge UP publishes second volume of *LEH* (1923–25).
2015   Cambridge UP publishes third volume of *LEH* (1926–29).
2017   Cambridge UP publishes fourth volume of *LEH* (1929–31).
2019   Cambridge UP publishes fifth volume of *LEH* (1932–34).

Selected Bibliography

For the works of Ernest Hemingway, see Abbreviations of Hemingway Works Cited, xxv.

• Indicates work included, excerpted, or adapted in this volume.

Scholarly Resources

Chamberlin, Brewster. *The Hemingway Log: A Chronology of His Life and Times.* Lawrence: UP of Kansas, 2015.

Ernest Hemingway Collection, John F. Kennedy Presidential Library, Boston, MA. www.jfklibrary.org/archives/ernest-hemingway-collection

Hemingway Society. www.hemingwaysociety.org/

Larson, Kelli A. et al., eds. "Current Bibliography." *The Hemingway Review.*

Oliver, Charles M. *Ernest Hemingway A to Z: The Essential Reference to the Life and Work.* New York: Facts on File, 1999.

Biographies

Baker, Carlos. *Ernest Hemingway: A Life Story.* New York: Scribner's, 1969.

Bouchard, Donald F. *Hemingway: So Far from Simple.* Amherst, NY: Prometheus, 2010.

Dearborn, Mary V. *Ernest Hemingway: A Biography.* New York: Vintage, 2017.

Donaldson, Scott. *By Force of Will: The Life and Art of Ernest Hemingway.* New York: Viking, 1977.

———. *The Paris Husband: How It Really Was Between Ernest and Hadley Hemingway.* New York: Simply Charly, 2018.

Fenton, Charles. *The Apprenticeship of Ernest Hemingway: The Early Years.* 1954; rpt., New York: Viking, 1965.

Griffin, Peter. *Less Than a Treason: Hemingway in Paris.* New York: Oxford UP, 1990.

Hutchisson, James M. *Ernest Hemingway: A New Life.* University Park: Penn State UP, 2016.

Lynn, Kenneth S. *Hemingway.* New York: Simon & Schuster, 1987.

Mellow, James. *Hemingway: A Life Without Consequences.* Boston: Houghton Mifflin, 1992.

Meyers, Jeffrey. *Hemingway: A Biography.* New York: Harper & Row, 1985.

Reynolds, Michael. *Hemingway: The Paris Years.* 1989; rpt., New York: Norton, 1999.

———. *The Young Hemingway.* 1986; rpt., New York: Norton, 1988.

Wagner-Martin, Linda. *Ernest Hemingway: A Literary Life*. New York: Palgrave Macmillan, 2007.

———. *Hemingway's Wars: Public and Private Battles*. Columbia: U of Missouri P, 2017.

Film Biographies

Burns, Ken, and Lynn Novick. *Hemingway*. Public Broadcasting System, 2021. 6 hrs.

Sage, Dewitt. *Hemingway: Rivers to the Sea*. Public Broadcasting System. American Masters Series, 2005. 1 hr. 30 min.

Letters

Baker, Carlos, ed. *Ernest Hemingway: Selected Letters, 1917–1961*. New York: Scribner's, 1981.

Bruccoli, Matthew J., ed. *The Only Thing That Counts: The Ernest Hemingway–Maxwell Perkins Correspondence*. Columbia: U of South Carolina P, 1996.

Miller, Linda Patterson, ed. *Letters from the Lost Generation: Gerald and Sara Murphy and Friends*. New Brunswick, NJ: Rutgers UP, 1991.

Spanier, Sandra, and Robert W. Trogdon, eds. *The Letters of Ernest Hemingway, Vol. 1: 1907–1922*. New York: Cambridge UP, 2011.

• Spanier, Sandra et al., eds. *The Letters of Ernest Hemingway, Vol. 2: 1923–1925*. New York: Cambridge UP, 2013.

Villard, Henry S., and James Nagel. *Hemingway in Love and War: The Lost Diary of Agnes von Kurowsky, Her Letters, and Correspondence of Ernest Hemingway*. Boston: Northeastern UP, 1989.

History and Contexts

Anderson, Richard F. *Ernest Hemingway and World War I*. New York: Cavendish Square, 2015.

Carpenter, Humphrey. *Geniuses Together: American Writers in Paris in the 1920s*. Boston: Houghton Mifflin, 1988.

Churchwell, Sarah. *Behold, America: The Entangled History of "America First" and "the American Dream."* New York: Basic, 2018.

Cowley, Malcolm. *Exile's Return: A Literary Odyssey of the 1920s*. New York: Viking, 1934.

Curnutt, Kirk. "'In the Temps de Gertrude': Hemingway, Stein, and the Scene of Instruction at 27, Rue de Fleurus." *French Connections: Hemingway and Fitzgerald Abroad*, eds. J. Gerald Kennedy and Jackson R. Bryer. New York: St. Martin's, 1999, pp. 121–39.

Dolan, Marc. *Modern Lives: A Cultural Re-reading of "The Lost Generation."* West Lafayette, IN: Purdue UP, 1996.

Donaldson, Scott. "Hemingway of the *Star*." *Fitzgerald and Hemingway: Works and Days*. New York: Columbia UP, 2009, pp. 233–50.

———. *Hemingway vs. Fitzgerald: The Rise and Fall of a Literary Friendship*. Woodstock, NY: Overlook P, 1999.

Fitch, Noel Riley. *Sylvia Beach and the Lost Generation: A History of Literary Paris in the Twenties and Thirties*. New York: Norton, 1983.

Florczyk, Steven. *Hemingway, the Red Cross, and the Great War*. Kent, OH: Kent State UP, 2014.

Gifford, James. *in our time: The 1924 Text*. Modernist Versions Project, Victoria, B.C.: U of Victoria, 2015 (available online via the University of Victoria Modernist Versions Project).

Hoffman, Frederick J. *The Twenties: American Writing in the Postwar Decade*. 1955; rpt., New York: Free P, 1965.

Joost, Nicholas. *Ernest Hemingway and the Little Magazines: The Paris Years*. Barre, MA: Barre, 1968.

Kennedy, J. Gerald. *Imagining Paris: Exile, Writing, and American Identity*. New Haven: Yale UP, 1993.

Kennedy, J. Gerald, and Jackson R. Bryer, eds. *French Connections: Hemingway and Fitzgerald Abroad*. New York: St. Martin's, 1998.

McAlmon, Robert, and Kay Boyle. *Being Geniuses Together, 1920–30*. San Francisco: North Point P, 1984.

Miller, Nathan. *The New World Coming: The 1920s and the Making of Modern America*. New York: Scribner's, 2003.

Moddelmog, Debra A., and Suzanne del Gizzo. *Ernest Hemingway in Context*. New York: Cambridge UP, 2015.

Moore, Michelle. *Chicago and the Making of American Modernism: Cather, Hemingway, Faulkner, and Fitzgerald in Conflict*. New York: Bloomsbury, 2018.

Olson, Liesl. *Chicago Renaissance: Literature and Art in the Midwest Metropolis*. New Haven: Yale UP, 2017.

Pizer, Donald. *American Expatriate Writing and the Paris Moment*. Baton Rouge: Louisiana State UP, 1996.

Wagner-Martin, Linda, ed. *A Historical Guide to Ernest Hemingway*. New York: Oxford UP, 2000.

Wickes, George. *Americans in Paris*. 1969; rpt., New York: Da Capo, 1980.

Selected Criticism of In Our Time

BOOKS

Benson, Jackson J. *Hemingway: The Writer's Art of Self-Defense*. Minneapolis: U of Minnesota P, 1969.

Cohen, Milton A. *Hemingway's Laboratory: The Paris in our time*. Tuscaloosa: U of Alabama P, 2005.

Comley, Nancy R., and Robert Scholes. *Hemingway's Genders: Rereading the Hemingway Text*. New Haven: Yale UP, 1994.

DeFalco, Joseph. *The Hero in Hemingway's Short Stories*. Pittsburgh: U of Pittsburgh P, 1963.

• Dudley, Marc Kevin. *Hemingway, Race, and Art: Bloodlines and the Color Line*. Kent, OH: Kent State UP, 2011.

Flora, Joseph M. *Hemingway's Nick Adams*. Baton Rouge: Louisiana State UP, 1982.

Grebstein, Sheldon Norman. *Hemingway's Craft*. Carbondale: Southern Illinois UP, 1973.

Gurko, Leo. *Ernest Hemingway and the Pursuit of Heroism*. New York: Crowell, 1968.

Hays, Peter L. *Ernest Hemingway*. New York: Continuum, 1990.

Lamb, Robert Paul. *Art Matters: Hemingway, Craft, and the Creation of the Modern Short Story*. Baton Rouge: Louisiana State UP, 2010.

———. *The Hemingway Short Story: A Study in Craft for Writers and Readers*. Baton Rouge: Louisiana State UP, 2013.

Moddelmog, Debra A. *Reading Desire: In Pursuit of Ernest Hemingway*. Ithaca, NY: Cornell UP, 1999.

Monteiro, George. *The Hemingway Short Story: A Critical Appreciation*. Jefferson, NC: McFarland, 2017.

Smith, Paul. *A Reader's Guide to the Short Stories of Ernest Hemingway*. Boston: G. K. Hall, 1989.

• Stewart, Matthew. *Modernism and Tradition in Ernest Hemingway's* In Our Time. Rochester, NY: Camden House, 2001.

Strong, Amy L. *Race and Identity in Hemingway's Fiction*. New York: Palgrave Macmillan, 2008.

Strychacz, Thomas F. *Hemingway's Theaters of Masculinity*. Baton Rouge: Louisiana State UP, 2003.

Svoboda, Frederic J. *Hemingway's Short Stories: Reflections on Teaching, Reading, and Understanding*. Kent, OH: Kent State UP, 2019.

• Tetlow, Wendolyn E. *Hemingway's* In Our Time: *Lyrical Dimensions*. Lewisburg, PA: Bucknell UP, 1992.

• Wyatt, David. *Hemingway, Style, and the Art of Emotion*. New York: Cambridge UP, 2015.

Young, Philip. *Ernest Hemingway: A Reconsideration*. 1952. University Park: Pennsylvania State UP, 1966.

COLLECTIONS OF CRITICISM

Beegel, Susan F., ed. *Hemingway's Neglected Short Fiction: New Perspectives*. Tuscaloosa: U of Alabama P, 1992.

Benson, Jackson J., ed. *New Critical Approaches to the Short Stories of Ernest Hemingway*. Durham: Duke UP, 1990.

———. *The Short Stories of Ernest Hemingway: Critical Essays*. Durham, NC: Duke UP, 1975.

Broer, Lawrence R., and Gloria Holland, eds. *Hemingway and Women: Female Critics and the Female Voice*. Tuscaloosa: U of Alabama P, 2002.

Cirino, Mark, and Mark P. Ott, eds. *Ernest Hemingway and the Geography of Memory*. Kent, OH: Kent State UP, 2010.

Flora, Joseph M., ed. *Ernest Hemingway: A Study of the Short Fiction*. Boston: Twayne, 1989.

Meyers, Jeffrey, ed. *Hemingway: The Critical Heritage*. London: Routledge and Kegan Paul, 1982.

Nagel, James, ed. *Ernest Hemingway: The Writer in Context*. Madison: U of Wisconsin P, 1984.

Paul, Stephen et al., eds. *War Ink: New Perspectives on Ernest Hemingway's Early Life and Writing*. Kent, OH: Kent State UP, 2014.

Reynolds, Michael S., ed. *Critical Essays on* In Our Time. Boston: G. K. Hall, 1983.

Sanderson, Rena, ed. *Hemingway and Italy: New Perspectives*. Baton Rouge: Louisiana State UP, 2006.

Svoboda, Frederic J., and Joseph J. Waldmeir, eds. *Hemingway: Up in Michigan Perspectives*. East Lansing: Michigan State UP, 1995.

Wagner, Linda Welshimer, ed. *Ernest Hemingway: Five Decades of Criticism*. East Lansing: Michigan State UP, 1974.

Wagner-Martin, Linda, ed. *Ernest Hemingway: Seven Decades of Criticism*. East Lansing: Michigan State UP, 1989.

CRITICISM OF THE WORK AS A WHOLE

Baker, Sheridan. "Nick—In Our Time." *Ernest Hemingway: An Introduction and Interpretation*. New York: Holt, Rinehart, and Winston, 1967, pp. 19–39.

Barloon, Jim. "Very Short Stories: The Miniaturization of War in Hemingway's *In Our Time*." *The Hemingway Review* 24.2 (Spring 2005): 5–17.

Beall, John. "Hemingway's Formation of *In Our Time*." *The Hemingway Review* 35.1 (Fall 2015): 63–77.

Benson, Jackson J. "Ernest Hemingway as Short Story Writer." *The Short Stories of Ernest Hemingway: Critical Essays*, ed. Jackson J. Benson. Durham: Duke UP, 1975, pp. 272–310.

Brogan, Jacqueline Vaught. "Hemingway's *In Our Time*: A Cubist Anatomy." *The Hemingway Review* 27. 2 (Spring 1998): 31–46.

Carey, Craig. "Mr. Wilson's War: Peace, Neutrality, and Entangling Alliances in Hemingway's *In Our Time*." *The Hemingway Review* 31.2 (Spring 2012): 6–26.

Cohen, Milton A. "Soldiers' Voices in *In Our Time*: Hemingway's Ventriloquism." *The Hemingway Review* 20.1 (Fall 2000): 22–29.

Cox, James M. "*In Our Time*: The Essential Hemingway." *Southern Humanities Review* 22.4 (Fall 1988): 305–20.

Fruscione, Joseph. "*In Our Time* and American Modernisms: Interpreting and Writing the Complexities of Gender and Culture." *Teaching Hemingway and Gender*, ed. Verna Kale. Kent, OH: Kent State UP, 2016.

Gajdusek, Robert E. "Dubliners in Michigan: Joyce's Presence in Hemingway's *In Our Time*." *The Hemingway Review* 2.1 (Fall 1982): 48–61.

Knodt, Ellen Andrews. "'Pleasant, Isn't It?': The Language of Hemingway and His World War I Contemporaries." *War Ink: New Perspectives on Ernest Hemingway's Early Life and Writings*, eds. Steve Paul et al. Kent, OH: Kent State UP, 2014, pp. 72–93.

• Moddelmog, Debra A. "The Unifying Consciousness of a Divided Conscience: Nick Adams as Author of *In Our Time*." *American Literature* 60.4 (1988): 591–610.

Nagel, James. "Hemingway's *In Our Time* and the Unknown Genre: The Short-Story Cycle." *American Literary Dimensions: Poems and Essays in Honor of Melvin J. Friedman*, eds. Ben Siegel and Jay Hailo. Newark: U of Delaware P, 1999, pp. 91–98.

Narbeshuber, Lisa. "Hemingway's *In Our Time*: Cubism, Conservation, and the Suspension of Identification." *The Hemingway Review* 25.2 (Spring 2006): 9–28.

Renza, Louis A. "The Importance of Being Ernest." *Ernest Hemingway: Seven Decades of Criticism*, ed. Linda Wagner-Martin. East Lansing: Michigan State UP, 1998, pp. 213–38.

• Reynolds, Michael. "Hemingway's *In Our Time*: The Biography of a Book." *Modern American Short Story Sequences: Composite Fictions and Fictive Communities*, ed. J. Gerald Kennedy. New York: Cambridge UP, 1995, pp. 35–51.

Smith, Paul. "Who Wrote Hemingway's *In Our Time*?" *Hemingway Repossessed*, ed. Kenneth Rosen. Westport, CT: Greenwood, 1994, pp. 143–50.

Strong, Paul. "The First Nick Adams Stories." *Hemingway: Up in Michigan Perspectives*, eds. Frederic J. Svoboda and Joseph J. Waldmeir. East Lansing: Michigan State UP, 1995, pp. 29–36.

Svoboda, Frederic J. "False Wilderness: Northern Michigan as Created in the Nick Adams Stories." *Hemingway: Up in Michigan Perspectives*, eds. Frederic J. Svoboda and Joseph J. Waldmeir. East Lansing: Michigan State UP, 1995, pp. 15–22.

Tyler, Lisa. "'Our Fathers Lied': The Great War and Paternal Betrayal in Hemingway's *In Our Time*." *Teaching Hemingway and War*, ed. Alex Vernon. Kent, OH: Kent State UP, 2016, pp. 30–40.

Vaughn, Elizabeth Dewberry. "*In Our Time* as Self-Begetting Fiction." *Ernest Hemingway: Seven Decades of Criticism*, ed. Linda Wagner-Martin. East Lansing: Michigan State UP, 1998, pp. 135–47.

• Wagner, Linda W. "Juxtaposition in Hemingway's *In Our Time*." *Studies in Short Fiction* 12.3 (1975): 243–52.

Wagner-Martin, Linda. "*in our time, In Our Time*, and Dimensionality." *Hemingway's Wars: Public and Private Battles*. Columbia: U of Missouri P, 2017, pp. 37–53.

Winn, Harbour. "Hemingway's *In Our Time*: 'Pretty Good Unity.'" *The Hemingway Review* 9.2 (Spring 1990): 124–41.

• Wyatt, David. "A Second Will: *In Our Time* and *in our time*." *Hemingway, Style, and the Art of Emotion*. New York: Cambridge UP, 2015, pp. 27–46.

CRITICISM OF INDIVIDUAL STORIES

"The Battler"

• Dudley, Marc Kevin. "The Truth's in the Shadows: Race in 'The Light of the World' and 'The Battler.'" *Hemingway, Race, and Art*. Kent, OH: Kent State UP, 2011, pp. 69–89.

Gerogiannis, Nicholas. "Nick Adams on the Road: 'The Battler' as Hemingway's Man on the Hill." *Critical Essays on Ernest Hemingway's* In Our Time, ed. Michael S. Reynolds. Boston: G. K. Hall, 1983, pp. 176–88.

Kyle, Frank B. "Parallel and Complementary Themes in Hemingway's 'Big Two-Hearted River' Stories and 'The Battler.'" *Studies in Short Fiction* 16 (1979): 295–300.

Monteiro, George. "The Jungle Out There: Nick Adams Takes to the Road." *The Hemingway Review* 29.1 (Fall 2009): 61–72.

———. "'This Is My Pal Bugs': Ernest Hemingway's 'The Battler.'" *Studies in Short Fiction* 23.2 (Spring 1986): 179–83.

Strong, Amy L. "Black Eyes and Peroxide in 'The Battler' and 'The Light of the World.'" *Race and Identity in Hemingway's Fiction*. New York: Palgrave Macmillan, 2008, pp. 45–58.

Stubbs, Neil. "'Watch Out How that Egg Runs': Hemingway and the Rhetoric of American Road Food." *The Hemingway Review* 33.1 (Fall 2013): 79–85.

Willis, Mary Kay. "Structural Analysis of 'The Battler.'" *Linguistics in Literature* 1.2 (1976): 61–67.

"Big Two-Hearted River," Parts I and II

Adair, William. "Landscapes of the Mind: 'Big Two-Hearted River.'" *College Literature* 4.2 (1977): 144–51.

Berry, Wendell. "Style and Grace." *What Are People For?* San Francisco: North Point Press, 1990, pp. 64–70.

• Cirino, Mark. "Hemingway's 'Big-Two-Hearted River': Nick's Strategy and the Psychology of Mental Control." *Papers on Language and Literature* 47.2 (Spring 2011): 115–40.

Civello, Paul. "Hemingway's 'Primitivism': Archetypal Patterns in 'Big Two-Hearted River.'" *The Hemingway Review* 13.1 (Fall 1993): 1–16.

Cowley, Malcolm. "Hemingway's Wound—and Its Consequences for American Literature." *The Georgia Review* 38.2 (Summer 1984): 223–39.

Florczyk, Steven. "Hemingway's 'Tragic Adventure': Angling for Peace in the Natural Landscape of the Fisherman." *North Dakota Quarterly* 68.2–3 (Spring–Summer 2001): 156–65.

Goodspeed-Chadwick, Julie. "Modernist Style, Identity Politics, and Trauma in Hemingway's 'Big Two-Hearted River' and Stein's 'Picasso.'" *Teaching Hemingway and Modernism*, eds. Joseph Fruscione and Mark P. Ott. Kent, OH: Kent State UP, 2015, pp. 10–20.

Johnston, Kenneth G. "Hemingway and Cézanne: Doing the Country." *American Literature* 56.1 (March 1984): 28–37.

Josephs, Allen. "The War in 'Big Two-Hearted River.'" *North Dakota Quarterly* 79.3–4 (Summer–Fall 2012): 9–19.

Justice, Hilary K. "Tragic Stasis: Love, War, and the Composition of Hemingway's 'Big Two-Hearted River.'" *Resources for American Literary Study* 29 (2005): 200–15.

Lamb, Robert Paul. "The Currents of Memory: Hemingway's 'Big Two-Hearted River' as Metafiction." *Ernest Hemingway and the Geography of Memory*, eds. Mark Cirino and Mark P. Ott. Kent, OH: Kent State UP, 2010, pp. 166–85.

Melling, Philip. "'There Were Many Indians in the Story': Hidden History in Hemingway's 'Big Two-Hearted River.'" *The Hemingway Review* 28.2 (Spring 2009): 45–65.

O'Brien, Sarah Mary. "'I, Also, Am in Michigan': Pastoralism of Mind in 'Big Two-Hearted River.'" *The Hemingway Review* 28.2 (Spring 2009): 66–86.

• Putnam, Ann. "On Defiling Eden: The Search for Eve in the Garden of Eden." *Hemingway and Women: Female Critics and the Female Voice*, eds. Lawrence R. Broer and Gloria Holland. Tuscaloosa: U of Alabama P, 2002, pp. 109–30.

Scafella, Frank. "'Nothing' in 'Big Two-Hearted River.'" *Hemingway: Up in Michigan Perspectives*, eds. Frederic J. Svoboda and Joseph J. Waldmeir. East Lansing: Michigan State UP, 1995, pp. 70–90.

Smith, Paul. "Hemingway's Early Manuscripts: The Theory and Practice of Omission." *Journal of Modern Literature* 10.2 (June 1983): 268–88.

Stein, William Bysshe. "Ritual in Hemingway's 'Big Two-Hearted River.'" *Texas Studies in Language and Literature* 1.4 (Winter 1960): 555–61.

Stewart, Matthew C. "Ernest Hemingway and World War I: Combatting Recent Psychobiographical Reassessments, Restoring the War." *Papers on Language and Literature* 36.2 (Spring 2000): 198–217.

Svoboda, Frederic J. "Landscapes Real and Imagined: 'Big Two-Hearted River.'" *The Hemingway Review* 16.1 (Fall 1996): 33–42.

Wells, Elizabeth. "A Statistical Analysis of the Prose Style of Ernest Hemingway: 'Big Two-Hearted River.'" *The Short Stories of Ernest Hemingway: Critical Essays*, ed. Jackson J. Benson. Durham: Duke UP, 1975, pp. 129–35.

Westbrook, Max. "Text, Ritual, and Memory: Hemingway's 'Big Two-Hearted River.'" *North Dakota Quarterly* 60. 3 (Summer 1992): 14–25.

See also McKenna under "Soldier's Home."

"Cat in the Rain"

Barton, Edwin J. "The Story as It Should Be: Epistemological Uncertainty in Hemingway's 'Cat in the Rain.'" *The Hemingway Review* 14.1 (Fall 1994): 72–78.

Bennett, Warren. "The Poor Kitty and the Padrone and the Tortoise-Shell Cat in 'Cat in the Rain.'" *The Hemingway Review* 8.1 (Fall 1988): 26–36.

Beuka, Robert. "Tales from 'The Big Outside World': Ann Beattie's Hemingway." *The Hemingway Review* 22.1 (Fall 2002): 109–17.

Chatman, Seymour. "'Soft Filters': Some Sunshine on 'Cat in the Rain.'" *Narrative* 9.2 (May 2001): 217–22.

Coleman, Hildy. "'Cat' and 'Hills': Two Hemingway Fairy Tales." *The Hemingway Review* 12.1 (Fall 1992): 67–72.

• Hagopian, John V. "Symmetry in 'Cat in the Rain.'" *College English* 24.3 (December 1962): 220–22.

Kennedy, J. Gerald. "What Hemingway Omitted from 'Cat in the Rain.'" *Journal of the Short Story in English* 1 (1983): 75–81.

Lodge, David. "Analysis and Interpretation of the Realist Text: A Pluralistic Approach to Ernest Hemingway's 'Cat in the Rain.'" *Poetics Today* 1.4 (Summer 1980): 5–22.

Steinke, Jim. "Hemingway's 'Cat in the Rain.'" *Spectrum* 25.1–2 (1983): 36–44.

Thomières, Daniel. "Being and Time in Ernest Hemingway's 'Cat in the Rain.'" *Journal of the Short Story in English* 60 (Spring 2013): 31–42.

Tyler, Lisa. "'I'd Rather Not Hear': Women and Men in Conversation in 'Cat in the Rain' and 'The Sea Change.'" *Hemingway and Women: Female Critics and the Female Voice*, eds. Lawrence R. Broer and Gloria Holland. Tuscaloosa: U of Alabama P, 2002, pp. 70–80.

"Cross-Country Snow"

• Daiker, Donald A. "Hemingway's Neglected Masterpiece: 'Cross-Country Snow.'" *MidAmerica: The Yearbook of the Society for the Study of Midwestern Literature* 41 (2014): 23–38.

Dömötör, Teodóra. "Absent Fathers, Homosexual Sons, and Melancholic Repression in Three of Hemingway's Short Stories." *Intertexts* 17.1–2 (Spring–Fall 2013): 69–89.

Edenfield, Olivia Carr. "Doomed Biologically: Sex and Entrapment in Ernest Hemingway's 'Cross-Country Snow.'" *The Hemingway Review* 19.1 (Fall 1999): 141–48.

Pfeiffer, Gerhard, and Martina König. "'The Bill Always Came': Hemingway's Use of the Epiphany in 'Cross-Country Snow.'" *The Hemingway Review* 16.1 (Fall 1996): 97–101.

Sanders, Barbara. "Linguistic Analysis of 'Cross-Country Snow.'" *Linguistics in Literature* 1.2 (1976): 43–52.

"The Doctor and the Doctor's Wife"

Fulkerson, Richard. "The Biographical Fallacy and 'The Doctor and the Doctor's Wife.'" *Studies in Short Fiction* 16 (1979): 61–65.

Grimes, Larry E. "William James and 'The Doctor and the Doctor's Wife.'" *Hemingway: Up in Michigan Perspectives*, eds. Frederic J. Svoboda and Joseph J. Waldmeir. East Lansing: Michigan State UP, 1995, pp. 47–57.

Nolan, Charles J., Jr. "The Importance of Hemingway's 'The Doctor and the Doctor's Wife.'" *Humanities Review* 5.1 (Fall 2006): 15–24.

See also Robert E. Gajdusek and Amy Strong under "Indian Camp."

"The End of Something"

Daiker, Donald A. "In Defense of Hemingway's Young Nick Adams: 'Everything Was Gone to Hell Inside of Me.'" *Texas Studies in Literature and Language* 57.2 (Summer 2015): 242–57.

Godfrey, Laura Gruber. "Hemingway and Cultural Geography: The Landscape of Logging in 'The End of Something.'" *Ernest Hemingway and the Geography of Memory*, eds. Mark Cirino and Mark P. Ott. Kent, OH: Kent State UP, 2010, pp. 69–82.

Kruse, Horst H. "Ernest Hemingway's 'The End of Something': Its Independence as a Short Story and Its Place in the 'Education of Nick Adams.'" *Studies in Short Fiction* 4 (1967): 152–66.

Stoneback, H. R. "'Nothing Was Ever Lost': Another Look at 'That Marge Business.'" *Hemingway: Up in Michigan Perspectives*, eds. Frederic J. Svoboda and Joseph J. Waldmeir. East Lansing: Michigan State UP, 1995, pp. 59–76.

• Tyler, Lisa. "'How Beautiful the Virgin Forests Were Before the Loggers Came': An Ecofeminist Reading of Hemingway's 'The End of Something.'" *The Hemingway Review* 24.2 (2008): 60–73.

See also Dömötör under "Cross-Country Snow."

"Indian Camp"

Bauer, Margaret D. "Forget the Legend and Read the Work: Teaching Two Stories by Ernest Hemingway." *College Literature* 30.3 (Summer 2003): 124–37.

Daiker, Donald A. "In Defense of Hemingway's Dr. Adams: The Case for 'Indian Camp.'" *The Hemingway Review* 35.2 (Spring 2016): 55–69.

Dudley, Marc. "'Indian Camp' and 'The Doctor and the Doctor's Wife': Deconstructing the Great (White) Man." *Hemingway, Race, and Art.* Kent, OH: Kent State UP, 2011, pp. 27–50.

• Flora, Joseph M. "The Boy." *Hemingway's Nick Adams.* Baton Rouge: Louisiana State UP, 1982, pp. 18–31.

Gajdusek, Robert E. "False Fathers, Doctors, and the Caesarean Dilemma: Metaphor as Structure in Hemingway's *In Our Time.*" *North Dakota Quarterly* 65.3 (1998): 53–61.

Hannum, Howard L. "'Scared Sick Looking at It': A Reading of Nick Adams in the Published Stories." *Twentieth Century Literature* 47.1 (Spring 2001): 92–113.

Lewis, Robert W. "'Long Time Ago Good, Now No Good': Hemingway's Indian Stories." *New Critical Approaches to the Short Stories of Ernest Hemingway*, ed. Jackson J. Benson. Durham: Duke UP, 1990, pp. 200–12.

Meyers, Jeffrey. "Hemingway's Primitivism and 'Indian Camp.'" *Twentieth Century Literature* 34.2 (Summer 1988): 211–22.

Stoneback, H. R. "Fiction into Film: 'Is Dying Hard, Daddy?': Hemingway's 'Indian Camp.'" *Social and Political Change in Literature and Film*, ed. Richard Chapple. Gainesville: UP of Florida, 1994, pp. 93–108.

• Strong, Amy. "Screaming through Silence: The Violence of Race in 'Indian Camp' and 'The Doctor and the Doctor's Wife.'" *The Hemingway Review* 16.1 (Fall 1996): 18–32.

Tyler, Lisa. "'Dangerous Families' and 'Intimate Harm' in Hemingway's 'Indian Camp.'" *Texas Studies in Literature and Language* 48.1 (Spring 2006): 37–53.

Watson, William Braasch. "The Doctor and the Doctor's Son: Immortalities in 'Indian Camp.'" *Hemingway: Up in Michigan Perspectives*, eds. Frederic J. Svoboda and Joseph J. Waldmeir. East Lansing: Michigan State UP, 1995, pp. 37–45.

See also Grimes under "'The Doctor and the Doctor's Wife."

"Mr. and Mrs. Elliot"

Comley, Nancy R., and Robert Scholes. "Tribal Things: Hemingway's Erotics of Truth." *Novel: A Forum on Fiction* 25.3 (Spring 1992): 268–85.

Dömötör, Teodóra. "Anxious Masculinity and Silencing in Ernest Hemingway's 'Mr. and Mrs. Elliot.'" *Hungarian Journal of English and American Studies* 19.1 (Spring 2013): 121–33.

Perloff, Marjorie. "'Ninety Percent Rotarian': Gertrude Stein's Hemingway." *American Literature* 62.4 (December 1990): 668–83.

• Smith, Paul. "From the Waste Land to the Garden with the Elliots." *Hemingway's Neglected Short Fiction: New Perspectives*, ed. Susan F. Beegel. Tuscaloosa: U of Alabama P, 1992, pp. 123–29.

Stewart, Matthew. "Why Does Mother Elliot Cry? Cornelia's Sexuality in 'Mr. and Mrs. Elliot.'" *The Hemingway Review* 24.1 (Fall 2004): 81–89.

Tanimoto, Chikako. "Queering Sexual Practices in 'Mr. and Mrs. Elliot.'" *The Hemingway Review* 32.1 (Fall 2012): 88–99.

"My Old Man"

Franke, Damon. "The Cardinal Lemoine Typescripts and the Narrative Cover-Up of 'My Old Man.'" *English Language Notes* 37.1 (1999): 64–72.

Phelan, James. "What Hemingway and a Rhetorical Theory of Narrative Can Do for Each Other: The Example of 'My Old Man.'" *The Hemingway Review* 12.2 (Spring 1993): 1–14.

Reynolds, Michael S. "Hemingway's 'My Old Man': Turf Days in Paris." *Hemingway in Italy and Other Essays*, ed. Robert W. Lewis. New York: Praeger, 1990, pp. 101–06.

Sipiora, Phillip. "Ethical Narration in 'My Old Man.'" *Hemingway's Neglected Short Fiction: New Perspectives*, ed. Susan F. Beegel. Tuscaloosa: U of Alabama P, 1992, pp. 43–60.

Somers, Paul P., Jr. "The Mark of Sherwood Anderson on Hemingway: A Look at the Texts." *South Atlantic Quarterly* 26 (1974): 487–503.

• Stewart, Matthew. "'My Old Man': A One-Story Interlude." *Modernism and Tradition in Ernest Hemingway's* In Our Time. Rochester: Camden House, 2001, pp. 80–84.

"On the Quai at Smyrna"

Long, Adam. "Ernest Hemingway in Turkey: From the Quai at Smyrna to *A Farewell to Arms*." *The Hemingway Review* 38.2 (Spring 2019): 75–86.

Smith, Peter A. "Hemingway's 'On the Quai at Smyrna' and the Universe of *In Our Time*." *Studies in Short Fiction* 24.2 (Spring 1987): 159–62.

Stewart, Matthew. "'It Was All a Pleasant Business': The Historical Context of 'On the Quai at Smyrna.'" *The Hemingway Review* 23.1 (Fall 2003): 58–71.

"Out of Season"

• Adair, William. "Hemingway's 'Out of Season': The End of the Line." *New Critical Approaches to the Short Stories of Ernest Hemingway*, ed. Jackson J. Benson. Durham: Duke UP, 1990, pp. 341–46.

Ganzel, Dewey. "A Geometry of His Own: Hemingway's 'Out of Season.'" *Modern Fiction Studies* 34.2 (Summer 1988): 171–83.

Johnston, Kenneth G. "Hemingway's 'Out of Season' and the Psychology of Errors." *Literature and Psychology* 21 (1971): 41–46.

Knodt, Ellen Andrews. "Hemingway's Commedia Dell'Arte Story? 'Out of Season.'" *The Hemingway Review* 31.1 (Fall 2011): 107–17.

Nolan, Charles J. "Hemingway's 'Out of Season': The Importance of Close Reading." *Rocky Mountain Review of Language and Literature* 53.2 (1999): 45–58.

Smith, Paul. "Some Misconceptions of 'Out of Season.'" *Critical Essays on Ernest Hemingway's* In Our Time, ed. Michael S. Reynolds. Boston: G. K. Hall, 1983, pp. 235–51.

Steinke, James. "'Out of Season' and Hemingway's Neglected Discovery: Ordinary Actuality." *Hemingway's Neglected Short Fiction: New Perspectives*, ed. Susan F. Beegel. Tuscaloosa: U of Alabama P, 1989, pp. 61–73.

• Strychacz, Thomas. "*In Our Time*, Out of Season." *The Cambridge Companion to Hemingway*, ed. Scott Donaldson. New York: Cambridge UP, 1996, pp. 55–86.

Sylvester, Bickford. "Hemingway's Italian Waste Land: The Complex Unity of 'Out of Season.'" *Hemingway's Neglected Short Fiction: New Perspectives*, ed. Susan F. Beegel. Tuscaloosa: U of Alabama P, 1989, pp. 75–98.

"The Revolutionist"

Groseclose, Barbara S. "Hemingway's 'The Revolutionist': An Aid to Interpretation." *Modern Fiction Studies* 17 (1971–72): 565–70.

Hunt, Anthony. "Another Turn for Hemingway's 'The Revolutionist': Sources and Meanings." *Fitzgerald-Hemingway Annual* (1977): 119–35.

Johnston, Kenneth G. "Hemingway and Mantegna: The Bitter Nail Holes." *Journal of Narrative Technique* 1 (1971): 86–94.

Martin, Lawrence H. "'The Revolutionist': Historical Context and Political Ideology." *Hemingway's Italy: New Perspectives*, ed. Rena Sanderson. Baton Rouge: Louisiana State UP, 2006, pp. 90–99.

Montgomery, Martin. "Language, Character and Action: A Linguistic Approach to the Analysis of Character in a Hemingway Short Story." *Techniques of Description: Spoken and Written Discourse*, eds. John M. Sinclair et al. London: Routledge, 1993, pp. 127–42.

See also Steinke under "A Very Short Story."

"Soldier's Home"

Azevedo, Carlos. "Oak Park as the Thing Left Out: Surface and Depth in 'Soldier's Home.'" *Ernest Hemingway: The Oak Park Legacy*, ed. James Nagel. Tuscaloosa: U of Alabama P, 1996, pp. 96–107.

Blazek, William. "All Quiet on the Midwestern Front: 'Soldier's Home.'" *War Ink: New Perspectives on Ernest Hemingway's Early Life and Writings*, eds. Steve Paul et al. Kent, OH: Kent State UP, 2014, pp. 169–89.

Cohen, Milton A. "Vagueness and Ambiguity in Hemingway's 'Soldier's Home': Two Puzzling Passages." *The Hemingway Review* 30.1 (Fall 2010): 158–64.

De Baerdemaeker, Ruben. "Performative Patterns in Hemingway's 'Soldier's Home.'" *The Hemingway Review* 27.1 (Fall 2007): 55–73.

• Kennedy, J. Gerald, and Kirk Curnutt. "Out of the Picture: Mrs. Krebs, Mother Stein, and 'Soldier's Home.'" *The Hemingway Review* 12.1 (Fall 1992): 1–11.

Kingsbury, Celia M. "A Way It Never Was: Propaganda and Shell Shock in 'Soldier's Home' and 'A Way You'll Never Be.'" *War Ink: New Perspectives on Ernest Hemingway's Early Life and Writings*, eds. Steve Paul et al. Kent, OH: Kent State UP, 2014, pp. 150–68.

Kobler, J. F. "'Soldier's Home' Revisited: A Hemingway Mea Culpa." *Studies in Short Fiction* 30.3 (Summer 1993): 377–85.

• Lamb, Robert Paul. "The Love Song of Harold Krebs: Form, Argument, and Meaning in Hemingway's 'Soldier's Home.'" *The Hemingway Review* 14.2 (Spring 1995): 18–36.

Lewis, Robert W., Jr. "Hemingway's Concept of Sport and 'Soldier's Home.'" *Rendezvous* 5 (Winter 1970): 19–27.

McKenna, John J. "No Homecoming for Soldiers: Young Hemingway's Flight from and Return to the Midwest." *MidAmerica: The Yearbook of the Society for the Study of Midwestern Literature* 36 (2009): 83–92.

McKenna, John J., and David M. Raabe. "Using Temperament Theory to Understand Conflict in Hemingway's 'Soldier's Home.'" *Studies in Short Fiction* 34.2 (Spring 1997): 203–13.

Trout, Steven. "'Where Do We Go from Here?' Ernest Hemingway's 'Soldier's Home' and American Veterans of World War I." *The Hemingway Review* 20.1 (Fall 2000): 5–21.

"The Three-Day Blow"

Kopley, Richard. "The Architecture of Ernest Hemingway's 'The Three-Day Blow.'" *The Formal Center in Literature: Explorations from Poe to the Present.* Rochester: Camden House, 2018, pp. 83–91.

• Tetlow, Wendolyn E. *"In Our Time* (1925): Before a Separate Peace." *Hemingway's* In Our Time: *Lyrical Dimensions.* Lewisburg, PA: Bucknell UP, 1992, pp. 61–65.

Vanderlaan, Kim. "Having It in Reserve: Secret Love and a Way Out in Willa Cather's 'Paul's Case' and Ernest Hemingway's 'The Three-Day Blow.'" *Journal of American Culture* 39.4 (December 2016): 426–37.

See also Daiker under "The End of Something" and Dömötör under "Cross-Country Snow."

"A Very Short Story"

Comley, Nancy R. "'A Very Short Story': The Italian Education of Ernest Hemingway." *Hemingway's Italy: New Perspectives,* ed. Rena Sanderson. Baton Rouge: Louisiana State UP, 2006, pp. 41–50.

Daiker, Donald A. "In Search of the Real Nick Adams: The Case for 'A Very Short Story.'" *The Hemingway Review* 32.2 (Spring 2013): 28–41.

• Donaldson, Scott. "'A Very Short Story' as Therapy." *Hemingway's Neglected Short Fiction: New Perspectives,* ed. Susan F. Beegel. Tuscaloosa: U of Alabama P, 1992, pp. 99–105.

Scholes, Robert. "Decoding Papa: 'A Very Short Story' as Word and Text." *Semiotics and Interpretation.* New Haven, CT: Yale UP, 1983, pp. 110–26.

Steinke, Jim. "The Two Shortest Stories of Hemingway's *In Our Time.*" *Critical Essays on* In Our Time, ed. Michael S. Reynolds. Boston: G. K. Hall, 1983, pp. 218–26.

CRITICISM OF *IN OUR TIME* CHAPTER VIGNETTES

• Cohen, Milton A. "Epilogue, The Fate of Experiments." *Hemingway's Laboratory: The Paris* in our time. Tuscaloosa: U of Alabama P, 2005, pp. 206–14.

Gradoli, Marina. "Hemingway's Criteria in Ordering the Sequence of the Vignettes in *in our time* (1924) and *In Our Time* (1925)." *North Dakota Quarterly* 76.1–2 (2009): 186–90.

• Hagemann, E. R. "'Only Let the Story End as Soon as Possible': Time-and-History in Ernest Hemingway's *In Our Time.*" *Modern Fiction Studies* 26.2 (Summer 1980): 255–62.

Thurston, Michael. "Reading the Paper: A Bibliographic Approach to *in our time.*" *The Hemingway Review* 38.2 (Spring 2019): 9–26.

See also Cohen under "Criticism of the Work as a Whole."

CRITICISM OF *IN OUR TIME* DISCARDED EPISODES

"Three Shots"

Grimes, Larry. "Night Terror and Morning Calm: A Reading of Hemingway's 'Indian Camp' as Sequel to 'Three Shots.'" *Studies in Short Fiction* 12 (1975): 413–15.

Nänny, Max. "New Light on Ernest Hemingway's Short Story Fragment 'Three Shots.'" *North Dakota Quarterly* 70.4 (2003): 88–93.

"On Writing"

Broer, Lawrence. "Hemingway's 'On Writing': A Portrait of the Artist as Nick Adams." *Hemingway's Neglected Short Fiction: New Perspectives*, ed. Susan F. Beegel. Tuscaloosa: U of Alabama P, 1992, pp. 131–40.

Renza, Louis A. "The Importance of Being Ernest." *Ernest Hemingway: Seven Decades of Criticism*, ed. Linda Wagner-Martin. East Lansing: Michigan State UP, 1998, pp. 213–38.

Smith, Paul. "Who Wrote Hemingway's *In Our Time?*" *Hemingway Repossessed*, ed. Ken Rosen. Westport, CT: Greenwood, 1994, pp. 143–50.